"Was I too soft in my verbiage?" Lenk asked. "Did you not feel the *chill* of death in my words?"

"Look." The guard captain sighed, rubbing his eyes. "I'll tell you what I told the tulwar: no oids, no adventurers, no...whatever the hell you are."

The captain looked him over with a glare that Lenk recognized. Usually, he saw it only a moment before swords were drawn. But the captain's stare was slow, methodical. He was sizing him up, wondering just how much trouble this was going to be worth.

Lenk decided to give him a hint. He slid into a tense stance, making sure to roll his shoulders enough to send the mail under his shirt clinking and show just how easily he wore the sword on his back.

"I don't see any colors on your shirt," the captain muttered. "I don't see any badge at your breast. I don't see coin at your belt. Which means you're not someone I want in my city."

"You're wise to be wary," Lenk said. "And I advise you to listen to that wariness and cut a path for me, lest I show you why my name in the old tongues means 'bane of death.'"

BY SAM SYKES

BRING DOWN HEAVEN
The City Stained Red
The Mortal Tally (coming 2015)

AEONS' GATE
Tome of the Undergates
Black Halo
Skybound Sea

THE CITY STAINED RED

BRING DOWN HEAVEN
BOOK ONE

SAM SYKES

www.orbitbooks.net

Copyright © 2014 by Sam Sykes
Excerpt from *The Black Prism* copyright © 2010 by Brent Weeks
Excerpt from *Promise of Blood* copyright © 2013 by Brian McClellan
Map by Lee Moyer

Orbit
Hachette Book Group
1290 Avenue of the Americas
New York, NY 10104

Printed in the United States of America

Orbit is an imprint of Hachette Book Group.
The Orbit name and logo are trademarks of Little, Brown Book Group Limited.

ISBN 978-1-62953-371-1

THE
CITY
STAINED
RED

the **Western Sea**

Harbor Road

the **Meat Market**

the **Sumps**

Sea Wall

the **Silken Spire**

Shict Town

the **Tribelands**

Silk
Town

the
Souk

the
Tower
Resolute

the
Horned
God

Temple Row

the
city
of Cier'
Djaal

the
Sovereign

FACTIONS

Fasha

Jackal

Khovura

Shict

Tulwar

Karnerian

Sainite

ACT ONE

THE HUMAN TIDE

PROLOGUE

Cier'Djaal
Some crappy little boat
First day of Yonder

Y ou can't lie to a sword.

It's a trait you don't often think of between its more practical applications, but part of the appeal of a blade is that it keeps you honest. No matter how much of a hero you might think you are for picking it up, no matter how many evildoers you claim to have smitten with it, it's hard to pretend that steel you carry is good for much else besides killing.

Conversely, a sword can't lie to you.

If you can't use it, it'll tell you. If you don't want to use it, it'll decide whether you should. And if you look at it, earnestly, and ask if there's no other way besides killing, it'll look right back at you and say, earnestly, that it can't quite think of any.

Every day I wake up, I look in the corner of my squalid little cabin. I stare at my sword. My sword stares back at me. And I tell it the same thing I've told it every day for months.

"Soon, we reach Cier'Djaal. Soon, we reach a place where there are ways to make coin without killing. Soon, I'm getting off this ship and I'm leaving you far behind."

The sword just laughs.

Granted, this probably sounds a trifle insane, but I'm writing in ink so I can't go back and make it less crazy. But if you're reading this, you're probably anticipating the occasional lapse in sanity.

And if you aren't yet, I highly recommend you start. It'll help.

I've killed a lot of things.

I say "things," because "people" isn't a broad enough category and "stuff" would lead you to believe I don't spend a lot of time thinking about it.

The list thus far: men, women, demons, monsters, giant serpents, giant vermin, regular vermin, regular giants, cattle, lizards, fish, lizardmen, fishmen, frogmen, Cragsmen, and a goat.

Regular goat, mind; not a poisonous magic goat or anything. But he was kind of an asshole.

When I started killing, it seemed like I had good reasons. Survival, I guess. Money, too. But the more I did it, the better I got. And the better I got, the less reason I needed until killing was just something I did.

Easy as shaking a man's hand.

And when it's as easy as shaking a man's hand, you stop seeing open hands. All you see, then, is an empty spot where a sword should be. And will be, if you don't grab yours first.

I'm tired of it.

I don't live in lamentation of my past deeds. I did what I had to, even if I could have thought of something better. I don't hear voices and I don't have nightmares.

Not anymore, anyway.

I guess I'm just tired. Tired of seeing swords instead of hands, tired of looking for chairs against the wall whenever I go into a room, tired of knowing lists instead of people, tired of talking to my sword.

And I'm going to stop. And even if I can't, I have to try.

So I'm going to. Try, that is.

Just as soon as I get my money.

I suppose there's irony in trading blood for gold. Or hypocrisy.

I don't care and I sincerely doubt my employer does, either. Or maybe he does—holy men are odd that way—but he'll pay, anyway. Blood is gold and I've spilled a lot of the former for a considerable sum of the latter.

Ordinarily, you wouldn't think a priest of Talanas, the Healer, to appreciate that much blood. But Miron Evenhands, Lord Emissary and Member in Good Standing of the House of the Vanquishing Trinity, is no ordinary priest. As the former title implies, he's a man with access

to a lot of wealth. And as the latter title is just cryptic enough to suggest, he's got a fair number of demons, cultists, and occult oddities to be
eradicated.

And eradicate I have, with gusto.

And he has yet to pay. "Temporary barriers to the financial flow," he
tells me. "Patience, adventurer, patience," he says. And patient I was.
Patient enough to follow him across the sea for months until we came
here.

Cier'Djaal, the City of Silk. This is the great charnel house where
poor men eat dead rich men and become wealthy themselves. This is the
city where fortunes are born, alive and screaming. This is the city that
controls the silk, the city that controls the coin, the city that controls the
world.

This is civilization.

This is what I want now.

My companions, too.

Or so I'd like to think.

It's not as though anyone chooses to be an adventurer, killing people
for little coin and even less respect. We all took up the title, and each other's company, with the intent of leaving it behind someday. Cier'Djaal is
as good as any a place to do so, I figure.

Though their opinions on our arrival have been... varied.

That Gariath should be against our entrance into any place where
he might be required to wear a shirt, let alone a place crawling with
humans, is no surprise.

Far more surprising are Denaos's objections—the man who breathes
liquor and uses whores for pillows, I would have thought, would feel
right at home among the thieves and scum of civilized society.

Asper and Dreadaeleon, happy to be anywhere that has a temple or
a wizard tower, were generally in favor of it. Asper for the opportunity
to be among civilized holy men, Dreadaeleon for the opportunity to be
away from uncivilized laymen, both for the opportunity to be in a place
with toilets.

When I told Kataria, she just sort of stared.

Like she always does.

Which made my decision as to what to do next fairly easy. This will be the last of our time spent together. Once I've got my money, once I can leave my sword behind, I intend to leave them with it.

Their opinions on this have been quiet.

Possibly because I haven't told them yet.

Probably because I won't until I'm far enough away that I can't hear my sword laughing at me anymore.

ONE

AN ARCHITECT OF BONE
AND MARROW

He smelled the corpses before they came.

That odorous smell of sun-cooked meat heralded the corpse-wagon long before the rattling of wheels and jangling of priestly chains could announce the presence. Captain Dransun pulled out the kerchief he wore beneath his Jhouche guard badge and held it over his unshaven face. He had not yet seen enough death to be inured to the stink.

But, then, it was only the beginning of the week.

"Hold up, hold up," he commanded the petitioners lining up before him, waving them aside. "Gevrauchians coming through."

No protests. Not so much as a word from the unruly crowd at the mention of the death priests. The press of flesh that had demanded to enter the city since dawn shuffled quietly aside. The impending procession required lots of room.

Before anything else, he saw the lanterns. Lit despite the noon-day sun and glowing with a cold brightness, the caged lights of the priests swung on long, willowy boughs strapped to their stooped backs like the lure lights of fish from a deep, dark place. Behind the glass circles sewn into their burlap masks, neither face nor eye could be seen.

This made them only slightly more unnerving than their cargo.

Drawn by the Lanterns, the corpsewagon groaned like an old man as it was hauled through the gates. The petitioners impolitely covered their mouths at the sight of burlap-wrapped bodies in various stages of dismemberment.

The Lanterns didn't care any more than the dead. Followers of the Bookkeeper were notoriously hard to offend.

As Dransun watched the cart thresh a wake through the humanity thronging the harbor, he became aware that he had been holding his breath. Whether from smell or some omen he had yet to give a name to, he began to release it, only to have it leap right back into his mouth when he felt a hand upon his shoulder. He whirled about, reflexively reaching for his sword.

The Quill, so named for the rank bestowed on those senior Gevrauchians, stared through tiny glass circles. The spear-long rolled-up scroll strapped to his back glistened with cleanliness not shown his black ceremonial garb. His glove, particularly rotten with grime and dried blood, thrust a similar, if smaller, scroll toward Dransun.

"Twelve bodies today," he said, voice flat behind his burlap mask. "Seven identified, dismemberments excluded. Please place this upon your notice board at your leisure, Captain, and remind families they have eight days to collect their loved ones before Gevrauch's Right is assumed."

"Right," Dransun replied, taking the scroll from him. "Will this be the last time you come through today or . . ."

"Death is an inevitability, Captain," the Quill reminded him. "As is our duty. We come when we are required. And we are required often of late."

"Yes, I *get* that," Dransun replied through clenched teeth. "It's just that the fashas are getting antsy. All this death and violence are bad for business."

"Your employers should consult those who make the corpses. We merely clean up after them. Death is our business, Captain. Business is always good in Cier'Djaal."

Dransun felt the color drain from his face. The Quill stared back for a moment before scratching the back of his head.

"That was a joke," the priest muttered. "We shall return later, Captain."

After the Quill departed, Dransun hesitated to wave the crowd back into place. Seemed pointless; this wouldn't be the last visit from the Lanterns today. They were always finding new victims in the Souk.

And yet, wave them back into line he did. These were the merchants, after all: the spice men, the artisans, the dust dealers, and the trade bosses. This was Cier'Djaal, where the only things more constant than death and odor were coin and protocol. The Gevrauchians could concern themselves with the death of the city. Dransun's concerns were for the life of it.

And more specifically, for those who would spill it on the ground.

"All right, then." Dransun tucked the scroll into his belt and produced his logbook. Sparing a quick glance for the towering petitioner before him, he flipped open the page and pressed charcoal to paper. "Name?"

"Daaru."

"Daaru." He jotted it down. "And what is your—"

"Saan Rua Tong Clan."

"No, I wanted to know your—"

"Born from the bleeding stomach of Rua, when the dead God earned His name, born from the sands—"

"Oh, son of a bitch..." Dransun muttered, it only occurring to him then to take a closer look.

A pair of yellow eyes, wide and wild as daybreak, didn't bother looking back.

A head taller than any man present, even without the jagged mane masquerading as hair, the creature was deep in the throes of reciting his ancestry. Hairy, apelike hands provided accompanying gestures. Lips peeled back with every word, flashing teeth so large and sharp as should only belong on an animal.

"Who the *hell* let a tulwar in line?" Dransun called out to his subordinates, who looked up briefly from their own lines and shrugged. "What do you turds think we have all these protocol meetings for?"

"—and painted the walls with his own blood," the beast called Daaru continued, "and when my father did dislodge the spear in a gout of—"

"No, no, *no*." Dransun held up his hands. "Didn't you read the signs? *No tulwar*."

Only at this did Daaru stop.

His glare ran a long journey down his face. Thick scars mapped the simian slope of his nose and overlong jaws in symmetry that Dransun couldn't quite grasp. Too smooth, too perfect to be from any battle, they began to fill with a wild splendor of red, blue, and yellow color as Daaru bared his teeth in a growl.

Dransun hid his fear behind an unblinking blue stare. The Jhouche were little more than the face of Cier'Djaal, but the fashas demanded they be an unflinching one.

"No tulwar," he repeated firmly. "No shicts. No vulgores. *No oids*." He gestured to the parchments plastered across the Harbor Gates. "Souk's on high alert. Unless you come in with round ears, flat teeth, and coin to trade, you don't come in."

"Trade." Daaru repeated the word with black enthusiasm. "I come with trade."

His hand settled on the grip of the long, curved blade strapped to his hip, a perfect match for the shorter one tucked beneath it.

"I come with swords." His smile was feral and unpleasant. "Your streets are awash with blood. The death priests come day and night. The city you built on the backs of my people begins to crack. Let the tulwar solve the human problem."

"The fashas have their own forces," Dransun replied. "*Human* forces. We don't need more swords. Let alone those considered..."

His voice and eyes trailed off the tulwar and onto the petitioners behind, attention caught on a short man wedged uneasily in line, glancing about nervously.

"Unstable," Dransun murmured.

Admittedly, the man might not have been planning to do anything. Men under six feet tall typically possessed an air of twitchy suspicion as a matter of nature.

Regardless, he rapped his gauntleted fingers upon his pauldron. His guardsmen spared a brief nod for the signal before giving their swords a shake to loosen them in their scabbards.

"The Uprising was in response to *your* city expanding," Daaru snarled, demanding Dransun's attention. "You brought *your* swords to *our* homes. And now that we have a taste for blood, you've lost your appetite?"

"That's life," Dransun sighed, glancing back at the twitchy man.

"*This* is *death*," Daaru snorted. "My father died in the Uprising so that I could stand here. And now you deny me the right to avenge him even as I do your dirty work. This is not over, human. Before I am done I will spill the blood of your—"

"Ancaa alive, I *get* it," Dransun snapped suddenly, turning his ire back to the tulwar. "Boo hoo, humans are so mean. The Uprising is over and you *lost*, oid. The city needs swords that'll answer to authority, and it doesn't pay for dramatic speeches unless they're on a stage. So either slap on a costume more ridiculous than what you've got on or *get lost*."

Dransun didn't bother paying attention to the threat Daaru made as the tulwar stalked away. His attentions followed the short man in the crowd, growing twitchier.

He was short, wiry to the point of being too skinny for the sword he carried upon his back. His face was far too young for the harsh angles of his jaw and nose and the many scars on his chin and bare arms. Far, *far* too young for hair the gray color of an old man's, but it hung around his face in poorly trimmed locks all the same.

And yet the cold blue eyes matched perfectly. Dransun recognized the stare of a man who had earned those scars, even from the Harbor Gate.

He knew the stares of men like these, just as he knew what ran through their heads. He laid a hand on the pommel of his sword and waved the next person forward.

— ·—ΞΞ·— —

Son of a bitch, Lenk thought. *He saw you.* He looked down at his hands. *Obviously. You're twitching like a dust-snorter three days clean.*

This was bad. This whole plan was bad. Why had he even listened to Denaos for this? What on earth would that thug know about breaking into a city?

Probably more than a little, Lenk admitted to himself. *But if this was such a genius plan, why isn't he here to see it executed?* He glanced over his shoulder, searching for a sign of his scraggly companion. *Likely because he doesn't want to be around to see* you *executed, the coward.*

He looked back up over the heads of the people in the crowd. The surly-looking guard at the Harbor Gate looked embroiled in an argument with whoever was trying to get through. His fellow guards looked equally busy with their lines.

Denaos was nowhere to be seen. His other companions were likewise worthless. Once again, it was down to Lenk to get everything done.

Right. Deep breaths. Try not to look crazy.

He pulled himself out of line and began to walk past people toward the gate. Head down, eyes forward, wearing a face he hoped looked at least a little intimidating. The only way this was going to work was if this no-necked guard believed Lenk was mean enough to not be worth stopping.

"Ah." A gloved hand went up before Lenk's face. "Stop right there."

Of course, he sighed inwardly.

"I didn't specifically *say* 'no mercs,' I know." The surly-looking guard angled his voice down condescendingly. "But I did say no unstable types, didn't I?"

Lenk's hand was up before either of them knew it, slapping the captain's hand away.

"Marshal your words with greater care, friend," he whispered threateningly, voice low and sharp like a knife in the dark. "Or I shall hasten to incite you to greater discipline."

What the hell was that?

The guardsman blinked. Once. Slowly.

"What?"

Well, don't change now. He'll know something's up.

"Was I too soft in my verbiage?" Lenk asked. "Did you not feel the *chill* of death in my words?"

"Look." The guard captain sighed, rubbing his eyes. "I'll tell you what I told the tulwar: no oids, no adventurers, no…whatever the hell you are."

The captain looked him over with a glare that Lenk recognized. Usually, he saw it only a moment before swords were drawn. But the captain's stare was slow, methodical. He was sizing him up, wondering just how much trouble this was going to be worth.

Lenk decided to give him a hint. He slid into a tense stance, making sure to roll his shoulders enough to send the mail under his shirt clinking and show just how easily he wore the sword on his back.

"I don't see any colors on your shirt," the captain muttered. "I don't see any badge at your breast. I don't see coin at your belt. Which means you're not someone I want in my city."

"You're wise to be wary," Lenk said. "And I advise you to listen to that wariness and cut a path for me, lest I show you why my name in the old tongues means 'bane of death.'"

The captain stared and repeated flatly, "Bane of death."

"That's right."

He blinked. "You're serious."

Lenk cleared his throat. "I am."

"No." The captain clutched his head as if in pain. "Just…just no. Back to the harbor, bane of death. No room for your kind here."

"What kind?" Lenk's face screwed up in offense. "A person of my…uh…distinct verbotanage must not be denied righteous passage into—"

"Boy, I wouldn't be impressed by this routine even if you *weren't* as tall as my youngest."

"Look, I don't see what the problem is." The bravado slipped from Lenk's voice in a weary sigh as he rubbed his eyes. "I've got business in the city. In fact, my employer got in shortly before I got here. His name is Miron Evenhands. We both came off the ship *Riptide.* If you'll just let me find him, he'll—"

"Here's the problem," Dransun interrupted. "You've got no colors and no affiliation, but you've got a sword. So you've got the means to kill people, but not the means to be held responsible." He sniffed. "Parents?"

"What?"

"Any parents?"

"Both dead."

"Hometown?"

"Burned to the ground."

"Allies? Compatriots? Friends?"

"Just the ones I find on the road. And in a tavern. And, this one time, hunched over a human corpse, but—"

"And *that's* the problem. You're an *adventurer.*" He spat the word. "Too cowardly to be a mercenary, too greedy to be a soldier, too dense to be a thief. Your profession is wedged neatly between whores and grave robbers in terms of respectability, your trade is death and carnage, and your main asset is that you're completely expendable."

He leaned down to the young man and forced the next words through his teeth.

"I keep this city clean. And you, boy, are garbage."

The young man didn't flinch. His eyes never wavered, not to Dransun's guards reaching for their swords, not to Dransun's gauntlets clenched into fists. That blue gaze didn't so much as blink as he looked the captain straight in the eye, smiled through a split lip, and spoke.

"*Human* garbage."

"And that's when he punched me in the face," Lenk said, as he covered his blackened eye. "So, anyway, that's why we're not getting in through the Harbor Gate." He added a sneer to the black eye he cast at his companion. "Your plans are crap."

"*My* plan?" Denaos's neck nearly snapped with incredulity as he whirled upon Lenk. "*My* plan was for you—not the bane of death— to go up, to wait your turn in line, to tell him you were a beet farmer come to sell your wares, and to go in."

"But I didn't have any beets."

"*It doesn't matter!*" Denaos threw his hands into the air. "You weren't selling beets to him, you were selling the *idea* of beets."

"I don't follow."

"Hence why you have a black eye. Look, it's simple…"

Denaos illustrated the plan with his hands, weaving an elaborate scene in the air as they pushed their way through the crowded harbor streets.

"Cier'Djaal is a city right in the middle of the desert. Something as mundane as a beet is rare and exotic to them and worth *coin*. They invite you in, you tell them you have hired hands with the actual product, we all grab some crates, pretend they're filled with the stuff, and follow in after you."

Lenk turned away from Denaos, looking over the bustling crowd that choked them and to the distant sea from which they had just arrived that morning.

"It was easier out there," he sighed. "In the wild parts of the world, chances were anything you stumbled across was an enemy. And even if it wasn't, you could solve most of your problems with it by jamming a sword in it. No rules, no laws—"

"No toilets," Denaos interrupted.

"Still."

"This is Cier'Djaal, Lenk," the tall man said. "People here don't have to kill for money. That's what you wanted, right?" At Lenk's meek nod, he sneered. "Then you should have stuck with the plan."

"Well, if this is all so easy, why didn't *you* do it?"

Denaos scowled at Lenk through eyes sharpened by suspicion and worn by drink. Or rather, scowled down at Lenk. The man stood infuriatingly taller than Lenk, with a long and limber body wrapped in the kind of black leather that usually accompanied drinking problems and knives in the dark. The fact that Denaos was frequently in the company of both meant that he wasn't the right person to deal with law-abiding folks like guardsmen.

"Fine," Lenk sighed. "My fault, then."

"So, Miron is somewhere over that wall with our money." Denaos gestured over the crowd. "And you fucked up our best chance of getting in. What are you going to tell the others?"

The shrug Lenk offered didn't satisfy either of them. It was too hot to think. Even as the sun beat down overhead, the crowd at the harbor grew ever more oppressive. Sun-skinned, sweaty, smelly, stretched, scorched, scarred, the press of human traffic was a noose tightening around the two men.

Sailors pushed their cargo up and down gangplanks, across harbor stones, over slow people. Guards of the Jhouche stood at the periphery, brandishing logbooks like blades at shrieking merchants. All of this done to the jaunty tune of prostitutes, beggars, and cutpurses plying their trades in a laughing, wailing symphony.

Ruffians, thieves, scum; Lenk had seen worse. He was an adventurer, after all. His were eyes used to noticing danger. But every time he did, he found that danger had already noticed him.

Tulwar, thick gray muscle left bared by their orange and red half-robes, scowls shooting down long faces knotted with gray folds of flesh, strode fearlessly through the berths the crowd gave them. Dark khoshicts lurked at the mouths of alleys and atop piles of crates, peering out from wild manes of braided hair with bright eyes and grins sharp as the necklaces of teeth they wore. Each one they passed gave him a look he knew well. The oids saw him as he saw them: weapons first, people last.

"So many of them," Lenk muttered.

"Of what?" Denaos asked.

"You don't see them? The tulwar? Shicts?"

"What of them?"

"I guess I hadn't expected to see so many of them here. You always hear tales of shicts stalking in the night, tulwar rampaging across the country. You never see them loitering."

"Teats get to choose who suckles them," Denaos said, grunting past a knot of sailors. "Carcasses don't get to choose what flies eat them."

"It just makes me wonder," Lenk said. "Why do they choose to be here instead of among their own kind?"

Denaos cast a sidelong smirk to his companion. "A little hypocritical of you, isn't it?"

Lenk narrowed his eyes on the man, even if it hurt the black one. "I'm allowed to be hypocritical about that particular subject."

"Why's that?"

"Because I know why Kataria chose me."

He hadn't intended that to sound as bitter as it had.

TWO

VERBAL DISEASES

Kataria drew in a slow breath. She closed her eyes against the glare of the sun. She felt pale skin grow pink under its heat. Under the braids of her hair, both of her ears—long and pointed as knives, three notches to either length—rose into the air.

She listened, growing anxious.

She shut her eyes tighter, held her breath, bit her tongue, denied her every sense but the most important one.

For three long breaths, she listened.

And still, she could hear nothing.

"Son of a wh—"

She couldn't even hear herself curse.

She could hear everything else, of course. A towering wall with spiked crenellations separated the tall ships and their docks from the Souk. Humans clambered to somehow cross over that wall and get to the trade on the other side. And the round-ears flowed, like a noisy tide, into every crevice of the harbor. She could hear *that* just fine: all their slurs, their curses, their jokes about genitalia. All their wasted words on stinking breath, she could hear everything.

Everything except *them*.

They stood two hundred paces away. Two of them, tall and limber, their ears long and sharp as spears, skin dark and hair black. Humans had cruder names for them, as they did for her: savages, beasts, *oids*.

She knew them by the name Riffid had given them.

Kho.

Shict. Like her.

They were standing right there. She could feel their dark eyes fixed upon her as she sat atop a stack of crates. They were but a quick stride away. And yet, they may as well have been across the ocean.

Their ears twitched like the antennae of insects. They were reaching out to her with the Howling, the language without words, the communicative instinct shared between all shicts as breath.

"*Hu'aish, pale sister,*" they were saying. "*How far from home are you? There are no trees here. Come and let us embrace you. Come and be away from these reeking kou'ru. Be amongst family. Be among your kind. Come to us.*"

At least, that was what she imagined them saying.

She could feel the intent in their stares. They were trying to speak to her. And she heard nothing. And, feeling the red-hot shame in her own face, she pulled her broad-brimmed hat over her head and looked down.

No one could say why a shict lost the ability to use the Howling. It wasn't something anyone ever talked about in her tribe when she left. There were theories, of course: consumption of black herbs, a weak bloodline, prolonged contact with humans. That was the most popular theory.

To breathe their air was to drink toxin. To take their gold was to invite infection. To feel the chill of their skin against the warmth of a shict's own vibrant flesh...

Well, she already knew what happened when she did *that*.

She hopped off her perch and disappeared behind a stack of crates. A flutter of movement caught her eye and she had to restrain herself from starting.

Gariath had been standing so still, his black cloak blending into the shadow so seamlessly, she almost forgot he was there.

One didn't notice Gariath in the same way one didn't notice a tree. One never *really* appreciated a creature of his size until he came crashing down on someone's head.

"No sign of them yet," Kataria said. "Hope you don't mind staying here for a little while longer."

"I didn't." Gariath's voice rumbled out of his hood in a deep growl. "Until you came back." Kataria glared at him and he snorted. "How much longer?"

"Infiltrations take time."

"Grabbing a rock and bashing someone's head in takes only moments. But for some reason we're trying to sneak in like rats."

"No one asked you."

"If they had, we'd be in already."

Kataria's sole response was an irate scowl. But it wasn't for Gariath; she didn't have the muscle for the kind of ire that he would warrant.

Her irritation was for the fact that, despite the roaring curses and hateful mutters of the human tide, she could hear the sound of footsteps. Light, wary strides moving quickly across stones.

His footsteps.

That she could always hear *him* might have given some other girl comfort. One who *wasn't* deaf to her own people.

It just infuriated her.

"I smell failure," Gariath muttered. "They've returned."

"I resent that."

She turned to see Lenk approaching. She didn't know what failure smelled like—she suspected fish and lemons—but he didn't look successful. The differences in his moods were subtle and it freshly irritated her that she knew them.

"If I smell like failure, it's only because I listened to *him*." The young man gestured behind him.

"A plan is only as brilliant as its executor," Denaos said, following after. "If you had just stuck to the story, we'd be in."

"You didn't go with beet farmers?" Kataria asked, quirking a brow. At Lenk's sheepish grin, she sighed and rubbed her eyes. "You did the 'bane of death' thing, didn't you?"

"Oh, *come on*," Lenk protested. "I figured that intimidation would be quicker than treachery."

"Yes, but all good intimidation is *steeped* in treachery," Denaos pointed out.

"And you have the height, mass, and silky locks of a little girl." Kataria plucked a single silver strand of hair from his head. "Terrifying."

"If he were a girl, we wouldn't have this problem." Denaos's eyes slipped over to Kataria with practiced appraisal. "In fact, perhaps the guards might be better persuaded by..."

He took her in with a few quick glances, from her bright green eyes to the lean archer's muscle left bare by the crop of her dusty leathers. He let out an approving hum, a plan coming to life behind his eyes.

Just as the snarl she shot him killed it dead.

"Think they'd like these?" She ran her tongue across a pair of overlarge canines. "They can strip a deer's femur in forty breaths."

Kataria fixed her scowl on Denaos as she reached up and pulled her hat from her head. Unkempt blond hair laced with long, dirty feathers tumbled to her shoulders. Her pointed ears shot up, rigid like arrows in a carcass.

"Or how about these?" They flattened against her head as she bared her teeth at Denaos. "What can I do to get us into this festering wound of a round-ear nest? The sooner we can get our money and are rid of each other, the better; am I right?"

"Pretty mu—"

Lenk cut Denaos off with a raised hand, looking warily at Kataria. "Is something wrong?"

"No, Lenk, I go into a spitting rant as a matter of routine," she snarled at him.

Lenk coughed. "Well, I wouldn't say it's a *routine*, but—"

"Never mind." She jammed her hat back on, tucking her ears beneath it. "At this rate, I'll be dead of old age before we get in and this won't be a problem."

"There is no problem," Gariath rumbled from his hood. "There are only three walking stacks of meat between us and your gold."

His black cloak parted with just a flash of dull crimson. A pair of clawed hands, broad and heavy, tightened into sledges of scarred flesh and trembled with all the wrong kinds of excitement.

"Let me shed this pathetic disguise and I'll finish this for you."

From beneath his hood, the dragonman's blood-colored snout split into a smile full of sharp teeth.

"We've discussed this," Lenk said with a sigh. "This? This stuff you say? This is why you have to wear the cloak."

Gariath's arms dropped.

"We never get to do anything I want to do."

"Because all you ever want to do is *kill* people," Lenk shot back. "And we're trying to *stop* doing that. That's the whole point of getting in there. Once we find Miron and our money, we're done."

"*We* never agreed to anything. *One* of us *decided* that," Kataria snorted. "You didn't ask anyone else."

"As you damn well noticed, adventuring isn't getting us anywhere and I'm not the only one who would say so."

"Oh yeah? Who else?"

"What about Asper?" Lenk asked.

"What *about* her?" Kataria demanded in reply.

"What about me?" a third voice chimed in.

The assembled went silent at the appearance of a tall woman in their midst. Though her robes were dusty and workmanlike and her long brown hair was wrapped in a businesslike braid beneath a blue bandanna, she carried with her an air of authority. Partly because of the silver phoenix pendant about her throat, a sigil of her station as a priestess of Talanas, but mostly because of the suspicious glare she shot them.

"You all went quiet very quickly. What were you talking about?" She must have seen something in their forced nonchalance, for her eyes widened. "Oh, for the love of…were you planning a murder?"

"*Discussing*," Lenk said, holding up a finger. "Discussing a murder. Not planning."

"We're not even in the city yet!" Asper protested. "You're not *allowed* to get us executed before we at least see the Souk!"

"It's not a crime until you actually do it," Denaos muttered. "And we entertained other options first."

"What happened to the beet-farmer plan?" Asper asked. "I was out trying to find crates we could use for it. I *liked* that plan."

"Most of us did," Denaos said, angling a sidelong glare at Lenk. "But now we don't have beets and, like most men deprived of edible roots, we turn to murder."

"I can't tell if you're serious or not and that always makes me uncomfortable." Asper tugged at her pendant. "I'm a priestess. A respectable member of society. I'm in."

"*You're* in," Lenk said. "We're still out here. And they're not going to believe we're with you."

Asper surveyed them: the short man with the sword, the tall man with the knives, the shict with the fangs, and…Gariath.

"Probably not," she said, sighing. "Well, maybe I could go in and find Miron and bring him back out? Or…" Her eyes lit up. "We could ask Dreadaeleon."

"But chances are good that he already figured out a way in and went without us," Lenk replied.

Kataria folded her arms over her chest. "He's a greasy little boy in a dirty little coat who spends more time trying to hide his erections than he does speaking. What use is he?"

"He can fly," Lenk said.

"Ah." She sniffed. "Well, he's not here, is he?" She shuffled her feet, glanced to Gariath. "So…murder?"

"*No murder*," Lenk and Asper shouted at once.

"Then let's get back on the ship we came in on and forget this whole cesspool!" Kataria snarled.

"We are *not* going back!"

Asper's eyelid twitched. She was aware of it, of course: the anger, the yelling, the hideously uncomfortable sexual tension. But she needed listen only for a few moments more. Meditatively, she counted down from ten breaths.

Nine...eight... She held her breath. A faint smile crept across her face. *Ah, there it is.*

The comforting numbness set in at the back of her brain, as it usually did when they started screaming. A marvelous self-preservation instinct, or maybe a hemorrhage that would someday kill her; either way, she wouldn't have to listen anymore.

Not that she didn't care. She had cared quite a bit when she set out with these people. Like all good servants of the Healer, she had cared a tad too much. She tossed her concern around like a rich man's coin, frittering it away on every problem she saw. Experience had taught her to be more frugal with her compassion. If they had a problem she could help with, she would.

Lenk and Kataria's particular brand of problem was not one of them.

But it had been well past ten breaths now. Their shrieking was a faint buzzing noise in her ear. And in her meditation, she noticed Denaos, likewise oblivious to the ruckus as he tended his nails with a small knife.

And an idea struck her.

Nonchalance to obscenity was a façade he wore well, usually because it was rarely a façade. But she had seen his many masks, and she knew how to spot the tears in them: his jaw was clenched; his body was taut and wary beneath his leathers. But the most telling sign was the fact that he was leaning against a wall that separated him from a world of whores, liquor, gold, and other illicit joys, trying to pretend like he didn't care.

"You're not looking well," she said, approaching him.

"You and I both know that I look amazing right now." He cast a glance at her from beneath unruly hair. "But what makes you say that?"

"I know you well enough, Denaos," she said. "And you know me."

She glanced at his fingers. "Also, you're trying to trim fingernails that you chewed away days ago."

"It's rather unfair of you to use obvious evidence against me." He hid his hand behind his back. "But then, I trust you're not actually concerned about my well-being."

"I am. But I'm more curious." Asper looked over her shoulder at Lenk and Kataria, as the former extended his chin, challenging the latter to take a swing. "You could have had us through the gate in no time. If you had been the one to lead the beet stratagem—"

"Let's not call it that."

"You could have gotten us past the guards in six words," Asper said. "But Lenk went instead."

"He's the leader." Denaos cringed at the sight of Kataria leaping atop Lenk, teeth bared and snarling. "Supposedly."

"In battle, sure. In other things…" She shared his cringe as she heard a decidedly unmanly scream from behind her. "Not so much."

"Point being?"

"Point being, you obviously know this city and how to get in," she continued, "and you're obviously not bringing it to anyone's attention, so you obviously don't care when or if you get into Cier'Djaal."

He said nothing. He didn't have to. She could see his mask fraying at the edges, in the crow's-feet of his eyes.

"But why?" she asked aloud. "Past that wall lies gold, women, liquor…everything you've missed from civilization. If you *don't* want to be in there, that must mean—"

"May I make a counterpoint?"

"Please."

"Shut up."

"That's not a counterpoint."

"Will it make you shut up?"

"Almost certainly not."

"Then what will?"

Denaos was not without his own knowledge of her. She knew he could see the answer in her determined stare. He sighed and slipped his knife back into a hidden sheath.

"Fine. I'll get us in," he muttered. He smoothed his tunic as he turned to walk away. "Tell the others to spread out and move in one at a time when I give the signal."

"The signal being?"

"You won't miss it," he replied. "Will this shut you up?"

"On this subject? Maybe for a bit."

"And do you ever stop to think about the ethical implications of getting things done by annoying people into doing them?"

Asper turned about and saw Kataria on Lenk's back, arm wrapped around his throat as he flailed behind him, trying to seize her to peel her off. She grinned triumphantly at Denaos.

"Only for the first ten breaths."

THREE

TO FLOW, AS THE RIVER

It had taken a lot of lost time and lost blood for him to figure out the great lessons of life, but Lenk had learned a few. And the most important and painful of them was that when Denaos said he had a plan and didn't immediately offer specifics, it was just wisest not to ask.

Perhaps it wasn't the best method of leadership. Certainly, such laxity wasn't the best quality in a leader. Proper commanders—the great generals and merc captains—would have had a better plan and an iron will to guide unwavering loyalties, their troops flowing like rivers toward their purpose. But those were men. Respected. Honored. Warriors.

Lenk was an adventurer. He had a thug, a priestess, a shict, an absent wizard...and Gariath. And between all of them, only one of them seemed to have a plan better than "run in and hope no one dies."

Perhaps they wouldn't flow in. But rivers did more than flow. They seeped, they flooded, and, in the worst cases, they simply rushed forward and everyone else got out of their way.

Not a good way for a man to lead.

But for an adventurer? It wasn't bad.

He stood at the edge of the harbor, his eyes on the Harbor Gate, directly across the human-choked road. The Jhouche guards spared him not so much as a glance. They had no idea what was about to happen.

Lenk would have taken more comfort in that if he had a better idea than they.

Beside the Harbor Gate, two massive stacks of crates bearing the sigil of a local fasha—an emblem of a naked girl upon a bed of coins—had been arranged with painstaking delicacy near the end of the lines of petitioners. It was behind these crates that his companions loitered: Kataria and Gariath lurking in the shadows on one side, Asper pretending not to notice them on the other.

And Denaos was nowhere to be seen.

Maybe he's not actually coming back. Maybe he's going to rat us out to the guards and ask for passage as reward. He bit his lower lip. *Not a bad idea, actually.*

He eyed the guard captain from across the way, the tall man with the hard chin, and wondered if he might be able to get that deal for himself.

It kind of makes sense, doesn't it? I'm the one who wants out of this. I'm the one who needs the money. Asper can always go back to the clergy. Denaos won't ever have trouble getting by. Dreadaeleon's a wizard; he'll never want for anything. Nothing could stop Gariath from doing what he wants. And Kataria...

His eyes drifted to her at the shadows. He knew she was staring at him before he even saw her. Pale and stark in the shadows, eyes vivid and sharp as spears, leveled right at him.

Even in the best of times, she always seemed to look at him the same way she would size up a chunk of roasted venison.

These were not the best of times. These were the times when all he saw was her scowl, her anger, her very large teeth bared in a snarl.

"Forty breaths..." he whispered. His face screwed up. "*Really?*"

"How much of a man do you suppose you can fit in a crate?"

At the voice, Lenk looked up with a start to behold a man standing beside him. Though how a man such as this had approached him without him noticing, he wasn't quite sure.

Clad in robes so white and unsullied as to be surreal, he stood painfully close, hands folded delicately behind his back. His face was long and elegant, cheekbones fine and lips thin. His skin, dark like any Djaalic's, was clean and free of blemishes, and his black hair glistened with a light sheen of oil.

His appearance unnerved Lenk, and not just because of how filthy it made him look by contrast. He looked too perfect, too serene to be in the harbor at all, let alone to have appeared out of nowhere as he did.

"You see how they all crowd around their possessions?" The man in white gestured over the harbor. "As though a man can take his heart, his lungs, his liver and wrap them in paper and stack them neatly atop each other inside a little box. As though, so long as those precious pieces of a man are in that box, he cannot be harmed."

He turned to Lenk. His eyes were alight with a curiosity that belonged on a dirtier man. His lips curled into a smile.

"For what else is there to harm once a man is in his box?"

Lenk blinked. He slowly looked for whom the man might be talking to, wondering if perhaps he had unwittingly come between *two* eerie, philosophy-spewing pretty men. With no such luck, he realized that the question had been posed to him.

"Uh," he said, "I suppose once that happens, a man starts looking to his box. His...box full of guts."

"And if there were no box? If it were far away or buried elsewhere?"

"Then...he can't be harmed, I suppose."

The man in white nodded carefully. He swept a thoughtful look from Lenk to the Harbor Gate, choked with people.

"You wish to enter?" he asked.

Lenk's first thought was not to answer. He was, presumably, supposed to be acting nonchalant enough for people not to assume that.

"A lot of people do," Lenk settled on saying. "There are a lot of boxes past that gate."

"A lot." The man in white spoke the words softly, tasting them. "So many lives tucked away in so many boxes. How many do you think?"

"A hundred, at least," Lenk replied, looking over the crowd.

"And they all funnel to that one tiny point guarded by three tiny men." The man in white made a gesture over the spanning Harbor Wall. "Seal this up, make it a wall with no doors, you will find men climbing it, burrowing under it, breaking through it in half the time that it takes to walk through it. Put one tiny hole, offer them that one escape, they'll go through it, no matter how long it takes, ignoring the many other entries."

Lenk let out a thoughtful hum, considering them. He scanned the crowd briefly for Denaos and found nothing. He had just begun to reconsider not trying to sneak in when he became aware of another stare fixed upon him. He turned to see the man in white, eyes brimming with something brighter than curiosity, darker than malice.

Lenk blinked and looked around.

"What?" he asked.

"Do strange men come and offer you cryptic advice as a matter of routine?" His smile piqued. "Are you not at all alarmed by this, my friend?"

"Well... I mean, a *little*, sure."

"Only a little?" The man in white chuckled. "Am I really that dull? Are you not utterly mystified by my presence?"

"Look," Lenk sighed, rubbing his eyes. "In case the scars and the sword aren't suggestion enough, I've lived a strange life. So strange, in fact, that I just don't have the energy to be utterly mystified by every weird thing I come across anymore."

He met the man in white's stare, and something within those dark eyes spurred him. He saw something steady, something that suggested it could handle what he'd wanted to say for a long time. And Lenk, without really knowing why, took a deep breath, and said it.

"I don't even think I can remember how many I've killed," he spoke. "People. Men. Women. Monsters, beasts... demons. Things that shouldn't exist. But they do. And I've killed them. I've killed... so many of them."

It wasn't until he said those last words, he wasn't aware of his heart pounding, of his breath gone short, of the drop of sweat forming at his temple. Images of them, his many enemies, the many bodies, their many faces, flooded his mind. He was aware, briefly, of the ache in a palm used to the grip of steel.

And then he let his breath out. He wiped away the sweat, told himself it was the noonday sun. And he was aware of the strange look the man in white affixed on him now.

And he remembered why he was here in Cier'Djaal.

"And when I told her...when I told *them*, they had exactly that look," Lenk said. "So, you're something that shouldn't be, or you're like me. A killer pretending not to be. Either way, I don't have the energy for you."

He turned back to the crowd. Before the man even spoke, Lenk could feel his smile boring into his neck, like a knife.

"You think you won't find blood in this city?"

He turned. A knife, it turned out, was an apt description for his smile. His lips were a small scalpel with a dirty edge, one used by a gutter-healer to cut arrowheads out of criminals.

"You think all these people, all the gold they trade behind those walls will make them less violent?"

"What?" Lenk asked.

"I've seen a great many things myself. A man used to killing is one I've seen often. The twitch of your muscles, the flex of your fingers, the way your voice raises just slightly when you think words are about to become blades..." The man in white's voice escaped on an unnervingly whimsical sigh. "Don't worry. It's not something you should be afraid of. Just something you should be aware of."

"What is, exactly?" Lenk asked.

The man folded his hands delicately behind his back again. He looked to the rivers of humanity crossing through the Harbor Road and smiled.

"Men don't become less violent when they store their guts in a box; they just become bolder. Men don't become civil when they're offered a hole through; they just become desperate. Men who can live without violence, without blood or gold, recognize the same thing."

"And what's that?"

Lenk's breath caught in his throat, his mouth suddenly too dry to speak; he was aware of just how bad he wanted the man in white to answer him.

And the man in white looked at him. And the man in white smiled broadly.

"That there's only one way to live," he said, "and that's without boxes or holes."

He walked out into the Harbor Road, floating like a specter. And like a specter, he moved with an unsettling grace. He didn't brush against a single hairbreadth of filthy, sweaty skin. His robes barely stirred at the press of people that seemed to part before him like a river before a ship.

And when he came to the Harbor Gate, he simply walked through. He looked at no one and nothing more than a simple glance was cast his way as he strode through the gate and disappeared into the Souk beyond as though he had never even been.

That, Lenk thought, was something strange.

Certainly not the strangest thing he had ever seen, though.

He was about to see that, or something close to it; he was certain. For at that moment, he spied Denaos walking toward the Harbor Gate.

Among the human tide, no one looked twice at him. Lenk, however, held his breath. He wasn't looking at Denaos, either.

And neither, Lenk saw, were Denaos's targets.

He spotted the tulwar right away; a gap that wide in the human tide was impossible to miss. Amber eyes set firmly forward peering out of the gray folds of his simian face, the brutish creature seemed to take no heed of the great swaths of humanity surrounding him, let alone the lanky, black-clad man who brushed past him.

Lenk tensed; no plan involving a tulwar was one he wanted to be a part of. But Denaos kept walking past the brute. Lenk felt his jaw and ass unclenching. He felt the urge to act passing.

At least until he saw the khoshicts.

Two of them, stalking down the Harbor Road, the crowd giving them an even wider berth than the tulwar. Lenk could see flashes of dark skin bearing dark tattoos beneath dark cloaks, shiny black hair braided wildly and woven with feathers. Behind their hoods, he could see their eyes, wide and white as their sharp-toothed grins.

Lenk cringed. They reminded him unnervingly of Kataria's own teeth. Still, they weren't quite as unnerving as the wink Denaos shot his way as the rogue brushed against the tallest khoshict.

His pulse quickened. His eyes widened. He felt his ass all but weld itself shut. Denaos stood between the tulwar and the sandshicts as they moved in opposite directions, a triumphant smile on his face. He held up a hand, a pilfered shictish dagger dangling between his fingers.

It happened too quickly for Lenk to notice. With a snap of his wrist, Denaos sent the dagger flying. Wordlessly, the rogue mouthed: "*Trust me.*"

No one would have heard him, anyway. Not over the howl of a tulwar trying to dig a hurled dagger out of his shoulder.

The human tide ebbed. The berth around the oids widened. Eyes awash in inappropriate excitement and horror looked on as the tulwar groped and grabbed blindly at the hilt jutting from his shoulder blade. A thick hand found it, pulled it free with a wrenching sound and a spatter of blood. When the creature whirled around, bloodied blade in hand, his eyes were alight with rage.

"*SHICT!*" His roar split the crowd, exposing the two creatures.

The casualness with which they turned to face him was almost insulting. One of their hoods fell back, revealing an impish female face piqued with curiosity. The second, taller, cocked a head at the tulwar. Ears, long like spears and notched with four deep ridges in each length, rose out of holes in his hood and twitched attentively.

"I assume you're talking to us?" A distinctly masculine, if hollow, voice rang out from beneath his hood.

"I see no one else here who would strike a proud warrior from behind like a rat," the tulwar barked.

"Are rats typically known for striking from behind?" the female khoshict asked. "Asp would be more appropriate, thematically."

"You insult us, monkey." The tall one pulled back his hood. A grinning mask carved from dark red wood stared out at the tulwar with frozen, unnerving glee. "Had it been us, you'd not be alive to scream."

The tulwar's lips peeled back, fangs bared. His face began to flood with color. A cacophony of yellow, red, and blue blossomed across the folds of formerly gray flesh. Lenk's eyebrows rose; he had always heard tales of the tulwar's distinctive facial colorations. "War paint," they called it, and with it came a fury that was legendary.

"I mean to do more than insult." His life slick on his palms, the tulwar's hands slid to the twin blades at his hip. "Before humans, before shicts, we stood on this land. Every son and daughter of Tul has bled upon these sands." They slid out of their wooden sheaths, long and hungry as the snarl painting the tulwar's face. "Their honor is mine."

The khoshicts' cloaks slipped back. They wore nothing but sandals and kilts, the long, dark muscle of their torsos wild with painted sigils. Their hands slid easily to the sickle-shaped swords at their waists. The one in the mask cocked his head to the side.

"We are nothing if not indulgent, *kou'ru*," he said. "If you feel this earth is thirsty, we are happy to slake it."

"Ecstatic," the female said, sliding blade into hand as her canines flashed in a grin. "Really."

This was your plan, Denaos?

Not that it didn't make a good spectacle, Lenk thought: Excited chatter rippled through the assembled crowd; shouts of encouragement and derision from the human onlookers collided in the air over the combatants' heads; money wagers began to change hands. All eyes were eagerly on the oid blood about to be spilled.

All eyes save the ones that counted, anyway.

The Jhouche guards at the Harbor Gate looked up with only passing interest. The rule of law in Cier'Djaal, it turned out, was really more of a loose guideline. And certainly the prospect of a few dead oids and a little stopped foot traffic wasn't worth disrupting their precious lines over.

He found Denaos in the crowd and mouthed the word: *What?*

Denaos shot him the same unnerving wink and mouthed a reply: *Watch.*

The rogue glanced to the edge of the Harbor Gate and gave a curt nod. The painstakingly stacked pyramid of crates bore a new passenger. At the very top, Lenk saw Kataria. Kataria didn't seem to see him, though. Her eyes were on the scene down below, on the khoshicts.

And she stared at them as she had stared at him. With longing. With anger. With sorrow.

Eventually, she noticed Denaos. With a nod, she leaned down and gave the crates a stiff push. Shict and crates tumbled down as one, the former scampering into the shadows as the latter split apart, scattering silks and spices upon the stones.

Lenk furrowed his brow in confusion. Nothing about this made sense.

Not until the earth began to shake beneath his feet, anyway.

The tide of people did not so much ripple as part in two tremendous waves to give path to the enormous shape that came loping up the road. Lenk's eyes went wide at the sight as he stepped back as far as he dared to let the creature pass without incident.

Resembling nothing so much as the product of a gorilla and a rhinoceros that saw admirable qualities in each other before they sobered up, a great beast lumbered toward the scene upon knuckles and feet the size of shields. Possessed of simian features with a long, twisted horn jutting from the center of its brow, it swept a pair of beady eyes around angrily.

The crowd shifted nervously, even the tulwar and khoshicts lowering their weapons. For had the monstrosity and irritability of the vulgores not already been legendary, it just wasn't a good idea to be too close to something with big, red tree trunks for arms.

Branded upon the creature's harness was the sigil of the naked girl atop the mountain of gold, the same that branded the crates shattered on the ground. It was only when people noticed this that murmurs of apprehension turned to whispers of fear.

The last one to notice this was the vulgore himself. When he spoke, his voice was that of a mountain. A mountain that had drunk far too much the night before.

"Kudj see many small squibs crowded around many small boxes. Boxes another squib paid Kudj to watch," the vulgore rumbled. "Kudj stack in very polite, very precise method so no squibs topple box. But squibs topple box, anyway. Kudj wonder if perhaps Mother right. Kudj wonder if civility only as strong as weakest person participating."

He drew in a long, deep breath. The crowd followed suit, holding it.

"But Kudj still believe in decency. Kudj believe in civilization. Kudj have faith in all people."

He exhaled, slowly, and nodded his massive, horned head.

"This why Kudj limit imminent rampage to six corpses or less."

And that, Lenk thought, *would be the sign.*

Further thought became impossible a moment later. An earth-shaking roar of fury and a screaming man flung from a colossal arm into the harbor provided a lot of distraction.

And apparently, that had been the plan all along, Lenk thought. For as the crowd dissipated into so much human froth, fleeing this way and that as the vulgore swung, smashed, and screamed across the harbor, the guards at the gate immediately drew swords and moved to intervene. In no great hurry.

Their lines shattered, with people grabbing as many goods as they could carry and making a mad rush past the gate. Among them, five undesirables would not be noticed, Lenk thought as his companions moved in and he moved to join them. They drew into a tight pack, heads low as they slipped in with the rest of the opportunists.

"I hope you realize this doesn't count," Asper said harshly. "I said no murder."

"You never forbid murder by proxy," Denaos replied.

"I *thought* that was implied."

He turned his nose up at her. "Looks like you have something to learn about communication." He smirked. "Anyway, I doubt he'll kill anyone. Vulgores are meticulous and tidy by nature, but the idea that they go into murderous rages when their things are touched is an urban myth."

Somewhere behind them, someone let out a short scream punctuated by a sharp squishing sound. Lenk winced.

"An urban myth, huh?" he asked.

"We're not technically in the city yet," Denaos said, "so it doesn't count as urban."

"And it doesn't count as a myth if he actually does it," Lenk said. "I'm pretty sure 'vulgores are violent' goes in the same category of fact as 'water is wet.'"

"Category?" Kataria asked, acid in her voice. "So, someone goes around from race to race, writing down their flaws, hopes, and habits in a summary page or so?" She sneered, flashing canine. "That's handy. Maybe you could buy one here."

Later. Lenk clenched his teeth. *Get angry later. Keep moving for now.* He swallowed his ire. It tasted bitter.

"Keep moving," he muttered, forcing his head down. "It's imperative that we don't draw any attention."

As they neared the other side of the gate, another guard stepped forward, hand held up. "Pardon, sirs and madams. There's been a disruption at the gate. We just need to—"

A thick red fist shot out, catching him in the face and sending him collapsing to the ground, unmoving but for a faint twitch. Lenk looked wide-eyed to Gariath as he drew his arm back into his cloak.

"You didn't have to do that," he said.

"I didn't *not* have to do that," Gariath retorted.

Lenk's face screwed up. "Yes. Yes, you did. What do you think 'imperative' means?"

"Some kind of fish, I'm assuming." Gariath impolitely stepped over the guardsman's unconscious body. "If that's all the trouble we see today, I'll be disappointed."

"Clearly," Denaos said, following suit, "you've never been to Cier'Djaal."

FOUR

Unto Heaven

There was no greater testament to man's devotion to making himself seem utterly insignificant than the Silken Spire of Cier'Djaal.

This was Lenk's thought as he looked up. And up. And ever up as the jewel of the city reached from the earth to knock at the door of the Gods.

By itself, the Spire was not so impressive. Just a trio of stone pillars at points north, east, and south of the great stone ring that was the Souk. Towering as they were, they were not so tall as to be what made Cier'Djaal famed across the world.

That honor belonged to the silk.

In red and blue, black and green, purple and white, flecked with gold and favored with the sun's caress, oceans of wispy silk swaths swayed in the breeze between the three pillars. And somewhere between the way the light sighed through it and the way the wind sent it rippling as waves murmuring on the shore, the Silken Spire told him why he had come to Cier'Djaal.

Here, he was small, insignificant. Not a man with a sword, not a man with so many bodies in his wake. Here, he was just a man.

Someone came up beside him.

"I came from a village so small," he whispered, "that the first time I saw a fountain, I stared at it for hours. I'd never even thought something like this could be made by men."

"It wasn't."

A sharp, harsh voice spoke, like an arrow sinking into flesh.

Kataria.

He saw her angle a finger toward a splotch of black silk upon the oceanic tapestry. Or what he thought was a splotch of black silk, anyway, until it started moving.

He stared and saw them more clearly: their many legs, their beady eyes, and their dark, hairy hides. Spiders, moving slowly across the silk sea like oil stains, trailed wispy strands of color from their spinnerets as they skittered across a massive tapestry that made sense only to them.

"Gods," he whispered, eyes widening. To be able to see them from so far away, he reasoned they must be colossal up close. "Monsters."

"Tourist." Denaos's sneer was as easy as his stride as he came up beside Lenk. "Sure, you think the Spire is great until you find out where it comes from. Then, suddenly, horse-sized arachnids that spew color from their anuses are *weird*."

"It *is* weird," Lenk said.

"What's the big deal, anyway?" Kataria asked. "You've seen worse before."

"Yes, and I've killed worse," Lenk replied. "I don't know how comfortable I am with the idea of giant bugs having careers better than mine."

"That's why this city bursts with gold while we scrape for coppers," Denaos said. "You see something that spews something useful and desirable—"

"Out its anus," Lenk interrupted.

"—and see something to kill," Denaos continued, unhindered. "The fashas saw an opportunity. Their ancestors have been breeding the beasts since before this city had a name. And the silk's made them—and, by happy coincidence, the city they live in—extremely wealthy.

"They gave the city the spiders." He pointed to the Spire. "The spiders gave the city the silk." He traced a line through the air, down from the Spire and toward the streets. "And the silk gave the fashas the city."

They found their eyes drawn to it, the beating heart of Cier'Djaal. And the Souk, with its thousand eyes, could not spare even one to look back at them.

It extended for miles in a vast ring, old stone walls rising around them, watching the goings on stoically as the people of Cier'Djaal steadfastly ignored them. Here the tide of humanity ceased to flow and started to churn. Here, it became a great, big, noisy, frothy, sweaty stew in a vast cauldron.

Merchant stalls and impromptu storefronts lined the cauldron in great spirals of canvas and wood, deals, pleas, and threats hurled from their stands like spears. People roiled like chunks of meat, bobbing from stall to stall to lose one thing and gain another so that they might lose it somewhere else. Above them, their own language boiled like steam in an endless, formless babble.

Even the tides of the harbor seemed cozy compared to the Souk's sprawling madness. And he had come here, of all places, to leave his blade behind.

To sell it to one of these greedy creatures in their caves of cloth and canvas, to get a price for all the blood it had spilled and the lives it had taken. To leave it to rust and eventually be picked up by someone with hands as soft as his had once been and never would be again. All so that he could be like them, these civilized people who never had to fight over anything more than a few coins…

The sun shone brightly overhead and Lenk felt a chill that belonged to an older, more tired man.

"So many people," Asper whispered breathlessly, moving to join them. "How are we to find Miron in all this?"

Of course. Miron. Their money. His future.

Somewhere within that writhing mass of humanity was the means for him to become part of it, to have enough coin to cobble together a life like theirs. All that remained was to find him. Miron. Just one man.

In a city of thousands.

"It won't matter if he isn't even in here," Lenk said, casting a disparaging look out over the cauldron. "He got past the gate hours ago. He could be anywhere in the city by now."

"He isn't."

The voice was nasal and shrill, like an insect's buzz except haughtier. The man—or boy; it was hard to tell these days—who spoke it did not seem any more impressive.

He sat upon the edge of a derelict wagon. Hunched over as he was, the boy looked like an amalgamation of leather, paper, and grease. A dirty brown coat pooled around skinny crossed legs upon which a book that looked far too big for him was opened. Stringy locks of black hair hung around a thin face that didn't bother to look up.

Instead, Dreadaeleon merely waved a hand over the book. A page turned of its own accord in reply.

Don't ask, Lenk told himself. *He wants you to ask.*

"How do you know?" Asper asked.

Gods damn it.

"A wizard's ways are his own," he replied. "One would hope we've known each other long enough that you wouldn't think I'd part with secrets so easily."

He looked up, a smug smile on a face that hadn't been punched *nearly* enough in its life.

"Look, Dread," Lenk said, rubbing his eyes. "Can we possibly just skip the coyness and get to the part where everyone acts impressed so you'll tell us what we want to know?"

The boy's face twitched, his smile dissipating. What settled over him next was cold and sneering.

"Make it good," he said.

"Everyone is indebted to the endless arcane power you command," Lenk said on a sigh.

"You truly make the rest of us laypeople look like simpering grubs," Denaos added absently, glancing at his nails.

"Soft, round women salivate at fantasies of burying their faces in your crotch," Kataria said through a yawn.

Dreadaeleon sneered at her. "Just because crassness comes as naturally to you as scratching yourself doesn't mean you should do either in public." He turned to Lenk. "To the point, then: I assume you were the root cause of whatever commotion just happened at the Harbor Gate?" He smirked. "And if so, you'll no doubt have already noted the state of alarm your antics have engendered."

He pointed at various spots on the Souk's wall, where gates leading to the other districts were stationed.

"Every gate leading out of the Souk has a guard and every guard has a line a mile long. Cursory surveillance suggests Miron isn't even standing in one. And thus, he has not yet left the area."

"Ah," Denaos said. "And so comes the part where you tell us you were able to cover every gate within the biggest part of the city by flying or using some other kind of magic?"

"How is it that you're still so unaware of how this actually works?" Dreadaeleon asked, haughtiness leaping comfortably into his voice. "Venarie—or 'magic,' to the common barkneck—is a precious gift, one not to be wasted on needless displays as fleeting as conducting examinations upon the gatherings of sweaty people."

He cast a wide gesture over the vast, churning populace of the Souk. "I could not spit without it hitting a merchant who would sell it for six coppers. I did not fly. I merely asked someone."

"Fine," Denaos said. "So how'd you get in here, anyway? Did you ask the guards?"

"Oh. No. For *that*, I did fly."

Lenk threw up a hand before Denaos could spit a retort. "That's not terrible news, then. If Miron's still here, picking him out shouldn't be too—"

He turned and looked over the Souk, surveying the miles-wide teeming masses. He hummed thoughtfully and sniffed.

"Or maybe we should split up."

"It would make it harder for any authorities to find us, I guess."

Asper forced a pained smile upon her face. "Of course, we probably wouldn't have that trouble if we weren't responsible for nearly killing a dozen people."

"*Later*," he snapped. "We'll make this quick and easy." He pointed a finger at Dreadaeleon. "You and Gariath check the gates to see if he's there." He eyed the boy warily. "Make sure Gariath keeps his cloak on." He turned his glare to Gariath. "Make sure Dreadaeleon doesn't call attention to himself. If either of you screw up, I want one of you to punch the other one."

Dreadaeleon's eyes went wide. "Now wait just a—"

"I like this plan," Gariath said sagely, stalking off, cloak billowing behind him. He paused, looking over his shoulder at Dreadaeleon. His snout poked out from beneath his cloak, his smile broad and unpleasant. "Well?"

The boy cast a baleful scowl upon Lenk for a moment before rising. The book fell from his lap, hanging from his hip by a thick chain. For a moment, he looked as though the weight of it might topple his skinny frame as he scurried after his hulking associate.

"That went easier than expected," he muttered. "So, Denaos, you'll search the stalls with Asper and—"

"*No.*"

She said it with such ferocity that Lenk started. When he turned and looked at Kataria, her eyes were alight beneath the brim of her hat.

"Asper always goes off with Denaos," the shict growled. "And I'm always with you." She seized Asper by the upper arm, pulling the priestess to her side with the same intensity she showed when someone touched her meat. "This time, this one is *mine.*"

Lenk merely blinked. He didn't dare do more. He had once touched her meat and he knew how *that* ended.

"Uh, all right," he said. "Why?"

"What if I want to spend time with her?" Kataria asked. "What if I want..." She made a brief expression like she was choking. "Woman...talk. Or something."

"Woman talk?" Asper asked, looking slightly worried. "Like…
what?"

Kataria furrowed her brow. "Hair."

"Hair?"

"Yes. I have concerns about hair. Hairs. Scalps. Manes. That sort
of thing."

Lenk looked horrified. "So, should I—"

"*You* should search *that* side." She made a vague gesture to the
northern half of the Souk. "We'll search the other."

Asper looked at him pleadingly for a moment as she was hauled off
into the crowd of people. Lenk could offer only an apologetic shrug;
to do anything more meant one of them would lose an appendage.
They vanished into the crowd.

"It would probably be wiser not to follow her," he muttered to
himself. That Denaos overheard was just his poor luck.

"Seems a little late to start considering wisdom a factor in this
plan," the rogue replied.

"Your harping on my plans is beginning to grow tiresome," Lenk
snapped, whirling upon him. "They've had sound foundations, and
aside from a few setbacks, things have gone better than I expected."

"Wisdom and intellect aren't the same thing," Denaos replied.
"Intellect bade you set your expectations low. And if you had more
wisdom, you'd have set them even lower."

Lenk felt a brief sensation at the back of his scalp, like a little hand
grabbing a fistful of the root of his hair and giving a sharp tug. He
found himself searching the crowd for a flash of blond hair, a green-
eyed scowl.

"Kataria didn't seem to be thinking clearly," he muttered. "Should
we go after her or…"

"When a wolf decides to chew on someone else instead of you,
you don't put your hand in its mouth," Denaos said.

"She's not a wolf," Lenk snapped. He rubbed his eyes. "She knows
I'm planning on leaving."

"How would she? Did you tell her?"

"No, and she's probably not too pleased about that, either." He shook his head. "It's hard to hide things from her. She looks at me and..." He tried—and failed—to illustrate with his hands. "She just *knows*. But it's not like her to be coy with what enrages her. She always lets me know."

"I see I'll be getting no end of opportunity to lecture today," Denaos said, walking past him and toward the crowd. "See, to appreciate a woman you have to appreciate a woman's right to change. And to appreciate a woman's right to change, you have to realize that she'll do it with maddening frequency, usually just to confuse you so that you'll never see her coming when she decides to rip your throat out and drink your blood."

"So, you think women are half-wolf, half-demon she-beasts," Lenk said, hurrying to catch up, "out to eat men alive."

"This is the source of most of our problems, yes."

"I see," Lenk hummed. "And you don't think it's distressing that between your alcoholism, numerous character flaws, and likely uncountable sexual diseases that you don't feel you have enough problems already?"

"Ah, my friend," Denaos sighed wistfully, draping an arm around Lenk's shoulder, "*this* is why you're not a romantic."

FIVE

The Cauldron

I t came out in a red-orange sludge, chunks of meat floating in it that were old enough that one would call them "dignified" just to be polite. The fever-reeking stuff sat before her, in a wooden bowl, on a lump of rice, looking quite smugly at her.

And the man behind the counter called it food.

"So, it's..." Asper's face screwed up in an attempt to comprehend. "Curry?"

"Yes." The merchant sighed. "It is curry. My daughter makes it." He gestured to the dark-haired girl stirring a pot behind him. "I sell it. It tastes delicious and sets your pasty northern behind ablaze. And it costs three zan a bowl."

"Zan?"

"Zan. Pennies. Copper."

"Oh." She fished three small pieces from her pouch and set them on the counter. "In Muraska, we just call them copper pieces. Seems simpler."

"Northerners give them simple names because you don't have respect for them." The man snatched away her coin. "Djaalics know better."

"Uh-huh." She didn't bother arguing. Instead, she held the bowl a respectable distance from her nose and sniffed at it warily. "It seems a little rank, though. Maybe you could add something to improve the aroma? Like raisins or something?"

The girl stopped stirring and looked up, eyes aghast. The merchant shot Asper an expression reserved for war criminals and people who had extremely sentimental opinions of sheep.

"Perhaps it's no longer my grandfather's time when you would be hanged for that sort of thing," the merchant said, holding up his hands. "But Ancaa help me if you bring such deviancy to my place of business again. Go. *Go.*"

He swept his hand out with such fury as to send her back a step. She felt herself collide with something, or someone, it appeared, as a pair of gloved hands set upon her shoulders to steady her.

She whirled about, befuddled at the man standing before her. In the north, someone like him—tall, pale, fair-haired—would be as common as someone like her. But among the dark skin and black hair of the people of Cier'Djaal, he would have been an odd enough sight even without his uniform.

Over creased trousers and a belted coat with brass buttons, a long blue overcoat hung from his shoulders, secured at the breast with a sigil of a six-pointed star of blue and red. If the insignia suggested it, the saber at his hip and the military-style tail of hair tucked beneath a three-cornered hat all but screamed "soldier."

He gave her a curt nod, the stiff incline of a neck that had any hint of friendliness beaten out of it by some corporal long ago. Pushing her aside gently, he marched to the curry stall, the merchant offering him an eager smile.

"Ah, the Queen's Finest come calling!" The merchant gestured to a blue and red banner hanging from his stall, the same six-pointed star displayed as on the soldier's breast. "The usual today, my friend?"

"Make it a bucket, aye?" the soldier replied, voice thick with a northern accent. "Convoy got held up by shicts in the north. Rations are lagging."

"Ah, yes. What better way to enjoy the cuisine I have spent my life perfecting than out of a bucket?" the merchant asked with a pained smile.

"Lively now, civilian," the soldier said. "Karnie bastards are afoot and I won't be caught out here alone."

He stood rod-rigid, staring straight ahead even as Asper stared straight at him. When he looked at her, the glare beneath the brim of his hat suggested he had been aware of her eyes upon him for some time.

"What?" he asked.

"Oh!" She shook her head. "Uh, nothing. It's just..." She scratched the back of her neck. "You're not the first Sainite I've seen today."

"Aye," the man replied. "We've a garrison in Temple Row."

"What for?"

"Everything you'd expect a garrison to be used for," he said. "Cier'Djaal's got gold for blood. A lot of both of ours went into it."

"And that involves going out for curry?"

"Ah, no," the soldier replied. "That's just my job as the chief S.C.Q. officer."

She furrowed her brow. "What do your duties include?"

"Just what's in the name," he said flatly. "My sole obligation is to wander around waiting for someone to ask me a stupid civilian question."

"Oh. *Oh*." Asper's face shifted seamlessly into a glare. "Well, did they also promote you to the head of the U.S.B., uh, W.M.S.P.Q.R.?" The soldier was no longer listening, nor even looking at her, and so she turned about, muttering under her breath. "Uptight, stupid bastard who molests..."

"Anything else today, Hand of the Queen?" The merchant grunted, hauling up a hefty bucket onto the counter. "If not, that will be forty zan."

"Why don't you Djaalics just call them 'coppers'?" the soldier muttered as he slammed a scrap of paper onto the counter and seized the bucket. "Recompensation slip. Turn it in to the garrison at your convenience; Watch-Sergeant will get you your money."

"I know what it is," the merchant grumbled. "I have a dozen more you gave me and so far none—"

The soldier, demonstrating a finely honed ability to ignore anything not in a uniform, spun on his heel and toted his burden away. The merchant murmured very carefully softened curses at his back.

"For years, the fashas' coin has bought enough mercenaries that we needed no army." He shoved the recompensation slip somewhere dark. "Now, because of that coin, Cier'Djaal has two."

"Two armies?" Asper asked. "Where's the—"

The merchant's eyes looked over her head. Faster than she could blink, he had torn down the Sainite banner from his shop and replaced it with a flowing banner depicting white horns on a black field. He raised his hand in salute and Asper turned.

In perfect rhythm, a small regiment of eight men came marching down the street, their harmoniously ordered step cutting a path through the crowds. Their breastplates and helms, the color of perfectly cut obsidian, reflected polished sunlight. Their spears rose proudly over their heads. And every muscle beneath dark, hairless flesh twitched in military unison.

Arms swinging as one, feet marching as one, sixteen eyes staring straight ahead as one, the regiment of soldiers marched down the street, through the crowd, and past the curry shack.

"Hail Karneria!" the merchant shouted after them. "Hail the Emperor and His Divine Mission! Welcome to Cier'Djaal! Buy a curry!" His enthusiasm faded as the soldiers did. "You cheap bastards."

Asper's eyes could not will themselves to blink. "The Karnerians? *They're* here, too?"

"Oh, yes, the 'Karnie fucks,'" the merchant said. "Here and ready to take our silks, same as the Sainites. The only thing stopping either of them from doing that is both of them."

"But they've been warring for years! They can't both be here." She glanced to the banner. "And you *can't* support both of them."

"I support whichever army will not kill me, burn my stand to the ground, and rape my daughter," the merchant replied. "And since neither of them will guarantee that, I hedge my bets."

"But that's horrible!"

"Yes, but not nearly as horrible as losing business because some northern woman won't get out of the way and let paying customers through." He made a shooing gesture. "Well? Scamper along."

She tried formulating a response that *wasn't* merely a bunch of angry-sounding noises. And had she more time, she surely would have. But as it stood, someone was waiting for her, and she turned and left.

Maybe it was her, she reasoned. Maybe civilization had always been this insane before she had followed Lenk to become an adventurer and she had just forgotten. Perhaps that would explain why she was busy buying curry instead of looking for Miron.

She should have been more concerned with his whereabouts, she knew. He was a priest of her order—a direct superior, even. He would doubtlessly insist that she stay here with him in the city to tend its many ills and heal its many wounded—just like she had always trained for. She couldn't explain why that thought sat unwell with her.

Maybe civilization hadn't changed. Maybe she had.

She found Kataria lingering near a derelict-looking stall brimming with curious knickknacks and dominated by a large portrait of a gentle-looking woman in repose. The shict looked up at her expectantly.

"Took you long enough," Kataria grunted. She snatched the bowl from Asper's hand and shot a disparaging look at its contents. "What's this?"

"Curry."

"What's that?"

"Something produced by assholes that goes into assholes and later comes out of assholes."

Kataria looked at the food curiously before leaning in and giving it a brief sniff. Her eyes widened in appreciation.

"Oh."

She pulled off one glove with her teeth and began to scoop handfuls of curry and rice into her mouth. She didn't look up until she noticed Asper staring at her. At the priestess's aghast expression, she wiped her hand off on her breeches and offered the bowl to her companion.

Perhaps it was the way Kataria tried to look friendly by smiling through those oversized canines, or maybe it was the way the glistening sauce of the curry so richly resembled blood smeared across her lips. Either way, Asper waved the bowl away.

"I'm fine," she said.

"It's not that bad," Kataria said, dipping back in. "And it's kind of nice eating something you didn't have to kill yourself."

"The joys of civilization," Asper sighed.

"What's the matter with you, anyway?" the shict asked through a mouthful of sauce and rice. "We're surrounded by your people. I thought you'd be happy."

"These aren't my people."

"They're human."

"They're Djaalics, Sainites, and Karnerians. Big difference between them and northerners."

"Like what?"

"They're rude, pushy, and try to force their way upon everyone else."

"So do you."

"Yeah, but I'm a priestess of Talanas. I do that as a matter of faith, not choice." Asper sighed. "I don't know. I guess I've just been away from civilization so long I forgot it wasn't the same thing as civility. It's hard to have to deal with someone when you can't physically assault them."

Asper had never believed Kataria's grin could be more unpleasant, but then she went and looked positively ecstatic.

"There was a time you detested violence," Kataria said. "You thought it violated your oaths as a healer."

"I figure if I help them after I punch them, I'm still doing the Healer's work." She returned the shict's smile. "And what's got you in such a good mood? We are, after all, surrounded by humans."

Kataria's smile faded. She licked her chops clean and snorted.

"We're always surrounded by humans."

"You looked ready to kill them all a moment ago," Asper said.

"Just the one," Kataria grunted, casting a glare toward Asper. "Not that I'd object to more if one of them kept asking questions."

Asper's sigh was bone deep. "Not that I couldn't get sarcasm and threats from anyone else, but if I were with Denaos, at least I'd be used to his. *You* were the one that wanted *me* to come with you, so obviously *you've* got a problem you want to unload onto *me*, so if *you* want to act menacing and belligerent, do it to someone *other* than *me*."

Kataria opened her mouth to retort. No words came out. She bared her teeth to snarl. No sound emerged. She clenched her fist to punch. And slowly, her fingers came loose with a long, slow sigh as her chin fell to her chest and her hair fell over her eyes.

"I couldn't hear them."

"Who?" Asper asked.

"The shicts. My people."

"Where?" The priestess looked around. "I thought nonhumans weren't allowed in the Souk."

Nonhumans not in disguise, anyway, she added mentally, eyeing the shict's hat.

"At the harbor. They reached out to me. I could feel them, trying to speak to me with their..." She looked up, mouth quivering with the need to explain. But she found no words in the empty air. "I couldn't understand it." She looked to Asper. "And that was *my* language. *Our* language. And I can't hear it anymore." Her ears quivered under her hat. Her teeth came out. "Because of *him*."

"Lenk?" Asper blinked. "How?"

"*I don't know!*" Kataria said, throwing her hands up. "I don't know how he did this to me, I don't know why I let it happen, and I don't know how to fix it!"

"Then what makes you think he caused it?"

"I don't know that, either." She ran a hand down her face, exasperation leaking between her fingers. "I've always heard that prolonged contact with humans causes these kinds of things."

"Well, we've been adventuring together for close to two years now," Asper said. "If it *is* caused by contact with humans, then aren't Denaos and Dreadaeleon and I all to blame?"

Kataria turned a glare upon her. "Not *that* kind of contact."

"Oh." A bashful smile crept across Asper's face involuntarily. "*Oh.*" She cleared her throat, seizing her composure and plastering it back onto her face. "So, did you ... *know* this would happen before you ... uh ..."

"Obviously not." Kataria sighed, leaning against the stall. "There are stories that are meant to make us feel better about shooting and killing humans," the shict replied with a shrug. "I mean, it feels *okay* as it is, but without a gripping narrative—"

"I get it," Asper interjected. "So, you're *not* mad at Lenk?"

"Not for *that.*"

"For what, then?"

Kataria gestured around her, to the teeming masses, to the sea of stalls, to the rhythm of clinking coins and pleading voices and guttering sounds.

"For *this,*" she said, scorn dripping from every word, "all of *this.* This gold, this smell, this noise." Her eyes narrowed to thin daggers. "These *humans.*"

"I see." Asper coughed. "You do know *Lenk* is—"

"He's *not.*" She spat the words upon the ground, a challenge she defied Asper to meet. "Not like them. Not safe, not greedy, not ... not *this!*" Her scowl trembled upon Asper, and she turned her gaze to her boots. "But he wants to be."

And when Kataria raised her eyes from the earth hesitantly, they were trying to cling to what anger remained, to keep the quivering fear behind it from showing.

"I gave it all up," Kataria said, no breath for the words, no anger for the voice. "My people. The Howling. Everything. I gave everything up for him. And now he's trying to become them, these people that aren't him, and he's giving me up for all this dirt and gold."

It all came so naturally to Asper, she was barely aware of it happening. The smile and the warmth it came with flowed to her face. The right hand extended and laid upon Kataria's shoulder. The fingers tightened gently about the bare skin in a sympathetic squeeze and she felt the tense, frightened pulse of life.

"He won't leave you," she said, voice so tender, words so soft. "You mean too much for him not to take you."

Kataria's eyes burst to bright, angry life. The teeth came sliding out like knives in a feral snarl. The ears came out from under her hat and flattened against the sides of her head. The arm swung, swatting Asper's hand away.

"Take me? *Take me?*" Kataria trembled, fighting to keep her fury restricted solely to her voice. "Take me where, round-ear? Why do you think I tuck my ears under this hat? Why do I not wear my feathers proudly? Why do I hide here, surrounded by humans?"

The shict leaned closer. Asper felt her breath, hot. Asper heard her voice, sharp and curt, each word the thrust of a stone knife with a rough edge.

"I. Can't. Live. Here. We are two different people. I left mine behind for him. What will I have left when he goes, too?"

Asper had no answer. Kataria had none that would satisfy her. The shict readjusted her hat, turned, and stalked away, muttering something about checking the other stalls for a sign of Miron. She disappeared into the crowd as though they were living underbrush.

Asper was left staring speechless at the roiling crowds, the flurry of thrust elbows, the forest of tramping feet, the beggars reaching out and the eyes looking away, the grunted curses and the muttered counter curses, the spewing and the snarling and the sand and the dust and the gold and the blood and all of them.

All the humans.

She looked down at the discarded bowl, remnants of rice and curry spattered on the dusty ground like the traces of some long-ignored murder. A man's boot stepped into the sauce, tripped over the bowl. He cursed at Asper and she never saw his face.

Sighing, she reached down and plucked up the bowl to return it to the curry stall. But a line had formed after she had left and it no longer seemed worth the trouble.

Instead, she turned to the derelict stall Kataria had leaned against. A collection of various sundries: jars, vials, amulets, pots filled with sludges, liquids, swirling gases, and what appeared to be a preserved head. Whoever it was, it didn't seem to mind Asper leaving the bowl there.

She placed it at the center of the stall's counter, before the great heap of black rags dominated by the portrait of the elegant lady. She looked up at it, meeting her austere, oil-based smile, and returned a sheepish grin.

"Sorry about this," she said. "I can accept the abuse, but I can't see myself standing in line to receive it."

With a slow, fluid turn, the portrait angled itself to regard her through a canvas stare.

"Your social commentary is noted and agreed upon." A flat, monotone voice responded from the elegant lady's unmoving lips. "You may proceed to jest about one or more aspects of the aggressor merchant's hygiene, if it so pleases you."

Asper would have fallen flat on her ass had she not staggered into someone as she backpedaled with a start. Her eyes so wide they forgot what blinking was, she stared as the heap of black rags stirred. And then moved.

They rose to a towering six and a half feet tall, unfurling to reveal themselves as a well-groomed, unadorned black robe. From their depths emerged a pair of long, pale arms ending in great, clawed hands. The appendages moved in slow harmony, one producing a bottle of wine, the other a pair of scales. Asper was so enraptured with their fluid movement that she scarcely saw the second, smaller set of arms extending from the robes, offering soft, childlike hands in a gesture of hospitality.

"Your expression suggests a lack of familiarity with the custom of greeting, *shkainai*." The flat voice emerged from behind the portrait, around which a hood had suddenly formed. "A prompt apology is delivered forthwith to precursor assurances that you are welcome among the wares of the couthi."

"You mean *you're* a couthi?" She had heard the name before, but never really imagined what they might look like.

"Your astonishment is noted for future reference. You shall be soothed to know that no emotional trauma has occurred to this one's demeanor." The portrait inclined toward her slightly. "Salutations are extended by one Man-Shii Kree, owner, proprietor, and employee of the month of *Man-Shii Kree's Curios and Wonderosities*."

All four hands gestured above the stall, to the plain, unadorned banner with words reading what was just spoken. Though right below, as the couthi neglected to mention, was the admonition: "*Safe for Human Consumption (Oral)*."

She thought to inquire, though not before he—or so she assumed the couthi was—spoke again.

"How may this one serve you today."

A long silence followed. She blinked and angled a curious look at Man-Shii Kree.

"Sorry, was that a question? It's just it's kind of hard to tell," Asper said, clearing her throat. "What with the, uh..."

Don't say "horrible, inhuman monotone," she thought.

"Accent."

"Ah. You are perhaps put at less ease by this one's lack of intonation familiar to the act of querying." The portrait bobbed as the head behind it nodded. "Research into your breed suggests that humans find confidence attractive. Questions indicate uncertainty. Uncertainty contradicts confidence. Statement, not question, is what establishes mercantile courage. Do you agree."

"Uh...yes?" She shook her head, searching for a spot to look on the portrait. "So, the...the painting."

"*Salvation's Mother*, artist unknown, acquired through personal commission."

"Right, right. So…is that your, uh, face or…or what's happening?" She extended a finger and made a vague, circular motion around the portrait. "With, ah, all this?"

The couthi said nothing, clearly offended.

Perhaps not "clearly," she reasoned. Maybe just obscurely offended.

"Our research in regard to your species suggests that the particulars of our facial structure were deemed"—he paused, considering—"unpleasing to a subset of our customers. Research indicates that humans prefer more soothing images, such as human females smiling, landscapes, or stationary bowls of fruit."

"Ah," Asper said, "so that's a mask?"

"If it soothes you to call it such a thing, *shkainai*, I am pleased to confirm it." He steepled all of his fingers at once. "Engage your eyes, please, to browse at leisure." One of his larger hands swept over his display of vials, while a smaller one slid a glass of red liquid toward her. "The Bloodwise Brotherhood is pleased to offer complimentary samples on all beneficial and mostly beneficial products, to better offer an understanding of our services."

Amidst that entire pitch, the *mostly* had been slipped in quietly, like a needle in a neck. And like a needle in her neck, it was all she could think of.

"Er, no, thank you. I was actually wondering if you might be able to tell me if you had seen—" She paused and stared at the portrait-mask for a moment. "If you had *noticed* a certain person around."

"Praise is heaped upon your face for attempting to invoke the tradition of associating mercantile prowess with helpful rumormongering. But research has indicated that indulging in such trains of thought have often led to missed sales and lowered productivity."

She frowned. "So, I have to buy something first?"

"It is without hesitation that this one informs you as to the Brotherhood's peerless information-gathering and information-dispatching prowess. But such a display would violate employee conduct."

She glanced over his wares, trying to decipher among the many vials and pots which liquid was the least disgusting. She pointed to something a pleasant rose color. "How about that? What's it do?"

"Your eyeballs are undoubtedly fiercely endowed to spot such a quality product, *shkainai*." One of Man-Shii Kree's larger hands plucked the vial gingerly off its shelf, passing it to his smaller hands to extend to her. "Among our multitude of legitimate customers, Essence of the Rose is popular for virility and fertility issues."

She peered closer, squinting. "What is it? A love potion? Or a cure for a man's slumbering groin?"

"Love potions are a myth, *shkainai*. And while the Brotherhood certainly possesses the knowledge to correct a human male's malfunctioning genitals, it is an invasive and costly procedure that we neither offer nor perform in public sectors with stringent decency laws." He gestured to the bottle with all four hands. "It is a heavy sedative, used to render a human into a drowsy and suggestible state."

"Heavy sedative...suggestible...virility..." She eyed the couthi suspiciously. "Just what is this used for?"

Immediately, Man-Shii Kree's hands went into a flurry. One of the smaller appendages snatched the bottle back as the other thrust up a cautioning finger, and the two larger ones immediately produced dense-looking scrolls with waivers and statements written illegibly on them.

"Employees of Man-Shii Kree and all members in good standing of the Bloodwise Brotherhood neither condone nor condemn nor possess a strong opinion on the subject of human copulation. All grievances may be directed to heads of societies and/or local authorities, presuming execution sentences are not considered."

Man-Shii Kree's larger hands reached beneath the stall and returned with a scroll that unfurled over the edge of the counter.

"Terms are negotiable and reasonable," he replied.

Just as his smaller hands produced a quill and inkwell and gingerly dipped it in before handing it to her, his portrait shifted. Asper followed his gaze—or what she thought was his gaze—and beheld Kataria approaching.

"I didn't find anything," the shict said, snorting. "Also, I didn't find a reason *not* to punch someone in the face. Not that I'm admitting to anything. Just that it's something we might have to deal with."

Asper sighed and muttered what she thought was under her breath. "Shicts."

Man-Shii Kree's portrait swiveled back to her. Digits trembled, deftly rolling the scroll back up and replacing it and the quill and inkwell back beneath the stall. His arms retreated back into his robes. He stood stock-still, apparently heedless of the curious looks Asper shot to him.

"Something the matter?" she asked.

"Ten thousand apologies heaped upon your face, *shkainai*," he replied. "It was this one's fervent belief, ardent hope, and private joy that the shict had departed for good. An unclean presence renders business impractical."

Kataria licked curry from her lips. "Who're you calling unclean, bug?"

"Wait, you two know of each other?" Asper asked, lofting a brow.

"The couthi race is granted such a beneficial position in mercantile culture owing to our lack of a homeland," Man-Shii Kree said simply. "Which we accredit to our many wars with perfidious, unclean, treacherous shicts."

Asper glanced at Kataria. "This is true?"

Kataria shrugged. "I don't know. Probably."

"Probably?"

"Well, *I* didn't do any of it!" Kataria snapped back. "Shicts have been around for a while. We've had wars with every race under the sun. Our fights with the bugs don't make for good stories, though."

"This one possesses no home." Man-Shii Kree's voice began to strain, cracks forming at the edge of porcelain glass. "This one possesses no face. And *that* one complains about possessing no story about how its people burned our land and took our scalps."

"Takes two to fight a war," Kataria snarled. "And we're kind of busy fighting the humans now."

Asper winced before turning back to Man-Shii Kree.

"All right," she said, holding up hands for peace. "We don't want any trouble. We'll just get out of your way. Sorry for…" She waved her hands about. "You know, all of this."

Man-Shii Kree's portrait tilted slightly. His arms came slithering out of their robes.

"For what, *shkainai*? There is no reason we cannot complete our transaction."

"What? After what she just said? After what *you* said? All that stuff about unclean ones?"

"Ah. Apologies. This one had hoped the shict was going to be away from you so you would be spared the explanation as to why we are now permitted to conduct business."

Asper had just opened her mouth to question that when she heard the cry. She turned around to see Kataria's hat lying in the streets. Its wearer was a good twenty feet away and fading, seized, struggling and snarling in the grasp of five burly-looking Djaalics in armor as they hauled her through the streets, crowd parting before them with astonished expressions.

The priestess whirled back on the couthi, scowling.

"You called guards on her?"

"In fairness, this one *did* offer statement as to the information-dispatching prowess of the Brotherhood." He held up the rose-colored vial once more. "Please, accept a 'slightly-guilty-of-treachery' discount of ten zan."

Asper made a move to dart away, then paused briefly.

She tore her pouch from her stall and slammed it on the counter, seizing the potion and tucking it into her medicine bag. She spared another moment to scowl at the couthi before snatching up the hat and taking off after Kataria.

Man-Shii Kree's voice chased her delicately, like flower petals on the breeze.

"Embalming services are also available for soon-to-be-severed heads of dearly departed associates. Reasonable rates."

SIX

THE SERPENT AND THE POET

Having known many, and a few quite well, Gariath had come to realize that humans were, by and large, a simple race.

They loved gold, swords, themselves, and each other, in that order. They guided themselves first by fear and second by lust. They called their cowardice practicality, their greed ambition, their love weakness. They were a simple people possessed of few surprises. And he thought he knew them well.

Then they had to go and do some weird crap like this.

Bedraggled, downtrodden, besotted, and degenerate. High-nosed, glittering, haughty, and grinning. Clad in rags, festooned in robes. Marked with dirt and gold and stains and beards. They were different, but he could tell this only because of their varying degrees of filth. Without that, all humans looked the same to him.

And all of them crawled through the Souk on their bellies like worms. In a slow-moving river of filth and flesh, they crawled on elbows and knees, between stalls and under feet and over sunbaked stone. They crawled, to a far-distant place, and their numbers were endless.

And they all wore bright, shiny smiles suitable for shoveling shit.

Only their scent truly differentiated them. And their odors filled his nostrils in noxious disharmonies. He could smell their fear, their desperation, the loathing they hid behind those broad smiles.

For years, Gariath had never cared to know much about humanity, this race that teemed across the land. And until two years ago, when he had met Lenk, he never had to. Two years later, he wasn't any closer to understanding them.

Despite the many he had known and the many he had killed, he could not stare at them as he did now without feeling something like hatred.

But sharper.

"Magnificent, no?"

Gariath turned at the voice. Too firm and full of itself to be the skinny little human he was supposed to be with; Gariath had a vague memory of the boy in the dirty coat saying he was going somewhere. Somewhere obviously not worth remembering.

This human that had appeared at his side was scarcely any more impressive. A robe that once had been fine, a mustache that once had been groomed, a smile that belonged on a man who smelled not quite as bad. Gariath regarded him carefully, making certain his hood was pulled up far enough to mask his face. Not that it seemed to matter; the human's eyes were solely on the humans upon the ground crawling through the Souk's streets.

"And this is but a trickle," the man said brightly. "To become a stream, then a river, and then a flood of worship that flows continuously to the temple of Ancaa."

Gariath said nothing. The man appeared somewhat befuddled by his silence.

"Have you not heard of Her?"

Truthfully, Gariath had not. He had heard a number of names humans had for these "god" things they loved so much, but he assumed them largely to be something akin to a bodily function. A noise they made when they were excited, aroused, or frightened.

"Ah, I see," the man said, sighing. "A northerner would not know Her glory, would he? She only became known to us in Vhehanna in the past ten years. Pilgrims came from the Forbidden East and brought Her words. Of such beauty and power were they, they spread like a plague."

"A plague?"

"Well, you know, a *good* plague. A plague of knowledge of char-ity." He turned his vast, consuming smile up toward Gariath's hood. "Have you known suffering, brother?"

Gariath looked away and said nothing. The man didn't seem to notice or care.

"Have you known what it is to be left wanting? To be left desir-ing? To feel a vast emptiness where something should be?"

Gariath lowered his gaze to the earth.

"I have known that," he said.

"As have we all, brother. As Ancaa has taught us."

The man raised his hands, as though trying to paint a picture with his fingers in the dusty air.

"She spoke of many things, and chief among them, of wealth. She told us that it was not made to be hoarded as the fashas do. Wealth is there to better mankind, and coin was only as good as the man who carried it. And so long as one man was too poor to rise above the filth, so too would all mankind."

He gestured to the river of the flesh.

"And so, until every man can rise above poverty, no man shall. And we shall all crawl, as the lowest man shall."

The look on the man's face was delirious. But the scent he exuded was treacherous, a kind of noxious blend of aromas that wafted into Gariath's hood and filled his nostrils. A sickly sweet odor of excite-ment clashed with the wafting stench of desire, but neither were nearly as prevalent as that most common, stale stink of humanity.

Fear.

"Join me, brother," the man said, breathless. "Join me in this great endeavor."

Gariath didn't. The man didn't bother to look as he threw his belly to the stones and joined the other worshippers in crawling as their lowest member to whatever distant goal they hoped lay at the end of their river.

And this, he thought, was why he hated them.

To them, suffering came from neither loss nor tragedy, but from desire and denial. To them, suffering was no famine or drought. Suffering was a belly not yet full to bursting, a mouth that drank water instead of wine. To them, suffering was something temporary, to be overcome, to be put aside and placed on a mantel with all their other things made of metal.

To a human, suffering was a novelty.

To a *Rhega* like him, it was uncooked meat.

To a *Rhega*, it was the scar that taught him to watch his back. To a *Rhega*, it was precious blood spilled and every drop counted. To a *Rhega*, it was as constant as the sun and as unforgiving.

To Gariath, last of *Rhega*, suffering was constant.

Below his cloak, his wings felt stifled, constrained. His tail ached from being coiled up to avoid dragging on the ground. His skin felt hot and itchy and his claws tensed, ready to rip this puny cloak asunder and give these weaklings something to really fear.

It was hard to think here—too many noises, too many smells, too many *humans*.

But he kept himself calm. He forced himself still. Lenk was depending on him to do just that. And while Lenk's desires never really superseded Gariath's, he respected the man enough to at least spare a moment of consideration before rampaging.

And so Gariath held on to that moment as long as he could. He breathed deeply, in and out, in—

And that's when he caught it. A stray scent on the breeze. Something stronger than fear, something stronger than a human. Anger tinged with hate, hate blended with derision, derision caked upon sorrow. It was a powerful scent. A familiar scent.

A scent of true suffering. Like the *Rhegas'*.

Pushing effortlessly through the crowds, Gariath followed it, through the river of flesh and into a forest of canvas and wood.

⊷ ⋯ ⊶

The fortieth time Dreadaeleon found himself nose-to-groin with some sweaty, belligerent barkneck, he wondered if it wouldn't be easier to just burn the whole Souk down and find Miron by sifting through the ashes.

Granted, his quarry would doubtlessly be consumed in the inferno, as well, but surely no court would convict him. Men could be pushed too far, and being pushed into someone's sweaty lap was at *least* twelve paces past too far.

He muttered something between a curse to the person who had shoved him down and an apology to the person whose belt his face had brushed against. Neither seemed to notice as he hauled himself to his feet and dusted himself off.

Again.

It's not right, you know, he told himself. *They look at you like some vagrant. Do they not see the book? Do they not* sense *the palpable purpose seething within?*

He looked down at himself. He saw a boy in a dirty coat and dirty trousers, a book too heavy for him hanging from his hip. He thought he could sense purpose seething within, though that might just have been the curry he ate earlier.

Or perhaps, it was something else entirely. A familiar pang of dread that welled up inside him, seized his heart, and twisted. He felt it as he picked his way through the crowd, suffering the jostling and the shoving with numb acceptance.

Perhaps some manner of disturbance as pertains to the disconnect between the body and the Venarie that flows through it, he surmised. *It's feasible to surmise that an aftereffect of magical use has lingered, some disturbance that's resulted in heightened tension, bowel disorder, and general anxiety.*

At the edge of the crowd, he found a long, wooden bench. And when he sat upon it, he found himself suddenly much heavier.

It's also possible that you're just a colossal coward.

That felt more plausible with every passing moment.

Every moment he wasn't out searching for Miron. Every moment he labored under the masquerade of being friend to Asper and the others. Every moment he spent out here in the tide of people instead of doing what his duty as a wizard and member of the Venarium commanded him to.

It was all so easy when you planned it out, wasn't it?

It was, by design, going to be a relatively simple endeavor. When he arrived in Cier'Djaal with his companions, he would use a simple spell to go over the Harbor Wall and leave them behind.

It was, by execution, even simpler. Breaking off from Lenk and the others was no more difficult than the spell itself.

It was, as ever, only in hindsight that everything completely went donkey's-balls.

Because nothing involving magic—by design, execution, or hindsight—was ever simple. And it never didn't go donkey's-balls.

That was duty. The duty his fellow wizards had put upon him. The duty he was supposed to be performing right now.

He rubbed his eyes. That was a mistake. He could feel it every time he closed his eyes: a steady pressure, a fluctuation of temperature, a subtle arc of electricity that sent the hairs on his neck standing on end.

Magic.

The Venarium.

They were here, in Cier'Djaal.

Exactly thirty-four degrees east, nine hundred and fifty-one paces in a straight line, he could feel the pull of Venarie surely as compasses felt north. It didn't call to him, of course; magic didn't work like that. It wasn't flighty or seductive. It was constant, a fact of life. And so it merely made him aware of the fact that it existed and always would.

And with that awareness came the creeping reality of his situation.

He should be going there now. Protocol dictated that every member in good standing of the Venarium—as every wizard living was—should report to the nearest sovereign tower and give a detailed listing of their discoveries as to the properties, practices, and executions of magic in their travels.

Yet he did not make a move to rise, let alone to go.

It was hardly his fault that nearly every item in such a listing involved a transgression against nearly every protocol, rule, and bylaw—all punishable by incarceratory punitive research until such a time as he expired and his organs, skin, and bones were suitable for harvesting.

As outlined in article sixty-six, item D of *The Seven Noble Laws*.

And because he had read that article several times, because he knew exactly what awaited him when he arrived at the Venarium, here he was.

On a dirty bench in a dirty coat among dirty people, ignoring a task given to him by friends that he intended to abandon. Trying to figure out how to best manage his time between doing a task for imbeciles and avoiding imminent and painful death by protocol.

I should start keeping a tally for every time this happens, he thought. *Every third time, I could reward myself with a treat. Something really nice, like—*

"Excuse me."

He turned to his left. A pair of bright green eyes greeted him, shining through a dusky, unwashed face, stars against a dark sky.

"This isn't a bench you want to sit on."

He blinked. For a moment, he failed to register her as a girl. Her dress was tattered and dirty, her hair hung about her face in thick, black strands, and there wasn't a bit of dusky skin that didn't bear some desert grime.

But he noted by the angle of her face and the weariness of her eyes that she was a young woman. Though she seemed more young than woman.

And more dirt than human, he noted.

At his intent scrutiny of her, she leaned back, regarding him down the slope of her nose.

"Unless someone told you this was the bench for creepy boys who stare too long," she said.

He stared, shaking his head. "Oh! Uh, sorry. I didn't..."

His words and his gaze alike drifted off, over her head and down the bench. A number of other people of various ages and common grime sat upon it, heads bowed, bodies bent. At the very end of it sprawled a wooden platform before a gathered crowd, not unlike a stage.

"I'm, uh, not from around here," he said, offhandedly.

She took him in—his pale skin, his lanky build, his dirty coat—with eyes that battled between unsurprised and unimpressed.

"You don't say," she said.

"So, what is this? Some sort of play? Should I move?"

"Yeah." There was a deep weariness in her laughter. "A play. It's a production of *To Wed and Be Bled*."

"Highly unlikely," he replied. "*To Wed and Be Bled*—or its original title, *Red Sheets Weeping*, as it's still known in its native Karneria—is a stage performance that benefits from more organization and pomp."

He pointed past her to the stage and its bare wooden planks.

"The orchestra should be well-warm by this point. The curtains should be hung. The paper dragons should be ready to go ablaze to introduce Lady Liaja, the Djaalic princess offered to the Karnerian emperor. Her entry sets the tone for the entire piece."

"It's a humble production," the woman said, lips straining to contain her smirk. "The director had a minimalist vision."

"Lunacy," he said with a sneer. "Even a functioning illiterate could look at the script and realize that it was intended to be presented with fanfare and flowers and fire."

"It's highly inconsiderate to critique a performance before it's gone on," she replied down her nose.

"Well," he responded, puffing himself up like a poorly endowed bullfrog, "it's high crime to premeditate the murder of such a classic work of theater."

And she laughed.

And she ceased to be anything that he knew. No longer a girl, nor even a woman. Her smile, white and wide against the dusk of her skin, made her altogether something else. She was something too warm to be ethereal, something too distant to be smoldering. She was...she was...

"Funny."

He blinked. "What is?"

"You, little northern boy," she replied. "You make me laugh."

"I hardly see where the humor lies in turning a theatrical masterpiece into a massacre."

Her smile faded. Her brow furrowed. She looked at him incredulously before shaking her head.

"No, we aren't actually—"

Her voice drifted off with her eyes as she looked over her shoulder to the stage. A glance became a gaze became a long frown that would have fit better on someone much older.

Perhaps she was getting into character, he reasoned. He fidgeted briefly in his seat before rising to leave.

And that was when she touched him.

Hers were not delicate hands, used to firmer flesh than his, and she did not let him slip through them. When he turned to her, her smile was back. No longer wide and cheery, it was something sad and subdued. Silk curtains in a stiff breeze.

"Stay and rest your feet, northern boy," she whispered. "My cue isn't for some time. The Lady Liaja has not yet emerged."

He looked out toward the crowd, where he should be searching. He looked thirty-four degrees to the east, nine hundred and fifty-one paces in a straight line, where he should be going.

"I should go. I've got..." He searched for an appropriate word, found only one. "Uh, people...to meet."

That was embarrassing. Not *quite* as embarrassing as the ease with which she pulled him back to the bench, though.

"One does not *meet* people," she replied. "One leads people, one kills people. One ignores acquaintances, one betrays associates, one avoids lovers. One only *meets* friends." She leaned back against the wall, tapping her chin in a show of contemplation. "But you didn't *say* 'friends,' so you're not meeting anyone, you're just trying to get away."

He furrowed his brow. "That seems a massive leap in logic."

She chuckled. "Am I mistaken?"

He wasn't *quite* sure which part about that question bothered him the most. Her logic defying leaps, her tremendously assumptive arrogance, her aggressively unspoken accusation...

If it wasn't clear to him, though, it certainly was to her. She ate the flush of his face through a wide, feline grin. She leaned forward, elbows on her lap, chin cradled by her hands.

"So where are we running to, northern boy?"

"I'm...I'm not...there's nowhere to—"

"You know what your problem is?"

"I am aware that my list of problems is growing by the breath, yes," he muttered, fixing a glare upon her.

"You have no love of lying," she replied, heedless of sour word or sour look. "You believe what everyone else does, that lying is something you're supposed to use as a last resort, if at all. You take no joy in the act or the feeling it creates."

"The feeling it creates being a hollow sense of fulfillment and a fleeting sense of security?"

"Only if you're an amateur of the art," she said. Her smile strained at the edges, chips on a porcelain plate. "If you feel hollow, then you didn't love the lie. If your security is fleeting, then you didn't believe it."

"And if you love it and you believe it?"

Something on her, something in her, broke. The porcelain shattered, the curtains hung still, the grime of her face peeled just slightly as a tear fell at the edge of her eye. And beneath the sand, beneath the dirt, she was soft, and she was dark, and she was a warm night at the crest of a grassy hill.

"Then," she said, "it's not a lie, is it?"

He stared at her, at that corner of her eye, at that long line of skin wiped clean by tears, at that fragile, soft, silk-and-porcelain smile. And just as he could not turn away, she could no longer bear to look at him. She looked past him and her smile diminished. He followed her gaze and saw the man approaching.

A small, slender fellow in silks and gold chains approached. His smile was strong and false below a waxed mustache. He gave a cursory glance at Dreadaeleon before turning his smile to the woman.

"My dear," he said, making a long, false bow. "They await your debut."

He gestured down the bench of broken people. She nodded once. She turned back to Dreadaeleon and offered him a soft look. It faded as she rose. Her shoulders stooped as she walked. Her body shuddered as she placed a foot upon the step.

And then he remembered to call after her.

"Wait!" he cried. "What is your name?"

And he saw the smile once more as she looked over shoulder.

"My name? Why, I am Lady Liaja, to be offered up as sacrifice for the adoring masses."

"No, you're not," he replied.

"Love the lie, northern boy. I cannot bear for you not to."

She ascended the steps. She walked to the edge of the stage, where another man in silks was waiting. A number of hands went into the air, a number of words were hurled at her, a number of peering eyes lay upon her. The man in silks hurled words back, pointed to people, nodded and shook his head, and laughed in their faces.

Dreadaeleon watched, far away and with ears too small to hear what they were saying and eyes too big to turn away.

"You like her, my friend?"

He remembered the man in silks at his side. He looked to him briefly. He saw only the false smile before he found his gaze drifting back to her.

"The bidding has only just begun," the man said. "If you've coin enough, you may try to purchase her for yourself."

"What?" Dreadaeleon asked, incredulity on his face.

"Ah, I see. You have never seen a debt auction before?" He made a gesture over Dreadaeleon's face. "Your skin. Of course. This must look strange to a northerner."

"Strange is one word for it, yes," Dreadaeleon replied. "'Illegal,' 'amoral,' and 'disgusting' are other good adjectives for slavery."

"Slavery? No, no, sir." He held up his hands, shaking his head. "She merely owes more money than she can pay. To whom does not concern us. She came to us to find her a respectable buyer and she has the final say in who purchases her." He glanced over his shoulder at the crowd. "At the moment, it looks like the bathhouses have taken an interest in her. Good prospects. Wealthy clients."

"What the hell's a bathhouse?"

"You may call them something significantly more crass in the north. Whorehouses? Pleasure-dens? Here in Cier'Djaal, we respect a business's dignity."

"How can you speak of respect when you *sell* people? *People!* What about *their* dignity?"

"Indeed, *northerner*." The man's tone turned hostile as his mirth faded. "And how can *you* speak of dignity? I have heard tales of what happens to the poor in your cities. They are offered mercy from a church that wants their servitude; they are offered respite in an army that wants their lives. If they are truly allowed dignity, they get to beg on the streets and watch their families starve to death. Here, at least, a man or a woman has a choice in the matter."

"How can they have a choice if the only way out is selling themselves?"

"You don't like it?" The man sneered, turning away. "Buy her yourself. Show her what a gentleman you are."

As a matter of fact, he wanted to do something along those lines.

Save that his method involved more fire and ice. He could feel the power at his fingertips, burning behind his brow, singing beneath his skin. The magic inside him begged to be released, to show these heathens what it meant to cross a wizard, to show Liaja, whatever her true name was, that he could save her.

And then he felt it: the electricity, the fluctuating temperatures, the pressure bearing down on him. He was aware of the wizards who would eagerly kill him for unleashing his magic over so trivial a matter.

Thirty-four degrees to the east. Nine hundred and fifty-one paces in a straight line.

And he let go of his anger. And he let the power dissipate inside him. And he sighed, let his shoulders stoop, and said only what came to mind.

"This is horrible."

"This is business," the man in the silks replied and moved to pick up the next person from the bench.

Onstage, Liaja was being taken down. A man in a black suit emblazoned with a crest depicting a curling black cat took her gently by the arm and led her away. She never looked up to see him watching her, to see his eyes fixed impotently upon her and growing ever smaller as she vanished into the crowd. She could not see him hold his hand out, strain to reach after her, and fail to take even a step forward.

She did not see him.

There was small comfort in that.

And growing ever smaller.

A shadow fell over him suddenly. He didn't bother looking up. There was something distinctly familiar, almost comforting, in the aura of contempt that heralded Gariath's presence.

"Who was that?" Gariath asked.

"A woman," Dreadaeleon said. "I don't know what her name was."

"It doesn't matter."

"Oh." Dreadaeleon frowned. "Right."

The shadow shifted as Gariath turned to go. "I found a scent. Come."

"Of Miron?" Dreadaeleon asked without looking up.

"I don't know. Maybe. Come and find out. Or you can stay here and wait until I solve all our problems again."

As good a reason as any to leave, the boy thought. He did desperately want to put this place behind him. He did want to forget this happened.

But as he turned around, he felt paralyzed. There was not enough blood left for his legs to move. It all swelled in his chest.

Gariath, at some point, became aware of this. He turned and looked at Dreadaeleon.

"I watched her disappear," the boy said. "And I didn't do anything. I could have set fire to something. I could have frozen them where they stood and made off with her. But I'd have been breaking the law. So I sat here and I just watched her go."

Gariath said nothing. Gariath did not move. And so Dreadaeleon felt something stick in his craw and spoke in a choked whisper.

"Should I have done something?"

"Whatever you could have done, you didn't." Gariath's voice was flat as he stalked away. "So, what's it matter?"

SEVEN

THE BRASS LADY

He couldn't see himself in her face.

There was too much there already. Her eyes were too full of purpose to reflect someone else's desires. Her chin was too strong to be bent under the weight of someone else's needs. Her lips, the enigmatic tug of a smile at the edges, were for someone else. Not him.

And for that, Denaos was grateful.

He felt distant as he watched her, even though she was two feet away. She was that kind of woman, though: the kind who bore a purpose too big for most men to contemplate, let alone understand. He had always felt dwarfed by her, in awe of her, of all she did. Just as he did now.

And still, he stared. He cleared his throat. He offered a nice smile. "You look good."

His voice cracked.

"I mean, considering." He looked away, up to the chipped and smoke-stained stone that framed the shadowy alcove she stood in. Refuse crowded her sandaled feet. Sand hung like a shroud over her shoulders. "I remember this place being nicer, at least.

"But you," he said, looking at her again, "you are more beautiful than I remember. And there hasn't been a day I haven't remembered." He squinted as he leaned closer. "Except it looks like a seagull shit on your head or something. Let me get that for you."

He withdrew a handkerchief from his belt and began scraping

away the dried filth from her hair. Not a single lock moved beneath his finger. Nor did she blink as he pressed himself against her. And she continued to say nothing.

Denaos wasn't quite sure what he expected a brass statue to say.

But Denaos hadn't quite expected to see this statue. Not today, anyway. He wanted to come at night, when there were fewer people, when he could have been alone, when he could have apologized and wept and begged her for forgiveness.

As he had begged her once before, on a cold night when she drew her last breath in his arms, her blood on his blade and a gaping wound he had torn in her throat.

Through careful meditation, steadfast reflection, and lots and *lots* of alcohol, he had learned not to let his thoughts drift too far back. If they did, he would feel the shiver of that night. He would feel the warmth of her blood on his hands. He would feel the urge to scream.

And then everyone would know. They would know everything.

Even now, they stared. The people of the Souk would slow as they walked past and saw this pale northerner polishing her statue, sweeping refuse from her alcove. But they would do nothing more than make certain he was not defacing her.

Perhaps they had forgotten who she was. Perhaps the younger among them weren't quite sure what she did. But all of them could still remember her name.

Houndmistress.

Of the many names they gave her—Savior of Cier'Djaal, Thief-slayer, Punisher of Sin, Bitch Queen—and the many names she loathed, that was the one that stuck. It didn't capture the entirety of her deeds: her love of the people, her love of the city, her hatred of the fashas that wanted to abuse them both.

But the people would only remember how she stood against the Jackals, those thieves, those assassins, those thugs, and triumphed. They would remember how she and her crusaders had smoked them out of their dens and sent them running into the streets, out the gates, and into the desert.

And they would remember when the Jackals returned.

They would remember that cold night when the heralds every-where lined on every street and said to every person that the Hound-mistress had been murdered. The night a single stone hurled from the crowds had killed her herald. The night of the riots.

Days later, so many buildings burned and fourteen hundred people dead, everyone knew the Jackals had returned and things were going back to the bad old days. They would remember that.

They wouldn't remember him, though.

He was confident of that. He was darker when they had seen him at her side, his skin covered by time spent in the sun and patched with false pigment. He was pink and pale and northern now. His hair had been dark and glossy back then, dyed thick and groomed meticulously to fool them into thinking he was one of them. Now he had red-brown stuff growing in unruly messes out of scalp, chin, and jaw.

That had been another man when he was in Cier'Djaal last, when he stood beside her. That was a man who had had a wife and a heart and a soul. That man vanished on the night she died and was never seen again. That man was dead.

And only Denaos remained.

They didn't know him. They didn't know his face, or his name. But they knew his deeds, as they knew hers. They knew his death, as they knew hers.

But she had a name.

He knelt down to the plaque upon the pedestal where her statue stood. He pulled a dagger free from his belt and meticulously began to dig every grain of sand from each letter until he could see it, sum-marized in a few short letters, an afterthought of a story of a myth.

He spoke her name.

"Imone."

And he tried hard not to hate himself for doing so.

"Who is she, anyway?"

Lenk's voice. Right behind him. Denaos paused, took a breath. In a single twitch, tears retreated, breath steadied, a smile returned. He turned around and saw the young man standing, arms folded over his chest, staring up at the brass lady.

"I've seen little shrines of her all over the place," Lenk said.

"The Houndmistress," Denaos replied. "Local heroine. It became required by law for all places of business to feature an icon of her after the work she did for the city."

"Huh." Lenk shook his head. "They do things weird in the south, don't they?"

Denaos coughed. "Yeah."

Lenk responded with a curious loft of his brow. "So, uh, why were you—"

"How long have we known each other?" Denaos interrupted.

"About two years."

"And how many times have you found me hunched over in a dark, smelly corner somewhere?"

"Well, I . . ."

"And have you ever wanted to know what I was up to in any of those times?"

"Not really."

"Well, if you haven't shown an interest in my hobbies before, why the hell should I tell you what this one was all about?" Denaos snapped.

Lenk looked back at him with an expression somewhere between apology and perplexity. It was as true now as it had been then, Denaos realized: The best defense to inquiry was semi-coherent rants and accusations.

"And where have you been this whole time, anyway?" the tall man asked. "You said you found a lead an hour ago."

"Sort of," Lenk replied. "It's more that I had an idea."

"That's not the same thing as a lead. And it doesn't take an hour to form an idea."

"No, but it took me an hour to find a Talanite beggar." Lenk grinned at his companion's befuddlement. "See, I found a lot of beggars clinging to the sides of the Souk. They're all carrying holy symbols, begging in the name of one God or another. Most of them are for some 'Ancaa' God, but I finally found one begging in the name of Talanas."

"Miron's a priest of Talanas," Denaos replied, realization dawning on him.

"A Lord Emissary of the High Church of Talanas," Lenk replied. "Duty-bound to aid every suffering soul…"

"With special consideration to the faithful." Denaos's grin grew wide. "Clever."

"That, my friend," Lenk said smugly as he strode down the streets, "is why I'm the leader."

"You're the leader because no one else wants to be held responsible when we're finally caught," Denaos replied, striding alongside him as they pushed their way back into the crowd.

⊷ ▰◆▰ ⊶

At the edge of the Souk, Lenk and Denaos found them.

The pious beggars sat in a long row, pressed against the Harbor Wall for want of pews. They knelt upon the stone or discarded rucksacks, for want of prayer cloths. They scrawled crude holy symbols upon the street and wall in chalk and coal; they made crude effigies out of whatever they could find; they muttered quietly to men and Gods for alms.

They knelt in a long line. Too poor for priests, too pitiful for Gods, the beggars of Cier'Djaal held sermon to a sky that offered nothing.

"That's him?" Denaos asked, gesturing to one soul with his chin.

Lenk looked and saw him, one sullen face among many. He was a northerner, paler than they, his skin the color of curdled milk rather than the tarnished bronze of the Djaalics. That was only barely noticeable, though; poverty had painted them all the same color.

Upon the dirty streets before him, he had scrawled out a picture of the Phoenix, the sacred sigil of the Healer and patron beast of Talanas. His head lolled as his lips dribbled out a wordless plea.

"Yeah," Lenk replied. He pointed to the wooden bowl at the man's feet. "He's got a few coins, too. Someone's been by. Maybe Miron."

"So go ask. I'll wait here and keep watch."

Denaos watched as Lenk carefully made his way toward the northerner. But it wasn't long before he found his attentions pulled toward the people of the Souk. Though he suspected all had seen him at one point or another, back when he still lived here, nary a one looked at him with anything more than the contempt they held for a man standing in the middle of foot traffic.

And he, in turn, knew none of them. Silf the Patron, God of Thieves, held anonymity as a virtue as valuable as infamy but less precious than ignorance. With every passing moment Denaos knew that wisdom. There was comfort in staring out over a sea of faces, each one as meaningless as the last.

Except that guy, Denaos thought as he caught sight of someone uncomfortably familiar. *I know him from somewhere, don't I?* He squinted for a moment. *Back in the old days . . .*

And the moment it dawned on him, the blessing of ignorance died in his eyes.

He couldn't remember the man's name. But he remembered his face. And he remembered the vile deeds that man had done with a dagger. And he remembered the dark clothes he wore and the sandy hood that he gently tugged up around his collar as a pair of similarly clad men met up with him.

Jackals.

He remembered them. Every blade in the dark, every house burning in the night, every cold dawn that rose to find more corpses of debtors and squealers hanging from the Harbor Gate. The Jackals ruled Cier'Djaal's underworld with such cruelty precisely so that every man would remember them.

But he was among the few men that the Jackals were certain to remember, themselves.

Keep steady, he reminded himself. *They don't know what you look like now. They don't know you're back. You're just another fellow standing in the Souk, minding his own business... and slowly reaching for a dagger. Stop that.*

He became aware of his fingers unconsciously wrapping around the hilt of the knife, just as he was aware of his heart crawling into his throat. He steadied himself as the Jackals glanced about warily before disappearing into the crowd.

He knew that look. They were planning something. Which meant that his immediate plans should involve getting as far away from here as possible. As soon as Lenk was finished with—

"YOU!"

Dagger came to hand easily. He whirled about as a voice screamed from somewhere, but the scream was not for him.

He saw Lenk holding out his hands, mouth fumbling in explanation as the northern beggar backpedaled, thrusting a quivering finger at the young man.

"Demon!" the beggar screamed. "Murderer! Stay back! *STAY BACK!"*

For a man who came from a part of the world where begging was an occupation instead of an art, Denaos noted, this northern fellow seemed to have the act down cold. He sprang to his feet and scooped up his bowl in one breath, turned tail, and took off running in another.

He sheathed his blade as he came up to Lenk, who stood dumbfounded, staring at the chalk drawing where the beggar had just knelt.

"You spoke to him for all of thirty breaths," Denaos noted, "and he took off screaming and cursing your name. This is a new record for you, isn't it?"

"I knew him," Lenk whispered into the dry, hot air.

"What?"

"I knew him. I... was speaking to him, trying to make nice, and I asked him where he was from. And..." Lenk stumbled over his voice, picking words up as he found them. "He said 'Steadbrook.'"

Denaos raised a brow. "Your hometown."

"Burned to the ground. And I recognized him. I knew his name. Gathwer. He owned a farm at the edge of the village. I said his name."

"And?"

"And that's when he started calling me a demon."

"Well, maybe he meant something different." Denaos glanced over his shoulder. He saw more hooded people, more Jackals, dispersing throughout the crowd. "We should really be—"

"How many different ways are there to interpret someone calling you a demon?" Lenk asked, glowering at the man. "We need to go after him. He's our only lead on finding Miron."

"We can find others." Denaos swept his gaze around. Everywhere, he could pick them out. Sand-colored hoods. Figures slinking in shadows. Knives covertly drawn. There couldn't be this many here for any other reason. They knew he was here. "Later. *Much* later. For now, we need to—"

"Ain't no good running, pinkie."

The voice, sharp and low like a bent blade, stuck in their ears. Neither man had any trouble discerning from whence it came, for neither man could ignore the ochre stare fixed upon them from the nearby wall.

Far apart from the other beggars, with no God to feign patronage to, the creature crouched upon thin legs, resting thin arms on thin knees. Every bit of him swaddled in dirty rags, a scarf wrapped about his head, all that was visible was a pair of eyes without a face.

"You seen 'em, you already dead." His eyes were impossible to read, but the upward inflection of his voice suggested he was quite amused by this fact. "If only there was a mysterious stranger with an air of opportunism around that could help you."

"I assure you, the scent of desperation that led you here was coming from someone else." Denaos cast a look down to the empty stone before the creature. "And a beggar without a bowl is less than useless."

Lenk held up his hands. "Sorry, I seem to have missed... *everything*." He glanced at the rags-swaddled creature. "Just what the hell are you?"

"This, Lenk," Denaos interjected, "is a saccarii, a creature that stands distinct in a city full of scum by somehow being too loathsome to let in and too shifty to keep out."

"Among the human carrion do we humbly thrive." The saccarii offered an incline of his head on a neck far too long. "And for a mere favor, can the services of one such as Khaliv," he tapped his chest, "be yours."

"What kind of services?" Lenk asked.

"Wrong question," Denaos muttered, taking his companion by the arm. "You don't ask a saccarii for favors, you don't owe the saccarii favors. Better that way."

"Better than what, pinkie?" Khaliv replied, voice full of mirth. "Wandering around until you're cut down in the streets?" At Denaos's wary glare, he seemed to grow even more amused. "You seen 'em? They're everywhere. You want to get what you're looking for and get out alive, you listen to me."

"How in the hell would you know what we're looking for?" Lenk asked.

"Not hard to find out what people want," the saccarii said. "Even less hard when people are a pair of pink northerners who say everything that comes into their head with no care for who might be listening."

That statement made Lenk hesitate before asking again. "And why should we believe you can help us?"

"Who else gonna help you?"

"There's plenty of people to ask."

"You don't go to people to get information. Souk's full of them. From above, they all look like starving rats crawling all over each other. To know what's going on, you go to the ground." Khaliv's ocher eyes narrowed. "And the saccarii have lived underfoot for a long, long time."

Lenk barely had a moment to look thoughtful before Denaos placed a hand on his shoulder and took him aside.

"You don't want to do this," he muttered into the young man's ear.

"I *want* to find Miron and get paid," Lenk retorted sharply. "As I thought you did."

"And in order to do that, I want to stay alive," Denaos replied. "Dealing with a saccarii has never been conducive to that." He glanced over his shoulder toward the creature. "They're the native race of Vhehanna. When Cier'Djaal was built, it was built atop their homes. They do *not* have fond memories of humanity."

"I travel with a shict, a thug, and ... Gariath," Lenk replied, plucking Denaos's hand off his shoulder. "If I went around judging people by their race and profession, I'd be a lonely man."

"Then judge him by the fact that he's a freaky little thing skulking in the shadows staring at us," Denaos hissed. "Or by the vague threats he's spewing at us."

"We get threatened all the time," Lenk said. He affixed the man with a suspicious stare. "Or do you know of a reason why we should take this one seriously?"

More than you know, runt.

Denaos opted not to say that and the whole messy story that went with it. He merely held his hands out to the side, inclined his head, and made a note to rub this in later when it all went to shit.

Lenk, satisfied, turned back to Khaliv.

"We're looking for—"

"I can find him."

The young man blinked. "I haven't told you yet."

"Talanite, right? Northerner, I'm guessing? Ain't hard to find someone like that in the Souk. Coins to curses says he's at the fountain."

"*This* is why you don't trust a saccarii," Denaos interjected. "There's no fountain in the Souk."

"There *wasn't* until the Lady Fasha Teneir found the love of Ancaa and had one commissioned for the poor to have water," Khaliv replied. "'Course, the poor aren't allowed in the Souk, so it's just a nice place to visit if you're a foreigner."

Lenk eyed the saccarii carefully. "Show me. Then you get paid."

"You suspicious of me?" Khaliv asked.

"Very."

"Smart."

The saccarii rose with joints popping and bones creaking. He rolled his head on his neck, rotated his shoulders, and cracked his knuckles, his body groaning in protest. Neither man could see what expression he wore beneath his raggedy veil, yet neither would doubt that he probably took great pleasure in the disgust present on theirs.

He bowed low, extending a long arm out toward the crowd.

"After you, sirrahs," he said.

With a hesitant look, Lenk began walking. Denaos had just begun to follow when he noticed a pair of eyes on him. Between two stalls, so distant as to be a memory, a man in dark leathers stared right at him. The tall man froze, as if all his problems would be solved if he simply held still enough. Maybe it actually worked; the man in leather drew up a tan hood and turned, disappearing into the crowd.

"They ain't here for you, adviser."

A word. A title. As common as any. Yet it was one that made Denaos stiffen like a blade. Because it was one that Denaos hadn't been called in years.

"You been gone from Cier'Djaal too long," Khaliv whispered. "Lot's changed since you stood by her and spun your sweet lies."

"And what," he whispered, "do *you* know of that, saccarii?"

"I know who you are. I know who you were. I know who you killed." He adjusted his veil, pulling it up over his eyes. "And I didn't tell nobody."

He flexed his fingers. The skin on his joints sloughed off and fell as a pale shedding, leaving glistening dark flesh behind. He shoved his hands into his pockets and pushed past Denaos.

"You gonna owe me a favor."

Denaos wasn't sure how long he stood there, staring at the empty space where Khaliv had just squatted. But when he turned around, the saccarii was gone, Lenk was gone, the Jackals were gone, and everyone was gone but the human tide.

And he wished that he were as alone as he felt.

EIGHT

NATIVES

Just as Lenk had begun to grow used to Cier'Djaal's Souk and its seething tide of humanity, the metaphor proved painfully apt once more.

Where before it had ebbed and flowed, it now receded, parting before him as though he were a prophet. Though the wary gazes cast his way with varying amounts of scorn were anything but reverential.

The vast majority of glares, however, were not for him.

Khaliv's slow, ambling gait cut a path through the crowd. Even if Lenk could have seen his face past his veil, he doubted the saccarii gave much notice to those whispering about him. And as Lenk overheard some of the more threatening ones—ones revolving around ropes, mostly—that began to worry him.

"You're too tense, pinkie," Khaliv said reprovingly.

"Yeah, I get that way when I get the feeling everyone wants to kill me," Lenk replied.

"Every predator is always aware of prey," Khaliv said. "Humans ain't no different. You show 'em fear, they're gonna show you teeth. So toughen up."

There was an obvious truth there, Lenk knew. *He* was the one with the sword, after all. And yet, for all his steel and scars, they looked at him as if he was meat instead of a warrior. While Khaliv, with his rags and filth, bade them move by presence alone.

And when he stopped and looked around, the entire crowd stood stiff.

"Ain't got much time," Khaliv said. "Jhouche'll be here soon. They ain't gonna show me the same courtesy as these fine folk."

His gaze settled on a nearby lamppost and he gamboled toward it, sending people scattering out of his way with a gasp. He shimmied up, perching upon its iron hood and staring out over the crowd. A long, bony finger extended, pointing out to the crowd.

Lenk followed. Lenk saw.

A ghost stood among the living. His white robes were too white, unsullied by sweat or sand. His back was too straight, his chin too proud, his features too gentle for this cauldron of stooping, weary people. Upon his breast, he wore a pin of Talanas's Phoenix.

Miron Evenhands. Chatting away with a merchant as the world idly ebbed around him. As though he didn't even care that people were looking for him.

Lenk looked up and found Khaliv staring down at him expectantly.

"I should have told you," the young man said. "I don't have money."

"Nor I, friend," Khaliv said. "Saccarii don't trade in coin."

Lenk couldn't see it, of course, but somehow, through veil and filth, he could feel Khaliv's long, crooked smile.

"You'll owe me."

And with that, the saccarii leapt off the lamppost and landed lightly upon the cobblestones. Thrusting hands in pockets, he took off at a jog. The crowd opened before him, closed behind him, and swallowed him whole.

Lenk glanced behind him. Denaos was absent. Unsurprising; the rogue had a good instinct for sensing when a bad idea was about to go wrong. Fortunately, Lenk had an equally good instinct for realizing when bad ideas were the only options.

And he chose to listen to it once more.

Hiking his sword up, he took off, weaving through the crowd. As if they sensed his attempts as one collective entity, the people pressed closer together, impeding his progress.

Miron stood not far away, chatting away the day. His laughter was long and crystalline in the din, inviting others to join in. His smile coaxed out grins all around him.

The Lord Emissary was, indeed, a pleasant enough fellow to be around if he didn't owe one money.

"Evenhands!" Lenk called out.

Miron twitched slightly, looking around for the source of the voice. Lenk cried out again, leaping up to be seen over the heads of the crowd and waving his hands.

"Evenhands!"

From beneath his cowl, Miron looked at Lenk. His eyes twinkled brightly, a pair of stars set in a soft, pale dawn. The smile he offered was soft, slow, and gentle. Lenk saw it for just a moment before the priest turned smartly on his heel and departed.

"Hey!"

Lenk pushed a body aside, ignoring a curse upon his family. He elbowed his way past a portly woman, suffered a slap for his efforts. He ignored the sweat and filth and noise as he pushed his way through the crowd.

"Get back here, priest!"

Miron gave no sign that he had heard the young man. Miron gave no sign of stopping. Without weaving, without shoving, he seemed to flow through the crowd, a line of white froth amidst the tide.

That wasn't right. How did he move like that? Lenk wondered. The tide barely even seemed to acknowledge him.

Lenk grit his teeth, suffering the elbows and curses of the crowd as he shoved his way through. He kept his eyes upon that froth, that man too pristine to be among the Souk. Miron would not walk away with his money, his new life, again.

"PRIEST!"

———◆———

"Demon."

"She-beast."

"How did it get in here?"

She could hear them. As they crowded around the fountain, held back by the guards in black clothing, they whispered to each other. Her ears rose, taking in every sound.

"I thought the Souk was supposed to be safe."

"Look at her. She's not the same color as the others."

"Is that blood around her mouth?"

And she could see them. She could see their wide-eyed stares peering over the guards' shoulders. She could see the fear, the curiosity, and the faces they would show only in the presence of a beast.

"Who let a shict in here?"

"Why don't they just throw her out?"

"Filthy oids. Why don't they just leave?"

As she looked at them, as she heard them, their terror, their hatred, she found she could not hate them.

No more than she could hate any maggot for crawling from a diseased corpse.

That, Kataria knew, was what they were. Blind, grubby little things that knew nothing but rotten flesh and putrid meat, terrified of the world outside their homely corpse. Their corpse may have been of stone and sand, their meat may have been gold and silver, but they were maggots all the same.

And she could not hate them for that.

She could only hate that her companions had come from the same kind of corpse, possessed the same appetites and the same fears. She could only hate that her companions would leave it all behind, leave *her* behind, for this corpse. These maggots.

That was a flimsy hate, though. She needed something stronger, hatred she could hold on her tongue, sharpen on her teeth, and jam into someone's eye.

She forced that hate up from her heart into her mouth. And there she held it behind clenched teeth, staring across the square at the first one who would die.

"Khutu," she had heard them call him: a maggot that had learned to walk and dressed himself in blue silk to hide his flabby body. His face, cherubic and overhungry, was painted with gold and white and blue. He tilted his nose up as high as it would go as he looked over her bow, handling the weapon like it was some charming piece of antiquity and not something she would use to kill him.

She made a note to savor the surprise on his face later.

For now, though, the only thing on his face besides all the paint was arrogance, the cautious pride one shows a caged beast. And he showed it to her in a broad, blue-lipped smile. Perhaps he sensed the hatred boiling in her mouth; she made little enough effort to hide it. She didn't care. As he tossed her bow aside, he made a fleeting gesture.

"Bring her unto me."

Eight gauntleted grips tightened on her arms and shuffled her awkwardly toward the small man. The guards moved her warily and she could feel the tremble in their steps as they did. It was a point of pride that it took four men in armor with swords to restrain her. It would be a bigger point of pride when they realized four men weren't nearly enough.

Khutu raised a hand, slowly, as if to cup her chin in his manicured fingers. He cringed, though, as he spied the blood around her mouth. His hand, instead, slipped into his sleeve and withdrew a long, thin wand of ivory wood. He bent it daintily between two soft hands as his kohl-painted eyes slithered over her.

He turned about, glancing to the armored men ringing them, keeping the crowd at bay. His eyes settled on a large tent on a raised wooden platform that squatted ominously beside the marble-carved fountain. Ten shirtless, brawny slaves stood at its sides, eyes straight ahead. The sunlight caught the black fabric of the tent, painting in shadow a massive shape within the tent that raised a hand and waved.

Khutu nodded and turned back to Kataria, blue lips coiled into a smile.

"You will note, first, her savagery." His voice came gentle as song, high-pitched and uncomfortable in her ears. "A treasure such as this is not meant to linger in the tender grip of lord or lady fasha. She demands a ferocity to match her own. She demands a fury. Such is the nature of the shict."

The men's grips on her arms were overly tense, hard with fear, and they only grew tighter at the description. Bowstrings drawn too taut; they would snap if pulled hard enough.

"And it is this natural aspect to the shict that must be treasured," Khutu continued. He waved his wand at her, glancing back to the tent. "You see how she barely follows? No doubt, the tongue of civilized men eludes her. This feral grace she exudes is unpracticed, undisciplined." He absently chewed the tip of the wand between two blue lips. "Untested."

Kataria looked over at the tent, if only to look away from Khutu for a moment. The figure within trembled with an emotion Kataria dare not venture a guess about. But her eyes caught it for only a moment before they were drawn to the sigil painted in white upon the tent's fabric. A naked girl atop a bed of coins, just the same as the vulgore at the harbor had been wearing.

She felt something tap beneath her chin. Her eyes crossed to see the wand's tip, still slick with saliva, tilting her head upward.

"Note the angle of the jaw," Khutu said, tracing a line across her chin. "Perhaps in our own civil society, this might be considered mannish. But in the shict, it is a marvel of nature. Jaws such as hers are required for the gnashing of bones and meat that provides the she-beast with such anatomy."

He tapped the wand against his cheek, mouth open in thought as his eyes drifted lower. Her abdomen contracted instinctively as she felt his eyes settle upon her midriff.

"Correct her posture," the man said.

The men tightened their grips on her arms; she could hear the clanking tremble of their gauntlets. They were growing tired, held too tense for too long. Not enough, though, to make her move and not enough to keep them from hoisting her to her feet and forcing her spine erect.

Khutu's wand followed his gaze, coming to a slow and gingerly halt beneath her sternum. She could feel the brush of the finer hairs on her body as it slipped down, tracing a delicate line down the center of her belly.

"The rare quality of such musculature is never seen in the women of civilized lands," Khutu hummed, the wand tracing a slow circle about her navel. "Nor even in the khoshicts, who strive so much to be like us. In the north, the shicts of the forest make no apologies for their restless savagery."

Her breath caught in her throat, the muscle of her abdomen contracting as she felt the tip of the wand gingerly slip into her navel. He twisted it idly between two fingers, pressing at tender skin. She kept her teeth hidden behind her lips, but nothing could hold back the growl boiling up in her throat.

"But they can be tamed," he whispered, "given patience...and time."

He looked over his shoulder to the tent, smile broad and blue.

"I trust she meets with your approval, O fasha?"

The shape within nodded once. Khutu beamed beneath his paint.

"Outstanding," he said. He looked to the men holding her. "Have her taken to the palanquin and we'll..."

His voice trailed into an undignified cringe as he caught sight of something awry. A single, waxed eyebrow rose in query.

"Did I not send *five* of you out?" Khutu asked.

She heard the rattling of armor from the nearby crowd, the groan of pain. And from the wide eyes on Khutu's face, she could guess what he had seen. No doubt the fifth guard had just found his way back, stumbling out of the crowd with a red smear upon his neck and a pulpy stump where an ear had once been.

Khutu's eyes drifted down to her face. As they noted once more the smear of blood at the corner of her mouth, they grew wider still. She smiled, showing him the crimson staining her overlarge canines. He opened his mouth to say something.

She spat.

Something flew into Khutu's mouth. He flailed briefly, choking on words and spittle alike as he bent over and coughed something out onto the stones. The better part of a human ear glistened with blood and saliva, the same that trickled over Khutu's painted lips.

"Ancaa alive!"

His voice quavered into a shrill squeal, hands flying up. The men's grips on her trembled at his fear and anger.

And she saw her opportunity.

With blood on her howl, she tore away from the guards. Their hands snapped; they cried out as she jerked away and lunged for Khutu. The painted man held up his wand in a defense barely as feeble as his voice and skinny hands.

She tore the implement from his grasp, seized his arm, and rammed it down. The wand split through the tendons of his wrist, splintering as it burst out the other side. She seized him by the shoulders and threw him, screaming, into the pack of guards.

The men at the perimeter, holding the crowd back, reached for their swords. But they took no further action as Kataria seized her bow from the street and drew an arrow in a seamless movement. Khutu flailed amidst a tangle of guards, screaming for someone to do something.

She obliged him, her response in the shriek of a metal arrowhead biting the air.

It flew into the gang of men, missing Khutu only by his fortuitous squirm, and lodging itself in the collarbone of a guard who went down gurgling. The others advanced warily, held at bay as she drew another arrow and swept its point about, silently challenging anyone to step closer.

"Stop! *STOP!*"

Someone did. Someone she didn't feel the urge to put an arrow into.

Yet.

Carrying a dirty hat in her hand and breathing heavily, Asper pushed past the crowd and into the square. She interposed herself between Kataria and the guards, hands thrown out wide as though they would be a suitable shield for either arrow or blade.

"Just *stop!*" the priestess cried out. "It's very obvious that you're not going to take her without losing more than ear, so let's just calm down for a moment."

"She...she *killed* one of the house's guards!" Khutu cried out, disentangling himself from the men.

"You kidnapped her," Asper countered hotly.

"She did *this!*" The painted man held up his impaled wrist. "She *bit off* an ear!"

"You kidnapped someone prone to stabbing and biting!" Asper snapped. She waved a hand at Kataria. "Did you not *see* the teeth and bow? What the hell did you *think* was going to happen, halfwit?"

"I'll tell you what *I* think is going to happen."

Kataria's voice was accompanied by the creak of her bow as she drew her arrow upon Khutu. Asper took her by the wrist, drawing her close and growling.

"There are at least a dozen of them," she said harshly.

"And there's two of us," Kataria replied. "Handle three of them and I'll take care of the rest."

"And what'll you do about the rest of the city when it comes down on us?" Keeping herself close enough to interfere with Kataria's aim, Asper turned and addressed Khutu. "Look, obviously, there's been some"—she glanced at Khutu, bleeding atop a dead man—"misunderstanding. We can work this out! Maybe!"

"I agree entirely."

The voice was long and low as it came from the tent. A pair of the shirtless men drew back the curtains to expose what appeared to be something between a man, a grub, and a pillow that couldn't quite make up its mind.

Kataria had seen humans before that were merely fat. Kataria had seen humans that were merely gargantuan. There was nothing mere about this human.

His many rolls of flesh, wrapped in a blue silk robe that was somehow both voluminous and straining at the same time, blended indistinguishably with the many silken pillows that he sat among. Burdens of gold and silver wreathed his shoulders, his chubby digits, his many chins. And atop it all, the peak of a mountain of excess, a head shaved of all hair and painted in wreaths of white and blue colors crowned the face that stared down with a smile as vast as his person.

"May the House of Ghoukha, Fasha of Cier'Djaal, extend fondest welcomes to you, northerner."

His voice flowed like a river, something deep and resonant that did not expect to be resisted. His gaze, though, was something darker that settled upon Kataria like a hungry night.

"Please, accept my humblest apologies for our misunderstanding," the man called Ghoukha boomed. "I trust that we need not prove the northern repute for unreasonableness correct today, yes?"

Asper's face screwed up slightly. "Pardon?"

"Of course." Ghoukha nodded, sending his chins jiggling. "There is no need to let the relations of our regions be dictated by senseless melodramatics, yes?"

Kataria glanced over her shoulder, at the tears streaking Khutu's face, at the dead man lying next to the severed ear. She snorted.

"What has happened here is no more than a mistake, a cut thumb on a paper's edge." Ghoukha chuckled, rippling. "And do we all not look foolish when we spill blood over a mistake? Of course, we apologize for trying to take the shict."

"Well." Asper visibly shrank with the force of her sigh. "Good."

"We had no idea she belonged to you." He placed his massive hands together and inclined his head in apology. "We shall, of course, pay for her."

Asper's eyes went as wide as Kataria's went narrow. The priestess held up her hands.

"Uh, well, I'm flattered—"

Kataria whirled her scowl upon the woman. "The *hell* are you flattered for?"

It would be hard to explain to anyone, Asper thought, how after so many years of being assumed to be the weak one in the group, someone thought of her as strong enough to own someone. It would certainly be no easier to explain to a shict trembling with barely contained fury. She cleared her throat, looked back to Ghoukha.

"She's not mine. She's not yours. You can't have her for any amount."

Ghoukha stared at her blankly for a moment. The lower lids of his eyes, painted blue, rose beneath his eyes, giving the impression of an enraged reptile.

"Northerner." His voice no longer flowed, but boiled in his throat and emerged as hissing steam. "I am fasha. My family owns spiders. My family owns silk. My family owns *this city*. I am gentle enough to spend coin as pleasantries and, like pleasantries, I have no difficulty withholding them if I find them inconvenient."

The fasha was trembling now as his voice boiled inside him, sending his body quivering. Kataria saw his men responding, reaching for blades, inching closer. She drew her arrow, began picking targets.

It would have been much easier had Asper not stepped in front of her.

"*You* will not do anything," she said, her voice a rock to break the waters. She thrust her symbol, the silver Phoenix of Talanas, toward the fasha. "*I* am a priestess of Talanas, associated with the Lord Emissary of the Church of Talanas, Miron Evenhands. *She* is my associate and *your* men will step aside and let us pass unless you want trouble that'll make severed ears seem a pleasantry."

"You dare speak to me in such a way?" Ghoukha snarled. "You *dare* utter a God's name at me? No God reigns over a fasha and no *northerner* tells a fasha what he shall do!"

He made a wave of a massive hand. The guards began to close in. Kataria took stock of targets—exposed throats, wide eyes, men without helmets—as she counted the arrows at her quiver. Not enough for clean kills all around. But that was what she had a knife for.

Asper backed up against her warily. A solid woman with a speech,

Kataria knew, but not much use without a weapon. If she was lucky, the priestess might be a good distraction.

"Miron! *MIRON!*"

Then again, there might be a better one.

She heard him long before he came stumbling out into the cobblestones. There were only so many voices that bore so much frustration, confusion, and anger at once. It wasn't exactly a relief to see Lenk come pushing through the crowd into the square. But people in need of distractions couldn't afford to be choosy.

"Miron, where the hell did you—"

The young man's voice cut off as he became aware of his surroundings. He looked behind him with an uncertain expression upon his face before he became aware of the armed men surrounding him. He glanced at Kataria and Asper, bow drawn and backs pressed together. He threw his hands up in the air.

"How the fuck did *this* happen?"

"We were just fine until you came along," Kataria snarled.

"Clearly."

"And fine time you took, too," she snapped. "Didn't you hear me? Didn't you hear me being taken away?"

"How *could* I?" he roared right back.

"Because I can *hear you!*" she said, voice strained at the edges. "I can't hear anything *but* you!"

He flinched, as though struck. He looked away from her, to the men surrounding them. "Look, we can talk this—"

"Already tried that," Kataria interjected.

"Of course." Lenk's sigh was matched with the hiss of steel as he drew his sword. He held it warningly before him as he moved to join his companions. "How many?"

"A dozen, at least," Asper replied. "Where's Denaos?"

"Where do you think?" he asked.

"Of course," she sighed.

"It's not that bad," Lenk replied. "They might kill us, but not before we—"

"*Kill* you?" Ghoukha laughed from his tent. "Oh, my friends. We are Djaalics. *We* will not kill you." He smiled broadly, folding his hands over his massive belly. "We have people to do that for us."

He looked to Khutu and inclined his head. The small man turned a spiteful sneer upon the companions as he slid a hand into his sleeve and produced a delicate crystal bell. He flicked it gently, releasing three crystalline notes into the air. They carried over the hushed crowd, ringing through the sky.

Kataria's ears twitched. She looked at Khutu and drew her bow.

"I like this game," she said. "Now tell me what this sounds like."

She paused as her ears rose up of their own volition, a faraway sound filling them. Something deep, like the sound of thunder. It came again and again, growing louder. By the fifth time it came, she did not hear it.

She felt it.

Under her feet, the ground quaked. Before her, the crowd parted, flinging themselves to the sides as something tremendous came striding forth.

A shadow fell.

A dragonman. Perhaps ten feet tall—perhaps more—the color, size, and density of a large rock towered over the scene. Thick gray scales interlocked like plates over a body bound by a thick harness and kilt. Limbs like tree trunks hung from shoulders broad as an ox. Upon a dense neck, a reptilian head with a prodigious underbite and a very vast, very sharp horn affixed to a thick snout swung back and forth.

Black pits for nostrils twitched as he drew in a scent. Only after a moment did the great dragonman think to look down. Black eyes, wide as fists, took the companions in. Kataria saw herself reflected in the obsidian orbs, saw her vast, astonished gaze staring back at her.

Slowly, the dragonman looked over to Khutu.

"You can't be serious." His voice was slow, unstoppable, a rock rolling down a hill. "There are only three of them."

"They're animals, Kharga. *Savages!*" Khutu held up his bleeding wrist. "See what they did to me?"

"I can't bend down that far," the dragonman boomed.

"The fasha *pays* you that he need not subject his men to such barbarism," Khutu shrieked to be heard. "Do as you are commanded."

Kharga looked to Ghoukha, who gave an approving nod.

The dragonman sighed, reaching over his shoulder to grip a massive haft. He pulled free a broad ax in the shape of a cleaver, gripping it in two massive hands. The companions backed away, huddled together, raised weapons.

"Oh, Gods," he rumbled. "Let's not make this messy." He hefted it over his head. "I don't get paid enough."

They began to scatter, found Ghoukha's men herding them back toward the dragonman. Eyes desperately swept the square, searching for reprieve and, finding none, looked to heaven for a miracle.

It never came. Not from heaven, anyway.

But neither did the blow. The ax never fell. Instead, Kharga looked up, over the companions. His nostrils swallowed a great gulp of air. His eyes narrowed to spearheads. A growl rumbled in his throat.

"Have my scent, scum?"

A familiar voice spoke. Not as loud as Kharga's. But just as vast and brimming with a fury Kataria knew well.

The crowd rippled away from the figure, towering defiant over the humans in a filthy black cloak, that had spoken as Kharga's gaze swung toward it. Kataria saw him and felt a grin creeping across her face. Lenk saw, too. She could tell by his groan.

"Oh, no . . ."

Not an unreasonable response. Despite his timely arrival, things rarely got simpler when Gariath showed up.

"How long has it been since you caught the scent?" Gariath roared beneath his hood. "How long have you choked on the human weakness, *Drokha*?"

"*Rhega* . . ." Kharga rumbled, the word a bone that stuck in his craw. "*Rhega*."

"*DROKHA!*"

Two great arms, red as blood and ending in vicious claws, flew out of his cloak and seized it, tearing it from a body thick with crimson muscle wrapped in a dirty leather kilt. Vast wings spread behind him like a cape, sending people scattering. A reptilian head, topped with horns, flanked by ear-frills, ending in a snout full of razor-sharp teeth, threw back and let out a howl.

A howl met, matched, and swallowed by Kharga's roar.

The great gray dragonman thundered forward, heedless of the companions leaping out of his way or the guardsmen crushed beneath him. Gariath met him, falling to all fours and rushing forward with a horrifying laugh in his mouth. He leapt, seizing Kharga by the throat and tearing with his claws while his foe tried to dislodge him.

"Damn it, damn it, *damn it*!" Lenk snarled. "How the fuck did this happen?"

Kataria had answers for that, of course. Most of them involved punching him in the face. Satisfying as that might be, she held her fist as something caught her ear.

Somewhere distant, a bell tolled. The scent of flames rose to fill the air with black smoke. Someone screamed; a name went up on the smoke and fear.

"*Khovura!*" they screamed. "*Khovura are here! Run! RUN!*"

NINE

GLORY TO GOD

The Souk was dying before Lenk even knew what was happening. Screams choked on smoke that rose in black plumes. People cloaked in shadow slipped as black serpents among the human tide, blades in hand and blood underfoot. Flames rose in bright blossoms through merchant stalls. Everywhere, fire was rising. Everywhere, steel was flashing. Everywhere, people were running and screaming and falling.

And Lenk was left to wonder why it was that, whenever everything went straight to hell, it could never do so in a calm, orderly manner.

He wasn't certain what was happening as the world caught ablaze around him. No more than he was certain what was happening as one of Ghoukha's guards fell down before him.

Until he saw the long-bladed knife jutting from the man's back.

Thin fingers wrapped about the hilt of the weapon, wrenching it free from the guard's back. A man wrapped in shadow-black clothes twirled it about to reverse his grip on the blade. Above a dark veil, eyes burned narrow and bright and full of hate.

"*Deshaa fasha*," he hissed, stepping over the guard's body. "*Asathu deshaa*." He broke into a charge. "*KHOTH-KAPIRA!*"

Through instinct and only a bit of luck did Lenk's sword come up in time to meet the shadow-clad's blade. The man moved with such fervent speed that anything short of snap reflexes would have found Lenk with an opened throat. Their steel kissed in a shriek, the man trying to push Lenk's guard forward and receiving only a boot to the belly.

He did not so much stagger backward as slither. In one fluid movement, he shed fervor from his stance and slid into a fighter's poise, hands up, blade held at the ready, eyes alight.

Lenk tightened his grip on his blade, stepping into a swing as he brought an arc of steel to bear against the man. And with that same serpentine confidence, the man slithered out of the way. Lenk followed with another cut and another, as much to test the man's defenses as to keep him back. And each time, he was met with empty air and a frustratingly fluid foe.

He chanced another swing, fast and light. And he found flesh. But no joy to go with it.

The man recognized the strength behind the blow and caught it in his palm. Lenk found his blade trapped between fingers that most impolitely refused to be hacked off, even as blood oozed between them.

"*Deshaa fasha,*" the man repeated, fighting for control of the blade as he drew closer to his foe. "*Deshaa, nejiru.*" He snarled, whipping out his blade and catching Lenk on the cheek, drawing a thin red line. "*KHOTH-KAP—*"

It was, as it turned out, hard to scream gibberish when one's mouth was full of blood. And it was hard to keep one's mouth free of blood when a short man with a thick skull slammed it into the bridge of one's nose. The man sputtered, red spattering out beneath his veil as he staggered backward.

Lenk tore his blade free, drawing a shriek of agony.

"I heard you the first time," he snarled.

The pommel of his blade came down, smashing against the man's face and driving him to his knees. Lenk flipped his sword in his hand, angling the blade down into the man's collarbone and thrusting.

The scream lasted for but a moment. The spasming of his corpse, even shorter. The hatred, though, the fury that burned in his eyes lingered long after he slumped to the stones in a leaking pool of red.

"*DESHAA! DESHAA!*"

He whirled, saw another man in black sweeping up through the panicking mob. He raised his sword, saw the long scimitar in the man's hand come flashing out silver and red. He gaped and saw the man spring into the air and sail over the crowd to come descending upon Lenk.

But when he saw the man sent spinning awkwardly in his flight to crash upon the ground, unmoving, he merely cursed.

He looked from the dead man on the ground and the arrow quivering in his throat to the woman who had launched it. Kataria came stalking up, ire in her eyes and bow in her hands.

"The hell were you during that last fight?"

She spared a scowl for him, briefly, before gesturing over her shoulder to the three other dead men lying on the stones with arrows in their corpses.

He cleared his throat. "Ah. Well, thanks for that."

Kataria tore the arrow from the most recent corpse. "I do it all for the gratitude." She grunted, slipping it back into her quiver. "Where's Asper?"

"I was busy. You didn't see her?"

"No." Kataria looked over his head. "But I do now."

Sure enough, Lenk thought as he followed her gaze, there the priestess was. Though she was easy enough to miss in the mayhem as she valiantly tried to fight her way through a roaring tide of screaming civilians, fleeing this way and that in a mad panic.

Ghoukha's tent was fast disappearing, the many shirtless men hoisting it up by its platform and waddling off with it as the remainder of his guards closed in around him, protectively. They vanished, swallowed up by the tide of humanity.

Asper was left, struggling and fighting and screaming to be let through.

And, like a snake from the river, another black-clad burst from the torrent of people, blade aloft and scream on his lips.

"ASATHU DESH—"

Whatever he was about to say next trailed into wordless agony.

And that, too, was drowned out by the sound of fire roaring as the man was suddenly enveloped in flames. He fell back to earth, a brimstone mortal, flailing wildly. The crowd parted with instinctual fear, giving him a wide berth as he shrieked and tried vainly to bat out the flames before he collapsed in an unmoving pyre.

Callous laughter drew their eyes upward, to the top of a nearby stall. A man, short and fat, stood wrapped in black leathers with a sand-colored scarf smothering his entire head. A pair of wooden goggles peered out from below, the only thing to escape the smothering wrap besides a gruesome, excited cackle.

He reached for the bandoliers lining his chest and pulled free a small, gourd-shaped flask. He snapped his fingers, two flint rings sending sparks to catch upon the linen rag poking out of the flask's lid. It caught ablaze in an instant and, with an athlete's aim and a madman's abandon, was hurled into the streets below.

A wall of fire rose up where it fell, crackling as it coiled up into a spiral of crimson, sending civilians screaming away. Asper disappeared from sight—swallowed by flame or by crowd, Lenk had no idea.

"We've got to go back for her," he shouted to be heard as he scanned the crowd for a break that wasn't there.

"What about Gariath?" Kataria cried back.

A cacophonous roar brought his attention back to the brawl at the other end of the square. Gariath clung to Kharga like a parasite, clawing at his scales, biting at his throat, while the gray hulk tried to pry him off to no avail. Neither dragonman seemed particularly bothered by the carnage going on around them.

"He can take care of himself," Lenk muttered. He winced as Gariath let out a mad howl. "Probably. For now, we need to—"

"Get down!" Kataria cried, hurling herself against him.

Something shrieked overhead, biting the air where his skull had just been. A crossbow bolt struck the cobblestones and clattered off.

Lenk looked up and suddenly, they were everywhere. Men and women alike, clad in black leathers with sand-colored hoods, stood on every roof of every stall. Crossbows in hand and firing, fireflasks flying from their fingertips, they aimed for the men in black but seemed to take no particular care for who got hit.

"*Bleed, scum,*" one of them cried. "*BLEED!*"

"*Cier'Djaal belongs to the Jackals!*"

"*Die for your God, cultist shits! Tell 'im it was the Jackals who sent ya!*"

So many death threats, so many fires, so many *people*; Lenk couldn't tell what was happening, who was attacking whom, who was dying and who was killing. Kataria seemed to have a better idea, though. She hauled him to his feet.

"We get to cover," she grunted. "Now."

"What about Asper and—"

"We can't find her if we're dead," she shrieked, shoving him forward. "Now, *MOVE!*"

—◆—

Above the roar of fire and the shriek of people, she could still hear her pursuer. Closing in on her.

He was saying things: horrible things, Asper imagined, but she couldn't be sure. All his words were smothered by the scarf wrapped around his head. He was looking at her—with malice, she thought, but she didn't know. Every time she looked around, only the two wide, unblinking glass circles of his goggles stared back.

All she knew was that he was chasing her. And enjoying it far, *far* too much.

She heard the sound of glass shattering at her heels, of flames blossoming as his fireflasks sprouted red flowers behind her. They consumed the stalls, the fleeing people, and the black-clad men with indiscriminate glee. And that same glee was reflected in his voice as he pursued her, racing on short legs atop the stall roofs.

"*Hfy wrmrn!*" he called out, words smothered in his scarf. "*Crtch!*"

"*What does that even mean?*" Asper shouted back without breaking stride.

She wasn't sure why she asked. Every question only had the one answer. Another fireflask shattered behind her, another wall of flame roared to life. And the man on the roofs cackled wildly as the world burned behind him.

There was no telling where Lenk and Kataria were. No telling whether Dreadaeleon and Gariath were safe. No idea where Denaos had gone. And there was nothing she could do for the people fleeing around her, cut down by blade or impaled by crossbow bolt. She would help them, she vowed, as soon as she could. But for any of that to happen, she had to survive.

A prospect that grew increasingly paler as the flames continued to shepherd her through the rows of stalls. She would tire, eventually. She would trip, eventually.

"*Nk mse, wrmrn*," her pursuer cackled. "*Thf tfmf.*"

He snapped his fingers. His iron rings set the fireflask ablaze. She looked over her shoulder, saw him draw back his arm to throw.

She never saw the knife being thrown until it was lodged in his shoulder. He screamed into his scarf, dropped the flask. It exploded at his feet, bathing him in his own fire and sending him into a shrieking, flailing inferno. Just one more among many.

She slowed down as the fires relented, straining to catch her breath through the smoke.

The crowd had thinned out the farther into the Souk she had gone, most of the civilians either having fled or lying on the streets around her in puddles of their own blood.

There was a time when she would have stopped to mourn them. A time when she would have wept over the senseless loss of life, prayed over the bodies, sought out the living relatives.

Those were days born from her youth in temples and monasteries, when protocol and faith were synonymous. Those were days for youthful optimism, passion, and anguish in plenty. Time and suffering had tempered her.

She came to a halt beside a dead body, a young woman facedown on the stones, tucked neatly in a small square of the Souk flanked by stalls as though someone had left her there as a gift. Asper wondered then, as she sometimes did, just what she had lost when those flames were extinguished. She wondered how much more useful faith was as a weapon than as a source of warmth and light.

And, as she often did, she felt a tingle in her left arm.

Something within her that she had no name for felt her doubt and fed upon it. It hissed inside her left hand, flowed through her body like fiery blood to grow hot in her veins. She resisted the urge to claw at it, to whisper at it to stop, to beg Talanas to silence it.

She knew not what it was; she hadn't known when she entered the monastery, hoping that service to the Healer would cure it. So many years later, she still knew nothing of it, save that faith could not remove it.

And only suffering could calm it.

She closed her eyes. She forced her breath to slow. She bit back the agony welling up inside her arm. Temperance, she reminded herself. Iron. Stillness. Pain was fleeting.

"Deshaa…"

Eyes snapped open. She saw the black-clad man approaching, knife clenched in his hand, blood on the blade. His eyes were wild above his veil. They caught sight of the pendant hanging from her neck, the Phoenix of Talanas, and went even wider.

"Oppressor…" he hissed. *"Slave driver. Betrayer."*

"We can talk this out," she said, doubting it.

"Death to oppressors!"

He swept up to her, quick as shadows in candlelight. She was slow, without weapon or warning. Before she knew it, his hand was about her throat, his knife was above his head, and his scream was wild on his lips.

And before she knew anything else, the blade was coming down.

She caught him at the wrist, but barely, the knife's edge a finger's length away from her eye. Her windpipe closed beneath his grip. Her life stalled under his fingers. She fought the urge to panic, to scream and waste precious breath.

Easy, she cautioned herself. *He's not a man. He's a body, organs and bones and sinew. You're a healer. You know how bodies work.* She found her free hand going to the one around her throat. *He's not a man. He's a thumb.*

She found him, in his chubby digit atop her windpipe. She grabbed it and twisted, hard. He snarled, grip loosening, blade quivering. Distracted, she could feel his knife-hand slipping.

It's not a knife, she reminded herself. *It's a wrist.*

And she pulled it away, twisting the wrist as she did so. A snarl became a squeal as his joints groaned. She could see each one in her mind, each tendon she pulled, as she had seen in every corpse she had dissected before. She twisted until the blade dropped, then shoved him away as she kicked the weapon aside.

He hardly seemed to notice his weapon gone. He threw himself back at her, tackling her by the shoulders. His voice was alive in a howl as they tumbled to the ground.

"*Deshaa! Death to the oppressor Gods! Deshaa! DEATH!*" he screamed.

He rained blows upon her with such fury and fervor that she could not keep up. She couldn't find joints to twist or wrists to grab. She couldn't see, she couldn't think, she couldn't control her thoughts as they raced through her head or the thundering beat of her heart or the pain rising in her arm.

Oh, no.

Her left hand snaked out, the curse taking control, desperate to soothe itself. A surge of anger and fear and doubt and hate carried it from the stones to the man's throat. Her fingers tightened about his neck. A searing panic controlled them now.

"No, no, no . . ." she whispered.

The man didn't stop. He might not have even felt it.

But she did. She felt the fire in her veins, the fear in her heart. The curse had gorged itself on her doubt and now hungered for something meatier. Her arm tightened in agony. Beneath her sleeve, her skin burned bright red, painting the bones of her arm in pure black.

Something inside her whispered. It was a voice and not a voice. It was a stream of consciousness without language or breath. And it was not hers.

Don't like you can't help you want you gone go away.

A silent voice. And yet she couldn't hear anything else. She wondered if the man in her grasp heard it.

And, as the man's throat withered to a gray, thin stem in her grasp, she wondered if he even felt it.

He hung limp, tumbled lifelessly off of her as she shoved him off and lay there. He looked almost comical, his veiled head wobbling on a neck suddenly six sizes too small for it. She would have laughed, had she not been torn between crying and vomiting.

This wasn't fair. She had taken so many pains to hide it from everyone: her companions, her clergy, her God. She had been so *careful* with it. Yet every time faith wavered, the suffering began and like a hungry hound, the curse returned.

"This wasn't supposed to happen anymore," she whispered. She grabbed her left arm, hissed at it. "You were silent all through the trip here. Why now? Why again?"

"Deshaa…"

"What, *again*?" she screamed.

Indeed, again. And four times over.

She turned and saw a quartet of black-clad men slipping from the shadows, blades in hands, eyes alight. Yet perhaps they had seen what she had done, for they approached cautiously. She got to her feet, backed away, found the wall of a merchant's stall behind her. They raised their weapons; they hissed beneath their veils.

"Death to—"

"Cier'Djaal for the Jackals!"

Eyes went up. A trio of people in dark leathers and sand-colored hoods stood upon a roof. She caught only a glimpse of movement as they drew back their arms and hurled fireflasks to the square below. A collective scream went up from them as they shattered upon the ground.

Nothing more came of it. No fire. Not so much as a spark. Nothing but a wet, sticky sensation on her hands and face. Something red dripped down her brow.

Blood? She hadn't felt any pain. And it was far too thick, too chunky for that. She took a dab upon her fingertip and, curious, tasted it. Blood; but not hers. This was thick, greasy, almost like gravy.

"Animal blood?" she asked no one in particular.

And something in particular answered her with a low, guttural growl.

Blood-soaked, Asper and the black-clad men whirled upon one mouth of the square to see more hooded men wheeling forward cages. Behind their bars, canine creatures with arched backs, fur clinging to half-starved bodies, bared teeth.

"Oh," she whispered.

No answer this time but the groan of metal as the cages rose. The canines came streaking out, howls on their teeth, hunger in their eyes, and the scent of blood in their nostrils.

And Asper was running.

She could hear the excited cackle of the beasts, the ripping of flesh, the screaming of the black-clad men as the hounds tore into them. She didn't bother to look. Because she could also hear the tap of claws on cobblestones, the panic in her breath, the growl of a bristly beast as it closed in on her.

No chance of fighting it. No chance of outrunning it. She felt its breath on her heels. She felt its cackle in her spine. She closed her eyes; she prayed quietly; she thought of nothing else.

Certainly not of the hands reaching out from a nearby alley to seize her.

Brawny hands took her by the shoulders and hauled her in, slamming her against a wall of a stall. She screamed, of course, but more for the beast that came bounding in after her. One of the hands errantly flicked a handful of powder into the hound's eyes. The beast let out a shriek of alarm, pawing wildly at its snout as it collapsed to the ground. Unable to get out whatever was in its nose, it turned and scampered away, wailing in pain.

It was only when it was gone that she had time to appreciate who had just seized her and quite how peeved she was to see him.

Denaos turned and looked at her, blinking dumbly. "What?"

"*Do not* do that again," she snarled, shoving his hands off of her. "What the hell were those?"

"Hounds."

"Hounds? *Hounds?* Why the *fuck* do they call themselves the Jackals, then?" She wiped blood from her face with her sleeve. "And where the hell were you when we were at the fountain?"

"Avoiding tangling with a fasha. What was I supposed to do?"

"I...stab him, maybe? That's what you usually do."

"What I *usually* do is survive," Denaos replied.

"*At whose expense?*" she all but roared. "Who could you have helped by not skulking and hiding in the shadows? Who could still be alive if you were there so I wouldn't have had to—"

She didn't need to see his face grow concerned. She could feel the tears on her face. They burned upon cheeks that were already alight with heat. Her hand trembled at her side; she clenched it to force it to stop. But it was too late.

"You...used it, didn't you?" he whispered. "You killed someone with your arm."

"I had no choice," she replied, knowing it was a lie.

And Denaos knew. And Denaos said nothing.

Because, she knew, Denaos faulted no one for lying.

"Are you all right now?" he asked.

"Yeah..." She sighed, knowing that, too, to be a lie. "You?"

"Obviously not. I'm in the middle of a war."

"Between who?" she asked. "Who are they? Why are they killing everyone?"

"Because thugs like us don't fight fair," Denaos replied. "We don't have battlefields and we don't have armies. Not traditional ones, anyway. We fight wherever we want and hope that the society we use as a battlefield hates them more than they hate us. That's how the Jackals do it, anyway." He glanced warily out the alley's mouth. "As for the others..."

"No one knows."

Someone spoke from the shadows. They turned and saw no one there in the darkness, nothing but the glow of eyes lit by the bud of a smoking cigarillo. The man stared at neither of them, his gaze off at some spot in the darkness and fixed upon a shadow within a shadow.

He stood perfectly still, the only movement the plume of smoke escaping from mumbling lips.

"The Khovura speak no language we understand. Their tongues are meaningless, their Gods are unheard of. We share only a few words—blade, blood, fire—and we share them liberally."

"Yerk?" the word sounded uncertain coming from Denaos's mouth.

The man's head swiveled. A long, slow smile, perfectly white against the gloom, lit up the darkness.

"Hello, Ramaniel. You do not look well."

Asper shot a glance to Denaos that went pointedly ignored. She had never heard this name before. But she owed it to him to ask as little as he had asked her.

"Better than you," Denaos replied. "And considering I'm in the middle of a footwar, that's saying something." He offered a grin bordering on cruel. "Though, speaking fairly, you didn't look that great when I left, either."

"Ah, you wound me." The cigarillo tumbled from his lips with a sigh, fading into the shadows. "Let us not grieve your delicate company overtly. Suffice to say, much has changed."

"So I see. I saw Sandal's handiwork earlier. I thought the Debt Squad stayed out of footwars."

"Magnificent, wasn't he?" Yerk replied. "The things that man does with fire transcend poetry to become faith." There was a brief movement in the shadows as he began to roll another cigarillo. "My last report suggests, though, that lady flame turned on him."

Asper felt her blood freeze as she realized who they were talking about. She had been there to see him, this Sandal person, engulfed in flame.

"And?" Denaos snorted. "He catches on fire every other day. Or did, anyway. He'll be fine."

"Assuming the Khovura have not found him yet," Yerk replied. "What they do to Jackal prisoners is neither art nor faith, but crudely human."

"Who *are* they?" Asper asked. "These black-clad...Khovura?"

Yerk fixed a heavy-lidded, slow stare upon her.

"They are our enemy," he said simply. "And we are at war."

"Yerk," Denaos pressed. "There are four others with me."

"We saw your run-in with the honorable fasha Ghoukha. Unwise to make that kind of enemy in Cier'Djaal."

"Unwisdom has a long been a hobby of ours," Denaos replied. "I need to find them and I need to get all of us out of here."

"You will find the gates barred. The Jhouche guards themselves do not deign to enter a footwar, but their obligations to the fashas command them to keep the battles contained." A spark of a match and Yerk took a deep puff of his cigarillo. "I can keep you safe, so long as you stay here by my side."

"The boys and girls know me, surely," Denaos said. "They remember what I did for the Jackals."

"In war, blood is coin, Ramaniel. You trade the ones you covet the most and get new ones to fill your pouch. You've been gone too long. Even the old members we retained remember you as a dark Djaalic"—he gestured to Denaos—"not this pale northerner.

"Stand beside me and I can help you," Yerk said through a puff of smoke. "Go out there and you are one more coin slipped through my fingers."

Asper glanced at Denaos. Secrets he had aplenty, still. But the years had taught her to read him. In small, fleeting glimpses between the wrinkles at the corners of his eyes and the slight purse of his lips. But she could see him well enough, then, and see that he was dearly considering taking up Yerk's offer.

That, she resolved, was something he would consider alone.

She moved to go, found his hand on her shoulder. She whirled upon him, ready to brush him off by hand or by foul language. Instead, she found him in step with her, a sigh on his lips.

"Hang on," he muttered. "You'll get yourself killed out there without me."

"I haven't so far," she replied coarsely.

"Well, yes, but if I go out there and get killed, I'd like to have someone other than myself to blame."

He pulled ahead of her, making a pointed effort of not looking behind him. Yerk's voice, however, followed them out of the darkness on a slow, lilting tune.

"Anielle would love to know you're safe," he called out. "You left on such sudden terms, Ramaniel, she feared you dead."

"Ramaniel *is* dead," Denaos said, terse. "I go by another name now."

"As you will again when whoever you are now dies," Yerk said. "Out there, tomorrow; it doesn't matter. To men like us, lives are no more difficult to part with than suits."

Denaos put his head down and kept walking. Asper hurried to catch up.

"Where were they when you last saw them?" he asked.

"At the fountain, a little ways west," she said. "They've probably headed for the gates by now, if they're able to, though."

Her stare remained fixed on him. She opened her mouth to speak. He did not look back at her when he cut her off.

"You don't want to ask," he said.

She looked over to the distant flames, the Jackals silhouetted against the sheets of crimson, firing bolts and falling to blades. She glared at Denaos's back.

"Just how many secrets do you want to die with?"

"I was intending to go with all of them," Denaos replied with a sideways glance. "Of course, you went and ruined that."

She shot him an indignant look. "I saved your life. A few times, in fact."

"Don't get me wrong, I'm grateful," he said as he ducked between a pair of stalls, heading for the square. "But I should point out that if you had let me die, I wouldn't be facing this awkward conversation right now. So we're kind of even."

TEN

RARE MEAT

Around him, war was raging.

Crossbow bolts flew through the air as birds to find nests in bone and sinew. Fire rose in sheaves around the bodies that fell beneath them. And everywhere—under his feet, in his nostrils, stained on his hands—was death.

That did not matter. Today, Gariath had something more precious than all of that.

Today, Gariath had someone to hate.

All that mattered was the blood on his teeth; the scent of silk and soft, clean, civilized things burning in his nostrils; and the shudder of earth beneath his feet as a tremendous shadow fell over him.

Kharga's ax came crashing down, no war cry to herald it. It struck the earth as Gariath leapt away, no curse to accompany the shattered stone. The massive dragonman turned upon his smaller cousin without a single word.

There was nothing but the tremendous ax in his hands, fragmented stone sighing from its blade as he pulled it free. Nothing but the gashes from Gariath's claws painting his armored hide. Nothing but the hatred burning between him and his enemy.

This was Kharga, *Drokha*. This was Gariath, *Rhega*. These were dragonmen.

Their hatred for each other was something altogether too beautiful to be sullied by words.

Gariath's language was in his claws and his teeth and the roar he loosed as he fell to all fours and charged. In a twitch of wings, he leapt. And he scrawled his words across Kharga's flesh as his claws raked the bigger dragonman's flesh and drew gouts of blood.

Scratches. Nothing more than fleeting fragments of pain, half-smudged in red, running ink. Kharga's hide was too thick for his claws to do any true, lasting damage. To truly maim, to truly damage, Gariath would have to strike tenderly: a claw in the eye, a ripped nostril, a place where the colossus was vulnerable.

But Gariath did not do this. Not yet.

Anger was an ugly limerick. Despair was a droning speech. Hatred, however, was an argument. Arguments demanded that someone concede.

And only when the *Drokha* did that would Gariath grant him the death his breed so richly deserved.

Each finger worked its way between scales. Each clawtip drank greedily of the blood that wept. Kharga's flesh groaned beneath, drawn to a twitching spasm as Gariath ripped and tore.

Even then, Kharga made no sound. Though his body shuddered and his hand trembled, he reached up and seized Gariath. He tore the red parasite from his face, heedless of the flesh and blood that came away on Gariath's claws. He accepted Gariath's bloody argument, its many points and its many persuasions, and offered a single retort with one great swing of his arm.

And Gariath flew.

Gariath, who had killed dozens of humans, beasts, and worse, tumbled through the air like a leaf. Gariath, last of the *Rhega*, was—

He struck something hard. Thought left him, hammered from his skull.

Coughing on ash, he pulled himself free from the shattered embers. The remnants of the stall collapsed behind him with a shudder of ruined silks and dying wood.

Across the square, Kharga stood, unmoving, awaiting a retort.

Embers stung his nose. Ash smeared his skin. There was a

decidedly uncomfortable ache where a shard of blackened wood had decided to lodge itself.

None of that mattered. Gariath had blood on his claws. Gariath had ashes in his eyes. Gariath had a response.

"KHOTH-KAPIRA!"

That wasn't it.

That wasn't his voice, either.

He turned and saw the human running toward him. A walking sack of meat wrapped in black cloth pretending it had business challenging him. A sword was held high above his head, a shriek was caught in his throat, and something was in his stare that should have been in the eyes of disease-maddened beasts.

The human rushed toward Gariath, deftly leaping over the bodies fallen on the cobblestones. He swung his sword wildly. He started to scream.

"KHOTH-KAPIRA—"

He never finished.

A thick red hand wrapped about one's windpipe would do that.

"I'm *busy*," Gariath snarled.

A quick jerk, a twitch of claws, something red and glistening came out of the man's neck and into Gariath's hand.

Gariath let the human fall and stepped over his corpse, heedless of a distant cry and the hum of crossbows preceding a shriek of falling bolts. The battle raged around him, blades flashing and crossbow bolts flying as the humans waged whatever pettiness they decided to call a war.

He broke into a sprint, hoping to pass beneath the bolts as they flew. He caught one in the arm, another in the thigh, but those didn't matter. Nothing else mattered but Kharga. The *Drokha*. The hatred.

The air shimmered before him, almost imperceptibly. Easy to ignore. He crashed against it as though it were a solid wall. Less easy to ignore.

The crossbow bolts struck the same barrier, ricocheting off empty space with but a ripple in the air and clattering to the ground. Gariath snorted, reached out, and touched the invisible wall before him. It quivered at the touch, and through it, he could see a distorted figure in the distance.

Kharga.

Turning and leaving through the Souk gates.

Only then did Gariath make a sound.

A long, angry sound born from his chest and torn out of his throat and punctuated with a lot of soundless cracking as he smashed his hands against the barrier, the air rippling with the impact. Perhaps Kharga heard him. Perhaps Kharga had a smile across his gigantic face. Gariath couldn't see.

The thought alone was enough to make him roar louder, longer, angrier.

"Yes, yes. How terrible it is that I saved you from being impaled and crushed beneath a giant reptile's foot."

The human. The skinny one. The only one he knew better by the shrill condescension of voice than the reeking scent of weakness.

He whirled upon Dreadaeleon. The boy stood a few feet away, hand aloft in some arcane gesture, eyes bright red and leaking with the magic that held the invisible barrier up.

"Bring it down," Gariath snarled.

Dreadaeleon glanced up. He looked thoughtful for about as long as it took another volley of bolts to strike the barrier and bounce off. The boy frowned and shook his head.

"We could also do something that doesn't get a foot of iron and wood in our skulls," Dreadaeleon offered. He glanced over his shoulder; the barrier quivered with a moment's lapsed concentration. "There's cover back there. We can regroup, find the others, and then—"

"*He's getting away!*" Gariath snarled, smashing his fist on the air.

"Who? The big dragonman? What did you call him? Drugga?"

"*Drokha,*" Gariath snarled. He thrust an accusatory claw at the boy. "That is *our* tongue. It doesn't belong in your mouth." He pointed that claw across the square, toward the slowly vanishing hulk of Kharga's shadow. "And *he* doesn't belong outside of a funeral pyre."

"You're awfully worked up about this, I can tell. Regardless, there's still the whole—"

The barrier rippled. There was a thick sound of flesh striking a wall. A man in a sand-colored hood was pressed against the intangible wall, a knife jammed in his neck and trailing a red smear as he slid down the barrier to the ground.

"Yeah, that," Dreadaeleon said. "So. Back to cover?"

"Bring it down. You seek cover. I'll handle the killing, as usual."

"The incomprehensibility and self-importance of that statement is only vaguely overshadowed by the sheer hilarity of you wanting to walk out into an open war to try to kill someone twice your size. Which, given the fact that you are about twice *my* size, is just... just..." He shook his head, trembling. "Either way, no. The barrier extends about ten feet around me and it goes where I go."

The expressions of dragonmen were often inscrutable; long reptilian snouts and black, dead eyes didn't leave a lot of room for nuance. Still, there was a crack in the everyday fury that Gariath wore, just enough to let slip a clear, thoughtful look leveled at Dreadaeleon.

"Around..." he repeated slowly, "you."

"Yes. And that means—"

What he might have said was irrelevant and thus ignored. In any event, Gariath clearly disagreed. What it meant, as far as he was concerned, was that he was perfectly justified in seizing Dreadaeleon by the lapels of his coat, throwing him over his shoulder like a sack of flour, and taking off at a sprint after Kharga.

As near as Gariath could tell, magic largely revolved around the flailing of limbs and the screaming of a bunch of words incomprehensible even to humans. And while the flailing limbs were certainly present, the words that came vomiting out of the boy's mouth were all too human.

And entirely rude.

Humans were dying around him. Ones with black cloth around their heads fell into pyres, crossbow bolts jutting from their chests, necks, spines. Ones with sand-colored cloth around their heads were dragged from rooftops, cut beneath many hungry razors.

Thrown knives were flung at the barrier; ash parted against the barrier; ash-kissed corpses were shoved aside before the barrier; an errant bolt came through the barrier, sank deep into his shoulder, and chewed eagerly on the muscle beneath his skin.

That was annoying.

"If you're going to be obstructive, be *useful*," he snarled to his human cargo.

"*I am a wizard, you red turd!*" Dreadaeleon screamed. "*I am the apex of human knowledge! I am the product of* years *of careful study and raw, natural talent! I am—*"

"And if you're not going to be useful," Gariath interrupted, narrowly ducking beneath another bolt that had penetrated the barrier, "be quiet."

Through the smoke and the bolts and the wails of panic, Gariath saw Kharga. At the far edge of the Souk wall, he waded among the last trickles of a tide of panicked civilians through a great stone archway. Gariath could see the colossal dragonman's head tilt up, nostrils quivering at the scent of the approaching *Rhega*, just as Gariath could smell nothing but *Drokha*.

Kharga looked over his shoulder. His smile was infuriating, even more so than before. He offered a wave of a massive hand at a pair of guards wearing Ghoukha's sigil as he strode past.

With grunts of acknowledgment and then effort, the two men seized a complicated-looking lever in their hands and pulled down. And with the sound of thunder, an iron portcullis came crashing down behind the *Drokha*, sealing him away.

Gariath's howl was almost everything in him: all his anger, all his rage, all his frustration. But not his hatred. He wouldn't waste that on a roar thrown at a wall of iron and stone. He saved his hatred for the muscles in his arms, for the claws on his hands, for the boy he took off of his shoulders and aimed upward with intent to throw.

"Wait! *WAIT!*" Dreadaeleon screamed, swaying as the dragon-man took a few practice swings.

"If you don't squirm so much, you'll clear it fine," Gariath grunted. "Just open the portcullis on the other side and we'll—"

"Damn it, I said . . ."

Exactly what the boy said was no language Gariath knew. But the red light leaking out of his eyes, the wave of his hand, the ripple in the air that sent the dragonman flying, slapped away by an invisible wall of force . . .

He understood that.

He leapt back to his feet in time to see Dreadaeleon clambering back up. The boy was breathing hard, as he usually was after hasty expenditures of his power. Buckled at the waist, hands on his knees, the boy looked at Gariath beneath a brow creased with sweat.

"Look," he said, breathless, "I've known you long enough to not ask what makes you want to kill people. I've been around you long enough to know that you're pretty good at it. But why *this* one? There's dozens of people around to kill. What makes that one so important?"

"Complicated," Gariath said.

Dreadaeleon furrowed his brow.

"You know, for *most* people, murder tends to be complicated." He glanced up at the portcullis. "He's a dragonman, right? Like you."

"*Not* like me," Gariath snarled. "Not like us." His lip curled backward, all teeth bared. "*Not* like the *Rhega*."

Dreadaeleon fixed him with a curious glance. Gariath said nothing more. For a moment, hate had seeped into his voice. He had nearly wasted it. He needed all of it.

"There aren't many of you left," Dreadaeleon said, "your people. Right?"

Gariath said nothing.

"How many are there left of him? The gray dragonmen?"

"Too many."

"Right. So, he goes away to whatever happy, gigantic home he has with his happy, two-ton wife, and you waste your time trying to get over this wall while your friends," Dreadaeleon tapped his chest, "die in smoke and blood."

Gariath snorted. The boy's tone suggested there was a downside, but he was having a hard time seeing it.

"By now, everyone who saw you will be talking about red-skinned, horned demons. If you want to kill that dragonman, you're going to need help."

"I have killed bigger than him. With less than you."

"Then you'll do it alone. And when you kill him, when we're dead, you'll still be alone."

Gariath said nothing.

Because if he opened his mouth to voice his scorn, to scoff, to tell the boy just what he was about to rip off of him and where he was going to stuff it, something would tumble out on his voice. Something that would prove to Dreadaeleon and to himself that there were, indeed, worse things than not killing a *Drokha*.

And so Gariath growled, turned around, and began to stalk back toward the Souk.

He heard Dreadaeleon stumbling over bodies and ashes as the boy tried to keep up.

"So, what'd he do?" Dreadaeleon asked. "The gray dragonman?"

"Nothing."

"Nothing? You hate them for doing nothing?"

"Doesn't work that way," Gariath muttered. "You can only kill people for what they do. You can only hate them for who they are."

"And..." Dreadaeleon glanced over his shoulder at the portcullis. "Who are they?"

Gariath snorted. Ashes fell from his snout to lie upon the empty faces of dead men.

"Family," he said simply.

There was a brief pause after he took a breath. He touched his lower lip to his teeth and he stole a fleeting glance at her. That was how she knew he was about to ask a stupid question.

"How's it look out there?" Lenk asked.

Kataria took her hat from her head and placed it on the tip of her bow. Ducking low, she raised her bow, the hat peeking over the top of the abandoned merchant stall they had taken cover behind.

An instant later, a crossbow bolt was quivering in the wall in front of her and a neat hole had been punched through her hat.

"Not good," she replied.

In truth, "not good" was a bit of an understatement. But it would have taken too long for her to say "we're pinned down by a sniper who might just be a better shot than me and surrounded by people stabbing the people who are shooting them and if we ever get out of this alive I want to know exactly what makes this asshole of a city worth abandoning me over."

Her head hurt. She shut her eyes and drew in a breath.

One problem at a time.

She elbowed the wood of the stall; fire-kissed as it was, it crumbled away easily enough and gave her a small hole to glimpse out of. There, she saw her foe.

Far away and on the highest point in the Souk atop one of the few permanent two-story buildings, a woman, thin and tall like a stalk of corn, knelt upon one knee, balancing a weapon on her shoulder. To call it a crossbow would have been like calling a tiger a cat: technically accurate, but likely to end in blood and tears. It was a monstrosity of metal and wood, driven by a fiendish-looking crank and topped by what appeared to be a small tube on its grip.

Kataria squinted, observing quietly as the woman cranked back the weapon's string, loaded a yard-long bolt, and scanned the battle below. The men in black had scaled the stalls and dragged their opponents down, and blades had been drawn to make the fight more intimate.

The sniper adjusted the tube atop her crossbow and Kataria saw just what it was for. The setting sun reflected a beam of light upon a tiny circle of glass: a tiny spyglass to guide her shots. One of the men in black, undoubtedly, realized this as well once he found a bolt lodged perfectly in his collarbone.

"Clever little monkey," she muttered.

Envy, it was often said among shicts, was the mother of human invention, with them creating such contraptions as that monstrous crossbow to compensate for their natural inability with the bow. The pride from that thought was a small comfort compared to the hole that machination would put through Kataria if she stepped into its line of fire.

Still, Kataria thought as she nocked an arrow, *it's just a human*.

"What's out there?" Lenk whispered, leaning close.

The sniper had cranked another bolt and was searching for a new target.

"It's Asper," she said, never taking her eyes off the sniper. "She's coming this way. Looks bad."

"What?"

The moment Lenk leapt to his feet, she started counting.

One.

He put his head over the stall.

Two.

He looked around.

Three.

A pinprick of light flashed in the distance.

She seized his belt and pulled down sharply. He grunted as he fell to the floor and the bolt slammed into the wood where his head had just been. Kataria leapt up, drawing her bow back in a seamless motion and taking aim.

One.

She squinted.

Two.

She held her breath.

Three.

Her arrow sang, a long, lilting tune that carried it over the heads of the men in black and their hooded foes and ended in a short, bloody note.

A morbid grin creased her features as she heard the sniper scream. The arrow had only found a shoulder instead of a more satisfying target. But the woman slinked away from the edge of her perch before Kataria could draw another arrow.

One less problem.

"Did you just try to kill me?" Lenk demanded as he climbed to his feet.

Funny how there's always one more.

"I used you as bait to make the sniper shoot," Kataria replied.

"That's the same thing."

"No, I willingly put you in a situation in which I knowingly exposed you to something that would probably kill you. Not the same thing as trying to kill you," she said, clicking her tongue. "But it's close, I'll give you that."

"I take it by the passive-aggressive mincing of words that asking you to tell me what's bothering you would be futile."

"Just about," she grunted.

"Look, if you'd just stop fuming—"

"I am not *fuming*, Lenk." She whirled upon him, teeth bared, eyes ablaze. "I am *seething*. When something fumes, it stops when it dissipates. When something *seethes*, it doesn't stop until it explodes."

He touched his lower lip to his teeth. She cut him off with a sigh.

"When you said you wanted to leave swords and blood behind, I tried to understand," she said. "When you said you wanted to stay in Cier'Djaal, I tried to understand. But only now, today, do I understand everything."

"And what's that?" he asked.

"These people...they looked at me like I was an animal. They treated me like I was a hide they could trade. I defended myself from being kidnapped and they called *me* a savage." Her sneer was dark. "I can't live here, Lenk."

Somewhere in the distance, someone cried out. Lenk winced.

"We can talk about this later, can't we?"

"We can't," she said sternly. "We can't talk about it now, either. There's nothing to say. Deny whatever you want, say whatever you want, but I can see it in you...you want to be here. You want to put down your sword and count coins and pretend you're normal.

"I've walked into fire with you, Lenk. I'll do so again," she said, drawing her bow. "I'll walk with you out of here. But once we're out, I'm going to keep on walking until I can't hear you anymore."

There was a brief pause after he took a breath. His jaw hung open for a moment as his eyes struggled to speak and his mouth struggled to hear.

That was how she knew something inside him had broken.

He shut his mouth, as though the shards of that something might tumble out at any moment. He looked over his shoulder and she saw him find his resolve, as he did, in the usual places.

The bloodshed. The ashes. The violence.

"There's a gap ahead." He spoke firmly, curtly. "We run toward it. We run through it. We get to the Souk gates. Anyone else who survived will have headed for..."

A brief crack in his voice. A fragment in his mouth. Blood on his tongue.

"For there," he finished.

A part of her, not small, not hidden, wanted to say something. Something that would make him find a voice, that would make her put a hand on his shoulder, that would make everything she had just said meaningless and tell him that was all going to be okay.

But it was another part of her, something small and jagged like an old arrowhead lodged in a femur that just hurt too much, that bade her keep her mouth shut and stand by what she said.

His sword was in his hand. The feathers of an arrow ran between her fingers. They crouched beside the edge of the stall. They exchanged a brief look, their eyes searching each other's. His, searching for any doubt, any reason to believe she was lying just then. Hers, searching for any understanding, a compromise that would let her know he was ready to leave this city and its disease behind and come with her.

And in each other's eyes, they saw only one thing.

"Ready?" he asked.

She nodded.

And without another glance, they ran into hell.

Any semblance to a civilized war, with drawn-up sides, battle fronts, and casualties, had been dispensed with in favor of the much more satisfying ease of an all-out slaughter. Men in black dragged hooded foes to the ground to be hacked to thick, screaming chunks under curved blades. Hooded thugs kicked their dark-clad adversaries into burning stalls, firing bolts into them as they emerged, howling, from the inferno as walking holocausts.

"*Khoth-Kapira!*" they were shrieking. "*Saccaam ashal thuru! Khoth-Kapira!*"

"*Quit screaming and burn, you heathen sons of bitches,*" one of their foes shouted back.

Every thought was saved for the eyes that looked up from carved corpses to her. Every instinct was reserved for the thicket of blades and bolts overhead and all around. And everything in her was in her legs as she ran, trying not to hear the murderous screams hurled her way.

Harder to ignore were the bolts that flew from the stall rooftops. But these were wailing, warbling shrieks. The rhythm of her bow's song was something smoother, lyrical, in perfect time.

One.

She felt the feathers in her hair rustle as a bolt wailed past her ear.

Two.

She felt arrow in hand, string between fingers as her eyes picked up the crossbowman on the roof.

Three.

She felt that brief rush of wind as her bow sang and sent a steel-tipped note into the crossbowman's throat.

He tumbled off the roof, his scream caught between his throat and the arrow lodged in it, to plummet into a burning stack of silks. A dramatic death, she thought. That was a shot she might have liked to take in with greater leisure, had she not so many more to make.

Arrows hummed, answering every crossbow bolt with a shot that sent bodies tumbling to the flames and stones below. All the while, she kept the wind at her back, the arrows at her fingers, and Lenk at her side as they rushed through the carnage.

At the end of the stalls, the walls of flames, the packs of blades and bolts, she could see a large, sloping arch leading out of the Souk. It was barricaded with crates, barrels, and carts in some hasty effort by more levelheaded citizens to keep the battle from following them out.

Difficult, but not a problem, she thought.

"KHOTH-KAPIRA!"

The man in black charging toward her, sword in hand, scream in throat, though? That was a problem.

The rage in the man's voice spread through him like fever. His legs pumped with steady fury, heedless of the crossbow bolt lodged in his thigh. His sword was a curtain of steel around his head. His eyes were wide and wild and full of the hate that came spilling out of his mouth with every shriek.

He was fast. Incredibly fast. By the time she had an arrow in her hand, he was already upon her. By the time it was strung, the blade was above her head. By the time she thought to cry out, it was coming down.

She felt the blade's kiss, but only just a kiss. It caught her against the arm, an errant and haphazard blow from arms that were suddenly flailing. A blade lashed out from beside her and caught the man in black at the hamstring, cutting momentum and sinew alike.

The man in black went flying, the wound in his leg painting a crimson arc as he planted facedown upon the stones. The sword clattered from his grip, the blood wept from his leg. Yet he still tried to rise with the vigor of a man hale and unbloodied.

"*Khoth-Kapira*," he muttered. "*Shaalacc, Khoth-Kapira. Shaalacc.*"

He staggered to his knees and reached for the blade. He fell upon the stones just as the hard heel of a boot smashed between his shoulder blades.

Lenk stood above him, flipped the sword in his hands, and aimed the sword down. And for a moment, he was someone else.

In the moment when the blood-slick sword caught the light of a hundred pyres, in the moment when the screams were made silent, when two blue eyes were wide and wild with a desperate need to protect her.

Lenk became sound and color and steel.

And there he was, the man who put her above all else, the man who killed for her and no one else.

That man existed only until his grip tensed and he plunged the blade into the back of the man's neck, before he was lost in a spatter of blood.

He looked at her with the blue eyes of a desperate man, wholly human.

"You all right?"

She looked at her arm; a gash marked her flesh, but the pain was the steady ache of a nonlethal wound. She nodded, shouldering her bow as she looked toward the barricade.

There was no sign of Asper or the others. Yet. But they could wait. First, she and Lenk would have to clear the barricade. First, they would need somewhere to run to.

The archway loomed closer as they took off at a run again. The hail of bolts had thinned to a few stray shrieks. The screams of the dying and the roar of flames dimmed to a distant cackle. She could hear the thunder of her own breath as she rushed toward the gate.

And a single man stepped out of the wreckage to stand in her way.

She recognized him as human only because of how unimpressive he was. Short, slender, and with a sand-colored hood drawn low to

smother his face in shadows, he stood heedless of the carnage surrounding him. The red bud of a cigarillo burned in his mouth as
he lazily took Kataria in: her swift stride, the bow in her hands, the
arrow pointed right at him.

She drew back the arrow. She aimed for the only part of his face
she could see. She saw the long white scar of his teeth as his lips
curled into a smile.

And then, suddenly, she saw the rest of them.

They were everywhere, hooded men above her, around her,
behind her. She skidded to a halt as they rose upon the rooftops,
crossbows trained upon her and Lenk. She backed away as they crept
out of the ashes and shadows, cruel, short blades in their hands. She
felt herself press against Lenk's back; she felt him short and strong
and bristling against her as the hooded men encircled them.

And her ears twitched as the man with the cigarillo said in a low,
raspy voice:

"You must be new here."

ELEVEN

THE DISCIPLE

They weren't attacking.

Their crossbows were trained on him, fingers trembling on triggers. Their swords were drawn, each one wet with red life. Their eyes burned beneath drawn hoods, drunk with violence and looking for more.

But they weren't attacking.

And the man with a shadow for a face, who took a long draw on his cigarillo, wasn't saying a word.

Not for lack of encouragement. The hoods, with all their blades and bolts, glanced eagerly at him, looking for the slightest curled lip, the lowest muttered word, anything they could interpret as permission to start the butchery.

And still, the shadowed man said nothing as he dropped the cigarillo to the ground and crushed it beneath a polished boot. Not until he took another one from his pocket, lit it with a match, and inhaled deeply.

"They have a point, you know." His voice came out on a gray cloud.

"Who?" Lenk asked.

"The Khovura," the shadowed man replied. "They are a heathen breed, bereft of virtue or faith, but they know one or two truths. When they seek out foreigners in the crowd, for example, one finds oneself hard-pressed to fault their priorities."

He took a deep draw of his cigarillo and looked skyward to the Silken Spire hanging over the Souk. It wafted against the smoke-stained breeze with a serenity that belonged somewhere else, over a happier city with wives baking pies and children playing in streets not choked with corpses. The spiders were impassive to the suffering below as they ambled lazily over their rainbow-colored web.

"It's the silk," the hooded man said. "No other city makes it. And so the foreigners and their armies come to ours and buy it, steal it, fight for it, as we have bought it, stolen it, fought for it. They become entangled in our affairs. They live lives in Cier'Djaal, but they are not Djaalics, and so everything becomes vastly complicated.

"Case in point," he said, gesturing to Lenk's bloodied sword. "This is our footwar. You should have stayed out of it."

"I can agree with that," Lenk replied. "I tried telling them. But people kept trying to kill us. So I told them again." He hefted his blade, a drop of blood painting a thin red line as it wept down the steel. "They listened the second time."

The hooded man's laugh was bleak.

"You're funny." He glanced at Kataria. "And you're dangerous." He smiled broadly at the scowl she shot him. "I love these traits in a man." He held up his hands to Kataria in apology. "Or a woman. I encourage them in my own Jackals." His voice grew darker on a cloud of smoke. "But disrespect is something I cannot tolerate.

"You come to our city. You shoot our people. You leave them dying in our streets." He bobbed his head, thoughtful. "You kill the Khovura, too, and I applaud you for this. But I cannot abide someone killing my soldiers, my people, in my city and not suffering for it. It sets a poor precedent for anyone who may be watching."

"So, does the suffering come from us getting shot," Kataria asked, eyeing the crossbowmen, "or from listening to you go on?"

"People call us thieves. They assume we have no law." He shook his head. "Every man has a code. Every Jackal has a law. And mine tells me that it is an honorable thing to inform someone why they must die when I say they must die."

He raised his hand.

A dozen crossbows were raised in response. A dozen short blades twitched in anticipation.

He drew a long, smoky breath.

Lenk raised his sword. Kataria drew back her bow. Neither had any hope of either of those actions doing a damn thing. Neither had any intention of dying without the other at their back.

"Farewell, northerners," the shadowed man whispered. "Bad day for us all."

"Kapira Kapira Kapira…"

It was nothing more than a whisper. Less than a whisper, even— too hasty, too fevered, too completely nonsensical. It was a slurry of words, some that Lenk knew and some he did not. Yet one was spoken louder than the others.

"Kapira Kapira Kapira…"

At that sound, everything stopped. Yerk's hand froze above his head. The crossbowmen lowered their weapons and looked down to the streets. The hoods' grip tightened so hard on their blades as to send the steel quivering like stalks of grass.

"Kapira Kapira Kapira…"

"Son of a bitch, it's one of *them*," one of the hoods whispered.

The circle that had been formed around Lenk and Kataria broke suddenly, parting to give a vast berth to a figure emerging from the devastation of the Souk.

It was a man. Nothing more to him than a dirty black robe and eyes that looked like they had not blinked in days. His lips moved in rapid hushes, speaking gibberish.

"Ahmalaa, Kapira, protect me, I have served you, ahmalaa…"

Nothing but a man speaking nothing but gibberish.

And this, apparently, was the most terrifying thing in the world to the hoods.

"Run. *RUN*."

"Gods damn it, they always bring these things out."

"Don't look at it. *Don't look. It sees you if you look at it*—"

Their words dissolved into panicked screams, chasing them on soot-stained skies as they turned and fled, vanishing from rooftops and slithering into shadows. The hooded man was the last to go, shooting Lenk a pitying glance before vanishing behind a stall.

In their wake, Lenk felt the silence. There were no more cries of the dying and the fearful. The blades that had tolled like steel bells had fallen quiet. The flames smoldered with contented sighs.

Everything—all the violence, all the chaos—had stopped for this one man.

"Ahmalaa, spare me, Kapira, Kapira, Kapira…"

"Are you…well?" Lenk asked. He took a cautious step forward, sword lowering, but only a fraction.

"Look around you," Kataria spat, glancing around. *"No one* here is well." Her ears pricked up, hearing something his own couldn't detect. "But I don't hear fighting. Let's find the others before anyone else shows up."

Lenk looked to the man, as though he might plead for help. But nothing was forthcoming from his lips beyond the same lilting madness.

"Come *on,*" Kataria snarled.

Harsh as she might have been, she was talking more sense than anyone present.

"Kapira, Kapira, Kapira…"

Not that *that* was all that big an achievement.

Lenk flashed the man a wasted apologetic look. The man's face twitched, a sort of mad serenity settling upon his face before he hunched over and vomited upon the stones. Lenk cringed, turning away to follow Kataria as she began to walk back toward the center of the Souk where they had lost their companions.

You tried, he told himself. *You would have helped him, if there was anything you could have done. If he was even aware of you—*

"Help…" the man choked out.

Oh, come on.

"Help me." The man looked up as Lenk looked behind. Life left him out his mouth as thick gray chunks of an unknown substance dribbled out of his lips. "I wasn't prepared. I thought...I thought he would be pleased." He clutched at his belly, rocking back and forth. "But I wasn't. It's so..."

His arms hung at his sides. His robe fell open.

"Heavy."

Stretched to a smooth, hairless sphere, the man's belly bulged out of his robes, hanging heavy over his waist and pulling him low. The great sphere of flesh quivered as Lenk stared.

As though the sight of a pregnant man just wasn't weird enough.

"It hurts..." the man moaned, taking a ponderous step toward Lenk.

"Get *back*," Kataria snarled, suddenly at Lenk's side, arrow drawn.

"It hurts," the man said with another step.

Lenk held his sword up as he moved back a step with Kataria. Neither of them was quite sure what exactly they would need weapons for. But this was hardly the type of situation where one let down their guard.

"Make it stop," the man groaned. "Make it st—"

The man's voice died in his throat. No more words slipped from his mouth.

What began to slither out between his vomit-stained lips was something else entirely.

At a glance, they looked like serpents: four thin, gray tendrils that reached out of the man's mouth to curl over his lower lip. But they were too bony, too rigid, ending in sharp black spikes, drumming gently on the man's chin.

No, Lenk noted. *Nails*. His eyes went wide. *Sweet Khetashe, those are fingers.*

And as though they had been waiting for someone to notice, another four curled up and over the man's upper lip. Four of them groped searchingly across a face contorted in agony as a panicked scream tried to escape through the man's mouth, to no avail.

And that was when they began to pull.

Lips stretched to their limit and beyond. Skin tore like paper. There was a short, sickening snap as a jawbone became forcibly unhinged. The fingers pried the man's mouth open, farther and farther. The bulbous gut shrank to a withered pouch of skin. His head snapped backward, his mouth gaped to the size of a door.

Lenk and Kataria could but stare in horror as the man's throat grew bulbous as something slithered out of his mouth.

And stared back.

A head the shape, color, and texture of a crumbling column of a long-dead building peered out of the mouth. A face stared at the two: the withered, pinched, ancient face of a grandfather who had lived too long to think life was any blessing. Its eyes were black scars, as though someone had taken a coal pencil to its face and simply scribbled them out.

And yet, in some old, animal part of themselves, Lenk and Kataria knew it was watching them.

"Run," Kataria whispered, voice too terrified to make itself louder. "*Run.*"

And they did. To where, it was not certain. Nor did it matter. They couldn't stay here. They couldn't let it look at them.

They dived behind the sturdiest-looking stall they could find, peered out as much as they dared. And yet, even that seemed not nearly enough to protect them from the thing's gaze.

And whatever it was, it wasn't done yet.

The man might have been dead, or perhaps still alive. His eyes were locked in some wide, unthinking stare that knew only horror as the thing continued to crawl out of him.

An emaciated torso followed, old man arms on old man's body, gray skin sagging over visible ribs, glistening with bodily secretions. The thing drew itself free, shedding the man as a snake sheds its skin. And like a snake, it sat on a long, serpentine coil that began where the last vestiges of macabre humanity ended. It rose on its tail. It surveyed this world of color, its many reds and blacks, through a face made colorless with age.

And it spoke. In a voice old and horrible, it spoke.

"The sleeper awakes."

And in that voice, so ancient and so terrible, did Lenk finally realize what he was looking at.

A demon.

Old enough to have seen the world born, plucked from the same myths where mankind learned to fear the dark. Lenk knew demons when he saw them, as he had known them when he fought them. And he knew this one was real, alive, strong.

And searching.

Its scrawled-out gaze swept from side to side with a ponderousness that suggested the weight of its tall, flat forehead might cause it to teeter over at any moment. Its wizened face was unreadable; no sign in its scribble-black eyes that it could see anything at all.

And yet neither Lenk nor Kataria dared to move.

"I know you are there." Its voice was something ground and gravelly, echoing in the cavern of its own mouth. "The scent of your sin is pungent."

It trembled from its poise, falling to a street stained by blood and ash. Its arms trembled out, fingers sinking into the cracks between the cobblestones, and hauled its serpentine bulk across the cobblestones. From withered lips a trident-pointed tongue, the same color as a week-old bruise, flickered out.

"I taste the men you have killed," it groaned. "I taste their last pleas to Gods long gone deaf." Its head slipped from side to side, contemplative. "This place chokes on despair you have wrought. Come out."

With the sound of old bones creaking, the creature turned toward Lenk's hiding spot and leveled its scribble-black eyes upon him. Its tongue flicked out.

"Let me taste your sin."

Lenk all but hurled himself to the stones to get away from those eyes. He might have tried digging through the rock with his bare hands if he had looked into the thing's un-stare for one more moment.

As it was, he pressed himself against the stall with his heart thundering in his ears.

He nearly leapt out of his flesh when Kataria laid a hand on his shoulder and fixed him with a panicked stare.

She mouthed the word, voice too frightened to show itself.

Demon.

No question. No uncertainty. She had fought the same battles.

He nodded his head.

She tugged at her bow once, mouthed another word.

Fight?

Her pupils were rimmed with fear at what his answer might be. He imagined she saw the same in his own stare at that moment.

One never *fought* a demon. One merely survived them, if one was fortunate enough. They could be harmed, certainly, but not by any mortal weapon. They were once mortal, but that had been lost to them long ago. The only thing that tormented a demon, the only thing that could kill one, was a memory of their former lives.

Kataria knew this as well as he did.

And yet there was something else within the fear in her eyes. And when he saw it, he was certain he thought the same thing she did. They were not totally helpless.

He had fought demons before, yes. And he had done more than survive them. There were ways to slay one . . . if one was willing to pay.

He shut his eyes. He forced that thought out and forced his blood warm again. He shook his head sternly.

Kataria did not look at him. Perhaps she would have been ashamed for him to see the relief on her face as she mouthed two more words.

What now?

He bit his tongue. He pointed to the ground.

Stay here.

He held a finger to his lips.

Stay quiet.

He pointed over her head toward the distant gate. He mimicked walking with two fingers.

Then run like hell.

She nodded before she looked at him and whispered, voice nearly inaudible over the sound of the demon's slithering bulk as it dragged itself farther away from their hiding place.

"The others?"

He offered what he could: a hapless shrug.

He could tell by the anger in her scowl that she hated that answer. Just as he could tell by the defeat in her eyes that she couldn't think of anything better.

And so she looked at the ground. And she said nothing.

He was content to do the same.

"Lenk!"

At least until he heard someone cry out in the distance.

"Lenk! Kataria? Where are you?"

Even if he hadn't recognized her voice, he would have known it was Asper calling for them. No one else had either conscience or stupidity enough to go back into a battlefield to look for her friends.

Just as no one else had quite the bad luck needed to go screaming with a demon about.

"I hear your cry, child," the thing beyond the stall rasped. "Let me soothe your fear."

A scrabble of nails on stone. A slither of skin on sand. When Lenk dared to peek out to see what was going on, he only caught the last traces of a gray tail disappearing around a nearby corner. The demon had gone. They were alone.

With nothing but ashes and silence standing between them and the way out.

⊷ ⊷≻⊰⊹ ⊶

"They've probably already gone, you know," Denaos muttered, glancing warily about the abandoned Souk.

"And when I know that for sure, we'll go after them," Asper replied before cupping her hands over her mouth. *"Lenk! Kataria! Dreadaeleon!"*

"This isn't done," Denaos said. "Footwars are no-man's-land. If you're not fighting, you run away. You see nothing, you survive. That's the rule the Jackals live by."

"Forgive me for not trusting thieves to play by the rules," she replied coarsely. "*Lenk!*"

"If they find us here—"

"You talked us out of the last problem we encountered," Asper snapped. "If you can't talk us out of the next, then everything you've ever done for these murderers to make them respect you will be for nothing."

"Well, what's made you so snippy?" he asked, indignant.

"I was nearly killed by your friends, for one."

"They're not my—"

"And for two, you're trying to keep me from stopping your friends kill the rest of *my* friends," Asper said. "We are not leaving until we find them. Or their bodies." She tapped the Phoenix pendant at her throat. "I took an oath."

"An oath to engage in wanton stupidity in the name of mercy?"

"To engage in *any* stupidity in the name of mercy," Asper whirled on him, snarling. "And even if I hadn't, I'd do it anyway because it's the right thing to do. I'm a *font* of *compassion, asshole.*"

In truth, Denaos had a point. Cowards often could be counted on to deliver frustratingly reasonable advice. Even though the battle-field *looked* clear, nothing about its charred stalls and many corpses suggested it was safe. Beyond that, the fight had ended so abruptly, the Jackals fleeing the scene hotly while the Khovura slunk back into the shadows. Something had to have happened to cause that.

Something that they shouldn't go looking for.

And still, she pressed on. She was a priestess of the Healer. Oath-bound to do what she could to help the sick, the wounded, and the dying.

Though, as she passed the twelfth body, lying unmoving in an ash-tinged pool of blood, she knew everyone here was beyond any-thing she or Talanas could do.

Almost everyone, she corrected herself. *Focus. Ignore the dead. You can't help them now. Look for the others.* She looked around to the many bodies, the many ashes. *If they're dead, too,* then *you can worry about what you could have done.*

They walked in silence through the remains of a dignified anarchy. The stalls nobly held fast just long enough for them to pass before collapsing in whispers of soot. The ashes formed a soft carpet for them to walk upon. Even the victims, in their final moments, appeared to have climbed somewhere quiet and out of the way.

From the stalls, they emerged into the Souk's center, where they had first been separated. The fountain still babbled gently, bubbling with the red leaking from a body draped over its side. A morbid tranquility settled over the field. The bodies of Jackals and Khovura had been taken by their fellows, leaving only bloody smears where they had lain, and the civilians that hadn't been fast enough.

"When I was young, they called Cier'Djaal the City of Centers." Asper's voice was choked. "It was where every great thinker, scholar, and priest would congregate. It was always a dream of the Talanites to move their prime temple here, to be at the heart of humanity."

She turned around and beheld Denaos, standing amid the smoke and the bodies, a trail of sodden ash sprawled out behind him. He blinked absently.

"What?"

"This doesn't bother you at all? Seeing what your city's become?"

"I wasn't born in Cier'Djaal. It's not my city."

"But you lived here."

"Under it, maybe. Around it, at its fringes and in its shadows like any thug, but even the others never saw it as home." He turned and surveyed the destruction. "Just a place with a lot of people with a lot of money."

The easy way he shrugged his shoulders, the way he stifled a yawn, the way he looked it all over like it was a painting done by a bad artist; she couldn't say what it was about him that made her turn away. But she had to. She couldn't bear to see him like this. So calm. So cold.

Like this fountain.

She hadn't time to notice it before. It was ringed with stone children, hand in hand, dancing around a pillar formed of sculptures of women and men intertwined in joy. Their faces wore ecstasy like masks, hollow and false. Their hands were outstretched to catch the water as it babbled down from the top and became red in the basin.

It didn't belong in this city. It belonged in the City of Centers, that mythical, imaginary place where scholars that didn't exist would gather around it to talk about things that weren't real. This was stone: uncaring, frigid, perfect.

And moving.

Wait…

Something at the top of the fountain: some imperfect cut, some impure stone. She squinted. What was that supposed to be? An old man? A serpent? She inched closer to get a better look.

Her mouth opened. A withered hand ending in black nails lashed out and smothered her scream. She felt her feet leave the ground as she was hauled to stare into two coal-black scars where eyes should be. An old man's face, pinched into a frown, stared into her as the thing uncoiled itself from around the statue and slithered to the ground.

"Look at it, child," it rasped with a voice from somewhere dark and old. "What terrible tribute I awake to."

Revulsion, terror, sheer animal panic: There was too much inside her to render thought possible, let alone to struggle. She was carried, a trembling, weightless husk, in the thing's grasp as it slithered through the destruction.

"In my darkest slumber, I still dreamed of light," it spoke. "And I awake to a world still sleeping." It swept its head about, as though those scars-for-eyes could see more than darkness, more than light. "Nothing but the crude and primitive thought that has guided you since you crawled out of the muck."

And suddenly, those scars were turned on her. And suddenly, she couldn't feel herself breathe.

"He will fix everything. You will see, child. Khoth-Kapira will remedy the errors of your creation."

She felt its claws draw tight around her jaw. She felt its nails dig into her skin and her blood run cold beneath its grasp.

"Even if it must be done body by body."

For a brief instant, she felt one panicked, fleeting thought.

Denaos.

And like a cloud on a sunny day, there he was.

Denaos appeared over the thing's shoulder, arm looped around its neck. He held his free hand out and with a flick of his wrist, a blade sprang from the hidden sheath beneath his palm. The rogue whipped his hand forward and jammed the shiv deep into the beast's temple.

The thing flinched, as though it had just remembered something important.

Denaos hid his befuddlement beneath a snarl as he tore the blade free and stabbed the creature, over and over, again and again. A few moments later and the creature had several holes that wouldn't bleed.

"Oh," Denaos said, soft realization in his voice. "It's a *demon.* Well, *that* would explain—"

It was difficult to be witty when one was screaming, apparently. The demon's hand shot backward and plucked Denaos from its back like a tick. With another snap of its withered arm, it sent him flying into the charred husk of a stall.

"It is natural to fight back, to resist," the demon rasped, its attentions turned back to Asper. "That part which still yearns to walk on four legs demands it. Do not fear. This can be remedied."

With a delicacy belonging to hands more tender, it gingerly peeled back the sleeve of her left arm.

"I can cure you."

And promptly sank its nails into the flesh of her arm.

There was a scream. Not hers. But in her, flashing in her head, banging against her skull, trying to claw its way out of her eyes. But her mouth was sealed shut by its hand, her eyes were locked on the nails, sunk with needle-fine precision, and her flesh was on fire.

Skin began to alter, ripple, boil beneath its touch. Small bubbles blossomed across her skin, popped silently and exposed bloody sores. She felt agony. She felt terror.

But she was not the only one. The curse inside her felt it as well. And it spoke in shrieking nightmares.

Don't like this what is it make it stop kill it get rid of it go away leave us alone don't like it hate it hurts hurts hurts HURTS—

In two desperate breaths that faded, along with her terror. It felt as though she breathed in fog that slowly coated her mind, smothering thought and fear alike. All that was in her drained out of the sores the demon had opened in her arm. Nothing was left but the rasping.

"This crude thought, this vulgar flesh," it whispered, "you can be more. I can fix you. I can shape you. I will heal the scars your creators left upon you and when I am done, you will be—"

Silence.

Then pain.

Feeling and fear returned to her in a glorious, reverberating scream. She landed hard upon the stones, and her body reacted to the feel of solid stone beneath her, sending her scrambling away.

The demon was on its chest, pulled to the ground, face pinched in anger. A noise of annoyance that sounded something like milk boiling in a rusty kettle rose in its throat as it looked over its shoulder.

Demons could not be killed, or even harmed, by mortal weapons.

And perhaps Gariath had only just annoyed it.

The hulking dragonman was at the creature's back, hands wrapped around its tail, hauling it to the ground. His scowl was resolute, his claws sunken into the beast's tail, his grip unwavering.

"The unwashed"—a hint of anger crept into the creature's voice—"may not lay hands upon the *learned*."

It sank nails into stone, bracing itself. Its tail cracked like a whip, lifting Gariath up and smashing him down onto the stones. The dragonman offered nothing more than a snarl, more irritated than agonized. And as the beast continued to whip its tail around in an attempt to dislodge him, as he smashed against the stones time and again, he would not let go.

Tenacity was Gariath's strong suit. Timeliness, Dreadaeleon's. A skinny, frail figure came stumbling out of the stalls, narrowly avoiding tripping on the tails of his own dirty coat.

Despite the carnage and the presence of a thing that should not be, Dreadaeleon's first thought, and first glance, were for Asper.

"Are you all right?" he asked, breathless from his hurried flight over.

She looked at her arm. Four perfect circles glistened upon it. She tugged her sleeve down, as much to hide it from herself as from him.

"I'm fine," she lied.

"Lovely," the boy replied. "I suspect Gariath will need your attentions shortly after I'm done."

"And Denaos," she said, looking over her shoulder to where the rogue had fallen.

"If you must."

She glowered at him, but ignored the jibe. She clambered to her feet. "Tell Gariath to let go and make a run for it. We can still escape."

"Escape?" Dreadaeleon pulled back his sleeves as though exposing stick-thin arms was something to fear. "Why on earth would we do that?"

"It's a *demon*, Dread. What the hell are you hoping to do to it?"

He closed his eyes, drew in a deep breath.

"Oh, you know."

When he opened them, they were alive with a bright red light.

"Stuff."

The light began to spread, through his veins, into his voice. He spoke words that were painful to hear. He held his palms out as they began to steam and glow bright red. His stride was calm as he approached the flailing demon. His voice was soft as he spoke the power. His hands were outstretched as if he were about to ask for a hug.

And then, he unleashed hell.

Flames erupted from his palms in roaring gouts, reaching out to devour wood and cloth and flesh in great, crackling jaws. Sound and air were eaten alive. All other light dimmed. The world and all of its dead people and all of its charred wood somehow seemed meaningless against the boy and his terrible fire.

Gariath flung himself away just in time to see the demon swallowed by two great red sheets. The fire cackled, chewed ancient flesh, and spat black ash.

The demon snarled, writhing within the flames. But there was no pain behind its sound or movement. There was only a throaty fury, the groan of an old man's impatience with a young upstart. It writhed. It shrieked. It roared.

But it did not stop. It did not die.

And Dreadaeleon, grinning from ear to ear at the display of his own power, didn't even notice.

Asper began to shriek something to him when she felt hands around her arms, hoisting her to her feet. She instinctively lashed out and struck a cheek with a flailing fist. A very familiar snarl met her.

She whirled and saw Kataria standing behind her, glaring.

"You're all right," Asper said.

"Yeah." The shict drew back a fist and smashed it against Asper's jaw. "You, too."

"Are you not seeing this?" Lenk appeared a moment later, gesturing to the demon. "Why the hell would you hit her *now*?"

"She hit me first!" Kataria spat.

No time to respond, he turned to the inferno raging before them. "We need to move. Grab Denaos, tell Dread to break off, and we'll run for the gates."

"*Run?*" Dreadaeleon shouted to be heard over his own fire. "Did we not already discard this idea?"

"It's a demon," Lenk screamed back. "You can't kill it with fire!"

"The common misconception of the common man, I assure you,"

the boy shouted louder as his magic burned brighter, hotter, stronger. "*Fire. Solves. EVERYTHING!*"

The boy's laughter was loud and triumphant and lasted as long as it took for a great, serpentine tail to lash out of the curtain of flame. It struck him squarely across the ribs and, in an instant, a wizard was turned into a firefly, an insect fluttering on smoking wings and sputtering lights as he was hurled through the air, trailing black smoke behind.

"What now?" Kataria asked, watching him crash into a nearby pile of salt. "Retreat?"

"We'll never outrun it unless we leave Denaos and Dread to—" Lenk began.

"We *aren't*." Asper cut him off with a glare.

The look he shot her in return bore no anger. Only weary resignation.

"Second plan, then," he said with a sigh.

"That being?"

He hefted his weapon, sniffed a little. "Hit it with a sword. Hope we don't die. You know."

"What do you hope to change, child?"

A voice rose from the smoldering inferno of Dreadaeleon's magic. And with it, a shape painted black against the flames.

"I have awoken to a world alive with suffering. Would you ask me to sleep through more?" The demon came slithering out of the fire, unscarred, unshaken. "Khoth-Kapira calls us to the waking world. He will show you a world beyond your crude dreams. And his Disciples will call you to him."

The demon spread its withered arms in benediction. Its nails glistened obsidian.

"Come to me, child."

Only one of them did.

And he came from behind.

Swiftly.

Gariath's howl drowned out the thunder of his charge as he rushed forward on all fours, leaping atop the demon's back and driving its face to the stones. He stood there, one foot lodged between its shoulder blades, the other hammering a heel down upon the back of its skull.

Its arms lashed up, bending behind it with unnatural ease. Gariath caught it by the wrists, jerked its limbs backward, and pressed his feet against its spine, prying it up from the stones. He shot a desperate look to the companions and snarled.

"Go."

And they did.

Sword in hand, Lenk took off at a charge, Kataria close behind. A pair of arrows shrieked past his ear to sail unerringly into a gray collarbone and cheek. The demon did not flinch at the shafts embedded in its flesh. It barely twitched as it opened its mouth wide.

A long, purple tongue came lashing out, striking against the stones as it streaked toward the companions. It lashed across Lenk's shoulder and cut through the cloth of his shirt. He felt the warm splash of blood as it took flesh with it. He could bite back pain; he could ignore it.

But he could not ignore the shriek that followed.

He looked over his shoulder and saw the tongue wrapped around Kataria's leg. She fell to the ground, a bright red circle appearing around her calf as the tongue bit through leggings and into flesh. The tongue snapped forward, pulling her along the stones before Lenk even had a chance to raise his sword against it.

The demon's mouth gaped impossibly wide, jaw unhinging as it drew the shrieking shict closer. She abandoned her bow, clawing at the stones in a desperate bid to slow herself down. And as she did, Lenk picked up speed, too quick for a single thought as to how stupid this was.

He sped past her. He ignored the tongue drawing her closer. He took up his blade in both hands. He leapt.

And in a spurt of black blood, he landed.

He drove the weapon deep into the beast's chest. Where fire had failed, where mortal steel had faltered, his blade, his hands, his fury splashed black life across the sky. He had no fears that the only way to kill demons was to pay a price. He had no concerns for the blood splashing upon his face. He had no worries for the fact that he felt his body grow cold and his thoughts empty.

At that moment, with the steel in his hands and the blood in his nostrils, he felt something he had hoped to never again feel at the scent of metal and violence.

Complete.

The demon's shriek tore Gariath from its back, released Kataria from its grasp, and sent Lenk flying backward. But the young man was on his feet again in an instant, rushing back toward the creature. He couldn't let go of the steel. He couldn't stop the bloodshed. If he did, Kataria would be in danger. Kataria would suffer. They would all suffer if he did not keep killing.

This is what he told himself.

He took the blade's hilt in both hands and twisted it in the creature's chest. It writhed upon the ground, coiling up and thrashing as it tried to dislodge Lenk. But its claws were too weak. Its limbs flailed helplessly as he drove it to the earth, as he raised a boot, as he brought it hard upon the sword's crosspiece and the blade burst through its back.

But the demon was not screaming. The demon was barely struggling. Its voice was soft, almost mockingly gentle, a parent chiding a boy with his hand in a pastry jar.

"What have you changed, child?" it asked. "Did you honestly believe the Disciples did not plan for this as well? Did you think Khoth-Kapira would be so shortsighted as . . . as . . ."

Speech died. The demon died. In a pool of its own black blood, it coiled up into a tight ball, covering itself with its withered arm. There was a crackling sound as its skin grew hard and brittle, like old stone.

In another instant, a breeze blew hard across the Souk, carrying the scent of fire with it. The body of the demon, its skin and its many bones, sloughed and became as sand and was carried upon the wind into Lenk's face. It crusted upon his blood-painted visage, filled his nostrils, filled his senses with the scent of hatred.

He stood there, as his companions staggered to their feet.

He let out a trembling breath, as his sword clattered to the ground.

He let the world around him go dark, as a voice in the cold part of him that dreamed of dead men said to him a single word.

Glorious.

TWELVE

PAGES IN THE BOOK

How often, Dransun wondered, had he ever really stopped and looked up at the sky since he had arrived in Cier'Djaal?

Since the day he had set out from his father's little rice farm on the outskirts of the city, he had always been staring at something in front of him: the sword they put in his hands, the women they pushed him toward, the badges and promotions they pinned on his chest. But rarely had he thought to look up over the bustle of people and the clink of coins and stared at the sky until tonight.

Up there, the stars burned like lamplights hung from a thousand doorways of a thousand cozy homes. Through the webs of the Silken Spire, they seemed to shimmer like diamonds as the spiders, ever-aloof, crawled lazily across a sea of stars and silk.

Pretty, he thought as he looked at what was in front of him.

Down here, there were also stars. But they burned ugly, like dead moths around a candle flame. And while there weren't nearly as many down here as there were up there, there were still far too many for his taste.

In the darkness of the ravaged Souk, the yellow glow of the Lanterns bobbed precariously. Gevrauch's faithful, as befit their duties to the God of Death, combed through the ashes without a sound among them. The glow of their namesakes, bobbing over their heads like anglerfish, reflected against the glass circles sewn into their burlap masks. All throughout the Souk, they looked like morbid little fairies dancing over corpses.

When they found a body, they pulled what remained from the rubble and silently dragged it to a nearby tarp. Dransun's Jhouche guardsmen stood watch—or rather, stood, trying not to watch—as the Quill glanced over the body and wrote, in a very large book, details about the victim: gender, apparent age, cause of death, how many limbs were missing, how much blood was lost and other gruesome details.

Dransun couldn't bear to look back up at the sky again. The sight of light, he thought, would make him sick. So he stared down between his legs as he sat upon the bench. He laced his fingers behind his head and made a low, groaning sound.

If it turned out the footwar wasn't over, if a Jackal thug or Khovura radical came up behind him and gutted him right there, that would have been fine with him. Then he wouldn't have to go to the families of the dead tomorrow, and the next day and the next. He wouldn't have to see their faces.

Anguish didn't bother him. But there was never anguish on the faces of the bereaved.

Sometimes, there was rage, angry questions about what kind of fools this city had hired that they couldn't protect its own citizens. More often, there was greed, inquiries about how they would be compensated for the unlawful death. But these days, the most common look was one of acceptance, as though this sort of thing were just one more inconvenience of living in the city along with big rent and small living space.

As though this, all these bodies, were somehow normal.

This city is sick, his father had once told him. *It eats people and craps out gold and people pick the filth up off the city streets and shove it in their faces and smear it on their lips.*

Dransun often thought of his father when he reached for the flask of whiskey hidden in his boot. Usually because, at times like this, he often wondered why he hadn't followed his father's noble footsteps and become an alcoholic.

No sooner had he uncorked the flask than he saw a pair of black boots standing before him. He didn't bother looking up as he took a swig. He already knew who they belonged to, even before he heard the calm monotone of the Quill's voice.

"Good evening, Captain," the priest said. "We believe we have recovered the last of the bodies."

"Uh-huh," Dransun replied, taking another swig, a longer one.

"At a tally thus far, we have recovered forty-three corpses. All human. Twenty-six were men, eleven were women, and—"

"Stop."

The Quill's feet shuffled slightly. "I beg your pardon, Captain?"

"I can count, priest. I know what you're about to say, and if I hear it right now I'm going to pour the rest of this liquor on me, light myself on fire, and burn to death." He held up his hands, trembling. "I...I'll get to it. I just...I can't hear that right now."

The Quill said nothing. His boots did not move.

"Leave your report with one of my men." Dransun took another long swig. "Take the bodies. We'll inform the families. You can keep the ones that don't get claimed." He waved a hand. "You can go now."

The Quill still said nothing. But this time, his boots turned around. Dransun heard the scuffling of feet, briefly, before he felt a weight beside him on the bench.

"I do not believe you should be alone right now, Captain," the Quill said softly.

Dransun felt warm. That might have been the liquor. He handed the flask to the death priest, who took it gingerly. Only now did he look up to see the priest lift the flask up and study it through the glass circles in his mask, as though he wasn't sure what it did. Slowly, the priest lifted his mask just beneath his nose. There was a face under there, scarred and unshaven, but it was a human's face that was drinking.

The death priest was still a man.

"How do you do it?" Dransun asked.

The Quill coughed a little, wiping his lips with the back of his hand. He smoothed his mask out over his mouth and chin and turned his glassy eyes to the captain, questioningly. Or maybe that was the liquor, too; it was hard to read expressions through burlap.

"You follow Gevrauch, God of Death," Dransun said. "You surround yourself with corpses, the sick, the dying. You don't try to help them, like the Talanites. You just watch them die and then take their body for rites. How the hell haven't you killed yourself yet?"

The Quill looked away, back to his Lanterns as his subordinates began to load the dead bodies into a wagon.

"Humanity's reverence for life is misplaced."

Cold. Simple. The Quill spoke flatly.

"Life is fleeting, true. Precious, yes. But people act as though if they simply hold on long enough, they can hold it forever. But in holding on, they learn nothing but how to strangle life dead and leave it on the floor as an empty husk.

"In death, there is meaning, Captain. Sometimes, it is very simple. We learn much from the bodies donated to our temples, and we pass that knowledge along to the healers. And sometimes, it is very complicated. We sit and wait with a man who is ready to die and we listen to his biggest regret and we tell his children what mistakes his father made.

"But for life to mean anything, it has to end. And when it ends and another tally is made in the Bookkeeper's ledger, it is a meaningful stroke of the quill that scribes the name."

"But in all this?" Dransun asked, sweeping a hand over the devastated Souk. "In forty-three dead?"

"In three days, Captain, there will be more merchant stalls built over the ashes of the ones today. There will be new merchants to replace the old. There will be a hungry lust for gold, as powerful as ever, that keeps people coming back to the Souk even though a footwar rages in it near-weekly."

"And where's the meaning in that?"

"The meaning, Captain," the Quill said softly, "is that death does not stop life."

Dransun looked down at his feet. He was too drunk to see the wisdom in that statement and not drunk enough to take comfort in it. He took another drink from the flask and licked his lips.

"The dead," he said, "you said they were all human?"

"That is correct, Captain. The Jackals and Khovura took their dead, as they always do. We found no oids amid the dead."

"Figures," Dransun muttered. "Gods-damned couthi were probably the first out. The stupid bugs always know when a war's about to hit." He rubbed his face. "And I know the dragonmen made it out, because they were there with the fasha's men, preventing us from getting into the Souk."

"The fashas have condemned the footwar, though."

"They have, because it's expected of them. Everyone knows the Jackals are in tight with the fashas. The fashas let them run their footwar unopposed and the Jackals keep the markets running for them and keep the Khovura off their backs."

"The Khovura are decidedly not fond of the fashas."

"No. That's why they keep attacking the Souk. They think they're disrupting the fashas' coins, but all they do is kill people trying to make a gold piece. Radicals. Savages. Always the cause of—"

Dransun caught himself. He looked swiftly to the death priest.

"You said all human. You're sure?"

"I am sure, Captain."

"You didn't see a shict, did you? Sometimes they look like us, if you don't pay attention to the ears and teeth."

"I am acquainted with shicts, Captain. I would have recognized them. Why?"

"There were reports of a shict and a bunch of northerners causing trouble with Ghoukha's men." Dransun hummed, rubbing his chin. "They had a monster with them. Like a dragonman, but smaller... and red."

"You suspect them of having a connection to the Khovura?"

"Or the Jackals. It's not unheard of for footwar gangs to bring in mercs. And if these foreigners were messing with the fashas…" Dransun let his voice trail off into a nondescript hum as he scratched his chin thoughtfully.

"It sounds as though you've found some meaning in today's deaths, Captain," the Quill said, rising to his feet. "I will leave our report with your men. You may inform the families of the deceased at your leisure."

Dransun spared him a nod as the Quill left. Dransun did not look up or at his feet, and though he stared straight ahead, he seemed to see nothing at all. His mind was somewhere his eyes could not follow, somewhere with suspicious shicts and red monsters and mysterious northerners. He no longer looked anywhere but straight ahead.

Certainly, he did not look up and over his shoulder.

If he did, he would have seen a pair of green eyes staring down at him from the roof of a nearby stall left standing. He would have seen a pair of long, notched, pointed ears twitching as they slowly sank away, full of information.

And he would have known just how much meaning there was in these deaths.

      ⊷ ⊷≡◆≡⊶ ⊶

Kataria swept silently through the streets. It wasn't difficult to remain unseen; no one had yet returned to the Souk besides the guards and the death priests. It was easy enough to make her way to the outskirts, where more stalls stood unscarred and fewer torches hung.

And there were plenty enough shadows to obscure the five people huddled in the corners of a pair of abandoned stalls laden with cheap, cotton clothes.

Asper knelt beside Dreadaeleon, treating a gash across his brow from his rough landing. Gariath huddled toward the back, crouched on his haunches in quiet brooding. Lenk and Denaos discussed something between themselves, yet all looked up when she returned.

"They know we're here, but they have no idea who we are," she said. "I don't know how long that's going to last, though, since the human in the fancy armor sounded pretty interested in us."

"Did they say anything about the demon? Or about Miron?" Lenk asked.

She shook her head. At this, Denaos glanced lazily toward Lenk.

"Plan?" the rogue asked.

"Easy enough, isn't it?" Lenk asked. "We find out what happened to Miron, track him down, and get our money back."

"Easy," Denaos repeated.

"Simple enough, I mean."

"Track down Miron—who only *you* saw—and find out what happened to him—after he disappeared into nothingness in the middle of a battle—track him down—when he may be in the clutches of one of *two* groups that tried to kill us today—get our money back—assuming they haven't already killed him."

Denaos clicked his tongue.

"That's not simple. It's another word that begins with 's,' but not simple."

"It's simple enough if you still want to get paid," Lenk replied sharply. "If you're fine with throwing away all the blood we've already spilled for that man and getting nothing for it, feel free to stay here."

"Money aside," Asper began, looking up from her patching of Dreadaeleon, "I'd want to find Miron, even if we weren't getting paid. He's a good Talanite and has always looked out for us."

Denaos snorted. She glared at him before speaking louder.

"*But* Denaos has a point. Surely it can't be as easy as that."

"No," Lenk said, "but it can't be impossible. Cier'Djaal is a big city, but he wouldn't have been able to leave it just yet, would he? If he's been kidnapped, he's still here. And if he's left, we can go find him on the open road." At his companions' silence, he rubbed his eyes. "Look, I realize the task may seem enormous, but there are six of us. We can find him."

They exchanged brief glances. Asper looked uncertainly at the ground.

"There are bound to be temples here," she said. "He's the Lord Emissary of the Church of Talanas. If he escaped, he'll have gone there. I can ask around." She gestured toward Denaos. "And Denaos has his own contacts here."

"You do?" Lenk asked, looking to the rogue.

"Oh, let's not go acting like you're surprised that I know people in bad ways," Denaos said with a dramatic sigh. "Yeah. I'll ask around. Only because that's not money I want to throw away." He pointed at Lenk. "You owe me twice, though."

"Yeah. I sure am lucky you're both shifty and greedy," Lenk replied with a sigh. He looked to Dreadaeleon. "And how about you, Dread?"

"How about me what?" the boy muttered, holding a wadded-up bandaged to his brow.

"You mentioned there was a Venarium outpost here, didn't you? Couldn't you . . . wizard something up?"

"Wizard something up," the boy repeated, voice dripping with sarcasm. "Are you quite sure you wouldn't like to simply go barreling your way into the Venarium, slapping people about the face and demanding answers?"

Lenk sighed. "I assume there's a reason for this outburst beyond the fact that I have apparently committed a lot of sins against some passive-aggressive Gods."

"I could have stopped the demon," Dreadaeleon spat. "I could have *killed it*. I had near-limitless power at my command and you went and solved everything by hitting it with a big metal stick."

"Of course. How rude of me. Everything seemed to be going quite well until it threw you like filth from a monkey's hand."

"*You* don't *need* to be the one to save everyone," Dreadaeleon snapped.

"When they can't be incinerated, I do," Lenk spoke coldly, harshly. "If you'd rather we all have been eaten alive while patiently waiting for you to come back and try something else that didn't work, I'm sorry. But for now, I need to know if you're either going to help or leave, because those are your *only* options right now."

A tense moment of silence roiled between the boy's burning scowl and the young man's cold stare. It ended with Dreadaeleon sliding to his feet and sneering something at Lenk. He turned, he skulked, but he stayed.

Lenk permitted himself a sigh of relief. Thus far, it seemed as though everyone was at ease with the idea and everyone had something to contribute. Plans never went this well for him, he noted. Usually there was something to make things more difficult.

And that was when he found his gaze drawn, inexorably, toward Gariath.

His stare was scrutinizing at first as he appraised the dragonman. Slowly, it turned quizzical, then confused, then worried. The dragonman stared back at him blankly before slowly raising his right hand.

"I promise," he growled, "to kill only as many people as can reasonably be expected to help."

"I'll take it," Lenk said.

He would have said more, but at that moment, the sound of distant shouting and the authoritative tromp of boots silenced him. They huddled down low as the glow of torches gleaming off of polished helmets hurried by in disorderly fashion.

"If you're hoping this was all going to take place outside of a prison cell," Denaos muttered as they disappeared, "we should probably find somewhere to lie low for the rest of the night." He gestured toward the other end of the Souk. "There are some places between the harbor and the Souk that don't ask questions. We can make our way there and plan out further."

The rogue gave his companions a swift glance over and frowned.

"Probably better if we don't all move together. Make for the eastern gate and we'll meet up there."

With that, they broke, vanishing down alleys and into shadows as they hurried on. Lenk was about to head out on his own path when he felt the familiar pain of a pair of green eyes boring into the back of his neck.

He looked over his shoulder. Kataria hadn't made a single step. Nor did she move at his insistent stare.

"No part in this plan for me," she said.

"I figured you and I would go out and try to track him down ourselves," he said, "cover the places the others couldn't."

"I wasn't asking."

"If you don't want any part in finding Miron—"

"I don't care about Miron," she snapped suddenly. "I don't care about *humans*." The look she shot him wavered between fury and fear, both angry and nervous at once. "Not most of them, anyway."

"Then what is it? You just don't want to help?"

"Help you get your money? Help you find coin so you can settle down here and be like *them*," she snarled, sweeping a hand out over the Souk, "those *kou'ru* that called me an animal?"

"They've always called you an animal," he shot back. "They've called you worse. You've called *them* worse and *done* worse to them. You *bit off a man's ear* today and now you suddenly care what they think? What changed?"

"What changed is *you*"—she thrust a finger at him—"*you* want to be like *them*. *You* want money. *You* want to stop fighting. *You* want to scrape at dirt and be ruled by other people. *You* want to be normal and you're *not*."

"I'm one of them. I'm human."

His voice was flimsy, quavering at the edges. His words were trembling, a boulder teetering on the edge of a cliff. And in his eyes, something suggested he didn't quite believe what he said.

That suggestion was reflected in Kataria's eyes and amplified tenfold in her black, snorting laughter.

"One of them? No," she said. "And maybe not even human." She drew closer to him, holding out a hand warily. "You killed that thing, Lenk. You *killed* what mortal weapons couldn't. You're not normal. I don't know what you are and I've never cared up until now. But I know you're not one of them."

Her hand settled upon his shoulder. He did not return the touch. The smile he offered was soft, trembling.

Weak.

"And I liked it when you thought that, too," she said.

"Then, what am I?" he asked softly. "I can kill. I can murder. I can make things that don't bleed, bleed. And you want me to hold onto this?"

"I *want* you to be true to yourself."

"I don't even know *what* myself is," he all but roared. "Do you have any idea what it was like to kill that demon?"

She opened her mouth to speak; he cut her off.

"They don't bleed like people. They don't die like people. Because they don't remember what pain is like. And so when they get hurt, it's that kind of pain that only someone who thought he was invincible can feel. Their pain is so loud. It's so powerful. It's...it's *pure*." He looked at his hands. They were shaking. "When you cause that pain, you can feel it; you can *taste* it. And I did. You know what I felt?"

She didn't bother to speak this time. He looked at her, all cold, all quiet.

"Fantastic," he whispered. "I felt fantastic. Like everything else that I've been thinking and feeling just fell into some perfect shape the moment I feel blood on my face." His voice began to run hoarse. "And the more I do it, the more normal I feel and the more dead people there are in my dreams."

His voice faded. His lips went dry. His skin felt as though it were sand. The words hurt to speak, and the tears forming at the edges of his eyes felt unbearably hot as they slid down his cheeks.

"And I...I can't keep doing that," he said. "I can't keep killing people. I can't keep feeling this way. And for you to tell me that I have to choose between you and...and..."

Something deep within him shook as though it might break if he spoke another word.

"I might not be like them, now or ever," he said softly. "But I can't just live like I don't want to be."

And Kataria said nothing.

She looked at him, as she often did, with a gaze unwavering. There were no tears at the corners of her eyes. There was no trembling of her lip, no frailty in her body. What she felt, he knew, was not something one shed tears over. What she felt was something one shed blood over.

And so she was silent as she removed her hat.

She said nothing as she reached behind her head, wove fingers into the tousled mane of golden braids, and undid the bindings that secured the feathers to her hair.

She said nothing as she plucked a long, white one from her hair, took his hand, and laid it gently in his palm.

She said nothing. Not as she turned from him to walk away, never looking back as she vanished into the darkness.

THIRTEEN

SYMPHONIES FOR DEAD MEN

Mundas did not know the young man's name, nor did he care to.

They were all alike, these people. Their bodies may have been different, of course: some older, some younger, some men, some women. Mentally, though, they were all the same as that man who stood up as his name was called.

They were desperate. They were reckless. They had no idea what they were doing here beyond the fact that none of them could live another moment in the lives they had been born into.

It was that utter desire to be in anyone else's skin that made that young man rise from the crowd of hundreds that looked just like him. It was that sole trait that made Mundas continue to stand on the balcony and observe, as he had done for every young man, for the past two years.

"Kapira, Kapira, Kapira…"

The chant began almost immediately as the young man rose. Amidst the crowd of the black-shrouded Khovura, their many skins hidden behind many veils, a long gap appeared in the mass of flesh.

And the young man began to walk.

In the vast, rock-hewn hall, he was watched. By his fellow Khovura, kneeling upon the floor and staring with envy in their eyes. By the many hard-faced statues carved out of sandstone to march the walls of the hall, granite frowns observing his progress.

And by Mundas, from a spot wedged neatly between two of those statues, who watched him closely.

"Kapira, Kapira, Kapira…"

The chant followed him as he walked down the long gap. And as he did, he began to shed. His clothes were doffed scrap by scrap, until he was nude, leaving a black trail behind him. Dark-skinned and bright-eyed, his gait slowed as he drew closer to his goal.

The dais stood at the end of the hall, painted crimson in the sultry glow of the many braziers. Four tall pillars flanked it, each one inscribed with an ancient language the Khovura only barely knew. They could read a few of the words, to be certain.

"Kapira, Kapira, Kapira…"

And they certainly could regurgitate them at a moment's notice. But only Mundas could fully understand the script.

Flesh is the prison your ignorance is held in, the first read. *Know that in change there is truth*, said the second. *Within eternity, find Him*, the third. *Within Him, find eternity*, the fourth.

Cryptic. Ominous. Looking as though it had been wrought by the hands of some deranged naked prophet in the desert.

As demons tended to prefer.

The young man stepped upon the dais warily, as though it were sacred ground instead of dirty sandstone. He tapped his foot, possibly fearing that it might hurt to do so. Satisfied, he took a bold, triumphant step upon the dais and turned to present himself to his fellow Khovura in all his fleshy, vulnerable glory.

Whether the poor fool ever saw the long, gray limbs ending in long, black nails reaching from the shadows, Mundas was not sure.

Whether that was a scream of ecstasy or agony that tore itself from his throat as those black talons sank into his flesh, Mundas did not care.

The nails slipped into his skin like pockets, lifting him from his feet to hold him with ornamental reverence above the dais. From the darkness beyond, the Disciple emerged on gray coils. Its old man's face was pinched into a frown, its eyes scarred black staring holes into the weak creature it bore in its talons.

The Disciple was silent. Its sermons had been heard many times before.

The crowd was raucous, roaring the fragments of language they knew with the fervor they thought it deserved.

And the young man was screaming.

Within his body, beneath his tender flesh, the Disciple's power began to work. The young man's skin boiled, bubbled, burst, and exposed tender sores. His veins grew fat with blood, pressing against his face, his chest, his legs. His eyelids fled back into his skull, his white eyes bulged from their sockets, his lips curled up over his gums.

Sound burst from every contracting pore, seeped out of ears that were curling like burnt paper, ripped itself from rippling skin. The young man was crying many things, many confessions that he wasn't ready, many pleas for it to stop.

They all did that, at first.

But soon, lips became wires, tongue became porridge, language became meaningless. The young man was all sounds now: of bubbles bursting, of voices choking, of thick chunks of flesh made into stew sloughing off bones turning to twigs and plopping upon the floor.

It continued, the young man melting until he was but a saggy, shapeless blob in the Disciple's hands. His teeth were where his shoulder had once been, his hands hung as limp tendrils, his softened tongue lolled from a nondescript hole in his body. Only a single eye remained intact: wide and rolling desperately in its socket as it looked over the crowd.

Did he search for help? Mundas wondered. And what did he feel when he saw only adoring, envious eyes cast his way?

Mundas's curiosity lasted only as long as the young man did. Soon, the mass of dark skin, hair, and teeth slid off of the Disciple's talons. It lay there—for it was no longer a man—as a puddle of skin upon the dais.

"Unworthy," the Disciple rasped softly.

It slithered back into the shadows, disappearing and leaving the man-made liquid to cascade over the edges of the dais and seep into the sand.

Demons did not give. The power offered to the Khovura, the ability to resist wounds and fight their petty wars with petty thugs like the Jackals, came with a price. Not everyone was able to pay.

There would be more chants. There would be more writhing devotion. There would be more praise heaped upon Khoth-Kapira's name, invocations for him to return and alter the unworthy to a more pleasing form, more brave souls sent to the dais and more human puddles that someone would eventually remember to scoop unceremoniously into a jar and place with the other failed candidates.

Mundas hardly begrudged them it. Ritual was grass for the sheep, after all. But at that moment, he found himself in the rare position of having seen a man be turned into liquid too often for it to be a novel experience anymore.

He turned away from the spectacle below to retreat deeper into the halls. The Khovura were in every nook and cranny of the labyrinthine hall. Some prayed at small altars. Some sharpened their blades. Some rocked back and forth, hugging their knees and muttering to themselves.

More than once, as they often did, they raised their hands to him in reverence. He waved back with weary contempt.

He did not think them fools. Merely like children: all enthusiasm, no matter the cause. Children could be useful. Children could be taught. No matter how many bright, shiny lights and human puddles were needed to do so.

At the end of one of the many branching halls, he found his quarters: a humble cell furnished with cot, table, basin, and bookshelf. Crossing to the basin, he stared into the water: a stern-faced, dark man bereft of hair, eyebrows, or stubble stared back. He dipped a hand into the basin, drinking from his cupped palm until his thirst was quenched.

The heavy wooden door barred, the sounds of the Khovura muffled, he could hear the sounds of droplets striking the face of the water.

The only thing the tiny room offered in abundance was silence. And this was all he required.

"Miss me?"

Not that it's common enough to not be stolen by fools, he thought resentfully as he turned about to face Azhu-Mahl.

He squatted just at the edge of a shadow, thin as a dead tree. He would have been just as tall, as well, if he ever bothered to stand up straight. Azhu-Mahl, however, rested on skeletally thin haunches the color of a body six days dead, long fingers drumming impatiently on knobby knees. His face was bereft of any feature beyond a smile broad with teeth as long as fingers.

It always struck Mundas as odd that a creature without eyes or nose could look so smug. Even having undoubtedly spent hours waiting for this entrance, Azhu-Mahl was far, *far* too pleased with himself.

"You survived," Mundas noted.

"Easily," Azhu-Mahl replied. "The Khovura provided ample enough cover for me to slip away."

"And the adventurers you hired?"

"Likely dead."

"And if not?"

"They likely assume I am dead and have gone off to lick their wounds or rut in an alley or whatever it is they do," Azhu-Mahl replied. He looked expectantly at Mundas for a moment. "I'm fine."

"Pardon?"

"I said I'm fine. You know, having been away for all these many months, in near-constant peril, I thought you might be wondering."

Mundas stared back blankly.

"Do you possess the item?"

Azhu-Mahl sighed. He produced a small satchel, laying it upon the table and sliding it toward Mundas. The hairless man looked at it for a moment before opening the flap and easing out the item.

A book. Perfectly square, perfectly flat, perfectly black. It lay with an unexpected weight upon the table, as though it had been waiting its entire existence to be right here, right now.

The key to the gates of heaven and hell. One of the last records of the Aeons, those creatures that had become the demons. The Tome of the Undergates. A rare prize.

Mundas took it in both hands and delicately set it to the side. Azhu-Mahl frowned.

"You're not going to look at it?"

"Not now."

"You await the moment to be alone with it?"

"I merely await a moment I have to myself. It is a book. I will study it when I have quiet."

"It is not *a* book," Azhu-Mahl replied. "It is *the* book. The key to all that we have fought for. The reason I have been absent all these months. That which so many lives have been sacrificed for."

Mundas stared at him, then spoke flatly.

"A book. While rare, there are more like it. It is a book. A possible answer to a question with many possible answers and only one of them correct. A lead you were intent on pursuing, despite my advice. Something that likely did not require so many lives to be taken for which I am not at all regretful.

"That you have returned it is fortunate. I will study it at my convenience and reveal my findings to you. If your travels were such a burden to you, you are more than welcome to take the time to recuperate."

A flash of anger twitched across Azhu-Mahl's features.

"I have handed you the end," the creature said. "I have seen seas red with blood. I have waged wars on less. I have watched people die in the thousands for what you so casually put aside." He slammed his hands upon the table, rose from his chair. "I have ruined lives and destroyed faiths to deliver enlightenment to you, Mundas, and *you are taking all the fun out of it.*"

Mundas had no eyebrows to raise in surprise. He trusted his usual, deep-set, unrelenting frown to suffice as apologetic enough.

"Would it soothe you if I were to read it now?"

"We stand between worlds." Azhu-Mahl spoke forcefully, his words pointed like a spear's tip. "The archaic past, rife with idolatry and stagnant philosophy, is at our back while a glorious new future awaits us, brighter than any desert sun."

Mundas hummed; the creature, as ever, seemed incapable of saying anything in less dramatic fashion.

"The Khovura are ready," Azhu-Mahl said. "They are hungry with victory. The people will follow. They will change, as we all do. Can you not hear them? Do you not share their hunger? Their glory?"

"I do not."

"Why?"

"Because I am not a fanatic," Mundas replied curtly. "I do not bow. I do not kneel. I do not pray. I trade faith for thought, zeal for action. I am in the business of enlightenment, not devotion. I do not traffic in deities. I abolish them. As I thought you did"—he paused a moment before he began to speak the next word—"my dear lord—"

"*NO.*"

Azhu-Mahl's frown deepened. His thin, gray lips were so used to smiling, baring finger-long teeth, that the flesh cracked with his displeasure. He held up a long, gray hand before an eyeless face and shook his head.

"Do *not* use that name."

Mundas inclined his head in acknowledgment. It was, of course, generally considered poor manners to speak a shape-changer's name. Doing so tended to offend them terribly.

But Mundas had a point to prove.

"The plan goes well," he said; "this much is true. The Khovura are dedicated. The Jackals are routed. The people are listening, watching, and willing." He closed his eyes. "My enthusiasm remains contained for one reason."

He opened them, looked into Azhu-Mahl's teeth.

"*He* has yet to contact us."

It was impossible for the demon not to smile. But there were certain indicators as to Azhu-Mahl's mood that Mundas had become attuned to over the years: the way his lips tugged at the edges, the way his ears laid back, the way his claws sank into the wood of the table in barely controlled anger.

"Usually, creatures like Him take a greater interest in their own release," Mundas continued. "Usually, they can't resist the allure of worship. Yet for all the pleas sent to Him, all the sacrifices made, all the followers assembled, he remains silent."

"He sent his Disciples, did He not?" Azhu-Mahl asked.

"The Disciples pride themselves on not being fanatical devotees," Mundas replied. "They are loyal, yes, but not unthinking. They indulge the Khovura and perhaps that's a signal that He is not displeased, but He has yet to make his presence known."

He laid a hand on the Tome of the Undergates.

"Hence why this is of limited value," he said. "We cannot roust from prison that which does not wish to be freed."

"He wishes to be free," Azhu-Mahl said blackly. "I have seen His prison. I cannot fathom a being that finds it comforting."

"Regardless," Mundas said, "the Khovura interpret His will as they choose to. He does not punish them, so they believe themselves to have pleased Him. I am not so certain."

"We are attempting to summon *Him*, Mundas," Azhu-Mahl said. "The God-King. The Shaper of Flesh who was ancient when mortals started crawling out of the muck. You would be forgiven for finding His motivations inscrutable."

"Motivation concerns me less than execution. We stand on the edge of a new age, free from superstition and petty concerns of mortal trivialities. We are so close to the next evolution of the world and we have invested much and risked more to come to this point. If He *does* not come when called, that is one thing. If He *cannot*..."

Azhu-Mahl made a hum of displeasure. "Then what do you suggest?"

"What I have always suggested," Mundas said. "We continue with our plan. We continue to shape and mold. We lay the foundation for the moment He decides to speak to us."

"And then?"

"Then..." Mundas leaned back, crossing his arms and staring flatly at Azhu-Mahl. "We hope He likes our vision enough to spare us when we pull Him out of hell."

ACT TWO

THE CIVILIZED PREDATOR

FOURTEEN

LEFT A BLADE

Cier'Djaal
Some crappy little inn
Second day of Yonder

*A*sk a Karnerian, and he'll tell you Daeon made mankind out of iron and flame to be the perfect weapon in his arsenal. Ask a Talanite, he'll tell you Talanas made mankind selflessly out of his own breath and tears that we might know life. Ask a Gevrauchian, he'll tell you we're just blood and meat and it's all we get so try not to die.

Ask me, I'll tell you mankind is made of sterner stuff than all that.

Because if you ask me, I'll tell you how surprising it is how much a man can take and still call himself a man. Gouge out his eyes, carve out his tongue, chop off his fingers, toes, legs; so long as you leave him one arm, he'll keep dragging himself through the dust and thanking whatever God he worships for the opportunity.

Likewise, it's surprising how little you can take from a man to make him just . . . stop.

I guess it's been about more than five hours since Denaos led us out of the Souk and into a little inn where they don't ask questions.

Two hours to shake any guards that might have followed us.

One hour to find the place.

One more hour to negotiate payment with the owners, for rooms and for silence.

And another hour I've been lying here in a cold straw bed with itchy sheets.

She isn't coming back.

I've been looking over my shoulder the whole time, thinking I'd see her. Then when I didn't, I'd let my gaze linger, hoping she'd be there when I turned my head forward again, smiling like it was all a big joke and I was stupid for falling for it, like she was always going to come back.

But I know that's not her.

And the more I think about her, the harder it is to think about why I should ever get up from this shitty bed.

I can't remember too much of what my life was like before I picked up this sword. I came from a village called Steadbrook. I had a family. Then there was fire, shadows. It was gone. So were they. All that was left to me was the sword.

And I just kept on dragging myself through the dust.

So it's not like I have a great idea of what life I was hoping to reclaim by getting the money Miron owed me. A farm somewhere. Maybe a shop, I don't know. All I knew was that I was tired of killing, tired of blood.

And now, my first day in the city I was going to start my new life in, all I have left is blood.

She's gone. She isn't coming back.

Money's gone. I don't know where it went.

I don't know if I can get it, either. The way Miron looked at me in the Souk. He saw me. I know he did. And he just kept walking. I don't think finding the money is going to be easy as finding him. Hell, maybe he doesn't even have it.

But I'm not a man of sterner stuff.

If I stop here, all I'll have for this is an empty bed and a lot of blood. What will it all have been for? How many more would I have to kill to make that kind of money back?

But if I keep going, there's going to be more blood. Wherever Miron went, he didn't go to safety. Blood's a sticky thing. A blade doesn't get easier to put down once it's caked in it.

I don't know. Maybe it wouldn't be so hard, getting up tomorrow, going to find a job as an apprentice somewhere. Some blacksmith's shit shop, maybe. I'm older than they like for the job, but I could persuade them. Maybe it wouldn't be so bad, just working for a living.

Maybe it wouldn't be the life I wanted. Maybe it's not how I wanted my last adventure to end. But it's honest. It's bloodless. It's clean.

It's a new life.

And it still wouldn't have her.

And I guess that settles it.

I can't stay here. Fortunately, everyone else agrees with me. We've decided to split up, scour the city for any trace of Miron. We'll meet back up at this crappy little room in two days. That ought to be enough time to try to dig up something.

I can't tell you what men are made of for certain. I mean, really made of. I can tell you what comes out when you stick a sword in them. I can tell you what comes bubbling out between their lips when you smash a pommel down on the back of their neck. I can tell you what godless screaming comes out of their mouths when you gouge out their eyes, cut out their tongues, chop off their fingers, toes, legs, arms.

I can tell you what stops a man. But I can't tell you what keeps them going. Maybe it's money or Gods. Maybe it's just a cold bed where there ought to be a warm body. Maybe it is killing.

I don't know. But I need one of those things.

Leave a man but an arm, he'll just keep dragging.

Leave a man but a blade, he'll just keep killing.

FIFTEEN

HIGH SOCIETY

*R*ed is for short war."

Lenk remembered what she had told him, all that time ago.

"We wear red when we go to kill. My father once said we wore the feathers when we used to fight rival tribes. But we mostly just attack your people now. No offense."

"None taken."

He could remember saying that. At the time, she had shot him a long, askew glance. He imagined, now, how odd it must have seemed to hear him dismiss a declaration of war upon his race so nonchalantly.

"Black is for long war. When one of us wears black, it's to tell Riffid that she's got a grudge she won't let go of until the source is dead. Hence, if she's wearing black, Riffid can't take her because her business isn't done."

"And what's white for?"

"White is for loss. It's what you wear when you mourn. You don't take it off until you're done."

"Done mourning?"

"Just done."

She had remained silent for a long, lonely moment at that point. He could remember the way she had looked down at the earth.

"That's funny," he had said. *"I would have thought the white ones were for peace."*

Her grin had been big, broad, and far too pleased.

"*That's stupid,*" she had said. "*Shicts don't have a color for peace.*"

⊷ ⊶⊠⊷ ⊶

In the numb sprawl of his mind, her voice was an echo of an airy dream.

Waking, sleeping, Lenk could think of nothing else. There had been no dead men in his dreams last night. That would have been redundant. From the moment he had awoken, he had been granted the experience of being one himself.

His feet moved stiffly beneath him, guiding him through streets whose names he didn't bother to look at filled with people with no faces. They were all too soft and unscarred to be distinct, all of them free of the dead dreams and broken memories that made a person a person.

After a time, he didn't even bother looking up. He just couldn't see the point in it. He devoted every thought to keeping his legs moving beneath him, knowing that if he stopped walking, he would be hard-pressed to find a point to that, either.

All around him, the people with gentle eyes spoke words he didn't know in a language he thought was his own. Words like "the price of eggs," "I loathe my neighbor," and "I'm not sure where I'm going to get the money for it."

To him, these all had the same answer and it was currently resting heavily on his back in its leather scabbard. Swords and violence, he understood. But merchants and stalls and streets and neighbors and eggs and pleasantries and morning teas and salutations and vendettas that required a man to smile politely and never once think about stabbing someone...

Every time he heard those words, he felt a little farther from the sun these people walked under. Every time he felt his hand shake, he touched the hilt of his sword to steady it. And every time he did, he felt the urge to pull it out and leave this city far behind and go back to her covered in blood with a smile on his face.

Of course, then, he'd have to throw away everything he'd lost her for.

And how terrible that would be, he thought as he moved along the streets. *To throw away this glorious life of being a penniless, numb degenerate.* The weight of his sword felt heavier, bent his back. *Killing was what you were good at. These people aren't yours. They have families, coin, things that you left behind when you picked up that sword.*

He cast a glance around. The various people milling about their daily tasks didn't do much more than look past him as he passed by something more interesting, like a merchant's wares or a particularly affable-looking pigeon.

He didn't merely not belong here. He was not here. He was a dead man, walking among the living on feet that couldn't feel and listening to words that didn't make sense.

But you can't go back, either, can you? What would you go back to? More corpses, more dead men in your dreams, looking at your sword like it's your wife until the day someone's lucky enough to stick you in the spine and you end up dying in the mud with only a long list of bodies to remember you by.

Consumed with thought, he barely even noticed the crowds thinning around him and the cobblestones turning to paved brick beneath him as the road began to arch. When his legs couldn't think of a reason to keep walking, he stood at the center of a long bridge spanning a wide river.

Alone, but for the single thought that echoed inside an empty mind.

What's the point of it, then?

The only answer he received was the sound of rushing water.

He peered over the edge of the expertly carved stone. Beneath him, the river yawned. It flowed a lazy, meandering path through the city, passively taking in the sights of Cier'Djaal on an unhurried trip to the harbor.

Lenk wasn't concerned with the speed of it. Unconsciously, he took in the numbers.

The river sprawled twenty-two feet beneath him. Twenty-three, if he stood atop the walled edge of the bridge.

It was only about four feet deep; he could just see past the murky water, a few rocks jutting from the sandy bottom.

And it was flowing fast enough that any man who fell—or jumped—would be swept out to sea in a little under two hours, leaving a city full of people who'd never remember him.

For a very long moment, Lenk stared into the river.

He closed his eyes. He sighed deeply.

We'll call that "plan C."

He had backed away only three steps when he bumped into something. Something big and soft, judging by the feel of it, and likely something he didn't want to irritate.

"Sorry," he muttered, turning around. "Sorry about…"

His apology trailed off into a bewildered curse. His eyes widened to unblinking circles. His jaw hung open with primitive awe. And, staring back at him, were eight faces aping his slack-jawed horror reflected in obsidian orbs.

If he knew how stupid he looked, he didn't care.

Nor, either, did the horse-sized spider standing before him.

Its knobby, chitinous head canted at him. Its mandibles clacked softly, making a chirruping sound that would have sounded like a question had he been just a tinge more unhinged at that moment. At his astonished silence, it hissed a wordless demand for an answer.

The spider was trying to talk to him.

That, he figured—as any sane man might have—was reason enough to turn around and run screaming like a child.

Something hard struck against the base of his skull.

Light exploded across his eyes. He felt the embrace of stone as it rose up to meet him eagerly. Breath leaving him, darkness closing in around him, the last thing he saw was eight reflections of himself, sixteen eyes closing all at once.

"Here's what I don't get," she had begun.

She had let that thought hang, as he had hung from his fingers at the edge of the cliff. She had peered over her legs, dangling over the edge, down at him as he had struggled to find another foothold to haul himself up as she had.

And he had hung there, as her thought had hung, glaring up at her.

"Yes?" he had asked.

"You said your family's dead," she had said, *"and that explains why you're not with them. But it doesn't explain why you're out here, doing…"* She had glanced at his fingertips, embedded in the soft earth of the cliff, desperately trying to hold on. *"This."*

"Because you won't help me up," he had replied.

"And that's my point," she had continued, pointedly ignoring the accusatory tone. *"Why here? Why with a shict? Why not with other humans?"*

"I guess I'd never thought about it too hard," he had said through strained grunts as he reached for a nearby rock. *"To me, it never seemed too difficult a choice."*

"Well, it shouldn't be. Shicts don't get along with humans, you know. You're a disease."

"Me, personally?"

"Well, by association. Point being, shouldn't you be with your own kind?"

"Should I be?"

"Well, why aren't you?"

"Because the world has no shortage of people who want to kill me." He had grunted, trying to pull himself up enough to seize the rock. *"Or at least, wouldn't care if I were dead. And by that standard, one race seems as good as any other."*

"So"—she had let that thought hang a little longer—*"why me?"*

And he hadn't had an answer for her. He had grunted, strained, reached for the stone. He had wrapped fingers about it. She had looked at it and shaken her head.

"That rock's not going to hold."

"It will."

"The soil's too soft."

"It's hard enough."

"You're not going to—"

He hadn't heard her over the sound of his own cry of surprise as he toppled backward and landed hard on his back. He had stared up at her as she had peered down at him and smiled.

"You make a lot of bad decisions, huh?"

<hr />

The last traces of her voice vanished from his head. The last cloud of darkness fled his vision. His eyelids fluttered open to take in a face he knew well.

Not the bearded Djaalic scowling down at him: Lenk had never seen this man before in his life. But he knew the twisted-frown, furrow-browed expression of anger that bore down on him like a lead weight.

Intimately.

"Nobody," the Djaalic said sternly, shaking a shepherd's crook at Lenk, "but the shepherds may touch the fasha's spinners. Not peasants. Not oids. And certainly not *northerners*."

Lenk craned his neck up and looked down along his body and past his feet. The horse-sized spider seemed to be fascinated at its reflection in the running water below, apparently not a thought for the injury it had just caused him.

"You know what it's punishable by?" The Djaalic seized his attention, thrusting his crook back in Lenk's face. He wore the garb of a servant, a fasha's sigil embroidered on his vest. *"Do you?"*

"I'm guessing death?" Lenk replied.

No other punishment seemed worth quite this much fuss.

"That's right, *death*," the Djaalic said, sneering. "If I got one of the fasha's people out here right now, we'd cool our dinner with the breeze made by your corpse swinging from the gallows."

"He's not from around here. He couldn't have known."

The face that appeared over the Djaalic's shoulder Lenk knew as well. The man it belonged to, though, he knew only slightly better. He remembered that neatly trimmed goatee, those bright, curious eyes, that haughty, ever-present smile of the man from the harbor.

The man in white.

"There's no excuse," the Djaalic muttered, not looking over his shoulder. "This spider, it is my charge. I have raised it well. With the Khovura, the footwar... the fashas would have my—"

"There aren't any fashas here," the man in white whispered into the Djaalic's ear. "No one will ever know."

"I'm supposed to..." A faint sheen of sweat appeared on the Djaalic's brow. Traces of belabored breath crept into his words. "The fashas said I..."

"You did all you were required to. Be at ease."

The Djaalic stiffened up suddenly. He clutched his crook tightly and mopped his brow. He opened his mouth as if to say something more to Lenk, but nothing came out of it but a few smacks of lips suddenly dry. He turned to the spider and, with a couple of gentle prods, guided it across the bridge.

The man in white stood beside Lenk, hands folded politely behind his back as he watched the shepherd and his many-legged charge skitter off down the road.

"Had he paused for but a moment, he might have noticed the sword on your back," the man in white mused. "At which point, he might have realized he was about to throw his life away on behalf of a fasha who likely doesn't even know his name. He probably would have just left his spinner here and fled back to his family." He clicked his tongue. "The spinner, meanwhile, would have taken off into the city, been stolen by thieves or a rival, and the fasha would have torn the place apart in a bid to get it and its precious silk back."

He turned to look at Lenk and smiled.

"Had that man paused to think about what he was doing for even an instant, this city would have been in flames by nightfall." His grin broadened ever so slightly. "Wouldn't that be interesting?"

"Yeah. Right up until I burned alive," Lenk muttered. He held out his hand to the man in white, who stared at it curiously for a moment. After a long, awkward moment, Lenk sneered. "Thanks."

The young man hauled himself to his feet and dusted himself off. Surprisingly little sand came from his clothes, though. He hadn't noticed until now just how clean the streets were.

"Well, I just saved your life." The man in white paused, a thoughtful look on his face. "Or at the very least, saved you from a slight inconvenience. You can't very well go asking a slight inconvenience of me. You'd owe me two debts, then."

"Khetashe forbid," Lenk said.

"Three, in fact, if I point out that you dropped something."

The man gestured to a white feather upon the street. In hindsight, Lenk realized that the speed and vigor with which he leapt upon it were a bit odd. But at that moment, he could think of neither his dignity nor his company.

There was something about the way the man in white raised his brows at that reaction. There was something that peered too deeply, saw too much. There was something that made Lenk uneasy.

"Has she been gone long?"

And that was it.

"How the hell would you know anything about that?" Lenk didn't bother to hide the ire in his voice, nor the movement of his hand as it slid to his sword.

"You leapt upon that feather as a starving man leaps upon a dead rat," the man in white replied smoothly. "Hence, I deduced you either had a lost lover, a dead relative, or a very special avian friend."

"That doesn't necessarily mean there's a 'her' involved."

"True." The man in white looked thoughtful. "Has *he* been gone long, then?"

"That's not—" Lenk flailed briefly, as though the man's words were gnats to be swatted away. "Just...stay out of my head. I don't need anyone reading my thoughts right now."

"Are you so unused to observation that you instantly assume mind-reading?"

"I've seen a lot of strange stuff. It usually saves time to assume the weirdest." He furrowed his brow at the man in white. "I've got this weird, annoying pain in the back of my neck when I look at you, but I don't think I've found a name for it yet."

"If it will lend enough significance to your suffering, perhaps my name would do?" He tucked one hand behind his back and made a long, sweeping bow with the other. "My friends call me Mocca."

"All right," Lenk replied. "Unless I think of something more accurate, I'll use that." He cleared his throat. "So, thanks, Mocca. I'll see you around, maybe."

He had taken only a few steps when Mocca called after him.

"Do you always walk away from someone of potential use to you? Too proud to accept help when you need it?"

"Exactly what is it you hope to help me with?" Lenk didn't bother slowing down.

"You're in unfamiliar territory, my friend. What manner of man ventures into the unknown without a guide?" An edge of bemusement crept into Mocca's voice. "Or hadn't you noticed where you are?"

He hadn't.

Even when he looked up, he wasn't quite sure where he was. The squat stalls and cobblestones that had begun to grow somewhat familiar were replaced with towering buildings and smooth roads. The boiling oppression of the Souk was gone, replaced by a lofty, arrogant openness.

There were great houses of smooth stone here with glistening lawns and green gardens. There were stables for horses and hills that hadn't been flattened to make roads. The gentry who walked the streets were dressed in clothes finer than all the wares he had seen for sale in Souk. Certainly, they were much finer than the retinue of servants trailing them. Even a few giant spiders could be seen ambling leisurely up and down the streets, tended to by small clusters of servants of their own.

Everywhere there was the scent of people too wealthy to act as if money mattered with only the vast encircling walls and gates and the roaming gangs of guardsmen wearing house colors to contradict that notion.

"Silktown. Where even arachnids live better than most."

Suddenly, Mocca was right beside him, matching the area's austere arrogance with a reserved smile.

"But why wouldn't they? They *do* make the silk, after all. You've shown up to the wealthiest part of the wealthiest city in the world." He cast a sidelong glance at the young man. "I trust you came here for a reason?"

"I'm looking for someone."

"And you only brought a sword," Mocca chuckled. "This is civilization, my friend. They use different weapons to get what they want here."

"And you've got them?"

Mocca's smile took on a nostalgic quality, something that would be whimsical on a man with less dignity.

"All I've ever known is these people," he said softly. "Reason enough to trust me, I should hope."

"Maybe. If I know what you get out of it."

Mocca rolled his shoulders. "I'm bored. You seem to be a man that makes things happen." His eyes drifted down to Lenk's hand. "Like so."

Lenk followed his stare to another one. A pair of bright white eyes looked up at him from a head wrapped in dirty cloth. He became aware of the child in fragments: her tiny, malnourished body swaddled in filthy clothes, the few strands of scraggly hair bursting out of her headscarf.

By the time he became aware of her hands, wrapped around the white feather and the pouch at his hip, it was far too late. And at that point, all he glimpsed was her tiny body fading quickly into the distance over the bridge as she took off running.

"Hey!"

Before Lenk had even taken a step, Mocca let out a wistful sigh. "I wouldn't."

Before Mocca had finished speaking, Lenk was already running.

The pristine wealth around melted him into a featureless tunnel of ivory and green as he darted down streets and past lawns. The noises of passing, well-clad strangers and their accompanying, well-armed bodyguards blended into nonspecific grunts and curses. The thoughts of Miron and money were still standing beside Mocca.

Everything that mattered right now was forty paces ahead.

And aggravatingly nimble.

Not that it would surprise him too much that a small child in dirty clothes should prove better than a mostly grown man in relatively shabby garb at navigating the streets, but the way the urchin moved—slipping ghostlike between people, ducking under passing palanquins—seemed downright unfair.

Or maybe it was just him. His body, so clumsy and useless. His mind, so sluggish and numb. His life, reduced to chasing a filthy child through streets while being chased by the curses of rich men.

All for a feather.

A feather that he couldn't take his eyes off and couldn't make his feet stop over.

The urchin took a sudden, sharp turn down an alley. He skidded clumsily as he turned and pursued her into the lightless crack between two towering buildings. A third stood at the end of a short corridor, blocking any possible egress.

That would have been more heartening, Lenk thought, had the urchin not been standing there with her arms crossed and a confident shine in her eyes.

"I'm not in the habit of pummeling children." His words were laden with heavy breath. He pressed a hand against the wall, leaning hard on it. "That said, it doesn't mean I couldn't..."

His threat vanished in the gloom. He didn't worry too much about it, for he suddenly had bigger concerns. And, after all, it was hard to appear threatening when one's hand was stuck to the wall.

He pulled at his appendage, to no avail. It was held fast by some kind of shimmering, sticky film.

"Spiderwebbing?" he muttered.

"Yeah," the urchin grunted. "The spiders leave it everywhere in the rich man's town. Usually the shepherds clean up real nice after 'em, but not here."

"So, your plan was to get me stuck and then rob me blind," he muttered. "Clever."

"Uh, naw," she said. "That was an accident. I was just supposed to bring you here so he could meet ya."

"Who?"

"Me."

Lenk craned his neck. A tall, gangly creature wrapped in rags even dirtier than the urchin's stood behind him, staring at him through heavy-lidded eyes. The young man squinted to make him out in the darkness, not that there was much to discern in him that wasn't wrapped in cloth.

"Khaliv?" he asked. "What are you doing here?"

"Told ya," Khaliv grunted, reaching into his pocket. "You owe me."

"Owe you what?"

Khaliv drew a small vial out of his pocket. "Forgiveness."

Lenk didn't have to ask. He didn't have time. But he did manage to open his mouth just in time for Khaliv to uncork the vial and throw a viscous, reeking liquid in his face. It slid down his mouth like a thing possessed. Immediately, he felt his stomach churn, boiling inside him, raking at his intestines.

He felt ill.

He felt dizzy.

He felt like he was about to throw up.

But as he slumped against the wall, eyelids fluttering and tongue swelling up inside his mouth, he felt nothing.

SIXTEEN

PREY

She didn't know where she was; the city streets and buildings were all alien monuments to concepts she didn't understand.

She didn't know who these people were; the creatures staring at her from the edges of the street, stepping aside as she passed, whispering words she didn't know.

She didn't know where she was going; every street stretched on for eternity, into far-away nothingness of more of the same monuments and the same creatures.

None of that was important.

"Shict! HALT!"

The men chasing her, though? With all the sharp swords?

That was important.

Should have killed them when there was just one, she thought between the pounding of her feet beneath her. *Hell, could've just shot him in the leg and run before he could call for more. But no.*

"Somebody stop that oid!"

You *had to be culturally sensitive.*

Nobody in possession of anything bigger than a coin—such as two coins—seemed willing to put it down to grab her. Anybody that might have thought to do so was quickly deterred after somebody seized her by the arm and was promptly rewarded with a thumb jabbed directly in his eye.

After that, everybody seemed quite content to quietly shuffle out of the way and let her run.

But there were still bodies. Human bodies. Everywhere.

Behind stalls and in front of stalls, lingering in doorways and walking in streets, buying, selling, arguing, cursing humans. One body for every brick in every wall of every building.

All of them staring, eyes wide and horrified, muttering about how someone should stop that savage, spitting words like "beast" and "barbarian" and "long-eared deviant."

She shut her eyes and flattened her ears and gritted her teeth and heard only the sound of blood pumping in her skull and feet thundering under her. It wasn't enough; she could still feel their stares, their horror, the scowls they reserved for wild beasts and other things that shouldn't be here.

And like the beast they thought she was, she could feel the panic that comes from looking up and not being able to see the sky through the looming buildings.

She wanted to collapse. Or vomit. Or just shoot them.

But any one of those actions would mean stopping. And so, for want of a better plan, she shut her eyes tightly and ran wherever the panic told her to.

She ran until she could feel her teeth ache in her gums and her feet bleed in her boots and her breath turn raw in her chest. And then she ran until she could feel nothing at all.

When she finally opened her eyes, she was breathless, senseless, and alone.

There were no humans here; somewhere in her blind flight, the river of people had dried up into a dusty bed. The ground beneath her was hard and sandy, bereft of cobblestones. Whatever merchant stalls remained here were hollow skeletons, bereft of silver flesh or golden blood. The next breath she took was a long, weary sigh.

Bereft of relief.

Humanity might have been absent, but it wasn't gone. The sky was no less choked by their legacy. The buildings here were wooden and hollow, staring down at her with black, empty window eyes. Their broken, splintered crowns loomed no less high. Human litter—shattered glass, empty bottles, raggedy dolls forgotten by children—lay everywhere, the last stains from civilization's giants long since bled out.

She found it calming, the absence of humanity and their staring eyes and their snarling whispers, but not as much as she should have. These, she knew, were Cier'Djaal's precursors and its husks. The humans had moved from here, the old city, when they figured out how much sturdier bricks were. The overall impression was one of a field after a swarm of locusts had moved through: barren and devastated.

She walked numbly through its streets. Her ears were open, but the silence was absolute. Even the sound of her feet on the sand seemed to echo off the shadows. No sound of her pursuers, of humanity, or of anyone.

Except...

Something like a faint buzzing, at the very tip of her left ear. The echo of a rapid heartbeat. The faint ache of memory. Of him?

Her ears flattened against her head, folded over themselves. She didn't want to think about sound right now. Or anything that might remind her of what she had left behind.

All her attentions were for what lay ahead of her.

And what lay ahead of her loomed large.

Towering, tremendous, and with all the wood of a forest's graveyard, a wall stood before her.

Though the word "wall" may have been too generous for the haphazard pile of shattered timbers, splintered logs, and sharpened stakes that blocked her. Wedged uncomfortably between two buildings like a thorn, it was equal parts obstacle and message.

And, judging by the sight of red stains upon the stakes and a few choicely placed skulls hanging from jutting timbers, she didn't think too hard on what that message was.

"Shict!"

She whirled at the sound and beheld them. Six men, all wearing the colors and armor of Jhouche guards, advanced upon her. Their hands were on their swords—still sheathed, for whatever reason. But whatever reason wasn't good enough for her; her bow was up, and her arrow was nocked and aimed at the lead one as she took a single step backward.

And promptly felt the sharpened tip of a stake prick playfully at her bare back.

"Easy, oid," the lead guard said. "We didn't come all this way to fight."

"Then someone gave you the wrong directions," she snarled. "Take another step and I'll put this in something tender."

"Don't listen to her, Commander," one of them muttered. "Don't let a savage talk to you that way."

"Is that even the one we're looking for?" another whispered. "She's too pale. I thought all shicts were dark like us."

"Doesn't matter," a third whispered. "Don't even talk to it. It's not going to talk without a fight."

She narrowed her eyes and bared her teeth. The bowstring creaked just loud enough to drown out a tiny voice in her head that advised her to go ahead and shoot them anyway.

"*I said*," the lead one snapped, "we're not here to fight." He fixed a steady gaze upon her. "Yesterday, oid, there was an event. You know what I'm talking about because fasha Ghoukha's men told us you were there." He held up one hand higher but kept the other on his sword's hilt. "A lot of people died there. A lot of people have died in this footwar, and a lot of people are going to die still if you don't help us figure out what's going on, oid."

"My name isn't *oid*," she growled. "And I'm not telling you anything. Go *away*."

"Told you," one of the guards muttered. "Just rush her, already. No need for this."

"Be careful, though," another said. "She's got teeth. They bite you, you get all kinds of diseases."

"We aren't leaving," the lead guard said. He lowered his hand, but remained tense, ready to draw his blade at any moment. "This concerns all of Cier'Djaal. And Cier'Djaal says that I'm allowed to take you in by force if you won't come peacefully."

"Take two steps further," someone very close and very dark whispered, "and you aren't in Cier'Djaal anymore."

Their eyes turned, as one, up to the wall of splinters. And there he sat comfortably atop the shards and the stakes, like he had been born in a nest of briars. A man, large and powerful and thick with dark muscle, who rose to sandaled feet and skipped down the pile of jagged points as easily as he might a grassy hill.

He landed on the sand beside her and, this close, she could tell he was a shict like her. Only by the long, notched ears poking out of a mane of black hair, though. Everything else about him was far too thick. The sandals he wore strained against the muscle of his calves and the simple silk kilt he wore about his hips bared most of his broad, muscular physique.

He looked like some hero out of a story. Not any story she had heard, though. The heroes of shictish stories were all clever, small, and agile. This male, thick and dense and bristling like the splintered wall behind him, looked like something fit for the tales of the humans before him.

The edge of awe that crept into their voices certainly suggested as much.

"Listen, Thua," the lead guard said, stepping carefully over the shict's name, "I meant it when I said we don't want trouble. But this oid has to come with us."

Thua nodded thoughtfully for a moment. He turned and looked down at Kataria. Between the veils of his mane, she could see a plain wooden mask, two perfectly round holes for eyes and a thin slash for a mouth, adorning his face. From within, his voice sounded disembodied and far away.

"I believe you said your name was not 'oid,' yes?"

"That's . . . that's right," she replied.

"Well," Thua said, turning back to the guards. "As you can see, nobody named 'oid' is present. If you'd like, you may take nobody back with you and ask nobody what they think."

"Don't try to be cute, Thua," the lead guard snapped. "Your little camp is still in the limits of Cier'Djaal and, at a word, I can have guards swarming it."

The large shict canted his head to one side, then the other. His ears quivered a little.

"Which word?" he asked.

"What did I just say?"

The guard's voice cracked on the last word. An edge of anger swept into his voice and cleanly lopped off any authority he might have carried. He was trembling now, his nerves apparent in the shake of his hand and the strain of the frown he tried hard to force onto his face and tried harder to look menacing.

And even though she couldn't see past his mask, Kataria got the distinct impression that Thua was smiling broadly.

"I am glad you came here without the intention of fighting, Commander," he said. "I would hate to sully our special relationship with violence in front of your family and mine." He glanced down at Kataria. "And make no mistake, she is one of us. If you wish to speak with her, you may come to camp tomorrow, when she has had time to recover from being chased through the streets by your men. If she feels like talking to you, you may speak to her."

Beneath the eyeholes of his mask, something tender flashed at her.

"Is this acceptable to you, sister?"

She nodded weakly, not quite certain why. And again, she could sense Thua's smile without seeing it as he turned back to the guards.

"There we are. A perfectly nonviolent solution, perfectly acceptable to men claiming they have no desire to fight." He canted his head to the side again. "Assuming they are genuine men and not filthy, lying *kou'ru*."

"We give you and your camp a lot of pull around this edge of town, Thua," the lead guard snapped. "And in exchange for keeping guards out, we expect you to help us out once in a while."

" 'A while' is a long ways away, yet," Thua replied.

"He's not listening, Commander," one of the guards muttered as his sword came free of its scabbard. "This is a waste of time."

"Hold your steel," the commander shot at his man. "Remember where you are. We're one wall away from Shicttown."

"And there's only one shict here, Commander." Another guard added his sword and his snarl. "This is our city. They don't own anything here."

"This is true," Thua said. "This is your city. These are your buildings." He angled a finger up to the two broad, empty wooden structures flanking them. "We merely take up space."

Kataria looked up along with the guards and saw the same thing they did. In every window, in every shadow, they were there. Smiling with wide grins, staring with hollow eyes, leering, scowling.

Watching.

Over three dozen wooden masks appeared in the windows, each one silent and still as the trees they had been carved from. Only the leering wooden faces were revealed, bodies and bows and blades still hidden within the shadows of the buildings.

That seemed to be enough for the guards. They instantly huddled together, pressing backs to backs, all blades out and at the ready.

"Easy, Thua," the commander said, "you don't want this much blood on your hands."

"I do not," Thua replied. "I do not want you here at all, dead or alive. Tomorrow, Commander. You may return then and ask questions of my people in my camp." He made a dismissive gesture. "Until then, I ask you to leave my sister in peace."

Despite the painfully palpable hostility that burst from it, nothing more than a baleful glare came from the commander. At a word, swords slowly found their sheaths, boots slowly found their sand, and Kataria watched the guards slip away, muttering to themselves.

"Can you hear them?"

She turned to Thua. The large shict's eyes were up on the windows, at all the wooden faces looking down at his.

"All of them? So close to you?"

He looked to her. She looked up to the windows, to the many empty eyes and the many empty smiles all fixed upon her. Her eyes moved from window to window, building to building. And she saw only wood and shadows.

"I can't hear," she whispered, "any of them."

Her chin suddenly felt very heavy. Her neck suddenly felt very soft.

"What does that mean?" she asked the sand at her feet. "What does that make me?"

He laid a hand on her shoulder. She felt the warmth from his overlarge fingers as he offered a gentle squeeze.

"Ah, sister," he said softly, "it makes you gullible."

She blinked, spoke flatly. "What."

"*Did she fall for it?*" a voice, light and airy as an arrow descending, cried out. "*She did, didn't she? I told you she would!*"

Kataria's ears grew wide and trembled, shifting from side to side as she tried to find the source of the voice. She narrowed her eyes upon the wooden faces in the windows and came to an insultingly slow realization.

Only one of them was moving.

It was far unlike the others. Its grin was big, broad, and eerily pleased with itself. Its eyes were in the shape of upside-down crescent moons. Where the other masks were hollow, this one brimmed with a life all its own.

A life that still managed to pale in comparison to its wearer's.

A body, short and dark and lean, slithered out of the shadows of the window. Legs swung out over the frame, and it fell from the gloom to land in a graceful crouch. Kataria's eyes widened as the body rose up to about her height.

A mass of black braids bundled above the mask, falling in serpentine strands around bare shoulders. Lean arms, trembling with toned muscle, crooked as hands set upon bare hips. The same silk kilt as Thua wore hung off of a spear-slender waist, the leather sandals of the same material entwined thin calves. The only other garment worn was a half-tunic resting over a modestly rounded chest, leaving bare a long, lean midriff.

A woman. Ears long and notched like well-worn blades, standing tall and proud before Kataria as though she had just sprung out of a legend.

A shictish legend.

There was a part of Kataria that said nothing at all, that merely stared, wide-eyed, at the woman. That was fleeting, though, and quickly gave way to another part of her. The part with all the snarls and cursing and stuff.

"And what the hell are you so smug about?" she growled.

"I *almost* didn't think you'd fall for it." The woman seemed heedless of Kataria's ire; then again, it was hard to read someone through a wooden mask. "I thought 'she's going to see the strings, she's going to use the Howling and realize it's a trick,' but *nope!*" A thin finger shot out, poked Kataria playfully in the chest. "You fell for it, just like they did."

Kataria restrained herself from biting that finger off long enough to turn her glare over the woman's head. She squinted and, as the sunlight shifted through the clouds overhead, she could just barely see silken threads holding the wooden masks in the windows. No bodies. No bows. No shicts.

No voices to hear.

Save for the woman's laughter, obnoxiously light and irritatingly soft.

"That's not as hilarious as you think it is," Kataria snapped.

"You're only saying that because you didn't think of it first." The woman laughed. "Don't worry about it, *shkainai*. It's a trick. The fact that you were tricked just means it's a good one."

Her long, dark fingers slipped out and gingerly tickled beneath Kataria's chin.

"I'm so terribly clever, you know."

Kataria snarled, slapping her hand away. There was an itch left behind, upon her skin and in her ears as the woman snickered.

This woman spoke and laughed in serpents, a voice that slithered through Kataria's anger and into her ears to coil comfortably at the back of her head. She found her ears twitching, irritably.

"Do not worry about Kwar," Thua said. "She set up this trick weeks ago and has been waiting for someone to stumble in." He paused, regarded Kataria carefully through hollow eyes. "Yet, that's not why you're upset, is it?" He leaned forward. "You weren't surprised that you couldn't hear them, were you?"

The coils tightened around her skull. The air suddenly felt very heavy around her. Thua's words hung a weight around her as he spoke.

"You can't hear the Howling."

At that, Kataria found herself missing the woman's—this Kwar's—mocking laughter. That was merely enraging. Thua's words and the iron silence that followed were unbearable.

She couldn't stand looking at their masks anymore. She couldn't stand not seeing their eyes as they fixed her with hollow stares.

They were staring at her like the humans were. She just knew it. Looking at her as if she didn't belong here, as if she wasn't welcome here, as if she should go away and never return. She just knew.

Because where else, she asked herself, would she be? Why would she, pale and weak against their dark muscle and bright eyes, be here if she didn't belong where she had come from?

She turned to go. A hand caught her shoulder. Warm like Thua's, but not comfortable. Itchy. Tingling. Coaxing fine hairs on her arms to stand on end and ears to go involuntarily erect.

It turned her with a hint of a tug. Kwar stood before her, her free hand sliding up to the back of her head. A quick tug and the mask fell, hanging around her chin by a pair of leather straps.

And Kataria met Kwar's eyes, wild and dark like a thunderstorm. The khoshict stared, but without judgment, without fear, without anything but the need to look, the need to be looked at.

She only vaguely took in the other details of the khoshict's face—her pointed chin, her puckish lips, the crinkle at the corners of her eyes—everything was in Kwar's stare, including Kataria.

"Don't go, sister," Kwar said softly. "You are home."

"I'm not," Kataria replied. She slipped out of Kwar's grasp. Her skin still itched afterward. "I don't know what that word means anymore."

"You're not going to find it out there," Thua replied, gesturing over her head. "The inner city isn't safe even for normal shicts. And *you*," he glanced Kataria over, "from the forests, yes? The…" He looked at her ears, counted the notches. "Sixth tribe? You stick out in the eyes of anyone, let alone the guards that are looking for you."

"Come with us." Undeterred, Kwar's hand seized Kataria's with a childish eagerness. "We're just over the wall. Stay with us until you're better."

"How am I supposed to know that when I don't know what's wrong with me?" Kataria asked. "I can't hear—"

"You must have," Kwar insisted. "This city is vast, and yet you found your way to us. How else could you have been drawn to your own kind? Come, stay with us until you figure that out."

"But how do I—"

"If you finish that sentence," Kwar interrupted, "my next reply will be 'stay with us while you recover from that nasty injury I gave you rather than listening to more self-important self-doubt.' "

Amazing, Kataria thought, *she even smiles when she's threatening bodily harm.*

Maybe that was why she herself couldn't help returning Kwar's smile.

Maybe.

"Come, then." Thua had turned and begun walking toward the wall of splinters. "I don't trust the humans not to return with more. They are more clever than we give them credit for."

He moved with a thoughtless confidence, up the shattered timbers, over the jagged stakes, across the smashed wood, and to the top of the wall of ruin. Not so much as a moment's hesitation, not so much as a splinter as he hopped off the edge and disappeared down the other side.

Kwar gave Kataria's hand a squeeze before moving to follow. She had just leapt up and seized one of the jutting stakes when she turned to look at her new, pale companion.

"What are you waiting for?"

It was at that moment Kataria became aware that she was looking over her shoulder, down the sandy road. It was at that moment she realized she didn't know the answer to Kwar's question.

No one was coming.

"Nothing," she muttered.

She approached the pile of splinters with the same vigor, laying hand upon one of the timbers and testing it for sturdiness. With a cry, she drew back her hand and beheld the long sliver of wood embedded in her palm. A lance of pain shot through her hand as she pulled it out and watched a bright red blossom form on her skin.

They did it without even trying, she told herself. *A shict could do this easily. A real shict could*—

"Hey."

She looked up. Kwar's hand was before her. A thin scar adorned the heel of her palm. A bright smile was on her face, teeth bright and bare.

"It takes a little help to get it right," she said, "unless you're terribly clever."

Without thought, Kataria reached up. Without sound, she took Kwar's hand. Without a word, she was pulled up onto the pile and felt the itch as Kwar's hand left her.

And without knowing why, entirely, she felt herself smile.

SEVENTEEN

ACCORD

The stories were all the same.

Somewhere in the heart of a city—any city, so long as it had shadows and scum—lay an ominous, shrouded fortress. Sometimes it was a wooden stockade laden with spikes and skulls. Occasionally, it was a vast, iron fortress with warning signs and black plumes of smoke rising over spiked walls. The vast majority of the stories seemed to think it was an underground labyrinth—usually a sewer or other water-themed deathtrap—haunted by traps, guardian monsters, and pits full of spikes.

Spikes were a recurring theme in any good story about thieves. Any told by the common man, at any rate.

And if that common man—or woman or child, he supposed; everybody loved a good thief story, after all—were here right now, he might find The Oxbow rather unlike what the stories described as a proper thieves' guild.

It was neither ostentatious nor destitute. A humble building of stone and brick and wood sitting comfortably between the Souk and Silktown, quite content to dwell in the shadows of elegance and live forgotten on a road that saw only the mildest traffic of strolling grandmothers, weary laborers, and shy children. And any of those people would have been more interesting than the middle-aged, graying woman sweeping sand from the steps beneath a swinging sign depicting an old ox pulling an older plow.

Her broom wasn't even spiky.

Pity, that, Denaos thought.

Denaos could have handled spikes. Spikes, at least, had the promise of a swift death. Whatever happened to him once he stepped through those doors would be something slow, something total, and something a long time coming. Because whoever was beyond those doors had been waiting a long time to see him.

No sense in delaying, then.

Well, at least in delaying any longer than the three hours he had already spent staring at the inn, wondering whether it might just be nicer to go walk to the harbor and jump in.

He tucked his hands in his pockets and walked to the woman, casting a glance up at the windows.

"Cats?" he asked.

"Pardon?" she replied, not bothering to look up.

"You got any cats in there?"

"Just two," she replied. "Cats kill rats."

"Prefer dogs, myself."

She glanced up at him through the creases of her crow's-feet before looking back down to the steps.

"Who?" she asked.

"Rezca," he said.

"Business?"

"Always."

"Important?"

"I wouldn't know his name, otherwise."

She stood up, looked meaningfully toward the house across the street and stretched, knuckling the small of her back.

"Back left corner," she said. "Order the curry."

He pushed the door open, pausing briefly in the frame and looking at her. "Is it any good?"

"What?"

"The curry. Is it any good?"

"Wait," she said, "did they add a new bit to the code?"

"No, but…I mean, I still have to eat it, don't I?"

She didn't bother replying beyond a snort as she returned to sweeping the steps. He didn't press the issue as he slipped inside.

Inside, The Oxbow had all the markings of a world in transition. The tables were still unvarnished, splintering wood but had been rearranged into the booths and privacy-curtain-ringed style that had been all the rage in Silktown when he still knew the city. Wine was served in cups made of cheap glass, curry was dished out on cracked porcelain to the clientele of Souksellers and unpatronized artisans, and every stain was strategically placed to lend to the carefully cultured air of mediocrity.

A few of the standard glances from all the people one would expect to throw the standard glances were thrown. The man standing at the bar offered a brief, courteous nod, as such a man would. He sat down in the booth in the back left corner. The girl in the silk dress with the patches one would expect on a woman with a low wage and three dresses to her name showed up after he had waited just long enough to be slightly annoyed with her, as one would with any serving girl.

"Welcome to our humble establishment, sir," she said, rehearsed. "What may I offer you today?"

"Curry."

"What kind?"

"Just curry."

A crack at the edges of her face; she hadn't expected that answer, but showed no real surprise. She hadn't been working here long, he deduced, but long enough to know what happened to those who screwed up.

"Half an hour," she replied curtly.

"For curry?"

"For business. Curry will be out shortly."

"Is it any good?"

"About as good as you'd expect."

He sighed and leaned on his hand. "Of course."

She walked away to the man behind the bar and whispered a few words. The man behind the bar nodded once and disappeared behind a door. The door remained closed for thirty breaths before he came back out.

And Denaos started to wait.

The average talk of the economy and the whores and the foreigners was talked. The Karnerians and Sainites were a menace; this footwar was trouble; the fashas were greedy swine. The same talk anyone would hear in any other bar. The wine was poured and the glasses weren't cleaned. The curry came and went.

It wasn't good.

He had been waiting for far over half an hour when another plate of curry was set in front of him. Then one more dish across from him. No explanation was given before the girl walked away. None was needed; the explanation came walking in a moment later.

A tall, pale man entered. A northerner with a stocky build and big hands and a head shaved meticulously clean. His clothes were made for a man who didn't belong in this place, made for someone smaller, wealthier. The spectacles he wore would look silly on such a big man if they hadn't been set over such cold eyes.

The big man sat down without a word, delicately folding a napkin over his lap and arranging his cutlery carefully on the table. He placed both hands upon the tabletop. Denaos did the same. They stared deliberately into each other's eyes for a long moment.

"Rezca," Denaos said respectfully.

Rezca was not this man's real name.

"Denaos," the big man responded politely.

Denaos was not that man's real name.

But there was enough civility between murderers to afford them the courtesy of lying to each other.

And their only words were those two lies for a long time as Rezca quietly shoveled forkfuls of curry into his mouth.

"How is it?" Denaos asked.

"Good."

Three lies seemed adequately civil before business.

But before Denaos could open his mouth, Rezca held up a finger. He reached into a satchel at his hip and produced a small idol carved of black wood. The image of Silf the Patron, with his familiar grin and hands clenching a bowl, was familiar. So much so that Denaos could but sigh.

"Are we still doing this?"

"Rules are in place for a reason."

"When we were kids, sure."

"Silf doesn't tolerate deals He's left out of." Rezca fished a copper coin out of his pocket and dropped it into Silf's bowl. "A bargain's a bargain."

He looked expectantly to Denaos, who muttered in reply and produced a copper of his own. A meeting more dire would call for silver or gold, but this was, after all, just lunch. He dropped it into Silf's bowl on top of Rezca's.

"A bastard's a bastard," he continued the rhyme.

"Luck for the worthy." Rezca tossed in another coin.

"Coin for the master," Denaos finished with one more of his own.

Satisfied, Rezca nodded and pushed Silf's idol off to the side. To look at him, one wouldn't think someone like Rezca would be so superstitious. But, then, as businesslike as he might appear, he was still a thug.

But, Denaos noted, a thug with answers.

"How long have you known I was in town?" he asked.

"Exactly one day before you came into it," Rezca said.

"That's impressive."

"Not really," Rezca replied. "All the ship manifests are available to us and I was there when you chose your latest alias. The only thing truly remarkable is that you haven't chosen a new one in all these years."

"I like the sound of it," Denaos replied. "It's romantic."

"Mm."

"I guess it's too much to hope you know I didn't come here by choice, then."

"You arrived with five other people." He covered his mouth, swallowed his food. "Pardon. Three people, a shict, and...was that a dragonman we saw yesterday?"

"Yeah. That's Gariath."

"Interesting. I thought they only came in the one size."

"So did I, until I met him," Denaos said, shrugging. "We're... *they're* adventurers I hooked up with on the outside. Once we get what we came here for, we, including me, will be on our way."

"Hence why you've called for me."

Rezca had not been Denaos's first choice. He was far too like-minded to be his first choice.

He, too, was an outsider among the dark and vibrant Djaalics, being tall, pale, and possessed of stern angles and a serious face. He, too, had come from the north owing to circumstances beyond his control and found a modicum of respectable success through disrespectable means. And he, too, was a man who owed every coin, sin, and nightmare to the Jackals.

In a lot of ways, Denaos thought that he and Rezca would be excellent friends, and he suspected Rezca also thought that the two of them were a very good match for each other.

That was probably why they usually tried to avoid each other.

"I called for *you* because no one else would answer me," Denaos said. "I can't reach Yerk or Sandal and the Scarecrow—"

"She's been to the cutter for the past day," Rezca said. "Took an arrow in the shoulder in the Souk's chaos. I'm told we owe that to your shict."

"She's not mine. None of them are. But the people who *are* mine aren't reaching back. Everyone says you're the man to talk to now. What happened to Rheniga and Headhigh? What about Yerk and Fenshi? What about the other heads?"

"Rheniga is a casualty. Headhigh is a statistic. Yerk is a head now.

Fenshi rarely leaves his den. The others are underground, far away."
Rezca regarded Denaos evenly through his rounded spectacles. "In
case you've not yet noticed, Denaos, we are at war."

"We've been at war plenty of times. The masters always commanded from the ground. Remember Hell's Harlots?"

"I do."

"Rheniga brought them down. And the Twilight Harpists? That's
where Headhigh got his name."

"I do," Rezca stated, plainly. "I remember the Isstacca, the Morose
Family, and Troublemakers, Associated, as well."

"Oh, yeah." Denaos leaned back, a grin on his face. "You know, I
always liked the Troublemakers. They had style."

"The Khovura are different. The Khovura don't play by our rules
because the Khovura are not part of the game."

That gave Denaos pause.

There was a certain kind of hypocrisy to crime in Cier'Djaal,
a shame that extended only as far as the terminology. It was perfectly fine to slit a man's throat in the dead of night for his coin
pouch, certainly, but to refer to it as such was considered crass and
unprofessional.

Hence, throat slitting was "collar-buying," burglaries were "gen-
tlemen callers," and doing things through less-than-legal means was
merely a part of playing "the game." Thus, the Jackals were elevated
from mere thuggery to esteemed experts of a widespread, long-term
sport whose participation was mandatory and whose rules were
ironclad.

Until now, it seemed.

"They were looking like any other team in a footwar," Denaos
said. "I saw them fighting, burning, and looting the same as anyone."

"They aren't after any of that," Rezca replied. "They don't want
Cier'Djaal's money; they don't want Cier'Djaal's rulers; they don't
want Cier'Djaal. They want its *people*. They aren't players. They're
revolutionaries, radicals, cultists trying to bring us down by making
us unpopular with the people."

That a system of organized crime could be considered popular in the first place was a phenomenon unique to Cier'Djaal. But as much as people hated being preyed upon by thieves, they more hated the thought of being preyed upon by strange thieves.

The game, to the citizenry, provided rules, structure, order. They may still be preyed upon, but only in certain ways, in certain places, as certain punishment, and always in a very timely, organized manner with a polite, professional representative.

And so they played.

"And it's working."

Until now, it seemed.

Rezca raised his hand for attention. The girl in the patchy dress took precisely too long to arrive. She leaned over. He whispered in her ear. She nodded briefly.

As she passed a table of Souksellers, she leaned over and whispered in their ears. They rose a moment later, leaning over and whispering in someone else's ears as they walked toward the door. They, too, rose, whispered, left. The door closed shut a moment later, The Oxbow empty of patrons, staff, and anyone but Denaos and the big man who leaned on his elbows and steepled his fingers.

"The first two months did not go well," Rezca said. "The game was played as it always was, at first: in the alleys, in stairwells, with knives in the dark. We didn't know their name. But it didn't matter. Not until they found one of our dens and set it ablaze, consuming twenty-two Jackals."

Twenty-two Jackals in a den. Five hundred Jackals in Cier'Djaal. Fifteen years he had spent in this city. Denaos did the math in his head.

He had to have known the names, faces, and lives of at least six of those people burned alive.

"The announcement was taken poorly. 'A cleansing fire,' it was called. 'An end to the tyranny of the fashas by burning out their hounds.'"

"The Khovura said that?"

"The Khovura never say anything. They barely speak the human tongue." Rezca chuckled ruefully. "No, it was the *people* that said that. The public that had played by our rules for so long saw someone cheating and they applauded it. They applauded the next den to go up in smoke and they cried foul when we responded by hanging sixteen Khovura upon the Harbor Wall."

Denaos said nothing. The public never took sides in a game. That was against the rules.

They might have disliked the fashas, sure; it was hard *not* to dislike someone with more money than most nations who also wouldn't let a few coins of tax go unaccounted. But the fashas were good for the Jackals, the Jackals were bad for other thieves, and so the Jackals were good for the public.

Thinking it over, Denaos had to admit that logic *did* sound a little contrived. But it was the logic the entire city had bought for as long as the Jackals had reigned.

"We tried to keep it a coinwar. Then we tried to keep it an alleywar. We tried to keep it quiet, but the Khovura insisted on making it public and now it's a footwar. What you saw in the Souk today was the latest in a long line of brawls that go poorly for us."

"I saw no shortage of Khovura dead."

"But they can always get more. The public is emboldened by their actions. No matter how many examples we make, there are always the poor, the disenfranchised, the freed slaves, and the oids that will sign on with them."

"Revenge," Denaos muttered, "for a lifetime under the game."

"I thought that, as well," Rezca replied. "The heads still believe that. But now I wonder if it's less a resentment of the game and more a resentment of not being allowed to play it. Maybe they don't feel pride at seeing us lose, but at having a chance to play for themselves."

He waved a big hand.

"It's irrelevant," he said. "The footwar continues to go poorly. The more we fight in public, the more the public suffers and the more they go to join the Khovura. And the more the public starts talking, the more the fashas start talking. Rich men talking have never been good for us."

"So... what are you going to do?"

"The same thing we always do," Rezca replied, leaning back in the booth. "We change the rules." He looked at Denaos over the rims of his spectacles. "This is where you come in."

"No."

The answer was reflexive enough that it surprised Denaos after he had unwittingly said it. What was a bigger surprise was that Rezca appeared unfazed by the answer. He merely quirked a brow and waited as Denaos drew in a deep breath and continued.

"You know I'm not one to shy away from the game." Denaos held his hand out before him, studying it as though he could see past the leather of his glove. "I was pretty good at it by the time I left." His fingers twitched. The hidden blade just beneath his palm sprang out. "And I've killed a lot of people in the time I've been gone."

He pulled a hidden latch, drawing the blade back in. Rezca was cringing. Not for the blade, but for the language. The word "kill" was too crude for his civilized ears, despite how many screams of dying men they might have heard once.

"But the shit we've done, Rezca... the stuff I did... the people I killed..."

Bronze statues in the Souk. A tall woman who spoke proudly. The last noble of Cier'Djaal to have earned the title. She had never backed down from anyone, especially not him, not even when he had put the knife in her throat.

He shook his head. He bit back whatever was rising in his throat.

"I killed her," he said. "I went too far. I... I can't go back to that."

"Acceptable."

He was surprised, yet again.

"I was there when the heads handed you down the orders," Rezca continued. "I was there when we came up with the words." He said them through a sneer. "'The Kissing Game.' To make thieves into wives and husbands, and politicians and leaders into corpses. Among the most abominable plots we've ever had in a long and storied history of abominable plots. To be so close to that again…if you don't wish to be a part of it, I don't blame you."

"Thanks…" Denaos swallowed the stuff back down. "Thanks, Rezca."

"The service you rendered unto the Jackals was great. For that, the deal you made with the heads still holds. You may walk away from the game anytime you feel."

Denaos paused. Rezca was too professional to make him wait long for the "but." He appreciated that.

"But then we are under no obligations to help you find the priest you're looking for."

"Should I ask how you know?"

"You shouldn't. We saw your friend—the short one with the gray hair—chasing a priest in white through the Souk. One tends to notice such things in a city full of dark-skinned Djaalics. We also saw no sign of the priest after the footwar. I suppose you have your reasons for wanting to find him."

"I do."

"And he can be found," Rezca replied. "Priests are important people. They can't stay hidden from us for long unless someone with more pull than we have is hiding them."

"A fasha?"

"We have our suspects."

Rezca reached into his vest. He produced a small bundle of cloth and set it on the table. It unfurled to reveal three fingers, long and thin and possessed of a sickly sheen that made them slightly more distasteful than the fact that three severed fingers were now brushing up against Denaos's curry.

"Notice anything?" Rezca said.

"Many things," Denaos replied, "and all of them completely vile."

"Be serious."

"They're saccarii fingers," Denaos said. "Scaly."

"The Khovura are predominantly saccarii, we've found. Unsurprising, considering their position in Cier'Djaal's social ladder."

Specifically, Denaos thought, buried in the earth ten feet below the lowest rung.

"Look closer," Rezca said.

Once Denaos got over a fleeting tinge of revulsion, he did just that. He stared at the three fingers, each one as long, as thin, as scaly as the last. Each one possessed of the same scar... and the same swirling print.

"They're... the same finger," Denaos whispered, brow furrowed in befuddlement.

"Of the same saccarii," Rezca replied. "We captured one of them a while back. We cut off one of his fingers to make him talk. Then, when he didn't, we cut off the same finger when it grew back the next day." He narrowed his eyes. "Something is going on with the saccarii, maybe all of the Khovura. And I'm willing to bet that something is expensive enough to involve the Bloodwise Brotherhood."

"You mean the couthi?"

Such was unthinkable. The couthi were quiet, thoughtful, neutral, uninterested in anything humans had to say or do that wasn't perfectly round and made of a precious metal.

Ideal, respectful players of the game, in other words. They wouldn't risk that prized position by selling directly to the Khovura. Rezca doubtlessly knew this.

"Regenerative potions aren't unheard of, if you're in the right circle," Rezca said. "But that circle costs over six thousand pieces of gold to even know the name of. No one but a fasha would have access to the Brotherhood's darkest secrets."

The pieces were beginning to come together, but Denaos asked anyway. Courtesy, and all.

"So, what do you want me to do?"

"Find out which fasha is supporting the Khovura," Rezca said. "Chances are good you'll find which fasha is stashing your priest. And if you don't, the Jackals will, as a courtesy."

"Where do I start?"

"There are only two saccarii fashas in the city," Rezca replied. "Teneir and Sheffu. Start with one and hope for the best."

"Will I have to kill anyone?"

"Only if you want to."

Nothing more need be said. Denaos got up, pushed his curry away, and began walking toward the door. He didn't feel like talking anymore, and Rezca was a man for whom words were a commodity to spend only when necessary.

"You didn't ask about her."

Until now, it seemed.

"She's well, if you're wondering," Rezca called to Denaos's back. "The footwar has left her largely unscathed."

"Largely?"

"The Jackals are Cier'Djaal's police, merchants, and kings, Denaos," Rezca said. "What affects us affects everyone in the city. I suspect you and she will both realize this before too long."

Denaos did not say another word as he walked out the door, past the woman with the broom, and into the road. He didn't so much as open his mouth until he was safely tucked away inside an alley.

And then, he bent over and let the vomit come pouring out to splatter upon the cobblestones.

EIGHTEEN

HOUSES FOR THE COMMON MAN

L ike an open wound, a thick red line ran directly through the middle of civilization.

No, Asper thought. *That might not be a completely fair comparison.* She had seen many wounds and few had been quite this ugly. Of course, none of them had been nearly so big.

Three feet wide in bright crimson paint, the red line extended from the gate she had just stepped through, across the cobblestones of the massive square, and into the horizon of the district. There it lay, spattered sloppily, applied hastily, its purpose a mystery.

Well, no, she caught herself again as she looked up over the district called Temple Row, *that's not entirely true, either.*

Two Gods dominated the skyline, each one vying to scrape the heavens and straining to dwarf the Silken Spire.

To the south loomed Galatrine, Lady Sovereign of Saine, towering forty feet tall, thick as the stone She had been carved out of, brawny body brimming with the carved spikes and feathers that made up Her armor. A broad stone sword in Her right hand, Her six-fingered left hand extended in a gesture demanding creation itself to halt before Her.

Or if not creation, then at least the God that towered over the north end of the Row.

Tremendous, vast, a colossus of iron and stone rose to meet the challenge. Entire body bound in cruelly edged armor, save for the head bearing a pair of impressive-looking horns sweeping backward from a scowl leveled across the district at His rival deity. Viciously jagged blade in gauntleted right hand, left hand extended to the north in a commanding gesture that mirrored His hated enemy. Daeon, the Conqueror, God of Karneria, challenged foe and follower alike.

At the feet of each God sprawled a temple. Or, Asper supposed, what *ought* to have been temples. Instead, they looked like fortresses. The Sainite's gray granite aerie towers rising up to Galatrine's calves, the Karnerian's black iron walls belching forge smoke surrounding Daeon's ankles.

War and faith were synonymous with both deities and the nations they represented. The sole difference between the Sovereign and the Conqueror, the saying went, was which direction they came from when they arrived to burn your house to the ground. Saine and Karneria both had a list of conquered territories, conquered peoples, and conquered riches as long as the reach of their Gods' arms.

Sometimes she wondered, with so much in common, why the two were such hated foes.

As if that question didn't answer itself, she thought, looking down at the red line.

She walked down the line, as useful a path as any. There were hardly any other markers in Temple Row. There was hardly room left for anything else. Absent were the other Gods: Zamanthras the Sea Mother, Silf the Patron, Khetashe the Wanderer. Those were anticipated. Their followers had their own places of worship, all of them far from civilized society. What was more worrying was the absence of other temples for more formal Gods within the main square of the Row.

Specifically, the temple of Talanas. The Healer, it seemed, was not needed between the two Gods of war. There was something rather impractical about that.

More than impractical, though, it essentially rendered her plan moot. She had reasoned that, if Miron had escaped the Souk, he would have sought sanctuary with his fellow Talanites. She certainly would, if she hadn't had more unsavory fellows to seek sanctuary with. But if there were no temple, then where would he go?

She didn't know.

But she wagered the man who loomed at the foot of Daeon's temple might.

Like an echo of his God, he stood towering, clad in black armor, gauntleted hands resting on the pommel of a massive sword thrust into the earth before him. All hair was shorn from his head but his brows, and those were knitted above a steely, unwavering gaze aimed across the line at the Sainite fortress.

Temple, she corrected herself. *Or… templeress? Forple? Maybe you can ask him which he prefers. Open up with a joke. That's what Denaos would do, right? Of course, this guy probably doesn't find that sort of thing funny. Or anything funny, really. People with swords as big as they are don't usually have great senses of humor.* She cleared her throat. *Look, just say something before this gets weird.*

"Er… hello?" she said.

The Karnerian said nothing in return.

Of course not, she scolded herself. *Why would he? "Hello?" What kind of greeting is that? He's a follower of Daeon. Conqueror! War God! Greet him like a warrior.*

"Hail, noble sword-bearer," she said, throwing her voice to the back of her throat, "have you knowledge of the battle-times?"

Nice.

"Look," she continued, rubbing the back of her head, "I'm just a little lost. I'm a priestess of Talanas and if you could just point me in the—"

"I can."

His voice was deep; the kind of effortless deep that came from men who had nothing to prove and just a little bit wrong with them.

"Oh," she said. "But I didn't even—"

"Daeon speaks through those that share His vision," the man said. "And it is within His power to give and to take whatever is needed. What you wish is irrelevant. It is His to give."

"I see. So, you can tell me if there is a temple of Talanas?"

"By Daeon's will, many share this square under His guidance."

"So there is one! Great." She clapped her hands together. "Can you show me where it is?"

"I am capable of all things that He wills," the man said. "For this moment, He wills me to keep my vigil."

"Uh-huh. And how long is that?"

"Eternal."

"That's, uh, not exactly helpful."

"'Helpful' is not a word known to Him." He never looked at her, even as he spoke to her. His eyes never once wavered from the temple to the south. "'Necessary' is. To watch our foes, to be ever ready for their incursion, to extend His will across a world that craves His guidance even should it be through the flames of our foes' cities and the blood of their children, this is necessary."

She blinked.

"Uh, all right." She cleared her throat. "Could you maybe just... *tell* me where it is?"

"You won't get shit out of him, darling." Another voice, this one with plenty to prove, spoke up. "You can't sway even the lowliest Karnie slave with pity or mercy, much less old Careus. Any victim of their wars would tell you that."

She glanced over to the woman on the other side of the line. Or at least, what she thought was a woman. Her hair was tucked up beneath a Sainite's typical tricornered hat, her face masked by the buttoned high-collar of a Sainite bluecoat, and any sign of feminine curves was smothered beneath the soldier's kit she wore. But her features and eyes were both keen as the saber she wore at her hip: sharp, flashing, and eager to see blood.

"So, can *you* tell me where the temple is?" Asper asked. "Miss..."

"Watch-Sergeant Blacksbarrow," the woman said, standing crisply at attention. "Seventh year of a tenner in this sand trap. I could draw you a map of a harbor tramp's asshole."

The priestess frowned. "Is... is that good?"

"My shift's over in another turn," Blacksbarrow said. "Temple's on the north side, so if you'll come over here, we'll double back out the Souk, jaunt through the Sumps, and come in through the northern gate."

"That sounds needlessly complicated. Why not just come over here?"

"Faithful and heathen alike are bound to Cier'Djaal's laws," Careus interjected. "Our military presence here relies on an adherence to their request that we delay the impending vengeance upon the followers of false Gods for a time."

"Cier'Djaal won't *let* you fight?" Asper asked. "I've not seen more than a handful of guards. I'd wager both of you have over twice that number in your forples."

"Our . . . *what*?" Blacksbarrow shook her head. "Obviously, if we wanted to mess up the Karnies, we could. And no Gods-damned Djaalics could stop us. They've got less than four hundred Jhouche, including their dragonman mercs. We've got over seven hundred pikemen, archers, and scraws ready to go at a moment's notice."

"Daeon's faithful possess eight hundred legionnaires and the revered Faithbreaker," Careus replied.

"Point being," the Sainite continued, "Saine needs silk. Cier'Djaal has it. We fight here, they stop selling to us."

"You can't just take it?"

"The heathen Djaalics alone possess the knowledge of how to weave the spider's offal into cloth," Careus spoke curtly. "What stores we could seize—and we could, if we felt inclined—would be minuscule compared to what we can purchase. Hence, we are obliged to honor the Death Line."

Asper looked down to the long red smear beneath her feet. And for the first time, the Karnerian looked away from his vigil, as did the Sainite. All three gazes focused on the painted line intently.

"First one to cross is first one to break the law," the Sainite muttered. "Trading penalties, heavy fines . . ."

"And swift retribution," the Karnerian added.

"Nothing for you to worry about, civ," the Sainite said, voice piping back up. "Just come on over to this side and we'll fix your shit."

Before Asper could even begin to formulate an answer, the sound of steel on stone rang out. The Karnerian struck the cobblestones with the tip of his blade, hefting it.

"The Empire's duty is to guide the weak," he said. "The temple of Talanas is on our side of the Line. It will be Karneria who guides the priestess to her destination." He extended a gauntlet that looked like it might hurt to touch. "Come, pilgrim."

"The hell she will, scalp!" Blacksbarrow snarled. "The Talanites are a peaceful people averse to violence. That means they belong to the Sovereignty of Saine."

"Now wait—" Asper had begun to speak when Careus boomed over her.

"Typical Sainite greed," he said, sneering. "You claim the faithful and the faithless as your own subjects and think yourselves superior for doing it in the name of a nation instead of a God. Your faith means nothing, your sovereign even less."

"Just hold on—"

"The Sovereign *is* the nation, scalp," Blacksbarrow spat. "She leads us in war and peace alike. Your priests throw you scraps and you feast on them like the blind zealot dogs you are. You're a nation of slaves trying to find slaves of your own."

For the first time, a flicker of emotion flashed across Careus's stern features. He wore his anger comfortably, as if it had been there all along.

"The Empire honors its oaths," he spoke, hard and swift. "And it is through that oath that your head remains on your shoulders. Run back to your birds and platitudes. Daeon's own shall handle this."

"The fuck it will." Blacksbarrow's hand shot out and seized Asper by the bicep. "She's going to come with—"

"Do *not* touch me!"

Asper jerked away suddenly, far more so than Blacksbarrow

seemed to have anticipated. The Sainite staggered forward, thrown off balance by the weighty kit on her back. For the briefest of moments, the barest hairbreadth of the toe of her boot set upon the red smear.

And once again, all eyes were on the Death Line.

In the next instant, Careus and Blacksbarrow were staring at each other with wide eyes across the line, accusation burning behind their scowls. For a short moment, Asper was granted the cold feeling that something was about to go terribly, terribly wrong.

And in the next moment, it did.

Karnerian and Sainite both retreated, reaching to their waists. In the Karnerian's gauntlets, a war horn was produced. In the Sainite's hands, a silver bugle. Dissonant songs of warbling wail and shrieking rally went into the air as both blew furiously upon their own instruments of alarm.

The noise rang throughout the Row, flowing over the walls of their respective temples to the ears of their stone Gods.

An instant later, their calls were met with shrieking squawks, banging gongs, and the slow groan of fortress gates opening.

From the south, the bluecoats of the Sainites came fluttering, bows and blades in hand as winged scraws, beaks open in shrill calls, came flying from the aerie towers.

Out of the north, the phalanx of Karnerian soldiers came rumbling, every step locked in order, every shield pressed together, every spearhead glistening with the crests of their helmets as they came marching out as a singular iron fist.

War cries flooded the skies. The thunder of boots shook the stones. And the wind trembled with the anticipation that it soon would be filled with the sounds of men and women dying.

Asper, for her part, tried her best to ignore that.

Because Asper, for her part, was walking away quite swiftly in the vague direction she suspected the temple of Talanas to be, if Blacksbarrow's information could be trusted. She resisted the urge to break into a run, however. That would look suspicious.

And a certain level of nonchalance was required of the woman who may or may not have just inadvertently started a war.

⸻ ⸎ ⸻

Well, this wasn't too hard to find, Asper thought as she looked up, and up, at the vast temple sprawling before—and over—her.

Long marble steps rose up into a ziggurat, marching heavenward to a tremendous house wrought of smooth, white marble. Pillars depicting people entwined together to become columns unto themselves marched the length of it, their stone hands reaching up to the sky. And at the very top, the crown upon the throne of marble, a fountain bubbled among a ring of stone children holding hands, its waters descending the steps to pool at a tiny moat at the base of the temple.

It wasn't the *most* ostentatious tribute to Talanas she had ever seen. The Healer, after all, was popular for a reason; everyone got sick at some point in their lives. Still, the sheer wealth with which the God—her God—was displayed made her slightly uncomfortable.

Really, she wondered, why couldn't they just have told her to look for the giant ziggurat made of water and marble?

She approached, following the tide of people marching toward the steps. As they reached the foot, however, they dropped to their bellies and began to crawl up instead of walk.

She knew the rituals of the faithful differed from region to region, but this was new to her. She regarded at the only man standing, an elegant-looking fellow in teal robes painted to resemble a river perpetually flowing from his shoulders. He welcomed her, as he did everyone else, with a broad, welcoming smile.

Right up until he saw the silver pendant around her throat, anyway.

"We beg your terrible pardon," the man said, holding up a hand and halting her where she stood. "While we welcome all worshippers to the house of Ancaa—and wish you great peace for having sought blessing of the Endless River—we must ask you to discard all other garb of…alternative Gods."

"Alternative…" She glanced down at her pendant and clutched it protectively. "I thought this was the temple of Talanas."

"Ah. No. Unfortunately, the people who turned to the Healer found him somewhat…deaf when the footwar began. Ancaa was made known to us, then, and She revealed that we had been suffering long before the thieves began to make sport of us." He gestured to the vast temple. "And as evidence that wealthy and poor stand alongside the Lady of Equality, the great fasha Teneir had this temple commissioned for the faithful."

"Oh, well…isn't that nice." She coughed. "So, where *is* the temple of Talanas?"

＊＊＊

Exactly half an hour, three wrong turns, one moment of being chased by angry dogs, and a toothless man propositioning her for the princely sum of three copper pieces and a dead rat later, Asper opened a dingy wooden door and was immediately greeted by the stench of stale bandages, overripe wounds, and the shrieks of people in agony.

Ah, she thought, *this is more familiar.*

At the very far end of the temple was a very small wooden statue of Talanas, a tall man with a stately beard in shoddy robes with His hands held out to His side. The old fellow looked as though no one had really thought to ask what He might think of this, His temple, but the slow warp of the wood had twisted His features into a modest, disapproving frown.

And between the statue and her lay over a dozen pews that had been hastily hacked, sawed, and repurposed as sickbeds, each one of them occupied. Elderly mothers sobbed and lay hands upon young men missing limbs, muttering prayers over their bandaged stumps. Weary-looking fathers cradled tiny daughters and sang soft lullabies into ears stuffed with gauze and eyes wrapped in bandages. Some had no one, lying in their hard, uncomfortable beds and looking long to the bearded man at the end of the hall.

The scent of congealed blood mingled with expired salves and poultices. The dull, constant groan of ache was punctuated with the occasional sob of agony. Suffering hung in the air like a shroud.

And Asper suspected most of it came from the three frazzled-looking people in blue robes wildly rushing from bed to bed, offering peace to the wounded and abuse to each other.

"Yes, mother Halfa, we are doing everything we can for your son," a stocky young man with dark circles under his eyes said to one woman before looking over his shoulder and shrieking. "Where the hell are my hecatines? He'll be bled out by the end of the day at this rate!"

"Six freshly wounded arrived today and I've barely stitched up two of them! Get them yourself, you son of a bitch!" came the harried response from a harassed-looking young Djaalic woman, who instantly turned on a weary smile to a small girl fussing with a spoon. "I know it tastes bad, little lamb, but it will help with your fever. Could you try once more for me?"

"Will both of you ignorant dopes keep your voices down? This is a place of harmony and peace, for fuck's sake!" That one came from a slender youth whose shoulders looked too broad for his dingy blue robes. His eyes were wide and wild as they turned upon Asper. "You! What the hell are you doing?"

"I, uh," she began.

"Speak up," the young woman shouted. "No one can hear you over these idiots!"

"MY NAME IS ASPER I'M FROM THE NORTH AND I CAME HERE TO ASK SOME QUESTIONS BUT IS THERE ANYTHING I CAN DO TO HELP OH GOD."

"Yes, for the Healer's sake!" the stocky man shrieked. "In the back! Get me my hecatines!"

"What is a, uh, heca—"

"The bugs, *shkainai*, the bugs!" He jerked his chin over his shoulder toward a door at the back. "Go grab one!"

She was off, her feet weaving between the beds even as her eyes weaved between the injured. Upon their bodies she could see the salves that had remained on too long, the bandages that had been faded by covert washing and irresponsibly redressed, the stitches that had gone crooked due to haste or weariness or both. She looked at their wounds, she looked at the shoddiness of their healers' work.

But never once did she look at their eyes.

She knew what she would see there: desperation, anxiousness, a fervent wish that she would look into their eyes and tell them everything was going to be fine. And she knew what they would see in hers: a solemn, solid uncertainty crushing a slim fragment of hope.

Perhaps if she were younger, more inexperienced, she would think that brief hope to be a worthy trade for the despair to follow when she couldn't tell them she didn't know. But she had seen too much blood, too many corpses. Her skills, she knew, were best used noting what she could fix.

Later.

After she had retrieved the hecatines.

Whatever those were.

And even when she laid eyes on them, she still wasn't sure. The stench of year-burning incense assaulted her as she walked into a small wooden room laden with smoke. From the shelves, dozens of compound eyes stared back at her, seated upon thin, trembling legs and attached to bulbous, throbbing abdomens.

Bugs. Just like the sleepless man had said.

But... what did he expect her to do with them?

"*Something just ruptured! He's bleeding out!*" came a cry from the main hall. "*Now*, shkainai, *NOW!*"

To hell with it. She reached out and seized one without looking. *Surely, you can't screw up too much when it comes to handling giant bugs, right?*

Said giant bug—this fat, six-limbed thing sitting complacently in her hands—didn't disagree.

She returned to the main hall to be greeted by a frenzy of movement among a spatter of red. A young man missing a leg was screaming, flailing his stump, and heedless of the blood spurting even as he grew paler with each moment. The young woman was busy attempting to readjust a slipped tourniquet as the stocky man tried to hold him down. The slender man with the wide eyes was struggling to comfort an old woman through the headlock he had put her in to keep her frenzied, pleading flails from interfering.

"Mother Halfa, please, let us do the Healer's work." He looked over to Asper, eyes wider than ever. "*Shkainai*, what are you waiting for?" He gestured to the flailing man. "The hecatine! Use the hecatine!"

"*HOW?*" Asper screamed back.

"It's a giant bug filled with blood; how much more obvious do you need it to be?" the stocky one spat.

She stormed forward, elbowing past him and thrusting the bulbous little vermin upon the man's shoulder. To her immense surprise, it immediately twitched to life. Its barbed legs hooked into the man's flesh. Its compound eyes glittered as it loosed an excited chirruping noise. Beneath its eyes, a long, needlelike proboscis extended.

She was so fascinated by the bizarre display that she scarcely felt the long, slender arms encircling her middle. Or rather, as she realized a moment later, reaching past her. A pair of wide eyes appeared at her shoulder as the slender youth looked past her.

"It takes a moment to wake up." His voice was warm and soft in her ears as he whispered. "They instinctively react to the presence of blood." He took the bug gently by its thick little head, guiding the proboscis to the writhing man's throat. "But the incense leaves them a little sluggish, so we must guide them to an artery and…"

The proboscis plunged in. Asper let out a cry and instinctively reached out to pry it off, only to find his hands gently taking hers.

"Just wait," he said softly.

The bug's bulbous abdomen trembled. The thick red liquid sloshing about inside began to empty, deflating like a bladder as it slid out of the insect and into the man's neck. The patient groaned softly as color began to return to him, his thrashing easing as the tourniquet was reapplied to his missing leg and the two remaining priests began to dress the wound.

Hands released from hers and she felt him step back. Asper turned and saw him just as he began to shrink. A long, weary sigh left his lips and seemed to take the rest of him with it. The broad shoulders stooped, heavy lids drooped over the wide eyes, and a sleepy sort of smile creased a face too young for the wrinkles it was inviting.

He looked, at that moment, like a very tired young man in only slightly bloodied blue robes.

"The hecatines drain blood to feed to their young," he said. "Something inside their bodies makes it a handy mixture. If we can catch them early, we can put them to sleep and save them for when we need it. Like now." He canted his head at her. "I take it you don't have these in the north, *shkainai*?"

"No, most of our medicine is relatively magic-bug-free," she replied, brows knitting slightly. "But then again, in the north, we also call each other by our names instead of . . . whatever that word I keep hearing is."

"There is nothing magic about the hecatines. *'Shkainai'* is Djaalic for 'stranger.' And you are completely correct. I tend to forget my manners after about the fourth day of no sleep. I am Aturach." He pointed to his two companions. "These are Savine and Malauch." An imploring look followed. "And I hope they can handle things briefly while I speak to our guest?"

"Of course." Savine laughed a black, hysterical chuckle. Her left eyelid twitched. "The blood is only neck-deep today."

"Be hours yet before we drown," Malauch muttered, securing the bandage around his patient's stump.

"Beautiful," Aturach said, turning toward a distant table occupied by surgical implements and a basin. "We can speak more freely over here, mistress . . . ?"

"Asper. Just Asper is fine." She glanced over at the two priests as she walked with him. "And really, I can speak to your high priest instead. You seem a little . . ."

She couldn't choose between "underinformed," "overworked," or "smelly," so she let the thought trail into silence.

"Ah, if you'd like to talk to him, I can show you to his quarters," Aturach said as he began to dip a cloth into the basin.

"Oh, you can just tell me where they are, if it's too much trouble to take me."

"Certainly." He nodded, gesturing to the door. "You just hang a right once you leave the temple, turn left when you reach the much-nicer temple of Ancaa, and then hang another right when you see the cemetery. He's buried in the northwest corner. Look for the flowers we left there yesterday."

She met his black smile with a frown. The scent of suffering was no more apparent than there, between the wrinkles at the corners of his mouth.

It always started in the smile. People grew too comfortable with suffering. They always found it too easy to grin around the dying. Then they stopped washing the blood from their hands.

Then they became killers. Or sometimes, adventurers.

He pulled the cloth from the basin and she saw it was tinged red with blood that had already been washed away from earlier proce-dures. Maybe some of her thoughts seeped through that frown. Or maybe he just noticed the lack of hygiene. He cringed and emptied the basin into a bucket beneath the table.

"I'm sorry," he offered meekly, not looking at her. "I'm...I'm not usually like this. This..." He made a vague gesture around his face. "I wasn't lying. High Priest Thaala was killed two months ago in the footwar. Seffa was with him. She's buried next to him. Jalu left the city shortly after, Maribi hanged himself, Khefka converted to Ancaa, and..."

He gestured over at the hall, to all the bleeding and the suffering and the dying.

"This is what's left of it. Of us. There are more injured every day and they come to us for healing because that's what we do—Talanites and all—but then they just go and say 'praise Ancaa' because that

shit's apparently great right now and they leave us with fewer supplies and . . . and . . ."

Asper became aware of it the same moment he did: the crystalline
tears forming in the corners of his eyes.

"Sorry, I suppose I should have offered you tea before I broke
down crying like an infant." He wiped a hand across his face. "As I
said, I'm not usually like this." He looked at her intently with those
quivering eyes. "Would you? Like some tea?"

The tears were ones she had seen before. The question, one
she had heard before. And thus, she knew, he wasn't asking for
her sake.

She shook her head gently. She smiled softly. And she asked, in a
very low voice:

"Would you?"

⊷ ⚎ ⊶

To mend the big wounds, sometimes you must mend the small ones, she
thought as she poured tea into a copper mug. *And sometimes, the
small ones are so small you can't even see them.*

A wise man had once said that.

Well, a wise woman, anyway.

Well, *she* had said it. Thought it, really. Just now, even. But it certainly sounded wise to her.

"This isn't necessary," Aturach said from behind her. "I mean,
you had questions to ask, right?"

"That can wait," she replied.

No, it can't, she told herself.

"There are more important things."

More important than a missing Lord Emissary of Talanas? Unlikely.

"Such as getting this temple in order."

A temple that isn't yours full of priests that you don't know.

She tried to keep the thoughts, small and harsh, little pinpricks at
the back of her head. Those she could ignore.

The images of all those dead people in the Souk, the knowledge
that she couldn't do anything for them, the utter stupidity in thinking

that, by helping this temple that wasn't hers, she might somehow be able to undo anything so terrible in a city as sick as this . . .

Yes, well, she thought, *more important things.*

"Look, I should really be doing this." She heard a chair scoot on the wooden floor as Aturach rose. "You're a visiting priestess and a guest of the temple. I should be the one to—"

"You'd screw it up."

She turned around. The hurt apparent on his face was the sort one typically expected to see in children who had just been slapped with their own puppies. The sunlight bathing him from the small dormitory window beneath which the table sat gave him something of an angelic glow.

"I . . . what do you . . ." He bolstered himself, gritting his teeth as she sat down across from him. "Look, we're doing the best we can."

"No, you're not," she said. "And if you are, you need to do better. I saw too many crooked stitches, too many old bandages. You're pushing yourselves too hard and you're making mistakes."

"These people need our help."

"And you won't be helping them if they get infected when they leave." She pushed the cup across the table toward him. "So, you're going to drink this tea. You're going to take an hour. Then you're going to make another cup for Savine and she'll take an hour. Then she'll do the same for Malauch. You'll do this in shifts until you stop killing people."

He stared into his tea for a moment, contemplating the darkened reflection. He drew in the plumes of steam on a breath, sighed them out.

"You're right," he said quietly. "I suppose we can't save everyone."

"You can," she replied. "But not this way."

"I know, I *know*." He rubbed his eyes. "It's just . . . I wasn't meant for this. I wasn't even Thaala's intended replacement. Khefka was. But his family always wanted him to be a priest for a major church and once Ancaa became popular . . ."

"Can't they help, then?" Asper asked. "They seem wealthy enough."

"Ancaa is about wealth, yes. They share their wealth; they share their fortunes; they share their bounties. But it's a young religion. The Ancaarans don't have the practical skills we do."

"What about the Karnerians? The Sainites? In the north, they look to us for medical advice and treatment and we can expect their aid in exchange."

"In the north, I wager they usually aren't crammed into the same city, much less the same district." Aturach shook his head. "No, we can't ask for the help of one without the other considering it a pledge of loyalty. Then, when the city goes to war, we'll be considered valid targets. Better to just ignore them both and hope they do the same for us."

"What?" Asper asked, furrowing a brow. "I thought the city already was already at war."

"The footwar? Nothing more than two gangs of thugs pretending to be nations." Aturach's face grew dark as he lowered it over his cup. "I've been inside the Sainites' temple. I've seen what they've been hoarding: ballistae, fireflasks, an entire flight of fully grown scraws, hundreds of troops, and enough crossbows to put a quarrel in the chest of every man, woman, and child in Cier'Djaal.

"The Karnerians are no better. Two legions, training day in, day out, each one led by a war priest who's seen no less than three campaigns. And there are rumors that they've brought in one of their siege-golems. Ten feet tall, feeds on human blood.

"The fashas play them off of each other, making sure neither grows strong enough to take over and convincing each that they need to buy more supplies from fasha warehouses. But with the footwar, each side has been bringing in more and more soldiers, claiming they need the extra defense. They're both just waiting for the moment they can drive the other out and claim Cier'Djaal for themselves."

"What if the moment never comes?" Asper asked. "They've been here for ages and haven't fought yet, right? A war in Cier'Djaal would disrupt their silk trade, wouldn't it?"

"It wasn't supposed to come, no. It still might not. There's to be a treaty discussion in a few days. High Priest Thaala was supposed to mediate, but then the footwar started and . . ." He sighed, rubbed his eyes. "An Ancaa priest is sitting in instead. It might work. It might fail. But a few months' disruption of silk trade against the chance of a lifetime supply is a good risk to take. Especially when the cost is only a few thousand lives."

His smile was small and hysterical, a very contained fit of madness, for it was quite apparent that if he hadn't allowed himself that, he would have flung himself screaming from the window.

"Their war spans decades. Their armies cover nations. Whatever the Khovura and Jackals do to each other will look like a slapfight in comparison to what *they* can do."

And there it was.

In the moment he stared into his tea and saw his reflection staring back up at him with wide, unblinking eyes, he must have realized how much of himself he had spent to accomplish so little that could be taken away so easily.

It was a moment Asper knew with painful intimacy. The words he spoke next were ones she had once asked heaven and been met with a silence that had echoed throughout her life.

"What's the point?"

In that moment, Aturach's wounds were no longer small.

And to mend them was no longer a matter of duty.

"The point is people," she said. "The people downstairs who are dying because, somewhere inside you, you're afraid to help them. You think they'll go back to Ancaa and forget you, you think they'll be killed anyway, so you stop trying."

"Wouldn't you?"

"I would. I did."

"And what happened?"

"Nothing," she replied. "Nothing changed. The world didn't stop. Wicked men with wicked blades kept killing. People kept dying." She stared down at her left hand, drumming fingers on the table. "Only then . . . I was the one killing them."

"That's ridiculous. You didn't drive the blades into them."

"I didn't stop the blades, either."

"Could you have?"

"Not all of them. But I could have tried. If I couldn't stop them, I could have healed the wounds. Or maybe I could have just given them a good burial, I don't know. It's not a matter of absolutes. You have to do something, anything besides just standing around and watching the world burn."

She looked up and smiled softly.

"Even if it's just making a cup of tea for someone."

He nodded slowly. He raised the cup to his lips and drank. He lowered the cup and frowned.

"This tastes terrible," he said.

"Yeah, I've never been good at making tea."

"Kind of... ruins the metaphor, doesn't it?"

"Only if you think about it."

"But—"

"*Anyway*," she interrupted, "about my questions. I'm looking for a Talanite. A Lord Emissary. We were separated from him in yesterday's battle at the Souk. I thought he might have checked in here, if he was able."

"A Lord Emissary?" Aturach quirked a brow. "We would have been informed of his arrival, surely. Usually we get word days before they come."

"You didn't this time? Could it have gotten lost in the chaos?"

He shook his head. "I'd remember something like that. What was the name?"

"Evenhands. Miron Evenhands."

Aturach nearly fell out of his chair, so quickly did he start. "*Evenhands?*"

"You know the name?"

"I do. Though I haven't heard it in years."

"So you know what he looks like? You could help me search for—"

"Let me rephrase that: I haven't *seen* it in years. The last time I read it was in an old record of the temples of the south. He was a low-ranking priest of no particular reputation in an old city lost years ago."

Something inside her unsettled. Somehow, she found the words. "How many years ago?"

"Asper," he said softly, "Miron Evenhands has been dead for three centuries."

NINETEEN

CIVIL MEN WITH
CIVIL NEEDS

By virtue of their very existence, everything wizards did had meaning.

The relentless protocol, the unyielding rules, the construction of their many towers across the world: Each and every action performed by the Venarium was an order of necessity.

Even a creation so vast and elaborate and slightly ostentatious as Tower Resolute served a purpose far more intricate than what the uninitiated would surmise as nothing more than a demonstration of power from arrogant wizards.

Not that such a demonstration *wasn't* one of those purposes; it just wasn't the most important one.

Towers such as Resolute served many functions. They were schools into which simpering, terrified youths who had just discovered their magical abilities by accidentally setting fire to their siblings would be ushered. They were libraries, sanctuaries of studies in which the most powerful women and men would become the most brilliant. But above all else, a tower was a graveyard.

Tower Resolute was built upon a ring of solid, unyielding stones. And each stone served as both brick and coffin. Encased in each perfectly hewn, flawlessly carved, ten-by-ten block was a corpse. Quietly decomposing inside a suffocating tomb, the remains of a former wizard lay interred. While it might have seemed macabre to an outsider, this, too, had a purpose. For while a wizard's body might fail, his Venarie, that special quality that gave him his power, lingered on like the perfume of a wealthy lady: unseen, potent, and completely impossible to ignore.

A wizard's skin, blood, bones, and hair all carried Venarie long after a wizard's death. And Venarie could be used for any number of things, all of which should be used by those who already had it, or so the Venarium thought. For only the Venarium knew how to use it.

Magic was something primal, born in the body from a place that no one knew and manifesting itself in ways that nobody could ever predict. And perhaps it was to combat this chaos, this inherent meaninglessness, that the Venarium created their relentless protocol, their unyielding rules, their rigid towers.

To combat meaninglessness, meaning must be present everywhere. Even in something as mundane as filing.

Dreadaeleon reminded himself of this, as he stood in front of the clerk's desk in the lobby of Tower Resolute. He found it increasingly harder to take comfort in it as the second hour passed.

"Your contributions are past due," the little man with the glasses said from behind the desk far too big for him. He didn't bother to look up; whatever file he had in front of him seemed far more important. "*Well* past due, in fact."

"I have an exemption." Dreadaeleon was surprised at the confidence in his reply. The novelty of finally meeting someone smaller and meeker than him, he suspected. "I'm an adventurer."

"Less than one-sixtieth of concomitants in good standing choose . . . *that* practice," the clerk said, as though testing to see if this were all a clever lie. "I'm not certain it's even still considered a valid method of contribution."

"Well, I suppose you could either go back into your files, dig up whatever ancient amendments and notations on the subject lie buried under undoubtedly years of misplaced paperwork and layers of dust that likely have their own ecosystems by now"—he paused to breathe—"or you can just take my word for it."

The clerk, for the first time, looked up over his glasses. He cleared his throat and sniffed.

"I'll be right back," he replied, disappearing into a door behind his desk.

After so much time already wasted, one would expect this would elicit more than a weary sigh. But Dreadaeleon couldn't find the nerve to be that upset. In the clerk's absence, thoughts began to seep into his head, the same thoughts that had kept returning to him since yesterday, thoughts so private that he needed to be alone in a room as vast and empty as Tower Resolute's main hall to think them.

And as soon as he was, her name came flooding back to him.

Liaja.

No, no. He shook his head. *That's not her name. But she wouldn't tell you her name, would she? And she doesn't know* your *name, either. What'd she call you again?*

He tried to pretend he wasn't desperate enough to have remembered every little word she had said. He failed.

"Northern boy." Like you're some kind of child. No, she was sweeter than that. She smiled when she spoke to you. There were tears in her eyes. Granted, she was about to be sold into prostitution, but still.

He remembered her tear before anything else, the sparkling drop that drew a thin, clean line through the dust upon her face. From that, he could remember the vibrant curve of the cheek it slid down. From there, the soft, warm smile that she had shown him. And then her eyes...

Which he could never remember fully. Why couldn't he? What was so special about that woman's eyes that he couldn't remember them? As though he was *afraid* to look at them again, to see them and the tears in them and realize that he should have done something to help her, anything, if he weren't such a—

Steady, old man, he warned himself. *We're not here to daydream about girls. Remember, the others are counting on you. If you can request the Venarium for access to their divination methods, you could find Miron in a heartbeat. Less than a heartbeat, even. Focus on that. Not on the woman. What was her name again?*

He tried to pretend he didn't know.

"As it turns out," a shrill voice, growing shriller, spoke up, "there *was* quite a bit of paperwork surrounding it." Dreadaeleon looked back to the desk, where the clerk slammed a heavy sheaf of papers down. "Fortunately, it was thick enough to stand out."

Dreadaeleon looked down at the papers with his name scrawled upon them. "That can't be right. My home tower is Tower Ardent, in Muraska. I wouldn't even get this much paper *there.*"

"All notations applying to one…"—the clerk adjusted his glasses, mispronounced the name—"'Dreadaeleon Arethenes' have been marked for worldwide report, justifying copies to be sent to every tower within reasonable traveling distance. Please acknowledge the receipt of each article of information as it is given to you."

Dreadaeleon stared down at the sheaf, only later becoming aware that the clerk was looking at him. He blinked.

"What?"

"I'm waiting for you to acknowledge."

"What, the introduction counts as an article?"

The clerk nodded. Dreadaeleon sighed. He would have cursed, but he doubted that would have counted as acknowledgment.

"Fine," he said, waving a hand. "Go on."

The clerk produced a long list, handed it over. "Policy update to Protocol Nine with regard to the handling of heretics of a non-flammable nature. Please acknowledge the receipt of this article."

"I acknowledge the receipt of this article."

Another paper, handed over. "Reminder as to contributions past due with summary penalties applied. Please acknowledge the receipt of this article."

"I acknowledge."

Another paper. "Reminder as to contributions past due with regard to proposal to study effects of Venarie use in the field. Please acknowledge the receipt of this article."

"Uh-huh."

Another. "Venarium newsletter. Please acknowledge the receipt of this article."

"I thought I told you to stop sending me these things."

Another. "Absentee vote for Arch Lector of Karnerian Outpost Tower Number Nine, alias 'Defiant,' please acknowledge..."

"Sure."

Another.

And another.

And another still.

He wasn't aware of the confirmations coming out of his mouth anymore. The clerk didn't seem aware, either. Through the mechanical routine, Dreadaeleon found his thoughts drifting again.

You know, he thought, *it might be possible to sell the idea of using the divinations to find out where she works. Liaja. Technically, divinations aren't to be used for personal gain, true—it'll be tough to persuade them that the Khovura are enough of a threat to Venarium sovereignty to let you use them to find Miron. But still, couldn't you try?*

Then again, maybe you should just ask. But what would that look like? A concomitant of the Venarium, scrounging for whores. He bit his lip. *Stop that. She's not a whore. She was just sold into it. It's the city's fault.*

But it's their culture, surely. It's a sound economic theory, applied judiciously. Surely, it's that not big of a sin, right? And even if it was, you don't believe in sin because you don't believe in Gods. And even if you did, *what position are you in to judge what they do? What she did?*

It's all fine. Perfectly fine.

He tried to pretend he believed that.

He tried to pretend he was okay with the idea of her, naked and lounging in silks, some strange man's fat fingers clumsily groping at her body like her breasts were oranges and her legs sausages. He tried to pretend he was all right with the idea of being stuck here in a lobby instead of out there trying to find her so he could tell her he should have done something. He tried to pretend he was perfectly calm and above this and that he wasn't so boiling with rage at the thought of more tears staining her face that he might just set fire to these papers in his hand and the little mole of a man handing them to him.

He failed.

"…and warrant for summary execution."

He snapped back to the waking world at that last part. He looked back down to the massive pile of papers in his hand, the topmost of which had several long, bold words printed across it.

Dreadaeleon Arethenes.

Heresy.

Wanted.

"What?" was all he could whisper.

"The notice, concomitant," the clerk replied flatly, "for the summary trial and execution of one…" He cleared his throat, didn't bother mispronouncing the name. "Well, you. On charges of heresy, misuse of Venarie, and association in the death of a Senior Librarian."

He looked up, adjusted his glasses, and smiled.

"Please acknowledge receipt of this article."

＋—＝◼＝—＋

As wizards were considered—by everyone who mattered—to be the paragons of humanity, it stood to reason that their legal processes would be more efficient and logical than the typically murky and fear-based judiciary methods of the common man.

It would come as no surprise, then, that, in their infinite wisdom, the Venarium simply assumed that any charged party was guilty to begin with and placed the onus of proving one was innocent—or at least justified—solely on the accused.

The theory behind the practice was that any member in good standing who was not intelligent enough to execute his own defense was of no use to a profession that demanded the utmost brilliance. And even a member who had violated a law could prove himself innocent if he had enough value to the Venarium.

Dreadaeleon thought it had all sounded much, *much* more intelligent when he explained it to his companions.

Not so much when he was standing in the middle of an empty chamber at the top of Tower Resolute, three scowling, accusatory glares leveled down upon him from a ten-foot-high podium.

"Dreadaeleon Arethenes," a voice was handed down to him from a ten-foot-high podium. "Aged twenty. Admitted to the Venarium at age seven. Trained non-communally under the tutelage of one Lector Vemire Rondash. Granted emancipation at age sixteen. Contributing member via field research, specializing in exploration, practical applications, and discovery."

A silence followed.

Dreadaeleon admitted to being a little struck. He had never had his life so eloquently summarized before. It felt a little discouraging that it took less than fifteen breaths to do it.

"Currently charged with heresy, disregard of protocol, failure to contribute, association with undesirable elements, and implication in the death of a Senior Librarian."

Ah, he thought, *just saving the good parts for last.*

"The assembled council of Lectors shall now hear the defense."

The voice—and the tone that suggested this would be a short trial—belonged to the goateed man sitting at the center of the council. A mess of hard angles, from the sharp corners of his eyes to the hard line of his mouth, Lector Annis seemed very much a man of minimalisms.

Not a spare muscle was used unnecessarily to set his frown, not a single word was gratuitous in his threats, and, if either of those were any indication, not a single moment would be wasted in summarily deciding to execute the boy before him.

"You may begin," he said.

And another silence followed.

Outside of Dreadaeleon's head, anyway.

AAAAAAAAAAAAAAAAAAAH! To his credit, he thought he kept the fear off his face. *What are they saying? What heresy? Which heresy? What'd you do? To whom? When? Are they talking about Bralston? Well, obviously. But what else? Netherlings? Dark magic? That time you tried to turn a pig into a woman? Think, old man, think! Wait! Not too hard! They might be able to hear your thoughts. Can they do that?*

The silence grew thick. Not so thick that he couldn't see the expectant faces of Lector Shinka and Lector Palanis. The former regarded him coolly, her face pristine and unharried between a frame of meticulously trimmed hair. The latter seemed to have been saving every drop of suspicion and spite in him for this moment, coiled over wringed hands, mouth hidden behind knotted fingers, brows set in a deep furrow.

They're all waiting for me to screw up, to confess, to say I'm irredeemable and should be harvested and buried in the tower to serve as an example for future students. I'm not going to do it. No. I'm not going to. Right. So what are you going to do? Cry for mercy? No, look at them, that won't work. Just cry, then? That might.

He glanced to the tiny desk beside the three great podiums. The clerk sat there, attentively jotting down everything, even when no one was speaking. What was he writing?

"The accused looks guilty," most likely. *"Probably going to start crying any moment."*

Not for the first time, Dreadaeleon glanced back to the doors leading out of the chamber. They were unguarded, of course. Three Lectors of the Venarium didn't need guards. If he tried anything, they would kill him with a thought.

"Let's begin with the obvious," Lector Shinka spoke, her voice soft and sharp. "You departed on independent field study barely over two years ago, according to the records of Tower Ardent. In that time, you've not reported to any tower nor offered any contribution to the Venarium, yet you've managed to accumulate an impressive list of charges." A single brow rose. "Exactly *what* have you been doing?"

"Uh, if it pleases the, uh, council," he stumbled over his reply, "I've been in the company of adventurers."

Lector Shinka nodded, as though this explained everything. Lector Palanis muttered scornfully, as though this were some great sin. Lector Annis frowned deeper, as though this justified the use of the muscle.

"It should be considered a crime in and of itself," Lector Palanis muttered behind his clenched fists. "All the power and responsibility Venarie imparts and you chose to waste it in pursuit of gold. Magic was intended for greater purposes than simple mercenary work."

"With respect, Lector," Dreadaeleon replied, struggling to find composure in his voice, "'adventuring' is not quite the same as mercenary work."

It's much less respectable.

He chose not to say that.

"Continue." Lector Shinka inclined her head.

"First and foremost, I considered it a more ethical approach at the time," Dreadaeleon said, clearing his throat. "My inquiries into the subject suggested that mercenary companies typically sold their loyalty to a nation, such as Karneria or Saine, while adventurers tended to accept work and coin from independent clients. As members of the Venarium are forsworn from pledging their loyalty to any country, I suspected there would be less of a conflict of interest in an adventurer's company."

"Logical," she said, another brow risen.

"And yet, the Sovereignty Pact exists to prevent the irresponsible use of magic," Lector Palanis muttered. "No king, emperor, or priest can be trusted with our power. I fail to see how placing it at the disposal of a profession only slightly more reputable than thieves and murderers could be considered *more* ethical."

Dreadaeleon swallowed hard, looking at Lector Annis, who said nothing and did not move.

"It was that very reputation that drove me to seek their company," the boy spoke swiftly. "I was certain that an adventurer's knack for trouble would lead me to situations in which I could see the effects of all different schools and practices. I learned much about the practical limitations of magic use in the field."

"So we heard."

Lector Annis's voice was quiet, his movement precise as he held aloft a single scrap of paper.

"Our information on you is limited, concomitant," he said, "but what we gathered from the observations of a Senior Librarian is that the limits of your abilities have not progressed beyond basic evocations."

"Mere channeling of fire and lightning is the work of an initiate, at best," Palanis said, sneering.

"Even if we were to assume the Librarian's information faulty," Shinka said softly, "it would seem reasonable to conclude that, if an adventurer's life is as haphazard as suggested, you would have pushed yourself well beyond the ability to escape unharmed. Surely, you would have contracted a disease like the Decay or Spontaneous Eruption."

"The diseases that afflict us are not ones from which we recover with milk and tea," Palanis growled. "And if your experiments produced acceptable results, we should have received the information long, *long* ago."

"And, of course," Annis spoke forcefully and pointedly, "the fact that you are standing here and our Librarian is *not* suggests that perhaps the experiments you undertook carried too high a cost. We must recoup our losses somehow."

"I must protest," Dreadaeleon replied, careful not to let his voice go too high. "Every concomitant is responsible exactly for his or her own self and no one other. Unless you have evidence that I was directly responsible for the disappearance of said Librarian…"

Annis exchanged a look—none too pleasant—with Shinka and Palanis. His eyes narrowed scantly.

"Protest accepted," he said, "tentatively."

"And yet," Palanis offered, "protocol allows for a reasonable conclusion to be drawn under the auspices of precedent. If one can prove that the accused demonstrates a pattern of recklessness, one can conclude that said recklessness would doubtless be a contributing factor."

"A fair point," Shinka noted. "So, do tell us, concomitant. Why did you not report to Tower Resolute upon entering the city?"

"And why," Annis added, leaning forward, "did you expend your power in a thieves' war?"

Damn it, Dreadaeleon thought, *they've got you now, old man. How do you justify this? How do you explain why you're here? How do you explain the Souk?*

And he looked up to the three Lectors. He looked from Shinka's cool impassiveness to Annis's iron stare to Palanis's twitching glower.

Do they even care?

"There remains but one point of contention."

Dreadaeleon would have missed it if he blinked. As Lector Annis spoke, there was a faint tug at his lips, a barely perceptible twitch at the corners of his eyes. What would be unnoticeable spasms in a normal human being were wild as seizures upon a man as composed and controlled as Lector Annis.

For a very brief, very fleeting, very significant moment, Dreadaeleon could tell that the Lector hated him very, very, very much.

"What happened to Librarian Bralston?"

Dreadaeleon had nothing to say that would not result in him being incinerated on the spot.

"You have nothing else to offer."

Lector Annis stated, rather than asked. Lector Annis already knew the answer.

Yes. I was there when Bralston died. I could have saved him. I could have done a lot that I didn't. I didn't do it because I didn't want to be here. I wanted to live. I want to live. I want to see Liaja. I want to see her—

"Very well." Lector Annis's voice was sharp enough to cut Dreadaeleon's thought from his mind. "On all charges, henceforth, is the concomitant confirmed complicit. The Primary Lector overseeing the case suggests immediate termination."

"The Secondary Lector suggests sparing the concomitant," Lector Shinka spoke as a soft contrast. "While the concomitant's results seem sound, it would seem an utter waste to disregard what he's said and what he's done in the outside world. The Secondary Lector adds, further, that we forward his methods as a means for future field research."

"The Tertiary Lector concurs with the Primary Lector," Lector Palanis muttered. "Any information that could be wrought from the concomitant would pale in comparison to the danger his recklessness and secrecy present. Immediate termination is confirmed."

Annis nodded, gesturing to the clerk.

"That our annals may be complete," Annis said, "we may take the final statement from the concomitant."

There's a girl that works in a brothel somewhere. Her smile is big and bright. She has eyes that have smiles themselves. I've never felt more awful or more alive than when I think of her tears. Her name is not Liaja. Please go find her and tell her all this.

He chose not to say that.

"Proof by Ordeal."

He should have chosen not to say *that*.

But by the time it had unconsciously come tumbling out of his mouth, it was too late to take it back. Perhaps it was a desperate need to survive, the animal part of him that would say anything just to live. Or maybe he really was that stupid.

The raised eyebrows on every Lector, including Annis, suggested that they seemed to think the latter.

"I formally request Proof by Ordeal."

As the paragons of civilization, the Venarium were expected to portray a higher class of bloodthirstiness than the lowborn swine over whom they towered. As such, there was nothing they loved more than watching two people fight each other.

They just called it by a different name.

In truth, Proof by Ordeal was as good as any death sentence. In a last-ditch effort to prove that the accused still had worth to the Venarium, he could request to display his magical prowess. And always, this display was a magical duel of staggering odds against someone much older, wiser, and more experienced than he who could choose the stipulations and conditions. The chances of him dying terribly would still have been strong even if he *weren't* staring up at three Lectors, two of which seemed eager to kill him and the third of which hadn't seemed to hate the idea.

As they were quick to prove.

"The Primary Lector confirms the request," Annis said, "and approves."

"The Secondary Lector approves," Shinka said.

"The Tertiary Lector approves and accepts the declaration of Ordeal on behalf of the assembly," Palanis added.

"The Primary Lector approves."

"The Secondary Lector approves."

YOU STUPID MORON! his brain screamed, for his mouth couldn't. He had requested this, after all. It would look awfully contradictory to protest now. Or beg for mercy. Or wet himself.

Not that he'd ruled any of those out.

"The Tertiary Lector selects," Palanis spoke slowly, "as the means to minister the ordeal…" The next word was forced between thin lips curled into a smile. "Broodvine."

And with good reason.

"The Primary Lector approves," Annis said.

"The Secondary Lector…" Shinka paused, casting a glance toward Palanis. "Approves with reservation."

Broodvine. He wants to use broodvine. Of course. Why wouldn't he want to use broodvine? He doesn't just want you to fail. He wants to annihilate you. He wants to render you into an inert, gibbering pile of meat ready to be harvested.

Admittedly, when it came to rendering people into inert, gibbering piles of meat, few methods were more efficient than broodvine.

The clerk crept carefully from the shadows of the chamber, a polished wooden chest in his hands and a terrified expression across his face. He approached Lector Palanis, drawing back the lid to reveal a pair of black seeds upon a purple velvet cushion.

It was quite a bit of reverence to unveil what, to the untrained eye, would appear to be just a pair of stale, inedible pebbles. But Dreadaeleon knew what these little seeds were capable of, and he found it hard to fault them for the fanfare.

Even to the rest of the world, broodvine had a reputation as a hallucinogen strong enough to be eschewed by even the most deviant smoke-eaters. It was a seed that began in a man's smoking pipe and ended in a man's forehead when the hallucinations caused him to use said smoking pipe to dig out his own eyeballs to extract the rats he thought were making nests in his brain.

It took a wizard to appreciate broodvine, because it took a wizard to weaponize broodvine. The common man would be slave to the illusions the smoke showed him, but a wizard could control them, shape his own dreams, forge his own nightmares, and inflict them upon those of lesser mind.

Some became addicts themselves, using the broodvine to shape their own imaginary worlds to escape into.

Others employed them to deadly effect, using the smoke of the broodvine to create nightmares to warp the minds of their foes.

More often, though, the only sanctioned use of broodvine was what Lector Palanis was doing as he stepped down from his podium, took a seed from the chest, and stood exactly thirty paces away from Dreadaeleon.

A broodvine ordeal was, quite simply, the most straightforward assessment of a wizard possible. A trial of fear and pain, during which the mind would be twisted, warped, and quite often shattered. Those who had the will to resist and control the nightmares heaped upon their tender brains would be found too useful to terminate.

Those who didn't...

"Concomitant?"

Only then did Dreadaeleon notice the clerk standing before him, chest presented, seed staring up at him. Only then did Dreadaeleon notice just how bad his hands were shaking as he lifted the seed gently from its velvet throne.

He looked thirty paces across the room. Palanis was smiling broadly, the morbid pleasure on his lips at odds with the ire in his knitted brows.

He looked twenty paces to his left. Annis and Shinka tensed in their chairs, hands stiff and flat upon their podiums.

Half a dozen eyes were upon him.

Waiting.

His hands shook as he pressed the seed past dry lips. It tasted of ash and dust on his tongue. Through trembling thought, he called to mind the spell. He bit down and felt sparks fly between his teeth and ignite his breath. Just enough to choke his senses with fever-sweet perfume.

His lips parted and a plume of smoke scintillated from his mouth. Across the room, Palanis opened his maw like a hellbeast of legend, great gouts of gray pouring forth. With every breath of Lector and boy, the broodvine smoke slithered from mouth and nostril. It painted the air, shimmered purple in sunlight seeping through the windows. It carpeted the floor, drowning tile in a lake of roiling wisps. In moments, it filled the room.

And then, the nightmare began.

With voices, at first: nonsensical, jibbering, wailing, cursing, crying, laughing. The sounds of uncontrolled thoughts given voice and shared between minds.

Next, reality bent. The floor quivered, rippled like liquid, a vast lake upon which men stood as insignificant as pebbles cast across the surface.

The smoke began to breathe without the aid of Dreadaeleon or Palanis. From its tendrils formed hands, wispy fingers brushing against the boy's cheeks. From its clouds formed faces, opening smoky mouths in wordless screams. From its veils formed bodies, writhing through space to brush against each other and dissipate into nothingness.

There was a scream. The clerk went running for the door. Wise, Dreadaeleon thought; in another few moments, it wouldn't exist anymore.

Dreadaeleon fought the urge to follow him. Dreadaeleon fought the urge to flinch, to blink, to do anything but breathe. The body was a primal thing, one that responded to animal impulses. The mind must be strong to control the body. The body must be strong to control the mind.

But in another moment, he couldn't control either.

Lector Palanis's smile grew broader as he seemed to grow taller. No, Dreadaeleon realized as he felt the tile turn to liquid beneath him. He looked down and saw his feet disappearing into the floor, the tile rippling and becoming nothing as it swallowed him up. Beneath it, the earth grew solid again, seizing his ankles, drawing him deeper into a coffin of stone and salt.

He felt it around his knees, crushing. He felt his chest slide into the tile, breath escaping him. He felt the tile splash as he clawed at it, struggling to pull himself.

Steady, he told himself. *It's not real.*

He looked desperately to Annis and Shinka. Their gazes trailed down, following him as he sank deeper. They could see it happening. He could feel it happening. Palanis was making it happen.

If everyone saw the same thing, how could it not be real?

Fight it. He slapped the tile. It splashed beneath his palms. *Assert your will.* He slid deeper. The floor seeped between his fingers. *You aren't this weak, are you?*

He clenched his teeth, drew in a smoky breath between them, and reached out as he sank up to his armpits.

The floor was solid.

He gasped, clawed his way out, and felt breath return as he emerged from the tile. He struggled to remember how to breathe normally. The floor felt solid beneath him.

But not for long.

Cracks appeared in the tile, spread across the floor, a spider's web of wounds. The floor groaned, split apart, and erupted into fragments. An arm of desiccated flesh clinging to ancient bones reached up into the air. Another followed. Another and another and another until a forest of limbs stood swaying between Dreadaeleon and Palanis, the Lector standing tall and smiling.

The withered hands groped blindly about the tile, seizing handholds in skeletal fingers and pulling. Dust-choked moans followed as bulbous heads with the thinnest veneers of ancient flesh rose out of the earth. One by one, corpses hauled their withered bodies from the earth to rise and fix empty black sockets upon Dreadaeleon. One by one, they began to shamble toward him, moaning.

He cried out, fell onto his rear, and scrambled to get away from the advancing horde. He felt something grab his wrist, looked down to see a skeletal claw wrapped around his hand, a desiccated face looking up at him from a dark crack. He shrieked, pulled away, and felt blood blossom across his skin.

It's not real, he told himself. *Energy that leaves a body cannot return to the body. It is impossible.*

He looked up at the horde. He rose to his feet. He saw them and all their gnashing teeth and their eyeless sockets and their shambling flesh. And in the instant he saw them approaching, he knew the truth.

It should *be impossible.*

But the broodvine made it possible. The broodvine wrenched the waking and dreaming worlds until there was no difference. Perhaps this was but a dream, but it was Palanis's dream, it was Palanis's will.

The only way to control the former was to be stronger than the latter.

The horde closed in around him. He raised his hands.

Skeletal claws, tattered flesh dangling from their bones, reached for his flesh. He drew in a long, sharp breath.

Warm blood began to trickle down his face; pain shot through him. He clapped his hands together.

And screamed for all he was worth.

The horde fell apart, dissipating into wisps of smoke. The floor was whole beneath him once more. The veils of smoke parted to reveal Palanis, standing not quite so tall and not smiling at all.

It worked. Dreadaeleon thought this only because he had no breath left to speak it. *Son of a bitch, it* worked. *You can't concentrate, you old fart, can you? You can't force this on me.*

The Lector's face tightened into a grimace, as though he could hear these very thoughts. His eyes narrowed to thin slits. Dreadaeleon felt something slither up his leg. He looked down and saw a serpent, one of many, writhing up his leg in a great swarm. That was frightening, he knew. But he did not feel fear.

He reached down, tore them from his body, and threw them across the room. There they pooled; there they gathered, twisted around each other, and coalesced into one massive, giant serpent.

And Dreadaeleon felt as though he weren't showing the proper professional respect by not being as afraid as he should be. But he had to hold onto that fearlessness, that will. This would be *his* reality.

A giant snake. Brilliant. Is he just mocking me now?

Dreadaeleon looked past the serpent. He saw Palanis's face contorted with concentration. No, it appeared that the Lector genuinely *was* putting a tremendous amount of effort into this.

And that's when it occurred to Dreadaeleon.

The Lector had achieved his position through years of research, locked away in a tower, surrounded by books to read, colleagues to debate, and pupils to practice on. In any other ordeal, be it fire or frost, his technique would be so refined as to reduce Dreadaeleon to a pile of ash in a heartbeat.

But here, in a world of illusion and imagination, Palanis knew only what he had read about in books. He knew only what he *thought* people found frightening.

And just like that, Dreadaeleon could see no more serpent, hear no more voices. He saw nothing before him but a cloud of smoke swirling about an old man.

And he saw his chance.

He inhaled; the smoke swirled. He twitched his fingers; the smoke danced. He closed his eyes. And the world changed around him.

The voices that had faded to a distant murmur grew stronger now.

Their laughter became shrieking cackles. Their wailing became agonized moaning. Their senseless jibbering became clear, coherent.
They had language. They had words.

"*Weak*," they whispered.

"*Pathetic.*"

"*Insignificant old fool.*"

"What?"

That last one had been Palanis, a whisper offered to the smoke
that swirled around him.

"*Couldn't harm anyone.*"

"*Useless. Just give up.*"

"*All that knowledge, wasted.*"

"No, I…it's not real, it's a trick…"

He was trying to reassure himself. Vocally, Dreadaeleon noted.
He dared not do it mentally. The boy suspected the Lector's mind
was becoming quite crowded.

Dreadaeleon willed the earth to move. It did. The tiles quivered;
the walls trembled. Across the floor, upon the ceiling and the walls,
pouting lips sprouted like plants, mouths opened in twitching whispers, and eyelids winked to life and focused upon Palanis.

"*What good are you?*"

"*You've done nothing with your power.*"

"*You're going to die alone, no fear, no love.*"

"Stop it," Palanis muttered. "Stop it!"

Dreadaeleon could only barely hear him. The voices were louder.
The mouths were twitching endlessly. The eyes were locked upon
the Lector as he bent low, cowering beneath relentless stares.

Dreadaeleon shut his eyes. The world disappeared. An eager mid-
night seeped in through the windows, drowning the sun, light, and
smoke. Annis and Shinka vanished into the darkness; Dreadaeleon
followed. The many mouths and many eyes disappeared. All that
remained was a quivering, cowering old man.

And the many, many voices.

"*Nothing. You are nothing.*"

"No wife. No child. No legacy. Nothing."

"Why go on? Why bother? Kill yourself."

"Kill yourself."

"Kill yourself. Kill yourself. Kill yourself. Kill yourself. Kill yourself."

And then, there were no more voices. No more words. Just one long, loud noise as Palanis collapsed upon the tile, screaming endlessly and unblinking into the void.

That, Dreadaeleon thought, was the value of his time in the world. Palanis understood theory, technique, and any number of things that could be learned in books. But the knowledge of how to break a man? That could only be learned in practice.

And Palanis was broken, perhaps to the point where he would not ever fix himself. Proof of Dreadaeleon's own value had been offered. He should stop.

But he did not.

He deserves this, he told himself. *He deserves to shatter. He thought he could break you. He thought you were nothing. Show him, old man. Show him how wrong he was.*

He was aware of that thought. He was aware of how petty it sounded. He was aware that he should care more than he did.

But he was unaware of just how broad his smile was at that moment.

"That's ENOUGH."

A great gale ripped through the chamber, twisting smoke and darkness into a columnar whirlwind that was sent writhing out an open window. The air was cleaned, the day was returned, and the chamber was once again whole and unbent.

And Lector Annis, standing at the center of it, was trembling.

His arms were spear-straight at his sides; his face was twisted up in a grimace as he stood between the boy and Lector Palanis, quaking on the floor. His eyes began to glow red, the crimson energy of Venarie seeping into his scowl.

"You are proving more costly than you are worth, concomitant," he spoke through clenched teeth. "A Librarian lost, a Lector disabled, and now..."

He didn't bother finishing that sentence. His magic did that for him. Power radiated out of him as the blaze in his stare grew brighter, more magic boiling up from inside him, leaping to his fingers, setting the tips ablaze with fire. The force of his will alone was nearly enough to knock Dreadaeleon back.

Certainly, it should have been enough to make him reconsider calling his own magic, letting his own power bleed out his eyes, stepping challengingly toward the Lector.

"Concomitant. Lector."

Through the roiling energy, Lector Shinka's voice cut like a blade. She stepped between them, coattails wafting about her legs, hands folded delicately behind her back.

"If we could perhaps cease comparing genitalia sizes?" She smirked. "The ordeal has been completed to the satisfaction of the law. The concomitant's value has been proven."

"The Primary Lector," Annis said angrily, "protests."

Dreadaeleon had to admit: It was admirable that Annis could restrain his rage enough to respect protocol.

"An inquisition may be arranged at a later date," Shinka replied. "Though it is the opinion of the Secondary that we'd find no grounds for anything other than approval of the concomitant's abilities." She glanced past Annis to Palanis, coiling like a serpent upon the floor. "That he could do... *this* to an initiated Lector proves the extent of his value to the Venarium."

This did not seem to soothe Annis. The Lector's teeth clenched tighter; the fires at his hands grew brighter.

"Further," Shinka spoke softly, "I would point out that we have much to learn from the concomitant and that killing him will most definitely *not* bring Librarian Bralston back."

Annis flinched. The light from his eyes faded. Smoking tendrils drifted from his fingertips as the flames extinguished themselves.

And an instant later, he was back to the very portrait of a composed, severe Lector: hands folded behind him, face set into fixed serenity.

"The Primary Lector accepts," he said, "with reservation."

"Acknowledged." Shinka turned a nod to Dreadaeleon. "You are free to go, concomitant. Under Venarium law, you are instructed not to leave the city until our conclusions as to your ordeal are drawn and made manifest."

"I came here to request access," Dreadaeleon muttered, "to divination—"

"If you'll pardon the coarse phraseology, concomitant," Shinka interjected pointedly, "do *not* push it. Lector Palanis requires our full attention, and we have further concerns as to your insubordination. Consider it reward enough that you are permitted to walk away with our admiration for your . . . field research."

He should have protested. He should have pressed them. Lenk would have wanted that.

Fuck Lenk, he decided. *Lenk couldn't have taken down a Lector. Lenk couldn't have done* any *of that. None of them could. And none of them will.*

Dreadaeleon nodded stiffly at the remaining Lectors before turning and heading toward the door. There was vigor in his step, a trembling energy coursing through him as he went to the door. He hadn't accomplished what he had come for.

He had accomplished so much more.

And now he was going to do more still, once he found her.

What was her name?

Liaja.

TWENTY

Company Men

I t used to be that thievery was an honest job.

Back in the day, if someone wanted to pull a job—a *real* job, not some pickpocket guttersnipe hit man trash job—one worked for it.

If one wanted a good disguise, he or she watched the target for hours, days, weeks; enough to get every last detail of their countenance down. Then there was the matter of acquiring—legitimately or otherwise, and no one ever acquired anything legitimately— the material to craft it. And then, countless favors were pulled and promised to make the ruse a success.

It was difficult, yes. But it was through the labor that thieves— honest thieves—proved their worth. It demanded time, it demanded money, and sometimes it demanded dabbling with the very lowest of scum: crooked smiths, Bloodwise Brothers, and, Silf forbid, actors.

And one false slip—and there were many false slips—would see an amateur hanged, beheaded, or worse, depending on which fasha caught him.

Denaos, by necessity and elimination, had not hung around with amateurs.

Those were the days.

Bloodier days, admittedly, but still.

Those were the days when the Jackals were just another gang on the street, one head of a serpent with many, continuously devouring itself. Those were the days when the Jackals had earned their gold and their blood with labor and steel…and more blood.

Now the Jackals were a guild, a single snake with a single head. No longer a gang, but a company. No longer thieves, but businessmen. And ones who knew nothing of labor.

Why monitor a target when the organization had carefully edited dossiers illustrating the manner and posture of every servant of every house? Why pull favors when one had a network of employees to draw from, all on the company coin? And why steal or craft a disguise when one could simply wander into a shop and buy one?

Efficient. Organized. Bloodless.

Dishonest.

Denaos had plenty of time to reflect on this.

Mostly because service at Man-Shuu Yon's Emporium of Washables for Creatures Great and Small (Bipeds Only) was so absent it might as well have been myth.

He leaned over the counter, trying to see into the darkness through a doorway that segregated a small lobby from the laundry proper. He could see racks of clothes, washtubs, scrubbing boards, and a variety of vials and jugs from which the scents of a variety of soaps and perfumes wafted. But there were no employees, no managers, and certainly no one who could answer him.

And yet, all the same, Denaos sighed and reached for a bell attached to the counter via a pull rope, next to a sign that helpfully read: "*Engage all digits and apply with conviction (mental).*"

He pulled the rope. The bell rang out a clear brass note. Unfortunately, that note did not read "*come to the fucking counter,*" so Denaos pulled it again. And again. And again and again and again until he was spewing curses along with the bell's song.

"You are heard, consumer."

From behind the counter, a featureless black shape rose to a towering seven feet tall. The higher it rose, the more its shape became clear: a robe fell neatly into place around a thin body complemented by four arms ending in four hands folding neatly before it. It peered down at Denaos through a tastefully framed painting of a landscape of rolling hills and apple trees.

Couthi? Denaos thought, incredulously. *We're dealing with couthi now?*

"Greetings and welcome to where dreams are made after nightmares have been scrubbed clean from silk, assuming all chemicals available function as intended."

Denaos didn't bother to hide his wince at the creature's chilling monotone. He *did* restrain himself from openly screaming when the couthi extended one of its arms to him.

"Your tender skin should have been entrusted with a scrap of paper exactly one-quarter-foot by one-quarter-foot with all pertinent details as to fabric and physiology. Please relinquish it at this moment."

"Er, no." Denaos held up his hands, as if to ward away the creature's limb. "I don't have a..." He regained his composure. "Er, I mean..." He leaned over the counter, businesslike. "I've come from The Oxbow."

The couthi merely stared back, unmoving. Or at least, Denaos assumed he was staring. How in the hell would anyone be able to tell? *This* is why no one sensible worked with couthi.

The landscape serving as the thing's face shifted. Denaos looked behind him to see the door closing; it unnerved him that he hadn't heard it open. A man wearing dark leathers and a dark look came in, eyes glancing over Denaos as he took a seat on a nearby waiting bench.

"You are a patron of The Oxbow." The couthi turned its attention back to Denaos. "This is acknowledged. What do you require, associate of the Jack—"

"Not so loud, moron!" Denaos snarled.

He cast a glance over his shoulder. The door opened and shut as a woman walked in and took a seat beside the man. He leaned closer, whispering harshly to the couthi.

"I need a servant's uniform," he muttered, "for the house of Teneir."

"Your request is acknowledged," the couthi said. "Dimensions."

"What?"

"Relinquish your dimensions. Height. Weight. Are you not familiar with thieves' cant."

"That's not—" Denaos caught himself as the door opened and closed again behind him. "Look, just get me something that would fit. A little more than six feet tall, broad in the shoulders, long in the leg. Make sure it has a veil."

He looked over his shoulder. Another four men and two women had entered. All dressed in the same dark clothes as the first, all eyes upon the counter. The door was already opening when he turned back.

"Do you have one or not?"

"For all associates of The Oxbow, we possess anything necessary. Place both feet firmly upon the floor and proceed to count breaths while I attend to the back and locate the specified garment."

"No, not here." The door opened and closed behind Denaos again. "Have it delivered. To this location." He shoved a folded-up scrap of paper across the counter. "And have it there in two hours. You've got runners, right?"

"We employ all flavors of human," the couthi said, plucking up the scrap of paper. "Here at Man-Shuu Yon's Emporium of—"

"Yes, great. I'd love to stick around and die of culture shock, but I really must go." He knocked on the counter. "Two hours, got it? No more."

The couthi nodded—or maybe he didn't; it was hard to tell—and Denaos turned around to go.

Going, of course, would be difficult, considering the gang of twenty men and women standing between him and the door, glowering at him beneath sand-colored hoods.

Denaos didn't move. He kept his hands visible and well clear of his daggers. There was no need and no way to win this fight—not yet, anyway. If the Jackals wanted him dead, he'd be dead already. The Jackals only showed up in numbers like these to send a message.

Whether that message was something more complicated than a severe beating, Denaos had no choice but to wait and see.

But he didn't have to wait long. The door opened and closed one last time. The Jackals parted as another man—a tall, thin Djaalic wearing his beard neatly trimmed and his long hair oiled back into a tail—strode forward. He stopped before Denaos, standing just a hairbreadth shorter, and looked him over, resting a hand on the pommel of a sword at his hip.

"I have heard the name of the Jackals used here," the man said, his voice as oiled as his hair. "Not smart. If you're using that name, you know how it hard is to come by. And if you know how hard it is to come by, you know that no one joins the Jackals except in extraordinary circumstances."

The fact that they were working with a Gods-damned *couthi* seemed to suggest otherwise, Denaos thought.

"Now, if you were once a Jackal, that'd be one thing," the man continued. "But then, you'd know that no one ever leaves the Jackals, except in the *most* extraordinary circumstances."

He looked over his shoulder, saw hoods nodding in agreement. Suddenly, his head snapped back and his hand shot out, seized Denaos by the jaw, and drew him closer. His eyes burned brightly and his voice forced out between clenched teeth.

And still Denaos still did not move.

"And if you joined the Jackals and then left the Jackals and were stupid enough to come *back*," the man said, "you'd know that *no one* has ever done that…"

He pulled Denaos close, his breath blasting so hot on the rogue's face that he wouldn't be surprised to see smoke coming out of his nostrils. And yet when the man pulled Denaos even closer, pressed his lips to Denaos's, and thrust his tongue into the man's mouth…

Well, it was hard not to be surprised.

The kiss was terse and angry, the sort of thing one received shortly before going off to war or the headsman's block. And when he was released and the man shoved him back, his face was deadly serious.

"Except," the man said, "for the most magnificent bastard to ever have graced us with his presence."

Denaos smacked his lips, ran his tongue around his mouth and looked thoughtful.

"Do I taste cinnamon?"

It was hard not to grin by habit. One never *didn't* grin in the presence of Fenshi.

"It was that or poison," Fenshi replied, returning the expression. "And poison is more than scum like you deserves, running into the city without telling me. I could do it, too, you know. Remember? I killed fifty-one men."

"Fifty-one men, yes," Denaos sighed. "Thirty in duels, twenty by poison, and one just because you hate even numbers."

Fenshi reached out and touched the man's face. His visage screwed up, as if he couldn't believe he was actually here.

"Gods, I've missed you, Ramaniel."

"It's been a long time, Fenshi."

"Indeed." He withdrew his gloved fingers with a light slap on Denaos's cheek. "So long I forgot that I can't stand to look at you without fifty-one drinks in me." He whirled about and gestured to the assembled Jackals. "Boys and girls, tonight is the luckiest night of your fucking lives, and maybe some of you will drink enough to not survive it!"

He began pointing to faces, bellowing commands like a general, not a care who heard. Just like he always did, Denaos noted. Great killer, Fenshi. Shitty thief.

"You two! Head to the Crane and clear out every layman and peasant you see! You four! Down to my den—you know the one—and grab everything liquid that isn't water and meet us there. Anyone who isn't there by the time I arrive will be *gutted* in the street. Break out Silf's statue! Break out the coins! Ramaniel's come home!"

⇥ ⇥ ⊫◆⊨ ⇤ ⇤

A coin clinked as Denaos tossed it into the bowl carved in the idol of Silf.

"A bargain's a bargain," he said.

Another clink as Fenshi tossed in his own. Gold, of course.

"A bastard's a bastard," he said.

Denaos tossed in a silver. Silf's grinning ebonwood face leered at him.

"Luck for the worthy."

Fenshi dropped an entire pouch of coins onto the idol, sending it toppling over into a pool of spilled wine. The man with the oiled hair threw back his head and howled with laughter.

"*WINE FOR THE MASTER!*" he howled, downing the rest of his glass in a single gulp.

Denaos followed suit, along with everyone else occupying The Quarrelsome Crane's once-clean commons room. The Jackals, hoods off and boots up, roared with laughter as they echoed the rhyme. Those who could still speak without slurring, anyway.

Now *this* was more like the old days, Denaos thought as he swept his grin around the room. Barrels of wine had been rolled out and lined up on the walls, their taps perpetually flowing as the Jackals staggered between them and their tables. Knives were embedded in wood where impromptu games of blade-tossing had broken out. Barmaids did their best to stay out of the thieves' way and step over people passed out on the floor.

Dice rolled. Alcohol stained the boards. And at least three different people were having a very good, very naked time somewhere in the back.

Surely, he could be forgiven for forgetting what he was supposed to be doing for a while. Surely Rezca would understand. Surely Lenk would understand. Surely Asper...

Well, Asper would curse at him, probably smack him around a bit. At least until she got a drink in her. Or two. It'd actually probably take a whole barrel to get her to relax.

But even if she wouldn't, he forgave himself for putting his feet up on the table next to Silf's fallen idol and holding his empty glass out. A Jackal came scurrying up, refilling it with his own, before slinking away.

"Now *this* is the way it's supposed to be." Fenshi sighed, leaning back in his chair. "When was the last time you remember us doing business like this?"

Denaos glanced around. "Years ago. How long's it been for you?"

Fenshi smiled bitterly, quaffed his wine. "Years ago."

"Really? Couldn't have a proper celebration without me? I'm flattered."

"Flattered by yourself and only yourself," Fenshi said. The smile left him. The bitterness remained. "This shit with the Khovura...it has us hiding like the old days. The days before the riots, when the Houndmistress still walked. Remember those, Ramaniel?"

It took Denaos a moment to remember that Ramaniel was no longer his name. It took him much less than a moment to remember the Houndmistress.

"After the riots, we *ran* this city. We reached a nice agreement with the fashas and the merchants. The fashas brought their goods in, the merchants sold them, the Jackals made sure nothing burned down. Simple. Elegant. Every night was like tonight." He glanced at Denaos. "Of course, you wouldn't know that, would you? You had to leave the city."

"I *was* a wanted man."

"Feh. Rezca was a fool to let you go. In another week, we had this city moving again. It remained that way for years." He smashed his glass on the ground, snatched another one from a passing Jackal. "Until the Khovura came."

"I saw the aftermath in the Souk today. It didn't go well."

"A few fights don't go well and Rezca gets scared. Sends all the heads underground, tells us to stay in our dens and not show up." He chuckled into his wine. "He'd shit himself if he could see us now. Yerk, too, nasty old smoke-eater."

He glanced up over the heads of the assembled as the door to the bar opened and a pair of people filed in.

"Speaking of which..."

Sandal came trundling up to the table, wrapped head to toe, face smothered by a scarf and goggles shielding his eyes. He still reeked of smoke and oil and still didn't seem perturbed when others went fleeing at his stench. Behind him was a tall, thin-looking woman with a long face made longer by the pain from the bandage on her shoulder.

"Sandal the Candle," Fenshi said, beckoning them over. *"And* Scarecrow Sashe? Yerk deigns to let his people out after dark now? Or did you just do all your chores like good little boys and girls?"

The woman, Sashe, grunted her disdain in reply. Sandal rolled his shoulders.

"Hfrd Rfmfnl hn trwn," he spoke, unintelligible through his scarf, nodding to Denaos. *"Whrf yw brrn?"*

"Would you fucking take that thing off?" Denaos asked. "You know I can't understand a thing you say."

"Only Yerk can," Fenshi said. "And only Yerk gets the Scarecrow to do anything." He glanced at the bandage around her shoulder. "Speaking of, looks like something went poorly for you, dear. And here I thought that crossbow of yours kept you well away from trouble."

It probably did, Denaos thought. Or at least, it did until she decided to turn it on Kataria back in the Souk. But he wasn't about to mention this. The Scarecrow merely grunted, seized a glass, and started chugging.

"Isn't this glorious?" Fenshi said. "The Candle, the Scarecrow, me"—he made an elaborate gesture toward Denaos—"and of course, the pride and joy. If Anielle were here, we'd have a lovely reunion of the Debt Squad. Gods, why can't it be like this all the time?"

"Because of the Khovura."

It was just a mutter, barely audible over the din of the room. Yet Denaos heard it very clearly. And because he heard it, so had Fenshi. The man with the oily hair leapt out of his chair and the room fell instantly silent. His eyes settled upon a Jackal—one of the younger members relegated to pouring wine and making sure no one choked on their own vomit.

"What was that, *pup*?" he demanded.

"Nothing, Fenshi," the recruit said, turning his head down.

"Gods, man, at least have the courage to stand for what you said. I can let you keep courage, which is more than I'll leave you with if I have to *force* you to repeat yourself."

"It's just that . . ." The recruit looked around for support, found none. "We shouldn't be doing this, gathering here like this. Rezca said not to. You know . . . because of the trouble."

"Trouble? *TROUBLE?*" Fenshi quaffed his wine and hurled the glass at the recruit. "What the fuck would a quivering rat like you know about trouble, you little shit?" He chuckled. "You flinch at a glass. You run scared from the Khovura." He waved a hand and turned to address the Jackals. "The Khovura are nothing. A bunch of upstarts wrapped in veils. Most of you runts joined when times were good and we were on top, so any footwar looks like trouble to you.

"But how many of you remember the riots? How many of you remember the Houndmistress? *Those* were troubles." He deftly leapt atop the table, reached down, and held up the idol of Silf, turning the deity's grinning face out over the audience. "Let me tell you why we call them foot*wars*.

"Back at the beginning, you wouldn't know her from any other fasha's daughter: some high-and-mighty runt with a stick. But she grew up, inherited her father's fortunes, and decided she was going to clean up this town, starting with us. So she hired some goons with swords, ratted out a few of our dens, and cut us up in our own holes.

"As though *we*, the ones who had this city scrubbed of every amateur guild and gang that ever squeezed an honest citizen, were the problem. But she rallied her dogcatchers and she rooted out our dens and she put us to the noose, the cell, the ax, sometimes staved in our heads with her big stick. And the city *loved* her for it. They spat on our corpses and screamed her name."

He looked at the idol of Silf and nodded slowly, as if the Patron were whispering to him directly.

"*Those* were hard times, my friend. Watching every friend you ever made on the street get caught and cut up and left to be eaten by rats...those were hard times. Rezca was still taking orders from the heads at that point, not giving them. So they told him to fix this problem and we formed the Debt Squad."

He gestured to his table.

"Scarecrow Sashe, who could put a seagull's eye out at sixty paces. Sandal the Candle, who burned her guards alive like stuck pigs in their own homes. And of course, you all know me, Yerk, Anielle." He glanced around the room. "But who do you think it was that brought it all together? Who do you think it was that had the honor of killing the Houndmistress herself?"

He stomped his boot on the table.

"Who posed as the man who would become her counsel? Who lied, weaseled, and wormed his way into her innermost confidence? Who played the game so well that when he finally cut her down in the night, they had no idea it was even him who did it?"

Fenshi whirled and leveled a finger at Denaos. His grin was manic.

"*This* man right here. This man, who is the reason we're still around. *This* man, who is the reason the fashas and the merchants and the people look to *us* to lead this city. *This* man whose presence demands we drink until we vomit! *THIS* man who will solve this Khovura problem once and for all."

He raised the idol of Silf over his head like a goblet. Countless glasses were raised with him—by Sandal, by Sashe, by the trembling recruit and every last Jackal in the room. And they all pointed to Denaos.

"The man who killed the Houndmistress," Fenshi said. "The man who caused the riots. The man who let us build in its wake." He held his hands out. "RAMANIEL!"

"*RAMANIEL!*"

The word—for it was no longer a name—was taken up over and over, drank to over and over, until every glass was dry. And Fenshi lowered the idol and grinned at Denaos.

"So, tell us, Ramaniel. Tell us how you cut that bitch's throat."

Denaos's cheeks puffed slightly. His lips pursed. He shrugged helplessly and waved his hands.

"Humble," Fenshi said, nodding. "Always humble. She saw that humility, too, right before he killed her. You don't remember her, of course, you little turds. Maybe you remember the riots that followed, when we killed every last loyalist in the city, and those were dark times, too. But we came out of them stronger than ever, just like we'll come out of *this* stronger than ever! All thanks to Ramaniel!"

"RAMANIEL!"

The word filled his ears.

"RAMANIEL!"

The word followed in his footsteps as he nodded graciously and excused himself out the door.

"RAMANIEL!"

The word chased him into the street as he stepped delicately into a nearby alley, placed his hands on his knees, bent at the waist, and vomited copiously.

Every ounce of wine, every bit of food, everything he had in him and then some came splashing out on the stones. And when he could vomit no more, he spat words into the puddle of puke.

"I'm sorry," he whispered. "I'm sorry, I'm sorry, I'm sorry. I know, I know, I know. I'm sorry, I'm sorry, I'm sorry."

He crumpled against the wall, buried his face in his hands, and wept hot tears. Through his fingers, he could see the puddle of vomit begin to stir. From beneath the greasy surface a hand emerged, thin and delicate. An arm followed, gripping the stones of the street. Another arm followed and, between them, began to haul a body out of the puddle of bodily fluids.

She rose out of the vomit, dripping with his bile, and smiling broadly. Her eyes were huge. Her hair hung down to her shoulders. And her throat was cut open with a gash as big and terrifying as the smile she wore.

"Good morning, tall man," she said to him.

And he shut his eyes.

And he prayed to Silf. Or to Talanas. Or to anyone who would listen.

And when he opened them again, she was gone. And only a puddle of bile remained behind. He breathed slowly and forced himself to his feet. He wiped his mouth with the back of his hand. He forced a smile to his face.

And slowly, Denaos turned around and went back to the bar and when he opened the door, the word greeted him.

"RAMANIEL!"

TWENTY-ONE

SCENT OF GOD

Gariath raised his snout into the night air. He took a long breath and drew in the scent of everything wrong with the world.

The stink of humans was everywhere and everywhere stank of fear. There was no scent more common, and it reeked sickly sweet in his nostrils. It was an odor he had no use for, and he quickly ignored it.

He smelled anger, of course. He got that in short, stagnant bursts as he wandered through Cier'Djaal's lamplit streets. It seeped into his hood and burst at the back of his mouth as though he had just taken a bite of a lemon. It was a stronger odor than fear, but far too common to be helpful.

He was looking for a rarer scent. And he drew in breath upon breath to find it.

He found resentment: common. Resignation: depressingly common. Desire: alarmingly common.

All of them useless.

Then, suddenly, he caught it. Just a whiff, at first, but it bloomed into something overwhelming. The aroma of floors scrubbed by hands raw with labor, books burning on pyres, breath thick with fever and words. It was an aggressively stagnant aroma that hung in a narrow, thick trail through the odors of the city.

Faith.

Fanaticism.

Rare. Useful. Uniquely human.

Faith, being a concept, could not be smelled. But the primal reeks that went into it—desperation, despair, fear, and hate—always followed people that prayed. He had never scented it in another race. Only humans seemed capable of looking at a mess of stone and sand as this city and convincing themselves it was worth anything, let alone worth dying for.

He called this mess of scents faith. Or delusion. Same thing, really.

The Khovura, as the humans had named them, had reeked of it. He had smelled it in the bloodstains and broken bodies at the Souk yesterday. He had found it again today in a thick, twisting scent that wound through the city.

And he had followed it here, to a uniquely human creation.

The archway that loomed before him on the western edge of the Souk's back-alley streets was something that had probably been very grand in its day. Here was where it had stood proudly rounded before crumbling in the middle; there were pedestals for statues long stolen or smashed; overhead was where bold letters of a bold name had been carved in the stone before time and wind and sand and neglect had worn them away.

In its place was a big wooden sign tied with a rotting rope and daubed with greasy paint that read, in letters that smelled of low education and malnutrition...

SUMPS. NO GUARDS. NO GODS. NO PROBLEMS.

Straightforward. He appreciated that.

He leaned into the archway, peering past the meager torches halfheartedly sputtering light against the encroaching shadows. Beyond the sign, though, light didn't even bother. No orange glow of torches or lanterns met his eyes. Slivers of moonlight slipped like rats between crumbling buildings and cracked windows, chased by ever-shifting darkness.

The scents here were deep. Not old, but constant and seeping, embedded in damp earth and drowning under stale water. It was the reek of things broken and dying, but not yet dead and far from forgotten.

Something old. Something sodden. Something altogether not human.

Yet there, amidst the scent of hundred-year despairs and drowned ambitions, was the serpentine scent he had been tracking all day.

The Khovura had come this way.

Of course, Gariath knew, as he trod past the archway and into the shadows of this place, that his precious time could be better spent elsewhere. Such as tracking down Kharga and ripping his head off. However, over the past year with his companions, he had come to appreciate the nature of teamwork as he saw it—that is, forgoing ripping the head off of someone he really wanted to in lieu of ripping the heads off of people other people wanted him to so that they would shut up when he ripped the aforementioned head of the original desire.

For tonight, he could rip heads off on Lenk's behalf.

Such was his nature. He was a giver.

And so he set off into darkness, following the odious reek of hatred with the distinct intent of killing someone tonight.

Dry land gave out three steps into the Sumps. Water rose gradually, first to his ankles, mulling over his presence before it decided to rise up to his calves and then, embracing him like a brother, up to his thighs. That, he supposed, was where the Sumps got its name.

The ground was an uneven plane of sand and shattered cobblestones beneath his feet. He splashed awkwardly through the water, his every movement heralded by the churn of froth. Stealth was impossible.

Which was fine by Gariath. Stealth was for cowards who had too little sense to know when their time would be better spent coming out to be killed by him.

Besides, he reasoned, any water that came up to his thighs would be up to a human's waist. They would be as loud as he was. Not that he needed sound here.

Out of the corners of his eyes, he caught glimpses of orange fire-lights. Shy flickers that knew they didn't belong here; they darted away every time he looked toward them, dark shapes vanishing into shadows as the light fled. That was fine. He didn't need sight, either.

The other, cruder stinks were stronger here. Wet dreams mired in the sodden earth, despairs that hung in the shadows. He didn't need these. He had the pure scent of hatred to guide him, the twisted knot that coiled through the Sumps, guiding him ever deeper, growing ever stronger.

And leading him toward a light that did not flee.

He saw it there, a bright orange halo painted upon the wall of a long-decayed building, walls torn and windows smashed, whose decrepit shadow looked like a grimace most displeased about being exposed to such light. And painted upon that light were shadows, unmoving.

Either someone hadn't heard him or they had and just hadn't started running yet.

Sometimes, fate rewarded the charitable.

He picked up his speed, heedless of how obvious he was. The scent was powerful here, overwhelming, intoxicating. The orange light grew brighter as he approached, the scent of anger rising on the smoke of torches, and through the hiss and crackle of flames, the sound of voices was clear.

"You're in the wrong damn neighborhood, oid."

They were talking to someone. Not him. And there was a response. Without words.

The scent grew stronger. The anger grew purer.

"Sumps, Souk, or Silktown, Cier'Djaal belongs to *us*," a voice, bitter and moist, hissed. "You come here, you pay."

Gariath turned a corner and gave a shape to the voice. Short, skinny, dark against the torch in its hand and accompanied by three other figures, each one wearing the same kind of malicious glare upon their faces.

"You deaf, oid?"

Humans reeking of hatred.

No surprise there.

What was surprising was the creature they had cornered against the wall. Taller and leaner than they, gray skin covered in coarse silver fur and topped with a wild mane of hair the color of dull iron. A face, sloping and knotted with thick scars, stared back with yellow eyes.

A tulwar. That was what the humans had called it, wasn't it?

That was less surprising than what the tulwar was currently doing. Or rather, not doing. He stood, knee-deep in the water, long arms folded across a long chest, unmoving. Even his scowl, amber-clear and blade-sharp, was unflinching as it fixed itself upon the lead human.

The one reeking most strongly.

"You got blades. Been doing merc work? Must've made something." The man waded forward, hand extended demandingly. "Just pay up and you can—"

And then, the tulwar moved.

"Seamless," Gariath decided, was a good word to describe what happened next.

Without hesitation, the tulwar's fur-covered hand slid to the long, wrapped hilt at his side. Without a sound, he drew a heavy blade. And before he could blink, the human's arm was not so much hacked as unseamed, rendered from an appendage into a bloodless, flopping fish that wobbled precariously in the air before splashing into the water.

Between the moment the appendage vanished beneath the inky waves and the moment when the screaming began, the tulwar moved again.

His face flooded with a riot of yellows, reds, and blues. The tulwar erupted out of the water in a spray of froth and a flash of steel. His foes brought their blades up to meet his onslaught.

Theirs were short, clumsy things made for quick and dirty stabbings. His blade, long and lethal, cut clean through cloth and flesh.

But fear, common as it was, was a useful emotion. It drove them to rush at him, blades flashing, sending him back against the wall with a deep gash in his shoulder.

He took it without complaint. The blood from his wound seemed pale next to the bright colors of his face. Each lunge they took at him was deflected by the deftness of his cuts. Fear was a short-lived thing, and soon they exchanged nervous looks, suddenly wary of a foe that wouldn't die so easily.

And this would have all been very impressive to watch, Gariath thought, had he more time to appreciate it.

But the reek of anger and hatred, the scent of the Khovura, was almost choking here amidst the melee. One of these creatures knew something he would very much like to know for himself. Or rather, something one of the humans would like to know and something Gariath felt just motivated enough to kill to get.

Ordinarily it would seem rude to interrupt a good fight. But this was taking far too long.

Want something done right, Gariath thought to himself.

He let his cloak fall from him as he waded forward, still courteous enough to at least give them a *little* time to kill each other.

And to the tulwar's credit, his blade arced upward, a sheet of blood trailing the edge of his blade and a human folding, neat as a piece of paper, over a red line carved in his chest.

One of the humans, after watching his cohort vanish beneath the waters, turned to run. His head turned well after his body, and when he saw Gariath—his long, tooth-filled snout, his onyx eyes, his curving horns, and earfrills painted by torchlight—the human's eyes went wide.

Gariath was used to this.

Eyes wide first, yes, yes, he thought, *then the babbling lips trying to find words—yes, just like he's doing now—and then he'll finally say…*

"You're…you're…" the human sputtered, "you're a—"

"I am." Gariath placed a heavy hand on the man's head. "I'm also in a hurry."

Gariath jerked his arm down, shoving the human beneath the water. A mess of bubbles and froth was all that surfaced before he brought up a foot and stomped it down on what he thought was the human's neck. The sound of bone snapping was muted beneath the water. But an instant later, he felt it grow significantly warmer around his foot.

So, apparently that hadn't been the neck. Good to know. He would be happy to take better care of the remaining two.

The scent was still strong. The drowned one wasn't the one he was looking for. That left the human with one arm—desperately trying to cinch his belt around his stump to stem the blood loss—or the human with two, desperately trying not to die.

Against the wall, the two-armed human struggled with the tulwar. The long blade was high above their heads, all hands wrapped around its hilt as the human fought to keep it out of his skull and the tulwar insisted that it would look better there.

The tulwar's face was colored with fury, his muscles trembling beneath the fur covering his arms. His lips split apart in a feral snarl, simian teeth bared. In another four breaths, the human was going to be quite messily dead.

That would make what Gariath was about to do very rude, indeed.

He stalked forward, seizing both combatants by their shoulders. The tulwar, he shoved away. The human, he drew closer. He caught a glimpse of a dagger reaching for a hilt poking out of a belt. An instant later, he caught a tender wrist between his claws, gave a quick twist, and—

"*MY HAND!*" the human shrieked. "*YOU JUST BROKE—*"

"You probably didn't hear me when I said I was in a hurry," Gariath growled. "Let's pretend you've already called me a monster and then begged for your life, and get right to the good stuff."

He hoisted the writhing human by his shattered wrist, dangling him out of the water like a pale, shrieking worm on a hook.

"You reek of the Khovura," he said. "Two chances to tell me where they are."

And Gariath got the first surprise of the night.

"You're after the Khovura?" the human laughed hysterically. "And you want *me* to tell you about them? Right." His grin was broad with manic terror. "You're just a monster. And the Khovura are—"

"Again," Gariath said, "in a hurry."

His hand found the human's throat. His arm found the room to swing. And, in short order, his captive's face found the nearby wall. A bright red halo spattered against the brick. An unmoving body peeled off of rock and slid beneath the water, sputtering crimson bubbles.

Gariath turned and looked to the human with one arm. He was cowering against another wall, clutching his stump. Even if he hadn't been ghost-white with blood loss, Gariath would have sensed him.

Because the scent that came from him as the dragonman pointed at him was definitely not anger.

"Same offer," Gariath said. "Speak quickly."

"S-*same*?" the human sputtered. "You said two chances!"

"I did," Gariath replied, gesturing to the blood-smeared wall. "That was your first one."

"I...I've seen men," the one-armed one stuttered. "Not from the Sumps, like us. Black clothes, hanging near the Harbor Wall on the northwest end. They come every night and are gone by morning. That's all I know."

Gariath nodded, jerked a thumb in no particular direction. "Go."

"My arm..." the human whimpered.

"If it loves you, it'll come back." His lips curled back, exposing rows of teeth suggestively. "*Go.*"

The human took off as fast as a one-armed human with severe blood loss wading through smelly water could. Which, when Gariath was around, turned out to be rather quick. In his wake, he left a few scents, most of them foul and fleeting.

The reek of anger and hatred lingered, strong as ever.

And all the humans were dead or dying.

"You let him go."

Gariath turned around and beheld the tulwar. The creature's color faded from his face with each ragged breath he took, leaving behind the knotted gray flesh beneath a wild mane of hair. Blood painted the gray fur on his body, but Gariath hardly noticed.

The scent of rage from this creature was overwhelming.

"I would not have," he said, voice rigid as the blade he held in his hands.

"If you want to go finish him, I don't think he's gotten very far," Gariath replied. "He was yours to kill, anyway. I just needed him for a moment."

The tulwar shook his head. He flicked blood from his blade and slid it back into its sheath. Heedless of the wound in his shoulder or the bodies floating in the water around him, the tulwar offered a short, stiff bow from the waist.

"It was an honor to have watched you kill." The rigidity of his stance was in his voice, as well, every word forced out with slow precision. "I had only heard stories and rumors."

About me?

Gariath couldn't keep the surprise off his face. Not that such information was *entirely* surprising. The *Rhega* were, after all, the stuff of legend.

Or at least the stuff of mass panic. That was almost as good.

"The outer city sings of your deeds in the Souk." The tulwar's eyes lit up: tiny, angry stars in the darkness. "The vulgore, the saccarii, the couthi, and my people all speak of the dragonman that defeated his own kind."

Gariath's earfrills twitched. "You mean Kharga? What do you know of the *Drokha*?"

"That is your word for them?" the tulwar asked. "We call them other things. Hounds of the fashas. Swallowers of gold. They take the humans' coins to keep the other races in check. We know they are our enemies. We know they cannot be harmed."

He grinned, all fangs and hatred.

"Until yesterday."

The reek was all around Gariath now, in his nostrils, in his eyes, in his ears. It was palpable, roiling off of the tulwar with every breath. A hatred too well-tempered, too finely sharpened to seem fitting on this creature.

This creature before him was strong, proud. Hatred was supposed to be something he merely felt from time to time, not something he honed, not something he practiced. That kind of hate, that keenly scented reek, was something that belonged to humans.

That's how it should *be, anyway*, Gariath thought.

"You called them... *Drok-ha*?" The tulwar spoke the word hesitantly; it always sounded wrong coming from someone who wasn't a dragonman. "What do we call you, then?"

"Gariath."

"That is your name or the name of your race?"

Gariath stared at him flatly. His voice escaped in a bitter growl.

"It no longer matters."

The tulwar nodded, stiffly. He tapped two long fingers to his hairy, gray chest. "Daaru. Saan Rua Tong."

So many names, Gariath thought. *Who needs more than one?*

Even though he knew the answer already.

"You hunt the Khovura?" Daaru asked. "The footwar is a human problem."

"I decided it was mine," Gariath said. "The building the human mentioned. Where is it?"

"I can show you."

"You can tell me, just as easily."

"The tulwar owe you a debt for striking against the *Drokha*."

"That's my fight. Not yours," Gariath growled.

"No tulwar fights alone," Daaru said. "All tulwar share blood. And tulwar blood spilled is tulwar blood avenged."

"I am not a tulwar."

"No. You are *shkainai*. Foreign. You don't know where you're going and you don't know what the Sumps are like." Flashes of color appeared across his face. "And I am still tulwar. I do not leave when I am needed." He pointed at Gariath. "You need me."

It was easy enough for Gariath to figure out why he wanted to hold the tulwar under the water until he stopped struggling. He was presumptive, insistent, and overall far too convinced of his own worth. All qualities Gariath found could be easily cured by violence.

Less easy was figuring out why Gariath wasn't moving to do just that. There was something about the tulwar that he found too hard to throw away. The earnestness in his yellow eyes, maybe; the very real, very obvious belief that he was absolutely right, no matter how stupid he sounded.

The stink of faith. Daaru was a fanatic, but not a human fanatic.

Gariath found it slightly irritating just how easy it was for him to accept that.

He said nothing. No request for help, no invitation to come along, no forbidding warning to stay behind. He merely turned around and began walking in the direction he thought was northwest. If the tulwar wished to come, Gariath would not stop him.

He heard nothing. Not the sound of another pair of legs wading through the water behind him. Not the chatter about subjects like family, honor, bloodshed—subjects the tulwar seemed to think he knew about.

But he couldn't help smelling. The scent of anger off the tulwar, a well-aged, hundred-year hatred, was impossible to ignore. It was pungent. It was pervasive.

And it was so terribly human.

⊷⊶⊷

In the utter silence of a city long drowned, Gariath still couldn't hear them.

He could see them, or flashes of them, anyway. Brief flickers of torches and lanterns, dancing like witchlights before fading into darkness. Faces peering around the corners of ravaged buildings and rotted-out stalls, disappearing the moment he glanced in their direction.

But never once did they make a sound. Even in the ever-present water of the Sumps, those watching him never made so much as a splash.

And they never lingered long enough for him to get their scent.

"Cowards," he muttered.

"Survivors," Daaru corrected. "When humans were just gluttonous instead of glutted, this was Cier'Djaal, the outer city. They built the buildings you see here and were content to live in the shadow of the sea." He pointed to the ground. "But they built it in a valley that was too low. The first Harbor Wall broke years ago and let in the sea. And when their buildings were ruined, they moved to dry land and built bigger."

"The Souk?"

"And Silktown. And Temple Row. What they call the inner city today. The outer city is where they throw out their undesirables: Shicttown and the harbor."

"And the Sumps?"

"Are where the outer city throws *its* undesirables," Daaru said. "Cier'Djaal is a great, devouring beast. The Sumps are where it throws its scraps. And so, its scavengers grow large." He waved a hand. "But they are not cowards. Most are saccarii and other unwanteds, willing to seize any opportunity to survive. Opportunists."

"There is no difference."

"A coward is craven out of opportunity," Daaru said. "A rat is craven out of necessity. There is little to fight over here in the Sumps."

"Then why are you here?"

"Because where my people come from, there is even less."

"Then go elsewhere."

Daaru hesitated, looking over his shoulder. "You have never seen civilization before, have you, Gariath?"

"Human words are of no concern to me."

"Nor any of us," Daaru replied, chuckling. "We were content to live in our deserts, grow rice, hunt, and ignore the humans. But humans hate to be ignored. So they build their cities, they take our rice, they hunt our game, and offer to sell our own property back to us at a generous discount."

His lips peeled back in a sneer. "So we played their game. We traded our rice for their gold, our strength for their steel. And once we began to amass power of our own, they changed the rules. They brought in the *Drokha* and put us down."

"You hate the humans, then."

"Who doesn't?"

"Then why stay in their city? Why not fight them?"

"I need to eat."

"Then stay out in the desert. Starve and die with dignity."

"And my children?" Daaru asked. "My grandmother? My wife? If the fashas do not bat an eye when I die with dignity, will they suddenly see a dozen dead tulwar and feel sympathy?" He shook his head. "I play their game. I survive."

"It's not enough for you to just survive."

"No." Daaru sighed. "It's enough that the tulwar survive."

It was, at that point, that Gariath decided that he didn't like Daaru.

Daaru was a coward who skulked at the heels of the humans and ate what scraps they threw him. Daaru was a weakling who had been tainted by humans to have their scents blended with his. Daaru was a pretender who spoke of strength, but never used it.

This is what Gariath told himself.

But that was not what Gariath knew.

Daaru was the coward who collected scraps for family and people. Daaru was the weakling whose hatred was strong because he must keep it controlled. Daaru was the pretender who spoke of strength and never had to use it.

Daaru Saan Rua Tong, tulwar, father, husband, warrior, was someone Gariath, long ago and in another life, had been. Someone who Gariath had dearly enjoyed being.

This was what Gariath knew.

But that was not what Gariath told himself.

"How much farther?" he asked.

In response, Daaru came to a halt. With one hand resting on the pommel of his blade, he pointed out to a distant shape.

Remarkable only because it was merely decrepit instead of a standing ruin, the building loomed large over the rest of the Sumps. Retaining most of its windows—albeit all of them at least cracked— and with its roof caved in only on one side, it looked a far sight better than the rest of the drowned outer city. Even the moon seemed less disgusted by its presence, a silver glare peering through the gloom overhead to light it.

And that's when Gariath saw the chains. Crossed over a door that looked far too solid to belong here, two dozen iron links were secured upon the door with a large, impressive-looking lock.

Suspicious enough, even without the lingering scent of fear around it.

He began to approach without a care for the sloshing of his steps, pushing past Daaru, who merely watched him.

"The saccarii say not even a serpent slithers in the Sumps without someone knowing about it," the tulwar warned. "They may know you're coming."

"Good," Gariath replied, coarsely. "This will be quick, then."

"Wouldn't it be wiser to wait? Scout it out first?"

Gariath paused and drew in a deep breath.

"There are people in that building that I intend to kill. If I can't, then I will die. I *could* wait. But it wouldn't tell me anything I didn't already know. Live or die, I have to go eventually."

He snorted.

"So, we might as well be messy about this."

He had hoped that would keep Daaru back. But he heard the sloshing feet behind him. Daaru was not staying behind.

That bothered him.

He approached the lock on the door and held it in his palm. The finer points of locksmithing had never been his strong suit— mostly because he had never cared about the duller points of locksmithing—but he knew a few things. He knew how to spot a well-made, mostly new lock, as he did then. And he also knew the surefire way to open any lock, as he was about to demonstrate.

Once I can find a big enough rock, he thought.

"Gariath," Daaru said from behind.

Or a thick enough head.

"GARIATH!"

He whirled around, ready to deliver a cursing and possibly a beating for good measure, but thought better of it.

He probably wouldn't have been heard over the sound of the giant rampaging through the water toward him, anyway.

The darkness kept him from knowing exactly what it was, but there was no darkness deep enough to hide its size. Tall as a tree, wide as a boulder, something huge came loping toward him on two massive arms and a pair of thick, short legs. Walls of water erupted with each massive stride, froth churning in its wake. Sand and stone were flung aside by arms big as trees.

It was impressive.

Not impressive enough that Gariath didn't leap out of its path, but still.

The behemoth smashed into the doors with the rattle of chains and the crumble of stone. Bricks came loose and fell around the creature as it slowly turned to face Gariath, settling on the knuckles of immense hands.

"Kudj acknowledge perceived cowardice of ambush," a thundering voice spoke. "Being honest, Kudj surprised Kudj not noticed earlier."

Gariath recognized this creature. He knew the massive, bulky frame. He knew the chitinous horn jutting from the center of his brow. He knew the sigil worn on the creature's harness.

"Perhaps squibs not blame Kudj when Kudj make milk's meat out of them." The vulgore reared back on his stumpy legs, raising his giant arms over his head. "Perhaps squibs blame own lack of awareness."

His fists came crashing down and Gariath was forced to leap

backward again. Frothy geysers erupted, sending waves roiling strong enough to force Gariath to fight to keep his footing.

A smile leapt to the dragonman's face. He felt his claws twitch, his blood rush, his wings draw tight against his back. The water beat against his legs as he walked toward the monster. The earth felt unsteady beneath his feet as the behemoth lumbered toward him.

That was fine. He didn't think about the water, the earth, or just how small he was in comparison to his foe. He had enough of thinking and feeling.

It was time to let violence solve everything again.

"Wait!"

Starting with Daaru.

The tulwar leapt in front of the behemoth, arms thrown out to the side.

"Stand aside, vulgore!"

"Kudj not paid to stand aside," the vulgore said.

"We have no wish to fight you."

"Kudj lament resort to violence. Kudj always thought true career choice would lie in cooking." The vulgore raised a massive arm. "Harsh economy makes demands of Kudj, though."

The most self-righteous gnat in the world, Daaru was swatted. He flew into the darkness, his cry ending in an unceremonious splash. Gariath suspected he ought to feel worse for not having tried to help. And he *knew* he ought to feel worse for smiling.

And he promised he would, right after he took care of this.

Kudj lumbered forward with an air of boredom, likely not at all convinced that even a dragonman could pose a serious threat. That was fine; Gariath had killed much bigger than him.

He rushed Kudj as the vulgore raised a massive fist, and darted aside as it crashed down. The ground shook, the waves roiled; these were concerns for people who reeked of fear.

Gariath's nostrils were filled with the scent of dirty water, the aroma of dying buildings and, as he slipped around the behemoth and leapt upon a colossal back, the scent of blood.

If the howl that followed was any indication, Kudj was no longer bored.

Gariath scaled the vulgore's spinal column like a ladder, wrenching his claws as he jerked them out of thick red flesh, twisting them as he plunged back in. Kudj shuffled beneath him, massive red arms swinging around him; Kudj roared, stomped, groped in a desperate effort to dislodge him.

And Gariath crawled inexorably up toward the neck. Like the rest of the vulgore, it was thick and covered in a dense rhinoceros hide. But amidst the flailing and the gnashing and the blood staining his hands and feet, Gariath could see his chance. A thick rope of muscle connected the shoulders to the skull, big and bulging and begging to be severed.

And Gariath, ever the giver, moved to oblige it.

His jaws opened, he leaned forward.

There was a great spurt of blood as he was pried off the vulgore's back, a writhing tick between five massive fingers. He clawed blindly at Kudj's hand for a moment before the behemoth roared, snapping his arm forward and dashing the dragonman upon the ground.

His bones rattled against the earth. Sound, scent, and sight vanished as he plunged beneath the water. Something inside him that should be solid felt loose and liquid.

He couldn't see Kudj's fist. But he felt it as it slammed into the ground right beside him. He supposed Kudj couldn't see him, either. Not that one needed to see too well when one's fists were the size of hogs. He could hear the muffled slam, feel the shock through his body as the fists came down over and over, each time narrowly missing him as he scrambled blindly beneath the water.

The pounding stopped for a moment. He rolled onto his back. Through the wavering moonlight, he saw the behemoth's simian face leaning down to peer beneath the shuddering surface.

Gariath came howling out of the water, froth and claws and blood rising up to attach to the vulgore's horn. The behemoth reared back, taking Gariath with him. The dragonman clawed at the behemoth's face, bit at his cheeks, kicked at his chest. He felt the warmth on the behemoth's breath, the spittle in his howl, the blood torn from his face.

And in another instant, he felt the sky.

The vulgore ripped him off with barely a flinch, seizing him in both hands and hurling him.

Gariath felt his wings flapping for purchase before he skidded against the water and slammed against the brick-and-lumber remains of a long-dead building in a shudder of stone. Whatever had come loose inside him now rattled around in his chest. When he coughed, it burned and his mouth tasted of copper.

He staggered to his feet, half-surprised that he was able to without being ground into paste. Kudj merely stood, resting on his massive knuckles, looking at Gariath with an inscrutable expression.

"You're bleeding," the dragonman snarled. "Step aside before you lose more."

"Kudj have lots of blood. Squib can have more, if he need." The vulgore shifted on his knuckles, peering at the dragonman. "Why not squib run? Squibs always run from Kudj. Make guard duty much more preferable than squish-dependent jobs."

"What you're guarding is something I'm willing to kill for." He sneered. "Do they pay you enough to die for it?"

"Kudj not privy to rationale behind fasha decision," the vulgore rumbled. "Kudj not even know what Kudj guard. But Kudj sure it not worth more blood." He pointed a massive finger over Gariath's head. "Squib go. No more blood today."

"Gariath disagree," the dragonman growled.

He took a step forward. It hurt.

It shouldn't hurt, he said inwardly. *You're* Rhega. *The strongest. You've fought demons. You've killed things that should not be. Why does this hurt so much?*

And as he took another step, as he felt that ache in his chest, he realized. Months ago, that spot had been empty, possessed of a comfortable numbness that sat quietly in his chest and waited for him to die. Now, something inside him wanted to live, wanted him to feel the pain and turn around and run.

Fear?

No. Fear was something cold to move weaklings. Whatever this was, it was warm, it was painful, and it was immensely annoying.

And whatever it was, he resolved not to let it get in the way of killing himself. He lowered his head and ran toward the vulgore, biting back the pain shooting through him.

Kudj settled squarely on his stumpy legs and sighed.

"Always violence," he grunted. "Kudj often feel like tiny posy, blown about by cruel winds of demand economy." He raised his hands and cracked his knuckles. "But, if squib wants—"

He stopped talking right about then.

It turned out that it was more difficult with a thick iron chain around his neck.

Daaru appeared atop the behemoth's shoulders, the chains from the door drawn tight in his hands, wild color painting his face as he bared his teeth in a savage snarl. Kudj flailed beneath him, staggering back and forth, torn between the need to smash and the need to breathe.

Daaru jerked hard on the chains, steering the behemoth toward Gariath. The dragonman backed up as Kudj staggered closer until his wings struck the outcropping he had been hurled against. The massive vulgore swung his head, throwing Daaru from his back. But the tulwar held fast to the chains, dangling from the vulgore's neck. For a moment, Gariath got the impression of a large, unruly cat with a fleshy, colorful bell dangling from its collar.

But only for a moment. In another breath, all he could see was the opportunity.

He leapt, seizing the chains and hauling Daaru back down to earth. He could feel his muscles strain and threaten to rip as he and Daaru dragged the gasping, flailing behemoth toward the wall of the ruined building. Chain in hand, Gariath leapt over it, suspending himself over the water as the chains pulled taut upon the wall's edge.

He braced his feet against the stone. He tightened his grips on the chain. He roared. He pulled. Hard.

And the stone shook beneath him.

He felt the chains shudder. He felt his body ablaze with the effort. He felt the bricks of the wall come loose as the chain pulled the behemoth's face into the wall and smashed it against the stones. Gariath gritted his teeth. He bit back the pain in his chest.

And he pulled again.

And again.

And again until dust clogged his nostrils and the stones lay in a crumbled heap and his palms bled. And when he dropped the chain into the water, Kudj lay before him. The chains hung loosely around his neck as he rolled onto his back and groaned. His eyelids fluttered against a face riddled with embedded chunks of lumber and stone fragment. He drew in deep, desperate breaths.

But he did not move.

Nor did Daaru.

The tulwar stood, staring at the dragonman with eyes wide, color fading from his face.

"No one has ever done that to the vulgore," he gasped, looking at the ruin of bloodied stone. "No one has ever done... *that*."

"Uh-huh," Gariath grunted.

He stepped over Kudj's massive arm and past Daaru, toward the building. The door hung off its hinges; the lock lay smashed where Kudj had rammed it. Fine steel, strong metal, and it lay in pieces now. Had Gariath just been a tad slower, tripped just a little, that might be him.

It might still be him on the inside, for all he knew. The pain in his chest hadn't grown any softer. He hurt. He bled. All for what was behind this door.

Kicking it open would have been dramatic.

Also painful.

Gariath settled for just shoving it, watching it collapse inward. Inside, darkness reigned. Moonlight seeped through shattered windows in thin slivers, choked by crumbling support beams and hanging mold. The ground was sodden and sandy, rising only a finger's length above the water.

And his nostrils were filled with the reek of death.

The third step he took was met with a thick squishing sound. He looked down. The stains on the sand were darker than water, darker than even the night. Blood. Lots of it.

He heard something in the darkness, the sound of slurping and chewing. He proceeded carefully. It didn't matter. What lurked in the darkness wasn't paying any attention to him.

A thick head attached to a bulbous body supported on eight spindly legs bent over a mess that glistened in the moonlight, eagerly slurping thick, quivering strands into a pair of mandibles.

Gariath wasn't sure what it was—the way he unconsciously backpedaled, the way he unconsciously gagged—that made the spider aware of his presence. But the creature twisted its thick head, turned eight bulbous eyes upon Gariath, and made a chittering noise that sounded almost embarrassed. Despite the fact that it was the size of a horse, the spider skittered away like a frightened child, scrambling up the wall and disappearing out a window to a pair of waiting servants, who quickly disappeared with it.

"W-work..."

A voice.

Weak, soft, pitiful. Yet in the silence, unignorable. Gariath looked down to the quivering mess the spider had been feasting upon. And the quivering mess stared back, still alive.

"They promised us work."

Not at him, though. The eyes that looked up hadn't closed in days; they were pried open and blind with terror. The voice that spoke to him was hoarse; it had screamed itself raw and red long ago. The body that lay before him was merely half a human; whatever else there had been had since disappeared down the spider's gullet.

"They... they promised us work."

Gariath knelt down beside the man. From the waist up, he was human. Wrapped in a dirty tunic, a wrist shackled to a nearby support beam, he looked fine but for the terror that had been carved into his face. From the belly down, everything that he was was red and glistening, flesh and sinew stripped away in a messy aftermath of a glutton's feast.

"Gold," the human whispered. "Fasha Ghoukha...he had so much, they...they said just go into the building...locked us in, said it was for the silk. They watched us...watched it...watched..."

The last of the human's voice bubbled out on a thin trail of saliva. His lips twitched numbly, speaking silent words to ghosts. In the gloom behind him, Gariath could see half a dozen others like him. Worse than him. Devoured completely, ripped apart with a child's delight, the less palatable bits left for smaller scavengers.

Clinking chains brought his attention back down. The man's shackled wrist groped blindly against the sand. It brushed against Gariath's knee and stiffened with a needy reach. Slowly, Gariath touched the man's hand. And instantly, he could feel the heat drain from it, all the desperate warmth of a dying man vanishing into the darkness and leaving behind something cold and half-eaten.

As though he had been holding on through the entire feast just for this touch.

Maybe there was more to the human than this cold meat before him. Maybe he had a family he needed to feed. Maybe he needed money to feed himself. Maybe he once had a face that wasn't frozen in fear, eyes that could still see, mouth that could still speak.

But Gariath couldn't tell anymore.

When he looked down, he could see only meat that should have been human. In his head, he could see other humans—*his* humans—made out of the same meat, dying cold and alone with only the touch of someone they couldn't see to comfort them in their time of death. When they died, he wondered, would they die the same way? Would they leave behind the same cold meat?

And leave him alone?

They were weak. They were pitiful. They were not *Rhega*. But they were more than meat. To him, they were much more. And he knew how much that realization should bother him, but he did not feel it.

He rose to his feet without realizing he'd moved. His feet felt numb and senseless as he waded out into the water. His earfrills couldn't hear anything as Daaru assailed him with questions. And his hands were cold when he reached down and gently took the sword from Daaru's scabbard.

All he could feel now was the pain in his chest. The pain that had grown worse when he saw the cold meat, when he realized that humans could do this to each other, when he realized that the human back there could be any human. His humans.

All he felt was pain. Not the water around his legs as he walked toward Kudj's prone body. Not the sword in his hands as he raised it over his head. Not the dryness of his unblinking eyes as he stared intently at the vulgore's throat.

"Gariath."

Daaru said his name. He couldn't hear that. He tightened his grip on the sword.

"Gariath, stop."

Daaru put a hand on his shoulder. He couldn't feel that. He brought the sword down swiftly.

"STOP!"

Daaru slammed his fist squarely between Gariath's shoulder blades. He felt that. The sword fell from his hand. And his hand whirled around to strike the tulwar against his face and sent him twirling into the water. Daaru made to rise but stopped as the dragonman leveled a finger at him.

"Don't." Gariath spoke flatly. "Don't get up. I will kill you."

"And him, as well?" Daaru asked, color rising in his face. "What did you see there?"

"People. Humans. Made into meals for monsters. There are some things in this world no one should die for." He glanced back at Kudj, reached for the sword. "And there are some things they should…"

"Don't," Daaru growled, beginning to rise.

"Go and see it if you're not convinced. Just don't expect me to wait."

"You can't kill him!"

"I assure you, I can."

"You let that human go when I should have killed him," Daaru snarled, hauling himself to his feet. "He tried to kill me. For money. You'd let a human go but kill a vulgore?"

"That was different." Gariath plucked up the sword, raised it again, closed his eyes. "This is different."

"It *is* different," Daaru cried out as the sword came down. "*HE'S ONE OF US!*"

A hairbreadth from the vulgore's neck, the blade stopped. The steel grazed the flesh with each labored breath Kudj took. But Gariath couldn't bring it down, just as he couldn't shut his earfrills to the tulwar.

"He's one of us," Daaru repeated. "He plays the humans' game. Look at his harness. Look at the sigil. He works for Ghoukha. Fasha. Human. We all do. We don't have a choice. Neither did he." His voice lowered. "He has nothing else."

The next thing Gariath heard was the splash of the sword dropping into the water. The sound of his own voice was strange to him. It was full of fury earlier, but now it sounded hollow, empty.

"Nothing," he repeated. "He has nothing."

"None of us do," Daaru replied. "We do what we can."

"Do what? Watch the humans feed each other to spiders? Beg for their gold while they make you do it? What life is that?"

"The only one we've got."

This place was ill. This world was diseased. These people were sick. And here he was, in it all, with his humans, the ones he was willing to kill for, the ones he was willing to bleed for. They wanted to come here. They wanted to live here. They wanted to stay here and grow as sick as the rest of them.

This, he realized, was the pain in his chest.

It was this city. It was this world. It was these humans. And this was what their illness was doing to him.

Without a word, he turned away. Without a scent to follow, he began to walk out of the Sumps, back toward the world where the humans pretended they weren't ill.

"Where are you going?" Daaru called after him.

"I am going to get a better life."

He could hear the water sloshing behind him as Daaru followed. "How?"

And when he spoke again, he could hear the fury in his voice. "By taking someone else's."

TWENTY-TWO

THE SUN AND ALL
ITS CHILDREN

Before she knew anything else, she knew she was warm.

For a very long time, she was content to feel only that, unwilling to open her eyes and admit that the night had ended. She felt it on the pelt beneath her, baking atop hard-packed sand. She felt it in the shafts of sunlight seeping in through the tears in her tent. She felt it in the *sosha* she had drunk settling contentedly in her belly.

It was the warmth of the glutted lion that bade her to forget things like morning and remember only the feast of the night before. The fires she had danced around with the khoshicts, the roar of the songs she had sung, the *sosha* dribbling down her chin. There was still a chill in her, though. That which came before the hunter put an arrow through the lion's gullet.

That which she had felt every morning she awoke next to him.

She resolved, groggily, to forget those mornings, as well as this one, and reached down to pull the furs up over her.

She found no furs upon her leg. Instead, her fingers brushed across flesh, bare, tense, and far warmer than hers.

Her eyes snapped open and stared into a pair of broad canines seated in a long blade of a smile.

Her first instinct was to leap to her feet and scramble away: impossible, what with the weight settling down upon her. Her second was to lay a fist into those teeth; even more difficult, what with her arms trapped beneath the legs straddling her. Her third was to scream and curse.

But she wasn't about to give Kwar the pleasure.

"How long have you been there?" she asked, keenly aware of how weak her voice sounded in a suddenly dry mouth.

"Good question." Kwar hummed, settling back on her haunches as her weight came down on Kataria's belly. "Maybe an hour?"

"I find that amazingly disturbing."

"Because you have no sense of commitment." Her grin stretched a little wider. "Except when it comes to drinking, anyway. I'm surprised you're still standing." She glanced down at the paler shict pinned beneath her and coughed. "I mean, figuratively. Either way, you act like you've never had *sosha* before."

"I haven't." Her voice felt uncomfortable in her throat, reluctant to pass her lips. "We never had any drink in the Silesrian."

"Really?" Kwar leaned down, peering far too intently at Kataria, as though the truth of that statement lay somewhere up her nostril. "My mother gave me my first taste of it when I went on my first hunt."

"Well, mine *didn't*," Kataria snapped, fighting the urge to crane her neck up and bite the khoshict's nose.

"I still use her recipe." Kwar's eyes glittered with the same predatory mischief in her smile. "Did you like it? Be honest."

"It was good."

"*Just* good?"

"You told me to be honest."

"I meant honest in a way that made it clear you were completely blown away by my magnificent prowess at fermentation."

"I was enjoying it a lot more before this part," Kataria snarled. She tried to tug her arms free and found them still firmly pinned between her sides and Kwar's legs. "Get off."

In response, Kwar drew her legs tighter and placed her hands on her hips. "Not until you say it. Say I'm a mistress of fermentation."

"You're a mistress of fermentation." Kataria clenched her teeth and felt her spine go rigid beneath her as she struggled more. "Get *off.*"

"No, not like that. Say it like you mean it. Poetic-like." Kwar rocked as Kataria squirmed beneath her, but looked otherwise inattentive as she scratched her chin thoughtfully. "Say that I'm as skilled as the canniest trapper, if my quarry were yiji-milk. Or, something like—"

"I said *GET OFF!*"

Both shicts were surprised. At the anger in Kataria's roar, at the sudden buck of her body beneath Kwar, at the way she hurled the khoshict and sent her tumbling to the sandy floor.

Kataria shot up onto her rear end and, as if it had been waiting until she was awake enough to appreciate it, the headache hit her. A slow, steady drum pounded in her skull, her body was painfully tense, and her heart beat with a terror that she was only now aware of.

But she could feel it as keenly now as she could a couple of days ago in the Souk, when they had seized her and called her a monster.

Only now, there was no warm body beside her to at least pretend to seek comfort from.

And so she leaned forward, placed her head in her hands, and pretended that the pain in her head was the worst thing she was feeling.

Against the pain in her head and the terror in her heart, she could only barely feel Kwar's touch as her fingers brushed timidly against her shoulder. Faint, too, was the khoshict's voice, the mischief fled from between her teeth and leaving something small and soft behind.

"Sorry," she whispered. "I'm sorry."

Kataria wanted to say something to that. Something soothing, like: "*It's all right. I'm fine. I'm perfectly okay.*" But there were only so many lies she could tell herself in a day, let alone in one morning.

"I...I went too far, didn't I?" There was tenderness to Kwar's voice starkly at odds with her hardness, the qualities that made her seem like a shictish legend. "I do that, sometimes. I don't really pay attention and I don't listen to other people. Thua says our mother was like that. He says it'll hurt me someday."

Her hand grew bolder, fingers sliding across Kataria's skin to let her palm come to a gentle, easy rest upon her shoulder.

It felt warm.

"I don't know what happened to you out there, in the humans' city," Kwar said. "But you're with us now. You're with your own. The humans are somewhere else, in their own world. This one is ours. Mine and yours."

Just a slight tension. A simple curl of the fingers. A gentle grip upon Kataria's shoulder. Kwar did nothing more than squeeze.

And the warmth became something else.

"But if you want me to go, I will."

The sand shifted as Kwar rose beside her. Her fingers began to slip from Kataria's shoulder. A chill set in.

And once again, both shicts were surprised as Kataria's hand reached out, seized Kwar's.

And did nothing more than squeeze.

⊶ ⊷

She stepped out into the sunlight and walked among her people.

Or so she had been told, anyway.

They certainly *looked* like her. Their skin and hair were darker than hers, their eyes sharper, but the people going about their business around her were, indeed, shicts.

There were grandmothers and grandfathers, weathered and gray, smoking pipes outside their tents. There were beast tenders, whispering soothing words to the horse-tall, hump-backed, snaggle-toothed yijis they guided through the sandy streets to picket-corrals. And the pups of shicts and yijis alike ran screaming and laughing through the streets in a singular, unruly pack.

There were muscular young men and women returning with bows and blades on their backs. Hunters, she recognized by their garb and hungry leanness. But they carried no snare or bait; nothing but their weapons and the wooden masks covering their faces.

Kwar had told her of them last night. A shict's nature was to hunt, but there was no traditional game in the city. So they made their food through coin and they made their coin through mercenary work. Cier'Djaal, after all, was just a different kind of wilderness.

And the kind of quarry that people paid to have killed was abundant within it.

"*Do you?*" she had asked last night.

"*Do I what?*" Kwar had asked in turn.

"*Kill people.*"

"*Hm. It's not easy to kill a human, is it?*"

"*Not as easy as it should be.*"

"*Yes. Very wily. It would take a terribly clever hunter to do such a thing.*"

"*I thought you were terribly clever.*"

"*Thank you. I thought so, too.*"

But they had spoken very briefly. That had been a night for dancing. These young hunters who came marching in, their faces hidden behind wooden masks, had been smiling last night, faces bright and alive with *sosha*-glutted vigor. Now, they scarcely looked like shicts.

But they were shicts.

And this *was* a shict camp.

The wooden buildings of Cier'Djaal's outer city had been burnt, smashed, or otherwise cleared away to open up a vast sandy field. Some sturdier timbers had been reappropriated to erect the tents or build pens for the yijis. The rest had mostly been used to fill in gaps in the walls segregating this section from the rest of the city.

This was Shicttown. She was a shict. These were her people.

So why weren't any of them talking to her?

They stopped and talked to Kwar, of course. Grandmothers would ask her how her brother was and she would assure them Thua was fine. Hunters would ask her what she thought of the coin they just brought back and she would say she had seen bigger. Children would ask her to chase them and she would tell them later, later.

And every one of them looked at Kataria, managed a weak smile, then squinted as their ears twitched, and turned away.

Without failure, deviation or alteration.

"They can't understand you."

She looked to Kwar, who gestured up to her own ears. Long, pointed, each length scarred with four neat, clean notches. A member of the eighth tribe, just like all of them.

"They reach out to you with their Howling," the khoshict said. "But yours is...strange. It screeches in a language they can't understand." Kwar sighed, smiling weakly. "It hurts their ears. So they turn away."

"Not yours?" Kataria asked.

"It does."

So, why are you still here?

Kwar froze, coming to a sudden halt as her ears pricked up, rigid as spears. For a short, curious moment, Kataria wondered if she had heard that thought. And for a much longer, terrified moment after, Kataria wondered what other thoughts she had heard.

But it soon became clear by Kwar's gaze, locked unerringly forward, that she had heard no thoughts.

At least none of Kataria's.

She followed the khoshict's stare. Thua stood before them, matching his sister's intensity with a barefaced glower. Without his mask, Kataria thought, he looked quite handsome. But his jaw remained too square, his chin too strong, eyes too dark, still too much like a human.

Still pretty, she thought.

And quietly hoped that the intense stare he cast her way didn't mean he had heard that.

But his gaze lingered on her only for a moment before flitting to Kwar. She held his stare there in hers, eyes narrowed to thin blades angled directly into her brother's forehead. Without speaking, without moving, without blinking, they stared at each other for a very long time.

Only their ears betrayed any sign of movement. They twitched, fluttered, trembled with skittish energy. Kwar's expression flickered, her braids dangling about her face as her ears twitched violently. Thua's jaw clenched, ears straining upright.

They were talking to each other, Kataria knew, through the Howling.

And she couldn't hear them.

When Kwar finally deigned to speak aloud, she was still bereft of words. Her ears folded flat against her head, her eyes were all but shut, and her lips curled back in an angry, bare-toothed snarl. She spat that noise, that anger, at her brother as she turned from him.

Her gaze lingered briefly on Kataria for a moment and in it, she felt the lingering traces of Kwar's fury turned upon her. Instinctively, as though just brushing the scantest hint of Kwar's Howling, her heart leapt in her chest and she tensed.

But just as quickly, Kwar's features softened with the gentle smile she offered as she laid a hand on her companion's shoulder and squeezed. She cast a final glower at Thua before stalking off, leaving Kataria alone with him.

"Where is she going?" Kataria asked.

"Away from me," Thua replied with a sigh. "She always gets this way when she knows Father wants something." He looked at her meaningfully. "And today, he wants to talk to you."

"Me? Why?"

"Well, given that you're a pale *shkainai* from the north who came here after being chased by the city guards and he's the chieftain concerned with our continued peaceable coexistence with the humans..." Thua shrugged. "Maybe he wants to borrow some smoke?"

If he's this sarcastic in the Howling, no wonder Kwar stormed off. At that thought, Kataria glanced over her shoulder. Kwar had found a ring of hunters and began to speak stiffly with them.

"She'll calm down, eventually," Thua said. He turned and beckoned her to follow him as he walked toward a distant tent. "She always does."

"Right," Kataria muttered, following. "It's just that I . . ."

"What?"

I'm worried that I probably should have said good-bye to her just in case your father finds out I'm a human-sniffing, not-a-shict who can't even hear the Howling and chases me out of your camp.

He didn't hear that.

It would have been easier if he had, though.

"I just wondered if I should have said something to Kwar," she went with, instead.

"You'll have your chance. If she likes you, she'll find you."

"She will?"

Thua's sigh was a little heavier. "She always does."

⊷ ⊷ ⊷

Sai-Thuwan was not the typical image of a shictish chieftain.

For one, he was wearing a shirt.

Her father had never worn a shirt.

Her father had been more hatchet than man: short, compact, every muscle tense as a flint blade beneath endless maps of scars and war paint. He had plaited his hair in a thick braid and his feathers had been wild: red, golden, black. All war feathers. All victory feathers. He never once wore a white mourning feather, not even when her mother had died.

And while Kataria had only known but one chieftain before this moment, she had always suspected most of them would look as legendary as her father. But Thuwan was long, lanky, and weary. His body was younger than those of the grandmothers and grandfathers in the camp, but his wrinkles were deeper and darker. His skin bore no scars, but his limbs creaked as he settled long elbows on long legs. His hair hung in a messy tangle about his face and he wore just one feather.

White.

Kataria watched him intently as he fixed his stare upon the tent floor. She could see where Thua got his features from: the strong jaw that clenched about the pipe stem, the big chest that grew bigger as he inhaled. But nowhere in Thuwan was there any of the twitching hardness, the feral life of Kwar.

This shict shrank with the force of his sigh. This shict's long hands trembled as he passed the pipe to Kataria. This shict's neck bent so low he didn't bother to look up as he spoke.

"The guards came back this morning," he said in a quiet voice.

"Ah," she said, accepting the pipe. "I should have been there. Sorry, I was…"

Don't say "trapped between your daughter's thighs."

"Drunk."

Good job.

Thuwan might not have heard her. Thuwan might not have cared. He waved a hand dismissively, but the smoke around him lingered.

"They left," he said. "We gave them *sosha* and hides and they did not press the matter."

"Thank you for that." She drew the pipe to her lips, tasted the weed in the wood. "For all of this. For last night, for the *sosha*, for the tent. I'm sure it would have been better for you to just turn me out into the city again."

She inhaled. The smoke was harsh; it burned her mouth and stung her throat as she held it in lungs that screamed at her to cough it out. She didn't, though. A real shict wouldn't do that. She was determined not to, either.

"It still would be."

Not until he said that, anyway.

The smoke came out in a hacking cough as she pounded her chest with a fist. Thuwan might not have noticed. Or he might not have cared.

"It took a lot of hides and a lot more *sosha*." Another sigh, growing in weight and weariness. "We have plenty of both, but it was still more than I preferred to give. They wanted you, *shkainai*. Badly."

She considered aplogizing. But it was more important, she knew, that she did not. Not for Thuwan, nor for his children or tribe. But for herself. She refused to apologize for not being given away to men who treated her like an animal.

"But it's only skins and liquor." Thuwan looked up for once. Dark eyes, sharp as blades in the deep scars of his wrinkles, peered at her as he smiled. "And there are too few shicts." He reached out for the pipe. "The price of living alongside the humans."

"So, why do it?" she asked, handing him the pipe. "Why live here?"

"They own the land. Outside of Cier'Djaal there is only desert." He shook his head as he took another puff. "Not only desert. There are tulwar. Some vulgore. Bandits, too, of all races and whatever else there is that wants to kill us. We would have to fight them for the desert, which gives nothing without a fight in the first place."

"There are no other shicts?"

"We're the eighth." He gestured to his ears. "The seventh and ninth are out there, somewhere."

"So why not band together? *Take* the land from the humans?"

"A bloody war that would leave both of us dead."

"So it's better that *you're* dead?"

"We're alive."

"But you live with them. You share their land, you *pay* them to be here. How long before you become them?" There was desperation in her words, as unstoppable as the words themselves. "You can't have both their land and your people. You can't play by their rules and still be a shict. You have to choose."

Like I did.

He paused mid-inhale. He held the smoke in his mouth thought-fully as he considered her across the firepit. When he spoke again, wisps of gray trickled out his mouth to rise delicately to the roof of the tent, veiling him in smoke.

"You are sixth tribe," he mused. "From the Silesrian? Who do you fight?"

"The humans," she replied.

"Which of them? There are many."

"Muraskans, Sainites, Karnerians. Any who touch the borders of the Silesrian."

"The Silesrian is called the Sea of Trees. There are tulwar tribes out there, as well."

"We have fought them."

"And the couthi?" he asked.

"Them, too."

"With the fourth and the fifth tribes?"

She shook her head. "Just the sixth."

"And what have you lost?"

"Nothing." A twinge of pride came creeping into her voice, growing bolder with each word. "Not a handspan of land has been yielded to the humans. The sixth holds."

"I am not talking about the sixth." Thuwan leveled the stem of his pipe at her. "I am talking about *you*, *shkainai*. The Silesrian is vast. Three tribes touch it and never see each other. There is room to wander, to roam, to disappear. But you are here, in your pale skin, among my people. So, I ask again . . ." He fixed eyes upon her. "What have *you* lost, Kataria?"

Her mouth hung open, bereft of words.

Because not a word entered her mind. Only a color.

White.

Like the feather they had handed her to weave into her hair when her mother's war band came back short one. Like the feather her father had refused to wear and never told her why. Like the feather she had left in a pair of hands and turned her back on and tried to ignore the last time someone stared at her the way Thuwan was staring at her now.

But those eyes had been blue.

She spoke no words. And Thuwan heard none. But his ears were upright, listening to something she spoke with another voice in another tongue. A language he understood. A language she thought she had forgotten.

"Ah." His ears lowered. "I see." He sighed and took another long inhale. "Just one. But far too much, isn't it?"

He blew out a cloud of smoke.

"We came here, once, as shicts. I was young, then. Kwar and Thua, even younger. And their mother, she was fierce. This is why she was chieftain before me. She traded with the humans, demanded their gold, their weapons for our hides. And she would never think to let them on our land. For their city was smaller, then. But humans hate small things. It reminds them of how small they are.

"So they came for our land. We fought. We fought their soldiers; we fought their dragonmen. My wife, Kwar's mother, she..." He lowered his head once again, clutched the back of it, as though he sought to drive it down and bury it in the earth. "So we lost ours. We made Shicttown. We trade with the humans in different ways. We trade lives now. We trade wars. For hides, they don't fight. For *sosha*, they don't come here.

"Thua does not blame me. But Kwar does. She hates me. She has not spoken to me in years. And every day I wake up and she does not speak to me, I know that I was right to do what I did. Because she is still alive to hate me and I still wear only one feather instead of two or three."

"But can you live with that?" Kataria suddenly became aware that she was only barely in her seat, ready to fall off. "How? How can you trade with them, be with them, and still be a shict? How can you live by their ways?"

"I don't. Not completely. No human has set foot in Shicttown since we created it. They never will. Because Shicttown is for *shicts*, not humans. I do not live for the humans, to kill them, to seek revenge. I live for my people, my wife, my Thua, my Kwar. Because we negotiate instead of fight, because we value lives more than pride, because we define ourselves and don't let our enemies or our fellow tribes do it, we are alive."

He was sitting straight as a spear now, his back rigid like an arrow. His eyes burned bright, alive, piercing the fog of smoke that hung between them.

"And we are still shicts."

But only for a moment.

"I will mourn for their mother until I meet her again in the Dark Forest," he said, collapsing back down. "And there was a time when I thought I could not stay here, without her. But I refuse to let the humans make me live for hate. I will live here. I will forever be a thorn in their side. My children will grow and live. And they will be more thorns. And soon, they will bleed enough to satisfy my wife."

But for as much as he shrank, for as weary and beaten as he seemed, she could sense something within him. A sound, the last noise of a dying animal. No words. No language. Nothing but instinct and emotion.

The Howling.

She could hear it.

So faintly, though.

Was it been because she had spent time in the company of shicts? Or was Thuwan right? Had it been there all along, waiting for her to realize she could use it, no matter whose body lay next to her in bed, no matter whose eyes stared at her?

Could she have been simply too convinced she wasn't a shict to realize she was, no matter whom she walked with?

Her head hurt. The smoke was too thick in here. She rose up with scarcely a word and walked to the flap of his tent. Without looking after her, Thuwan called out.

"Should I ask where you're going?"

She turned to him, stared silently. His ears pricked upright, hearing her.

He nodded once, turned back to his pipe, and proceeded to fill the tent with gray smoke as she left.

TWENTY-THREE

GENTLE NUDGES

Lenk knew their names.

My name is Aetros.

Because they were telling him.

I bled out in an alley and stained the mud red.

He knew how they died.

My name is Hargassus. I cut my fingers trying to pull the sword from my chest.

Because he remembered killing them.

My name is Langen.

He could remember their faces, twisted in fear and in pain.

I fell while running from you and you put your foot on my neck.

He could remember the wounds he painted on their bodies.

My name is Checho. I died screaming for my wife.

Men.

My name is Sharla. I tried to strangle you with my last breath.

Women.

My name is Gorle. I never wanted to rob anyone, but I needed money.

But not people.

When he walked past them, they were just bodies. They were bloodred wounds scored upon lifeless flesh. They were cloven skulls and missing arms and split-open chests. They were dead eyes staring out endlessly into the long, cold dark.

My name is Henju. I watched you kill my brother. Then I died with tears in my eyes.

He didn't stop to look at them. If he stopped, he would freeze to death. The darkness was cold. The darkness was everywhere.

There was nothing beneath his feet. There was nothing above his head. There was nothing beyond the rows of the dead marching in endless lines on either side. There was but darkness. Complete. Eternal. Cold.

He could see his breath as he trudged forward. He could feel it seeping up through his boots and into his veins. He could hear his skin cracking as his fingers went numb and turned black.

But he could not stop. If he stopped, he would freeze. If he froze, he would join them. He would forever be trapped in this cold, lightless hell, never again to have a warm body, to hear a warm voice. And so he kept moving.

And they did not stop talking.

My name is Waning. My name is Joge. My name is Kalri.

And they did not stop bleeding.

In the chest. Upon the plains. Couldn't stop screaming.

He was not a murderer.

Watched you walk away while I bled out. Begged for my life. Cursed your name, even if I didn't know it.

These were not innocent men and women he had cut down. These were villains. These were brigands, assassins, rivals. These were people who would have killed him just as swiftly. There was not an innocent among them.

My name is Arla. My name is Wil. My name is Gen.

But there were so many. Could they all have been guilty?

Could he say that his blade had never once been drawn in haste, that it had never once killed someone who didn't deserve it? Could he say that he was the innocent one here, when it was his blade that had painted them all red?

A small twinge of heat arose in his breast. It burned shameful, violent, painful. It had a light. It had a voice.

They deserved it.

Those words weren't his thoughts. Nor were they the voices of dead men. They were something worse. They were something— here where there should be nothing—heavy, meaningful, and ter- ribly warm.

Their deaths meant nothing.

Ahead, a pinprick of light split the darkness with a searing white.

Nor did she.

It erupted into an angry wound carved into the void.

There will be more ahead.

It opened up, consuming bodies and cold and him.

This, I promise you.

Lenk awoke to a chill on bare flesh, a burning breath in his throat, and a vision of pastel fruit in his eyes.

"You are alive." A voice strained to express surprise through monotone cadence. "You may erupt in rejoicement, if you so desire."

It was not a man that stood over him as he lay on the cold marble slab. It was a something. Something morbidly tall, wrapped in a black shroud, four bone-white limbs sliding from many sleeves. From behind a framed picture of fruit in a bowl placed delicately in front of a hood, the voice came again.

"Uncertainty is a quality clients do not find desirable, but this one must confess surprise that the procedure worked. You will desire to lie still for the moment."

Lenk disagreed.

His arms were numb and senseless as they flailed against the couthi's robe. His voice was a painful, wordless rasp in his throat.

One of the couthi's long limbs cradled his shoulders while another pressed a blue bottle to his lips. Water flooded past numb lips, cold in his burning throat.

"You have been without water for a day," the couthi said. "Humans require routine oral quenching to avoid catastrophic shriveling. Our diagrams confirm this." He released Lenk, leaving him the bottle. He turned to a nearby table rife with vials of varying shapes and sizes. "This one does not desire to push the limitations of human biology twice in one day."

Had Lenk heard it clearly, he likely would have been worried about that statement. But his thoughts were focused on the bottle. Every bit of him was consumed with ravenous thirst, leaving no room for fear or for wondering where he was or what had happened.

That came an instant later.

He saw, at first, his shirt lying crumpled next to his sword in a corner of a small stone cell with high, narrow windows. Not a cell, he realized; the windows were glass instead of bars; there was an archway instead of a door; and the various tapestries, furnishings, and portraits hanging from the walls made for surprisingly tasteful décor, as far as prisons went.

Beyond the whole "waking up half-naked with a couthi poring over a table full of strange liquids" aspect, it wasn't too bad. This likely explained why he wasn't panicking.

That, he was sure, would also come later.

When he stopped feeling so nauseated, anyway. Every drop of blood in him seemed to flood into his bowels, churning violently and leaving his limbs barely strong enough to support him. He felt as though any movement beyond the act of sitting upright would cause everything inside him to erupt onto the floor.

"What...what happened?" Even the act of speaking felt as though it would make something burst.

"The response to the query would be a lengthy process not suited for what humans deem tasteful." The couthi returned with a thin, purple vial. "It is guaranteed that your recovery is reliant on this one's expertise and your ability not to express oral amazement." He offered the vial delicately to the young man. "Consume."

He eyed it before looking warily at the fruit picture, which looked as helpful as a painting of fruit could.

"It will assist with your nausea."

A wary man, he knew, would think things through a little more before taking. A wary man who didn't have the luxury of feeling as though his insides were *not* about to explode out of many orifices couldn't be so picky.

He seized the vial and downed it desperately. A single swallow, yet the taste was unlike anything he had ever experienced. If one could bottle a dying man's breath and his widow's bitter smile, he imagined it would taste much like that.

The couthi placed a copper urn in front of him and turned back to his table. Lenk, gasping through a mouth suddenly quite dry again, stared at it.

"What's this for?"

"That," the couthi answered, "is for what happens next."

And he didn't have to ask.

His body screamed. The roiling of his bowels spread to the rest of him in an instant. His muscles contorted in agony. Blood rushed through him before suddenly thickening to a point where it felt stopped in his veins. His fingers knotted up, back arched, bones creaked. His pain had a life all its own.

Hurts. Hurts bad. Make it stop. Get it out. Stop stop stop. Not finished yet. So warm in here. So comfortable. Can't leave yet.

It had a voice.

A scream came out on a river of illness as he leaned over the urn and emptied his insides in thick bile. It splattered violently into the copper urn before it came to a sudden, uneasy halt. Along with his screams. And his breath.

Can't leave, can't leave, too cold out there.

He felt something stick in his craw, something thick, alive, and wriggling greasily. As breath struggled to get in, he struggled to get it out, failing both as he retched violently into the urn.

Can't leave, no, no, don't make me.

A hand seized him by the shoulder, too fierce to be the couthi's. Someone shoved him onto his back, pressed a forearm against his throat to pin him onto the marble slab. He stared up through vision blackening at the edges as the air left him. A pair of fierce eyes above a tattered veil stared down.

He had only a moment to recognize Khaliv. After that, he could see only the thin metal calipers.

The two prongs slid past his lips, over his tongue, down his throat. He felt the wriggling inside grow fiercer as the calipers found something and took hold. Hand steady as a stone, Khaliv slowly withdrew the prongs from Lenk's mouth. He felt something slimy slide up his throat and out between his lips as air rushed gratefully back into his lungs.

He caught a glimpse of it as it was drawn from his mouth and held high and wriggling in the calipers. It was thick and tuberous, like a maggot, black and glistening, like a tadpole. But unlike a maggot or a tadpole, it had a face.

And it spoke.

"*No, no, no,*" it squealed, "*too cold, let me back, I must go back, I am not yet finished.*"

Lenk could but stare in slack-jawed horror. Khaliv, for his part, seemed largely unimpressed. The saccarii dropped the writhing little . . . *thing* into the copper urn, plucked it up, and left the room with it.

The young man felt suddenly empty, as though the saccarii had just removed an organ instead of a . . . a . . .

"What the hell *was* that?" he gasped.

"It is considered rude among humans to ask questions as to the subject of what comes out of their orifices," the couthi replied. "This one wonders if the inverse of the consideration applies to what goes in."

Interrogating the couthi, obviously, was not going to be productive. Punching the couthi in his fruit bowl, likewise, would only be *merely* satisfying. While violence was almost certainly the solution, Lenk knew he needed to apply it selectively.

So he leapt off the slab, seized his sword and shirt, and stormed off after Khaliv. A marble hall, its opulence and portraits smothered by a thick layer of age, stretched before him as he strode down it, following Khaliv's footprints across a carpet of dust.

"Ah, there you are."

Even in a haze of rage and confusion, Lenk recognized Mocca's voice. He found the man in white at his side a moment later, hurrying to keep up.

"I trust everything went well in there?" Mocca asked. "I heard the most awful retching sounds."

"And you didn't come to see what was going on?"

"Me? No. Looked a tad creepy in there, what with the vials and calipers and the weird fellow wringing all four of his hands over your unconscious body."

Lenk came to a halt, stared at Mocca incredulously.

"For future reference," he said slowly, "when I am half-naked and unconscious, lying on a slab in front of a thing with a picture of fruit for a face, you have both my explicit permission and wholehearted encouragement to come in and ask what's going on."

"I trusted you were in good hands," Mocca said, hurrying to catch up as his companion took off. "This is, after all, the house of Fasha Sheffu. Bit of a reputation for eccentricity." He chuckled. "But then, what saccarii isn't eccentric? They only get a reputation for it when they have money."

Lenk was only half-listening now. The tracks in the dust took a sharp turn to the right and he followed the path past an antechamber and into a small parlor.

"Where are you going?" Mocca called after him.

"To get answers," he growled back.

"Ought you not put a shirt on first?"

And now, Lenk was not listening at all. His eyes were sweeping about the room and its dusty bookshelves and dusty cabinets, settling on the three figures assembled at the center.

He recognized immediately Khaliv in his tattered clothes as the saccarii set the copper bowl upon a table beside a dust-covered chair. The small urchin wrapped in filthy rags, too, he remembered from the streets of Silktown.

The saccarii in blue robes wearing an elegant indigo veil across his face, though, was new. He was cleaner than the other two saccarii, though not by much. His garb looked as though it had once been exquisite, but was now frayed at the edges. His veil was weighted with brass jewelry that had long grown tarnished. And his eyes, the color of petrified amber, looked too weary for a rich man.

He was clearly old, clearly tired, and clearly weak.

And here, Lenk thought, he was about to have another problem.

"There are ten feet between you and me." The young man leveled his blade at the saccarii. "You have that long to tell me what you just did to me."

The urchin let out a frightened squeak, slipping behind Khaliv's legs. The saccarii in blue, however, offered only a nonplussed stare.

"Tell me," he said, his accent thick, "I pull something like *this* out of you." He gestured to the copper urn. "And you still turn your blade upon me? Exactly what does it take to earn your trust?"

Lenk took exactly two steps forward. "A good place to start is by *not* kidnapping me and doing . . . whatever the hell you just did."

"All necessary," the saccarii replied. "Or at least, all expeditious. The procedure needed to draw this abomination from you was costly and required several concoctions of liquids far stranger. Administering them while you were unconscious was easier than explaining it to you." He sighed, settled in his chair. "Though, since I'm doing that, anyway, one wonders if that might not have been the more efficient route."

"Horseshit." Lenk took four steps forward. "How do I know you didn't put that in me to begin with? How do I know what that is? How do I know *what* the hell you did to me?"

"You do not. I barely understand it myself. I had but ancient texts to go by to formulate the alchemical concoctions needed to draw out the taint." He gestured to the vast collection of old-looking books around him. "The Bloodwise Brother I hired was only scarcely able to make sense of them—and not cheaply." He glanced at the thing wriggling in the urn. "Still, at least we know they work."

Four more steps. Lenk was across the room, the blade was at the saccarii's neck, and every drop of patience had fled from his voice.

"You poisoned me"—he forced his voice through grit teeth—"you brought me here; you have done...*something* to me. You either tell me everything right now or you tell my blade."

He could only see the other two saccarii out of the corner of his eye. He caught only glimpses of Khaliv's hand protectively shielding the urchin, only flashes of the terror in the little girl's eyes, only whispers of the words she called him.

"*Demon.*"

He returned his attentions back to the saccarii in blue. There was no fear in this one's eyes. He barely even blinked as he looked down at the tip of the blade without moving his neck.

"Interesting," he said. "It would be too typical to level your blade at my throat. Dramatic, yes, but one slip and I can tell you nothing. So you point to my collarbone. You could cut a little and still not kill me." His eyes widened in appreciation. "You wield a blade well. Did your father teach you before he died?"

At that, Lenk wanted dearly for his blade to have a "slip" and end that question and the saccarii with it. And he might have, if he weren't quite so shocked.

"How did you know that?" he asked numbly.

"No, he did not," the saccarii continued, as if he hadn't heard. "You were talented with it from the moment you picked it up, no? Though you had not so much as touched steel before you saw this blade, it felt easy in your hand. Comfortable. Made for you." He tapped his veiled chin. "What were you before you and this blade found each other? Merchant? Laborer? A soldier's son?"

"Farmer." Lenk found the word tumbling out between numb lips. "A farmer's son...before..."

"Before they all died. Horribly. Murdered in flames and fire, yes? I have read this before." He nodded slowly, glancing at his books. "Different beginnings, same ending. It does not get less tragic with repetition."

"How?" Lenk asked. "How do you know this?"

"A long story," he said. He rose easily, gingerly pushing Lenk's blade aside with a single finger. "One I intend to tell you when you have eaten, what with most of your food now sitting in a copper bowl."

He laid a hand on Lenk's shoulder. His blue sleeve fell back, exposing gray skin with a sickly sheen.

"Welcome to the house of Sheffu."

If Silktown was where money went to live, Sheffu's courtyard was almost certainly where it went to die. The trees were bare and sickly. The lawn was brown and parched. Cobwebs of aged silk hung everywhere, a single ancient, hairy arachnid making its way slowly across the courtyard.

While he had been assured that Sheffu, like all fashas, did own property in Silktown, Lenk found it hard to believe. The manicured lawns, glistening gates, and palatial manors he had seen seemed like a dream. This massive, ugly thing on eight legs seemed like a waking nightmare.

Free-ranging spiders were not only encouraged but mandatory in Silktown, he had been told. It was against the law to cage them, to interfere with their daily roaming, or—if one was poor enough—to touch them at all. Apparently, there was no law against keeping particularly depressing specimens, though, for Sheffu's solitary spider seemed as though it might just give up and die at any moment.

As a solitary upside, the scenery was so magnificently depressing as to keep Lenk's mind off the hunger pangs gnawing at his belly.

At least, until he smelled the food.

Khaliv set a steaming plate of rice and scraps of baked meats before him. Lenk had already started devouring it before he became aware of the fork that had been delivered with it. And by the time he was aware of that, he was also aware of Mocca, sitting in the other chair, looking horrified.

Lenk smacked lips stained red with sauce, noting the empty space before his companion. He made an offering gesture to his plate, which Mocca politely waved away.

"Are you sure?" Lenk asked. "It's pretty good."

"It's terribly rude to speak ill against one's host," Mocca replied. "Though not half as rude as lying. I can tell just by looking at that that it's less food and more war crime."

Lenk looked down at the dish. The rice was slimy. The meat was burned. The sauce had some kind of chunks in it that would probably raise a lot of questions later. But, considering that everything he had eaten over the past two days now lay within a copper urn along with some kind of wriggling demon, he was willing to accept it.

"I'll feel bad about it later," he muttered.

"Whatever you feel later is between you and the toilet," Mocca said.

"My apologies." Lenk glanced up to see Sheffu walking toward the table. "I employ only Khaliv and Eili to do my cooking and cleaning." He eased himself into a chair, creaking with the effort. "You may take the state of my home as proof that their talents lie elsewhere."

"So, you do this sort of thing often?" Lenk asked, glaring sidelong at Khaliv. "Kidnapping people, poisoning them, and pulling . . . some kind of—"

"Demon."

Lenk stopped at that word. Speaking. Chewing. Breathing.

"That was a demon."

It was just one word, an unimpressive five letters, spoken very shortly and simply. But short words were not always simple words. Some words should never be spoken simply. Because some words should never be heard, for the creatures that understood them were far from simple.

The silence that hung between the two men in the aftermath of its utterance told Lenk that Sheffu understood this. And the long breath he took as he began to speak again told Lenk that Sheffu was about to say something he dearly did not want to hear.

"They were called 'Khamut,' once. 'Undying.'" Sheffu raised his left hand and waved at Khaliv, who brought the copper urn over and placed it upon the table. "That was long ago. They have a new name, one they much prefer..."

Sheffu took the pair of iron calipers, clenched them tightly, and held the thing aloft. The demon, dark as the word itself, hung like a moonless night.

"Disciple," Sheffu said. "Followers of His will."

The demon wriggled in the tongs, alive and hissing. It jerked about with such violence that Sheffu visibly strained to keep hold of it. Lenk winced at the sight of it, but could not look away. The thing's grub-like body was composed mostly of fatty, sagging flesh, drawn tightly back at its head to expose a pair of scribble-black eyes and teeth bared to the gum.

It was an old man's face. A face he knew.

And his face was one the demon knew. It whirled on him with a shriek, gnashing its teeth at him, cursing him in some squealing black tongue.

"This one remembers you," Sheffu said. "Not so surprising. It was only two days ago that you killed it."

Lenk's eyes asked the question his mouth could not. That thing? That was the demon he had slain in the Souk?

"The Khamut's death does not mean it ends," Sheffu said, returning the creature to the urn. "They become as dust and are lost upon the wind. They are breathed in through the nose and mouth, they settle in the belly of those who are nearby."

The fasha waved Khaliv over.

"They feed upon the darkness within a man or woman," he continued. "And there is much to eat there. They grow strong on hatred, fat on fear. And when they are ready to emerge, they..."

Sheffu's eyes spoke the threat that his mouth could not. Lenk didn't need reminding. He remembered well the man with the swollen belly, shed like a serpent's skin.

Khaliv set beside Sheffu a jar of salt. The fasha uncorked it, took it up in his left hand, and held it over the urn.

"Memory is all that kills a demon," he said. "They do not fear steel, for they have never feared steel. But that which reminds them of what they once were, before they fell, is that which kills them. Before the Khamut became what they are, they were made to suffer. When they were brought low by mortals, they were bound tightly and buried alive."

He tilted the jar over the urn.

"In coffins packed with salt."

No sooner had the first white grains fallen than the demon's shrieking filled the night sky. Its howls were too great for such a tiny thing, its agony too vast for something so twisted. It writhed in pain, curling up into a tight ball, withering with a hiss of steam as the salt buried it.

"But of course," Sheffu whispered, "you already knew that, didn't you?"

When Lenk looked away from the horror in the urn, he found the fasha's gaze locked intently on him, his eyes sharpened to thin blades.

"This is not the first demon you have seen. Nor the first you have slain."

Lenk was hesitant to answer. To speak of demons was to acknowledge their existence. And as deluded a power as denial was, to relinquish it was still heavy. Sheffu must have known this.

But there was no fear in the fasha's eyes. There was only scrutiny, the kind of piercing appraisal that one usually reserves for a well-made blade. It was the kind of look that should never be fixed upon a human being.

"They were different when I fought them," Lenk said softly. "We called them Abysmyths. I've never seen things like these . . . Disciples before. And I had hoped to forget everything I ever knew about demons."

He leaned upon the table, looking across at Sheffu, matching the intensity of his gaze.

"You know things that mortals shouldn't know. And before you tell me what you want with me"—Lenk hesitated, for the eager scrutiny in Sheffu's gaze already told him that—"I want to understand what kind of mortal you are to know this."

"I am many things," Sheffu said. "To Cier'Djaal, I am a senile old fasha, content to let his fortunes dwindle to a decrepit estate, two servants and a single, hairy spider that does not spin silk anymore. But to the saccarii and the world, I am something far greater."

"And what's that?"

"He's a *yenthu*!"

The bright, chirping voice came from Eili. The little urchin came trundling up, ponderously carrying a thick book, easily as tall as she was, in her arms. With considerable effort, she hefted the book upon the table, letting it fall before Sheffu with a weighty thud.

"A storyteller!" she said, excitedly.

"Storytellers shouldn't be concerned with demons past using them to scare children," Lenk said.

"The word '*yenthu*' has many meanings," Sheffu said. "Storyteller is but one of them. *Yenthu* are concerned with history. And where history and demons are concerned, so are the *yenthu*."

The book seated before him was old, incredibly so, wearing a skin of dust that lingered on wrinkled leather even after Sheffu tried to brush it away. And yet, for all the age it exuded, there was something off about it.

Where's the damage? Where are the scars? Why does the leather still look so new?

Sheffu had just begun to thumb it open when he became aware of Eili standing nearby, staring intently at the pages. He lofted a brow at the urchin.

"Have you finished your studies?" he asked.

"They can wait," she replied casually.

"The ignorant wait, the intelligent act. Go now."

"But—"

"Must I send Khaliv to help you?"

Eili scowled at him a moment before she skulked away, muttering curses through her veil. Lenk watched her briefly.

"She has no parents?" he asked.

"Killed," Sheffu replied, thumbing through the book.

"How?"

"Same way all saccarii are killed. They had the audacity to be born. Khaliv was the same when I found him. I help how I can."

"You could help more than two if you used your money better," Lenk said.

"The day I discovered this book was the day I stopped being concerned with money," Sheffu said without looking up. "It is impossible to see value in gold when you are made aware of just how many things out there want you dead..."

Lenk turned the book toward Lenk and pushed it across the table. Mocca leaned over, quirking a brow curiously.

"And how close they've come to succeeding."

He had seen this before. Not this book, but this writing: symbols that hurt to read, images that looked as though they had been painted in painstaking detail from the most intimate of fluids. He remembered this, and the memory hurt.

"Where did you get this?" he muttered.

"It came to me. It was shuffled between collectors who could not bear its presence. They claimed it stared at them, spoke to them, and so they got rid of it. It stared at me, as well." His eyes lit up. "But I stared back. And when it spoke, I listened. It cost an immense amount, for there are only as many like it as can be counted on one hand. The Book of the Dead, the Deineireal Libram, the Tome of the Undergates..."

The realization burned at the back of Lenk's mind. He knew what Sheffu was about to tell him.

"This one," Sheffu said, "is His Word. It is the detailed history of the Vhehanna Desert in the times before the fall, when Gods were not so distant and men were not so deaf. There were servants in that age, those who lingered between heaven and earth to impart the will of the Gods and deliver the pleas of mortals. One day, they would be called 'demon.' Before that, they were—"

"Aeon."

Lenk knew the word. He knew the legends that mortals had forgotten. He knew the names that mortals should not know. He had heard them from mouths that should not have spoken them—most recently, Miron's.

And the priest's tale was one of a heaven stained red with blood.

The Aeons, the legends said, were the messengers of creation. Too godly to be all-knowing, too human to be all-powerful, they were blessed—or cursed—to linger trapped between two worlds, short of heaven and far beyond earth.

That, Lenk always supposed, would explain why they grew to hate both.

It was their own mortal emotions that proved their undoing, so it was said. It was their envy of the Gods' power, their resentment of man's mortality, their utter hatred for their lot in life that changed them. Like mortals, they could be twisted. But far different from mortals, what twisted an Aeon twisted them inside and out.

They fell and that name was lost to them. When they rose again, they were called demon.

They subjugated mortality in short order, assuming rule over what they saw as a world theirs by right. But, as all things must, this world, too, ended in blood.

The Gods sent forth their armies to strike back. The wars that followed, as mortalkind rose up, raged across the face of the world; and before the demons were cast into hell, their conflict had left scars seen and unseen. The most grievous of which sat before Lenk, in this book and many like it, this record of horrors that time had mercifully tried to bury.

It wounded Lenk to look at it. Not because he knew of the tragedies of which it spoke. Nor even because he knew what such books could be used for.

It hurt because he knew why Sheffu had chosen to show it to him.

"His Word is not so broad a history as other records of the demons," Sheffu said softly. "It reads more like poetry. It sings the praises of the Aeon who stood over this part of the world in ancient times. It gushes at length of His power at chasing away superstition and belief and replacing them with reason and logic as the basis of society."

"What a tyrant," Mocca said, stifling a yawn.

"But it goes on, in frightening detail," Sheffu continued, heedless, "as to how He accomplished this. His subjects were assessed in worth and either elevated or enslaved based on how He saw them. He became the first and last word in law and life. He learned the intricacies of the human body by cutting them open as they still drew breath and studying them."

He flipped through the pages, showing Lenk diagrams, paintings, charts, each one proving what Sheffu had just said. Here, a detailed drawing of a man in agony, each organ marked and labeled. There, an intricate essay on how to judge the quality of human stock.

"It goes on like this," Sheffu said. "The author falls over himself to paint him, this demon king, as the harbinger of utopia, despite his endless sins. I thought it odd until I reached the end."

He flipped to the final few pages. The script here made little sense to Lenk, even by the standards of the rest of the text. There were no elaborate drawings, no sprawling charts. Only a handful of notes, hastily scrawled, as if in passing thought.

At this, Mocca appeared to take an interest, leaning over to see. Lenk thought to ask if he knew what was written here, but Sheffu spoke first.

"These are reminders," the fasha said. "Small, detailed instructions as to how He did it and how He would do it again. He foresaw His own fall and He wrote contingencies, should He return from hell. They begin with creating a cult, a base of fanatics who are consumed by his visions and sworn to spread His name. They end with His name on the lips of everyone the world over."

"And what was that name?"

"You already know," Sheffu said. "All of Cier'Djaal already knows.

They hear it every day spoken from the lips of fanatics and murderers. And *they* know it well, for they have seen it."

Sheffu leaned forward intently.

"He speaks to them through visions. And the faithful know He is watching."

He tapped the book's pages.

"The return of the Disciples—*His* Disciples—the utterance of His name, the sudden appearance of the Khovura cult; it cannot be coincidence. The God-King, the Shaper of Flesh..."

Sheffu's voice grew dark. His eyes grew hard.

"Khoth-Kapira is returning."

At these words, Lenk felt his heart sink.

Not for their dire meaning. Rather, it was the fasha's eyes, rather than his words, that made the young man tense. Even as Sheffu's voice softened, his eyes grew harder, his scrutiny sharpening itself upon Lenk as the fasha studied him with stark appraisal.

And here it comes.

"But you," Sheffu said, "you can stop them. You have done so before."

He flipped to a page and pointed to some drawings of men and women with pale hair and empty eyes. They marched against twisted demonic shapes scrawled upon the parchment, swords in hands and fire at their backs. Surrounding them was written all manner of what Lenk assumed to be vulgar curses, if the harsh penmanship was any indication.

"They have no names," the fasha said. "Or perhaps Khoth-Kapira never wrote them down. But He describes them at great length. People whose hair is the color of an old man's, no matter their age. Weapons made to fight the demons, the only ones who can. They have no families, they have no Gods, they have no home; all three must be lost before they can be what they were made to be."

Sheffu's eyes lit up in a way that made Lenk shudder.

"They brought His Disciples low once," he said. "And they can do so again."

Lenk was already shaking his head. Sheffu was thrusting the book at him as if it was a weapon.

"Khaliv has seen you fight; he told me and I knew I must meet you. These warriors the book speaks of, they are *you*. And with you, we can preserve this world; we can save it."

And you *can get what you want*, Lenk thought. *And* you *can be whatever hero you thought you would be when you first found this book.*

"The book speaks of a city," Sheffu said, flipping to another page. "Far away to the Forbidden East, where the seat of Khoth-Kapira's empire once stood before your people brought it low. We can head there and—"

"Khaliv saw me fight?"

Sheffu paused, glaring at the interruption. "He did. He saw you dispatch the beast quite handily."

"Is that true, Khaliv?" Lenk turned to a nearby tree, where the saccarii bound in rags was standing. "Did you see me dispatch it handily?" At the saccarii's silence, he pressed. "Did you see what it did to my friends? Did you see what we had to do to kill it?"

"I saw."

Lenk nodded. "And did you hear it?"

"I heard."

"And what did it sound like?"

Khaliv fell silent for a moment. His stare softened and when he spoke, it was but a whisper.

"Like a child."

"Like a child," Lenk repeated. "Demons are ruled by memory, it's true. And maybe they remember me, or what I was. I don't know. But they don't remember what pain is like. So when they get hurt, it's like watching a child skin his knee for the first time. He has no idea what he's feeling, but he knows it hurts and he wants it to stop. So he screams out to his parents' Gods, if they taught him. But if they didn't, he screams out to his mother, his father. He begs them to make it stop."

"They infest humans like disease," Sheffu said sternly. "You saw the hell they wrought upon the Souk. You saw what the Khovura did. They are one and the same, thralls of Khoth-Kapira. He is no child and neither are they."

"I'm not saying they didn't need to be stopped," Lenk said. "And I'm not saying I regret killing them. I'm saying that this isn't a great, glorious cause just because demons are involved. And just because they don't always feel pain doesn't mean it's any less messy."

He looked down at the drawing of his "people," settled upon an illustration of a man that looked a little like him: the same tired face, the same empty eyes, the same scars and sword.

"What you want me to be is a blade," Lenk said, "something that cuts cleanly through a demon and comes out shiny and polished. But what I *would* be is a man fighting a war, as ugly, as bloody, and as dirty as any other."

"There would be blood," Sheffu said. "There would be loss. Look at what I have already given up to take steps to secure a future for this city." He swept his hands around the desolate courtyard. "Money I have spent, time I have given poring over this book, learning everything I could so I could be prepared when the time came. And now, it is upon us and you express doubt because it will be difficult?"

"All wars are," Lenk replied. "And for as much money as you may have and as much knowledge as you may possess, you're still asking me to do all the killing. You're looking at me like I'm a weapon. I'm not. I don't kill and feel nothing. I feel..."

Complete.

Whole.

Good.

Lenk buried his head in his hands and sighed.

"It takes a lot to kill anyone," he settled on saying, "let alone demons. And go back to all that killing, all that blood..." He shook his head. "I came here to get away from that. I've given up..." He caught himself and sighed. "All that I lost will mean nothing if I pick up my sword again and go back to it like nothing's changed."

"And what," Sheffu asked with a cold hostility, "have you lost?"

A girl.

A friend.

Everything.

Lenk said none of this. Sheffu didn't wait for him to say something different.

"Because whatever it is, you stand to lose much more, along with everyone else, if you do not act." He held his left hand out to his side. "Because if you do not, then who will?"

Lenk looked up. He met those sharpened eyes of Sheffu, now dripping with scorn, and stared flatly at him.

"Are you going to make me?"

And, for the first time, Sheffu looked away.

"I am not," he replied.

Lenk said nothing beyond a mumbled gratitude as he rose from his chair, turned, and left. He didn't hear Mocca rise from his, but the man in white was beside him in an instant, walking with him to the nearby archway, turning into the hall, and trying to ignore Sheffu's scowl burning into their backs.

"I was rather proud of myself back there, you know," Mocca said finally.

"You didn't say a damn thing," Lenk said.

"To my inestimable credit," his companion shot back. "I doubt I could have opened my mouth without laughing in his face." Now that he was out of earshot, he saw fit to indulge himself with a chuckle. "Demons. And he expects you to kill them?"

"I've killed them before."

"Then why is he surprised that you don't want to do it again?" Mocca sighed dramatically. "Don't worry yourself overmuch. What would she say if you abandoned her only to go back to killing?"

Lenk stopped dead in his tracks, turning a glare upon his companion. "I never told you about her."

Mocca smiled. "You talk in your sleep. I put the pieces together myself."

That made sense, Lenk thought, resuming his trek toward the

door. Though it was hard to feel at ease knowing that Mocca had heard what he hardly spoke of himself. The man in white stopped at the door, making a gesture inviting Lenk to go first.

"*Shkainai!* Hey, *shkainai!*"

The young man hesitated, hand on the knob, when he heard Eili approaching. The little urchin came rushing up, stopping before him and reaching out to take his hand. She placed something in his palm and curled his fingers over it.

He didn't have to look to know what it was. He could feel its quill, its barbs. Still soft, still warm, still white, still hers.

Kataria's feather.

"Thanks," he muttered. "For not keeping it."

"Figured ya'd want it"—she turned and stalked down the halls, muttering over her shoulder—"since ya'd kill us all for it."

TWENTY-FOUR

ASSASSINS

Asper walked on a dead woman's legs.

There were people all around, laughing and singing praises to various gods—though mostly just one—as they ran through Temple Row. She walked through the shadows of looming cathedrals as the sun waned overhead. She stepped over a river of people crawling on their bellies as they scaled the steps to Ancaa's church.

And she noticed none of it, consumed by a singular echoing thought.

Miron is dead.

The man she had been searching for after nights of sleepless worry and muttered prayers to a God she wasn't sure would even listen.

Miron is dead.

The man she had spent countless nights discussing what it meant to heal to and who convinced her that treating a scraped knee was as important as treating a head wound.

Miron is dead.

The man who guided her through a world filled with blood and corpses and companions who were eager to make more. The man who helped her hone her skill as a healer. The man whose presence made her never doubt that the Healer was always watching over them.

That man was dead.

And she had just spoken to him four days ago.

But Aturach had shown her the logbook. Miron Evenhands had never reached the rank of Lord Emissary. Miron Evenhands had been a priest of no great notoriety who had studied briefly at various temples in the north and south before dying quietly and leaving no estate or relatives.

Could it have been mistaken? Could it have been lying? Could the scribe making the entry have been overworked, thinking of soft women and warm wine and simply... fucked it up?

No, she thought. *No, how could that have happened? If Miron hadn't been dead, then they would have amended the record when he showed up again, wouldn't they? He would have returned to the church and they would have known they'd made a mistake. But he never returned to the church.*

Her head was pounding, each thought a hammer blow to her skull.

Then who have you been talking to all this time? Who took you to Cier'Djaal? Who convinced you that healing people wasn't a waste of time? Who convinced you to stay with Lenk and the others even though you knew it was wrong?

Her skull seared. Her left arm itched. The curse inside her reacted to the tumultuous thought and grew agitated. She looked down at her arm and winced. She had never told him about it. But he had told her so much else.

He knew my problems. I told him about how my parents turned me over to the clergy on my eighth birthday. I told him about the time we sneaked out of temple and I met a boy and I loved him for that night only. I told him about... about Taire and... and about sneaking wine into our dormitory and... and...

"He *knew* me," she whispered. And she tried very hard to ignore how that statement now made her skin crawl.

She rounded the corner and saw the Death Line that bisected Temple Row. And for a brief, merciful moment, she saw something horrifying enough to take her mind off of her own problems.

Painted like tributaries from a river, smears of blood mingled with the Death Line. Some were small, puddles after a drizzle. Others were great abstract portraits in a single color.

On either side of the Death Line, Karnerians and Sainites went about the grim work of cleaning up. The dead and wounded they carried out on stretchers without so much as a flinch. The corpses of their foes that had happened to have fallen on their side, though, they took great care to leave burning or impaled or otherwise desecrated.

There was no air of suffering here, as there had been in the temple of Talanas. Nor was there a basking fervor, like at Ancaa's temple. There wasn't even a trace of the tension that had been present when she first arrived.

It was a casualness that fell over the court like a heavy, woolen blanket. And it was the casualness that unnerved her. Here, men and women looked past the dead without tears, reverence, or horror. They plucked up their dying comrades like baggage, trod over their dead foes like litter. They moved with a weary familiarity that suggested they had done this all before and would do it all again, so who would bother getting upset that they had just seen so many people die?

If Miron were here to see this, she wondered, *what would he say?*

The man she thought was Miron, though, would have lamented the loss of life. He would have told her to keep her chin up, to not take the sign of such casualness as indicative of all humanity. He would have said that there would be at least one soldier in his bunk at night, weeping into a pillow because he had just seen his best friend die, and it was for *that* man that she must continue.

But the man she thought was Miron was a fraud.

Was everything he had said also a lie? How could she trust the words of a pretender? A liar who wore another man's identity as his own? How could she take his comfort when the comfort he gave wasn't his?

She sighed and walked along the Death Line. Not a soul looked up to challenge her as she began to trudge wearily toward the gates of Temple Row and, ultimately, back to the others.

Lenk would want to know.

Well, that's not true, she thought. *Lenk* would *want to know where Miron was. Lenk* won't *want to know that Miron doesn't exist and he's never getting paid. Should I even tell him?*

She paused at the gates, thinking.

Should I even go back? Miron was the one that told me to stay with them. And he's... She shook her head. *But they need to know. They need* me. *Don't they?*

To do what?

Make more corpses?

Listen mutely to her lectures?

Ignore her when she prayed quietly to a God that might not be there?

Not too far away, the Souk's distant hum of coins and lives changing hands was quieting as the sun continued to sink. It felt like a long, lonely road back to the inn and her companions. A road made all the harder by the dead woman's legs beneath her.

Absently, she pondered just sitting down here and quietly waiting for someone else to come along and tell her what to do, so she could at least be ready when she was disappointed again.

Or maybe she would die first. That might be nice, too.

"Shkainai! SHKAINAI!"

Of course, she thought with a sigh. Someone *would* have to go and interrupt *that*, as well.

It was a Djaalic man who came running up to her, pale and sweating. Not a rich one, either. His clothes were shabby and his eyes were sunken. When he skidded to a halt before her, his breath was desperate and short.

"Healer? Yes?" he gasped, gesturing to the pendant about her neck. "You're a healer? Talanite?"

For a brief moment, she wondered if it might be better if she pretended to be someone going to a costume party with a religious theme. Her weary nod, however, was automatic.

"Please, come," the Djaalic said, frantically. "My brother, he fell.

He can't get back up, he won't stop shouting, and...and I don't know what to do." He looked up at her, pleading. "I left my wife and cousin with him. Please, you must help."

"The, uh, the temple of Ancaa is just behind—"

"Ancaa can't do anything! Her followers don't know anything other than how to talk pretty and spend money!" The desperation on his face pooled in his eyes, glistening. "No one else can do this, *shkai*—" He caught himself and winced. "Priestess. *Please.*"

That, she was certain, was almost definitely not true.

Even the Karnerians and Sainites had field medics. The Ancaarans probably had a few people who knew a bit of healing. And there were always the Quills and Lanterns of Gevrauch.

But they were far away. And she was here.

And this, apparently, was reason enough to start moving.

The Djaalic fell over his feet and his words as he stumbled ahead, leading her down the cobblestones, babbling gratitudes the whole way. She barely heard him. The dead woman's legs were gone and her thoughts with them. Returned were the old familiar habits of the healer.

She was here. She could help. Even if Miron was an impostor, even if her companions were savages, even if there would be more suffering, more bodies, more blood tomorrow, she would always be able to do something, no matter who told her she was capable.

Not much of a reason.

But enough.

The outskirts of the Souk were notably more rustic than the core of the city. Its homes were largely well-worn, uncared-for wood alongside a few very old houses of carved stone. Sunset seemed to arrive sooner here, with windows shut and only a few old men and women on the street, who disappeared into their doors as she and the Djaalic passed.

"Here," he said, pointing down an alley. "We live down here. He collapsed on our doorstep."

A narrow confine of walls and doors greeted her as she rounded the corner. Huddled together at the center, a woman and another man crouched and sobbed hysterically over a dark shape.

"Get back!" she barked. "Give him some air."

Muttering pleas, they fell back, leaving her room to kneel over the man. He was clad in a thin robe, curled up on his side, trembling with contained agony. She laid a hand on him; even through the robe, she could feel the fever in his flesh.

"Who...who?" the agonized man gasped.

"It's all right," Asper replied. "I'm a Talanite. I'm here to help. Tell me where it hurts."

"T-Talanite? Was once...once..." He shook his head, droplets of sweat falling. "Didn't listen...couldn't ignore the v-visions, what he s-said..." He drew in a sharp breath through a choked throat. "W-wasn't ready. *I wasn't ready!*"

Delerium. Fever. Shortness of breath. Diseases and suffering sometimes seemed like the only bountiful things in life.

One despairing thought at a time, she cautioned herself. She took him gently by the chin, pressed a hand against the back of his skull and raised his head up. *Choked voice. Something must be swollen.*

"Open your mouth for me," she said softly.

"Burns...hurts...wasn't..."

He either hadn't heard her or couldn't do it on his own. With a little bit of pulling, she was able to pry his lips apart and open his mouth. She stared down his gullet and saw everything looking perfectly pink, unswollen, and healthy. Past his tongue, there was only darkness.

And it was from this darkness that an eye, wide and white and bloodshot, stared back at her.

She fell back with a shriek. The man groaned in reply, rolling onto his back. His robe parted, exposing a tremendously swollen belly, spherical and quivering as his groan became a scream.

His agony grew louder. His mouth opened wider. Long gray fingers ending in dirty black nails curled over his lips as something inside him reached out.

And ripped his mouth into a doorway.

Asper's heart was pounding, her breath was short, and her limbs were flailing beneath her as she scrambled to her feet. As she whirled about to run, she saw them. The woman and two men were pulling black veils over their faces, drawing knives from their clothes, fixing wild stares upon her.

"*Kapira*," they whispered in lilting, crazed harmony. "*Kapira, anshaa.*"

She froze before them, even as they advanced. She didn't dare retreat, for she could already feel black eyes upon her.

"They looked upon us as Gods, for they knew not the difference between God and learned man." The demon's rasping groan came to her ears, carried on the thick, glistening sounds of flesh stretching and snapping. "The burden of knowledge was one we did not wish upon them. The agony of thought was one we were content to spare them."

Its words slithered across her flesh, into her ears. She knew then that if she didn't turn to face it, she would run screaming into the daggers. And so, when she whirled around, she did so biting her tongue, hoping the pain would be enough to distract from the fear.

No such luck.

Rising like a plume of smoke from a fire extinguished, the demon emerged from the man's mouth, stretched unnaturally wide to let the expanse of its gray, withered coils escape. Through scribble-black eyes pinched between a columnar skull and the wrinkles of an old man's jowls, it stared at her.

"Would you take our burdens, priestess?"

She felt her body grow tight beneath its gaze, as though every drop of blood inside her went still, fearing that they might be spotted if they moved. Her eyes were locked wide open. Her jaw was clenched tight. Every bit of her was frozen in fear.

Save her left arm.

Skin twitched beneath her sleeve, sinew burned beneath her skin, blood beneath the sinew. And beneath all of that, she could hear it, the pain of the curse in her arm.

This thing, hate it, want it dead, keep it away from us, hurts us, want it dead.

She couldn't speak to it. She couldn't move. Not even as she heard feet scuffling behind her and felt the iron stares of knives pointed at her back.

The demon raised a hand. Behind her, the Khovura halted.

"We have sensed your thirst," the demon said. It shed the dead man from its flesh as it slithered forward slowly. "It is rain on parched lips, priestess. You seek answers into matters beyond your concern. Such was our way before we were turned."

Was it just that demons were incapable of *not* being cryptic, she wondered?

"But knowledge is a terrible sin in the eyes of the Gods you serve," it hissed, drawing closer. "To know is to be without fear, and to be without fear is to know no God. What lies did yours tell you?"

The temple, she realized. *They know where I've been. They've been following me.*

That was her last thought before thought, too, froze with fear. The beast leaned close and she could see past the black scribbles of its eyes to the bloodshot orbs buried beneath the darkness.

"You know that which you should not," it rasped. "You keep company of slayers, the cold-eyed heretics who slew us for our sins of knowledge."

"Lenk?" she whispered.

"They have no names, for they have no souls. When they go, they shall be one of many taints expunged."

She watched a long, thin arm rise up around her. She felt thin fingers wrap around her neck, the tips of black nails prod at the tenderness of quivering flesh. She heard a voice rasping, a long tongue flicking against desiccated lips with every word.

"Let this knowledge soothe you," it said, "as you learn the price of knowledge."

"BACK!"

A single thought made into a single word spoken from a single voice. And none of them were hers.

Not entirely, anyway. It was her left arm that reached up and dug fingers against the gray flesh of the demon's wrist. It was her pain that raced through her veins, down into the marrow of her bones. But it was not her choice to do so.

Nor was what happened next.

Her sleeve split apart in a burst of crimson, erupting in a hellish light that painted her skin red and her bones black. It lasted for but a moment, an eye into the keyhole in the door between earth and hell that closed shut in a breath.

But the scream that followed lasted much longer.

The demon's grasp slipped from her as it fled down the alley, chased by its own wail. It coiled over itself defensively, clutching the blackened, smoking flesh where her hand had touched. Between its coils, it scowled spitefully from a withered face.

"You *dare* to touch the learned Disciple?" it snarled. It leveled a thin black fingernail at her. "She is a vessel, tainted! Unfit to hear His word! *Rend her.*"

"*KAPIRA!*"

She turned and saw the Khovura's eyes first, wide and crazed. She saw the blade second, held high overhead as he rushed her, its steel quivering with his screeching charge. He was coming at her fast. He was crazed. He and his knife wanted her dead.

He's not a knife, the thought came instinctively. *He's a wrist.*

A wrist that she caught, pulled, turned as she forced the momentum of his charge into the nearby wall. She drew fiercely on his arm and planted a boot at the base of his spine; she heard a snapping sound as the limb came free from its socket, and a scream as the man dropped his blade and fell to the stones.

She turned to face her remaining two opponents. They were warier, holding their knives defensively, not willing to give her any more momentum to use against them. She drew in a deep breath and steadied herself.

They're not knives, either, she told herself. *They're just—*

Something lashed against her back. A sharp pain lanced through her. She felt cloth split and blood weep. She turned and saw the demon's long tongue, wet with her life sliding back into its mouth as it began to claw its way toward her.

Or maybe we just run this time.

This she did, guarding her face with her arms and barreling between the two Khovura. She felt the blades nick her, kiss her flesh, and paint her further scarlet. She could run through that; she could bite that back. Pain could have her attention later, after fear had its turn.

She burst out of the alley and into the streets, breaking into a sprint. She heard feet behind her, screams of a name she didn't know on the lips of the Khovura.

And then just ordinary screams.

She glanced over her shoulder; the demon came howling out of the alley, smashing the Khovura out of its way as it slithered after Asper, clawing toward her upon black nails.

Don't think about that. She forced herself to look forward. *Don't think about the pain.* She forced herself to ignore the searing lash upon her back. *Don't think about what it'll do to you if it catches you in its claws and finishes what it was about to do last time when it—*

She felt her arm burn. The wounds where the last demon had dug its nails into her flesh quivered, as though they knew she was thinking about them.

I said don't *think about that.* She picked up speed, biting back pain. *Think about escape. Get back to Temple Row. Get help.* She nodded to herself. *Right. How'd we do that again?*

The buildings were a blur of ancient wood and decrepit stone as she sped by. She couldn't remember how she had gotten here, where she had been led. She certainly didn't know where she was going, save for away from the—

Something caught her ankle. Her chin hit the stone. She watched a trail of her blood grow as she felt the ground moving beneath her.

She whirled onto her back and saw the tongue lashed about her ankle and the cavernous maw to which it pulled her ever closer.

Asper shrieked, clawing futilely at the stone for a moment before remembering her arm. As the demon's tongue drew her toward its body, she lashed out with her left arm, hoping that the curse would act then.

But when the beast caught her by the wrist in a withered claw, her arm remained painfully, unbearably mortal. The Disciple hauled her up, heedless of her screaming as it lifted her off the ground. Its scribble-black eyes scowled over her arm spitefully, looking at the burned flesh upon its own limb.

"We remember the first vessels," it rasped. "When we sought to improve the frail mortality by sealing our kin within them. The ungrateful hosts repaid our gifts with betrayal, turning to our foes and turning our gifts upon us." It drew her closer. "Now, we reclaim what we gave you in blind generosity."

The demon's free hand rose and made a beckoning gesture. And instantly, Asper's flesh was alight with pain. The wounds in her arm that had been struck by the first demon in the Souk began to tremble and burn as they were called to agonizing life. She felt her flesh ripple like liquid, watched it bubble and boil at the beast's behest.

"Such frail gifts your creators gave you," the demon mused through her agonized shrieking. "What love could they have had for you? See how it springs to life at our command? We used much the same techniques in crafting the first vessels."

Asper could form no question as to what a vessel was. For Asper could form no thought amidst the pain that wracked her body, sent her writhing in its grip. Between the shrieks pouring from her mouth, the bright flashes of pain clouding her mind, the fiery heat lancing her body as her flesh danced at the demon's command, she knew nothing but agony.

"Come to us, brother," the demon whispered. "Be free of your prison."

And certainly, she knew not what her arm was doing.

Not until it had burst to fiery life. Not until it seared with a pain sharper than any the demon could coax from her. Not until it answered the demon with a voice that shrieked long and loud.

The demon was aware of it before she was: the steam seeping between its fingers, melting its flesh to her own and devouring it into its red light. The Disciple screamed and shook her, trying to dislodge her, but its fingers locked tight by a will stronger than its own. Its limb, already withered and twisted, deformed further. It grew bloated, then shriveled, sinew and flesh and bone dissipating and becoming as steam that faded on the setting sun.

Asper knew what was happening only when she felt the pain fade from her, drain from her body and flow back into her arm. A glowing beacon to which all agonies, demon and mortal, were called to pay tribute.

The demon's arm was too withered and pitiful to hurl her, to even lift her. When she fell, the arm fell with her, an ugly, blackened strand that shriveled into a black stain.

When the demon recoiled, clutching the stump where once had been a limb, it was not with fear, nor with anger.

"Brother, you . . . choose her over your own? What did we . . . *why*?"

And for a moment, Asper saw an agony upon the beast's face that seemed greater than any she could have inflicted upon it. Betrayal, astonishment, hurt: the fringes of human emotion strained to make themselves known in the spiteful wrinkles of an inhuman face.

There were no curses as it fled, no promises of vengeance. It slithered into a nearby alley, leaving behind only a black stain upon the stones, the lingering whispers of a clash of agonies, and Asper.

Alone.

But alive.

She reminded herself of that with each breath as she sat there, bleeding from the chin, her robe's sleeve tattered, her head pounding behind closed eyes.

I am alive, she reminded herself. *I am still alive.*

You're welcome.

A thought not her own, but painfully close. For a moment, she wondered if this was the moment Talanas would reveal Himself to her, if this darkest hour was when she would finally be told that everything she had suffered for was worth something.

But only for a moment.

Because in the next, she felt something in her left arm: a tingling, itching, crawling sensation. It was as though something beneath the skin rotated slowly and, through the muscle and blood and flesh, looked straight at her.

I sense your alarm, child, those thoughts said. *We've not yet spoken properly. Forgive me; I have been too famished to concentrate. But now that I am fed…*

And with the same skin-crawling certainty, she could feel something beneath her arm form a smile just for her.

We may be properly introduced.

TWENTY-FIVE

SHARED BLOOD

It was only when he stood absolutely still and took a deep breath without the scent of blood that Gariath realized just how injured he was.

He looked down at his hand and watched the scars on his knuckles turn pink as he curled his fingers into a fist, each joint popping as they did.

"As far as I know," he said, "I am the last one."

He put his hand on his shoulder and rolled it. The joints creaked in protest, its pain smothered by a layer of muscle.

"I could be wrong, of course," he said. "Even when there were more of us, we never had much contact with each other. It was mostly just families, living on their own where they could. Once in our life, we'd wander off, find a mate..." He sniffed and drew a thumb down a long scar that ran from his collarbone to the left side of his chest. "And then beat the shit out of each other."

His wings twitched on his back, stiff from being folded so tightly to his body. Didn't matter; those were mostly used for attracting said mates to beat said shit out of. That hadn't been a problem for him in a long time.

"I suppose, at some point, we started dying off." His sigh was vast enough to have scars of its own. "Humans taking our land, fighting each other, not breeding enough; who knows. I didn't. And I didn't care, so long as I had my sons."

He drew his legs up and down, feeling the muscle strain beneath his skin as he forced blood back into his calves, sensation back into the soles of his feet.

"And when they died..."

He stood still. He took a deep breath. And he held the scent of blood in his nostrils again. And rain. And damp, cold earth.

Like he was still there.

He shook his head. No. His sons weren't a part of this story. They—their lives and their deaths—would be for him alone.

"I've always wanted to believe that we died for good reasons," he said, breaking the silence. "Going down fighting for something we believed in, stopping a great enemy; legendary deaths, ones that made ours more important than other peoples'." He shrugged. "Maybe some of us did die good deaths."

He stared down at his hands once last time. He squeezed them into fists so tight they trembled and saw the blood weep out from his palms as his claws dug in.

"But it's taken me this long to realize that the *Rhega* can die for stupid reasons, too."

When he looked up, Daaru stared blankly back at him.

"Uh, all right," the tulwar said. "Why are you telling me all this?"

Gariath leaned down and plucked up a heavy burlap bag, a sticky liquid and accompanying reek seeping out of it. He tossed it over his shoulder.

"I thought that was obvious."

He ventured out of the alley onto the lamplit harbor streets. No cloak, no disguise, nothing but a dragonman and a smelly bag. Those few people still on the streets—those not yet drunk enough to know what they were looking at, anyway—started at his approach and fled without a word. Whether alarmed by him or his macabre baggage, Gariath didn't care.

His business was with the building looming at the end of the lane.

Daaru was talking again. Something about "another way," "this is really stupid," "pummeled into a fine paste." Distractions he didn't need. As with any argument, concentration of mind, body, and purpose was needed. And for that sort of focus to be maintained, one needed to have at least some semblance of disregard for personal safety.

He came to a halt before a looming building of shoddy stone and plaster and set his burden down at its door.

Thunder House, as it was known, was one of the few establishments in Cier'Djaal capable of providing any sort of service to *Drokha*. Largely by virtue of its truly colossal doorway opening into a gigantic room where a dragonman's dark shape towered over the human rabble of the bar, assisted by a pair of servants who hauled barrel-sized tankards to him.

Gariath drew in the scent. The odor of liquor, ash, and desperation clouded the smoky room in abundance. He glanced at the doorway and saw Kharga's weapon—a massive hunk of metal battered into a vaguely ax-like shape—leaning against the wall.

He was here. A ten-foot giant, heavy as a house and brimming with muscle beneath a thick hide, bristling with scorn, skilled—or as skilled as one needed to be—with a weapon the size of a human male, of which there were more than a few inside.

None of whom would likely have many nice things to say about a *Rhega*.

Gariath could feel Daaru standing behind him, but he did not look at his companion. He was relatively certain that he already knew what the tulwar's expression would be, because he was certain just how crazy he looked as he drew in a deep breath and roared.

"KHARGA!"

The scent changed almost instantly from desperation to rage. He knew Kharga had picked up his own scent at that moment and knew exactly who was waiting outside for him.

The sound of thunder followed shortly after.

"You might want to leave now." Gariath directed a grunt behind him.

He felt Daaru's resentful stare for a moment before he heard the shuffle of feet on stone as the tulwar took off running.

The earth shook beneath his feet; every grain of sand that had settled upon the stone trembled, rising and falling and giving the impression of a liquid earth, quivering like waves.

A storm was coming.

And it wasn't alone.

Kharga emerged a moment later, his great ax slung lazily over one shoulder, black eyes staring contemptuously down a horned snout. Gariath turned his scowl upward. Scant evidence of their previous fight in the Souk remained: Kharga's cuts had faded; Gariath's claw marks had withered into tiny little gashes in a thick hide that had seen much, much worse.

Behind him crowded five others. Humans, bearing the same badge of the naked human on a pile of coins that he did, wielding spears and wearing masks of quivering confidence that would turn to liquid and drip off their faces if they didn't have Kharga with them. Even then, they made a clear effort to keep the giant between them and Gariath, content to throw only scowls and muttered curses at the smaller dragonman that still dwarfed them.

"Son of a bitch," one whispered. "Is that the thing from the Souk?"

"Looks just like ours . . . except smaller."

"Kill him, already. Our food's getting cold."

Gariath would only barely notice them, even if they weren't lingering in Kharga's shadow. It was likewise apparent that Kharga didn't notice them, either. They were unimportant. What they saw, undoubtedly, were two monsters staring at each other when they should be killing one another.

What they didn't see, what they could never see, was why it was crucial that bloodshed not be the first resort here.

Gariath drew his leg back and the humans tightened their grips on their weapons. He kicked the smelly bag forward. It fell open, a small pile of glistening meat and blood rolling out to settle before Kharga's massive feet. The *Drokha* looked down, impassive.

His human company, less so.

"*Ancaa*," one said with a hiss, "what is that?"

"Did…did *he* do that? Should we…should we get help?"

"Gods, it *reeks*."

"It is—was—a human." Gariath spoke firmly. "He was eaten alive by a spider. Your human master owned that spider. You protected the human who did this." He leveled a claw at Kharga. "This is what your world creates: a snake that devours its own tail and calls itself sane."

Kharga's nostrils flared. "And?" He waved a hand. "You call humans inferior and worthless in one breath and then toss a dead one at my feet as though it's some great loss. Which is it?"

"This is not about that." Gariath snarled, kicking the bag. "This is about *you*. *You*, who kill them. *You*, who serve them. *You*, who take their coin, drink their drink, and live in their cities like you're one of *them*." He snarled. "You and your entire breed. The *Drokha* all snivel at the boots of humans and think to wear them for themselves."

"There are few *Drokha*." The fury building behind Kharga's voice was tempered by frigid contempt. "And fewer *Rhega*. Does the fact that you are all dead make you so noble? Did you think I did not see the humans *you* walked with in the Souk?"

"I protect them from their own stupidity," Gariath growled. "I keep them alive when they are too weak to do so. I do *not* beg for their coin."

"Then what is it that drives you to stay with them?" Kharga rumbled. "What is it you feel for them? I take the humans' coin. But they are not my family."

Gariath fell silent at that. There was no answer to offer. What could he say? That the humans viewed him as an equal? As a *friend*?

"Look around you." Kharga gestured to the harbor, the lanes lined with buildings, the ships bobbing at the docks. "This city was built by strong hands, keen minds. Even the *Drokha* could not stop it, even if we tried. You do not hate us for living here. You hate us for *living*." Kharga fixed a cold stare upon Gariath. "You hate us for not dying out in the wilderness until only a few of us were left."

He narrowed his eyes, spat the words.

"Like you."

Gariath had suffered many wounds in his days. He had lost track of even the most life-threatening ones. But barely could he remember a time when he felt more winded, more numb, more wounded than he did at that moment.

Kharga's ax did not rise. Gariath's scent had already given away his weakness.

He had no answer.

"Here, *Rhega*, we have a future," Kharga spoke, voice dripping with scorn. "We don't stand in this city. We are a part of it. We do not work for humans. We work *with* them. We are equals here."

A long silence ensued. Neither Kharga nor the humans behind him said a single word. And for a very long time, Gariath found it hard to meet the *Drokha*'s eyes. When he spoke, it was soft and it was weak.

"Do you drink with them?" he asked.

"What?" Kharga rumbled.

"Do they sit at a different table when they drink?"

Kharga said nothing.

"When they talk to you, do they call you 'Kharga'? Do they call you '*Drokha*'? Or do they call you 'dragonman'?"

No human would notice the change. The shifting of emotions from contempt to hatred to fury would have only been apparent in the wall of scent that assailed Gariath as Kharga's own weakness was revealed. The humans, staring dumbly as though watching two dogs try to have a conversation, wouldn't have known anything was the matter at all.

Not until Kharga's ax came hammering down.

Stone shattered. Earth screamed. A cloud of sand and pulverized cobblestones went flying into the air and cloaked the many bodies that fell, the road torn out from under them like a rug.

And Gariath was still alive.

Or so he thought, anyway.

Kharga's blow had barely missed, but he felt the shock of it in his bones as he stumbled to the ground. The pain in his chest resonated with a dull ache. Maybe he hadn't slept off earlier wounds. Maybe he was getting older, weaker.

Or maybe Kharga was just that angry.

That was easy enough to believe, even before Gariath felt a shadow fall over him. He narrowly tumbled aside in time to avoid Kharga's foot as it came crashing down, sending the stones shuddering.

Gariath clawed his way to his feet as the humans tried to find their footing. When he came up, he found himself snout-to-face with one of them. Eyes wide, hands trembling, the human made a grab for his spear, thrust halfheartedly at Gariath.

"S-stay back."

The flimsy attack was an insult. Gariath thought he should have done more than just smash his fist against the human's nose and send him unmoving to the ground. But, the dragonman thought as he reached down to pluck up the spear, he was in a hurry.

"DIE, MONSTER!"

Gariath whirled and saw it. Not the human leaping at him, sword drawn, mouth wide in a war cry. That, he barely noticed. Rather, Gariath saw something else. Something that made him duck low.

Kharga's ax swung wildly over his head with enough force to cleave through the human in midair. Two twitching pieces fell to the ground.

A fine red mist mingled with the sand and dust in the air. The humans were screaming, some running, some grabbing weapons. Gariath didn't care about that. Nor, it seemed, did Kharga. Their eyes were on each other, brimming with hatred.

Kharga's swing had left him open and Gariath leapt at him, hanging from the giant's horn with one hand and driving the spear forward with the other. He drove it to the haft into Kharga's collar. Thick hide split. Blood wept. The shaft shattered in his hand.

And Kharga did not so much as flinch.

Unsurprisingly, it was difficult to read emotions through a reptilian snout. Between dragonmen, scent was everything.

And at that moment, Kharga's scent was rage. There was no room for anything else: not the spear in his collarbone, not the blood weeping down his chest, not the foe hanging from his horn. A massive hand reached up and seized Gariath by the shoulder.

And flung him to the ground like so much filth.

He didn't hear the sound of his body striking the stones. Nor the sound of the humans cackling. Nor even the sound of coughing as blood spattered from his mouth onto the ground.

"Maybe they hate us," Kharga rumbled. "Maybe they look down on us. Maybe we take their coin. But we are better for living with their stink than dying out there like *you*."

Even if Gariath hadn't smelled the anger and desperation on the bigger dragonman, it was clear his words had struck deeper than any spear could. That would be more satisfying, he thought, if he could actually hear whatever Kharga was saying.

His earfrills were filled with a ringing sound. His body felt numb as he staggered to his feet. His own scent reeked of fear, panic, pain. Agony tinged his senses and through it he could think of only one word.

Run.

It was only through that panic that he willed his legs to work, picking him up on a swaying stagger and sending him forward. Or at least, he assumed his legs were working. He couldn't feel them moving under him. He couldn't feel the pain in his chest.

Nor could he feel the earth tremble as Kharga let out a howl and came charging after him.

He hurt with every step he took. Blood worked itself back into his legs, sensation returned to sharp, agonized splendor. Without panic to cloud his thoughts, every stab of pain became all the more exquisitely pronounced.

Good.

Fear was poor motivation. It came and went of its own accord with no respect for who might need it the most.

Pain lingered. Pain reminded. Pain taught a lesson.

One Gariath was eager to share as he took a sharp turn down a nearby alley. The houses here were unfinished, their stonework stacked around lumber frames like granite skin flayed from wooden bones. Carts full of mortar and bricks lined the street. A large wooden crane hung over a taller building, toting a heavy load of stone and lumber.

This was where Gariath chose to make his stand.

He whirled. Kharga was not far behind. The dragonman was charging without roars, without words. His ax rose without a curse or a snarl to accompany it. Everything he had to say filled Gariath's nostrils.

Gariath forced himself to look away, despite how stupid it was to do so. He forced himself to ignore the scent of Kharga's fury, despite how impossible it was to do. He cast a look up at the crane, up to the yellow eyes that looked down upon him.

He gave a brief nod.

A blade flashed in the dark.

And stone rained from the sky.

There was a howl barely heard under the roar of falling earth and shattering wood. Dust and sand erupted in a cloud; Gariath shielded his eyes as it swept over him. When it dissipated, the giant dragonman lay unmoving, a two-ton child tucked ungently beneath a heavy quilt of bricks and timber.

"Is he dead?"

Gariath glanced up. Daaru hung by one long limb onto the severed rope of the crane, his blade in his spare hand. With simian dexterity, he swung to the crane itself and began to clamber down to the streets below.

Despite the smothering stone, Kharga still drew breath, however faint, through twitching nostrils. His eyes were closed, his body was still, but he was, indeed, still alive.

Admittedly, Gariath hadn't expected this to work.

At first, he hadn't trusted Kharga to even take the bait. And when he had the spear in his hands, he hadn't trusted himself not to drive it a little deeper and aim for the heart. And finally, when the stones fell, he hadn't trusted even the crushing weight of hewn earth to stop the giant.

But, he thought. *It worked. I stopped him. Without killing him.*

"Waste," Daaru said, casting a sneer down upon Kharga. "It's these creatures that keep the other oids at bay. They're not like Kudj, you know. Not simple paid labor. Their sole purpose is to spill our blood. Even *one* dead dragonman would improve the lives of every tulwar in the city."

"I can't."

"Why? He's not one of us."

"He's one of me."

He didn't look at Daaru. He didn't need to know the kind of resentful glare the tulwar shot him. Resentment, Gariath knew, born from not understanding. Gariath only barely understood himself.

He did not know anything about Kharga. All his thoughts were pains, as keen and bitter as the dull ache lingering in his chest. And he knew that to kill Kharga would be to kill another dragonman.

And that thought came with more pain.

"Should have done it better," Gariath muttered, mostly to himself. "Should have fought him." He sighed, looking over the bricks. "This wasn't the right way."

"No," Daaru agreed. "Did you learn that from your humans?"

Only then did Gariath look at the tulwar. And he did not know the look that Daaru turned upon him.

"You heard that," he observed. No question, no defense.

"I was on the roofs, watching. Is it true?"

"It is."

"Is *all* of it true?" Daaru asked, gesturing to Kharga. "What makes you any different from him, then? You hang around humans, same as he does."

"I don't serve them."

Daaru's lip curled back, exposing long canines. "You either kill them or you serve them. They don't know any other way to exist with us. Or you."

"Mine are different."

Daaru looked back down to Kharga. "Maybe he thought his were, too." He shook his head. "I don't know. Maybe yours are. But they're only different for *you*, Gariath; the rest of us have to live with them as we know them."

And when he looked to the dragonman again, Gariath's face was twisted into a frown, an echo of pain playing across his features.

"You can't be one of us," Daaru said, "and be one of them, as well."

Gariath stared back at Kharga, unconscious and wounded. The humans—Kharga's humans—would come searching for him eventually. Even now, they might be raving with tales of a ravenous dragonman, except small and red instead of a gray giant, to their fellow guards. Even now, they might be coming back, seeking the dragonman—*their* dragonman.

Kharga had chosen his people.

And Gariath hated him for it.

But at least Kharga had chosen. At least Kharga had declared himself to stand with the humans instead of keeping one foot in their world and one foot in the world Gariath occupied. At least Kharga knew who he was.

He growled. His chest hurt. His head hurt. Everything hurt.

Daaru said nothing at that. Daaru had turned around and was already walking away, sheathing his sword.

"Where are you going?" Gariath asked.

"There is no work in this city. I must find another way to feed my family. And to do that, I must go back to them." He glanced fleetingly over his shoulder. "Where I belong."

Gariath said nothing in response.

For a long time, though, he looked at a fallen brick and thought, not for the first time, that if he flung it just right at Daaru's head, it might kill the tulwar. That wouldn't help, he knew, even if it would spare him future lectures. That which Daaru had said would still be said, no less true.

And so, Gariath watched him go, leaving him alone with Kharga and the pain in his chest.

TWENTY-SIX

THE LADY AND THE ROGUE

This is how they trick you."

The house guard patted the hilt of his blade, the sword rattling against his armor.

"'Be a house guard,' they say. 'Serve the fashas! Good pay and you'll have a sword handy if the Jackals come sniffing after you.'"

He reached to the stove, plucked a satay of beef from the skillet, and took a bite out of it. He warned off the servant who looked curiously at him with a glare before snatching a bottle of wine from a nearby table and taking a long swig.

"Lies," he muttered through a mouthful. "Pay's shit. Fashas're shit. They don't even *let* you use these swords. Put it in your hands, make you feel like a big man, but anytime there's actual fighting to be done, they call in their dragonmen to do it. My uncle was defending Cier'Djaal in the Uprising, you know? Never even drew his blade. Dragonmen did all the fighting.

"Worst part?" He looked around the kitchen warily and fell silent as another set of servants walked past the doorway, before leaning over and whispering. "This blade isn't going to do *shit* if the footwar spills into Silktown. The Jackals have always had an understanding with the fashas, sure, but they're still a pack of dogs. What do they do when they start getting squeezed by the Khovura like the curs they are? They're going to turn on us is what they're going to do."

The servant made a noncommittal hum beneath his veil, not

looking up from his work of assembling a meal of satays and apricots from the sizzling stove. The house guard kept his glare upon him, regardless, as he took another bite from one of the satays he'd purloined.

"Why you think I've been hired?" he muttered. "Teneir only hires saccarii, right? She and that freak Sheffu. But now she's got a need for extra guards, just like all the other fashas. They've locked themselves up in their homes with their spiders. They want to be ready for the Jackals—or the Khovura, whichever comes knocking. No more parties, no more harems, no more feasts. Just my fucking luck, eh?"

He took another big bite, another big swig.

"Could've signed on with Ghoukha. He's still spending money like it's water. Hear his silk is stronger than ever. Huge demand from the merchants. Parties every night, slave girls running around naked." The guard sighed wistfully. "Could be bending over some little thing right now instead of watching Teneir's snakes slither around."

He fell silent as one of the saccarii servants came in and glanced between the servant, the guard, and the platter. In a thickly accented language that sent the guard cringing, he asked the servant something, who nodded briefly in reply. At that, the platter was collected and spirited away.

"Snakes," the guard spat again. "Can't ever get around that accent." He glanced at the servant left remaining. "What'd he ask you, anyway?"

The servant said nothing, turning his attentions to the dirty dishes left over and beginning to scrub them. The guard sneered.

"You think you're better than me or something? Too good to talk to a human, *oid*?" He reached out for the servant's veil. "You stupid piece of—"

His fingers had barely grazed the cloth when he found a palm at his throat. And his mouth had barely opened to swear when he heard the click of a hidden spring.

When the blade leapt from its hidden sheath beneath the wrist and entered his throat, he barely knew what had happened.

Denaos was already cursing himself when he rushed to catch the falling guard. He seized a nearby cloth and jammed it up against the neck wound to halt the spurt of blood. Careful to leave not a drop upon the floor, he hurriedly hauled the dead man toward the pantry.

The hell'd you do that for? Sure, he was an asshole, he told himself, *sure, he was about to tear off your veil and blow this whole thing. But there had to be a better way.*

This much was true. Even as Denaos hid the man behind a few barrels and stacked some sacks of rice atop the body, he knew he had just turned an hourglass upside down. He had only between now and the moment someone found the body—which might be anywhere from two breaths to two hours, depending on whether anyone got a craving for curry—to locate some evidence linking the Lady Fasha Teneir to the Khovura and, hopefully, Miron's disappearance.

He wiped his hidden blade clean and tucked it back beneath his sleeve by drawing the latch back until it clicked into place. He adjusted his veil, walked out of the pantry, and emerged from the kitchen with the quick, poised stride that would be expected of a servant.

No one looked twice at him as he moved through the carpeted halls of Teneir's manse. No one ever would.

In the mind of the common man, infiltration was an art form. Stories were rife with tales of unseen assassins and shadowy thieves, moving like ghosts from shadow to shadow, hidden from sight until the time came to strike and they would leap from the darkness like creatures from hell to slay their targets in a single thrust.

Those stories were popular for a reason.

Because in the mind of the practical rogue, hiding in shadows to get into a rich lady's home was a bunch of horseshit. For one, there weren't any; rich people could afford lights in every corridor. And besides, this was Cier'Djaal, where wealthy people had accountants to tally every coin with cold-blooded covetousness. These people were always wary of thieves, always ready for assassins.

A shadow in Cier'Djaal would have a thousand eyes on it.

But no one would ever think to look twice at the help.

He heard the sound of armor rattling as he turned the corner down another hall. He had only a moment to catch a glimpse of the cluster of house guards, armed with blades and spears and clad in mail and silks, before he fell to his knees and pressed his head to the floor in dutiful obeisance.

When they passed, he had a moment to look up and see the slight figure they guarded. Legs hidden behind skirts laced with gemstones, face and hair cloaked behind elegant crimson veils, the Lady Teneir was a silken scarf wrapped about the hilt of a blade. Where her bodyguards stomped, she floated. Where they scowled, her austere stare never wavered. And wherever she walked, her servants bowed in genuine reverence.

You wouldn't think someone like her would support the Khovura, would you, he mused to himself.

Honestly, he hadn't expected that any fasha would be in league with them. They were as old and established in Cier'Djaal as the Jackals. And like most well-to-do families, the thieves and the nobles tended to have much in common. With the tacit understanding that the fashas' considerable assets would never be levered against the Jackals, the rogues agreed to keep their distance from the fashas' operations.

It was a contract penned in blood a long time ago.

And it had plenty of fine print.

What made the alliance between the Jackals and the fashas so elegant was the understanding that both were predators. Either one would watch the other die in a fire if it meant earning a few more coins. And for a long while, this had been a prosperous situation: the fashas would covertly send the Jackals against each other, thinking themselves rulers of the thieves while the thieves saw themselves gradually weakening the only rival power in the city.

And as with any deal between predators, everyone was keenly aware that there would come a point when one partner saw the other as meat. And it wouldn't be hard to imagine a fasha seeing an opportunity in the rise of the Khovura. Predators were beasts of opportunity, after all.

Even one as elegant as Lady Teneir.

He listened until the sound of clinking mail faded entirely, then took off down the hall toward the *houn*. Not much longer now, he knew. He had to be quicker about getting out than he was getting in.

To a fasha, there was no more important room than the *houn*. An older Djaalic word for "boast," it was the room where they greeted every petitioner, broker, and fellow noble and, thus, the room that would send a statement to the world.

That statement would usually be "Look at how much more money I have than you, you stupid, poor bastard."

Teneir, however, seemed intent on saying "Look at how much more money I have than you and how much more pious I am than you, you stupid, poor, blasphemous, possibly ugly bastard."

The rugs were woven to display a river of humanity crawling across the floor on their bellies. The pillars were carved to resemble people twisting into columns, hands extending to support the walkway on the upper floor. The sigil of Ancaa, a wreath of human hands bound together by each other, was everywhere. In every tapestry, in every sculpture, in every graven image: a forest of limbs in silk and steel and stone.

Denaos's eyes drifted up to the walkway ringing the upper floor. No servants were in sight, which suggested that this was a place where servants should not be seen. Which, in turn, suggested he should work even faster than he thought he might.

He swept up the stairs, holding himself still and quiet as he heard another pair of guards come rattling past down below.

"All I'm saying is," one of them muttered, "if it comes down to war, we're better off enlisting with them."

"Which one?" his companion asked. "The Karnerians or the Sainites?"

"Doesn't matter. They both pay better than this oid."

"Because they expect you to die for that coin, moron. Fashas just want you to look pretty. Besides, if the mediation goes as planned, there's not going to be a war. Think of how many lives would be lost."

"The mediation is a myth. They've been planning for months and haven't done shit. Besides, this is Karneria and Saine we're talking about. When have lives lost ever concerned them?"

He waited until he couldn't hear them anymore, then swept about the upper level. He cracked open each door, peering inside.

Silks, bed, mirror—guest room. He moved to the next. *Table, window, jug—breakfast room.* He slipped to the room at the far end of the walkway. *Papers, chair, desk—there we go.*

The people who suspected that a good rogue stuck to the shadows were the same people that probably thought a good rogue would go straight for the vaults. True, there had been some good thieves who had lifted a few precious things from a few unwary fashas in the past. Those were freelancers, though: unguilded, unmade, and usually killed quickly. Denaos was a professional.

And professionals knew that the bulk of a fasha's wealth was wrapped up in deals, trade agreements, and arrangements made with other merchants. Professionals knew that the most valuable things in a fasha's house lay sprawled out on the desk in sheaves, like those Denaos saw when he slipped into the room and shut the door behind him. Professionals knew that the most dangerous men in the world were accountants.

Lady Teneir undoubtedly knew this as well. The desk was a mess of papers without a single lick of organization to them. A clerk who had his own system—especially a messy one—was a boon for paranoid fashas. It made his notes harder to root through, as Denaos quickly found out.

Fortunately, messy clerks tended to leave their most recent

business close at hand. And this one had left the most important part of any fasha's fortune: the trade manifest.

He pored over the numbers, searching for any sign of mysterious payments, donations or expenses with suspicious names and found little.

Little of Teneir's expenses, anyway: nearly every coin she had spent had gone directly to the Church of Ancaa or artists specializing in Ancaa-inspired decor. But what her rivals were doing was of greater interest.

It wasn't surprising that the fashas should keep tabs on each other's expenditures. It was a practical necessity for staying competitive. Teneir's lists were accurate to the last copper. The relatively skimpy lists of Fasha Mevuum and Fasha Mejina—and the shamefully short list of Fasha Sheffu—looked like little minnows on the paper, fit to be swallowed by the massive fish that was Fasha Ghoukha's expenses.

The bulk of it was rather standard fare for a fasha known for such excesses: crates of fine wine, Muraskan cheeses, fruits shipped from distant lands...

New house guards: twenty-six, one hundred seventy gold pieces weekly, Denaos read. *Wine, food, arms, and armor for them and an additional one hundred: two thousand gold pieces. Weekly income: four thousand?*

What had that guard said? Ghoukha's silk was stronger now? In high demand? Enough that he could afford hiring a small *army*? There were expenses listed for architects, engineers, and laborers that suggested he intended to build even more lodging to house even more guards.

Or... what everyone thinks *are guards.*

Could that be it, he wondered? Could Ghoukha be hiring an army of paper guards whose identities existed only in the ledgers of accountants? Could the real bodies filling his halls and carrying his weapons be Khovura agents?

Obviously, he half-thought, half-cursed to himself. *Look at this.*

Everyone's profits are down but his. The Khovura are targeting other businesses, ones not under his protection. They might be behind this powerful new silk, as well.

The Khovura *did* have a fasha on their side, and they were rigging the economy to make him the wealthiest, most generous, and soon-to-be most-well-armed man in Cier'Djaal. Rezca would want to know this. Rezca would *need* to know this.

And Denaos committed to tell him once he resolved the little matter of someone pressing the tip of a dagger against the back of his neck.

Just as soon as he figured out how to do that, everything would be coming together.

"Well?"

A voice ran down the blade like cold water, settling at the base of his skull.

"Well, what?" he asked.

"*Well*, there is a certain way we do this sort of thing," the voice at the end of the blade said. "It usually concludes with someone bleeding out on the floor. But before that, there's a little shameless begging. Before *that*, a few empty threats. And before *that*, a bunch of ridiculous lies as to what a *shkainai* dressed up as a saccarii is doing in a fasha's accountant's office." A throat cleared behind him. "So, you know, whenever you're ready."

"It sounds kind of like a waste of time, doesn't it?" he asked. "If you were going to kill me, you would have done so already. And since you know I shouldn't be here, you probably already know what I'm doing here. Which means either you're a self-absorbed, loathsome individual who enjoys threatening people with knives purely to get a sadistic shot of confidence at the expense of someone else's fear," he sniffed, "or you're a good friend of mine."

The blade slid from the back of his neck, scraping at the finer hairs, before tapping lightly on his shoulder. A tongue clicked behind him and the voice, languid and liquid, whispered.

"Can't it be both?"

When he turned around, the first thing he saw was her smile. It wasn't a beautiful smile, not naturally: thin lips, curling up at the corners not unlike the way a cobra's mouth naturally curved. But it was beautiful by design, coiling with rehearsed spontaneity, meticulously crafted and honed to look as natural and unfinished as possible. It was a painted, pretty picture that told men that she was so very happy to see them.

Everything else about her was built around the fraud upon her face: the smooth, slow curves fit into tight black leathers, the long, dark hair that pooled with a carefully carefree grace around her shoulders, the eyes that glimmered like cut gems. She was as slender, as honed, and as beautiful as the blade in her hand, but even that didn't look half as dangerous as her smile.

He saw Anielle's smile first, because Anielle wanted men to see her smile first. And back when they had run in the same circle, it was her smile that men had always seen last.

"Ani," he said, softly. "It's been a while."

"So long that I don't even know what to call you now," she replied, lofting a black brow. "When you fled the city, you were still Ramaniel. Now I hear you're calling yourself Denaos. But that was a day ago. You might have picked out something new since then."

"Ramaniel's dead," was all he offered in response. "He died in the riots."

It would have to be a remarkable thing to make a smile so elegantly sharpened waver like hers did at that moment. But there hadn't been anything quite so remarkable as the riots. She had been there, with him, behind the scenes, holding the knives that had made them happen.

"A lot of people did," she replied, voice heavy. "No one else came back, though. Must have been someone special that made you."

She didn't finish that thought. She didn't have to. The gleam in her eye, the breathless rasp that came in on the end of her sentence made her question clear. Denaos was merciful enough not to make her say it. Just as he was cruel enough to shake his head, *no*.

"I run with a new crew right now," he resigned himself to answering. "This is just a one-time favor for Rezca."

And suddenly, that smile returned. But there was an edge to it this time, one of morbid joy.

"Yeah," she said. "Sure. Yerk had the same thought as Rezca, which is why I'm here." She glanced over his disguise before pulling a hood around her head. "Of course, I came in the *real* way."

"What? Sneaking in? Like some kind of fairy-tale cutthroat?" He rolled his eyes. "*Please.*"

"It's classic!" she protested. "In like a breeze, out like a shadow. Also?" She gestured to her hood. "This right here? *Amazing.*"

"A moving shadow, a talking breeze," Denaos replied. "People tend to notice those. Disguise, at least, has the benefit of not drawing attention to itself."

She opened her mouth to reply. All that was heard was the distant clang of an alarm bell followed by the clomping of boots and the rattle of armor as guards rushed to assemble.

Someone, apparently, had gotten a craving for curry.

He nudged the door open and peered out into the hallway. Guards were rampaging up the steps; veterans, they knew exactly where a thief would be heading.

"Damn it," he muttered. "Let's hurry up and—"

No reason to finish the sentence, he realized as he looked over his shoulder. Anielle already had hurried up. The window hung wide open, leaving only shadows and the breeze where she had just stood.

All right, he admitted to himself as he rushed to the window, *so it's a classic for a reason.*

⸺ ⋯⋙⋯ ⸺

"All right, all right," Anielle said, pointing to the upper-left window, where three guards swept through a parlor, looking behind couches and wardrobes. "Look at this guy, trying to be all thorough, tearing up pillows. As though there's a two-foot-tall assassin hiding under them."

"I'm watching this fellow here," he replied, pointing to the window just below, where another pair of guards searched carefully through a bedroom. "You can *just* barely make it out from here, but he's waiting for his friend to leave so he can drop his trousers and claim to have been naked in Lady Teneir's bed."

She laughed.

And he found himself smiling.

Not for the sound of it, of course—she had the sort of laugh that only ever came out when old people got hit in the head with bricks—but rather because it was the only part of her that she had never been able to hone, to perfect, to disguise.

When she laughed, she was just Anielle. And he was still Ramaniel.

And it was almost like the time back when neither of them had killed anyone yet.

"You remember when we first did this?" she asked him.

He leaned back on his hands and felt the tile under his palms, cooled by the night sky. The roof they sat upon was part of some other fasha's home that overlooked Teneir's manse, every window filled with shadows as guards searched for a murderer they'd never find, unaware of the two people watching them from the outside.

"Dark Croi's gang," he said, "squatting in a warehouse on the docks. We snuck in, lifted his favorite ax, sat on the roof of the warehouse next door, and watched him through the windows, threatening all his boys, and tearing the place apart looking for that thing. What'd he call it again?"

" 'Kiss of Death.' Remember what happened then?" she asked, grinning broadly. "We had it blunted, painted it pink with big, googly eyes and lips and renamed it the 'Kissy-face of Death.' "

"Hung it at the Harbor Gate. Dark Croi thought a rival gang was coming for him and disbanded." He laughed. "Never even crossed his mind that it was just a couple of kids."

Anielle sighed, pulling her knees to her chest and resting her chin atop them. "That was about two months after you came in on the boat and begged to join Rezca's and my gang."

"I remember that," he said, lying back against the tile. "A gang made up of a nervous little fat kid and a girl that looked like a boy. What was I thinking?"

"Likely, you were thinking that we were your only hope for survival as a *shkainai* boy in Cier'Djaal."

"Doubtful. You kept calling me 'pale boy' and laughing at the way I sunburned."

"Well, you had it coming. You *were* pale and you smelled like bacon when you got burned." She fell back alongside him. "More than anything, we wanted to be Jackals."

That was the only part that was missing: the desire to be a Jackal. Everything else fit just like it had when they were young.

Here they were, lying down next to each other on a roof, staring up at a night sky that still didn't seem half as big as the city. Here they were, laughing about doing terrible things to other people, talking about Jackals like they were creatures of myth and not a gang of thugs. Here, on cold tile, the heat of her body next to him and... and then...

What happened next, again?

He felt feather-soft fingers slide alongside his neck and trace the path of a blade's tip down to his collarbone.

Oh, right.

He should have said something, then, as she rolled on top of him. He should have listened to a voice not between his legs as she spread hers across his waist and leaned down upon him. He should have been thinking of other things than the fingers sliding into his hair, the warmth of her breath as she drew close, how easy it was to recall the circle of her mouth and how his lips fit around it and how very, very nice it was to shut his eyes and pretend that this was all he ever wanted.

He didn't, though.

Some men made mistakes in their lives.

And then some men lived mistakes.

Denaos was that man now, just as Ramaniel had been that boy.

The boy who never wanted anything more than to impress her, the boy who would piss off Dark Croi just to hear her tell him he was stupid and brave. That boy was here, eyes shut, breathing in the ink-and-leather scent of her skin, feeling the curtains of her hair brush against his jaw, feeling the way her fingers remembered the curve of his cheek as she pulled him ever further into her.

That boy's fingers were back, as well, fumbling at the belt that hung from her hips, trembling as they tried to concentrate despite the rise in his trousers screaming for him to hurry. That boy's fingers had only ever shown up once before. Only ever with her. But there was no avoiding it; he would have to look to see what he was doing, just like he had then.

And when he opened his eyes, that boy was gone.

So was Anielle.

Straddling him was Imone, the woman they called the Hound-mistress, eyes wide, grin wide, throat slit open in a bright red slash, a river of blood pouring down her breasts, slithering over her belly to stain the fingers that trembled terribly and pulled away.

He shut his eyes again. Opened them once more.

Imone was gone.

And so was the boy.

"I can't," he whispered into her mouth.

She pressed her lips a little closer, shut her eyes a little tighter, gave a gentle moan as an answer, and pretended she couldn't hear him. They couldn't lie to each other—never had been able to—but they could deny. They could pretend.

Or she could, anyway. He had to pull away and mouth a silent apology to her as she looked down at him. No anger in her stare. She had known this was going to happen, even if she pretended she couldn't have. She was just sad that he couldn't have, as well.

"You shouldn't have come back, Ramaniel," she whispered.

"I hadn't planned on seeing you."

"Do you seriously think I'm concerned for me?" she asked. "Were you entertaining fantasies of me sitting by my window, waiting for you to come back?"

He shook his head.

"I was happy when you left," she said. "I knew something was going to kill you if you stayed—it was either going to be the Houndmistress's supporters or it was going to be yourself. When you disappeared, I knew you'd at least die far away and I'd be able to tell myself I couldn't have done anything to stop it.

"But you don't get to come back and act like things have changed, Ramaniel," she said, rising off of him. "You and me, we scarred this city when we were done. You coming back is just putting a knife back in that old wound. You don't get to choose to stay out of it. Not after what you did here."

"Like I said, this is just a one-time favor," Denaos replied. "When I'm done, I'll be gone forever."

"You were supposed to be gone forever last time," she said, walking to the edge of the roof. "And you know that there are no one-time favors when it comes to the Jackals. You're a veteran and you came back during a war. You really think they're going to let you sit this one out?"

"They aren't going to do to me what they did back then," he protested, clambering to his feet. "This isn't going to change who I am."

"That's why you shouldn't have come back."

He knew, again, that he should have done something. He should have rushed her, stopped her before she could leap off the roof. But he didn't. And when he looked down off the edge, she wasn't there. Nothing below but shadows and a breeze.

TWENTY-SEVEN

THE LOW ROAD

L enk was ten when he drank his first ale at a harvest festival. Mere moments after that, he had met his first alcoholic in the form of a widower who traded his barn for a barrel. And while he would have more ale and meet more drunkards during the years that followed, he had always remembered that festival when he had staggered home drunk and been given an earful from his grandfather.

"Some men live at the bottom of a tankard," Grandfather had said, *"and down there, it's dark and cold and quiet. A man hears nothing, sees nothing, and feels nothing."*

During all the years that had followed, Lenk always knew his grandfather had a point.

It was only now that he was beginning to realize that the alcoholic might have had a better one.

He tilted his head back, drained the rest of his tankard, and set it back down on the rotting wooden table, next to the other two empty ones. He wiped his mouth and, with foam-stained fingers, made a beckoning motion across the table.

"All right, I'm ready," he said. "Tell me again."

Asper's frown deepened, as it had progressively deepened with every tankard. A furrow of irritation marred her brow.

"Miron has been dead for centuries. Whoever owes us money isn't who he says he is. The Khovura know we're looking for him. The demons are with them and they are all trying to kill us."

Lenk returned the stare. He nodded slowly. He looked down at his empty tankard and hummed.

"No," he said. "I was wrong. That's not going to do it." He slid the tankard to the side. "One more."

Denaos nodded, tilting the last of the fourth pitcher into the tankard. "You're buying the next one," he said. "The man drinking shouldn't consume more than the man paying. It offends Silf."

"Silf is a god of thieves whose rules change when it's convenient."

"He's good to His own," Denaos replied.

"So I see," Lenk muttered, eyeing the small pile of coins before the rogue. "Did He give you that?"

"No."

"Then what is it?"

"A loan."

"From who?"

"Friends."

"Which friends?"

"Additional evasive answer."

"What?"

Denaos looked up. "Sorry, I just thought I'd save us both some time there." He slid the tankard back to Lenk. "Drink up."

A hand caught it. Not Lenk's. The young man looked up at the tankard in Asper's grasp. Then he looked up farther at the scowl scarred across Asper's face. Then he looked down as she slowly upended the tankard and poured the ale onto the floor.

"Well," he said, "I shouldn't have to get the next one after *that*."

"Shut up," she snarled. "And listen. I've told you three times already. If I have to tell you again, I'll use this"—she shook the tankard—"to smash a new hole in your head to shout into. The Khovura know who we are. They know what we're doing. They know who we're looking for and *we don't*." She slammed the tankard onto the table. "Miron Evenhands, the Lord Emissary, the fellow with *your* money does *not exist*."

"Which means we won't be getting paid." Lenk gestured futilely to the empty tankard. "Which felt like reason aplenty to drink heavily."

"You're not drinking over money lost. You never do." Her voice was hard and edged like a rough blade. "You'll kill over it, but never drink. You're drinking because it's been two days and Kataria still hasn't come back."

His left eyelid twitched. She set the tankard down heavily upon the table.

"And if you're going to be absolutely useless until she does, then could you please let me know so the rest of us could figure something out?"

It was an iron-and-straw silence that hung between them, something vast and heavy balanced precariously on something small and flimsy, teetering between the man and woman, waiting to see which of them would push it upon the other.

Outside, there was a rumble of thunder. The clouds that had gathered as evening fell began to mutter and complain to each other. A droplet of rain fell upon the window of the cramped, dingy room that separated the other cramped, dingy rooms they had bought from the innkeeper.

It was Lenk who pushed the silence over. He leaned across the table and rubbed his eyes.

"Look," he said, "it's not that I don't *get* what's going on. Obviously, payment aside, people trying to kill us is bad and demons trying to kill us is worse." He glanced at Asper, who rubbed at the torn sleeve of her robe. "But it's a little difficult to find someone who doesn't exist."

"You seemed pretty confident that we could find him before," Asper shot back. "All we need to do is stop looking for Miron and start looking for whatever man or thing is *pretending* to be Miron."

"Thing" might be too generous a term to describe whatever was masquerading as Miron, Lenk mused. Nothing ever was so simple as that when demons were involved.

He sighed. "And how do you suggest we do that? You didn't

find any leads on where Miron—sorry, Not-Miron—actually is, did you?"

"No. But *I* at least found out that he wasn't who he said he was. Did you find anything?"

"Not pertaining to Miron, no," Lenk said. "And since Dread and Gariath aren't back, I don't think we'll be hearing from them."

"Kataria might still—"

"If you finish that sentence, you had better hope I don't get hold of that tankard again."

She sank into her chair, crossing her arms. "Well, where does that leave us, then?"

In the silence that followed, the long, deliberate sound of slurping echoed in the musty confines. They turned toward Denaos, who drank noisily from his own still-full tankard, smacked his lips, belched, and set it back down on the table. He folded his arms, stared pointedly out at nothing, and said not a word.

"Yes?" Lenk asked.

"Oh," the rogue replied, "nothing. I was just thirsty."

"Just say it," the young man said with a sigh.

"No, no. It's quite all right. You two go on striking your foreheads together, hoping to get enough of a spark to light a tinder." He plucked up his tankard. "I'll just sit here and, you know..."

He took another agonizingly slow slurp.

"Denaos," Asper pressed.

"Fine," the rogue said with another belch. "If you can both agree to trust me enough to hear what I have to say without interruption or asking how I found out or questioning my methods, I can tell you how to find Miron."

"Agreed," Lenk said.

Asper did not say anything, fixing the rogue with a glare. He met her gaze with an expectant look. With a mutter, she relented.

"Fine."

"Lovely." Denaos leaned over the table. "All right, so, if we know that the Khovura have a reason to stop us from finding Miron, would it be safe to assume that our best link to him would be through finding them?"

"If they're attacking us like Asper says they are—" Lenk began.

"They are," Asper snapped.

"—then it would at least be smart to know where they are."

"In that case," Denaos said, "we need to find a way into the house of Fasha Ghoukha."

"Ghoukha?" Asper asked. "Why do—"

"You already agreed not to interrupt," Denaos replied, holding up a finger. "There's a fair amount of evidence to suggest that he's housing, aiding, and abetting the Khovura. Get into his house, you can find where they are, what they're doing, and maybe Miron . . . or Not-Miron. Whatever."

"But how—"

"You *also* agreed not to ask how," the rogue said. "Fortunately, the parts that you're not allowed to know also suggest that Ghoukha is in the habit of throwing large parties. And they aren't too difficult to get into."

"They are when they're full of rich people," Lenk said, "and we look the way we do."

"It's easier than you'd think," Denaos replied. He glanced over his shoulder as fat drops of rain continued to strike the window. "Probably even more so now that the weather's turned. Rain's bad luck in Cier'Djaal. For fashas, anyway."

"Why's that?"

"Free water," Denaos replied, "is bad for business. They like to throw themselves feasts and remind themselves that they still shit gold. Lots of money, lots of liquor, lots of guests. We can think of something."

"Can you think of something to get rid of that giant dragonman he keeps with him?" Asper asked. "I can't imagine it's easy with him around."

"It won't be a problem."

Every ass cheek sprang off wood at the sound of Gariath's voice.

They craned their necks to the bed pressed up against the wall, where what they had assumed was a large pile of blankets had been. The dragonman lay on his stomach, eyes closed, arm draped over his head.

"How long have you been there?" Asper asked.

"Long."

"Why didn't you say anything?" Lenk asked.

"Because."

"How do you know the dragonman won't be a problem?" Denaos asked.

Gariath cracked open a single black eye to regard the rogue. Then he snorted, rolled onto his side, and said nothing more.

"Well, there you have it, I guess," Lenk said.

"There we have what, exactly?" Asper asked. "Cryptic gibberish from a drunk and a dragonman is hardly anything to base a plan around."

"And yet, we've done more with less," he replied with a shrug. "If Gariath says it's not a problem, I believe him." He glanced toward Denaos. "Whether or not I believe *you* is another matter. What's your plan?"

"Simple enough," he replied. "Find the Khovura, find Miron. Find Ghoukha, find the Khovura. That's the second plan."

"What's the first?"

"To sleep now and tell you later." The rogue yawned, scooping the rest of his coins into a pouch and drawing the strings tight. "I'd rather spring it on you when there's less time for you to think about it."

"That doesn't give me any confidence," Lenk said.

"Then let's forget about the money, Miron, and Cier'Djaal altogether," Denaos said. He rose to his feet, tossed the coin pouch up, and caught it again. "Hardly makes a difference to—"

The door opened and slammed shut. They looked to the entry of their dingy room and saw a boy in a dirty cloak, hair wet with rain, a wild look in his eyes. It was only scarcely recognizable as

Dreadaeleon. There was something much too unrestrained and inelegantly twitchy about him for him to be *their* wizard.

"You took your time," Lenk muttered as the boy stalked in. "Where the hell have you been?"

"Out," Dreadaeleon replied.

"And did you find out any—"

"No," the boy interrupted without looking at Lenk. His eyes were firmly fixed on the pouch in Denaos's hands. "Is that gold?"

"It's a loan," Denaos replied, drawing it against his chest protectively.

"Give it to me."

"Fuck off. Why should I?"

"I need to buy a woman," Dreadaeleon said.

Asper's eyes went wide, jaw hanging open. Lenk's brows went up in disbelief. Gariath stirred slightly but made no move to rise.

It was only Denaos who moved. Slowly, he circled around the table and stood before the boy. He stared down his chest into a pair of eyes that were wide, wild, and untrembling. His mouth set in a frown, his eyes half-lidded, Denaos took the pouch in hand and held it up.

He gave it a brief toss, testing its weight, before he took Dreadaeleon by the wrist, held his hand palm-up, and dropped the pouch into the boy's grasp. He put his hands on Dreadaeleon's shoulders, looked him square in the eye, and drew him in for a long, close hug.

"I'm so proud of you," he whispered softly into the boy's ears. "Go with the Gods, my child."

"Thanks," Dreadaeleon muttered as he turned to walk out the door.

"Wait!" Asper called after him. "You can't just—"

"Don't you ruin this moment," Denaos growled over his shoulder. "It's *special*. This is a *special* day."

"But we're about to plan something for—" she began to protest.

"I'll hear about it later," Dreadaeleon replied.

He waved a hand. The door opened of his own volition as he walked through it. Another wave and it shut behind him.

"How could you let him do that?" Asper snapped at Denaos.

"Do what?" Denaos asked. "Go perform something perfectly legal, however expensive?"

"He isn't ready!"

"That's his decision, isn't it?" Denaos gestured with a hand as he turned to disappear into one of the side rooms. "You can catch him and try to convince him of the error of his ways, if you want. But you'd better hurry. I've seen that look before. He'll be sprinting."

Without another word, he vanished behind a door, leaving Asper no one else to direct her outrage toward but Lenk.

"And you have nothing to say about this?" she asked.

"Do *you*?" he replied.

She looked very much like she wanted to have the comfort of flying into a sputtering, half-verbal rage. But the expression that came across her face was despairingly aware.

"I don't know," she said, slumping back into her chair. "It's just... what's happened since we got here? Dreadaeleon is buying whores, Denaos is sneaking around, Gariath disappears for days at a time, Kataria's gone, and you and I are..." She rubbed her left arm. "Is this what you wanted, Lenk?"

He looked down at his empty tankard with an intent that seemed to suggest he thought it would talk back when he spoke into it.

"You know, I'm not sure what I wanted." He leaned back in his chair. "I mean, I guess that's a lie. I had this vision of us walking through the Harbor Gate, Miron handing us our money, giving us a firm handshake, and parting ways forever. Then we'd all get a drink together—just one—and make a few jokes and one by one, we'd leave.

"In my mind, Dreadaeleon was always the first to go. He'd say something about magic, reporting into the Venarium or some such, call us all barknecks, and then leave. Denaos next, just getting up to take a piss and then never coming back. Then you, going off to accompany Miron to the church or something. Then Gariath, who would just wander off and maybe I'd hear about him in legends, some kind of monster terrorizing the countryside or something. And then it'd be just me and..."

With that last word came a quaver in his voice, and he chose to go no further. He glanced up from his tankard. Asper was staring pointedly at his forehead, too courteous to look into his eyes and make him finish that thought.

"Then Miron disappeared and the Khovura happened and all this happened and it all went right back to killing," Lenk said. He laid his head upon the table and rubbed the back of his neck. "Maybe that's how it was always going to be. Maybe it just comes too easy and everything else is just too hard. Maybe it's always going to be killing."

"No."

One word. Uncertain. He looked up at her. She was no longer looking at him, any part of him.

"If it was always going to be like that, we wouldn't even try," Asper said, rubbing her left arm. "We'd just accept it." She leaned her elbows onto the table. "I guess that's why I didn't want Dread to go. Even if he's not doing anything terrible, I guess...I just had to try to do something."

"You know, whatever Denaos has planned, it might end badly," Lenk said, looking intently at her. "Could be more killing."

"Could be," she said. "I'm not going to say that it's all right, either, that we're doing it for Miron...or Not-Miron or whatever. I know it's still killing. But there's got to be some kind of difference between killing for the sake of money and maybe killing for the sake of something else." She flinched. "Right?"

He felt something spatter across his brow. He looked up and took a drop of water in the eye. He scooted his chair back and balanced his tankard on his belly to catch the water dropping from the leak in the ceiling. There was a rhythmic echo with each drip, an endless sound hanging between fleeting moments.

"We could leave it," he said. "Whoever Not-Miron is, he doesn't want us to find him. The Khovura wouldn't chase us outside of

Cier'Djaal, probably. We could just leave. Go try again somewhere else. That'd be doing something else, wouldn't it?"

"Yeah," she said, looking down. "Yeah, it would."

For the first time that night, their eyes met. Only for a single echo, a moment during which a drop of rain hung over an empty tankard. But echoes could last forever, if the emptiness was big enough, and sometimes cups ran deeper than most people knew.

So they stared at each other, and in that echo they realized that they both knew only one way to try. And that way didn't involve them leaving behind the city, leaving behind everything they had pushed for, everything they had lost.

Or maybe they were drunk and angry.

Lenk didn't know.

He said nothing as he set his tankard back on the table, rose up, and walked to another of the side bedrooms. Asper didn't watch him as he went. Their echo was over. Water splashed against the floor with a dull rhythm. Tomorrow, they would be going back to what they did, back to trying the only way they knew how to.

Lenk wondered, as he opened the door to a dark bedroom, if it would end in killing.

Lenk tried to tell himself, as he closed the door behind him, that he didn't know.

TWENTY-EIGHT

AND HER

A human was a finite resource.

The bulk of him went to his fears. More went to his hungers. A few stray drops were spared for his loves and his devotions. Whatever scraps were left went to his senses.

All that was left of Lenk that night was wordless, shapeless thought.

The roof of his room was leaking. Rain came through on a tone-deaf chorus, a dozen little tin notes ringing out as drops fell into tin mugs, pans, other things that didn't matter.

The sheets of his bed were of poor quality. Overeager, inexperienced bed mates, they scratched at his naked flesh, brushing passionlessly against old scars, enthusiastically groping new wounds that aspired to be as old, as twisted.

He hadn't bothered to turn off the lamp. It sputtered out on its own ages ago. He didn't care. He didn't mind the dark. Or the rain. Or the itchy sheets. Or the way his body ached and begged him to just lie back and stop thinking.

He didn't have the sense to mind.

He rolled onto his side and stared at the corner where he'd propped his sword, the tatters of his tunic hanging from the crosspiece like a blindfold. It didn't matter. The sword could still see him, blind and in the dark. The sword was still staring at him, looking at him as though it was the answer to everything.

It didn't talk. Of course it didn't talk. That'd be stupid.

Talking implied that there would be a rapport. Swords didn't do that. Swords made statements. This one's was very simple, very clear.

Pick it up. Put it in something warm and screaming. No more thinking. No more problems.

Thinking was a problem. Swords were answers.

He rolled away from the sword, lay on his back, and tried to hate himself for thinking that the sword was actually making a lot of sense.

He stared up at his weeping ceiling in the dark. He listened to the bickering rhythm of the falling droplets. Thunder muttered somewhere in a murky city alley. He closed his eyes and tried to drift off into a numb, senseless sleep.

Tried.

His eyes twitched behind his lids. His nostrils quivered. The scent of rain grew strong, odorous. It carried with it the smell of sunbaked earth, of night skies stained by fire, of sweat and cinders and...

And...

Something wet brushed against his cheek.

He opened his eyes.

And there she was.

Looming over him, legs straddling his, hands placed firmly on his shoulders. Her fingernail scraped with a rhythmic fondness against an old scar near his throat: a scar she had given him. He didn't feel it.

Rain mixed with sweat upon her brow and trailed across her cheek to travel the slope of her neck, slide beneath her tunic and down the center of her belly, falling to dampen already moist sheets. He didn't notice.

The smell of her hair was thick and wet as damp braids hung about his face in long blond curtains, drawing him into a world that consisted solely of her as she leaned forward. But he didn't care.

He had only enough left of himself to look up and see her eyes, bright and vivid and wild with green, and convince himself he wasn't dreaming.

"Hey," Kataria said.

"Hey," he said. "When did you get in?"

"Just now."

"How?"

"I'm very clever."

"How'd you find me?"

"You're not."

"Where did—"

Two fingers pressed against his lips. Two green eyes bade him to be silent.

"I need to tell you something," she said. Her voice was slow, halting, raindrops in a tin cup. "I've been thinking about it all day and I've been walking back and forth between here and Shicttown and I keep thinking how I'm going to say it or what's going to happen when I do and I know that I'm either going to say it or hit you, so I need you to just...shut up for a bit."

She looked intently at him.

"All right?"

He nodded. His neck ached where she had scratched.

"I came back," she said, "for you. But not because of you." She looked past him, to the scar on his neck, to her finger retracing the groove in his skin. "Not because of them, either. It's not going to be about you or them anymore, choosing between you. I don't...I can't..."

A sigh shook her. In the fading light of a storm-shrouded moon, Lenk saw the tremble of her body, skin painted silver by the rain clinging to her skin.

"When you're here, I feel like...like we have to keep running. Like if we stop, we'll start thinking about everything we're doing and we'll realize how stupid it is and we'll just die. So when you say you want to sit here and live like this, then...I don't know.

"But when you're not here, I feel sick." Her voice stopped quaking. She spoke with certainty and with sadness. "And I thought that was going to be my choice. I was going to choose which way I was going to die. But then, when I was out there with them, with Kwar, I...they told me..."

She clenched her teeth, shook her head, as though words were something she could force out of her mouth if she merely tried hard enough.

He said nothing. He had not the sense to. His senses were filled with her, with her scent and her touch and the warmth of her body as she leaned closer and pressed herself against him and lay her hands on his cheeks and drew him close, pressing her forehead to his.

"I'm not going to choose anymore." She spoke the words into him. "No one's ever going to make me. I'm never going to be afraid and I'm never going to be sick and I'm never going to run."

She drew in a sharp breath through her teeth. He felt her body shudder against his, felt her draw tense upon him, felt her hold her breath in her belly like it was all she could hold onto.

"But if you want to," she whispered, "you should do it now."

The dark shroud of the sky shifted outside his room, casting a few scant traces of blurred moonlight through the window. Caught between shadows and silver, she looked like a beast from a dark wood: tense, wide eyes watching him.

Without knowing quite why, he lay a hand upon her naked side. She grew tight beneath his hand, her muscle bunching beneath her skin. He could feel her warmth, fever hot, following his hand, muscle twitching beneath his fingers as they ran up her side, past a subtle swell of trembling breast.

His fingers found her face, cradled her jaw, thumb brushing gently against her cheek. Even here, she seemed far from delicate. She pressed into his palm and seized his fingers in her own; and he could feel the same fever heat in her face, in her fingers, in her hair. He found a single, damp blond lock hanging before her face, took it between his thumb and finger, and gently ran them down, raindrops on his fingertips.

She needed more than rain.

As did he.

His free hand slid beneath his pillow and scrabbled across itchy sheets until he felt the prick of a sharp quill. He withdrew it and held before her, between his fingers, a single, white feather.

She leaned down. His hand welcomed her, drew her face to his. She hesitated just a hairbreadth over his lips; the warmth of her cinder-scented breath fell over him for but a moment.

Her lips found his, hesitantly at first, a light kiss, as though she wanted to see if he would run. Then deeper, her tongue sliding out to brush against his. He returned the favor, his tongue brushing against her canines. Her lips twitched, she bit down. A faint copper taste filled his mouth.

And then, he knew her. As though his senses had been waiting for him to wake up in case this was some terrible ale-soaked dream, they sprang to life.

He knew the fever of her flesh beneath his fingers. He knew the scent of smoking fires and rain-soaked sand flooding his nostrils, making him dizzy, making him fight to hold onto her scent. He knew her taste on his lips, on his tongue, and it was of blood and sweat and hunger.

And he forgot how long it had been since he had lain with her.

And soon, he forgot everything else but the need to be here, for this not to be a dream.

He felt cold metal against his belly as her hands were at her belt, fumbling with the buckle, tearing it from her waist. He felt her wriggling against his body as she slid free of her breeches. He felt the sudden blast of cold, rain-soaked air as she pulled the sheets from him and exposed him to her.

Nothing was left of him to know what was happening, what it all meant. No more fears to tell him that this would end badly as she spread her legs to straddle him. No sense left in him to feel her knees digging beneath his ribs as she tightened her thighs about him and guided him into herself. Nothing left for love or hate or thought or sense.

Only need.

Rabid and desperate and nothing else.

She rocked upon his hips. He arched beneath her. He felt her warmth in her hands as she pressed them upon his shoulders, pushed him into the bed, as she brushed past the old scars and dug her nails into his skin and began to make new ones. He jerked beneath her, the pain acute.

She let out a sharp gasp, and a growl caught in her throat as her head snapped back. In the silver, wavering light of the rain-soaked night, her canines were big and white and animal. She drew tighter about him, knees in his flanks, nails in his skin, scent in his nose, and snarl in his ears.

And he could not lay still.

He had to move. He had to seize her. He had to hold her or else he might simply slip away.

His arms shot out and wrapped about her middle. He drew her close to him, felt her fire blaze against his skin, felt her breasts press through the coarse cloth of her tunic against his chest. He stood, felt the cold floor beneath his feet, the sheet about his ankles, her legs wrapped around his waist. And a moment later, he felt the impact of the wall shuddering as he pushed her against it.

There was blood. There was pain. The sounds they made were of hunger, of need, of thoughtlessness. He knew none of this as he pressed against her, hips bucking forward, feeling himself thrust deeper inside her. He didn't feel the blood drawing beneath her nails. He didn't feel the chill of the air or the rain falling upon them as his movement sent a tin cup spilling to the floor, the water pooling around his feet.

Raindrops fell upon them from the roof, between them, mingling with their sweat and disappearing where their bodies clung together. His hands were shaking with their grip upon her. His knees were bloodless, numb beneath him and propped up only by need as he thrust inside her, pressing against the wall, feeling her tighten against him, around him.

The growl in her throat shook through her body, into his skin, into his blood. He could feel her voice inside him, as he felt him inside her. He could feel her breath on his ear, her warmth on his flesh, her fingers knotted in his hair, jerking his head back sharply to expose his neck.

And her teeth were there. And he was growling as well. And he didn't care that it hurt. And he didn't care that she burned at his touch. And he didn't care that when this was all over, everything that had driven her away before would still be there.

Swords.

Blood.

Bodies.

Problems for a thinking man.

Not for him. Not for the creature driven by need, holding onto her as if she was all that was keeping him here on the ground. Not for the man who felt himself erupt inside her, who felt his knees turn to liquid and fall to join the rain splashed upon the floor.

This man would have problems later. For now, he had her. For now, he had her hair in his fingers and her scent in his nose. For now, he had her warmth burning him and the cold biting him and her lips whispering soundlessly words that he could hear inside him.

For now, he had her.

And her fingertip on his back, tracing the old, jagged flesh of the first scar she had ever given him.

A Gold Coffin for a Poor Man

TWENTY-NINE

BAIT FOR A
TWO-LEGGED FISH

Cier'Djaal
End of the first week of Yonder

*I*f not money, Miron, or self-respect, we at least have a plan.

    As it's been made known to me, parties aren't a matter of celebra-tions for the wealthy of Cier'Djaal. Celebrations are for poor people. People with money throw parties purely for business. Well, in the same way that a dog humping a man's leg is purely business.

    The relationship between the fashas is quite close, dangerously so. As Denaos phrases it, they all stand in a circle, with their right hands on each other's genitals and their left aiming a dagger at each other's backs. When they need to discuss business, they can't meet privately for fear of inciting suspicion among their fellow fashas and sparking off a trade conflict—or a more old-fashioned conflict, with knives and stuff.

    So, they throw massive parties, invite every dignitary, statesman, ambassador, merchant, military man, and, most importantly, each other. They throw these as an opportunity to discuss business while at the same time lording their own wealth over each other.

    Fasha Ghoukha has much to lord these days.

    It's said he's got a new silk, thicker and stronger than his rival fashas', which has been allowing him to consume the others' markets. This new surplus in wealth is being dedicated to expanding an already sizable estate and house guard force. While it's true that a bigger fortune would require more men to guard it, there is a point at which a man ceases to use his men to secure his own fortune and starts using it to secure the fortunes of others... usually, for himself.

It is, in fact, both possible and likely that Ghoukha is in league with the Khovura. If he controls them, after all, he has his own private shadow army with which to strike at the mercantile machinations of his rivals while appearing clean and the Khovura, in turn, have a powerful and wealthy backer.

It's also possible and likely that having one's own private army in Cier'Djaal these days is just plain sensible. Asper gave me the gory details, but this morning, news of the conflict between the Karnerians and Sainites was on the lips of every citizen in the Souk. Their battles are becoming more heated, more aggressive. This is fine, so long as they keep to Temple Row, but people are worried that war will strike when they're out in the taverns, out shopping in the Souk, out traipsing Cier'Djaal.

There will come a moment when a war becomes too big to be contained to one district. And when that moment comes, I suspect an awful lot of people will wish they had the foresight of Ghoukha.

But it's been said, as well, that Ghoukha has given his full endorsement to the mediation about to take place between the Karnerians and Sainites. He's even offered to provide the use of his own manse as a staging area for the Ancaaran priest to negotiate between the two factions.

For what purpose?

Maybe that's just a wealthy man's concerns.

Mine are simpler. If the Khovura know we're searching for Miron... Not-Miron... whatever, then they'll try to protect him. If Ghoukha is in league with them, then his estate makes the most sense to hide Not-Miron at. And if we can't find him, then we can find something we can use to track him down.

After all, it'd be hard to get into a heavily guarded rich man's house.

Unless you've got someone like Denaos on your side.

As it happens, tomorrow night, Ghoukha will be throwing another party. According to rumor, it's mostly to showcase where he plans to stage

the meditations and court Karnerian, Sainite, and Ancaaran approval.
Though, of course, it might also be to flex his gold cock a little and show
his rivals what's what.

Which means that he'll be seeking new servants.

New, half-naked, subservient people with which to flay verbally, pay
scraps, and possibly abuse for his amusement.

I trust I don't need to expound further; suffice it to say that I under-
stand why Denaos didn't bother explaining until the day before the feast.
There's just no time left for a better plan.

And if we can go in and find Not-Miron, we can finally figure out
what's going on and how we can get our money.

And yet, the more I think about it, the more it seems like such an
awful lot of work.

Admittedly, I had thought it was the only way out, at the time. With-
out that money, I can't start my new life, free of bloodshed and killing.
But to go in, there will almost certainly be danger, possibly more killing.
I tell myself it'll be necessary, the last time, but...

How many times do you get to call it "the last time" before you're just
lying to yourself?

And I wonder if it's worth it. I wonder if I do need that money. More
than I need her, anyway.

We've never had money before, after all. Adventurers get by.

But whenever we've not had money, we've always had killing.

I don't want that. Money, murder, Kataria; I only get to keep two.

I tell myself that this is why we need to go into Ghoukha's estate. I tell
the others as well. Not all of them believe me.

Gariath refuses to talk about it, but he's become antsy. The mention
of Ghoukha, of gold, of anything civilized makes him angry. Angrier.
Perhaps he's wondering where he, with all our goals in sight, fits into it.

Perhaps he's wondering what he can force to work.

Asper and Denaos are all in favor, at least. Denaos, for his own rea-
sons. Asper, for finally getting to the bottom of Not-Miron's identity. At
least, she is right now. She's yet to learn what Denaos has planned for
getting into the estate.

Dreadaeleon, too, seems enthusiastic. Not for us, Khetashe knows. But whatever—or whoever—he is enthusiastic for is making him pliable enough to just agree to whatever we suggest. Anything to get more money, he says.

Bless him, the greedy little rat.

Bless us all.

Please.

THIRTY

TRUST THE NAKED PEOPLE

Let me ask you something.

Asper knew that wasn't her voice speaking in her head. She knew the sound of it from the dreams of unsound slumber, and she knew that she was wide awake. She knew ignoring it wouldn't make it stop.

Still, what was a religious woman, she asked, without a healthy grasp of denial?

You're supposed to be the clever one, right? Thoughtful, perceptive, intelligent. The "voice of reason," if you will.

She closed her eyes and called to mind a meditative hymn. She had recited it often when she was younger, a mental ward against constant stress. It had always been useful for directing frantic thought into something saner.

She found herself thinking of it often lately.

I'd ask why you aren't in charge, but I think I understand. I imagine controlling this rabble would be rather like attempting to herd shaven apes. Rather amusing to the casual observer like myself, but I doubt you'd find it as hysterical.

Shut up.

Now, that last thought *was* hers. It was her voice in her own head, screaming at the unwelcome invader, unsurprisingly impotently. And yet, the virtues of denial...

Shut up, shut up, SHUT UP.

Still, I can't help wondering. The invading voice continued with this line of thought, undeterred. *With all that intellect and wisdom… why is it that they make* you *dress like a tramp?*

"I AM *NOT* A TRAMP!" she shouted.

"Well, you and *I* know that, darling," someone said. She looked over her shoulder to see Denaos peering out through the curtains behind the stage she stood on. "But we're rather attempting to convince others of the idea, which isn't helped if you go around screaming contradictory self-assertions. If you wouldn't mind holding onto that white-hot shame until we get everything done?"

His head slipped back behind the curtains. She felt her cheeks go red.

Redder, anyway.

The aforementioned shame had actually been quite mild—considering her usual standard—when Denaos had explained the plan. It had gotten a tad warm once he showed her the costume he had cobbled together. It had slowly grown throughout the long walk to the Harbor Road, until she had arrived at this point.

Standing on a flimsy wooden stage.

Surrounded by various unwashed people with various diseases.

Wrapped in a flimsy sheet of silk about her breasts, a similarly scandalous skirt hanging from her hips.

White-hot shame wasn't quite severe enough a description for it.

Though, really, it wasn't as if anyone else was taking stock of her undress. In fact, very few people of the Harbor Road seemed to looking at her at all. Not that she could blame them; she was far from the most interesting thing here.

To call it a road was slightly misleading. True, the entirety of the bazaar had been formed on the western edge of the harbor, where the odorous scent of the Sumps wafted over broken walls to mingle with the stink of flesh and cooking meat. But only a narrow spit of the stone path was available to walk upon. The rest of it was full of merchants.

Too unsavory for the Souk, too legitimate for a back alley, the air of dubious morality surrounding the Harbor Road's sellers choked the sky as surely as the stink of their wares. Some were common odors: laborers selling reeking oxen or rutting swine, bootleggers hawking homemade whiskey straight from the still.

But mingled within these everyday reeks were more exotic stinks: a shifty-looking fellow at a stall brimming with vials of bubbling red and green potions, a dirty man wearing a dirty Talanite's robe selling hecatines doped to the gills on incense, and at least one couthi whose wares she couldn't see but who stood under a sign reading EXCESS BODILY FLUIDS? WE PAY!

One would think—at least, she did—that among so many opportunities to be profoundly disturbed, the sight of slavery wouldn't be the worst of it. But her twisting stomach suggested otherwise.

They stood huddled in cages or corrals, some of them chained to posts, more than a few on stages and blocks like the very one she stood upon. Some of them cast looks of keen resentment from prospective buyers to the dirty men and women trying to slap a price on them. But many more simply stared at their feet with empty eyes. They were humans and shicts and tulwar, advertised as laborers and house servants and bodyguards, sold for copper and silver and gold. Just a few heated words of negotiation, a quick changing of hands, a jangle of chains as one of them was led off the block and away by his new owner was all that took place.

Asper had never seen people become property before. Somehow, she hadn't imagined it would be so efficient, so...very casual.

Her stomach turned again. Something got caught in her throat. The nausea had begun when Denaos had first told her of this plan and it hadn't stopped. All of what was going on around her was perfectly legal, perfectly acceptable, perfectly casual; yet somehow, all parts of her felt dirtier for standing here.

Some parts more than others.

Why do you take orders from them? The curse's voice spoke within her head. *Why do you stand idly by and let them do this? Do they have power you do not?*

She clenched her teeth and shut her eyes tight.

Just stop thinking about it, she told herself. *Stop thinking about it and it will go away.*

Something beneath her left arm itched.

Pardon, what was that? Speak up, dear girl. I'm not a mind reader, you know.

"You're in my head," she snapped back. "How can you not hear my thoughts?"

Technically, I'm in your arm, not your head. And even if I were, it would be terribly impolite to read your thoughts without your consent, wouldn't it? There is, after all, a certain way these things are done.

"These things? *What* things?" She seized her left wrist as though it were a neck and forced her hand to look at her, pausing only a moment to reflect on how insane that looked. "Who are you? *What* are you?"

Have I not introduced myself? the voice asked. *I'm certain I meant to. You may call me Amoch-Tethr.*

"My concern was really for that last bit," she replied. "I don't *want* to know your name. I don't *want* you at all."

I'm hurt. The voice—Amoch-Tethr's voice—certainly didn't sound it. *After all we've been through together?*

"We've been through nothing," Asper spat. "*Nothing*. You're not my friend. You're a curse. You kill people."

Given your current company, one would think a penchant for murder was a prerequisite of becoming your friend. The voice chuckled and it burned inside her wrist. *And we have seen much together. Since the day I awoke, trapped inside your flesh, I have seen everything.*

That word resonated through her. She stared intently at her palm, as though she could see through it, to the voice within and whatever mouth it spoke from.

"Everything?"

Every body that I consumed for you, and every sleepless night that followed. When you whispered your prayers and begged the darkness for an answer, the only one that heard you . . .

Again, she felt it: that slow twisting of sinew beneath her flesh that made her absolutely certain that this thing was smiling at her.

Was me.

At that moment, Asper felt hollow. It was as though everything inside had been devoured, leaving nothing but a vast and dark emptiness throughout which those words would echo endlessly.

"Why now?" Her voice was an agonized whisper, razors in her throat. "Why are you talking now?"

Ah, yes. Pardon, you heard only the starved whispers of a maddened beast before. I cannot subsist on the meager flesh you fed me.

"Flesh?" she asked. "Those were *people*! I didn't feed you; you *destroyed* them."

Technically, I consumed them. And it'd be more accurate to say that we did. *I am merely a passenger in this vessel. I can do nothing without your permission.*

"I didn't tell you to do that!"

Well, not with words, no. Suffice it to say, I acted on your behalf, such as when I ate of that Disciple earlier.

"You mean the demon?"

Rather a coarse term for so learned a scholar. He recognized me, you know. I imagine we might have enjoyed a pleasant chat, had he been more reasonable. Regardless, his sacrifice sated my pangs. I can carry on a more civil discourse.

"Then tell me what you are," she snapped. "Tell me what you're doing. Tell me…" She bit her lower lip. "Tell me how to *get rid of you.*"

No response, from its thoughts or hers. The vast emptiness inside her was filled again with the sounds of rushing blood and a beating heart. The mutter and rabble of the Harbor Road filled her ears again. The arm she stared at was just a limb, without eyes to see or ears to hear.

"Careful there, dear." Denaos emerged from the curtains. "We're not going to be able to get you sold if you appear touched."

She wasn't sure how much he had seen. She didn't enquire,

dropping her hand, folding her arms over her chest, and retreating away from the glancing passersby.

"Unless, of course, we offered a discount," he hummed, twiddling an elegantly long mustache that wasn't there this morning.

"Why are you wearing that?" Asper asked, scrutinizing the handlebar wisps.

"Clearly, you know nothing of disguise," he retorted. "I am attempting to convey the character of a sleazy flesh trader." He gestured to a loud purple shirt and painfully tight-looking breeches. "Such a role requires a fair bit of villainy. And as every fool knows"—he smoothed out the false whiskers upon his lip—"mustaches are inherently villainous."

She squinted at him. "There is something sincerely wrong with you."

"There's something sincerely wrong with this whole *plan*!"

Lenk came out from behind the curtains. Kataria followed, clad like Asper. The shict glanced her over and offered a sympathetic grunt.

"Sending two people into a dangerous situation," Lenk continued, "unarmed and naked in all but name? This was the *best* we could come up with?"

"You've got a better idea?" Kataria leaned against the railings of the stage. She tugged at the skimpy wisp of silk bound around her chest. "Did *you* want to wear this thing?"

"What I *want* is to do something that would involve less silk and more steel," Lenk replied.

"So," Denaos hummed, "in the face of a vast, unknown estate brimming with countlessly well-armed cultists, house guards, and goodness knows what else, your first plan of action is to run into them headlong, spitting war cries and swinging a sword?"

Lenk looked down at his feet. "Well, when you say it *that* way, of course it sounds stupid."

"It all sounds stupid."

Dreadaeleon's voice was low, brimming with a dark authority. The effect, likely, would have been more powerful had he not emerged wearing dark-shaded spectacles and a bright red fez. His face was set in a cold smirk as he drew his hands behind his back.

"We could end this all so easily," he said. "We know where the Khovura are. Show me. I will handle the rest."

Some chuckled at that, some didn't appear to notice. Only Asper affixed the boy with a stare.

He had always boasted, of course. But usually they were the overly verbose gloats of an inexperienced boy. Since he had returned from his...excursion, something had fallen over him. He walked taller, he spoke less, and his boasts sounded more like threats: short, terse, and spoken with a dreadful certainty.

That was another worry for another time. At that moment, her eyes, along with everyone else's, were drawn down the Harbor Road to Gariath striding toward them, wrapped up tightly in a thick black cloak.

"They're coming," he grunted before hopping onto the stage to join them.

"Right, right." Denaos began flitting his hands about, directing them. He pointed to Asper and Kataria. "Merchandise, on display." He gestured to Dreadaeleon. "Accountant, at the ready." He nodded to Gariath. "Muscle, look ominous."

"What should I do?" Lenk asked.

"In the back." Denaos gestured with his thumb. "You didn't like this plan and we're out of costumes. Be there in case something goes wrong."

"Are you sure?" The question went to Denaos, even though his gaze went to Kataria.

She snorted in reply. "Piss off."

He opened his mouth to reply before Denaos waved him off behind the curtain. Asper winced, glancing to Kataria.

"A little harsh, wasn't that?"

"Yes," the shict grunted. "Yes, it was."

With so much skin left bare by the scanty silk, it was easy enough to see that Kataria was tense. Asper supposed that was only reasonable. It had been only a few days, after all, since the shict had almost been dragged off by the very people with whom the plan now called for her to go with willingly.

She couldn't blame her for being anxious.

She probably wouldn't blame her for whatever else she might do today.

"Places! Places, people!" Denaos announced. "Here they come. Let me do the talking and for Silf's sake, act professional." He stroked his false mustache. "We're slavers. Not lowlifes."

Their targets came down the road a moment later. Among the crowds on the street, the sign of Ghoukha's house, the naked girl on a bed of coins, was stark against his servants' clothes. A quartet of house guards flanked a woman with elegant hair, blue robes, and a face painted in elaborate designs of indigo and white. She strolled slowly down the cobblestones, surveying the various wares—flesh and fleshless—on display. A pouch hung heavy at her sash.

"She hasn't bought anything yet," Denaos noted. "Not good."

"Why not good?" Asper asked.

"It means she's picky. She's looking for quality."

"Oh." A moment passed before it struck her. "Oh, you can go fu—"

"Shh! Here she comes!"

Ghoukha's envoy, a look of vague uninterest playing beneath her painted face, passed slowly beside them. Her gaze drifted up and over Asper and Kataria. Unsure of what to do, Asper offered a weak smile, to which the envoy flashed a puzzled look. Denaos quickly swept in front of her, a sleazy grin broad beneath his mustache.

"Searching for Cier'Djaal's finest?" he asked in a greasy lilt. "Then look no further. Before you are—"

The envoy didn't bother offering anything ruder than a roll of her eyes as she moved to walk away. Denaos flashed an accusing stare at Asper, who shrugged helplessly.

In another moment, though, Gariath pushed between them. He

came down off the stage in front of the envoy, who skidded to a halt and looked up into the darkness of his cowl with wide eyes. Her house guards reached for their weapons, though seemed in no hurry to draw them. Or to get between her and the massive cloaked fellow.

Gariath lowered his scowl upon her. "Buy something."

The envoy cleared her throat and took a few steps back to the stage.

"You were saying?" she asked Denaos.

"Ah, forgive my dear brute's mannerisms," the rogue replied. "He simply could not bear to let you leave before I paid due compliments to the servant of the Fasha Ghoukha. Obviously, you are of particularly keen discernment to be entrusted with the purchase of servants for his feast."

"Is that street knowledge already?" the envoy asked, quirking a brow.

"Only for select pairs of feet," Denaos replied. "I have heard rumors. Yet here you are, with a full pouch."

"Then you doubtlessly know that Ghoukha's feast will collectively shame every other noble in the city from fasha to felon," the envoy replied. "Every noble, every dignitary, every Karnerian, Sainite, and priest of worth will be there."

"And you've found your staff a bit short?"

"A bit unimpressive. The fasha strives to impress." The envoy's eyes lingered over Asper. "He has a . . . taste for the exotic. Perhaps a northerner would do the trick."

"Ah, if it's exotic you seek, look no further." Denaos swept up behind Kataria and laid his hands on her visibly bristling shoulders. "I defy you to find any trader here with flesh half as enticing as a forest-dweller's."

The envoy's painted lips curled into a frown as she surveyed Kataria. "A bit gamey, isn't she? All that muscle, nary a curve. What statement are we making with this one?"

"One of power, of strength!" Denaos plucked Kataria's arm. A low growl rumbled in her throat as he raised it for inspection. "Witness this, the product of years of dwelling in the wildlands on a diet of flesh and blood! She is the very essence of a predator! Note the muscle!" He reached up and brashly pulled back her lip to expose overlarge canines. "Note the teeth!"

She drew in a long snort, then spat a thick glob of phlegm at the envoy's feet.

"Note," he muttered sharply, "the . . . the accuracy."

"A moment." The envoy's finger thrust accusingly at her ears. "Those! What are those? *Is that a shict?*"

"Why, yes, she—"

"Oh, no, no, wastrel!" The envoy shook her head and hands as one. "The fasha has had . . . an incident with a shict in the Souk. Too much trouble. No shicts."

"But, she—"

"No. Shicts."

Kataria half-shrugged, half-shoved Denaos off and slipped back toward the curtain. The rogue shot her an accusing glare. She shot an unpleasant grin in response before disappearing.

"Just as well," the envoy said, sneering. "One could hardly expect the fasha's guests to see the charm in that, no matter how exotic." Her attentions turned back to Asper. "Tell me of this one."

"Of course, of course," Denaos said, returning to her. "Abundant where the shict was lacking, rounded where she was sheer, this one is certain to fulfill all desires."

Asper furrowed her brow at the description, but said nothing.

"But is she smart?" the envoy asked.

"Literate *and* substantial," Denaos replied. "Reads, writes, performs arithmetic, knows a dozen poems and a few prayers."

"To northern Gods, most likely," the envoy said, blanching. "Still, part of the package when you buy something so pale, I suspect. How much?"

"For you? Twelve."

"*Twelve?*" The envoy looked at him as though he had just dropped his trousers and thrust profusely at her whilst singing operatics.

That is, she looked offended on an entirely different level. "Do you possess some manner of seeing condition that makes me appear as though I am made of gold?"

"No, but I do note your fat pouch," he said, gesturing to her sash. "You have clearly been waiting for the best. I am offering her to you at a very reasonable twelve."

"Northern or not, she's worth no more than seven."

"*Seven?* Were we in Temple Row, they would burn you for blasphemy! Eleven!"

The numbers flew back and forth. There were curses exchanged and polite rebuttals. And Asper heard them all, but only barely. It was, after all, rather difficult to hear one's attributes and roundness so thoroughly described, labeled, and priced.

At that moment, she couldn't help looking over her shoulder to where Kataria had disappeared. Should she have followed, she wondered?

It was a ruse, of course. She knew it wasn't *really* demeaning. Was it? But surely, she could have thought of something better. Surely, she could have put together something more sensible. Lenk was right, she was about to go in hostile territory, unarmed and half-clad and apparently, now, alone.

She looked down at her left arm. Maybe it wasn't too late to listen to Amoch-Tethr. But he—whatever he was—remained silent.

"Nine."

Her attentions were suddenly snapped back to the envoy as she began counting out coins in her hands.

"Or we walk," the envoy said.

"Fine, fine." Denaos sighed, taking the coins and tossing them off to Dreadaeleon. He gave Asper a wink that was not nearly as comforting as he intended it to be before nudging her off the platform.

She suddenly became aware of the house guards closing in around her, regarding her with cold iron stares.

It might have been just nerves dancing beneath her skin. It might have been her imagination. But she couldn't shake the idea that whatever dwelt in her left arm was, at that moment, sighing disappointedly at her.

—⊷⊱⊰⊶—

"You got turned down?" Lenk asked, bewildered.

"That's what I said," Kataria muttered. She unabashedly tore off her silk skirt as she reached for her breeches draped across a nearby barrel. "Something about a bunch of trouble in the Souk." She grinned at him, flashing canines. "I think I might be famous now."

Lenk rubbed at his eyes. "You spat on them, didn't you?"

Her smile grew distinctly more unpleasant. "Like a champion."

"You"—his voice came out on an angry breath—"have fucked up *everything*."

"Don't ask me to feel bad about not having to go into that den of monsters." She stripped off the silk barely covering her breasts and shrugged on her shirt. "I was willing to go along with this, but I'm not going to waste time crying that it didn't work out." She glared at him. "And if you ask me to, *you're* going to feel a lot worse than you already do."

"Do you honestly not understand what's happening out there?" He gestured over to the curtains. "The only reason I came onto this plan was because I thought you'd make up for whatever weapons we couldn't sneak in. It's a two-person job. Or it was. Someone needs to be in there to watch Asper's back."

Kataria stared at him for a moment. She narrowed her eyes at him, less in anger and more in appraisal. She pulled her hunting knife from her belt and advanced slowly upon Lenk. He backed away, gaze wary, hands up.

"What," he said softly, "do you think you're doing?"

In an instant, she was upon him. She seized him by the tunic and dragged him close enough that he could feel the tip of her blade against his belly. She hissed through her teeth.

"Fixing it."

There was a violent tearing sound. Lenk felt cold metal brush against his flesh. He looked down to see the knife's edge racing upward, ripping his shirt in two. Before he could protest, she tore the rent garment from his back.

"I, uh..." He stared down at his own naked, scarred flesh. "I'm not sure I understand."

"Give it time." She seized him by the belt and angled her blade toward his trousers. "It's a two-part plan."

· · ✦ · ·

"Admittedly, I didn't think that was going to work." Dreadaeleon counted through the coins, covertly palming a pair of them into his own pocket. "I thought your haggling had ruined it. Surely, there wasn't a need for that."

"Says you." Denaos stroked his mustache as he watched Ghoukha's guards depart, Asper in tow. "She's a dear friend of mine. I wasn't about to sell her for a pittance."

Dreadaeleon lifted his spectacles to watch. "Do you...do you think she'll be all right?"

"No." Gariath rumbled from beneath his cloak. "Selling humans as meat, sneaking around like cowards; this city is making us as sick as it is. No one in it is all right."

"Oh?" Denaos rolled his eyes. "So you don't like this plan, either? Would you have us go along with Lenk and rush in and burn down Ghoukha's entire estate?"

"No." Gariath turned toward the rogue. The white of his teeth was bright beneath his cowl. "I wouldn't stop there."

Any concern Denaos might have voiced at that was lost in the sound of a scuffle behind the curtains nearby. Their eyes turned to Kataria as she emerged, hands on Lenk's bare shoulders, shoving the young man—now clad only in a crudely wrapped silk breechcloth about his waist—toward the stage.

"So..." Denaos watched the scene with vague alarm. "Is this... something I should know about?"

"It's a two-person job," Kataria said, struggling to keep Lenk at the stage's edge. "And we only sent one out."

"All well and good." Denaos glanced toward the skimpy cloth

hanging from Lenk's hips and cringed. "Or at least, all well. But the envoy's already taken off with—"

"HEY."

Gariath's roar carried across the Harbor Road, commanding the attention of the envoy, as well as several other merchants. He seized Lenk by the back of the neck and shoved him forward, waving him at the envoy like a child's toy.

"Buy this one, too," he bellowed.

"This isn't—" Lenk began to stammer, looking helplessly from Kataria to Denaos. "I didn't mean—"

"Do you want this plan to work or not?" she snapped back.

"Well, yeah, but not with *me*!"

"But it was fine when it was *me*?" she snarled. "Denaos is the one they talk to. We obviously can't sell Gariath. And clearly, I'm not good enough to be someone's half-clad, simpering flesh-slave. Poor me."

"What about Dreadaeleon?" Lenk demanded, pointing a finger at the boy.

"No one's going to pay for him!" Kataria growled.

"Hey," the boy protested meekly.

The envoy trotted up with a bit more vigor in her step. A groomed eyebrow rose in appreciation as she swept an appraising look over Lenk.

"Well, well." Her voice came lilting out between the faintest curves of a smile. "You old hoarder, were you holding out on me?"

"Ah, yes," Denaos began, "well, this one is a recent arrival—"

"Buy him," Gariath interrupted tersely.

The envoy took her time in surveying the young man. She hardly appeared to notice him squirming beneath her gaze; if anything, it made her grin more broadly, though the eager greed playing in her eyes was quickly smothered by her appraising, businesslike stare.

"He's a bit torn up, isn't he?" Excitement was tempered by caution in her voice. "Is he a warrior? Has he seen many battles?" Her eyes slithered across the expanse of his chest. "He certainly looks fearsome, doesn't he? Will he take orders?"

"I don't know," Gariath grunted. "Maybe." He snorted. "Buy him."

"Very well," the envoy said, tapping her cheek. "I'll give you... eight."

"Ten," Gariath retorted.

"Nine."

"Eleven."

"What?"

"Four."

The envoy furrowed her brow. "Is... this some northern haggling technique?"

"You want him or not?"

"As you wish." The envoy shrugged and counted out the coins. "Four, you said?"

"Who cares."

Gariath didn't even wait for her to hand the coins to Denaos before he shoved Lenk off the stage. He cried out as he stumbled, colliding with the envoy. She let out a soft giggle, placing hands on his shoulders to steady herself.

"Oh, my," she said, sliding her palms across his skin. "Usually, we don't get them this excited." With an intentional slowness, she slid her fingers off of him. "Ah, ah. But we mustn't let instinct get the better of us, must we? Civility and all."

She gently nudged him toward Asper and her guards, who enclosed around them both. With a curt nod to Denaos and Gariath, she took off once again down the Harbor Road, giggling as Lenk cast a worried glance back to his companions.

In another moment, they rounded a corner and vanished.

"So," Denaos said, twirling his mustache, "the pieces are in play. The trap is set. Our little keys are behind the locks. We need but wait for dusk to begin act two of our dark performance." He sniffed and took the moment to scratch himself discreetly. "So, what do you guys want to do until then?"

Kataria looked up at the noonday sun and shrugged. "Get some curry?"

"Always with the curry," he said. "They have more than just that here, you know."

"Fine," she replied. "We can get whatever you want once you lose the mustache."

Denaos narrowed his eyes at her. His fingers twirled about the tips of his false facial hair.

"Curry it is."

THIRTY-ONE

Rich Men and Their Dreams

There was, Asper decided, a certain cynical satisfaction in knowing exactly how much, by the current value of the Djaalic coin, the sum of one's body, mind, and soul was worth.

Just as there was a certain fear in knowing that there existed a bottle of wine that was worth more than one's life.

"To spill a drop," the headman, an elegantly trimmed and dressed servant, said as he filled each goblet on her tray, "is to invite misfortune." He stared at her intently. "To spill on a guest is to invite death."

He replaced the bottle upon the table and gently pressed the tray into her hands, wincing as the goblets trembled precariously. He made a sweeping motion out toward the *houn* and the throng of guests thereon.

"Be careful out there," he warned. "I know you're northern, but I'd rather not see you executed on your first night for offending one of the fasha's guests."

She crept timidly out of the antechamber, pausing at the archway to peer out into the massive *houn*. A sea of silk and painted faces greeted her, hardly any space left between bodies to navigate through. She glanced over her shoulder and suddenly felt a jostle. A servant with an empty tray pushed past her without so much as a look of acknowledgment. She panicked, briefly, as the goblets

swayed on her tray before settling. Holding her breath, she took a
slow, careful step into the den of luxury.

Every nobleman worth his silk in Cier'Djaal, she had been told,
had a *houn* like this. Well, not like *this*. Ghoukha's *houn* was said to
be twice as big as the second biggest in the city.

She believed it. She would have believed any story about
Ghoukha's estate because, as she looked around it, she sincerely
believed that the human imagination was too limited to make up a
story grander than this kind of wealth.

The massive chamber—bigger than most temples—stretched
impossibly wide, forming a vast field of polished marble. Its ceiling
was a balcony-laden vaulted dome painted with elaborate depictions
of Ghoukha's lineage—lots of spiders, lots of burly men, and lots
and *lots* of naked women. Bearing the burden of this art, golden
pillars marched the length of the hall, each one carved to resemble
a statuesque female, elegantly holding up the ceiling with delicate
hands.

Tapestries hung from every wall, each one woven of silk from
Ghoukha's spiders. And the artisans themselves were in attendance.
The horse-sized arachnids could be seen skittering up the pillars,
leaping gracefully from balcony to balcony or crawling across invisible strands of silk they had woven as a net beneath the ceiling. Each
display of arachnid agility was met with laughter and applause from
the legion of guests below.

Strange, she thought, since the upper class of Cier'Djaal was perhaps the only thing weirder than giant, free-roaming spiders.

As was all the rage in the city, nearly every face was painted
with a riot of colors: blue cheeks, white scalps, red eyelids, green
noses. Across the *houn*, their faces wrought a nauseating rainbow
with their colorful silks and jewels. Some foreigners were present as
well. She recognized the staunch military bearing of Karnerians and
Sainites and a few other minor priests. A swaying, jewel-encrusted
headdress of a priest of Ancaa commanded the attention of several
Djaalic guests.

House guards, clad in armor painted with Ghoukha's emblem, stood at various corners. Rather than guarding, though, a great number of them seemed to be imbibing and showing off their weapons to excited guests. She suspected they were likely here as another display of wealth, rather than as effective protection.

Among all this, and in stark contrast to the ostentatious wealth, was the common man. Servants, half-clad in scanty silks and bearing laden trays worth more than they were, darted expertly between the guests, filtering in and out of the antechamber with empty and brimming trays of food and wine. One of them emerged between a pair of noblemen, leaning over as he passed by her.

"Hey, northern," the servant whispered. "Fair warning: New meat has to tend to the oids. Try not to stare."

"What?" she asked.

He offered nothing else as he quickly strode toward the antechamber. Asper felt a cold shadow fall over her a moment before she heard the jarring monotone.

"Greetings are heaped upon your face, *shkainai*."

She looked up. A couthi, four hands folded delicately upon perfectly smoothed black robes, stared down at her from behind a rather elegant portrait of a young lady in springtime. His smaller hands reached down to pluck a goblet from her tray, passing it off to his larger hands.

"It is both surprising and pleasant to see you in such conditions," the couthi said. "Your contribution to the economic fortitude of the human city will be commended. This one wonders, though, what happened to deliver such a status to you."

"Do we..." She let the question linger.

"Apologies. This one did not engage all adequate mannerisms." He swept both left arms out in a bow. "Man-Shii Kree. We exchanged pleasantries in the Souk. When last seen, you were a free female."

She stared blankly, struggling to comprehend the monotone. She racked her brain for her cover story.

"Uh, I...made some bad decisions," she said. "Debt slavery was the only way out."

"This one accredits your fortuitous rotation to the city," Man-Shii Kree said. "All serve the greater function here. The downtrodden trod upward on economic stability. The system is to be praised."

"Uh-huh." Her eyes were locked, dumbfounded, upon the couthi's portrait-face.

"You are staring, *shkainai*."

"Oh, sorry," she said. "I just...hadn't seen any oids. I mean, non-humans here."

"Privilege is the harvest of the seeds of civility planted by the couthi," Man-Shii Kree replied. "Our ability to provide the enigmatic warrants invitation by the humans possessed of gold. The unwashed tulwar and shicts remain uninvited." He swiveled his portrait toward her. "A memory. How fared your shictish company."

"She..." Asper paused, forming a lie. "Gone. Disappeared."

"This one mars no face with tears," Man-Shii Kree said. "A shict is no friend to the couthi and all have earned death. This one is pleased to have hastened hers, though this one regrets inconveniencing you by alerting the humans to her presence."

"Yeah, well..."

Man-Shii Kree looked up, casting his gaze—or so she assumed—over the assembled crowd.

"This is not our home." The slightest edge of emotion, something as cold and bitter as the winters that never came to this city, crept into his voice. "These are not our people. We lost both in our wars with the shicts. Because of them, we are here, mongers and floor-scrapers among those who would have trembled at our might."

All four of Man-Shii Kree's hands trembled, clenched into fists at his sides and around the goblet he grasped.

"They want more war, these humans. They will not listen to us. Another home will be lost to us again." From behind his portrait-face, Asper had no doubt that Man-Shii Kree was snarling. "And the couthi shall once again preside over a court of ashes."

For a long moment, he stood completely still. His hands slowly relaxed and hung limp at his sides. He inclined his portrait toward her respectfully. She quivered beneath his unseen gaze.

"Apologies upon your face, *shkainai*. This one should be more considerate."

The crowds of guests and servants parted before him as Man-Shii Kree glided across the floor, a looming shadow in a room filled with bright, golden light.

She forced his words from her mind. She was, after all, working.

She maneuvered her way through the crowds, offering wine and being waved away enough to make her disguise look plausible. Through the rumble of conversation, fragments of phrases assaulted her ears.

"—if you ask me, we should just kick them out. Mobilize the dragonmen and evict the Sainites and the Karnerians and every other *shkainai* in—"

"—then in two months, they bring their armies here and turn Cier'Djaal into a battlefield. Don't be such an—"

"—never had it this bad in his time. My grandfather built his fortunes from two coppers and a sack of salt. Sure, the criminal guilds were bad, but *this* is—"

"—not thieves. The Khovura are something else entirely. I've heard talk of monsters...*demons*. They're worse than the Jackals, mark my—"

"—it's the shicts, you know. Always those damn oids making trouble. Either them or the tulwar. Remember the Uprising? Why'd we ever let them—"

"—and Ghoukha's brought us here to boast again. Does he ever get tired of this? The glutton's got a new silk and suddenly he thinks he's Ancaa incarnate?"

The fear that had been burbling at the base of her spine since she had woken up this morning and heard Denaos's plan had now crawled up to her neck. To hear the nobles talk, Cier'Djaal seemed as though it was on the brink of three different apocalypses. She tried not to worry about that as she maneuvered closer to the massive doors of the *houn*.

There were enough guests milling around the doors that it wouldn't seem odd if she were to linger there long enough to hear what she was supposed to. Three slow knocks, then three swift ones. That was Denaos's code, the sign to let the rest of them in.

All she had to do was wait and hope nothing else particularly alarming happened.

"Priestess?"

One out of two, she thought with a sigh as she turned to face whoever had just spoken to her.

She was astonished to see Watch-Sergeant Blacksbarrow standing before her, if only because the Sainite actually looked like a woman this time. Her dusty overcoat and tricorn hat had been exchanged for a set of elegant breeches and jacket in Saine's colors and her hair had been combed into a tail with a matching bow.

While the garb was flattering enough to accentuate her more feminine qualities, she was still every bit the warrior, even without the ceremonial saber at her hip.

"Watch-Sergeant," she said, not bothering to keep the surprise out of her voice.

"Wing-Sergeant, actually," the Sainite replied. "Promotion after W.S. Scarmont died in the latest scuffle with the fuckin' Karnies." Blacksbarrow's eyes traveled the length of Asper's half-clad body. "So...this is new."

"Debt slavery," Asper blurted out as she made a vague attempt to cover herself with her tray. "Bad decisions. And...uh, yeah."

"Fuckin' Djaalics." Blacksbarrow took a long sip from her glass, then tossed it aside and watched it shatter upon the floor to be scraped up by another servant. "Puts people in chains and then lectures us about civility. If High Command would approve deployment of a proper Wing into the city instead of the shit garrison we've got stationed here, we could change that." She snorted and took a goblet from Asper's tray. "But they want us to play nice with the

Djaalics, so we have to come here and see where this 'mediation' shit is going down."

"Survey it well," a deep voice boomed from nearby. "It will be the grave He buries you in."

Asper was not as surprised to see Careus approaching, even less surprised by his garb. Strict followers of Daeon, the Conqueror, diplomatic dress for Karnerians was only slightly less intimidating than their battle armor. His giant hands were wrapped in black gauntlets; plates of black metal glistened from beneath the pitch robes he wore. A tremendous silver sign of the Sacred Horns of Daeon hung from his neck as the only color in his wardrobe.

"Er...wine?" Asper raised her tray to be met with a gauntlet held upright in refusal.

"Daeon demands strength of mind and body, and thus Daeon demands abstinence. If we are to make His will known in these trifling mediations, we must remain in control of every faculty."

Asper mouthed the word *we* silently. She suddenly caught sight of them, two more Karnerians in equally severe dress, looming nearby with scowls fixed on the conversation. A quick sweep to the other side saw three Sainities in military dress, equally attentive and hostile.

Every hand was on a sword—ceremonial dress, but still bladed and ready. Every brow was locked in a glare—beneath shaven Karnerian pate and Sainite warrior tail. To survey the scene, one might have thought they would wage their own war right there, mediation be damned.

Fitting, Asper thought. Far from this conflict, the priest of Ancaa, his robes trimmed with gold and his headdress a sea of emeralds and sapphires, laughed long and loud with the guests surrounding him as he drained a goblet of wine in one swallow, completely oblivious to the imminent disaster.

"You should drink while you can, Karnie," Blacksbarrow snarled. "If this mediation scrawshit falls through, the only thing you'll be possessing is a three-foot blade in your throat."

"Your threats are as empty as your faith, Sainite," Careus replied, voice black as his garb. "You rage against that which cannot be shaken. You rail against that which has no ears for such shrillness."

"Is that so?" She swigged the rest of her wine and threw the goblet aside, heedless of the servant who collected it as she reached for her saber. "Do you need a few new holes in you to hear with, then?"

Careus pushed aside his robes to reveal a long, serrated blade at his hip. "The Emperor and Daeon shall shed no tears if I uphold honor here."

Asper swept a fervent glance around. The other Karnerians and Sainites moved forward, beginning to draw their blades.

"Wait!" she all but shrieked. "*WAIT!*"

Both of their gazes—as well as those of a few guests—turned toward her.

"Do this," she said softly, "and all you'll have proven is that you couldn't control yourselves. How will you ever convince these people you could control their city?"

Hard as iron, their stares all but creaked as they turned them from her toward each other. Their thoughts were seared across their faces in scowls, neither willing to show cowardice by backing down, nor willing to show recklessness by drawing first blood.

Slowly, hands were eased off of hilts. Slowly, heels were turned upon. Slowly, a bloodbath was averted as priest and soldier consigned themselves to ignoring each other.

Asper breathed a sigh of relief. She hadn't actually expected them to listen. A priestess had few armaments at her disposal. Fortunately, guilt and shame were both well-honed tools of her trade.

She started at the sudden sound of a heavy knocking at the door. Three swift, three slow. The signal.

She looked around; all servants who might know better were otherwise occupied. Slowly, she moved to answer the sound. Ghoukha's massive, gilded doors were far too huge to be feasibly opened, spanning at least ten men tall. A smaller, more accessible door set at their foot slid open soundlessly as she pushed it.

And for about the thirtieth time that day, she suspected she had been wrong to assume Denaos's madness might just be a misunderstood brilliance.

Three figures in black of varying height stood before her. Their clothes were made of black burlap; masks covered their faces with glassy eyes sewn in. Two carried lanterns hanging upon rods they carried on their back; the tallest wore a heavy book on his. A long wagon loomed behind them.

"Gevrauchians," she said. "You disguised yourselves as death priests."

"Yes?" Denaos asked from behind his burlap mask. "And?"

"I was expecting you to be dressed as nobles. So you would fit in. You're aware the goal of a disguise is to *not* attract attention, aren't you?"

"We're wearing shoddy clothes, we smell like corpses, and we worship a God who eats souls," Dreadaeleon muttered in reply. "Who, exactly, is going to want to spend time with us?"

"Besides," Denaos spoke up, "noble disguises cost money. Stinky burlap costs nothing." He canted his head to the side. "Now, are you going to invite us in?"

She made a move to step aside, but paused. "There was a gate around Ghoukha's estate. Weren't there any guards?"

"Maybe," Denaos replied. "But is anyone really going to question why Gevrauchians smell like blood?"

She resisted the urge to shut the door on him. But then, it seemed a waste to go walking around half-nude for no reason. With a sigh, she stepped aside and let them and their wagon rattle in. Fortunately, even the smaller door was ostentatiously large enough to allow the wagon entry.

Almost unanimously, the guests turned to see the newcomers. And, with the same precision and much, *much* more haste, they instantly turned away.

"Who invited the corpsers?" someone impolitely called out.

"Shut *up*!" another one scolded. "They're priests of the Bookkeeper. Do you want to offend the Death God?"

Asper had to admit to herself, the disguise was cannier than she had suspected. Guests turned aside to let them through without looking at them; servants took extended routes to avoid them as they rattled toward a deserted corner—or rather, a corner that quickly became deserted—to park their wagon.

She followed, as a polite servant would have, and the other slaves seemed grateful for it. That was how she noticed something stirring beneath the wagon's burlap cover. Her eyes widened.

"Gariath?"

The dragonman offered a low, disgruntled growl in reply from beneath his cover.

"Don't *talk* to him, idiot," Kataria said, whirling upon her. "He's supposed to be a corpse!" She slapped the burlap. "And corpses don't growl." Through her glassy eyes, she surveyed the *houn*. "Where's Lenk?"

"He managed to sneak upstairs." Asper pointed to the twin staircases snaking up to the estate's second level. "He thought Miron might be hidden up there."

"Makes sense," the shict grunted. "I'll go see what he's found."

"Upstairs is off-limits to guests," Asper protested.

"Anyone who wants to try to stop me is more than welcome to try," Kataria growled before stalking off.

"And have you found anything?" Denaos asked.

"Not yet," she replied. "Ghoukha is supposed to be coming down within an hour to make his announcement and showcase where he'll be holding the mediation. I thought I'd be able to sneak around at that point."

"A problem." Denaos pointed to the various house guards stationed everywhere. "Have a look at that."

"What? I've been watching them all night. They aren't doing much more than talking with the guests and showing off."

"Exactly. They're too handsome to be guards." Denaos scratched his burlap. "Ghoukha wants his most charming ones down here for his guests. The ugly ones—that is, the real ones—will be upstairs and other places where people like us ought not to be."

"What about Kataria?" Asper asked. "And Lenk? Are they in danger?"

"They wouldn't be, if you'd let me do something." Dreadaeleon's voice was low and menacing. "These barknecks have never seen a member of the Venarium at full force. A bit of fire here and there and they'll scatter like flies from a corpse and we'll have free run of the place."

"Until the other guards come down," Denaos sighed in reply.

"Then we kill them, too," Gariath muttered from under the tarp.

"Corpses don't talk," the rogue replied. "Just...hold on. Give me a moment to take stock of where looks like a good place to stash an impostor posing as a priest. If Ghoukha's announcement draws enough attention, we'll have an opportunity to go looking later."

Asper frowned at him. "And if it doesn't?"

"Then we make our own opportunity." Denaos rapped his knuckles on the wagon. "Or did you think I brought this just to impress the help?"

"What do we do in the meantime, then?" Dreadaeleon asked.

Denaos pulled his burlap mask up enough to reveal his mouth twisted into a wide grin. He plucked a goblet from Asper's tray and took a long swig.

"It's a party, Dread. Try to enjoy yourself."

THIRTY-TWO

GILDED GOBLETS OVERFLOWING

It wasn't until Lenk discovered the toilet that he decided he truly hated this man.

Carved into the wall of an amply rounded room made out of marble, fitted with bronze trimming, and built solid, sturdy, and tremendous for a man of the fasha's gravity, the toilet possessed a smugness not befitting something one shat in. It seemed to glisten as though it were a throne, its golden seat a crown.

Lenk wondered how much this had cost Ghoukha.

Admittedly, indoor plumbing—to the immense and smug delight of Djaalics—was still something of a novelty in the north. In his home village of Steadbrook, four walls around a hole in the ground had been high luxury. Perhaps his view of the subject was tainted by the fact that he understood this toilet only slightly better than he did witchcraft.

But still...

A man ought not to pay more to shit than he does to buy a human.

He heard the sound of armor rattling, boots treading on marble. He ducked into the lavatory, eased shut the door, and waited for the patrol to pass.

This was quite encouraging, he thought.

Not hiding in a toilet—this just happened to be the closest room to hide in. But before this, he had hidden from guards in an accountant's office, an upstairs kitchen, and a room he could only describe as a garden of shaven delights.

Why so many guards? The upstairs were supposed to be forbidden to guests and servants alike, but surely that would require only a few token guards to watch the halls. He had counted, by sound of boot, no less than fifteen men up here.

He supposed he could chalk that up to Ghoukha's wealth. Gold toilets notwithstanding, the upstairs was still worth more than most villages. Every imported wooden door with gilded knob concealed behind it a parlor, an office, a room filled with more wealth in silk, art, and furnishing than Lenk had ever seen. There wasn't a bare spot on the walls of the halls, either. Spiderwebs coated the walls in elegant, abstract tapestries.

Lenk knew enough about Djaalic nobility to be aware that even by the standards of fashas, Ghoukha's wealth went well past obscene and touched blasphemy.

Just as he knew the only thing fashas liked more than having wealth was showing it off. *Houn* was something ingrained in their culture, Denaos had said; in the north, dominance was decided through war, in Cier'Djaal people accumulated gold, spiders, silk.

So why forbid guests from being up here to see it all? Why keep them relegated to the fabulously ostentatious *houn* when they could just as easily be given two entire floors to be dazzled by?

Unless Ghoukha had something to keep hidden. Or someone.

Lenk pressed his ear against the door and listened. The footsteps faded into the background. Nothing else was coming. He eased open the door and leaned out.

A pair of eyes, wide and startled, met him.

His fist lashed up instinctively, but stopped just short of a goateed chin. Instead, he settled for pursing his lips and glaring at the smiling face set within the white hood.

"How the hell did *you* manage to get up here?" he asked.

"It's very hard to keep me out of places I want to be in," Mocca replied. His eyes drifted over Lenk's half-clad body, one nostril flaring in distaste. "I do believe the story of how *you* found yourself up here might be more interesting."

Lenk glanced around the upstairs hall to make certain no guards were coming. "You need to get lost."

He slipped out of the toilet and began to creep down the hallway. He paused at a corner, peering around the corner. There was no sight of armored body, no sound of heavy boot. The upstairs was dead silent.

"Oh, are we on a *stealth* mission?"

Was.

"How exciting!" Mocca whispered, creeping up behind Lenk and mimicking his posture—albeit with a flair intended to exaggerate sneakiness. "What are we doing? Searching for lost treasure? Angling to *assassinate* someone? Should I have worn black?"

"Shut *up*," Lenk whispered angrily. "What are you even *doing* here? This is a party for the nobility of Cier'Djaal. You know, the wealthy? The influential?"

"My friend"—Mocca's smile came out on the slow lilt of his tongue—"I am more influential than you or this city will ever know." He cleared his throat. "I got bored of the party down below. I noticed our dear host hadn't yet shown himself, so I got curious."

"That's it? You waded past guards just because you were curious?"

"Why's that so hard to believe?" Mocca offered a nod behind Lenk. "Clearly, I wasn't the only one."

Lenk looked up. Behind them, standing like a particularly impoverished ghost, was the slender form of Fasha Sheffu. The fasha had dressed up for the invitation to Ghoukha's house, though not with any real conviction, changing his threadbare, ragged blue robe for a threadbare, ragged gray one.

"How'd he sneak up on us?" Lenk whispered to Mocca.

"Clearly, you're not as good at this as you think you are," Mocca replied.

"Things have taken a turn for the worse for you, my friend,"

Sheffu said, striding toward Lenk. "Debt slavery? Low funds? Perhaps you just liked the feel of the breeze?" He stopped a few feet away and canted his head at the young man. "Or perhaps, as a novelty, we could choose to not lie to each other this time."

Lenk met his gaze. The fasha's amber eyes possessed an unnatural, heavy-lidded calm to them.

"You first," he said.

"It took a bit of persuasion to get me in here," Sheffu replied, an edge of bitterness in his voice. "Invitations do not often come to my house of late. But this was an event I had no desire to miss."

A long silence hung between them. Lenk sighed. "Are you waiting for me to ask?"

"I suspect there's no need," Sheffu said. "Just as I suspect you're here for a similar reason." He glanced about the opulence of the hall. "There is something awry in the house of Ghoukha. He has always been wealthy, and yet this is not the home of someone merely wealthy, is it?"

True, Lenk had to admit to himself, if not to Sheffu; a man who literally shat gold—or on gold, anyway—transcended mere wealth.

"Where did he get it all?" Sheffu pressed. "And how much does he have that he can afford to hire so many guards and buy so many weapons?"

"They say he has a new silk," Lenk said. "Something stronger than anything else out there."

"And where did *that* come from? What has he done to earn it? There are rumors, of course. The silk is made strong by feeding the spiders human flesh. How is he doing it? Who is lending him aid?"

"I'm guessing you have an idea."

"As do you," Sheffu replied; "otherwise you would not be here." He drew closer. "Can you not feel it? It is as the beat of a heart in decay, the pulse of black blood through a dark vein. Something vile stirs beneath this home."

"I don't feel anything but increasingly uncomfortable at how close you are," Lenk replied, gently shoving the fasha back a step. "I came here to find someone who owes me money. Nothing more."

"There is always more, fool," Sheffu growled behind his veil. "Do you honestly think someone with your ability and your legacy was meant for coveting coins? Do you not think a greater power had a hand in your coming here?"

The fasha's left hand shot out and seized Lenk's wrist. His eyes shot open to wide ambers. Lenk saw movement behind the man's tattered veil, a tongue lashing against the silk. Mocca cringed away, blanching.

"Understand this," Sheffu uttered. "The footwar, the Karnerians and Sainites, whatever Ghoukha has planned, *all of it* will pale in comparison to what Khoth-Kapira will do to this world when He breaks free. You are not here for money, Lenk. You are here because you *need* to be here."

"I suspect this might be flattering if it weren't so terribly awkward," Mocca murmured from behind a bemused smirk. If Sheffu heard him, though, he paid him no heed.

Lenk pulled at his arm. "Let go."

Sheffu narrowed his eyes. "Will you at least listen? Will you at least hear what must be—"

Whatever it was that must be heard was drowned out in the clanging sound of a silver serving tray being smashed against the back of a veil-wrapped head. Sheffu's grip went limp, along with the rest of him, as he slumped to the floor with a groan. A slender figure wrapped in smelly black garb stood over him, a tray in her hand and a grin on her face as she pulled off her burlap mask.

"I swear, every time we do that, I never think it's going to work," Kataria chuckled. "Then *bwong!* Down they go." Her mirth dimmed—but didn't die—as she looked up at Lenk, who stared back at her, shocked. "What?"

"*The hell did you do that for?*" he demanded, pointing at Sheffu's body.

"Do what?" she asked. "He was grabbing you! I thought he was a guard."

"Does he *look* like a guard?"

"Well...he's ugly! Denaos told us to look out for the ugly ones."

"You can't just dent a tray on a man's skull for no good reason."

Kataria opened her mouth to retort but steadied herself with a deep breath. "I thought you were in trouble," she said softly, "and if you disagree that that's reason enough, there's room on this tray for two dents."

"That's not..." Lenk sighed and looked to Mocca, who shrugged helplessly in return. "Yeah. Thanks." He glanced down at Sheffu. "Is he dead?"

"Look at him breathing. He's fine." A small droplet of blood pooled upon the floor from beneath Sheffu's veil. "*Mostly* fine." Another one followed. "Look, maybe we'd just better move him before he's even less fine."

"Right, right. You get the legs. I'll take the—"

"*Shkainai!* Stop!"

They looked up. At the end of the hall, several swords were being drawn and several pairs of boots were thundering across the marble floor.

And they were running.

True, Lenk felt bad about abandoning Sheffu. He felt slightly worse when Mocca fell behind. But as he glanced over his shoulder, he saw the guards rushing past the white-clad man, ignoring him in favor of more spirited quarry.

Lenk had about as much energy for confusion as he did for sorrow. Everything was concentrated on the cold marble beneath him and the ostentatious hall around him. He turned down a corridor, then another, then another.

He was lost in opulence, every gilded door and silk-spun hall looking the same. He wasn't even sure how far he had come or where he had turned or whether Kataria—

Kataria.

Had he lost her? He couldn't hear her next to him. He couldn't—

Wait. A dark shape appeared in the corner of his eye, rushing to catch up with him. He breathed a sigh of relief as it came closer, toward him, at him.

That sigh of relief exploded in a great burst of air as the house guard came careering around the corner and tackled him at the waist. He fell to the ground in a heap, skidding along the marble with the weight of armor bearing down upon him.

Breathlessness did not mean senselessness, however. He jerked his elbow back behind him and caught the guard's jaw. He twisted his hand across his body in a shot to the kidneys, finding a gap beneath the man's breastplate and driving a fist into it. With a deep breath and a sudden spasm, he hurled the man off his back and rolled up to a sitting position.

Where he was promptly met with a boot to the chest.

The kick drove him back to the ground, just in time to find another leather-covered toe jamming into his ribs. Breath became a distant dream, not even enough to groan as he rolled onto his stomach, attempting to curl into a protective ball.

As it turned out, it was hard to protect oneself from several more boots stomping simultaneously. He felt them strike his back, his arms, and his legs. None of them were quite so bad as the one that struck his temple, though, causing his head to crack against the floor.

His vision faded. Everything felt cold, even the hands grabbing him by the arms and hauling him up. The last thing he saw before a halo of darkness swallowed his sight was a dark red drop of blood dripping from his brow into his eye.

⊷ ⟞⟝ ⊶

By the time she saw that she was alone, she didn't dare call out for him.

Somehow, she had lost the guards. She didn't know how. Most of them went after Lenk when they turned different ways down that one corridor, but two had followed her and . . . and . . .

Now Kataria was alone.

She tried to catch her breath, looking down the hall she had just come from. Her ears pricked up, twitching left and right, searching for a sound. No boots, no armor, no warning shouts. No bare feet, no hard breathing, no calls for help.

No guards.

No Lenk.

Nobody.

Maybe the silk covering the walls smothered his sound. Or maybe he was already dead.

She should go back, she knew. She should call out for him.

No, she told herself. *They'd hear you first. There are more of them than there are of him. Just go back and... I don't know, listen for him? Yeah. You know the sound of his breath. You know the sound of his feet. You can go back down the hall quietly and wait until you can hear... you can hear...*

She was distracted. She shook her head; her ears twitched like a cat's. It didn't help.

She could hear *something*.

What was that, she wondered? Something faint, like a fly, buzzing right beside her ear? No; more like a heartbeat, felt through someone else's chest. Or maybe the sound of a song heard through many soft trees and many stiff breezes and many, many miles.

It grew louder with each breath, shrieking, roaring, screaming. She couldn't hear anything else. She couldn't concentrate. She couldn't—

She felt someone rise up behind her. An arm went around her neck. She snarled, reached up to seize it, and made no move beyond that. The tip of a dagger pointed beneath her chin was enough to discourage it.

"Move, you die," a voice threatened in her ear. "Do what I say, though..." The steel kissed the tender flesh beneath her jaw. "You just might live. Understand?"

She nodded as much as the blade allowed. Fear raced through her, demanded she struggle. Nerve steadied her, though, as she was all too aware of the metal scraping against her skin.

"Good," the voice purred. "Now, answer me this." A hot breath blew against the tip of her ear. "What happened to your last shirt?"

She blinked. "What?"

"That little green thing. I liked that one."

Her brows furrowed. "*What?*"

"This black thing here kind of smells. Couldn't you cut the middle out of it or something?"

Kataria broke free in a flail of slapping hands. The knife fell away from her chin almost immediately, a morbid chuckle following it.

When she turned around, a wooden face greeted her, a broad, impish grin and a pair of eyes like upside-down crescent moons carved into it. Even if she didn't see the braided, feathered hair or the long, pointed ears, she would have known who stood before her by the chuckle alone.

Kataria narrowed her eyes at Kwar. "That," she growled, "was not funny."

Kwar pulled her mask up. Somehow, the wink she offered some-how more unsettling than the half-moon eyes of her mask.

"You liked it."

"Because who *wouldn't* like having a knife jammed up under their chin?" Kataria snarled. "It's not as if this place is crawling with people trying to kill me, after all."

"All right, all right, fussy-ears, I'm sorry," Kwar said, laughing. "To be honest, I didn't think I could actually sneak up on you." She pointed to her ears, twitching attentively. "Didn't you hear us?"

She *had* heard her, Kataria realized. That buzzing in her ear, that beating heart, that distant song; had that *all* been Kwar? It had been so loud, so much so that it had consumed every other sound around her.

Kwar's Howling.

A language meant only for her.

For a moment, Kataria found herself breathless at the memory. Though still not enough to miss the word Kwar spoke.

"Who's 'us'?"

The question was answered a moment later as two dark shapes came trundling out from around the corner, dragging something behind them. She recognized the other shicts almost immediately, and not just by their grinning masks or their pointed ears. She could hear their Howling, as well, but theirs was fainter than Kwar's, distracted and meant for other ears.

She might have been more worried about that if she hadn't recognized the two shapes they were dragging behind them. Maybe they weren't the humans that had been chasing her, but they were house guards, and they were quite dead. Their cloaks were laid out behind them like blankets to keep the blood from their slashed throats from weeping out onto the floor.

The two shicts dropped their burdens next to a window, pushing its blinds open. Absently, their ears twitched, hearing her unspoken Howling. They looked up at Kataria through their grinning masks and waved with a decidedly unnerving air of nonchalance.

"Good evening, sister," one of them called as he grabbed the ankles of one of the guards.

"Glad you found us," the other, taking the guard's arms, added. "We'd been calling for you."

"Sorry," Kataria said, watching with morbid fascination as they dumped one and then the other guard out the window. "I was distracted."

"Apparently," Kwar said. She reached out to take the hem of Kataria's tunic, sniffing at the material and making a disparaging snort. "Maybe I'm just old-fashioned, but I don't understand the shicts of today. Running around in fancy houses, dressing up in smelly black burlap..."

"It's complicated." Kataria slapped away her hand and smoothed her tunic out.

And it just got more complicated now that you're here.

Kataria resisted the urge to say that. And at that moment, she regretted even thinking it. Kwar fixed a steady stare upon her, looking past the burlap, past the skin, into some other part of her entirely.

And even as her eyes remained steady as stones in a riverbed, her ears twitched excitedly.

Kataria grew tense under her gaze. She was ready to run, if necessary. She was ready to come up with some half-assed excuse for her presence, if necessary. But Kwar's stare betrayed no action; Kwar's ears betrayed no discovery on her part.

Hence, when the khoshict burst out laughing, Kataria nearly jumped.

"Fine, then," Kwar said. "Be all mysterious and secretive. I'll find out later." Her grin curled into an impish *v*. "I always find out."

"What are *you* doing here, then?" Kataria asked. "Or is that a secret, too?"

"Not at all. Everyone is welcome on a hunt!"

"And...who are you hunting?"

"Oh, you know." Kwar's lips split apart and her canines glistened in the lantern light of the hall. "Prey."

Kataria cast a sidelong glance at her. "And is Thua with you?"

Instantly, the smile faded. "Thua doesn't need to know about this."

Kataria did not ask. For at that moment, her ears caught a sound. The patter of feet on marble, a sharp gasp of air, an unsteady breath that accompanied the hair standing up on the back of one's neck. She saw by the upright ears around her that the khoshicts had heard it as well.

"Ah," Kwar said softly. "And there it is now."

Her ears twitched and her companions responded to the unheard command, crouching near the corner of the hallway. She looked at Kataria and grinned.

"Coming?"

Kataria froze. She knew that she ought to refuse, that she had already wasted enough time that she should use searching for Lenk. But what would she say to Kwar?

Sorry, I have to go back and find a human that you probably really would hate and also I'm sleeping with him; hope that doesn't bother you or your friends here? If you end up finding him, would you please come get me and, you know, not kill him?

If Kwar heard *that*, she didn't say anything.

"Right behind you," Kataria whispered.

This made sense, she told herself as she followed the khoshicts to the corner of the hall. Lenk could handle guards better than he could a shictish hunting party. At least if Kataria was with them, she could stop them from killing him if they found him first.

Or she could try, anyway.

Her ears went spear-straight as she heard the sound. Footsteps were drawing closer. Soft on the marble: shoes or barefoot. Not a guard, then. A servant, perhaps. Or even Miron. It didn't sound like Lenk's footsteps, but it was hard to concentrate here.

She looked down at the dagger clutched in Kwar's hand and tensed, ready to grab that wrist if needed.

The footsteps were loud now, almost deafening to their sensitive ears. They tensed collectively, ready to strike. The other two shicts slipped hatchets and short, curved blades into their hands. They drew breath as one, held it as one, waited.

Until their prey rounded the corner.

The human woman had been frightened before she even saw them, and thus she was ready to run. She evaded the shicts' grasping hands as they lunged at her, whirling around and sprinting down the hall she had just come from. Kwar leapt over her companions, flipping the dagger in her hand to grip it by the tip. She stood at the mouth of the hall, drew her arm back, and threw in a single fluid motion.

A soft *thud*. A screech. A body hit the floor.

And Kwar was laughing.

"Ha!" She leapt into the air, triumphant. "Didn't think I was going to make that, did you?" She turned to her companions, pulling her mask over her face. "*Did you?*"

"Horseshit," one of the khoshicts muttered, rising to his feet. "You got lucky."

"Lucky, clever, *and* charming," Kwar said smugly.

Kataria followed the khoshicts down the hall. Their prey hadn't gotten far; she lay upon the marble, a dagger's hilt jutting out of her left buttock. The fear in her eyes was new, but Kataria recognized the rest of the woman.

The envoy. From the Harbor Road that morning.

"Please," the human gasped on the floor. "Please, don't kill me. I have nothing. This is all the fasha's."

"Ah, see, that's where you're wrong." Kwar knelt down beside the woman, gently thumbing the hilt of the embedded dagger. "This is yours, human. All this land is yours. It was once ours, once, but not anymore. It's not fair, but that's the way it is." She looked at the human thoughtfully. "Now, doesn't that seem reason enough to kill you?"

She pushed the hilt about with two fingers, wiggling it inside the wound. The envoy's scream was stifled as Kwar clapped a hand over her mouth. Tears streamed down the woman's eyes, streaking her face paint as she shrieked into Kwar's palm.

But even muffled as it was, Kataria could hear the scream as clearly as if it had come from her own mouth. She shook her head and made a move to step forward, but Kwar released the dagger before she could.

"Lucky for you," Kwar said, "I don't care about your life tonight, only what you know. You will tell me what I want to know. This is not a request, nor a command. This is what will happen. That part is out of your hands. It may take a moment, it may take an hour. That part is up to you. Do you understand?"

The envoy nodded a trembling head. Kwar nodded back.

"Where is the sewer access?" she asked.

"Down...downstairs," the envoy replied. "In the basement." Kwar's mask betrayed no emotion. The woman drew in a sharp gasp. "I...I can show you."

Kwar nodded. She slipped a small piece of leather into the woman's mouth. "Bite down. This will hurt."

The envoy shrieked into the leather as Kwar pulled the dagger free and wiped it clean on her skirt. The wound bled a little, Kataria saw, but didn't gush. The envoy looked up at her, the only unmasked shict, with a glistening plea in her eyes.

No recognition at all.

Kwar grunted at one of her companions. He swept forward and plucked up the envoy, slinging her over his shoulder. She stared at the envoy through the slits in her mask.

"Any noise aside from direction, things go bad," she warned.

The envoy nodded weakly. And they were off.

They went quietly down the halls, removing the leather from the envoy's mouth long enough to get directions, navigating their way to a second set of servants' stairs tucked away in a tiny corner at the rear of the house.

Guards rambled about, unaware of their passing. Before any of them ever heard the sound of tramping boots, Kwar was there with ears and hand up, signaling a halt. Before any of them could react, Kwar's dagger was out, ready for blood.

And, more than once, Kataria looked at her carefully and wondered who this woman moving like a shadow was.

Where was the coy, playful khoshict that she had awoken to find sitting atop her? Where was the laughing, capricious woman who danced around the fire with her? Where was her impish smile, her glittering eyes, her laugh?

This woman was a stranger, her movements were careful and precise instead of carefree and easy. This woman's stare was cold instead of warm. This woman moved less like a woman and more like a predator, alive only in the hunt.

And Kataria was not the only one to see it.

In those moments that the envoy dared to look up, her gaze was split between Kwar and Kataria. The fear in her eyes was everpresent, though there was only a bright, glistening desperation when she looked to Kataria. A wordless plea that babbled down her face in shining tears that she didn't dare show Kwar.

And, at that moment, Kataria could understand why.

Regardless, she followed Kwar and the other two khoshicts down the stairs. They avoided the rush of servants to and fro and slipped past stray guards and guests to another set of stairs leading to the basement.

Even Ghoukha's cellar was magnificent, its narrow brick tunnels well polished, its many, *many* larder doors well oiled. Almost *too* well oiled—the pungent reek of grease was everywhere. They must be close to an oil store, she reasoned, and quite a bit of it.

They followed the envoy's directions farther down to the end of the cellar. In a small, round room lit by a dim lantern, a thick iron grate barred a hole the size of a man leading into darkness. The sound of rushing water reached their ears: not the cheerful nonsense of a babbling brook, but the ugly, curse-laden mutter of a sewer.

Kwar swept in and took a quick survey of the grate. She glanced at the envoy. "It's locked."

"Keys!" the envoy shouted as she was set down before Kwar. "I have the keys!"

The khoshict canted her head to the side, glancing at the woman's sash. She reached past her arm, ignoring the frightened whimper that emerged, and plucked out an iron ring laden with keys. She held them up before her, inspecting them.

"It's the copper one," the envoy spoke up, voice quavering. "The copper one unlocks it."

Kwar nodded slowly, tucking the key ring into her belt. "Anything else I should know?"

"I . . . I don't think so."

"Think hard."

The envoy shook her head. "N-no. Nothing else. I swear."

"Good." A flash of steel, Kwar's dagger was in her hand. "Then you get to die quick—"

"WAIT!"

The dagger's blade paused a hairbreadth from the envoy's throat. Kwar visibly stiffened as she looked over her shoulder. Through the moon-shaped slits in her mask, Kataria should see her dark eyes aflame.

"Kill her and there's too much blood," Kataria said. "Too easy to track."

"We dump her in the sewer," Kwar replied. "No mess."

"If the humans find out it was you—"

"They won't."

Kataria opened her mouth. Nothing came out but a single word, pathetic and weak to her ears.

"Don't."

During the moment Kwar held her gaze, Kataria swore she saw something in the deepness of her eyes. Not a fiery scowl, nor even a cold glare of contempt. What burned in those eyes was something bright and desperate, a wordless howl that pounded at the wooden mask like a prison door, begging to be free.

All that came from Kwar, however, was a long sigh. The tension fled her body as the dagger slipped back into her belt. With an almost petulant ease, she smashed the back of her hand against the envoy's face, sending her limp in her companions' grip.

"Go hide her in a room somewhere," Kwar said.

"That doesn't sound smart," one of the khoshicts replied with a wary glance.

"No, it doesn't." Kwar lifted her mask and regarded Kataria through a face softened by a frown. "Do it anyway."

Kataria could feel the khoshicts' glares keenly, even through their masks. Still, their enmity for her seemed to be outweighed by their respect for Kwar. They plucked up the unconscious envoy and hauled her out into the hall.

Kwar didn't look up as she went to work unlocking the grate. She didn't make a sound but for a strained grunt as she tried to lift it. Slowly, Kataria crouched down on the other side of the grate and took a grip.

"Humans keep access to their sewers in their houses?" she asked.

"Rich ones do," Kwar muttered.

A breathless moment passed between them.

"Thank you," Kataria said softly, "for that."

"Yeah, well..." Kwar sighed. "What's another human running around, anyway? Not like you'd solve the problem just by killing one."

"It must have been difficult." Kataria stared down at her own hands wrapped tightly about the iron bars. "Your father told me... about your mother."

There was only the sound of rushing water. At her silence, Kataria finally looked up at her companion. For the second time that night, she saw someone different.

The laughing young woman and the silent predator were both gone. What remained was someone who looked uncomfortable under all her muscle, who looked too scared to look so strong.

"I remember when she died," Kwar said, her voice a whisper against the water's burble. "I was just a child, but I remember. The humans were trying to fight us. She, my mother, stood up before them and raised her blade and dared them to come get her and they..."

She closed her eyes. Her lips tightened into a thin scar.

"She dropped her blade and I ran to pick it up," she said. "Thua tried to stop me, ran up behind me and grabbed me. But I was always bigger and stronger than him. I kicked him hard, so hard it made his shins bleed. Then I bit his fingers. He was crying, so I called him a coward. Then I used Mother's blade and cut him on his arm and he let me go.

"I was going to kill the humans." She growled. "All of them. But Father, he—"

She shook her head.

"He wanted to make peace with them. He said it's what Mother would have wanted. He's a liar. Thua is just a coward; he can't help that, but he believes our father. My mother wanted the shicts to be safe. And for that, I would kill every last human, no matter how long it took."

When Kwar finally looked up at Kataria, her face was soft. Her eyes were wet. Her smile was sad.

"But," she said, "I suppose I can let a few live if it'll make you happy."

It was so rarely that Kataria ever found herself without a retort. Very cruel of Kwar to do that to her, she thought. Very cruel of her to make her feel as if something was caught in her throat as she opened her mouth.

And yet, Kwar's ears twitched all the same, hearing something unsaid.

But not for long.

Kataria's ears pricked up at a distant sound. Voices from below, feet sloshing through water. Far away, growing closer. Someone in the sewer.

"Ah," Kwar said. "We should hurry. Our contractors won't be happy if they find their way in still blocked. Give me a hand with this, will you?"

Kataria nodded. With a grunt, they strained to haul the grate up, opening the manhole in the ground. It fell open with a crashing sound.

"Good," Kwar said. "Now, let's get out of here."

"Why? Don't you need to be paid?"

"Payment was arranged beforehand," Kwar replied. "We don't want to be here when this place gets ugly."

She made a beckoning motion for Kataria to follow, but the shict hesitated. She leaned closer to the hole, the voices growing clearer. It was a language she didn't understand, but one whose fervor and harshness were all too familiar. She turned to Kwar with wide, accusatory eyes.

"Who hired you?" she asked.

"It's not important."

"Who?" Kataria demanded.

Kwar's stare was firm. "I know they are violent and crazed. Frankly, I'm counting on it. If the humans want to kill each other, who am I to stand in their way? Fasha, Khovura…" She sneered. "They all look the same to me."

Kataria's mouth hung open for a moment. She hadn't a word to offer, not that any could be heard over the sudden thunder of her heart.

The Khovura.

The Khovura were coming.

Kataria looked to the grate. Too heavy to lift on her own, and she knew she couldn't convince Kwar to help her. The sound of the fanatics echoed through the tunnels. Even a round ear could hear them now.

There was no time to explain why she suddenly took off running. And certainly no time to stop and wait when Kwar called after her.

But if she hurried, if her lungs held out and her legs held firm and someone up in heaven decided to put aside racial differences and stop hating her for just a single moment, there might just be enough time to find Lenk before the house of Ghoukha was painted scarlet.

THIRTY-THREE

THROUGH GILDED VEIN

*F*ish eggs?

Asper shook her head.

No. But they are eggs, aren't they? All glistening and…quivering and…and… She forced a visible cringe into a visible frown. *Do I really want to know?*

Whether she did or not, when she looked up from the tray to the headman who had just handed it to her, she was met with a glare and a rather forceful gesture to return to the guests.

She did so, eyes never leaving the glistening green sacs quivering upon flatbreads. She delicately evaded guests, pretending not to hear their calls or notice their reaching hands. She made her way to the corner of the room where the corpsewagon lingered, still given a large berth.

She glanced around the room and, once she was sure no one was watching, pulled up the tarp covering the wagon and slipped the tray in.

There was a faint rustling from beneath, followed by a low growl.

"What's this?" Gariath muttered beneath the tarp.

"I don't know," Asper said. "Spider eggs, I guess? Ghoukha likes to make an impression."

"I told you to bring me meat. Why would you bring me this? Did you want me to hit you? We could have worked something out."

"It's all they serve here!" Asper retorted, trying *not* to look like she was talking to a corpsewagon that should definitely not be talking back. "Just eat it."

"What is this room called again?"

"The *houn*. It means 'boast' in Djaalic."

"What's it made of?"

"Mostly gold. Other expensive stuff."

"And they eat things that come out of a bug's anus."

"That's what you do when you're rich," Asper whispered. "Look, if you don't like it, you can just wait until we're out of here. It won't be long now. Probably."

She looked across the *houn*. Dreadaeleon and Denaos would be easy to spot even if they weren't dressed in sheer black, just by the total absence of people around them. True to the disguise, though, every guest and servant seemed to be taking exceptional pains to avoid even looking at them, let alone interacting with them.

They had taken positions at various doors at the walls of the *houn*, ready to disappear once Ghoukha appeared. There had been murmurs of activity upstairs, which she could only assume was Ghoukha preparing to come down.

Either that or something had gone terribly wrong with Kataria and Lenk. That worried her. But, with so many things with so much potential to go wrong, she could but trust in their ability to handle themselves. Not like she had much of a choice, anyway.

"I smell fear."

"That might be me," Asper whispered back.

"It's everywhere. I smelled it back in the city. The scent of people who cling and grasp." There was a long pause. "You say the room is made of gold?"

"It is."

No response. Not so much as a growl. Gariath was completely silent.

That, too, worried her.

Almost as much as the hand that shot out to seize her by the arm and drew her close.

"Hey, northern," one of the servants, a young girl with a tray of wine, snapped, "do me a favor and take this to Fasha Teneir."

"What?" Asper grunted as the tray was shoved into her hands. "Why can't you?"

"For one, you're new. For two, you're northern. For three, you haven't had a chance to understand why no one else wants to do this." She gave Asper a swift slap on the rump, shoving her out onto the floor. "The saccarii with the Ancaaran. Just nod and smile."

Sparing a wary glance for Gariath's hiding place, Asper made her way out to the floor. She hadn't ever seen Teneir yet—though various whispers floating between guests and servants had given her a good idea of what to expect, even before she saw the ornately dressed Ancaaran priest and the veiled woman standing beside him.

The only person in the room who was given a wider berth than a wagon purportedly full of dead corpses.

The moment she crept within range, a pair of amber eyes, sharp as knives, was whirled upon her.

The woman's eyes were as lit and lively as fireflies, flitting from Asper's face to Asper's hands to Asper's middle to Asper's shoulder. Wherever the saccarii's gaze lingered for longer than a breath, she felt a flinch of pain, as though the woman's eyes could prick as surely as any needle.

"This wine." Teneir's voice came scalpel-thin from beneath her veil, an elaborately stitched green ensemble that matched the rest of her dress. "It was made from grapes grown in the shadow of a tall building whose windows are cracked and where people huddle together?"

It hurt to hear her voice. It hurt to look her in the eyes. Asper could but do as she'd been advised, forcing a trembling smile to her lips and nodding.

"And was it crushed by the washed feet of a poor mother with a bent back? Were her children hungry and her husband gone on a holy day?"

Asper forced her grin a little bigger, for fear that it might collapse into a grimace at any moment. She nodded again.

Teneir's slit gaze lingered on her for a moment longer before she reached down to pluck the wine from the tray. Asper caught but a glimpse of her delicate hand before it retreated back into its sleeve: It was gray, almost scaly.

"At least Ghoukha manages to show some respect to Ancaa, if only in drink," Teneir muttered to her elaborately dressed companion. "I should renew my objections to his plans for mediation."

"Your passion for the faith is admirable, Teneir," the Ancaaran priest replied through a smile as sparkling as his headdress. "But there is no need. Peace between the foreigners will bring glory to Cier'Djaal. Why should it not be made in the most glorious home of Cier'Djaal?"

"And what of Cier'Djaal's people?" Teneir asked sharply. "Ancaa loves the poor most of all. If this peace is to benefit them, then why not do it where they can see it? The Meat Market lies between the Souk and the Sumps, at the heart of—"

The Ancaaran priest made a face as though someone had just broken wind. "The Sumps! Fasha, you cannot be serious. So much dirt and grime."

"Dirt is the cloth of the impoverished. Grime is the cloak of the oppressed. Let the people witness the peace Ancaa delivers them! Let them know She is no deaf Goddess."

"I'll hear no more of it!" he replied. "Please, let us speak of other things." Instantly, the grimace was wiped clean by a silken sleeve. In its place was a simpering smile. "Now, as to the donation you were speaking of…"

"Yes, yes," Teneir replied. "I have already instructed my accountant to—"

Without even a pause, Teneir's eyes cut to Asper, drawing thin as razors. Asper didn't know if yelping was as dignified as smiling and nodding; at least she managed not to use the tray as a shield.

"Do you require my attention, *shkainai*?"

Asper shook her head, trembling.

"Then *go*."

Asper didn't know if there was a dignified way to flee, either. She turned sharply on her heel and left, all the same. She felt Teneir's gaze chase her, the pins pricking with every step she took, until she felt the guests and servants close in around her once again.

Asper cast a glance over her shoulder. Everyone was behind her. No one was behind her.

She turned to head back to the wagon and felt a sudden jolt as another body collided with her.

"Your pardon," she said, making sure to throw in an exaggerated bow. "The fault was all—"

She looked up into darkness.

He had a face. She knew this, only because she knew he had eyes. And everything he was—the tall thinness of his body, the narrowness of his mouth, the slope of his shaven head—was swallowed within a wide, unblinking stare.

"I didn't mean..."

She emptied her words into those eyes, watched them drift into aimless whispers. She caught the rest of him in periphery, unnecessary details of a body there only to bear the burden of his stare. His clothes were threadbare and coarse. He wore no shoes. His skin should have been dark, but looked drained and pale.

He did not belong here.

She did not belong before him.

"Haven't..." she whispered, "haven't I..."

"You have." His voice was soft, deep, a yawning hole into which a lake slowly drained. "You will not again."

He blinked. The world blinked with him. When it opened its eyes, he was behind her.

"Noisy in here," he observed. "Do you think Talanas will hear you when you pray to Him?"

She asked him something that she couldn't hear. The *houn*'s noise was eaten alive by the sound of a loud gong. When she turned around, the man and his eyes were gone. But everyone else's were turned to the stairs and the man upon it.

The gong rang out with every step of the servants that carried him along the upper hallway to the top of the stairs, as if to suggest that his coming was thunder and his smile was the sun. A burden of gold sat upon his neck and shoulders, just as his burden of flesh sat upon the palanquin his servants set down upon the marble.

As vast and painted and glistening as she remembered him from the Souk, Fasha Ghoukha surveyed his golden land like a glutted god.

"Friends," he bellowed over their heads, "esteemed emissaries, men and women of all Gods." He swung his meaty arms over his *houn*. "Be welcome to the House of Ghoukha."

Light applause. Just loud enough to hide the spiteful whispers exchanged among a few more envious attendees.

"Long have we fashas led by *houn*," he continued. "By our ambition, by our gold"—he gestured to the ceiling, where the source of his wealth skittered across on eight legs—"by our friends who have, in turn, led us to be the voice of Cier'Djaal. For years, our voice has been *houn*. And only *houn*.

"This was the way of our fathers." He held up a thick finger and waved it. His chins shuddered. "But not ours. Our fathers could count the luxury of isolation. But we, their sons and daughters, live in a different Cier'Djaal.

"We are a city of many races"—he swept a hand to Man-Shii Kree, who bowed respectfully—"of many faiths"—he found Blacksbarrow and Careus in the crowd and met their scowls with a smile—"of many people. No longer can we speak with only one word.

"Let us therefore, find a new way to speak," he continued. "Let us add to our vocabulary. And let the first word be—"

His lips shuddered. A loud belch slipped between them. Noses crinkled in distaste. He offered a nervous laugh.

"Peace," he continued. "Let us speak of peace. Let us speak with peace. Soon, we shall meet with our gracious Karnerian and Sainite guests present, in the House of Ghoukha, to discuss matters of—"

He was interrupted. Another raucous belch burst out of his lips.

A murmur of disapproval went out, smothered quickly by a louder, more nervous laugh.

"Pardon. I do believe I shall be having a word with our chefs after this," he said to unenthusiastic laughter. "With war brewing beneath the Silken Spire, we cannot allow ourselves to continue to play this game. We must stand united against the Khovura, against the Jackals and soon, against any—"

Another belch. Flecks of white spittle chased the noise from his lips. His belly shuddered with the force of the explusion. Now the disapproval became open, scorn plain on their faces. Ghoukha's face seemed to melt with his frown. He held out his hands.

"Please, excuse me, but I—"

Another. Drool began to stream out from between his lips. His belly trembled, squirming like a living thing beneath his flesh. With each belch that followed, it grew in intensity, rippling across his flesh, prodding at his flab.

Through the quiver of skin, perhaps no one else noticed it. But Asper had seen it before.

Against his tremendous belly, the impression of a long, thin hand pressing the flesh.

"Oh, Gods. Please, help, it hurts so—"

His mouth craned open. The belch came again.

A river of blood followed.

<hr />

Lenk watched two red droplets fall. They fell softly upon the cold, white tile of the floor and spread into ugly smears.

Almost like they're reaching toward each other, he thought, staring at his own blood. *Like they want to be together.*

And with that thought, Lenk was pretty sure he had a concussion.

Before he could share either of those conclusions, though, another fist cracked against his jaw. He felt himself go limp and be propped up again by the gauntleted grip of the guards. He took in the scowl of the other two—wait, no, there was just the one hitting him, he realized as soon as his vision stopped swimming.

He surveyed the room they had brought him in. A nice little parlor, off to the side of the hall; the low-slung table, demure purple tapestries, and knee pillows suggested it would be a nice place to take tea. Lenk wouldn't have thought it'd be an ideal place for pummeling a man to death, but what did he know?

"Look," the guard said, rubbing his knuckles, "we get paid the same no matter what happens, but I prefer avoiding unnecessary labor. If you die, we have to deal with your corpse and we have to get our asses chewed about why we didn't find out who you were working for. But if you just *tell us*…"

He let the implication hang, as another drop from Lenk's bloodied nose hung from his upper lip. He snorted it back in, looked up at the guard. The taste of copper filled his mouth.

"So, who was it?" the guard asked. "Sheffu? Mejina? Teneir? She's always been keen to cut off a piece of Ghoukha's ass."

"There isn't a knife big enough," one of the guards holding him chuckled.

"I'm not working for a fasha," Lenk said.

The guard drew his fist back. "If you're going to lie to me, it better be a good one."

"If it is, do I not get punched?"

"Maybe."

Lenk lowered his head and sighed. "Actually, we were looking for evidence of cult activity that would have led us to the location of a priest who owes us money and who may or may not actually have been dead all along."

He heard the crack of knuckles against his jaw. He swayed in the guards' grip, snorted, and spat an artless glob of red onto the floor. He looked up and sneered at the guard through a bloodied nose.

"Well, what the *fuck* was wrong with that one, then?" he demanded.

The guard didn't answer. And frankly, Lenk didn't care. Through his swimming vision, something over the guard's shoulder caught his eye.

Dark shapes. Two legs. Moving swiftly and silently. He caught glimpses of their black clothes, their thick veils, their wild eyes.

Khovura.

Dozens of them rushing past in the blink of an eye.

And striding softly amidst them, a single white lotus floating upon a black river, was a man tall and elegant and clad in white. He felt the urge to cry out, to demand something. But there was no need. Just as he noticed the man in white, the man in white noticed him.

And Miron Evenhands turned to regard Lenk and smiled softly an instant before a pair of Khovura swept forward and slammed the doors shut.

"The hell?" The punchy guard turned and rushed to the door. Finding it barred from the outside, he pounded a fist against the wood. "Hey! Hey! Open the door. We're not finished in here. Who's out there? Deresk? Is that you? This shit isn't—"

He interrupted himself with a sudden cry of alarm and a leap backward. Black liquid began to seep under the door, filling the room with the acrid reek of oil.

"Come on," the punchy guard muttered, waving a hand. "Help me break this down."

"What about him?" one guard asked, looking at Lenk.

"*Forget* him," he snarled, whirling on his companions. "Do you want to die here? Why do you think they're pouring oil in if not to—"

He didn't have to finish that question.

The fire did it for him.

An orange spark raced across the pool of oil, eager as a child with a hot red giggle sneaking into a room it ought not be in. And before anyone could think to do anything about it, it reached out to tug at the oil-stained hem of the guard's cloak. Too excited to calm itself, it leapt onto the guard for a piggyback ride.

And within an instant, its crackling laughter mingled with the guard's screams. The flame ate him, sending him flailing across the room to spread its fire to tapestries, pillows, rugs, and the other guard he was grasping in a desperate plea for help.

Lenk and the remaining guard backed away, leaping to keep clear of the rapidly spreading flaming oil and the fiery embrace of the two guards as they tumbled to the floor. They lay there, the flame settling upon the heap of molten flesh and armor.

Lenk and the guard exchanged a brief glance, just enough to let each other know that neither of them gave a shit about each other anymore. That and a quick shove was all the attention the guard was willing to spare Lenk before rushing to the window.

A crash of glass. A flail of arms. A loud scream, growing softer.

Lenk ran to the shattered window and peered over the edge. A narrow ledge ran around the wall of Ghoukha's house, beneath each window. The guard had probably thought he could use it to escape.

Or maybe he had just thought he'd survive the fall to the courtyard below.

Of course, he'd been wrong about that, too.

In truth, Lenk noted, it wasn't a bad idea. The ledge was barely wide enough for a man's feet, but it might be done. The guard hadn't been stupid, just scared. Fear frayed nerves. Frayed nerves made for stupid choices.

Now, Lenk thought as he climbed out onto the ledge, when you made a stupid choice with perfectly intact nerves, *that* was called "strategy."

The flames devoured the room behind him. They licked out over the broken glass, nearly catching him as he crept away. He held his breath against the smoke and sidled his way slowly along the ledge.

He wanted to move faster. This wasn't a matter of escape. He had to find another way in, another way to find Kataria before the Khovura did. He had to save her. Then the rest of them. Then find Miron. All through an inestimable tide of Khovura who were probably all better armed and definitely better armored than he.

How he planned to do that with nothing but a breechcloth, he wasn't quite sure. But one problem at a time.

He glanced into the first window he came to next. A gang of Khovura hunched over screaming guards, hacking them to death with long knives. He hurried past, hoping they hadn't seen him.

The window to the next room revealed a more welcome sight, even if it was full of dead guards. They lay upon the floor of another parlor, their blood staining the rugs, making swollen the elaborate designs stitched into them.

There would be time to feel bad about that later. Time, too, to feel bad about him tearing his breechcloth from his hips and wrapping it around his hand. Looking away, he smashed his swaddled fist against the glass, carefully so as not to cut himself or make too much noise. And carefully he made his way into the room.

Through the walls and the open door, he could hear the sounds of dying men and fists banging against heavy wooden doors. The air was toxic with the scent of oil mingling lazily with the pools of shed blood upon the floors.

The Khovura were dousing the entire upper floor in oil, locking people in their rooms, and barring the doors not already secured from within. This was no mere impulsive attack, then; this was going to be a slaughter, efficient and messy and of who knew how many people.

And though he could think of only one of those people right now, he forced her from his mind for the moment. Fear could speak when instinct was done talking. Right now, he had to think about getting a weapon.

He found one of the house guard's swords and pried dead fingers loose from its hilt. That was one problem solved. And as he glanced at the guard's waist and tried to guess what size breeches he was wearing, he was about to solve another when he became aware—as naked people did—of eyes upon him.

He looked up. In the doorway a Khovura stood, sword in hand, eyes wide and locked upon him.

Lenk felt a stiff breeze. He sniffed a drop of blood up into his nose.

"Hey," he said.

"*KAPIR*—" the Khovura started to reply.

Lenk cut him off with a punch, batting aside the Khovura's blade and driving a fist against his jaw to silence him before he could raise an alarm. The man looked hardly put off by this, immediately lashing out wildly with his blade, aiming for Lenk's torso.

He danced backward, careful to remember where the dead lay, careful not to trip over them as the Khovura drove him back with frenzied strikes, broken glass cutting into his bare feet.

The Khovura lunged at him, blade out and seeking blood. He caught it with his own pilfered sword, retreating another step as the Khovura drove his blade forward, trying to shove Lenk toward the broken window. He growled, feeling the jagged shards of glass cut into his skin as he was driven back another step, and then another until he was arching his back just to avoid being impaled. The Khovura bore his weight down, trying to shove him onto the glass—or out the window.

"*Kapira, Kapira, Kapira…*"

Maddened whispers were on his lips, slithering out from beneath his veil, giving him fervent strength as he pressed his weight against Lenk, unbearable, inevitable, impossible to hold back.

So Lenk didn't bother.

He twisted to the side suddenly, the glass scraping against his flesh as he tumbled away from the embrace of blades. The Khovura's momentum carried him forward, downward, aided by Lenk's hand as he seized the man about the neck and shoved him down. Hard.

The ensuing squelching sound was satisfyingly messy. And then, it was silent. The Khovura hung limp, a jagged shard of glass jutting out of the back of his neck.

Lenk took a moment to breathe.

That was a mistake. He had clarity enough, then, to appreciate the situation. He could feel the blood oozing out of his face, his back, the soles of his feet. He could hear the sounds of screaming from Khovura fanatics and dying guards. He could smell oil and cinders and smoke in the air.

And he had just enough lucidity of thought to know that somewhere, in all of this mess of death and flames, people needed him. Sheffu, if he hadn't woken up; Mocca, if he hadn't escaped; Kataria...

If she wasn't already dead.

He tried to fight down that thought. He tried to fight down the pain in his feet as he walked out the room. He tried to fight down the dizzying scent of oil and the fear gnawing at the base of his skull.

He tried.

For he could do nothing else.

━━━◆≡◆━━━

This can't be happening.

In the moment between when she inhaled screams and exhaled denial, she closed her eyes. When she opened them again, the world was drowned in darkness and everything gold was painted red.

Somewhere, in the breaths between the bodies falling and the knives rising, Asper's denial became prayer.

Don't let this be happening.

She didn't know where they had come from, where they had been hiding, how they had gotten in. But they were everywhere. Flickering at the periphery of her vision, shadows cast by a trembling candlelight, they ran among the crowd with their long knives and their fanatic cries.

"KAPIRA!"

Khovura.

Everywhere.

Please.

Nobles were carved, their painted faces smeared as Khovura hands dragged them down and cut them. Servants fell, offering upheld hands and pleas as ineffective shields against Khovura knives. The house guards flailed clumsily with blades meant for harder hands than theirs before they, too, were dragged to the floor and crushed under Khovura boots.

Ghoukha presided over the slaughter from the staircase, sprawled out, body jiggling with convulsions. Blood poured from his mouth in a frothy spray, descending the steps in an elegant, undulating waterfall. No longer a God but a fallen idol, his palanquin bearers had either fled or lay bleeding beside him.

The convulsions ceased for a moment. Long enough for him to look up to his silk-strewn ceiling and his golden naked women and let out a long, desperate wail to any God who would listen.

Asper couldn't hear what he said over the cries on the floor. Nor did he ever finish his plea. Accompanied by the sound of bone snapping and flesh tearing, a long gray limb ending in polished black claws reached out from the red-rimmed hole of his mouth and groped blindly upon the red-stained gold.

She had no idea where Denaos was, where Dreadaeleon was. Any one of the black-clad figures rushing through the crowd could have been them. She had to find one of them. She had to get help. She had to find—

Gariath.

She turned and saw the wagon where he still lay hidden. She saw a man in black rushing toward her. And then she saw nothing but the big knife he drew over his head and drove down toward her heart.

She caught his wrist with her right hand, his throat with her left. She couldn't tell one from the other. He wasn't just a knife, he wasn't just a wrist. He was a demon in black, fury in his eyes and on his lips. His words were choked as she tightened her grip around his throat; his arms quavered as she jerked the knife down and away, but he wasn't stopping; he wasn't backing down.

But she could feel herself giving way. She could feel blood beneath her feet. She could feel herself retreating step after step before his frenzy.

And she could feel her lips moving in silent, frenzied prayer.

"Please, please, please…"

It wasn't a prayer. She didn't have the wit to spare for anything proper. It was the desperate chant that people only ever uttered when they wanted to wake up from a nightmare. It went to no God. It would receive no answer.

Except this time.

There is no need to worry.

She heard his voice from within her. As bright and cheery as a funeral pyre. She could feel Amoch-Tethr's heat in her flesh as he stoked himself to an inferno inside her arm and poured his bright, cheerful hell into the Khovura's flesh.

The man dropped his knife and fell to the ground. His mouth was open in a scream, but nothing except white clouds of smoke emerged from beneath his veil. He reached for her wildly and she could not tell if he was trying to kill her or begging for help.

She could feel Amoch-Tethr watching this.

She could feel him smiling.

Panic seeped into her like a poison, settling in her bowels, solidifying in her spine. They were everywhere. She watched a fleeing woman trip and be set upon by three people in black with long knives. Khovura stalked the floors for hiding victims, leaving bloodied footprints where they walked. She needed to do something. She couldn't do anything. She needed help. She needed—

"KAPIRA!"

Run.

She was off as the shadows descended upon her. At least three—maybe four? She couldn't tell. They all blended together as they pursued her, a tide of night with wicked stars twinkling silver and red in the darkness. She searched the crowd. Was that Denaos or a Khovura? Where was Dreadaeleon? Why wasn't anyone helping her?

She almost knocked the wind out of herself, so hard did she run into the wagon. She whirled and saw them descending upon her. One rushed toward her, a cry beneath his veil, a weapon in his hands, blood on his fingers. He leapt.

"KAPI—"

His cry died in the air, choked out of him by the clawed red fingers that caught him by the throat. His legs kicked; he slashed wildly with his blade to no avail.

Gariath rose up, shredding the tarp with his horns. The Khovura still squirming in his grasp, he stepped out of the wagon, without a cloak, without hesitation. No one seemed to notice something as trivial as a massive red dragonman in the carnage.

But Gariath noticed everything. His eyes went wide with wonder—or was that revulsion—as he looked around the battlefield that had once been a *houn*.

"So much gold," he whispered, awestruck.

A knife caught his bicep, drawing a thick red line. He glanced down and suddenly became aware of the captive Khovura. Almost as an afterthought, he drew his arm up and slammed the man head-first upon the marble floor, stepping over his twitching body as he continued to stare with wonder.

"Where did it all come from?" he asked no one in particular. "Where did they get it? How does this much even exist?"

War cries tore mouths open. The other two Khovura charged Gariath, heedless of their companions' fate. He caught them, one in each hand, and casually pressed their faces together until two bodies shared one head. He let them fall before him.

"Who did they take it from?"

He appeared to stare past the carnage, or so Asper thought. He had seen more and better than this before; perhaps it wasn't all that exciting to him. Or maybe he just had no interest in who was dying.

He stared past the blood; he stared past the bodies; he watched the people falling beneath the knives and heard them begging for their lives and didn't care.

But he saw the *houn*.

He saw the gold glimmering as the tendrils of blood wept down them, the silk fluttering, painted with the shadows of knives descending. Pillars of gold towered around him, but he didn't seem to notice the bodies stacked at their bases.

He was surrounded by death.

And he didn't even care.

The hairs on the back of Asper's neck rose. She felt someone behind her. Her arm acted before she did, lashing out to wrap around a black-clothed throat. She felt a pulse racing beneath her thumb. She felt Amoch-Tethr grow giddy at the feeling.

Denaos held up his hands. The fear present in his blood wasn't on his face.

"It's me," he said gently. "It's me."

She released him and grabbed her arm to keep it from trembling. "We have to do something."

"Agreed," he said. "Gariath's the best equipped for this. He should stay here and find Dreadaeleon while you and I go upstairs and find Lenk and Kataria. We'll meet up outside."

"What? No." She cringed. "I mean, yes, them, too. But these people"—she gestured to the carnage—"are being slaughtered! We have to help them!"

"There's too many of them and not enough time. We're going to have to abandon the search for Miron as it is."

Asper's face set into a hard scowl. "It can wait."

"What about Lenk and Kat, then? Can *they* wait?"

"They'll take care of themselves." She shook her head. Too hard to think. Too much noise. "We can't just...we have to help whoever we can. We can't let all these people die!"

"What do we do? The house is crawling with Khovura. They're everywhere."

"I don't know. We'll...get them out? Evacuate them, maybe. Hold off the Khovura until—"

"How? *How* are we going to hold off this many?"

A cry pierced the air. A cry to Kapira. It started as a war cry, but it ended as a plea. And it came from the Khovura who was raised high above the crowd, screaming and arms flailing, by an invisible force.

No God answered him. The air rippled around him as a magical grip tightened around his body. He was flung haplessly against the golden breasts of one of the pillars. With a sickening splatter, he peeled down the column, leaving the statue's naked body streaked.

The next words she heard, she recognized, even if she didn't understand them. Dreadaeleon's voice was a crack of thunder. A prelude to the arc of lightning that shot through the crowd, parting them and leaving twitching, electrified corpses in its wake.

Asper took off running through the gap presented, leaping over the lightning-struck corpses, trying to ignore the fact that some were not Khovura.

When she reached Dreadaeleon, he was surrounded by bodies. The corpses of Khovura lay, ashen and smoldering at his feet. His hands whipped about in gestures she couldn't understand, seizing Khovura from the crowd with magical grips and flinging them into the air with invisible force.

"Dread!" she cried out.

He didn't bother looking at her. "This is marvelous, isn't it?"

"*What?*"

"Look at me. I've killed two dozen so far and I'm not even breaking a sweat. But I suppose that's to be expected, isn't it?" When he finally looked at her, his face was painted with the biggest, smuggest grin she had ever seen. "I've been through a few changes, after all."

"How long can you do this, then?" she asked. "How long can you hold them off?"

"All night and into the morning, if need be. Are my services required?"

"Yes!" she shot back. "Do whatever you can. We need to protect these people. I'll find Denaos and Gariath and try to get the doors to—"

"Understood."

He drew a deep breath and closed his eyes. When he opened them, a red mist poured out. Magic, Venarie, whatever he called it: She recognized it coming out of him in bright ruby clouds.

"What are you doing?" she asked.

He extended his arms to the sides, palms out. He began to speak something in the terrible language of wizards. Bright pinpricks of light burst out on his palms. His fingertips began to smoke.

"Dread," she said, "you can't—"

"I can," he replied. His voice resonated with power. The red mist poured out of his mouth. "I can do anything. I can kill Lectors. I can kill demons. I can save everyone."

His hands burst into flames. They cackled wildly upon his flesh, eager to be put to use. His feet left the ground, the air rippling beneath him. He rose higher, the flames spreading up his arms; he resembled nothing so much as an angel falling from the sun, a halo of bright red vapor about his brow.

"This is it," he said. "I am the hero this time."

Asper looked around. The dark shapes of the Khovura ran everywhere. How could he possibly stop them all? There was blackness on every surface; they seemed to excrete it with every step, leaving it in puddles on the ground.

Wait.

She realized what they were, these pools of pitch black, glistening against the gold. On the banister. On the floor. On the silk.

Oil.

Everywhere.

And Dreadaeleon loomed overhead, his limbs ablaze, his flames alive.

She screamed something to him. Her voice was lost on the roar of flames as his great, fiery wings spread.

And so, too, were the screams of the dying lost on a whirlwind of ash and cinders.

THIRTY-FOUR

VERSES IN OIL AND ASH

It had begun like a song.

In a verse of smoke that hung thick, in a melody of cinders that carried red through the darkness, reaching a crescendo in the sheets of flame that rose around her in a thousand crackling voices.

"Lenk!"

Kataria's was just one more lost in the smoke.

She yelled his name into the flames. The flames responded with a cackle, as though she had just told a wonderful joke, as though the thought of him still alive was positively hilarious.

"LENK!"

And the flames ate his name, swallowed it into their symphony and consumed it. She couldn't even hear herself over the sound of the flames roaring, of the men dying, of wood creaking.

And rafters breaking.

She looked up at the sound of a groan. Red veins sprawled across the ceiling, burning against the stone and wood. She saw a fiery artery burst. She saw the rafter crack and a hail of cinders and stone and wood come crashing down.

She felt the wind explode from her as something tackled her from behind.

A spray of brimstone burst against her back, settled upon her clothes and in her hair. Firm hands swiftly patted her down, cinders extinguishing with a frustrated hiss. She struggled to catch her breath.

Those same hands took her by their arms, gently now, as they helped her to her feet. She reached behind her, trying to find those hands, his hands, and wrap her fingers about them.

She found someone else.

"Easy." Kwar's breath was soft and clear; it didn't belong here. "Breathe slowly. There's too much smoke." She tugged gently on Kataria's arms. "Come on."

Kataria turned around. "Where are the others?"

"They went back to guard our escape," Kwar said. "Every place that isn't on fire is swarming with Khovura. We need to leave."

"I can't go," Kataria said. "Not yet; I need to find..."

She caught herself a heartbeat before she said it. She couldn't let Kwar know. She couldn't say—

"Lenk?" Kwar asked.

Kwar had heard. Over all the hell surrounding them, Kwar had heard her scream.

"Who is Lenk?"

Kataria's mouth hung open, soundless. Kwar's face fell, her frown a deep shadow painted across her skin by the firelight.

Wood groaned. Stone cracked. Somewhere else, someone cried out.

"Whoever it is," Kwar said, "you're not going to find them if you die here. We must go."

Kataria could hear her voice before it even left her lips, all the denial and desperation to fly out into the fire and try to find one man in a sea of death and ash. But she let those words die in her mouth before she could voice them.

Kwar knew the right thing to do.

She could but hope that Lenk knew, too.

They ran through the halls. The smoke grew thicker around them. Kataria could see shadows in the shroud: humans running every which way, some screaming, some falling, others descending upon them with knives. The Khovura lingered behind to kill, even as flames licked at their heels and danced at their fingertips.

Above them, the rafters continued to groan. The fire grew hungrier, eating at everything it could. The house of Ghoukha seemed as though it was holding its breath against the smoke coursing through it and, when it exhaled, everything would come down with it.

Perhaps Kwar knew this. Perhaps that was why she ran so swiftly. Perhaps that was why she didn't let go of Kataria's hand as she led her along the twists and turns of the hallways.

They rounded a corner and the smoke grew thinner, streaming out through an open window. She saw the other two khoshicts standing there, a rope at the ledge. Kwar shouted a command to them and they obeyed, hopping over the ledge and shimmying down to the courtyard below.

Kwar swung one leg over the window's ledge and paused, looking back. Kataria stood nearby, staring down the halls, searching. And not moving.

"Are they that important?"

She turned. Kwar stared at her intently.

"Are they worth dying for?"

Around them, the fire sang. Its harmonies raced down the web-lined walls. Its dirges were accompanied by the groaning of wood and stone. Its notes smoldered in pools of burning oil.

And above it all, through it all, Kataria could hear Kwar.

"Is he?"

And the pain in her voice was a song all its own.

The house shuddered. Something snapped overhead. Wood cracked, stone shrieked, and a hail of fire came crashing down from the ceiling.

"*KATARIA!*"

She could hear Kwar's cry as she leapt backward, as the stone smashed where she had just stood. It carried through wood and flame and smoke. It echoed in her head.

And it hurt to hear.

Over the sound of the last fragment of rock settling and the brimstone smoldering, over the sound of bare feet padding down the hall toward her, she could hear someone approaching.

Lenk emerged from the smoke. A sword was in his hand. Blood spattered his bare skin. He was completely nude. None of this appeared to bother him.

"Hey," he gasped.

She looked him up and down. "Naked," she observed.

"Long story," he replied. "Not the place. Have to go." He pointed down the hall with the sword. "That way. There's a window with some hedges at the bottom. We can jump, I think."

"What? Are you sure?"

"No. Not at all. Let's go."

He started running. After a moment, he became aware of her not following him. He reached back, took her by the hand, and started pulling. His grip was rough, bloodied, desperate.

She yanked her hand from his and ran alongside him.

Behind her, the symphony of fire grew louder. The groan of the collapsing ceiling became a scream as rafters continued to break. The song swelled to a cacophony, agonized, a thousand cackling voices straining to be heard over each other.

And through it all, she could hear Kwar's voice.

"KATARIA!"

Calling her name.

"KATARIA!"

———— ❊ ————

Everything was silent.

Only a moment ago that there had been so much noise. The people had been screaming. The Khovura had been screaming. The knives and the wounds and the spiders and her own voice had been screaming.

But now, all the voices had been seared out of scorched throats, and all the pain wafted away on dissipating plumes of smoke rising from smoldering cinders like the sighs of satisfied lovers.

And everything was silent.

When Dreadaeleon had spread his wings, Asper ran. She had dived behind the corpsewagon and turned it upside down over her. She had shut her eyes and prayed empty words into a world of fire.

Maybe he wanted to frighten the Khovura. Maybe he was thinking of a plan she couldn't. Maybe he wasn't thinking at all.

But the fire had spread in only a few moments, engulfing the *houn* and racing up to the upper floor and spreading everywhere. In a roar of ecstasy, it had opened its maw to consume everything it touched.

And now she walked in the wake of its feast.

The floors were black. The pillars carved like women were black, their golden faces and breasts dribbling down their bodies in molten slag. The silk tapestries still burned, shedding embers like tears as they wafted upon the walls and ceiling. The flames that remained smoldered in little patches on the floor, upon the bodies.

She could have thought this place hell were it not for the silence. There was an air of desolate tranquility about the place, as though peace had only settled for want of anything left to kill. The fires burned contentedly, misplaced hearths offering cozy light and gentle warmth. But their gentleness was the fat, lazy placidity of a glutton too fed to move. The fires had eaten.

And the people were dead.

They curled up on the floor like little black snakes, limbs twisted into serpentine coils, almost as though they were asleep beneath blankets of ash. Had Dreadaeleon's fire done that? Or, in their last moments, had they curled up to try to protect themselves? Had they prayed, then? Could she have heard them?

Could Dreadaeleon?

There was no sign of her companions. Maybe Denaos and Gariath had escaped. Maybe others had, too. Maybe Dreadaeleon had burned himself up in all this. They hadn't fled through the door. It currently hung from its hinges, a barrier of burning wreckage, releasing smoking sighs into the world.

Maybe they were all dead.

"In days long escaped, they used to cower before us. It was our fire they feared before they even knew why it burned. They coveted it, for it was something unknown and magical to them. Do you remember?"

She turned at the sound of the voice, looked to the top of the stairs and the demon looming over them.

The doors leading to the upper floor still exhaled fire and smoke, weaving curtains of gold and black behind the Disciple. It rose up on its coils and stared out over the blackened *houn* at her. Slowly, down a staircase painted with cooked-on blood, it slithered toward her. Its tail flicked behind it, shrugging free the last vestige of the sack of split skin and burst fat that had been Ghoukha.

"In those days, would they have turned this kind of fury upon each other?" the Disciple mused aloud. "Would they have turned it upon us?" It chuckled; the sound was like water being sucked into a patch of dry earth. "'Despots,' they called us, those who would abuse power to control them. But look around you." It extended its arms to encompass the ruin of the *houn*. "Without us to guide them, they abuse themselves more than we ever could."

Its voice numbed her ears, the darkness in its words draining the thought from her. To her, it sounded like twisted babble, the ravings of a madman. But there was something in its stare: in the way its black gaze looked at her, in the expectant set of its old-man face.

It looked into her, not at her.

It wasn't talking to her.

It made a low bow, sweeping one arm across its chest in a display of respect. "Amoch-Tethr," it said, "the presence of the learned brightens this dismal scene."

She felt him stir beneath her skin.

So nice to be recognized, he whispered into her thoughts. *Though to my utter shame, I don't quite place this one's face.*

"You knew him?" she whispered back.

Hmm? Oh, I suppose it's possible. It was rather fashionable to know my company back in the day. I expect this one came to learn at my feet at one point or another.

"And he...sees you?"

Not "he." It's an "it," dear girl. Whatever thin threads held it to mankind were cut long ago. You do it a disservice by referring to it as such. She felt Amoch-Tethr sigh within her. *And no. It cannot look past your flesh, if that is what you fear. Nor can it hear me now. It merely knows my presence.*

"Tell me, master." The Disciple leveled a black talon at her soft, pink flesh. "What is that you are wearing?"

She took a defensive step backward.

Have no fear, Amoch-Tethr assured her. *I have no intention of letting it harm you.*

What, exactly, she wondered, did he intend to do about it?

"Come, master," the Disciple said, slithering toward her. Its black nails grew long upon its fingers. "Let me free you from that cage. Gaze upon this, our glorious conclusion, with your own eyes."

Ask it what it's so proud of.

"What?" she asked.

Stall it.

"What 'conclusion' is this?" she asked. Boldness edged her voice, cutting through the quavering fear. "Is this funny to you? All these dead people? All this destruction? All because of *you*?"

It halted.

She hadn't expected that to work.

It frowned.

"No," it said simply. "Knowledge is virtue, yes, but it is burden above all else. The learned were not placed here to sow discord, merely to observe it." It gestured to the deflated and eviscerated Ghoukha behind it. "I did not force my way into this one. I was invited. His greed, his envy, his pride, presented before me like a sumptuous banquet laid out for myself alone. I fed, every bit the shameless glutton as my host, as he plotted and schemed.

"And his schemes were as endless as his hatreds. He despised his rivals, wealthy men who traded knowledge for precious metals. He loathed the interlopers, those who heaped sacrifices upon Gods not his own. He craved control and yet felt it slipping through his grasp, watching his city fall into ruin, rent by blades and claimed by infidels.

"And I?" It crossed its hands over its withered chest. "I watched. I saw his world collapse around him and how he struggled to prop it up. He sought to be the shield his people craved. He called men to his side; he gave his fortunes to arms and his destiny to metal, to seize back the fate of his people from reaching hands."

She narrowed her eyes. Inside her, Amoch-Tethr chuckled.

How interesting, he said. *Ghoukha's army was not for the Khovura, nor even for Ghoukha, but for Cier'Djaal. His first selfless act and it earned him this.*

"You were watching," Asper said, "waiting to strike. And you killed . . . all these people."

Well, technically, it didn't, Amoch-Tethr chimed in. *Not all of them, anyway.*

She tried to ignore him.

"And the wealthy fell," the Disciple said. "And the powerful fell. And the unlearned, no matter how much silk they wrapped themselves in, no matter how much gold they sat upon, discovered that they, too, were tiny under the eyes of heaven."

"This was all to send a message, then? Not for gold or blood? Just . . . to make a statement?"

"It is the weakness of mortality to confuse word for thought, action for meaning," the Disciple said. "It is the burden of the learned to make them harmonious. The people of this city, with all its prisoners, choke themselves on gold, deafen themselves with prayer, cloud their minds with greed and hope and claw at the walls as the water rises over their heads. We can bring truth. We can establish order."

At this, she dared to sneer. "Tell me something," she said. "Why is it that everyone in this city is so damned afraid to admit they're killers? Why is killing people a game? Why is it all for Gods or order or knowledge? If it's such a burden, who asks you to take it? Humanity can handle itself."

"Does it?"

It swept its scribble-black eyes across the *houn*. It looked from the pillars, their golden faces molten to grotesque masks, to the bodies, ashen piles upon the floor. Embers drifted down from silk webs ablaze overhead to settle upon its shoulders like snowflakes.

"Can it?" It slithered closer still. "When a man kills, is the blood on his hands? Or is it on the Gods'? Did he kill on his own behalf or did a rich man make him? Was the knife in his hand or was it in hers and she put it to her own throat when she rejected him? When he faces judgment, does he claim that he did it for himself or for a God who did not stop him?"

It canted its head at her.

"When you gaze upon the hapless dead, whom do you blame?"

She had no answer for that. None that she could admit to herself or the demon.

"This is why it is our burden." It extended its arms in a sign of benediction. "This is what Khoth-Kapira taught. There will be more blood. Many will die. The world shall be cleaner for it."

There was no conviction in its voice.

No fervent desperation to be right, no fanatic thought fueling maddened speech, no prayer, no boast, no insanity.

It spoke with the voice of a cold, dark night, as certain as the sun setting and the moon rising. It spoke without enthusiasm, without love, without bloodlust. It spoke, and thus it would be so.

Many would die.

Because it said they would.

And Asper felt herself go cold.

It lurched toward her.

"Come, Amoch-Tethr. Let me be the one to show you."

She began to backpedal, feeling her knees giving out beneath her. Its stare was upon her now, on her weak flesh, on her trembling eyes. It looked at her the way it would look at a lid on a jar. Or a box. Or a coat. Or anything that was trivial and in its way.

She staggered. Inside her, she felt Amoch-Tethr speak.

Do you want to live?

She nodded *yes.*

Do you want to stop this? All of it?

"Yes."

Do you trust me?

At this, she hesitated. At this, she did not answer. At this, she stood still, feet upon an ashen floor, and stared up into the eyes of the demon.

Then let it take you.

Was it fear she felt, she wondered, as the Disciple's tail coiled about her ankles, her legs, her waist? Was it a prayer that escaped in that last breath as the demon brought her up to stare into its withered face? Was it resignation that made her arm limp as a pale white fish in the demon's grasp, its black nails rapping upon her skin?

And when her eyes closed that she might be spared the horror, she wondered if it was her or Amoch-Tethr who did that.

It didn't help. Even if she couldn't see it with her eyes, the hellish red light flashed bright in her mind. She could feel the skin of her arm peeling back, the red light burning too brightly to ignore. She could smell the stench of burning, stronger than even the fire had been.

She felt her left hand clamp down over the demon's hand.

And she heard its scream as the single long toll of a church bell in autumn.

"Master." The certainty in its voice now quaked, cracking at the edges. "I do not understand. I only wished to share with you the glory of the design."

Apologies, my dear friend. Amoch-Tethr spoke no longer in thought. Now, his voice was her flesh. His prayer was her fire. His laughter was her agony. *I've become attached to this body. It's cold out there, you know. It sounds as though you intend to make it much colder than I like.*

She could hear him clearly. Over the sound of the demon's bones snapping. Over the sizzle of its flesh burning. Over the black sigh of flesh and sinew disintegrating and vanishing into red light, she could hear him. And it.

"Khoth-Kapira would have wanted you to be there when it happened," the demon rasped. "He will not be pleased."

I suspect I'll deal with that if He ever comes back.

A loud snap.

"When He comes back."

A long, black sigh.

And Amoch-Tethr's dark chuckle.

She felt the demon's limb turn to nothing in her hand. When she opened her eyes, it was but a gray and twisted husk, shrinking around her, lowering her to the ground. Soon, it lay at her feet, as ashen and indiscernible as any of the corpses standing around her.

She felt no stronger. She looked down at her right arm, saw its flesh dead white. All her blood, everything inside her, burned within a bright red left. She felt bloodless legs give out beneath her, send her to the floor. She felt her head swaying, vision swimming, breath running short.

Amoch-Tethr had eaten more than his fill.

She looked up to the ceiling, as though she could see past it and into heaven, but she hadn't breath to pray. Her gaze drifted to the fire and smoke belching from the upper floor. There, painted black against the flames, she could see a figure.

She didn't know his name. She didn't know his face. But she knew his eyes, those vast, swallowing orbs too big to be drowned out in shadow. He had asked her if Talanas would hear her down here.

She had an answer for him now.

He didn't wait to hear it. Without so much as flinching, he turned around and walked into the flames.

And she collapsed, her world disappearing into soot, carried into darkness on the sound of Amoch-Tethr's glutted sigh.

⊷ ⊱⊰ ⊶

She heard their anger before she heard their words, though the latter came quickly enough.

"It wasn't easy," a female voice said, silk wrapped around a blade. "The Karnerians and the Sainites were already there, searching in every corner. And she was just lying there, taking a nice nap in the middle of it all. You want to tell me how she was the only one who survived?"

"I don't want to, no." Another voice, familiarly warm. Denaos's. "And in return, I don't want you to tell me why the Jackals arrived too late to stop anything. I told you something was up at Ghoukha's house. I expected some backup."

"The word came late. We weren't sure which heads were being sent until it happened. I thought it was Yerk; Yerk thought it was me. Rezca smells a rat."

"I said I didn't want to know."

"You don't get to make that decision anymore, Ramaniel." Blade cut through silk; her words turned harsh. "This wasn't a *favor* I did for you. This is a loan. You're going to have to repay it."

"Later."

"Tomorrow. Rezca's calling a new game. He wants you to be there."

"I'm not—"

"You are. Whether you want to or not. New rules, Ramaniel." A pause, cold. "Who is she, anyway?"

"My sister."

"Horseshit."

"Obviously. The only way I'm ever going to tell you is if one of us has a knife in our throats. I think she's coming to, anyway. Take off."

"Remember, tom—"

"Yeah."

Asper's eyes finally caught up with her ears, fluttering open. A dark face framed by dark hair was looming over her, a woman whose features were too hard to be hidden by the soft cheeks and gentle smile.

"Ah, so she is. Up we rise, darling." She reached down, took Asper by the arm, and hoisted her up. She felt herself drawn against the woman's slim body, bare skin brushing against her leathers. Her whisper was a needle in Asper's ear. "You've got a good friend looking out for you, girl. Take care of him."

And she was gone, trotting off into the night. Asper watched her step lightly down a hill, vanishing behind a hedge. In the distance, black against the moonlight, the house of Ghoukha stood, a charred and bitter husk of what it once was, its last breaths sighing into the sky on clouds of smoke. She could see figures moving amidst the darkness, hear them screaming at each other, hurling accusations instead of the spears in their hands.

"They survived."

She turned and saw Denaos standing behind her. Farther up the hill, Lenk and Kataria and Gariath sat. There was no sign of Dreadaeleon.

"Once the Khovura showed up, the Karnerians and Sainites got the Ancaaran priest and a few fashas out," Denaos said, pointing out to the ruined manor. "Trying to curry favor, I guess. Gariath and I had to fight our way out. We thought you had run. If we had known—"

"It's fine," she said. "Did anyone else make it?"

"I didn't see anyone else." He laid a hand on her left shoulder. His touch felt painful, as though he grazed new skin. "What happened in there?"

"A lot." She shrugged his hand off. "Did they find Miron?"

"Lenk said—"

She didn't wait for him to finish. She was already moving. Up the hill, she found them sitting, applying charbalm to fire-kissed skin and wrapping up scrapes and cuts. She stood over Lenk. He looked up.

"That's everyone, I guess," he said with a sigh. "You good?"

"Better than the people in there," Asper replied. "*Lots* better. What did you find?"

"Nothing."

Her eyes widened. "Denaos said—"

"What? That I saw Miron long enough to know that he was walking with the Khovura? That he looked at me as I was about to die and smiled?" He snorted. "Yeah, I found that. Whoever he is, he's with them."

"He could have died in there with them, the guards and everyone," Kataria offered. "There were so many dying..."

"If he was coming in with the Khovura, he knew what they were doing," Lenk said. "And if he knew what they were doing, he probably had a way out for himself." He rubbed his temple, touching a wound there and flinching. "How did they get *in*?"

"They used him to talk their way in," Kataria said. Her ears twitched. "Maybe."

"Doesn't matter. We lost him again." Lenk sighed and rose to his feet. "At least we know that the Khovura and Ghoukha aren't together, anyway."

"At *least*?" Asper's outrage carried across the night. "How many people died in there? How much blood was spilled? And you're trying to pass it off like it was *worth* it?"

"I'm making the best out of a bad situation."

"People are *dead*. This isn't a 'bad situation,' Lenk, it's—"

"Justice."

Gariath spoke softly. But even a whisper from a dragonman was a rumble of the earth, something born deep. He crouched on his haunches nearby, staring down at the ground.

"Whatever died in there, it wasn't people. The humans in there don't deserve the name. All that gold, all that wealth...while their 'people' starve and drown in their city?" He snorted derisively. "What died in there was hungry animals carrying a disease. The world is cleaner for having them gone."

"They weren't all wealthy," she countered. "Some were servants, *slaves*."

"Daaru was right."

"Who the hell is—"

"This whole city has the disease. They all chase the same scent, all crave the same meat. The animals that died in there get the biggest pieces and everyone else slavers and spits for the scraps." His anger came out in a low growl. "You weep for their lives. They died begging for meat. They weren't people."

Asper turned around. For to look at him—that inhuman, monstrous piece of filth—for one moment longer would make her want to hurt him. And to try to hurt him was pointless.

What could get through a skull that thick?

"You said everyone made it out? All of us?"

"Not without issue," Lenk said, "but yes."

"Where is he?"

He didn't answer right away. Perhaps he could hear the acid in her voice. And because of that, he didn't need to ask who she was talking about. With a sigh, he pointed down the other side of the hill.

And she was off.

She found Dreadaeleon sitting halfway down, his knees drawn tight against his body, his head held between them, fingers knotted in his hair as he clutched his skull. With every step she took toward him, she thought of a new way to kill him, to make him suffer for everyone he had slain.

By the time she was within three paces of him, she had decided a quick blow to the back of the head would be the kindest option.

By the time she was within two, she wasn't sure if she wanted that.

And by the time she was close enough to strangle him, he spoke.

"I wanted to be the hero."

His voice quavered. And she stopped.

"I thought... I thought I'd make everything better," he continued. "It was so easy in my head. The fire would scatter the Khovura, send them fleeing and give me more room. Then I could just use lightning or something to take them out individually. I didn't account for... I couldn't..."

His voice trembled at the edges, weak.

"And then I went and ruined everything."

Her mind, at that point, was in staunch disagreement with her body. She could hear the tears in his eyes, the tightness in his throat. She knew he was remorseful, in agony over the lives he had taken.

But he had still taken them, her body reminded her. He had still acted like an idiot and killed everyone, her trembling fists objected. What good were good intentions, her clenched jaw asked her, if they still killed everyone? How many times did someone get to say they were sorry, the fever burning behind her eyes asked as it tinged her vision, before the words didn't mean as much as the deed?

She closed her eyes and tried to release the rage through a long breath. She tried that many, many times before she felt she could speak without bludgeoning him.

"I understand," she said.

"You don't," he said. "That's why I ran. I couldn't face you. I couldn't let you know that—"

"But I did." She laid a hand on his shoulder, squeezed it, resisted the urge to do more than that. "I saw. It happened. We can only move forward and try to make this right."

"We can?"

"Yours wasn't the only sin committed this night. Someone has to answer for...all of this. You can try to make things right by helping with that."

"I can." No question this time. Hope crept into his voice. "I can do that. Next time, it will go flawlessly."

"Next time?" She quirked a brow.

"Right. We'll call it a learning experience, won't we? My lack of foresight was...disappointing, but explainable, considering previous circumstances. I'll have a better handle of things next time. Casualties will be minimized."

"Minimized? What are you—"

She lost her voice as he looked up. There was something on his face, but it wasn't despair. There were no tears, no sorrow, no remorse etched into his wrinkles. Only worry, only stress, fleeting emotions that vanished under a broadening smile.

"Naturally, I made a few mistakes and there were consequences. But all the same? Better to overreach and fail than remain…"

She couldn't hear him anymore. He was speaking a language that no longer made sense, and his face was a mask she didn't recognize. He looked too hopeful, too contented with himself. His eyes were already bright with childlike wonder, his hands already gesturing the grand schemes he had laid out; his smile was already full.

Of her fist.

With the first blow, he staggered backward and looked at her as though she had made a mistake, like she had just spontaneously lost control of a limb. The second left no doubt, knocking him flat on his back.

She wasn't angry.

Not as she straddled him. Not as she struck him, her fist moving back and forth with mechanical fervor. And certainly not as her knuckles grew red with his blood.

She didn't feel angry. She felt dutiful. This was something that had to be done. These were words that had to be said.

"You don't even care about them," she said. "You don't care about who you killed; you only care that it didn't go your way. You don't give a shit about those people you burned alive. You only care that they're not here to call you a hero."

He was crying out, begging for her to stop. Now she saw the tears. Now she saw them running down his cheeks, cutting glistening scars through the blood painting his face. But she didn't stop.

"You're not a hero. You're a tiny, weak, selfish, cruel, *useless* little boy. You laugh at Gods and Their teachings, but They at least teach us to feel sorry for what we've done. They at least teach us that humans are more than just a 'learning experience.' But you didn't listen, did you? You just sit there and fucking think about how great it'll be when you can swoop in and make a great, flaming ass out of yourself so everyone will pay attention to you."

"I didn't mean it!" he cried out. His voice was stuffy with a shattered nose and thick with his own blood. "Please, Asper! I'm sorry!"

"No."

She hammered her left fist against his cheek.

"You."

She smashed her right fist against his jaw.

"AREN'T."

She raised her left hand.

Do it.

And froze.

End it.

Her heart beat in time with the thoughts running through her head.

He said it himself. He'll just do it again. Amoch-Tehtr's voice purred within her. *Remove him. Think of how many people you'll save with one more menace gone.*

Her arm quivered over her head. Her eyes weren't blinking. She suddenly realized those weren't Dreadaeleon's tears streaking down his cheeks. She wasn't sure when she started crying. She wasn't sure if he was crying now.

She wasn't sure whose thoughts were going through her head.

"ASPER!"

Hands grabbed her. Lenk and Denaos pulled her off. She turned around and stared wide-eyed at them; shock was painted on their faces. Kataria frowned with concern. Gariath merely snorted as if he knew she would do this all along.

She looked down. Dreadaeleon was weeping, cowering, hiding behind skinny, trembling arms. His blood was painted on the hill and on her hands. It felt warm between her fingers.

She spoke to no one.

"Sorry, I…" She stared off at the lights of the city. "I need to… I'll see you all. A little later."

And numbly, trailing blood and horrified stares, she walked off into the night.

THIRTY-FIVE

TALLIES

Whiskey was expensive in Cier'Djaal.

Arable land was rare in the desert and typically was used to grow grapes for wine. Harsher northern drinks had to be imported, and even ones so rancid as to be more grain than liquid—such as the one sitting in front of Lenk—were expensive.

That didn't stop him from pouring another, though.

Six coins a bottle. Six pours to a coin.

He downed the liquor.

That'll be . . .

He counted all the drinks he had had so far.

Two coins I piss out later.

His stomach rumbled as the liquor hit it.

Or vomit.

He poured again.

If Miron—or whoever—owes us one thousand coins . . .

He took another drink.

And we buy one bottle for every person dead tonight . . .

He poured.

And we didn't even bother counting the dead . . .

He drank.

And they're all dead because of us . . .

Pour.

And we allow for anyone we might kill tomorrow . . .

Drink.

And I just wait for everyone else's life who touches mine to turn to shit...

Pour.

Spill.

Shit.

He threw his cup to the floor. The whiskey that splattered across the unwashed boards would have looked like a bloodstain to him, were he not aware that blood came cheaper. He signaled to the barkeep nearby without looking up and heard a brief grunt as confirmation.

The greasy, hairy lout who owned a shitty little hole in the harbor like Swigslips, one would think, would be a little more eager to serve. Its tables were splintering; its chairs wobbled; its windows were cracked; and its patrons—all three of them, including Lenk—were the sort of people who had little regard for the quality of their drink, their purses, or their internal organs.

The fact that it took as long as it did for him to get another glass might have bothered him on any other night.

But the past few hours had been far too sobering. And the only cure for hours far too sobering was hours far too drunk.

The logic was foolproof.

"Ugh, are you *really* doing this?"

He didn't bother looking up. No matter how badly he wanted that to be someone else, he recognized Mocca's voice even before the man sat down across from him—making certain to tuck his pristine white robes so that they didn't touch anything they didn't have to.

"In a dingy little bar drinking cheap whiskey to drown one's sorrows," Mocca continued to chide. "Really, don't you feel the *slightest* bit ashamed for how clichéd this is?"

"You're alive," Lenk noted by way of response.

"I am. Once you so ungraciously took off with guards in tow, I suspected there might be trouble on its way, so I excused myself from the festivities."

"Sheffu?"

"As far as I know, he fled shortly after me. I saw him and that monstrous little child he calls a servant returning to his shack of a manor before the . . ." Mocca cleared his throat. "Well, you know."

"Yeah." Lenk poured another finger of whiskey. "I do."

Mocca watched with a cringe. "Look, I can appreciate the theatrics of drinking yourself to death, but it's not going to solve anything."

"Shows what you know. A specific problem has a specific solution. And a problem as specific as mine requires the solution of pouring into my mouth what tastes like if a hyena had diarrhea fermented in day-old bathwater." He stifled a belch. "Specifically." He downed the drink and looked pointedly across the table. "How'd you find me?"

"I observed you on the hilltop," Mocca replied. "The tall woman bludgeoned the little fellow, then you all appeared to exchange words and everyone went off in a different direction. I followed you here—after you had gone and retrieved some clothes, anyway." A well-trimmed eyebrow rose. "Difficulties?"

"No. What you observed was us planning our outfits for tomorrow. See, we wanted to coordinate and we realized none of us had anything to match this." He tugged at his dirty tunic. "So everyone went off to try to find something a little more presentable. It didn't have anything to do with the fact that there are a lot of dead people who didn't deserve it and it's all our fault and you're definitely not a fuck-witted imbecile for not thinking of that."

"Are you always this hostile to people trying to help?"

"You're not helping."

"I'm alerting you to the notion that if it was this easy for me to find you, it might very well be even easier for, say, a systematic sweep of guardsmen looking to solve the mystery of why the house of the wealthiest man in Cier'Djaal just burned down with him inside it."

"Good," Lenk said. "Let them come. I'm ready." He poured another. "Or I will be, soon. Just hold them off until I can drink the rest of this."

"It was a hollow threat. The guards are all sitting around with their fingers lodged firmly in crevices better left unnamed. The Sainites and Karnerians won't let them get near Ghoukha's house."

"Pity."

"That's the theme of tonight, isn't it?" Mocca sighed, leaned on the table. "Precisely what are you so upset about, anyway?"

"Did you not hear me just now?"

"I did. I hope you'll forgive me for pointing out the hypocrisy in taking so many deaths so gracelessly, considering how many you've had a direct hand in causing."

"That was different."

"Probably not for the dead people."

"No, it's..." He shook his head as if he could throw the thoughts from his skull. "Do you ever think that when you get good enough at something, you just do it as a matter of instinct?"

"Pardon?"

"My grandfather, back when he was alive, he did this thing where he could spit a seed into an empty bottle from five paces. He got better and better at it: ten, fifteen, twenty. Pretty soon, he was just doing it without knowing, every time he passed a bottle, empty or not, seed or no seed. He'd just see a bottle and spit and hit it, dead on."

His eyes were heavy as he looked at Mocca. Too heavy to blink.

"What if... what if killing's the same way? What if you get so good at it, if it's so easy, that you just do it without knowing? What if people just die around you because that's what you do?"

"That sounds a little—"

"Well, how the hell do *you* explain it, then?" Lenk shouted. The two other patrons looked up at his outburst before cringing and returning their attentions back to their drinks. "How the hell is it that the lives of everyone that comes near mine turns to shit?"

"You *are* an adventurer. You carry a sword. You lead a violent life."

"And that's just it. Even when I'm naked, I've still got the sword. I can find a blade in a burning house. If I can't, I'll find another way to kill people. My sword's always there, even if it isn't. And if it's always there, how do you get rid of it? Because every time I try, I keep killing people. This whole thing was about getting money from

Miron to stop this, the killing, but how many people have to die so I can stop killing them?"

He slouched back in his chair. He reached for the drink and pushed it aside instead. His head found the table a splintery-enough pillow, one fit for the specific breed of half-drunken, fevered slumber he felt himself drifting in. He pressed his forehead to it, closed his eyes, and hoped that his dreams would be terrible enough to make the waking life look a little better by comparison.

Of course, that was hard to do with Mocca staring at him.

He felt the man's eyes on the back of his head, like an itch that couldn't be scratched. And with each passing moment, he could feel Mocca's stare boring deeper into him. The air grew so still that, by the time he finally deigned to speak, it came as soft and sharp as a needle in an eyelid.

"Tell me," Mocca all but whispered, "is the whiskey more delicious than the self-pity?"

"Don't mock me," Lenk mumbled into the wood. "I don't find it funny."

"Nor should you. It's not funny at all. This…" He made a flippant gesture at Lenk. "This isn't even sad. This is merely pointless."

"The *point* is that I ruin lives and I'm helpless to stop it."

"That's the pointlessness of it. You claim you're helpless, yet in the same breath ascribe such meaning to your life as to render all those around it moot. Are you an insect or are you a God?"

"I'm just a man."

"Men are not yet so powerful that they can kill people just by existing, nor are they so insignificant as to be incapable of change." He ran a finger around the sleeve of his robe, flattening it against the table. "This world was not made for them. It existed long before they were of any particular consequence. They can but stand on one particular plot of land at any given time and make do with what happens upon it."

"And mine is soaked in blood and ashes."

"As though suffering is so rare as to be the luxury of just one man," Mocca scoffed. "The Khovura did not come after you, specifically, you know. You were there, of course, and maybe you tend to be around when trouble begins, but those people were going to die anyway, regardless of who happened to be there."

"Why is it that the only way we can ever feel better about people dying is to say it doesn't matter? If it doesn't matter, then what's all that shit about standing on a plot of land, then? Why bother with anything?"

"I didn't say it doesn't matter."

"You just—"

"No, I said it *didn't* matter." Mocca raised his arm and began to draw his sleeve back. "Man—no, *anything* that ever had a right to call itself a person—is determined to devote every fraction of his being toward the task of destroying himself.

"He eats food only in the anticipation that he will one day starve. He worships Gods so that he'll know where to go when he dies. He makes love with the desperate knowledge that, on the day he dies..."

His sleeve fell, exposing a long thin arm patterned with scar tissue. Designs cut of perfect angles ran from wrist to elbow, a madness of fleshy ziggurats.

"He will be alone."

He glanced at Lenk. His smile was tightly coiled upon his lips, even as Lenk's mouth hung open at the sight of the scars. He looked around, as though incredulous that he should be the only one to see this. If the other patrons noticed, though, they didn't care enough to look up from their cups.

"And when he drinks, he takes a string of bad luck and makes a melodramatic noose for himself." Mocca slipped his sleeve back over his arm. "Tell me, then, if you're so certain to kill anyone you touch, why strive for something else? Why linger near people you claim to care about?"

Lenk stared at the whiskey across the table, pointedly avoiding Mocca's stare. "Because if I don't, then there would have been no point to any of it."

"So, if you stop now, will there be a point? If you drink yourself to death tonight, would you be anything but one more body to add to the list? Would anyone weep for you as you wept for them?"

"I wasn't *weeping*, I—"

"It's your plot of land," Mocca continued, ignoring his protest. "It's your dirt under your feet. The ashes and blood you choose to stand upon are yours now. The lives are yours now. If you do nothing but lie in it, you will have nothing but ashes and blood."

"Then what's the alternative?"

Now he met Mocca's eyes. Now he saw that the man's smile was gone, replaced by something hard-edged and precise as a scalpel. He held Lenk in that look for a long time, eyes perfectly steady as he peered into something that wasn't there. Then he waved his hand.

"You and I, we don't stand on the same earth," Mocca said. "Though, if you're looking for direction, I should point out that you weren't the only survivor last night. The others aren't drowning themselves."

"Barely. The Ancaaran emissary got out, protected by the Karnerians and Sainites."

"Before the killing began in earnest, even. He must be a subject of particular desire." Mocca stroked his chin thoughtfully. "He *is* at the helm of an effort to avert open warfare, is he not?"

Lenk paused, his thoughts drifting back to a previous conversation. "Asper said . . . back when she told us about Miron, she said that the Talanites were going to mediate originally, but their envoy was killed by the Khovura."

"Many people were killed by the Khovura."

"Yeah, but what if it's not an accident? What if it's . . ." He tapped the table. "The Khovura are murderers, anarchists, but they're not an army. Not yet. They can't challenge the Karnerians or the Sainites." He looked up. "But the Karnerians and the Sainites can challenge each other."

Mocca furrowed his brow. "You'd think they'd try to incite a war? Just to build on the ashes of an empire?"

"Ashes they'd control," Lenk replied. "It makes sense, doesn't it? They killed Ghoukha, the wealthiest man in the city. If they can remove the two foreign armies—or at least bring them to a point where the Khovura can fight them on even terms—they can swoop in and claim this city for...for..."

"Khoth-Kapira," Mocca said. "You realize who you sound like, right?"

"Sheffu was chasing ghost stories," Lenk replied, waving a hand. "This is flesh-and-blood stuff. Men, not demons."

"The men *have* demons."

"One problem at a time. If this *is* their plan, then the obvious course of action is to find them before it can happen. They'll strike at the mediation. We can stop them there, find Miron, figure this thing out, and then—"

"The people will still be dead," Mocca pointed out. "And more will die, as well. Are you prepared for that?"

"Death is the only thing I am prepared for now. If it has to come, and if it has to be my earth on which it stands, then maybe I can at least stand in its way."

Mocca offered a light applause. "Half-drunken poetry is the most honest kind of poetry. Too slurred to be eloquent, not slurred enough to be witless."

Lenk grinned as he tossed back the whiskey. It tasted sour on his tongue. "Let me ask *you* something," he said, pointing at Mocca. "What's with you?"

"Pardon?"

"You showing up here, helping me like this, helping me all those other times. What's in it for you?"

"Mankind fascinates me."

"Be serious."

Mocca's smile fell slightly, becoming something soft and faraway. "There's no such thing as fate, you know. No divine plan, no scroll upon which your life is written. All we have, you and I, is earth to stand on. The only way we keep it is through choice. And consequence."

"How can you be so sure?" Lenk asked. "That there's no plan?"

"Because," Mocca said as he eyed the bottle, "I can't imagine any God would be boring enough to want to know how everything ends."

THIRTY-SIX

MACHINATE

It was gears—not blood—that lay inside humans.

Asper knew this now.

And when the Gods—or the world, or the people in it—broke down a person, removed all the layers of skin and sinew, that was what was left.

This was what was left.

Someone who could move only like a machine: one foot in the front of the other, no matter the road; one breath after another, no matter how hard they came; one red-stained hand curled into one red-stained fist, pounding on a door, forever.

Or until it got answered.

"All right, all right, *all right!*" a voice shouted peevishly from the other side of the door. "I'm up! If you've got a broken hand, though, I'm going to lose my—"

The door swung open. Aturach met her with suspicion, as though he didn't recognize her. And then astonishment, as though he *did* recognize her. And then despair, as though he'd rather go back to the first part.

She saw herself in his face.

In his cringe, she saw the grime-black of the soles of her feet, the soot clinging to her belly and arms. In his frown, she saw the tatters of her silks and the ash-choked locks of her hair. And in his wide, wide stare, she saw the furrows that tears had gouged in her cheeks, dripping from eyes as red and wet as her knuckles.

She sniffed. "Hey."

He grimaced. "Hi?" He flinched, as though suddenly aware of her presence. "Um, would you like to come in?"

She stared at him. He glanced around nervously before stepping aside. One foot in the front of the other, she entered.

She felt the emptiness of the temple, the absence of people filling her like a breath of air too cold and too thin. Every pew converted to sickbed lay empty. There wasn't so much as a stray bit of stitching or scrap of bandage left. The floors had been scrubbed clean of blood. One might never know how much suffering occurred here if one hadn't seen it.

Or if one didn't know what kind of suffering there went on out there.

"Oh!" She heard Aturach scurry excitedly up behind her. "You noticed? We took your advice, worked in shifts. It took days, but we finally did it." He gestured to the empty pews. "Every last man, woman, and child in here was seen back to their family alive. Honestly, I'm a little surprised we managed to do it. Even for all that I prayed, all the work I did, I doubted that we could save all of them."

He breathed in that vast, empty air. He exhaled it in a long, grateful sigh.

"I guess Talanas really is looking out for Cier'Djaal," he said, turning to Asper, "isn't He?"

She turned to look at him.

She smiled weakly.

And then vomited on his feet.

＋—✠✦✠—＋

Directly to the right of the wooden idol of Talanas, incense burned. The smoke was, according to the hymns, the last words of the dead. What the forgotten, the ill, and the dying whispered before their suffering ended lingered in the world between this one and the next. In the embers of the incense, in the scent that filled the air, in the curl of the gray plume, the lost words were made visible.

Directly to the left of the wooden idol of Talanas, a bell rang with a gentle tap. It was a hollow bronze cylinder, unadorned but for a single engraving of the Phoenix, the Healer's symbol. The sound was a low, constant hum that faded over the course of long moments. It was the sound, according to the hymns, of Talanas drawing in a deep breath and holding it that the rest of the world might breathe for a little while.

Directly before the wooden idol of Talanas, two people knelt in meditation.

Beneath the robe that didn't quite fit, Asper's freshly scrubbed skin still tingled. Or so she assumed. She could barely feel it, or the pillow under her knees, or the presence of Aturach beside her.

She watched in silence, waiting for the moment when she was supposed to feel her breath come as Talanas's left.

If it came, she didn't notice.

She observed the tip of the incense curling, the embers traveling down the stick and leaving a gray twist behind. She watched it as it broke under its own weight, a trio of gray coils of ashes lying beside the idol. They reminded her of the bodies, coiled upon a blackened floor, like children slumbering beneath blankets of soot. She watched as the incense continued to burn, as more bodies fell.

She continued watching it as the sound of the bell went silent and Talanas released his breath.

This was what was left of the dead.

This was what was left of her God.

Ashes and silence.

"I think it was right after my parents died that I first asked myself."

Aturach had waited until after Talanas had released his breath to speak. His eyes were locked on the idol.

"Not in so many words. I don't think anyone really ever looks up to the sky and says 'do you even exist?'"

I do, she thought.

"It happened right after the riots," Aturach said. At this, he looked down at the floor. "The Houndmistress was going to put an end to the Jackals and the thieves and bring this city back to its people. But she didn't. There were riots. A lot of people died. I guess you might not have heard of it."

I did, she thought.

"Anyway, my parents died. Not a huge surprise, I guess. Lots of peoples' parents died. People. They were Talanites—not devout, but no one on our street was, what with work and all. But they were people. And I wondered, 'was it us? Did Talanas not save us because we were too faithless?' Which is ridiculous, I think."

I don't, she thought.

"So, maybe I joined out of fear. Fear that I'd be next if I wasn't a better Talanite or something." He rubbed the back of his neck. "Stupid, right?"

"No," she said. She looked back to Talanas. "I think the only reason we worship is out of fear."

"Come again?"

"Maybe we don't say it, but we do it to make ourselves think someone is looking out for us. Because we don't think anyone else will." She looked to Aturach again. "And we're right to do so."

He held her gaze. "I heard what happened. Even before you told me, I knew what happened at Ghoukha's house. I was a little surprised that we didn't get any of the wounded over here. I suppose that they're rich, and they have their own private healers to—"

"There weren't any wounded."

"Oh?"

"They were all dead."

His gaze fell. "Oh."

"All of them. Servants. Nobles. Fashas. Anyone who didn't get out."

Aturach said nothing. Neither of them did. Nor did they turn away from the idol. Talanas appeared unfazed by this news. His arms were extended in benediction. His smile above His beard was enigmatic. His eyes were turned upward to a hopeful heaven.

But above Him, there were only the gray wisps painted across the air by the burning incense. The last words of the dead.

Funny, she thought, how Talanas, patron of the suffering and healer of the wounded, always looked so upbeat.

He was just the Healer, after all. Maybe He didn't care so much about the dead.

"I asked myself tonight," she said suddenly, the words tumbling out.

She heard the shift of Aturach's robes as he looked at her.

"Not in so many words, like you said." She watched the gray wisps dance over Talanas's head. "In words that meant something else. I was . . . praying."

"What, in the middle of all that fire?"

"No, not like that. I was *really* praying." She gestured to the idol. "This is just ritual. This is hymns and incense. What I was doing, it's like . . . like a reflex, like wincing just before someone slaps you, even if you know it's coming. I wasn't praying to Talanas, but to anyone. I was just saying things and I really wanted them to be true."

She felt a smile creep across her face, unbidden. To hear it said like that, she thought, it sounded a lot like lying. Maybe there wasn't much of a difference.

"And then?" Aturach asked.

"And then everyone was dead," she said. "And there was . . ." She rubbed her left arm, tried to ignore the whispers in her head. "I got out, somehow. And then I saw the house burnt down and they—my friends—told me everyone was dead and I already knew that."

She sniffed. A wet sigh.

"I never once asked Talanas where He was. I never once blamed the Gods. I never looked to heaven. I just looked at the embers of that house and thought, 'What did I do wrong? Why am I the only one who cares? What was I supposed to do?'"

"That's reasonable," Aturach said. "We all look back on tragedy and wonder what we could have done differently."

"It wasn't *wondering*." The force of that word surprised her as it came out. As did the heat behind her eyes as she turned on him. "It wasn't a *wonder*, it was a *need*. I *had* to do something. I *needed* to do something right there and then or I was just going to…I would have…"

Her hands had balled into fists without her even noticing. She looked down at them. The scrapes on her knuckles were a bright ruby red against her scrubbed skin. They didn't sting now. No more than they had when they had been smashing against Dreadaeleon's face.

"You don't belong here, you know."

These words, too, were a surprise. But not a shock, like hers had been. The words that Aturach spoke were more a stinging sensation, like she had just been slapped across the cheek. And it hurt.

"What, you mean here in Cier'Djaal?"

He shook his head. "Here. In this temple. Before Talanas."

"I've been a priestess all my life," she protested.

"You were born into the clergy?"

"I might as well have been. I became an initiate when I was very young."

"I joined when I was fourteen," Aturach replied. "I needed to do something, too. For me, that was prayer. For me, that was attending a temple, taking oaths, doing the Healer's work. That was doing something. But it's not for you. Prayer isn't enough. The Healer isn't enough. You need to save everyone. You were just too young to realize it before you knew it."

"Don't tell me what I am." Her fists were still curled unconsciously. "Don't talk down to me." She gritted her teeth without knowing it. "Don't be horrible like everyone else."

The moisture rimming her eyes, the way the tears stung her cheeks. She was aware of those.

"Please."

He inched off the pillow, closer to her. She trembled as though she might strike him, and he flinched as though he believed it. Yet his hands were steady as they reached out and took hers; his voice was calm as he whispered, the words of the dead hanging between them.

"Asper," he said, "I couldn't. I can't. I'm not. And that's what I am. I'm a person of 'nots.' But you…" He looked over his shoulder to the empty pews. "I would have thought prayer was enough for those people. I would have said that I did my duty and fulfilled my oaths and I would have slept soundly in my room as they died down here.

"But you…it's not enough for you. Talanas isn't enough for you. Faith isn't enough for you. You need more. You need living people. That's why you don't belong here, Asper." His smile was soft, weak, a flickering candle in the dark. "But I'm glad you are."

A long tendril of smoke slithered in the air between them. The thick scent of the incense cloyed her nostrils. There was nothing more to it than that: just an aroma and some smoke.

This smoke wasn't the words of the dead.

That wasn't Talanas on the altar.

Those people were still ashen heaps on the ground.

Gods didn't listen. People were scum. Steel was worth more than gold. Gold was worth more than flesh. Blood was everywhere. People died in the streets and nobody cared. This city was shit. The world was shit and no words a man with a soft smile could say would ever change that.

But sometimes, it was nice to feel good about them anyway.

Or at least to try.

Aturach looked over her head. The moonlight shone stark through the window, waning.

"It's getting late."

At the end of that sentence, he squeezed her hand. She smiled at him, withdrew hers, and felt his fingers brush against her palm.

"Yeah," she said. "My friends will be worried about me."

Liar.

"And I should be resting in preparation for tomorrow," Aturach sighed as he rose. "The mediation will take—"

"The mediation? It's still going ahead?"

"You hadn't heard?"

"I hadn't heard and I was *there.* How did you?"

"Word travels swifter than bare feet on cold stone," he replied. "Swifter still when it's carried by fear. The Karnerians and Sainites are at each other's throats with accusations as to who sent the Khovura. If the mediation doesn't go ahead soon, we'll see war before the week's out."

"That can't be right." Asper hopped to her feet. "There was just an attack. They shouldn't rush into this. It isn't safe."

"All of Cier'Djaal won't be safe if we *don't* rush into this," Aturach said. "With Ghoukha no longer around to oppose her, Lady Teneir's recommendation that it be held on the border of the Sumps, closer to the poor, was approved. They're already setting up. It'll be at sunset."

She held a hand to her temple. "How does everything move this fast in the city? Back when I was adventuring, it all seemed to be from moment to moment."

"Who can afford to wait?" he said, sighing. "Regardless, if there's trouble, I should be there." He looked at her meaningfully. "You should, too."

"Two armies squaring off? If there's trouble, there's not a lot either of us can do."

He continued to stare. He blinked once. The incense smoke began to dissipate around him. She sighed, rubbed her eyes. She needed sleep.

She needed a lot of things.

Most of all, she needed not to say what she was about to say.

"Sunset, then?"

THIRTY-SEVEN

SIX COFFINS, NEATLY ROWED

Silf was a God of necessity.

Men born to prestige worshipped Daeon, the Conqueror. Men born to compassion worshipped Talanas, the Healer. Men born to skill worshipped Arexes, the Smith.

Men who should never have been born at all worshipped Silf, the Patron, God of Thieves.

No one chose to worship Him, of course. He merely accepted whoever was willing to pay for His blessing: a scoundrel God, but an ironically honest one. And since His worshippers were often less than willing to part with coin to begin with, He was rarely called upon outside of the most desperate circumstances.

And to invite a thief into one's house, one's circumstances must be especially desperate.

Denaos sat across the table, staring at his God as Rezca pushed him forward. Up close, Silf didn't look so impressive: tiny ebonwood idol carved to resemble a thin man with two faces reclining on a throne made out of knives. One face was a smile, coy and terse, the other a frown, vaguely disapproving. Mild emotions, both deprived of any great mood; Silf parted with nothing, not even an emotion.

Not without pay, anyway.

There was a jingle of coins as Rezca dropped his purse on the table and reached in, fishing out a bright golden piece. He placed it in the wooden bowl carved in Silf's lap.

"A bargain's a bargain," he said, sliding the idol to his left.

Yerk looked out from under his hood and slid a hand into his vest. He produced a second gold coin and set it in the bowl. "A bastard's a bastard."

He slid Silf to his left. Anielle pulled her glove open, withdrew another gold coin, and set it in. "Luck for the worthy."

She slid the idol to Denaos. The two faces of Silf stared up at him expectantly, echoed in the expressions of those seated beside him. He reached into his pocket, clasped the heaviest thing he could find, and placed in the bowl.

A piece of copper, tarnished and ugly, lay flat upon the gold coins like a wart.

"Gold for the master," he finished.

Yerk looked at the copper coin, then up at Denaos. His eyes were wide and white. "Unwise to start a meeting with blasphemy."

"It's not blasphemy," Anielle said with a pointed glare at Denaos. "It's just bad luck."

"It's a rhyme," Denaos muttered under his breath.

"Same thing," Yerk said, ignoring him. "Luck, disrespect, blasphemy...all the same to Silf. These are harsh times. Times when we'd be lucky to have the Patron watching our back."

"It's a rhyme," Denaos said again, louder.

"He's just a little rusty. He hasn't played the game in years and we haven't whispered the pact in longer," Anielle said to Yerk. "Besides, no one told him—"

"IT'S A FUCKING RHYME." The coins jingled as Denaos slammed his fist on the table. "It's something made up by gutter-priests to bilk dumbshits out of their money. It didn't do anything when we were young, it didn't do anything when we were older, and it's not going to do a fucking thing to save us from our own stupidity *now*."

He thrust a finger across the table at Rezca so fiercely it might as well have been a blade.

"Ghoukha's dead. A *lot* of people are dead. The fashas are scared, the Karnerians and Sainites are preparing for war, the Khovura ran wild in our yard, and we're here spitting rhymes like they mean a fucking thing." He leaned across the table. "Where was my backup? If we had had Jackals there to fight the Khovura, they'd...they'd..."

Anielle and Yerk looked at him, waiting for him to finish that thought. The flat stares that met him suggested that they knew as well as he did what would have happened.

They'd probably be dead, all the same.

"It could have been different," Denaos muttered, settling back in his seat.

"As I recall..." Yerk paused to fish a cigarillo out of his vest and lit it. "It was you that suggested Ghoukha might have allied with the Khovura. Is it not better he is dead if that were the case?"

"I wanted you there in *case* that were the case," Denaos retorted. "And in case he was a target of the Khovura, I would have wanted you there to protect him so we could have figured out what they wanted and gotten in good with the richest fasha around while we were at it."

"We were already in good with him and every other fasha." Yerk took a puff of his cigarillo. "The Jackals have had an understanding with the fashas since the riots. Whatever fool errand led you to believe that it was any fasha, let alone Ghoukha, was—"

"Our 'understanding' with the fashas goes as far as agreeing not to hurt them too badly if they pay up," Anielle interrupted. "We've been squeezing them for years. Why wouldn't they try to take a chance to put us down if they had it? Especially if we can't even keep the Khovura out of their houses. I've heard Ramaniel's theory. It adds up. It was a good bet and we should have been there."

"His 'theory,' yes." Yerk sneered. "We've all heard it. Accountancy and some errant addition do not make for a reason to go trying to upset the order of things."

"Where did he get the money, then?" Anielle snapped. "He was rich, but he wasn't magic. He couldn't have pulled the money out of thin air. He must have been getting it from some—"

"Spiders."

Rezca finally spoke. His voice was soft, lips pressed against his hands as he studied the idol of Silf carefully. His sigh was long and weary as he leaned back and adjusted his spectacles.

"His spiders were producing a very strong silk. The silk was made strong by a change in diet. The diet was people." Finding them too uncomfortable still, he removed his spectacles and rubbed his eyes. "We found the carcasses in the Sumps and pumped a few gutter runners for information. He's been feeding his spiders human flesh for years now. The Khovura had nothing to do with it."

"How did we not know about that?" Denaos asked. "When I left, a rat didn't *shit* in this city without us knowing about it."

"Things change," Rezca said, replacing his glasses. "Standards become lax. Recruitment goes up. We have enough eyes to watch the city and not enough to watch ourselves."

"Traitors?" Yerk tapped the ash from his cigarillo. "Impossible. This city knows who we are. They know what we do to those with swaying loyalties."

"How else do you explain it?" Rezca shot him a sidelong look. "I sent word out to both of you to get to the house of Ghoukha. Did either of you receive my messages?" When no answer was forthcoming, he nodded. "And I didn't receive word about Ghoukha's deals, either."

"Deals?" Denaos asked. "What deals?"

"The deals that are the reason Silf is at our table, Ramaniel," Rezca replied. "This is a meeting and a funeral."

A hush fell over the table and persisted for a long moment. Rezca seemed content to let it sit for a while, at least, in no great hurry to continue. His hesitation was plain on his face, a sharp wince and long frown preceding his words.

"Ghoukha was growing an army, it's true," he said, "an army to oust the foreigners. He aspired to be a hero to the city. But he was still a businessman. He had no desire to go against the rules. He wanted the Jackals' support, reached out to a few of our heads, detailed every interaction, and kept the records in his house."

He leaned forward again and ran a finger along Silf's frowning face.

"And those details, along with you, were the only things to survive that fire. The Khovura found them, used them to ferret out our cells, our dens, and our hideouts, and killed every last player inside."

"How many?" Denaos asked.

"Of the rank and file? I don't know. At least one hundred fifty. Of the heads, though? Ten."

"How can you be so sure?"

"Because we received their bodies this morning. Most of them, anyway. Their heads and hands had been cut off, jackal heads and paws sewn in their place. Their bellies had been cut open and stuffed with dead rats."

"With no heads, how can you be sure it was them?"

"Because those arrived two hours before you got here." Rezca sighed, rubbed his temples. "Jon-Jon, Radical Teshke, Afre, Kuromar..."

"Fenshi?" Denaos almost croaked the name.

Rezca nodded. "Ghoukha reached out to them. Any word they might have sent to me, I never received." He stared thoughtfully at Silf. "Someone was intercepting their runners, keeping them quiet."

"Who would do it?" Anielle asked. "Who *could* do it?"

"Difficult to say. I didn't catch on even when most of my heads *weren't* dead. With Fenshi and the others gone, it's impossible to track down who was doing what while this was going on."

"My men won't like that," Yerk hissed. "The Jackals are the masters of this city. We do not sit idly by while the Khovura tear apart everything we've worked for and our leader speaks of difficulties and impossibilities. I want a name; I want a head; I want *revenge*."

"All of which I fully intend to give to you," Rezca replied calmly. "This game is best played in harsh conditions, after all." He cracked a smile, something that was too warm to belong at this table. "Anielle, do you remember the riots? Remember when you swore that would be the end of us? The end of the city?"

She nodded, hesitantly. "Yeah."

"And remember how we formed up, bigger and badder than ever? It was those riots, the death of the Houndmistress, all those people..." His words trailed off. His smile faded. "We made our mark then and there. We emerged from the ashes. We built this game, we built this city, and we ran it. Priests work well in silence. Scholars work best in solitude." He looked meaningfully at Denaos. "Thugs like us? We need a bit of noise to distract people. I've taken care of that."

Denaos did not look away. "What did you do?"

"The mediation is going to occur at sunset," Rezca said. "In about an hour. Get word to your people. Tell them to stay off the streets."

"What did you do, Rezca?" Denaos repeated.

"We'll meet up again in a week. I'll have a plan for us by then. Until then, anyone caught in the open is as good as dead, understand?"

"Understood," Yerk said.

"Understood," Anielle echoed.

"Rezca. Please." Only Denaos's voice defected from the air of professionalism in the room. His words were edged with desperation. "Tell me what you did."

Rezca adjusted his spectacles. He laid his hands flat on the table and spoke simply and flatly.

"What any of us would have."

THIRTY-EIGHT

TRUE NAMES

Try as he might, Gariath found he could not expel the scent of ashes from his nostrils.

Which seemed odd to him, not least because he was currently surrounded by a throbbing, burbling throng of humans, whose collective sweat, fear, breath, and desire should be overpowering.

He found it easy enough to block out their chatter behind the thick black hood covering his face and head. He found it easy enough to avoid touching them behind the accompanying black cloak. He supposed it ought to be easy enough to ignore their stink as well.

And why wouldn't it be? Human words, human touch, human stench: a lot to do little. He cared little for humans, as a whole, much less dead ones.

Which is why he found it so puzzling that he couldn't ignore them: the odor of ash, the sweet reek of burned, melting gold, the mouthy stench of charred flesh an instant before it became cooked meat.

Still, he tried. He held his breath. He closed his eyes. He ignored the babble of the surrounding human throngs until everything was silent.

"You heard, then?"

Except for the two humans standing right beside where he was sitting.

"Everyone's heard. How many dead was it, anyway?"

"Thirty? Fifty? Of the nobles alone, even. Who knows how many other servants and house guards. You know what this means, don't you? If the Khovura can kill Ghoukha in his own home, what hope do the rest of us have? How bad can it get?"

Gariath exhaled. His breath felt stale beneath his hood.

"It can always get worse. The Karnerians and Sainites are on edge. The Ancaarans had to beg them to come down here. Have you seen the square where they're setting it up? Guards everywhere. Crossbows on every roof. They aren't going to let it turn into another massacre."

"You think it'll work? Ghoukha bought his own army and it didn't save him from the Khovura. You know, I even heard there was some kind of monstrosity, some manner of demon—"

"Don't tell me you believe that oxshit. The fashas want you to think that it took a demon to kill them rather than admit that they're as vulnerable as the rest of us."

"Maybe you're right. He had enough money to hire one of those huge dragonmen, after all, and where the hell was it? Seems like a two-ton scaly son of a bitch would have been pretty handy in that situation."

Gariath inhaled. He tasted smoke on his tongue.

"Guzzling ale by the gallon, probably. Fucking oids. Only good for one thing and they're not even around to do it."

"This is what happens when you trust them. The one time they might be *useful* coming into our city and they aren't around. Fucking oids."

The scent finally changed when he caught a whiff of his own blood. He felt, suddenly, his hands trembling under his cloak, his claws dug deep into his palms. He hadn't noticed exactly when that had happened.

That, too, was puzzling.

"Hey, how long have you been sitting there?"

It took him a moment to recognize Lenk's voice. Longer, even, to recognize Lenk's scent. He looked up halfway, careful not to let his hood slip. The young man and the tall, brown-haired woman both stood before him, looking at him curiously.

"Hours," Gariath replied with a grunt. "You said to be here by noon."

"Right, I did," Lenk said. He glanced from Gariath to Asper. "I told everyone to be here by noon, didn't I? How come it's just us three?"

"Denaos said he had something to take care of," Asper said. "Though he specifically assured me he'd be here on time." She paused. "I suppose my first hint should have been that he used the words 'specifically assure,' so that's on me."

"Kataria said the same," Lenk replied with a sigh. "And I don't think Dreadaeleon's going to show up." He cast a sidelong glance at Asper. "Considering…"

She met his stare flatly, unflinching. "I'm not sorry."

He said nothing and looked out over the heads of the crowd. The tide of humanity had grown too vast for the Meat Market to contain and had spilled out into the streets of the Souk.

They called it the Meat Market, a tiny square surrounded by tall buildings between the Souk and the Sumps, because it was where many illicit deals and dead bodies were dropped as the Jackals did their business.

It was the site of the mediation because the Ancaarans had argued, successfully, that it was where the poor people and the wealthy people—but not the people so wealthy that they should be forced to endure the presence of the poor—were at their closest connection.

Gariath knew this because he had spent the past few hours sitting patiently, listening to humans.

And because he had spent the past few hours sitting patiently, listening to humans, Gariath had an overwhelming urge to start hitting things.

At that moment, a murmur of excitement swept through the crowd. Word from the front of the line had passed to the back. The Karnerian and Sainite delegations had just arrived. The mediations were about to get under way.

"No choice, then," Lenk muttered. "We go on without them." He glanced at Asper. "You still think you can get us in?"

She nodded. "If Aturach is here, then probably. Wait here. I'll go find out."

She turned on her heel and pushed her way into the crowd.

"Go where?" Gariath asked.

"In there," Lenk said, pointing toward the Meat Market. "I saw Miron walking with the Khovura in Ghoukha's house. I *saw* him. And I think the Khovura were going to try to kill the Ancaaran envoy. So, if they strike here, chances are—"

"Why?"

"Now, that part I'm not sure about. The Khovura want an unstable city, though. They want to sow chaos. But if we want to save these people—"

"No, why are we going in there?"

At this question, Lenk looked at Gariath as though he had just asked why they couldn't be sure the moon wasn't really the sun in disguise.

"Who do you think you can save?" Gariath continued. "The Khovura killed a lot of humans, but so did Dreadaeleon. These people are all going to kill each other one day, anyway. They'll knife each other in alleys or steal each other's money or leave each other to die in filth. Nothing can save them. Not you, not her, not Kharga."

"It's not just about them," Lenk said. "If we want to get paid—"

"You're not going to get paid. Miron isn't who he says he is. You saw him last night?"

"I did."

"And he saw you?"

"He did."

"And he left you to die?"

Lenk's face screwed up with rage. "Fuck, I have to *try*, Gariath," he snarled. "I have to find some way to end it all, to stop killing and try to live a normal life."

Gariath looked at him intently from beneath his cowl. "If you go in there," he said, "do you think you'll find less killing... or more?"

"What am I supposed to do, then? Go out into the wilds and starve to death with Kataria? With *you*? We'll only find more blood there. It's what we do."

"Then why are we trying to fight it?"

"Will you *stop* asking fucking questions?" Lenk all but roared. A few curious heads turned his way and he lowered his voice. "Don't you ever get tired of it? Don't you ever wish you could stop hurting people?"

Gariath inhaled deeply. His nostrils caught a new scent: of fear and fallen bricks and a great, heaving body buried beneath them that exuded a scent not so unlike his own.

"I do," he replied coarsely.

"Wouldn't *you* try to end it some way, if you could? Any way? With this gold, we *can*. Think of what we could do with it."

"Where? Here?" He stomped the earth. "In this city? In any city?" He looked long to the direction of the waning sun. "Out there, I am *Rhega*, the last. Here, I am an oid, one of many. Out there, I am strong. Here, I hide behind a cloak. Out there, all I had need for was food, rain, and..."

He paused and looked back to Lenk.

"What can I do with gold? What makes you think I care about it?"

Lenk met his gaze evenly. "Then tell me," he said, "if you don't care about gold or humans, why are you even here?"

Gariath stared intently into the young man's eyes. He was strong, as humans went: scars to boast a long life of battle, wiry muscles tense and ready to back up those boasts, the keen, thoughtful look of someone used to seeking weakness and finding opportunity in his eyes.

Yet, for all that, he was still human. It would not be a large matter to simply reach down and break him where he stood.

As he had broken Kharga. And Kudj. And so many others and been left with nothing but empty earth and the scent of ashes.

It was Gariath who looked away first. He saw the tall female's brown head bobbing through the crowd. She waved at them and beckoned them into the crowd to follow her. Lenk turned to go and paused at the edge of the mass of people. He looked over his shoulder at Gariath.

And after a time, with heavy footsteps and bent shoulders, Gariath followed.

Nothing was ever destroyed in Cier'Djaal. Things broke, things crumbled, things were forgotten: homes, buildings, people. But they were always built over; always did the new crush the old, always did the old support the new.

Not quite the drowned disaster of the Sumps, nor quite the modern splendor of the Souk, the Meat Market was a small square about three hundred paces in any direction from the center. Walls, haphazardly placed from a time before architecture had become an art, snaked across the sandy streets just as cracks and crumbles snaked through their stonework. Buildings, erected before treacherous foundations had rendered such heights unsustainable, rose up on shaky foundations to scrape the setting sun.

Between the worlds of the wealthy and the poor stood the Meat Market.

And between the worlds of the poor and the Meat Market stood a line of steel and flesh.

The crowds thinned dramatically the closer Asper led Lenk and Gariath to the square. While the mediations held the fate of Cier'Djaal and the attention of the city, very few looked actually invested enough in that fate to challenge the human barricade of Karnerian soldiers that had blocked the tiny gap between snaking walls that marked the entrance to the Meat Market.

Their spears were held rigid. Their tower shields were locked together. Truly, though, only the dead iron glares from beneath their helms appeared necessary to keeping the crowd at bay.

Most of the crowd, anyway.

"The hell do you mean 'forbidden'?" Asper snapped. "I was *just here!*" She gestured over the Karnerians' heads. "Did you not see the Talanite who spoke with me? How could you not? We were talking *through you.*"

"My orders come from Speaker Careus," the Karnerian replied, voice like cold metal. "His orders come from Daeon. None may disturb the mediation."

Unless they can afford it, anyway, Lenk thought.

Between the helms of the Karnerians, he could see people assembled in the Meat Market: finely dressed merchants, minor fashas with servants in tow, a few of the wealthier priests. Lenk was used to worlds where things were solved by harder metals than gold.

So, too, it seemed, were the Karnerians.

"You impudent piece of—" Asper trailed off as she caught sight of something over the Karnerian's head. "Aturach!" She waved a hand and hopped up and down. "*Aturach!* Over here!"

A thin Djaalic man wearing an expression that lay somewhere between worry and a concussion peered out between two helmets. He exchanged some words with Asper—his timid, hers decidedly not—before he bit his lower lip and looked to the Karnerians.

"She's with the temple of Talanas," the man named Aturach said. He spared a quick glance for Lenk and Gariath. "Her friends, as well. Please let them pass."

"I have my orders," the guard replied.

"Given the possibility that things may turn very, *very* ugly here," Aturach said threateningly, "whether or not we have an extra healer on hand could very much be what decides if you or one of your brothers lives or dies. Now please, *let her pass.*"

The Karnerian stood stock-still for a moment. "The big one in the cloak"—he nodded to Gariath—"stays here. The other two may pass." He cast a glance at Lenk's sword. "Unarmed."

Lenk turned and looked at Gariath. Slowly, he unbuckled his sword belt and shrugged the weapon off his shoulders. He stepped close to sling it around Gariath's shoulder, so as not to let a trace of red flesh be accidentally shown. And close as he was, he could feel Gariath's growl in his bones.

"Do you remember the times when we used to fight alongside each other?" the dragonman asked. "Before I was relegated to carrying your shit?"

"It's just for a little bit," Lenk replied. "You'll be here when we get back?"

Gariath looked at him flatly. "Where else would I go?"

The heat in Gariath's words made him consider the wisdom of leaving the dragonman alone. Yet Asper beckoned him to follow as the guards stepped aside, opening a gap for them to walk through.

He had scarcely taken five steps beyond them when Asper stopped abruptly and turned to face him.

"What is it now?" His voice was ringed with irritation.

"You're not getting paid."

"What?"

"You have to know that by now. Whatever happens here, there's no Miron, there's no gold," she said. "If you set foot here, it's either for revenge or to keep people from dying. And if it's the former, don't think I won't tell Aturach to get rid of you. So which is it?"

"I'm here to help," he said. The words sounded hollow on his lips, and in her ears, if her frown was anything to judge by. "Really."

Whether she was satisfied by that answer or not, she was at least moving. He followed her into the square, glancing up around the towering buildings. He hadn't noticed before, but as the sun faded beneath the city's horizon, he could make out blue coats stationed atop the roofs. He suspected he had found the reason there weren't as many Sainites on the ground as Karnerians. Standing at the ready, crossbows loaded and eyes locked on the Meat Market below, at least six Sainites stood on every roof.

Except for one.

At the east end of the square, upon the roof of one of the shorter buildings rising behind one of the taller walls, a small squad of Karnerians sat cross-legged. Clad in white robes, heads shaven, and a Karnerian numeral tattooed on each of their scalps, they stared straight ahead, lined up in numerical order, unmoving, unblinking.

"Who are those Karnerians on the roof?" he asked.

"Machine Cult," Aturach replied from ahead.

"What's that?" Asper asked.

"If the mediations go well, we'll never find out," Aturach muttered, pressing on through the grimy square.

The Meat Market, it had been rumored, was where the Jackals first got their start with the bloody mass execution of a rival gang. Since then, it had become a popular dumping ground for bodies, and Lenk could see why. The many snaking walls and alleys left a lot of hiding places, the plaster and stone still discolored with bloodstains long past.

An ideal place for an ambush.

He chose not to mention this to Aturach. The man looked as if he was about to shake himself to pieces as it was.

"I need to go and make sure Savine and Malauch got in all right," he said to Asper. "Can you be on hand? You know, in case something happens. I don't think it will, but…"

"I can and I will," Asper said, nodding to the priest as he slipped into the crowd.

Something would happen. Too many armed men for it not to. Lenk chose not to state this fact, either.

After all, no one else seemed bothered by it.

At the center of the square, all eyes were upon a well-polished table brimming with documents, pitchers of wine, and plates of food. It looked like it would be more at home in a *houn* than at a mediation. And its attendants looked like they'd be more at home on a battlefield with each other's swords in each other's throats.

A stern-faced, black-armored Karnerian and two soldiers sat at one end of the table, glowering across at the dusty glare of the Sainite woman, her spear leaning against her chair, flanked by a pair of Sainite bluecoats. Glares, for the moment, seemed sufficient to satisfy either party. They exchanged hostile words filtered through the Ancaaran priest seated at the middle of the table. Here, too, was a face that looked serenely bored with the proceedings.

This *was* supposed to be the mediations upon which war and subsequently thousands of lives hung in the balance, wasn't it? Yet no one present, from the mediator to the observers, seemed quite so invested in that outcome.

On *this* side of the Karnerian line, anyway.

It didn't sit well with Lenk. Too many weapons, not enough of a shit being given about using them. There was a proverb there somewhere, one he would think of after he told Asper. Her arms were folded, eyes upon the table. He reached out to seize her shoulder and her attention.

But something seized his first.

Striding like a ghost among the living, there he was. Each step so graceful that he walked through a crowd without touching a single soul, tranquility painted in the smile across his face, hands folded delicately before him, he paused and looked across the mediation table to Lenk and smiled as though it was the most natural thing in the world.

Miron Evenhands.

The priest's smile, once so warm but now so smug, lingered on Lenk for a moment longer before he turned and vanished down a nearby alley. The young man glanced at Asper. If she had noticed, she wasn't giving any sign that she had, her eyes still locked on the mediations.

He half-considered telling her. He half-considered asking her to help him. He half-considered taking her advice when she would doubtlessly tell him to leave it alone.

That was his sensible half talking. The other half, the half of him that was so tired of killing, the half of him that wanted to start over, the half of him that had poured so much blood and sweat into this moment already...

That half spoke much, much more loudly.

He said nothing. He ducked into the crowd. He did not look back.

"'You shall show no foe your back. You shall show no foe your feet. You shall show only the blade. They shall know you not as men, but as weapons.' This is the Conqueror's holy mandate. It is all we seek to enforce in this city. Whether you force us to choose that or not is on your heads."

They were not diplomats.

"The fuck it is. I've read your 'mandates,' ripped them out of a book, and wiped with them. A bunch of tripe stewed up by ancient old shits to excuse all the people they killed. We let you enforce this 'mandate,' Karnie, we might as well just let you burn the city to the ground. Fuck if we won't do it first."

They were warriors.

"Speaker, Wing-Sergeant, please. We can come to terms."

This was not peace.

"There can be no terms where the compromise is blasphemy."

This was a farce.

"Hard to fucking sign a treaty with a wolf that can't even wipe the blood from his paws."

Asper hadn't been here long, but the set of their scowls told her that little had been exchanged between Careus and Blacksbarrow that hadn't involved accusation. The table was littered with documents—rough drafts of treaties, maps of Cier'Djaal, holy scripts, mission statements. The food and drink provided, though, went largely untouched save by the Ancaaran envoy who even now proceeded to fill his plate.

"We have gathered here"—he waved a hand around the assembled crowd—"for the purposes of restoring peace. Surely, there is a way we can all get what we want here."

No demands for Cier'Djaal from him. No lines drawn in the sand. Not so much as a harsh word for either party threatening to destroy his city.

He had no interest in peace. He had eyes only for the crowd, all watching, all judging, all waiting for him to finish this and be done so that they could carry on with their lives. Yet only with as much attention as could be expected from a noble. The crowd began to yawn and mingle among themselves, as though this were an exceptionally dull party.

Out of the corners of her eyes, though, Asper could see there were those who were hanging on every word. The Karnerians and Sainites gathered in gangs at opposite ends of the square. Slowly but surely, they had been assembling into loose formation, ready to strike.

"Keep an eye on the Sainites"—she leaned over to whisper to Lenk—"and I'll watch the Karnerians. If anything happens, we find Aturach and the others and protect them. All right?"

Lenk did not answer.

Maybe he was as uninterested as everyone else.

Or, far more likely, it was because he was across the square. She saw his wiry form, his silver hair, his stare directed down an alley into which he quickly disappeared. And she felt her jaw clench together.

That son of a bitch, she thought. *He lied to me.*

Granted, she wasn't *certain* he'd lied. There was a chance—a small one—that he was heading that way for some other reason. Maybe he had seen someone in need of help. But then why didn't he tell her? Why wouldn't he have gotten her to help, too?

She would decide for herself, she thought as she took off after him, *after* she had pummeled him senseless.

"You will not catch him."

A voice spoke. It was not loud. It bore no emotion. It did not so much as change inflection. Yet Asper heard it very clearly, for it had been meant for only her to hear. It was made loud by the absolute certainty with which it spoke.

She turned and saw him. In Ghoukha's *houn*, he had looked out of place in his threadbare robe and his bare feet stained black and his wide, sleepless eyes. Here, he looked like an open wound on society: something dark and ugly and poor in a sea of wealth.

And yet no one seemed to see him but her.

And she wondered, as she approached him, if anyone else could.

"You can chase him," the man with the stare that saw everything said. "You can slow him down, this time. But you will never catch him. You will never stop him. He goes into dark places. He finds violence. This is what he does."

"Who are you?" Asper asked.

"And you," the man said, ignoring her question, "go after him. You are forever chasing. You are forever trying. You are forever failing. This is what you do."

"The hell is that supposed to mean?"

"You fail because you are made by the chase. You do not exist without something to pursue, without wounds to heal, without villains to slay. For you to be of any value, someone must first act that you may react. And for this reason, you will always be too late."

He looked at her. His eyes swallowed her. Voices around them faded. The light of the setting sun vanished into his stare. There was nothing left but her and a world that existed entirely within his eyes.

"As you were last night."

She found she had no answer for that, within or without. No words on her lips. No anger behind her brow. His words echoed within her, made her cold and empty.

"Ask me," he said.

"What is your name?"

"Mundas."

"Are you with the Khovura?"

"Yes."

That cold feeling welling up inside her became a spike of ice lodged firmly in her lungs, one that made it hard to speak. "What are you planning?"

"Nothing." He turned back to the mediations. They suddenly looked so unimportant, so puny. A boy and a girl fighting over tin soldiers. "I do not intend to lift a finger or move from this spot. There are no Khovura here and none will come. There are no demons here and none will be summoned.

"But very soon, many people will die. And shortly after, many people will swear that it was a good and honest thing that they did. They will praise Gods for what they have done and say it was the will of heaven, not their own, that killed so many."

"I'm here to stop that," she said.

"You cannot. I cannot. I have tried many times before. But each time, I fail, like you. Everything that happens now is out of the hands of Gods and men. The sole difference is that men actually bother to reach out and try to grasp events as they happen."

Her face fell flat, nearly sliding right off her head. It was something in his voice, the absolute conviction with which he spoke.

"What you're talking about, it sounds so..." She shook her head. "Sick."

"Do you intend to cure the illness?"

"I do."

"As do I."

Mundas blinked. The world went black for a moment and people ceased to exist. When he opened his eyes again, she saw the world rearranged. He was elsewhere, across the square, vanishing into the shadows of the nearby alleys.

Yet his voice was just as soft, as clear, as certain.

"When this is over and you speak to Talanas again," he whispered to her from so far away, "remember that even He was powerless to stop this."

And he was gone, leaving only the cold feeling in her gut to confirm that he had ever been there. The crowd in his wake seemed a writhing, nebulous thing, without individuality or beginning or end. So many faces blended together; so many voices rose at once; so little of it seemed to make sense.

She looked up because she could not bear to look at them anymore. And perhaps it was that tapestry of faces, that endless lack of distinction, which enabled her to spot the glint of the last fading light off of a steel arrowhead.

And she could see it, from so far away as to be able to be powerless to stop it.

A crossbow bolt aimed from the window of a nearby building, straight at the Ancaaran envoy's heart.

— ✦ —

Only a few passing glances were given to Lenk as he wound his way into the alley. Mostly bemused aristocrats wondering how someone in such filthy clothing had been invited, none nearly interested enough to call attention to him. He moved through the shadows of the alley, caught sight of Miron, stark white in the gloom, and instinctively reached for a sword that wasn't there.

He caught himself and cursed silently as Miron looked around warily.

Then cursed a little louder as Miron's shape began to twitch and ripple like liquid.

Miron's skeleton twisted, snapping into shorter limbs with a more compact spine. Clothes changed color, then cloth, and then everything as his white robes became a blue Sainite coat. Face trembled, shifted, and rearranged itself until a strong-jawed, stubble-cheeked, blue-eyed Sainite soldier looked out.

Miron—the thing that had been Miron and had never been Miron—looked over its shoulder warily. Lenk barely had the presence of mind to duck farther into the shadows. The creature's gaze swept the alley cautiously for a moment before turning and heading deeper into the maze of streets.

Lenk was not certain what made him follow. Perhaps it was that uncertainty that kept him going. The uncertainty of what he had just seen, of what it was planning, of what he was even going to do if he caught up to it.

Some things were so uncertain that the logical mind could not abide them. Some things were so uncertain that they must be made certain.

And if those things happened to owe a person a lot of money…

The alley twisted the farther he went in. He followed and kept his distance by the sound of the creature's footsteps. When they came to a halt, he peered out around the corner of the alley and saw the creature standing at the doorway of one of the buildings overlooking the Meat Market.

Another Sainite guard, a young man with barely any hair on his cheeks, stood at the door armed with a buckler and sword. He and the creature exchanged a few words in a crisp Sainite accent. The creature added something the guard chuckled at before waving it through, sending it into the door.

Now was the time to turn back, Lenk knew. Now was the time to acknowledge that whatever he had planned, whatever he thought he was going to do to Miron, was obviously not going to happen. Now was the time to walk away.

And give up on everything he had hoped to build in this city.

And surrender everything he ever wanted.

And go back to killing.

Over the wall, he could hear the discourse of the mediations growing louder and more heated. An excited murmur rose up among the crowd.

No, he told himself. *You can't go back now. That thing is plotting something, right? It has to be. How can you build a new life in the city it will destroy?* He looked up at the building it had just entered; three stories tall, plenty of windows overlooking the Meat Market. *You told Asper you were here to help, right? Are you?*

He answered himself in a single step as he walked out of the shadows and approached the doorway.

The Sainite guard held up a hand to discourage him. "Ease off, mate. This area's forbidden to all civs." He glanced Lenk over. "Which is what you look like. Head back the way you came."

"I need to get in there," Lenk said, gesturing to the door. "The soldier you just let in isn't who you think he is."

"Really? Because I certainly *think* that's my mate, Trescel."

How long has Miron been doing this? How many other lives does he lead?

"And I certainly *think* I'm not going to let a slack-jawed foreign dimwit spew shit about my fellow soldiers," the Sainite said. "Get back to where you came from, civ."

"I just want to take a look inside," Lenk said, taking a step closer. "That's all."

"Mate." The man's hand went to his sword. "Walk. Away."

Lenk hesitated. He became aware of the vast shadows behind him leading back to the Meat Market and how far he had walked through them to get here. He became aware of the door before him and how very little he knew of what was behind it.

Of the young man before him, of the sword in the scabbard, he was only barely aware.

He took another step forward. Steel hissed against leather. And a step became a leap. Lenk caught the sword's pommel and shoved the blade back in the scabbard. His hand went for the Sainite's belt and slipped into his coat. The soldier's buckler caught him in the chest. He fell back, feeling the dagger from the belt come with him.

The Sainite reached for his sword again. Lenk lunged, darting low as the sword flashed over his head. He flipped the dagger in his grip, pointed it upward, and drove.

Hard.

He felt warm life dribble out onto his hands. He felt a great weight go stiff and then settle on the blade. When he released the weapon, the Sainite fell to the ground and lay limp, eyes frozen wide as though he still hadn't realized what was going on even as the dagger was jammed up beneath his chin.

Lenk was a little surprised himself.

By how quickly at it had all happened, how very naturally it had all felt. Not a life taken, just a reflex, something neither of them had had any control over. Like a dance and only Lenk knew the steps. So he had done them.

And this man was dead.

It was just that easy.

This wasn't the first man he had killed. Nor even the first man who might not have deserved it. It should not bother him. He was doing this for a cause. It would all be worth it in the end.

And yet...

"Fuck," he yelled. "*Fuck*. Why'd you have to do that?" He wasn't sure who he was talking to.

He shut his eyes as he stepped over the body and pushed the door open to check the interior. Just inside, Miron, wearing the shape of the soldier, was sitting on the seventh step of a wooden staircase.

Just smiling.

"Would you like to know?" the creature asked.

"Who are you?" Lenk replied. "Who are you, really?"

"Not that." The creature gestured to the dead soldier. "Would you like to know his name?"

Lenk would not.

"Would you like to know who he was? What he wrote in the letters he sent back home? Would you like to know if he had a woman here or in another country somewhere far away? Would you like to know if they ever talked about marriage? Would you like to know if he ever promised her he would come back?"

With each word, the creature's grin grew broader, and the creature's eyes grew wider. When he fell silent, at last, his smile was too big for his face, eyes too wide for their sockets.

"Would you?"

Lenk shook his head. "No."

"I suppose you wouldn't." The creature's smile did not fade. "What difference would it make, anyway? You'd still be a murderer."

"It wasn't like that," Lenk said. "It wasn't murder. I had to get past him to stop you and whatever you're planning."

"What if I'm not planning anything?"

Lenk stared at him. "Are you?"

The creature's grin grew a little broader. "Yes."

Lenk reached down, took the dead soldier's sword, and stepped forward. "Sometimes you have to kill to make things better."

"I happen to agree," the creature replied. "And so does Khoth-Kapira."

"You were in league with all of this. I knew it. That makes this man here"—Lenk gestured to the dead soldier—"and everything else I've done worth it."

"Who are you trying to reassure, Lenk?"

"No more questions. No more games. No more running." Lenk pointed the blade at the creature and took another step forward. "Don't even bother explaining what the point of all this is. It ends now."

"In whose name?"

Lenk flinched. "What?"

"You claim that all the death, all the dying, is worth it. Who gets to decide that? You? Me? A God? When those dead people go to heaven, will they be reassured that they died for a good purpose? Will their widows understand? Will their children?"

"I don't know."

"Faith is a valuable thing, Lenk." The creature rose up to its feet. Its grin shrank to a razor-thin smirk. "If you can't trust yourself, trust that someone here knows what they're doing."

The creature whirled and rushed up the stairs. Lenk was after it in an instant, though for all the good it did him he might as well have waited. The creature was fast. Inhumanly fast. He took the stairs six at a time on legs that stretched with each step, leaping up the steps and disappearing into the building's upper reaches.

Lenk lost sight of it within seven breaths.

And seven breaths later, he heard the screaming.

Three short cries punctuated by three short gurgling sounds and three bodies hitting the floor. Lenk saw the blood weeping down the steps before he even made it to the landing of the first storey.

More Sainite soldiers lay twitching on the ground, hands clutching swords and slit throats as they bled out onto the floor. Lenk was almost tempted to ask which way the creature had fled. Somehow, he doubted they'd be of much help.

The groan of wood and iron caught his attention, the door swung open ahead. He rushed in after the creature and found only a small wooden room, bare of anything but draped crates and rotting furniture.

And a tall, slender woman at the window.

She looked over her shoulder at him, jaw agape in astonishment beneath her hood. A Jackal's hood, Lenk recognized. A massive crossbow rested against the windowsill, scope sighted down at the Meat Market. This was the woman from the Souk all those days ago, Lenk realized. The one who had nearly killed him and Kataria.

That would worry him more had he not been struck by a bigger concern.

Where the hell is the creature?

He heard the door groaning again. He whirled around and saw a Sainite soldier—or what appeared to be one—standing at the threshold, his grin as broad and as awful as the wound in his throat. With a delicate wave, he slammed the door shut behind Lenk.

He heard the sound of a lock clicking into place moments before he heard the sound of a crossbow being loosed, followed by a wrenching scream carried up from the Meat Market.

He whirled. The woman was already running, climbing up a stack of crates to disappear through a trapdoor hidden in the ceiling, the hatch slamming shut behind her, before Lenk even thought to pursue.

Instead, he rushed to the windowsill. The crossbow lay empty there, its sole bolt currently far away and embedded in the throat of the Ancaaran envoy slumped over the mediation table, bleeding out onto the treaties.

A hundred eyes turned up to him. Fifty fingers pointed at him. And a single voice tore through the air.

"Kill the assassin!"

THIRTY-NINE

A Heaven of His
Own Design

Dreadaeleon's father had been a strict Daeonist, the grandson of a convert in Karnerian-occupied land over a century ago.

And he had learned that Daeon's vision of the life eternal was one of emptiness. To be faithful to Daeon was to know joy by leaving behind guilt, worry, and desire to become one in the Conqueror's eternal army, to stand perpetually vigilant for the moment when Daeon's forces would sweep the land clean for Him to step upon.

At around four years of age, Dreadaeleon started to doubt his father. It seemed odd that such a fate would be considered desirable enough to wake up before dawn to pray to a God that he could neither see nor hear. At five, Dreadaeleon's magic had started to manifest itself, and his doubts as to godly powers had grown.

By the time he was six, his father had given him to the Venarium in exchange for twenty-five gold coins and Dreadaeleon had no doubts as to whether or not Gods existed.

But he often thought of heaven. He often wondered what it looked like to happier people.

He doubted that the *houn* of The Sleeping Cat bathhouse was it.

But it was probably close.

Incense smoke hung in the air in soft blankets, mingling with steam from the distant private rooms. Curtains of red and purple fell in cascades from polished mahogany walls. The Djaalic woman who came out from the hall at the end of the *houn* to greet him was very clean and pretty.

He couldn't remember how he had gotten here.

"Ah, young foreign master." The woman offered a deep bow. When she rose, her silk robe hung off one shoulder. "I am thrilled beyond words that you have returned to us so soon. Have you come far tonight?"

"I don't know." His voice was weak and dry in his throat. The incense smoke tasted so sweet in his nostrils.

"Mm. Such can be the effect of our various poets. Would you like to see a new one tonight?"

He shook his head. "No."

"Ah. You wish to see—"

"Liaja," he interrupted. "I want to see Liaja."

"Of course. She awaits you."

"I have gold."

"We may discuss payment later. But you are such a sweet young boy for offering." The woman flashed an impish smirk as she headed back toward the hall. "Would you follow me, sweet boy?"

Boy.

The word echoed in his head.

Boy. Boy. Boy.

Many times. And many times, it became other words.

Boy.

Boy.

Sweet.

Boy.

Tiny.

Boy.

Weak.

Boy.

Selfish.

Boy.

Cruel.

Useless.

Useless.

Useless.

Boy.

Boy.

"I'm not a boy."

She paused, looked over her shoulder. "Mm?"

"I'm not a boy," he repeated.

Her smirk became a smile. Something so very warm, so very lovely.

"Of course, my apologies." She gestured to the candles hanging from braziers overhead. "The light is so poor. I should have remembered that we only serve men here."

"Yeah. Yes. Men."

"Would you come with me, then, my dear man? She will be waiting."

She disappeared into the steamy shadows of the bathhouse.

He followed her.

He could not remember for how long.

⋯ ⋙✦⋘ ⋯

The water was hot. Dreadaeleon knew this because she had told him it was so before she had gently tugged him out of his clothes and eased him into the bath's sunken stone basin.

His body ached. Dreadaeleon knew this because he had not slept for a night and a day. He had only barely remembered to wipe the blood from his nose. The bruises on his face, he could not wipe away.

But although he knew these things, he did not feel them. He could not feel the water cascading down his shoulders and back as she filled a bowl and poured it over him. He could not feel the sting of his bruises or the pain in his body as she massaged his shoulders.

Every ounce of blood inside him was in his head, stewing around that word.

Boy.

"Boy?"

He winced. Struck.

"Are you all right?" Liaja's words were the water, flowing down him, dissipating into steam. "You're so quiet tonight. No requests?" He could hear her smile in her giggle as she leaned close to his ear. "Shall I be the Empress Garai tonight, moments before I ascend the throne on the backs of those who bowed before me? Or would you like me to be the slave Atrena, dancing for the Beast of the Wild Wood?"

He opened his mouth to say something. To tell her something. To tell her she was beautiful and that her touch hurt him so much, it was so soft. But he couldn't think of a reason, so he closed his mouth and pulled his knees to his chest.

"Northern boy," Liaja whispered, pulling a lock of damp hair from his ear, "talk to me. Tell me where you've been this past day. Tell me how you got so filthy. Tell me where you got those bruises." At his silence, she laid a hand on his cheek. "Northern boy..."

"I AM NOT A BOY."

The Venarie came surging out of him. The water exploded from the basin in a geyser, striking the ceiling before falling again as droplets of warm, steamy rain. He stood up in the tub and turned to face her, naked and trembling.

As she trembled, too.

What had she looked like when he first saw her on the slaver's block so long ago? Dirtier, he imagined. Scrubbed, scented, naked as she was now, she didn't look quite so delicate as she had that day. Her hair was soft. Her skin was soft. Her eyes were wide as she shrank away from him.

She had not known his power. She had not known what he could do.

But she did not cry out. She did not weep.

Even as he did.

"I'm not a boy." His fists shook at his sides. His tears were lost in the steaming drops of water falling from the ceiling. "I'm not."

She did not tremble for long. She rose up, instead, and faced him.

She was taller than him, he noticed. And soft. Her breasts were soft against his chest. The slope of her belly was soft against the concavity of his. Her legs were soft as she drew a thigh against his. And her voice, her words, her poetry was soft.

He knew this.

"You are," she said. "You are a gentle, sweet, northern boy. You are strong, but that is not what is important. That strength is for anyone." She slid her arms about his neck. She rested her forehead against his. "But your softness is only for me, northern boy."

And suddenly, he felt so very warm, so very pained, and so very, very tired. He sank to his knees with a crash. He wrapped his arms about her legs. And he wept.

"I did something terrible," he sobbed. "I hurt so many people. I said they shouldn't be treated like that, like you were, but in the end, I didn't care. I didn't care and she was right. I'm useless. I'm selfish. I'm cruel."

"Hush," Liaja whispered. She laid her hand upon his head, wound fingers through his hair. "She was wrong. She saw only your strength. She was frightened of it. Some women are."

"She was ... she is ..."

"It does not matter who she was."

Dreadaeleon swallowed hard. He looked up at her. His eyes were blurred from tears.

"I ... I did ..."

"That does not matter, either." She knelt down before him. She drew him close to her. Her voice was steam in his ear; her lips were water upon his neck. "What you did, what you can do, this is not who you are. I do not need to know that. I know who you are." She stroked his hair. "I know you, my northern boy."

When she rose to her feet, she took him by the hand and led him from the basin and onto the wet floor. She drew him to the bed with the silk cushions and the perfumed sheets that lay at the other end of the room. And there, she reclined. And there, she held out her hand.

"Come, northern boy."

He did not. Not yet.

He looked at his dirty coat, slung over the side of a changing screen. He went to it and rooted around in his pocket.

"I brought you something," he said.

"A gift?" She giggled. "Oh, you didn't have to." And yet she leaned forward. "What is it?"

His fingers wrapped around something pebble-small and pebble-hard. For a moment, he felt something tell him to let it go, to tell her he had lied. But then he looked at her, at her smile, and felt how very nice it was to see her smile.

Broodvine might have been sanctioned only by the Venarium, but one could get anything in Cier'Djaal if one looked hard enough. He took the broodvine seed out and placed it in his mouth. He focused his thoughts and turned his breath to fire. It burst into smoky life in his mouth.

"Tell me what your favorite scene is," he said.

"Of what?" she asked.

"Of *To Wed and Be Bled*. What's your favorite part?"

She made a show of thinking, leaning back onto her elbows and humming. "The moment where the Emperor sends his guard away and is alone with Liaja, when all the red curtains hang silent and only the statues are left to see them."

He remembered that scene. He remembered that stage.

He closed his eyes and felt the smoke build up in his mouth. He took a deep breath and then exhaled a shimmering mist from his lips. He heard her gasp, but he didn't hear her footsteps. She wasn't running. He felt the mist shape itself around him, turned thought to reality, reality to thought.

And then he heard Liaja.

"Oh, northern boy," she whispered.

When he opened his eyes, it was all there. The red curtains emblazoned with the sigil of the old Karnerian imperial court. The statues of the mighty emperors and empresses of old. The brass braziers burning red and the great gold chandelier hanging overhead.

Her scene.

Their scene.

"How did you do this?" she asked. "What magic—"

He crawled onto her. He tried to focus on how warm she was, on how soft she was. He tried to focus on how perfect the scene was, on how expertly he created it. He tried to focus on how nice she smelled and how very tired he was.

And not on how the Venarium would have him executed if they knew about this or how many people he had killed.

He asked her nothing else. He did not ask her if she was ready as he slid between her thighs. He did not ask her if this was perfect before he entered her. He did not ask her if he was a man as he lay atop her and felt her shudder beneath him and wrap her fingers in his hair.

If she spoke, then he couldn't hear her as she closed her eyes, laid her head upon the silks and whispered his name.

"Dreadaeleon," she said, "oh, Dreadaeleon."

FORTY

THE BREATHS BETWEEN

In the moment between a sword leaving a scabbard and entering flesh, there was a very narrow window of opportunity to appreciate just how badly everything had gone.

Lenk had seen many of these moments. He had a scar for each one.

People were screaming in the Meat Market below. The bubble of humanity turned into a roiling boil, people running toward the exit and being bowled over by the Karnerians running to the square. Through a choir of screams, notes of steel sliding from scabbards rang out in excited harmony.

The floor was rattling beneath him. Boots were thudding up the steps. He rushed to the stack of crates and clambered up it, reaching for the trapdoor he had seen the Jackal sniper vanish through. It held fast against his poundings; she must have put something heavy over it.

Asshole, he thought, hopping down. He glanced at the empty crossbow next to the windowsill. *Kind of her to leave the murder weapon, though.*

The door was rattling as someone kicked at it. He looked at the sword in his hand and brought it up before him as he backed toward the windowsill. The door splintered at the hinges with another kick. He drew a deep breath, steadied himself, and prepared for whatever was going to come through.

The door swung open.

He caught a glimpse of the crossbow.

He heard the trigger click.

And suddenly, something pierced his side and sent him tumbling out of the window.

He remembered seeing an arc of his blood painted on the night sky as he fell. He remembered an explosion of light as he hit the ground. He remembered slipping into darkness.

Everything else, all the voices that followed, he knew only as dreams.

"—sent an assassin! Their words are empty as their faith! Exterminate them. All of them! DEATH TO PAGAN—"

"—planned this all along! Fuckin' Karnies! Draw steel, boys and girls! Make me proud! Kill every last fuckin' scalp you—"

"—get up. Lenk! LENK!"

Another explosion. Pain shot through him, wakening deadened senses and wrenching a scream from his throat. He saw the bolt first, clenched in a woman's hand. He saw Asper shortly after, concern drowning under fury in her stare.

"What were you doing? What the *hell* were you doing?"

"Miron," he gasped. "Miron, he's here. He's somewhere. He's someone. He can..." He tried to stagger to his feet, found his legs swaying under him. "I need to find him. I need to stop him."

He steadied himself against a wall. A shadow danced at the corner of his eye, drawing closer. He saw the steel of a spearhead, the crest of a black helmet. The Karnerian came charging across the Meat Market, spear at the ready, shield upraised.

"Stop!" Asper threw herself between Lenk and the Karnerian, holding her hands up. "There's been a mistake! *STOP!*"

His shield lashed out, caught her across the jaw, and sent her sprawling to the ground. He stepped past her and thrust the spear. It bit the stone as Lenk narrowly rolled out of the way. The Karnerian slammed his shield against him, crushing him against the wall.

His wound seared, weeping blood. His head swam and grew dim.

Sword, he barely had breath to think. *Sword. Where's the damn sword?*

Metal hissed. A body shuddered. He found it—the blade of it, anyway—jutting through the Karnerian's armor.

The Karnerian looked down at the finger of steel jutting from his belly, as though he could scarcely believe it himself. He fell to the ground in a clatter of metal, leaving only a woman with wide eyes and bloodied hands behind where he had just stood.

Asper's hands trembled as she turned horrified eyes to Lenk and all but whispered.

"What did you do?"

"Nothing," he replied.

"You said you were here to help."

"I am."

"You said you wouldn't kill."

"I didn't."

She took a step back, shaking her head, looking at her hands, looking over her shoulder as though she were just now realizing what was happening.

Even then, maybe not.

In flashes of black and blue, they clashed amidst the crowd. Karnerian spears thrust, spattering Sainite blood. Sainite bolts flew, piercing Karnerian helms. Such merciful deaths were not for the civilians. Merchants were trampled beneath sandal and boot. Servants were thrown out as shields and obstacles between soldiers and fleeing fashas. The Ancaaran envoy's life wept out on the table as he lay facedown, a hand clutched weakly around the bolt in his throat.

"There he is! Kill the assassin!"

And yet there was ample bloodlust for a quartet of Sainites to break free of the melee and rush with swords drawn toward Lenk and Asper. He could see the broad grins painting their faces, the wildness in their eyes. He half-thought they might thank him, so eager were they to be back in a real, proper war.

Something tremendous and black swept out of the crowd and leapt. It landed upon the lead Sainite with four limbs, smashing him into the stones. It rose up on his back, seized the Sainite by the legs, and drew a broken, bloodied body from the ground.

Red arms flashed from beneath his cloak as Gariath swung the Sainite corpse into his compatriots. They fell, toy soldiers scattered to the ground and buried beneath their own dead.

More emerged from the brawl, Karnerian and Sainite alike eager to prove their worth by slaying the assassin and his shadowy new companion.

But courage was a flower, something that blossomed and wilted swiftly. And Gariath was a cold snap in winter.

He shredded his cloak beneath his claws, unfurling his wings and voice as one, his roar tearing through the crowd cleaner than any sword. The soldiers fell back, bravery faltering and hiding behind blade and shield.

Gariath wanted to pursue them; Lenk could see by the twitch of his claws and muscle. And whatever it was that kept him from doing that, he was thankful for. The dragonman turned and stalked toward the two humans, tossing Lenk his sword.

"What happened?" he growled.

"Do you care?" Lenk asked, slinging his sword over his shoulder.

"No," Gariath said, "but I thought you might like the opportunity to reflect on how useless you are without me."

"Later," Lenk said. "We have to get out of here. Now."

"No." Asper's words were as hard as her stare. "We have to find Aturach and the other Talanites. We came here to help."

"Look around you," Lenk said. "What can we do to help this?"

"I don't know, moron," she snarled. "The opposite of whatever you did to start it?"

"I was set up. Miron was there, and a Jackal and—"

"I already said I don't care," Gariath snarled. "Now which is it? Are we leaving or fighting?"

Of course, had he the presence of mind to think of it, Lenk would have known that such decisions were rarely left to him.

Of this fact, he was reminded as Speaker Careus stood atop the mediation table, sword held aloft and voice booming as crossbow bolts fell like rain.

"*Wash clean this city of the unworthy! Let the unbeliever gaze upon His works and tremble!*" He pointed to a distant building. "*Brothers, speak His name and He shall be with us! Summon the Faithbreaker!*"

They had been sitting stock-still this whole time, enough to escape the notice of everyone. But at that moment, Lenk saw the white robes of the Machine Cult flutter as one of them stood up on the roof a far building. The Karnerian numeral for "one" scrawled into his scalp, he stepped to the edge of the building and held his hands out wide.

"*I AM CHOSEN!*" he shrieked, hurling himself off the edge and disappearing behind a low-slung wall.

The earth quaked. Stone, far older than that of the Meat Market's, groaned to waking life. The body of the Machine Cultist rose up over the wall, twitching and impaled upon a horn of carved marble.

All screams and sounds of battle fell silent before the explosion of rock as the nearby wall crumbled. From the rising cloud of dust stepped something tall, powerful, eyes alight with bloodred fire and earth shuddering beneath its feet.

Daeon, Lenk recognized.

He knew the face: hard and angular and curled up into a cruel frown and crowned by a pair of curling horns. He knew the body: thick with muscle, carved from stone to naked, godlike perfection. He knew this statue: he had seen it in every shrine, temple, and church dedicated to the Conqueror.

But those statues didn't move.

Blood from the impaled Cultist wept into the Faithbreaker golem's eyes as it craned its head about, surveying the battle through a red haze. From a stone throat, from an unmoving mouth, it spoke with the voice of a God.

"Death to pagans."

Commands rose from the Sainites; crossbow bolts followed, raining upon the golem from on high and below. And like raindrops, they did not so much as slow it down, clattering harmlessly from its stone flesh. It reached into the rubble of the wall and produced a heavy chunk of stone. It turned its baleful gaze skyward toward the Sainites on a nearby roof and hurled the boulder.

And so, too, did bodies fall like rain.

"Cleanse this city of the filth, brother!" Speaker Careus scowled at Lenk down the length of his blade. "Begin with their vile assassin!"

Lenk had seen many of these moments before. And he did have scars to prove it.

But as a set of red eyes settled upon him, he realized there was a moment when the sheer amount of shit a man could get himself in could be so great as to break the feeble mind that tried to comprehend it.

"Death to pagans."

That moment was now.

The crowd became a shrieking tide, desperately trying to part before the golem as it strode forward, heedless of the unfortunate crushed beneath it. It cared not for them. Nor did Lenk. He turned to run, trying to ignore the wound in his side, trying to ignore the earth shaking beneath him, trying to ignore the noise and the pain and the shadow falling over him.

Growing darker.

He threw himself to the side. When he struck the ground, he felt it shudder beneath him. He rolled onto his back in time to see the golem step through stone like a curtain. The wall of the building crumpled before its stride. Men strained to be heard above the groan of stone as the wall collapsed, chunks of rock falling like angels struck from heaven.

Lenk could do nothing but crawl and keep his head down and pray for it to be over.

And when it was, when he rose to his feet, he was not certain whether he was alive or dead.

He still drew breath and blood still wept blood from his wound. But what faced him was the nightmare he always saw when he closed his eyes.

Dust hung in the air in a great shroud, deafening the pitch of battle and blinding his eyes. But even through this, he could see the faces. Some stared up in blank, unblinking horror, wearing their last moments in their glazed eyes. Others lay half-pulped by boots and stone feet, only fragments of noses, teeth, and jaws remaining to prove they had ever been human. Fewer still moved, lips fluttering in numb prayers too soft for any God to hear.

So many of them. Every time the dust closed over one, it parted to reveal another. He could not turn away, could not shut his eyes to them or the stinging dust. He was meant to see this.

He was meant to look upon the dead and know that he had caused this.

Somehow.

The stone groaned behind him. He looked over his shoulder, up to the sky. Red eyes stared down at him, a shadow black against the cloud of dust, a voice echoing in the void.

"Death to pagans."

He was running, or doing something very like running. He clutched the wound at his side. He tried to breathe and coughed against the dust filling his nose and mouth. And he tried to ignore the golem's thunderous footsteps drawing ever closer behind him.

He saw a shadow stir at the edge of his vision, and rush toward him. Someone seized him and draped his arm around a firm shoulder, easing his weight. Asper's face was locked dead ahead as she hurried him through the cloud, looking anywhere but at him.

He wondered whom she had left behind to come for him.

An avian shriek cut through the dust, drew his eyes to the sky. Painted black against the night sky, he could see dark shapes, feathered wings, heavy armor.

"*Scraws inbound, Sergeant!*" someone shouted out.

"*Fuckin' FINALLY!*" He knew that voice. "*The area is now hot! Clear out, boys! The Karnies are about to drown in fire!*" Blacksbarrow's laughter and the scraws overhead shrieked as one. "*TASTE MY TAINT, YOU SONS OF BITCHES!*"

Fire glimmered bright red upon the evening, falling like bleeding stars cut from heaven. From the wings of the scraws, fireflasks whistled as they fell, shattered against the stone, and erupted into patches of flaming oil.

More screams cut through the square: Djaalics, Karnerians, the few Sainites who hadn't been swift enough. The shadows that had been painted black against the curtains of dust burst into bright orange pyres, flailing wildly in vain attempts to scrape the oil from their flesh. The golem strode on, unimpeded by the flames rising up around it.

"Keep moving," Asper snarled, tightening her arm around Lenk's waist, forcing him to march faster. "Don't stop. Don't look behind."

That was probably meant to be reassuring.

That would have been more reassuring if he hadn't felt the earth shaking.

His wound bled. His legs ached. His lungs burned. His eyes stung from the dust, but he dared not close them. All he had left was the sight of a distant gate, the way out, growing painstakingly larger with each agonized step.

He tripped over something: a fallen helmet, maybe with a head still in it. Asper struggled to haul him up and called him a foul name he couldn't hear above the sound of stones breaking behind them.

He looked over his shoulder. Before he saw anything else, through flame and dust, he saw the great stone hand reaching down for him, fingers outstretched and trembling.

Slowing.

Stopping.

It hung over him, a foot away from crushing him like an insect, frozen. He looked past the tremendous hand to red eyes that had gone dark. Atop its great horn, the impaled cultist, blackened by flame, sloughed off. The blood he had wept upon the golem's stone flesh flaked off and disappeared in the dust.

And Lenk understood the difference between a golem and a statue.

"He returns to slumber!" Another cultist, scalp marked with the second numeral, came running naked toward the golem. "I must wake him. I was chosen! He must live again!"

A red arm lashed out of the dust to snatch him by the throat and haul him from his feet. The cultist's eyes were still upon the golem, his hand still reaching out for the stone flesh, when Gariath's arm tensed with a snapping sound. A limp body struck the stone.

"Those bird things are coming back to drop more fire," Gariath grunted as he emerged, cuts mapping his skin. "We should go now."

"How many are dead?" Asper asked.

"Who cares?"

"Did you see any Talanites? People in blue robes like mine?"

"I see one now," he replied. "If she would like to come back later, there will be plenty of bodies to sift through."

Asper turned a look of hard appraisal upon Lenk, as if measuring him against all the bodies in that square. And whether she found him worth it, he did not want to know.

"Come on," she muttered, readjusting his weight across her shoulders and hurrying him toward the gate.

They rushed across the cobblestones, heading for the gate leading out, stepping over the bodies. Lenk counted them as they went. One eye, staring up glassily as dust settled upon it. One arm still twitching, reaching out from beneath a stone. A mass of blackened skin and tar that had once been a man, trying to pull itself across the stones. One after the other after another.

Until he finally closed his eyes.

FORTY-ONE

SHICT

There were no fires that night in Shicttown.

One would know it was a village only if one had been there to see it before. No shict walked its sands. No yijis bayed at the moon. No fires were burning, no songs being sung. Many tents had been rolled up and carted away. Only a few remained, standing silent and dark in the night.

Kataria walked between the tents that still remained, the crunching of her boots upon the sand the only sound in the night. No one had come to greet her when she arrived. No one had come to speak to her since. Occasionally, she thought she caught a glimpse of shadows moving at the edges of her vision. Frequently, she felt eyes settle upon her and follow her between the tents.

She didn't call out. A shict wouldn't call out.

She closed her eyes. Her ears went spear-straight. Concentrating, she reached inside her and touched the Howling, held her breath, and waited for a reply.

In the long dark of the Howling, she could hear sounds: growling, mutters, whispers. But these were not words. And they were not for her to hear. No voice reached out to acknowledge her.

But there were people here. There were shicts here. She knew that now, even if they didn't know her.

Eyes shut, ears twitching, she followed the susurrus through the

Howling. It guided her around tents, over extinguished firepits, across the sand until she heard the sound of scratching.

She opened her eyes. A yiji, two heads taller than the three shicts gathered around it, buried its canine snout into the sand. Its paws worked dutifully, excavating a small hole. One of the shicts beside it muttered a command and stroked the beast's mane. It giggled excitedly, stepping away from the hole and settling down upon its haunches.

Through the moonlight, Kataria recognized two of the shicts closest to the hole as the two that had accompanied Kwar to Ghoukha's house. They proceeded to toss bulging sacks into the hole, coins jingling beneath the burlap. One of them spoke a command to the yiji, who eagerly leapt up and began kicking its back legs, burying the bags beneath the sand.

"What's going on?" Kataria asked. "Where is everyone?"

The khoshicts acknowledged her with nothing more than a glance. They looked far more interested in the yiji as it filled the rest of the hole, sniffed briefly, raised its leg, and urinated over it. The two shicts began to stamp down the sodden earth, packing it tightly over the bags.

The third shict, also familiar, however, kept a cool gaze firmly on her.

"East," Thua answered.

She cocked a brow. "What for?"

"Those who cannot hold a bow have gone with the yijis and however many hunters needed to protect them." He looked long over the distant walls to the rising moon. "They will meet the Seventh Tribe in the desert and stay there."

"For how long?"

"Riffid knows. I do not." Thua said softly. "I do not know what humans will do when they are panicked. The last time, they burned our homes to the ground, they stole everything we owned that glittered, and they took my..."

He held his voice within a stilled breath. He closed his eyes.

"They are like any other animal. We tread lightly when they have the scent of blood." He gestured to the camp. "If they come to burn, they will find our fires cold. He gestured to the hole. "If they come to rob, they will find nothing. And if they try to kill us, anyway..."

Thua's ears flickered in time with hers. They heard the same thing through the Howling—a warning growl, the baring of teeth. Their eyes were drawn up to the black windows of the long-vacant buildings surrounding Shicttown. Arrowheads glinted silver in the moonlight; wooden masks peered out as pale, empty faces staring down.

"If this is because of what happened at the fasha's house," Kataria said, "I don't think they'd come here. They have no reason to."

"There are twenty of them for every one of us and each one of them is panicked and terrified. They do not need more reason."

"But why would they blame the shicts?"

Thua's eyes sharpened to thin blades. He grunted something at the other two khoshicts. They nodded, collected their remaining bags, and left, the yiji panting after them as they did. As soon as they were gone, Thua's ears flattened against his skull as he swept forward, a hairbreadth away from Kataria.

"How long have you listened to Kwar?" he growled, teeth clenched. "Do you believe her when she calls me a coward? An idiot?"

She said nothing that could not be said with the flattening of her own ears, the narrowing of her own eyes, the firm plant of her feet as she stood before him, arms folded and canines bared.

"There are *humans* out there," he snarled. "They have steel, they have fire, and there are *thousands* of them. They do not speak our tongue, so we speak theirs, and Kwar would call me a coward for doing so to keep our tribe safe.

"I know where this gold came from." He stomped on the sodden earth. "I know you were with her last night. She came home looking as she did when our mother died. Each time she goes out with her knife, she is looking for our mother. But our mother is dead, so she looks where death walks."

His hands fell to his sides and trembled into fists. It struck Kataria, then, how utterly petulant the gesture seemed with arms as big and strong as his.

"Is it any wonder, then," he said balefully, "that she found *you*?"

Kataria lowered her arms to her sides, inhaled sharply. She leaned forward and let the heat of her breath wash over Thua's face.

"Say what you want to say," she said, "hit me if you want to hit me. Then turn around, walk away, and never look back."

His flinch was minor, but all too visible. His eyes softened, his lips eased, and the tips of his ears quivered.

"I try to be like my father," he said. "I try to understand the humans. But you, I think, understand them too well." He snorted. "You want to find Kwar, I won't stop you. But if you are at all grateful to her, to my tribe, say what you will to her and then go back to the round-ears."

He turned too swiftly to convince her he was walking away of his own choice. His back was too rigid to convince her he was standing tall. And his hands still trembled, still looked so small at the end of his arms.

He had looked so very big when she first saw him him. He looked so stern, so serious. And now he looked so very worried, so very scared.

So very unlike Kwar, she thought.

It would probably be poor etiquette to chase after him and ask her where his sister *was*, of course. But then, it hadn't been the brightest of ideas to come to Shicttown in the first place.

She was already late, she knew. Lenk had told her to meet him and the others at some place in the city ages ago. And, of course, she had set out fully intending to do so.

Of course.

And as she walked to the place—this "Meat Market"—she had fully intended to try to keep her step steady, despite the night she had spent thinking instead of sleeping. That humans had died hadn't bothered her; none of them had been hers. That humans had died in great numbers hadn't bothered her; there were always more, after all.

Numbers hadn't kept her from sleeping. Numbers didn't bother her.

Names did. Specifically, her name.

Repeated over and over, hour after hour, echoing off of itself so many times she no longer remembered it as a word. Merely as a voice.

Kwar's voice, as fevered and frantic as it had been when the fire fell between them, had never left her through last night. Between every thought like a desperate comma in a slow poem, it had been there. She had heard it every time she closed her eyes. She had heard it when she set out to meet Lenk and the others. She had heard it when her feet had inexplicably turned her toward Shicttown.

And she heard it now, as it spoke to her across the Howling.

No longer a name, no longer a word. Now it was entirely Kwar's voice, speaking so soft and so close that it could be a language with a single word meant for a single person.

And she followed it here, to the flap of a modest tent rimmed with the light of a fire burning inside.

She ran a finger down the fabric of the flap, warm to the touch. She hadn't realized how cold it got in this part of the city.

Maybe Lenk was thinking how cold it was right now.

Lenk. You're supposed to be back there. You should go there now. Her feet steadfastly ignored her thoughts, however. *All right, just go in, show her you survived, and then leave. Lenk needs you. They all do. They're helpless without you.*

She drew in a deep breath.

In. Out.

She let it out.

Right?

That thought, like so many others, went unanswered as she pulled back the tent flap and entered.

Kwar sat on a yiji-hide mat, staring into the dying remains of a fire. She wore the shadows like war paint, black streaked across her dark skin, eyes bright against the gloom. She did not look up as Kataria entered.

But Kataria knew she had the khoshict's full attention. Her ears were trembling, sending out into the Howling, searching for answers. But as Kataria drew closer, their seizure slowed with each step until they finally lay still against Kwar's head.

Kataria sat upon a mat on the other side of the fire. Only then did the sound of the Howling stop; only then did a silence fill Kataria's ears. And that silence hung between them, cooking over the sighs and sputters of the flames, just long enough for Kataria to start thinking again.

Say something. In. Out. Remember.

"So," she said, "you didn't die."

Nice.

"I didn't," Kwar replied. The omnipresent boast that edged her voice was dull now, leaving her voice something softer.

Kataria nodded, staring into the fire. "I didn't, either."

Very nice.

"I see that."

Okay, then. Good enough. Let's get out of here.

And Kataria made to rise and do just that when a log crumbled into ash and the shadows shifted across Kwar's face. And there, Kataria saw it. Beneath the dark laid the same fear, the same quiver, the same weakness that had been on Thua's.

And yet, where Thua wore his fear like a mask, she wore hers like a wound: something lasting that she bled into the fire.

"Are you all right?" Kataria asked.

"I'm fine," Kwar said. "You can go now."

"I don't need to."

What?

"You should," Kwar said. "There'll be trouble soon."

She's right.

"There's always trouble," Kataria replied. "It'll wait until later."

It won't.

She knew this thought to be true, but only for a moment. Once Kwar looked up from the fire, across to Kataria, she knew only those eyes staring through the shadows.

"That's it?" Kwar asked flatly.

"That's what?"

"You disappear behind a wall of fire, then come ambling back to tell me it was all okay the whole time?"

"I...thought you knew. Or would have known, anyway. I do this sort of thing a lot."

"How would I know that?" The edge began to return to Kwar's voice. Her posture stiffened. "I know barely anything about you except that you're not like anyone here in Shicttown. And before I could know any more, you disappeared." Each word came with a flash of sharp canine. "Too many people have done that to me."

"I didn't mean to—"

"And *nobody* has seen me like *this*!"

Kwar all but roared as she leapt to her feet, and Kataria found herself scrambling to hers from sheer instinct. Kwar's muscles tensed beneath exposed skin, her entire body trembling, her eyes flashing like a wild animal's.

"I didn't sleep," she said, slowly approaching Kataria around the fire. "I didn't eat. I didn't talk to Thua, but he looked at me and he knew and I *hate* that he knew. I *hate* that he can still do that to me."

Kataria was tempted to take a step backward as Kwar approached. She felt her own body trembling, the fire suddenly not warm enough to ward off the chill that had entered the tent. She was aware of the fire in Kwar's eyes, the curl of her lip exposing bared teeth, the slinking stride that brought her ever closer to Kataria.

She felt the urge to turn and run.

She did not know why she didn't.

"I know you don't get along with your brother," Kataria said, "but that's got nothing to do with me."

"It does. But it shouldn't," Kwar said. "It's not that I don't get along with Thua. It's that I don't *get* Thua. I haven't understood him, my father, or anyone in this camp for years and I was *fine* with that up until you came along and things were..." She shook her head, rubbed her temples. "And you said words about Lenk, and then you disappeared and...and..."

Her head snapped up at Kataria suddenly. The last remnants of the fire lit her eyes wild. Her nostrils flared with each breath, and with each breath she only seemed to grow more tense, more angry.

And Kataria felt herself reflect that tension. Her hands tightened into fists and her jaw clenched, as if anticipating a punch. Her ears flattened and the silence between them grew loud.

"Well?" she asked.

And Kwar's hands were up, about her throat, fingers against her jaw. And Kwar's leg was forward, pulling her closer. And Kwar's eyes were closed, Kwar's lips were on hers, Kwar's scent was in her nostrils.

And the silence between them was no longer so vast.

Just as suddenly, Kwar released her, stepping away. She swallowed hard, breath disappearing into a body held taut as a bowstring. All the fear that Kataria had seen still flashed in Kwar's eyes, but it grew smaller each moment, vanishing behind something brighter, something bolder.

A challenge.

Kataria's ears were ringing. Her head felt very heavy and she rubbed the back of her neck to see if her skull was as thin as it suddenly felt. She swallowed hard and tasted Kwar's dusky scent upon her lips. She looked up and saw Kwar turning away, eyes downcast.

She saw Kwar walking away. She felt her own hand on Kwar's shoulder, turning her about, sliding behind her neck, drawing her closer until she tasted her once more.

She felt long, thin arms wrap around her torso, hands clasping her about her waist. She felt a handful of Kwar's thick braids between her fingers and the airy sensation of the sand slipping beneath her feet as she and the khoshict fell to the hide mats in a tangle of limbs.

Leg crossed over leg, hands grasped hands until she rose up atop Kwar, straddling her waist and staring down at her. And from down on the mat, sand clinging to her bare skin, the woman who had looked so strong when Kataria had met her now looked up at her, wide-eyed and breathless.

"So," she said, "are you . . ."

She let the question hang. Kataria did not know the answer. She smiled, shrugged. This was enough. The familiar grin returned to Kwar's face, impish and alight, as her fingers entwined with Kataria's.

Kwar's legs rose up behind her, gave her the momentum to send the two tumbling across the mats until they bumped against one of the tent's support poles. The khoshict rose atop Kataria now, her grin full of teeth, her eyes full of fire as she slid her fingers from Kataria's fingers to Kataria's wrists.

The breath left her as Kwar pressed them against the floor, leaned over, and let her braids brush against Kataria's cheek.

"What are you doing?"

What are you *doing,* she asked herself. *You shouldn't be here. You shouldn't be with . . . you should be with . . . you should . . .*

It was hard to think. Too hard to remember names.

Kwar's reply was a flash of skin that became a slither. She laid a palm upon Kataria's naked flank and drew her hand down the pale flesh slowly; each finger felt upon each rib until they swept across her belly and drummed upon the buckle of her belt.

"Trust me," Kwar whispered.

There was an urge not to, an urge that made Kataria squirm beneath the khoshict's legs, that made her grit her teeth as the sound of her belt sliding free of her breeches filled her ears. But never to cry out, never to resist as Kwar guided her hands behind the tent's support pole and deftly bound them together with her belt.

For a moment, she counted: breaths leaving her body, droplets of sweat sliding into the hollow of her collarbone, fingers clenching and unclenching against her bonds, braids dropping into her face as Kwar lowered herself closer.

And then, she felt her ears fill with her own breathless gasp.

Kwar's lips found a tender strand of flesh upon her neck. Kwar's teeth gripped it gently, bit down just enough to make her cry out. Kwar's tongue found the sweat in her collarbone, the tension down the centerline of her belly, the fine hairs rising in a halo about her navel. And Kwar's fingers found the waist of her breeches, pulling them free from her hips.

Kataria counted the kisses. One beneath her navel, again above her sex, and the third...

Her head fell back, too heavy to support. Her eyes snapped shut, the tent unbearably bright. She arched her spine, her hips steadied by Kwar's hands as her tongue slid between her thighs and spoke a language meant for her alone.

And through the sound of her breathless gasps, and through the sound of Kwar's lips upon her skin, and through the sound of a very loud silence, she could hear but one sound.

One voice.

Speaking one word, over and over.

FORTY-TWO

THE COMMON COLLECTORS OF MAN

When Dransun signed up for the Jhouche guard, they had given him boots. He had hoarded what little gold the city paid him to buy polish and new laces and to resole them when constant patrols had worn them enough to earn him a promotion.

When Dransun was made sergeant, they had given him a helmet. A meager pay raise earned him enough to have a smith to hammer out the dents that rioters had put in his helmet and to hire a Gevrauchian to bury those guards without helmets somewhere nice.

And when Dransun was made captain, they had given him a sword and a flask, because he would never need one and not the other so long as he stood guard for the City of Silk.

Never once in all his years had they given him an oath to read. Never once had they given him allegiance to swear. Never once had the city asked anything more of him than the skin to fill those nice boots.

It didn't take much more than that to be a guard in Cier'Djaal.

"But it fucking ought to," he snarled from beneath his helmet. "If I had my way, the only way you'd be getting past me is in a corpsewagon as the Gevrauchians haul you out to a charnel house."

The guards before him were not looking at his eyes. They were looking at his shiny boots, his undented helmet, or at the great archway leading out of the city that he currently stood under. He stood there, arms folded and glowering, as he had stood for the past half hour. And not one of his boys had looked him in the eye since.

"Come on, Captain, don't say that," one of them finally spoke. "We *want* to stay and help, but..."

"But what?" Dransun asked. "You could do it well enough when the city gave you gold and wine."

"Gold and wine were all we needed to deal with pickpockets and bar drunks, Captain," another of them offered. "What are we supposed to use against the Karnerians and Sainites?"

Dransun winced, stung. "You can't leave," he said. "I can't hold this city without help."

"Then come with us, Captain," another guard said. "The foreigners are tearing this place apart. It won't be here by next week! My father has a rice field outside the city and my family's already ridden off to see him. We've got room there. You could stay with us."

Dransun's eyes began to water. He sniffed and looked away to wipe the tears. He suspected that might be a more dramatic gesture if everyone else weren't also doing it.

Smoke hung heavy in the air. Another fire had broken out somewhere nearby. Possibly the Karnerians and Sainites. Possibly the Jackals and the Khovura. Possibly looters taking advantage of the chaos.

Duty called.

"Don't expect any fucking jobs when you come back," Dransun snarled.

He pushed his way past the small throng of his guards. Even as he left, they could not bring themselves to look at him. Even when he looked over his shoulder to see them joining the convoy of people fleeing the city with their belongings stacked on wagons and backs, they didn't look back at him.

Pity, he thought. The next time they looked behind there might not be a city left to see.

Broken glass and bloodstains greeted him as he turned the corner. Karnerian steel had shattered the glass, Sainite steel had spilled the blood, and Djaalic bodies had been left in the wake.

A naked corpse lay before him—likely a merchant. No sensible looter bothered stripping a poor man's corpse. Whoever had come after the fight was over had taken everything from the man save for the crossbow bolt in his chest.

Dransun wondered what this man had been doing when the fighting broke out between the foreigners. Fleeing, probably. Maybe trying to keep their battle from spilling into his home, if this was his home.

How many ways could someone be crushed between the foreigners, Dransun wondered. How many more would he find today?

"Hello, Captain," a familiar voice came. "Are you well today?"

The Quill approached quietly from a nearby alley, sparing not so much as a glance for Dransun as he leaned down, took the corpse by the ankles, and began dragging it away.

"Not well, Gevrauchian," Dransun asked. "Where are you taking him?"

"To join the others."

"He might have family nearby. We should wait."

"He does, Captain. I am taking him to them."

How a man could sound so unimpressed by death, Dransun suspected he would never know. Maybe Gevrauchians became inured to it over time. Or maybe they were just born that way and that's how they were chosen to serve the Bookkeeper.

Or maybe this was the only job these particular freaks could get.

Still, as freaks went, Dransun was fond enough of this one to follow him into the alley, carefully checking for anyone who might be following.

"It's not safe to be out here, priest," Dransun said. "The foreigners are at each other's throats. Thieves and looters are picking at the corpses they leave behind. I sent a couple boys to Shicttown to make sure everything was in order and I haven't heard back from them. If the oids start—"

"It was never safe, Captain," the Quill interrupted. "It is merely less safe now. There have always been thieves, foreigners, and shicts. There always will be."

They emerged from the other side of the alley and into a small square of shops. Their windows had been shattered and lay upon the cobblestones like leaves fallen from trees. Crossbow bolts kissed the wooden walls, reached out with broken hafts and heads. Smoke crept in shyly over the roofs to settle as gray eaves over the square.

Like a meadow, Dransun thought. Or at least, what he thought meadows looked like from the poems he had read; he had never gone far enough outside the city to see one. The square had been devastated, but there was a certain tranquility in the wake of destruction. There was nothing more to destroy.

It was almost peaceful.

And if he were *really* drunk, he might have been able to pretend that those bodies stacked around the corpsewagon at the center were just sleeping.

The Quill let the dead man fall amidst the others: a woman, a young girl, a younger boy. The Gevrauchian took a moment to raise his burlap mask long enough to mop sweat from his throat before leaning down and attempting to drag one of the bodies into his wagon.

"What happened to the Lanterns?" Dransun asked.

"They have fled," the Quill replied between grunts. "We discussed it at length last night. I urged them to do so."

"What? Why would you do that?"

"It was the will of Gevrauch."

The Quill gasped as he finally pushed the dead man into the corpsewagon. After pausing a moment to catch his breath, he attempted to throw the wife in after him.

"Horseshit," Dransun spat. "I don't know much about the Bookkeeper, but he wouldn't will his followers to abandon a city in need."

"That was not His will, no," the Quill grunted. The woman's dead weight, after loading her husband, seemed too much for his skinny arms.

"Then what was it?"

The Quill muttered as the corpse slipped from his grasp and

pooled in a pile of limbs and lolling head at the wheels of the corpse-wagon. The Gevrauchian fixed his glassy stare upon Dransun.

"Gods do not merely decide to will one thing or another, Captain," he said. "They simply will. One does not choose to disobey it at their leisure, regardless of soldiers or swords. Gevrauch's will is that we fulfill our promise to Him until we, too, are put into the books." He leaned down and took the corpse by the wrists. "One obeys the will or one does not. Those that did not are no longer His concern."

The Quill began to pull at the corpse's wrists again. He strained as he tried to haul the body up to the lip of the wagon. With a sigh, Dransun stepped forward, took the ankles, and helped him roll it up and over. He peered into the corpsewagon and cringed at the sight of flesh before him.

"How many have you found?" he asked.

"Many," the Quill replied.

"How many will you take?"

"As many as He will."

Dransun sighed and pulled his flask free from his boot. "Need some help?"

The Quill regarded him through the glass circles of his mask. "Are you offering whiskey or labor, Captain?"

Dransun uncorked the flask, took a long sip, and wiped his mouth with his sleeve before offering it to the Quill. "Yes."

The Gevrauchian accepted the flask and peeled his mask up to take a swig. The liquor dribbled down his chin and spattered upon the cheek of the dead boy at his feet. Dransun winced and knelt down to clean it from the pallid flesh.

"Gevrauch will not turn them away, Captain," the Quill said, replacing his mask. "This is unnecessary."

"Night like tonight, everything's necessary," Dransun muttered. Something moved at the corner of his eye. He was on his feet, sword in his hand and leveled at the mouth of the alley. "This isn't the meat you're looking for, vulture. Room in the wagon if you're looking for blood."

"Easy, friend." The man came out of the shadows slowly and steadily, hands held before him and smile on his face. His northern face. "I've seen all the blood I can handle for one night; I'm just looking for a way to avoid adding my own to it."

"Good luck with that, *shkainai*," Dransun muttered. "Your kinsmen were fighting in every district, last I checked." He squinted. "I've seen you here before."

"You have not," the man replied smoothly. "And they're not my kinsmen. I'm from Muraska."

Dransun could believe that. The man had that stubble-cheeked, hungry-looking alcoholic look that the northerners shared. He snorted and slowly lowered his blade.

"You can try Temple Row," the captain muttered. "The Talanites might be taking refugees. Wouldn't bother with the Ancaarans. Locked up tight after tonight's shitshow."

"As you say. I'll be sure to—"

"If I were you, though, I'd run for the gate. Or a ship, if they haven't all left by now. Once the foreigners drink their fill of each other's blood, they'll be ripping this city apart for the assassin." Dransun eyed the man carefully. "He was northern, too."

"Not every pale face is a northerner," the man said with a sneer.

"Maybe. But this one was. Had a head full of hair like an old man, they say." He glanced at the northerner's dirty locks. "You might not, but if they don't find him…" He sniffed. "They might not care what pale face they find."

Dransun squinted through the smoke. Something about this northerner was hard to make out, and Dransun had seen enough thieves and liars to know when it was by design. There was hair where there shouldn't be, dirt where flesh was used to being freshly scrubbed, and the eyes were more sunken, but…

"I *know* I've seen you before," Dransun said, raising his sword once again.

The man backed away for the first two steps, turned, and broke out into a sprint for the rest. Dransun moved to give chase but stumbled over something. He glanced down. The dead girl's glassy eyes looked up at him, her head lolling right next to his boot.

There was a bloodstain on the toe, he noted.

He'd have to polish them after he was done here.

"All right," Dransun sighed, leaning down to take her arms. "Lift with your knees, priest."

— ◆ —

Now, admittedly, that *hadn't* looked like the action of a man with nothing to hide. Men with nothing to hide didn't go running away when a guard started asking questions. And men *with* something to hide, the ones who were good at it, anyway, didn't run for ten city blocks before stopping to catch their breath beside a shady-looking building with shattered windows.

He looked up at the sign overhead. Barely legible through the soot, the image of two rodents copulating atop a beer keg marked The Rutting Rat swung squeaky on its hinges. This place hadn't even been respectable *before* it was looted.

Desperate circumstances, he told himself. *Desperate men adhere to desperate logic in desperate circumstances.*

He looked at the night sky. The feathery wings of a flock of scraws flapped in the darkness, painted orange by the illumination of rising flames. Their riders haphazardly hurled fireflasks over the sides, clearly too far up to hear the agony of those being burned alive below.

Denaos, however, was close enough to hear them just fine.

The scraws shrieked, wheeling overhead and flying in his direction. He wasted no time in crawling through the broken window, careful to avoid the shards of glass. He stepped lightly over the smashed barrels and broken chairs, and *very* lightly over the dead body at the foot of the stairs.

The inn's second upper looked no better. The banister had been broken and a dead Sainite lay sprawled in the hallway. Perhaps he had been sleeping here and the Karnerians drinking downstairs when the fighting had broken out. The looters had come afterward, tossing the rooms whose doors now lay open.

And to think it's only been three hours since the Meat Market inci-dent, he thought. *Say what you want about their cooking, but don't disparage the Djaalic's efficiency when it comes to rioting. Ha. That's funny. Laugh.*

He crept to the end of the hall.

You're not laughing.

He knocked lightly on the one door that was shut tight.

Wasn't that funny, anyway, I guess.

"Who is it?" a muffled voice demanded from the other side.

"Me," Denaos replied.

"What's the password?"

"I'm not saying it. You knew I was coming back and you can hear my voice. It's me, Gods damn it; now let me in."

No reply came from the door. He sighed, rested his head against it.

"Flowers in springtime," he said. "Pretty, pretty motherfucking posies."

There was the sound of several large and heavy things shoved aside from the door. It creaked open just enough for Asper to peer out at him, then just enough to let him see her glare.

"The swearing was unnecessary," she said.

"So was the password." He shoved his way in and slammed the door shut behind him. Asper was already shoving furniture in front of it.

"Were you followed?" she grunted, struggling with a heavy dresser.

"Saw a few patrols," Denaos replied as he moved to help her. "The Karnerians and Sainites only have eyes for each other, though, and this place was already hit before we got here. They won't be back."

"How can you be sure?" she asked. "We were there, Denaos; Gar-iath, Lenk, and I. And the three of *us* running through the streets aren't exactly inconspicuous."

"Which is why you were lucky I found you when I did," he replied as the dresser slid into place. "I know this city. I know its streets. And I wound us through enough of them that a Gods-damned jackal—quadrupedal or otherwise—couldn't track us."

He turned and had gotten two steps before he saw Kataria. The shict perched upon the windowsill, idly chewing a strip of dried meat. She raised a hand in greeting and spoke through a full mouth.

"Hey."

"When the hell did you get here?" he demanded.

She shrugged. "Little after you left, I think?"

"How'd you find this place?"

"You're not that hard to track."

"And just where the hell have you been this whole time?"

She stopped chewing. Her eyes grew hard as she swallowed. "Somewhere else."

"Where—"

"I'm here now, aren't I?" she snarled. She bit off another mouthful of meat and cast a glare to the corner of the room. "I know I *shouldn't* be surprised that things turned out like this in my absence. Still…"

Lenk met her scowl with one of his own. Or at least, it started as a glare before turning to a wince as he touched the bandages around his midriff. Whatever he might have said became a groan as he hauled himself to his feet and reached for his tunic.

"How's it look out there?" he asked.

"A little better than in here," Denaos said. "The Karnerians and Sainites are fighting in every district. Looters are roving in their wake; petty thieves and lesser gangs are using the battle as a cover to settle old scores." He clicked his tongue. "Wait here and I'll go see if I can find an artist to paint you a picture. I think I saw one writing on the wall in feces as I came in here."

"That's hilarious." Lenk pulled his shirt over his head. "You're hilarious. I swear as soon as I think it won't open my wound again that I'll start laughing." He fixed a sneer upon the tall man. "Once more, except without the bit where you're an asshole."

"What the hell do you want me to tell you, Lenk?" Denaos threw up his hands. "It's a fucking *war* out there and everyone knows you started it."

Lenk's face fell, leaving something white and shocked behind. "Everyone?"

"The Jhouche know, Lenk. In Cier'Djaal, the guards are the last to know anything."

Lenk's eyes turned to the floor, legs following as he collapsed back against the wall. He buried his head in his hands. His breath came out in a thin, airy sigh. The desperation in his eyes shifted to disbelief, as though he wished he could tear himself out of this reality as easily as he tore the hair out of his scalp.

"How?" he asked the floor. "How did this happen?" Upon receiving no answer, he looked up at the faces around him. "How the *fuck* did this happen?"

Well, it's really quite simple. See, the principle of distraction works as thus: when you are losing a fight and losing it badly—as my dear friends in the Jackals were—it often makes sense to point somewhere else and scream "Look over there!" and hope that your enemies—in this case, the Khovura—look and are suitably distracted by whatever you happen to point at—a massive war tearing the city apart, as it were— while you turn tail and run.

All reasonable logic, Denaos thought.

That wouldn't concern you, of course. But I imagine "wrong place, wrong time" wouldn't be of any better consolation.

But reasonable logic was for honest men, not desperate men. Desperate men stood quietly, said nothing, and tried to ignore the teary desperation of their good friends.

That sounded no less reasonable to him.

"Are you really so stupid as to be surprised?"

Denaos thought he could be forgiven for not noticing Gariath squatting and hunched in the corner. Among all the devastation he had seen today, a seven-foot hulk of scarred meat and anger just sort of blended in. Yet as the dragonman rose up and stalked forward, he demanded attention.

"How long have we known each other now?" Gariath rumbled.

"How long have I been proving myself right? How much longer are you going to keep from listening to me?"

Desperation faded from Lenk's face, replaced by irritation as he glared upward. "For all that I've listened to you, all I know is that you choose the absolute *worst* times to gloat. Did you have a point?"

"Look around you." Gariath swept his arms about the room. "Look out the window. This city is diseased. It eats itself alive. I could smell it; I *told* you, but you didn't listen. This happened because you were too stupid not to walk away from it."

"So that's it? Humans are just doomed? I was going to end up like this, anyway, just because I wanted stop killing?" Lenk rose to meet the dragonman, stared up into his black eyes. "Is that the only reason you hang around? To gloat when everything goes wrong?"

"No." Gariath said nothing more than that and his posture challenged Lenk to ask.

"This isn't helping." Asper shoved her way between the two. "Neither is staying holed up here. We need to do something."

"To do that, we need to get through the streets," Denaos replied. "A boy who could spit lightning and shit fire would be *extremely* handy for that."

Asper shot him a scowl. "Dreadaeleon isn't here. We'll think of something else."

"There is a way," Lenk said. "I know someone who can help." He looked to Denaos. "Can you get us to Silktown?"

"Won't be easy," Denaos replied. "They've probably got their guards patrolling, keeping the rabble out. Maybe a few dragonmen to keep the foreigners out, as well." He shrugged. "But...there are ways."

"I'm *not* leaving," Asper interjected. "I can't. Not when we're responsible for this."

"We *aren't*," Lenk snapped.

"No." She turned her scowl on him. "Not all of us."

"Fine, then!" He threw his hands up. "*I'll* get out. Do whatever the hell you want; I can't be here with an entire city hunting me."

She sighed, rubbing her eyes. "Agreed. But where do you think you can go?"

"I don't know. *I don't know.*" He leaned against the wall, looking very heavy. "Maybe I can find another town somewhere. Start over." He sniffed. "Again."

"With more people?" Gariath growled. "More humans?"

"Where else would I go?"

The dragonman stared at him as though this were substantially more stupid than usual. "Anywhere. Anywhere in this world, you could go. Any town, any city, any country infested by your breed." He tapped two claws to his chest. "Where do *I* go?"

"Gariath..." Asper placed a hand on the dragonman's shoulder and withdrew it as soon as he scowled at her.

"I've shed my blood protecting your worthless, weak body." Gariath turned his glare back to Lenk. "I've broken bones to keep you from dying. Every time you sat and gorged yourself on pity, I was out fighting, bleeding, killing." He jabbed Lenk hard in the chest with a single claw, pressing him against the wall. "Now that it's all done, you want to go somewhere else? Where do *I* go?"

"I don't know," Lenk replied.

"What was all that blood for? Why did I spill it?"

"Because you wanted to and it was useful."

"Useful? Is that what I am?" Gariath stepped closer to Lenk, shoving Asper aside. He looked down his snout at the young man and spoke through clenched fangs. "What am I to you?"

Lenk made no answer and moved to step past the dragonman. A red arm caught him by the shoulder and shoved him against the wall.

"Say it," Gariath snarled.

"No," Lenk spat, two hands needed to shove off Gariath's one.

"Say it. Say that word."

"*No.*"

"*SAY IT.*"

He didn't wait for an answer. He seized Lenk by the neck, lifted him off the ground with one hand, and smashed him against the wall.

"SAY IT! SAY OID! SAY IT!"

His roar shook the floorboards, though not quite as badly as Lenk's body did when he turned and hurled the young man across the room. Denaos, reasonable as ever, resisted the urge to follow Asper as she rushed forward and was promptly swatted aside as Gariath stalked toward Lenk.

Denaos knew he couldn't stop this.

A bowstring creaked. An arrow whistled. The dragonman howled in pain.

Kataria, on the other hand...

Gariath whirled on her. She already had an arrow drawn and aimed just a few fingers above the one lodged in his shoulder. No anger was on her face, no emotion at all. And when she spoke, every word was a promise.

"You take one more step, I put this in your eye," she said.

"You shouldn't have stopped me," Gariath rumbled.

"You were going to kill him."

He laughed blackly. "And if I did?" The smile he turned on her was something dark and unpleasant. "How do you think they look at you? What do you think they call you? How long is it going to be before he"—he made a gesture at Lenk—"starts calling you that?" He snorted. "Longer for you, maybe. You look like them, except for the ears. You even *smell* like them. But this moment came. So will that one."

He pulled the arrow out of his flesh and snapped it. Blood oozed from the wound.

"If I kill them," he said, "if I kill them all, what would be lost but that moment?"

It was funny, Denaos thought. He had often wondered how the world looked through Gariath's eyes. When they had first met, he suspected the dragonman often saw everyone as walking pot roasts. As they had grown to know—and loathe—each other, he had been forced to admit that Gariath's view of humanity was rather impossibly complex.

But still, as Gariath looked around the room, as he saw the horror in Asper's face when she took a step away, as he saw Kataria's arrow trembling as she drew it upon him, as he saw Lenk look up through an eye shut against the trickle of blood from his temple, Denaos wondered if the dragonman saw the same thing he did.

Three people utterly terrified of a monster who could rip them apart without a thought.

"If you can't cure yourselves," Gariath said, soft as a voice like his possibly could be, "then I will."

He turned and stalked toward the door, pausing to leer at Denaos, sniffing as though he could smell the lies hidden behind his lips. The rogue held up his hands and backed away.

Gariath snorted, seized the furniture stacked against the door, and hurled it over his head with scarcely any effort or thought. The companions scattered, trying to avoid being hit by a flying dresser, chair, or bed.

By the time any of them looked up, the door swung half-torn off its hinges. The scent of smoke and blood wafted in.

"Well, okay, then," Denaos said, clapping his hands together. "Silktown, was it?"

Asper shook her head at him. "You go. I need to get to Temple Row."

"It's going to be carnage out there. What the hell do you need to go there for?"

She smiled sadly at him. "We both know why."

In truth, he didn't. But this felt like the sort of thing he just shouldn't ask about. Questions, after all, were something he was trying to avoid tonight.

"I'll head out now," she said. "I know my way around enough to get there."

"Not unharmed, you don't." Denaos sighed. "I'll take you, then come back for the rest of the rabble." He glanced at Kataria. "You can handle things here, can't you?"

She nodded, taking another bite of her strip of dried meat. He squinted; for a moment, he felt compelled to ask where she had found it.

You know better than that, he scolded himself as he swept out the door on Asper's heels.

⊶ ⊷

The great thing about head wounds, Kataria thought, was that it tended to keep people quiet.

Lenk's record for silence post–getting bashed in the skull was two hours. So far, he had only remained silent, lying on the ground and staring up quietly at the ceiling for a half hour, but that was acceptable.

They both had a lot to think about.

Not that there weren't distractions still. Her ears picked up the sounds of the carnage in the streets: glass breaking two city blocks away, spears slamming against shields as Karnerian marched through the streets three blocks south, a woman whimpering softly in the alley next to the building next to this as a gruff voice bade her to be silent…

But Kataria didn't dwell on these. Even if she couldn't ignore them completely, she had greater matters on her mind.

I can't go with you.

She had been rehearsing for all this time, running the words she'd say to him through her head. She had tried a few versions, discarded most, but they always began with those five words.

And I can't tell you why, because I don't know why and you don't need to know. I don't know where I'm supposed to be in this world. I don't think I've known since I was born. And I was fine with you when it seemed like you didn't, either. But now, you want to belong to somewhere I can't and I…I want to find out if I belong somewhere else. With someone else.

And it always ended with these five.

I'm sorry. Be safe. Good-bye.

There, she decided; that was as good as it was ever going to get. All she had to do was say it to him. Now, while he was still silent, while he was still on his back and bleeding from his head and wondering what had happened. Then she could leave before he figured it out, let Denaos take him wherever he needed to go while she went back to Kwar and they could just keep on walking in opposite directions.

Right. So just say it.

She shifted on her haunches.

Now.

She rubbed the back of her neck.

Okay... now. Now.

Her ears twitched. Her mouth tasted dry as she opened it.

"Right before noon, at the Harbor Gate, right before you had to tell me."

She fell silent. She wasn't sure if Lenk was even talking to her, but somehow the option of not speaking felt much easier than interrupting him.

Coward, she cursed herself.

He held his hand up and looked at it: callused, cut, and dirty.

"That's when I should have walked away." He dropped his arm to the floor. "Right after the Khovura fight—hell, *during* the Khovura fight—that would have been a good time, too." He closed his eyes. "Any of the times that I was faced with a chance and just ignored it and everyone else and kept on going. I could have walked away anytime. Gone anywhere else. But it had to be here, in Cier'Djaal. I thought if I kept walking, I'd never stop."

He turned his head and looked at her.

"That wouldn't have been a bad thing," he said. "I know that now."

His eyes drifted back toward the ceiling. The long silence settled between them again, leaving ample room for her thoughts to echo in her own head.

Tell him now. Just like we rehearsed. Go, go, go—

"Even when I was getting the hell beat out of me, I didn't care," he said. "I just kept on going, thinking I could make it better." He rubbed his eyes. "Why is it that I only learn after everything has already gone to shit?"

Well, there you have it. Things can't get much worse for him. Go on and do it now.

"And now...I don't think I even know what I'm doing. What I'm planning, I don't know if it'll work. Where I'm going, I don't know if it'll end. What I'm leaving behind...I don't think I ever even knew what it was."

He rose to his feet slowly. She could hear his joints popping, the stretch of his scars upon his skin, the patter of a drop of blood falling from his temple.

The Howling—Kwar's Howling—was something eloquent, melodious, a sound composed solely for her. This sound, these noises Lenk made, were crude and inelegant and wholly honest. The statements of a man whose body didn't know how to lie and whose heart didn't know how to hide just how very terrified he was.

He knelt down before her, took her hand in his, and stared down at it as he traced his finger along the calluses from her bowstring.

"And because I don't know," he said, "I can't ask you to come with me."

Good.

"But I want you to." Something caught itself in his voice. "Because I know I'm not good at this; I know I don't listen and I'm useless at anything but killing people and..." He looked up at her. Tears glistened at the corners of his eyes. "And I don't know if I can go much farther."

Always with the crying, these humans.

They tried so hard to cling to sharp things with their soft hands and then seemed so surprised when they got cut. It would be kinder to let them be, to let them figure things out for themselves. It would be kinder to leave *him* here, to let him face this all alone. That would be kind. That would spare him from the worst of everything.

When she leaned forward and pressed her forehead against his, when she closed her eyes and breathed in the scent of his tears and his sweat, of his blood and his dirt, she knew she wasn't doing the kind thing.

Or the smart thing.

Or the right thing.

And maybe she never would know why she was doing it, any of it, here where she knew she didn't belong, aside from the fact that she knew the sound of his terrified heart so very, very well that it filled her ears and left no room for anything else.

And so she merely let her head touch his.

And held him.

And wondered, absently, if he could smell the scent of Kwar's flesh on her.

FORTY-THREE

SCRAPS FOR THE HOUNDS

Exactly seven hours after the world had ended, Asper emerged from a trapdoor onto the roof of the Temple of Talanas.

The first thing she noticed was the Temple of Ancaa nearby, its ziggurat standing a cold and dark shadow against the moonlit sky. No candles burned behind its stained-glass windows. She saw no bodies knelt in supplication within. If prayer was offered to Ancaa within, Ancaa was not listening.

But then, maybe Ancaa simply could not hear them. Cier'Djaal was a noisy place lately.

At the edge of the temple's roof, she found Aturach. His attentions were not on Ancaa, nor even on Talanas or any part of Temple Row. His eyes, glassy and heavy-lidded, stared out over the horizon of the city.

A false dawn had shed its light across the roofs of the city in many red wounds. Fires dotted the city below, a red canvas upon which shadows bled in inky blots. Through the streets, tightly ordered squares of Karnerian soldiers marched with spears aloft and shields glistening, unfazed by the carnage surrounding them. Above the roofs, the Sainites rode their scraws, raining fireflasks and crossbow bolts upon their foes below.

And everywhere, the people were fleeing. They darted in and out of alleys in the wake of the Karnerians. They took shelter in buildings when Sainite fire rained down upon them. They pulled bodies, some moving and some not, into darkness.

She couldn't hear them from here. Not their prayers, not their screams, not over the fire and the marching feet. She wondered, then, if Ancaa and Talanas simply had better ears than hers.

"Right about there," Aturach said. He pointed over the roofs to the Harbor District and the plumes of smoke rising from it. "Once we cleared the Meat Market, I found out the fighting first started there. Some dirty little bar called The Seahorse's Dream. Four Karnerians and six Sainites were drinking there and then started throwing punches."

He leaned back on his hands. His entire being shrank with his sigh.

"And it happened less than half an hour *before* the mediations began."

She sat down next to him and stared out over the carnage.

"They were fighting before they heard what had happened?" she asked.

"And in the next hour, more of them started fighting there, there, and there." He pointed to more fires burning. "It took less than three hours for them to get into armies and start tearing people apart."

"They were waiting for mediations to fail," she muttered.

"They never wanted it in the first place," Aturach said. "They never wanted peace; they never wanted to end hostilities; they never planned to obey anything that was agreed upon tonight. This was always going to happen."

She looked out away from the flames toward the Souk. Above the city, untouched by fire or smoke, the Silken Spire still hung tall in the air. Against the moonlight, she could see the horse-sized spiders skittering across their tremendous web, indifferent to the suffering below.

"They've left the Spire alone," she noted. "That's something."

"They've left Silktown alone, as well," he said. "And the temples. And the harbor warehouses. And everything else that can make them money once one of them has claimed whatever's left of this city."

"They aren't destroying everything, then," she said.

"Yes, how terribly blessed we must be." Aturach laughed, extending his arms to the sky. "Thank you, O Wise Healer, for in Your infinite wisdom, You have decided to kill only *most* of the people in this city. Let all who doubt Your mercy hear my cry." He cupped his hands over his mouth and screamed into the night sky. "It could have been worse, ingrates! Fall to your knees and be grateful that the Gods killed only *half* of your families!"

"You're not helping."

"And *you* are?" He whirled on her, incredulous. "For months, all anyone could talk about were these mediations, how they were going to fix everything. Forget the Jackals and the Khovura, forget the fashas. At the very least, we wouldn't be conquered or killed by foreigners. For *months* we prayed that Talanas would make this go ahead and send us even that small blessing. For months we—"

His voice cracked suddenly. He turned away from her and covered his face with his hands. His body shuddered with a broken breath.

"Savine is dead. She was crushed by the crowd in the Meat Market." He wiped his eyes with the sleeve of his robe. "Malauch ran away. I haven't seen him and I'm never going to again. We were the last Talanites in the city."

He looked out over the many pyres, the city's many wounds and many bruises. When it finally became too much, he let his head fall between his legs and clutched at his skull.

"For months, I prayed. For months, I did His work. And this is what Talanas sent me."

Asper stared out over the carnage for as long as she could tolerate it. After a few moments, watching people drown in fire or be crushed underfoot was too much. She looked skyward to a night stained orange.

"Do the hymns ever say if Talanas has bowel movements?" she asked.

"Don't try to be funny."

"I'm not. I couldn't. I'm just wondering if there's a reason that the

Gods sometimes just squat down and take a giant shit on us every now and again." She craned her neck back farther, peering up at the moon high overhead. "Presumably, if they *do* shit, then it has nowhere to go but down here."

"And if they don't?"

"Then this sort of thing was going to happen anyway," she said, sighing. "I know that's not helpful. Because I know there's not much we can do to help." She looked at him now and saw that he was staring intently at her, waiting for an answer. "But what else are we going to do? Pray?"

"What else *can* we do?"

She shrugged. "Try."

"Try what?"

"Just try."

Not a good answer, she knew. Not a helpful one, certainly not the sort of thing a priestess should offer someone in doubt, even if that someone was a fellow priest. But it was an answer.

And even if it was clumsy and unhelpful, it was not hollow.

"Yoooooo hooooooo!"

A call came from the other side of the temple. They exchanged a glance before heading to the opposite edge of the roof. Peering down, they saw a man in a guard's armor pounding at the door of the temple, swaying precariously as a Gevrauchian leaned against a wagon full of dead bodies.

"Hellooooooo in there!" the guard called out. "Captain Dransun is knocking. Captain of the city of the dead! Got a fresh load of corpses for you!"

"Are you...are you *drunk*?" Aturach called down.

At this, Dransun staggered backward and searched for the source of the voice. It took a few moments before he flashed a tipsy smile up to the roof.

"Very drunk," he confirmed. "Me and the...the, uh..." He flailed out a hand, gesturing to the Gevrauchian. "The Quill. We've been heading through the streets, trying to save the city."

"It doesn't look like you've been very successful," Asper said, eyeing the wagon full of corpses.

"That is why we are very drunk," Dransun replied. "Everything doesn't seem quite so awful anymore. But...you know... it still is." He removed his helmet, ran a hand through his greasy hair. "We've been telling people to head to Temple Row. Saw a couple of them heading this way. The foreigners' temples are empty and the Ancaarans aren't answering. Can you...you know, do anything?"

Rather than heaven, rather than Cier'Djaal, rather than Talanas, Aturach looked to Asper. She met him with a soft smile and a hand upon his shoulder. He sighed, leaned over, and nodded to the captain below.

"We can try," he said.

✦ ✦ ✦ ✦

When Dreadaeleon slept, there was only darkness.

All his dreams had emptied out his mouth on clouds of broodvine smoke. All the great palaces of gold, all the meadows of perpetual autumn, all the waves crashing on the beaches upon which he and Liaja had lain had dissipated and slid out the window on the smoky air.

When he slept, there was nothing left of him to dream. There was nothing but a darkness so deep, a silence so profound, he could hear the words echo through his head forever.

Boy. Worthless. Useless. Little boy. Selfish. Boy. Cruel. Boy. Boy. Boy. Useless. Useless. Useless.

He groaned in his sleep and rolled over, groping blindly at the bed. He felt no swell of breast, no soft, clean flesh beneath his fingers. The sheets lay cold and empty beside him.

At this, he awoke.

She left? Why had she left? He had paid, hadn't he? He had had enough to pay for this night, just one night more. She couldn't have left. Had she cheated him? Had she gone once he fell asleep? When? Where? She couldn't leave. Not now.

Not now, not now, not now, he thought, clutching at the cold sheets between clammy fingers. *Please.*

He whirled at the sound of breaking glass and breathed a sigh of relief. Liaja stood at an open door, peering down the hallway. He pulled himself from the bed, came up behind her, dutifully ignored the fact that she was taller than him, and slid his arms about her waist.

She started at the touch but grew soft in his arms, reaching down to place her hand in his. But her grip was tense, her body trembling beneath the flimsy silk robe she wore.

"What's the matter?" he asked.

She didn't answer.

She didn't have to.

Voices carried down the hall from the bathhouse's parlor, hot with anger. He leaned out, saw more doors open, more girls peering along the hall. Beneath their kohl makeup, terror shone on their faces. The rattle of metal and the sound of flesh striking flesh echoed down the corridor. The girls shrank behind the paper screens of their rooms' doors.

"Soldiers?" Dreadaeleon muttered.

"They didn't come for girls," Liaja replied. "And they won't leave."

"Mm." He smiled sleepily at her, gently kissed her neck. "Typical barknecks. Ignore them."

He leaned forward to kiss her again. She stepped away, her face darkening. He blinked stupidly.

"What?"

"Men with coin are civil, northern boy," Liaja said. "When they take something, they leave something behind. Men with steel are different. When they take something, nothing is left behind."

Dreadaeleon looked into the hall. "They're whores. Surely they're used to men making demands of them."

"They give." Liaja's voice grew as cold as her stare. "Do you think they have nothing that can be taken?"

He stared at her dumbly for a moment, at a loss for words. The look on her was as hard as a fist and struck him like one. He took a step backward, remembering the last time a woman had looked at him like that.

Boy. Boy. Useless. Boy. Selfish. Cruel. Boy. Little boy. Boy.

He shut his eyes, shook his head, and tried to fling the words from his thoughts.

No. No. NO. I'm not a boy. I'm not.

Something stirred within his head, sent electric anger racing across his skull, into his eyes. His palms itched; his eyes burned behind their lids. Other words came to him. Words much longer, much stronger than the ones that had been occupying his sleep.

"Stay here."

He found his trousers on the floor, pulled them on, and stormed down the hall. The girls followed him with their eyes, peering out from their rooms to watch as he came into the bathhouse's parlor. The glass from one of the windows lay shattered on the floor, voices carrying through the shards in the frame.

"I don't understand." He recognized the voice of the girl who had met him here earlier. "This is a bathhouse. I've seen some of your own men here before!"

"It is a den of filth and sin," a deep, masculine voice answered. "It will be purged."

"The other soldiers left us in peace. Please, try to see reason. We can work something—"

He heard a meaty smack and a shriek as a heavy hand struck a soft cheek.

"Do not test me, whore."

Dreadaeleon swept to the door and pushed it open. The girl recoiled from a wall of soldiers in black armor, all lined up neatly with spears and shields. One in the lead, stare as cold and hard as the iron of his helmet, stood with torch in hand. He looked up to regard Dreadaeleon.

"Collect your clothes and depart, civilian," the Karnerian commanded. "No lives need to be lost that are not already damned, but

Daeon teaches that strength comes from purity. This house must be burned."

Dreadaeleon met the man's stare for a moment before looking at the girl. Her dress was torn at the shoulder. A purple bruise was blossoming upon her cheek. Tears brimmed in her eyes as she hid her face from him.

"You have limited time, civilian," the soldier said. "Do not waste it."

Dreadaeleon didn't say a word.

Not at first, anyway. Not when he looked back at the man and considered, carefully, the slope and ridge of the black helmet he wore. Not when he extended a hand, palm flat and fingers stretched out. Not when his eyes burst with the red light of Venarie flowing through him.

He spoke only after all this: a single word with a single meaning that the soldier could not understand.

Not at first, anyway.

It only became clear once Dreadaeleon drew his hand into a fist, clenching all fingers together. The air rippled around the soldier's helmet and suddenly it, too, clenched.

There was the crunch of metal twisting, there was a crack of bone, there was the patter of blood as a great crimson fan burst from the helmet's eye slits. But there was no scream. For when the soldier fell to the ground and the torch clattered to the floor alongside, the fist-sized crumpled wad of metal that had been his head had no room left for screams.

"Consider this bathhouse under the protection of the Venarium," Dreadaeleon said. "Consider what just happened here very carefully before you decide what to do next."

With a ripple of metal and a cry of alarm, the soldiers broke their rank, stepping backward and looking warily at one another. Only one remained forward, huddling behind his shield as though it would protect him from whatever Dreadaeleon might do next.

"The...the Venarium are neutral!" he stammered. "There are oaths! There are—"

"You do not know about the oaths," Dreadaeleon interrupted. "You do not know their depth, their implication, or whether or not they allow me to do what I just did." His eyes burned bright, the red light leaking out of them to dissipate in the air like so much smoke. "What you *do* know is that I just crushed a man's head with a word. And whatever you do next, know this."

He folded his hands behind his back, stepped lightly over the dead man's body, and approached the soldier. The Karnerian flinched backward, staring down at Dreadaeleon over the rim of his shield.

"I have many, *many* more words." Dreadaeleon growled through clenched teeth, "*Leave.*"

The soldiers exchanged nervous glances, backing away steadily. Maybe it was pride or merely good military order that kept them from turning and fleeing outright as they disappeared around a corner. Maybe they would go to the Venarium and find out that what Dreadaeleon just did—using magic to interact in a non-sovereign military action—was in violation of all those oaths. Maybe they would return with Lector Annis, a dozen more soldiers, and an execution warrant that should have been served the first time.

Maybe.

Like a muscle tensed too long, his brain began to hurt. The light left his gaze, leaving behind eyes tired and mapped with red veins. His shoulders stooped and his body sagged as he dragged himself back to the bathhouse.

He didn't care about soldiers. He didn't care about the Venarium. He didn't care that the girl looked at him with more horror than she had at the man who had struck her.

All he cared about was soon in his arms. His lips were on her neck, her sigh was in his ears. But her body was still tense.

"What happened out there?" Liaja asked. "I heard screaming."

"There was screaming," Dreadaeleon confirmed. "Now there isn't."

She held him at an arm's length and looked at him intently. "What did you do, Dreadaeleon?"

He smiled lazily, reached into his trouser pocket and produced a broodvine seed.

"Please," he whispered, popping it into his mouth, "call me 'northern boy' again."

⁘

"You remember what he used to call himself? Back when we first met him and we weren't even a gang with a name?"

Denaos sniffed and instantly regretted doing so. The embalming tar had done little to curb the stink.

"Yeah," he replied. "He called himself 'Fearless Fenshi.'"

"Fearless Fenshi." A pause. "Bit of a prick back then, wasn't he? We'd always lay down the game, watch the marks, plan the heist, make sure we weren't stepping on any other gang's toes..."

"And he'd go charging in, sword swinging and screaming like it was a contest to see who could fuck things up the most." Denaos chuckled. "You remember what he called himself after we made it?"

"'Fenshi the Feared.' Had himself a new sword made and everything. Remember how he went around with that thing on his face?"

"Yeah, that stupid half-mask." Denaos laughed, trying to ignore the smell. "'So that my enemies may know only the barest hint of the legend who struck at them.' What an idiot."

"That mask, yeah." A sigh. "He always wanted to be a Jackal."

Denaos stared down into Fenshi's eyes, shut tightly behind stray globs of embalming tar. They had made him look as peaceful as one could with one's head severed and one's hands chopped off and one's belly hollowed out. At the very least, they had removed the various dead animals the Khovura had attached to him.

Still, laid out on the table in the back room of a cutter's office in a gutter in the Sumps, it was hard for anyone to look peaceful.

But those eyes, sealed so tightly, looked as if they were going to spring open at any moment and Fenshi would start cracking some kind of crappy joke.

Something like "*Hey, this is no way to get a-HEAD in life.*"

He'd have liked that. Fenshi liked shitty jokes. Only ones he told, though, because he always thought they were brilliant when they came out of his mouth. Arrogant turd.

"I'm going to miss him," Denaos said.

"And Rheniga? Headhigh?"

"Them, too."

"What about Stacco? Mahdula? Easy Erstwhile?"

"Sure, but—"

"The Candle? The Scarecrow? Rezca?"

"They're not dead yet."

"And what about me, Ramaniel?"

He turned to regard a face like a shattered mirror. Anielle's visage was cracking with every moment his eyes lingered upon her. At the edges of the eyes, the corners of the lips, the cheeks paling steadily, she forgot everything about the woman she was supposed to be and became, for once, embarrassingly honest about who she really was.

A small woman standing next to her dead friend, feeling alone and terrified.

"Are you going to miss me when I'm gone?" she asked, voice trembling. "Because it won't be long now. They got Fenshi. They got Rheniga. They'll get us all. Maybe slower, now that they can't hunt us on the street thanks to Rezca fucking with the mediations, but it'll happen."

The woman staring up at him was not the woman he had met those nights ago in Teneir's manse. She was not the woman who had pulled Asper out of the fire. She was not the woman who had played the Kissing Game with him and helped bring down the Houndmistress and plunge this city into riots.

This was not Anielle looking at him.

But he recognized her now, from so many years ago, when they were gutter trash on the streets of Cier'Djaal. He recognized the cracks in her face where the cocky little girl who looked like a boy had sometimes sat up at night and cried when she thought he was asleep and punched him in the throat if he asked what the matter was the next day. He recognized the face now as the one he had seen long ago, when he and she had stopped being trash and started being murderers.

"It's not going to happen," he said.

"You can't promise that."

"I'm not promising, I'm stating. This isn't going to happen." He stared down flatly at her. "I owe this city."

She shook her head, trembling. "No. You can't make up for what you did just by killing a few thugs. Don't tell me you're going to." She pulled a knife from her belt, held it by the blade. "You do this, you do it for us. Not for the dead. Not for your friends. No one else."

He looked down at the blade and saw that it was newly forged. Its leather scabbard was still stiff and rigid from being boiled recently; the polish on its wooden hilt was buffed to a high gloss; the cross-piece was perfectly free of any dents or blemishes. It was a virgin blade, one he'd never seen before.

Yet already he could feel how it would fit into his grasp; he could already feel its weight in his hand and hear the leather hiss when he would draw it out to cut a throat.

That sound, he could hear it in his sleep. No matter how much he drank, no matter how much he lied, no matter how many times he looked in the mirror and saw a woman with a slit throat standing behind him, he could never stop hearing it.

So maybe then, it was time to just stop pretending he ever could.

This was what he did. Maybe he'd do it for Anielle, maybe he would do it for the city, maybe he'd do it for the dead girl in his dreams who smiled at him through her neck.

He highly doubted the blade cared.

And when he held his hand out, palm up, and accepted the hilt Anielle laid upon it, it fit within his fingers exactly as he thought it would.

Some of them swore aloud. A few of them stepped out of the way or held their children a little closer. But most of them simply continued walking, head down and dragging whatever cart or sack or children they could as they trudged through the gate.

No one tried to stop him.

As he strode among them without his cloak, wings spread wide, head held high, teeth bared, and claws twitching, they didn't even think to look at a *Rhega* and know fear.

If they were smart, they would. They would be out with whatever swords they could scavenge. They would grab the spears of fallen guards and soldiers and come at him. They would look at him, at all his teeth and his claws and the hate in his eyes, and know they had to kill him, for he surely intended to kill them.

He was Gariath. He was *Rhega*. And he would kill them all, someday. Or save them all.

If they knew that, they would look terrified.

But they didn't know that. They didn't know him. They didn't know the word *Rhega*.

Here, in the slow-moving stream of refugees leaving the city, he was just another oid.

At a closer glance, the crowd wasn't even mostly human. Many were tulwar, carrying swords upon bent backs. More were shicts, leading great, hyena-like beasts by leather reins. Many saccarii, many couthi, even a few vulgore added themselves to the stream.

Many races. Yet to a one, their heads were bowed low, their backs were bent, and their possessions were meager.

There were no other dragonmen here. No *Drokha* strode among them. Gariath had heard they remained behind in the city, bought up as mercenaries by fashas who could afford them.

Perhaps Kharga was among them, Gariath wondered, cleaving humans apart for human coin. Gariath could see the *Drokha* in his mind, blood-slick ax blade, striding through the bodies hewn and heads smashed.

It was not hard to imagine one of those heads bearing a mane of silver hair matted with blood.

He snorted.

It was this city. This city made proud dragonmen fight over coins. This city made humans eat each other alive and not think it vile to do so. This city bent backs, bowed heads, made strong people weak, made weak words strong.

And no one else seemed to give a shit but him.

Fine, he growled inwardly. *That's fine. Always it's been me to solve this. They're too weak: Lenk, Kharga, the others. All too weak. They need me to save them again. They need me to solve this.*

He carried this thought with him long outside the gates, as he walked across the sand and crested a high dune. The city was so far away from here, something small and dark with a big, ugly spire jutting from it like a cancerous growth.

He would solve this.

He was the strong one.

Like always.

A harsh wind kicked up, carrying many scents with it: distant smoke, burning wood, ebbing fears. None were quite so strong, though, as the scent of meat cooking nearby. Pain gnawed at his stomach in protest, bade him to seek out the scent. He followed it over a few dunes before arriving at the site of a small campsite with a big occupant.

A vulgore sat hunched beside a rather dismal fire attempting to heat a rather intimidating pot. He swung a great, horned head up as Gariath approached, but did nothing else. Gariath couldn't remember the face, but he recognized the smell.

The vulgore, it seemed, didn't know any other *Rhega* to confuse him with.

"Kudj welcome wayward squib," Kudj grunted. He held up massive hands. "Kudj no want fight, if squib come bearing grudges. Kudj got no job no more, striking out to forge own destiny."

While Gariath did not outright deny that he wanted a fight, he made no move to attack. Seeming satisfied with this, Kudj gestured to the other side of the fire.

"Come, squib, sit with Kudj. Engage in beautifully awkward hospitality." He reached into the pot with a large finger and stirred whatever was inside. "Stew not hot. Fire not big enough. Squib is welcome to some anyway."

The stew smelled of old meat, old vegetables, old water. It felt lukewarm in his hand as he scooped it up. It tasted vile on his tongue as he shoveled it into his mouth. But food was food. He had no idea when he would eat next.

"Squib smart, like Kudj," Kudj said. "When human squibs get the jibblies, they always take it out on oid squibs. Oid squibs always hang around to get money from human squibs. Such is price of unspoken economic-induced caste system. Good to leave now, come back later when jibblies gone."

Gariath continued to eat the stew silently. Kudj stared at him, squinting.

"How far squib going?"

"Far," Gariath replied.

"Where squib going?"

"Away."

"Ah. Kudj see. Kudj have great appreciation for dramatic tension."

This, apparently, meant Kudj would fall silent as Gariath finished eating. After he swallowed a mouthful of stew, Gariath rested his hands on the rim of the pot and stared down into the broth.

"Ask me what I'm going to do when I get back," he said.

"What?" Kudj asked.

"I'm going to burn this city to the ground."

"How?"

He snorted. "I'll find a way." He turned and began to stalk away. "There's plenty of stew left. It tastes awful."

He had begun to climb the next dune when Kudj bellowed after him. "Squib know way around desert?"

"No."

He had reached its peak when Kudj called again. "Squib want help?"

He didn't say no.

Kudj took the pot in one hand and upended it into his maw. When it was drained dry, he hurled it aside, scraped sand over the fire, and let out a tremendous belch. He rose to his feet, rested on his knuckles, and came clambering after Gariath.

"Kudj not so fond of city life, after all," he said. "Kudj's mother paint inaccurate portrait of wonder and mystery." He glanced down at Gariath and the dragonman looked up, unused to the sensation of doing so. "Maybe squib need friend in the desert?"

Gariath did not "need."

Need was something that humans did. They needed their cities. They needed their coins. They needed their silks and their wars and their societies more than they needed air.

More than they had needed him.

Gariath did not need.

But as he trudged across the sand and as Kudj's shadow fell over him, he did not say no.

FORTY-FOUR

THE FASHA AND THE FOOL

As the world burned, they laughed.

Beneath a halo of lamplight, they giggled as they chased each other around the lamppost. He, young and carefree with hair as long and silky as his clothing. She, tittering behind an elaborately painted face as she evaded his reaching hands. She darted this way and then that; he tried to snatch her about the waist. Finally, she relented and was pulled into his arms, laughing.

Drunk on expensive foreign liquors—or maybe just each other's company—they spun in lazy circles, laughing merrily. They came to a slow stop, staring into each other's eyes for the briefest of moment before they came together in a kiss, smearing the paint on their faces as they did.

And they swayed in each other's arms as the breeze carried stray ashes from someone's home over the wall to fall on them like black snow.

Lenk supposed he couldn't blame them. They were nobles of Silktown, after all, as unaware of the violence going on beyond their walls as they were of him observing them from the manse's window.

And yet, he wondered: Had they not smelled the smoke? Could they not hear the screams? Could the bloodshed really be so far away that no one here could hear it? Or did they simply find it easy to ignore?

Here in Silktown, a wealthy man's moonrise was clear and quiet, painting silver light upon the houses that could afford peace.

There was a flash of movement from the nearby wall. A pair of skinny hands reached over the top, hauling up an equally skinny man. He tumbled over the top of the wall, landing on a lawn not ten paces away from the young lovers. He wore no weapons and there was no room for malice in his eyes behind the hungry desperation.

The two nobles did not look away from each other as the vagrant crept across the lawn and into the street. He seemed content to ignore them, as well, perhaps just as glad to be free of the rest of the city's own apocalypse. He looked around, presumably for a safe place to hide.

The stones shuddered with the force of a bellowing roar. From the edge of Lenk's vision, he saw one of the colossal gray dragon-men come charging down the street, ax in hand and black eyes fixed upon the vagrant.

The man held up his hands, lips babbling in a desperate plea. The dragonman's sole answer, however, was a tremendous upraised foot.

Coming down.

Even one story up and behind a pane of glass, Lenk could hear the thick popping sound as the vagrant was crushed beneath the dragonman's foot and left as a greasy red smear upon the pavement. The dragonman's lips peeled back in a sneer as he scraped the corpse from his scales.

With an effete delicacy unbefitting a creature of that size, he stepped aside as the two young nobles broke from their embrace and walked past. Hand in hand, lost in each other's painted smiles, the lovers strolled daintily down the street, heedless of the dead man they walked over to do so.

As soon as they were gone, contempt replaced itself on the drag-onman's face. His onyx glare swept upward toward the windows overhead. Lenk ducked beneath the sill and waited there until the thunder of the brute's footsteps faded.

In hindsight, coming to the house of Sheffu might not have been the wisest idea, he admitted to himself. True, out there, there were hundreds of foreign soldiers and many more looters and cutthroats and, in here, there were fewer than a dozen of the dragonman mercenaries patrolling the streets of Silktown.

But when it came to monstrous creatures the size of houses with axes the size of horses, how many did one really need?

Just one, he told himself. *Just one to see you, just one to recognize you. Then it won't matter who you try to hide behind. Even a fasha won't be able to save you.*

He leaned against the wall, covered his face with his hands, and breathed in the scent of smoke and sweat on his palms.

Seeking help here wasn't a very good plan, he knew. But all his good plans had burned away in fire and bled out on the streets. All that he had left were desperate measures and half-assed rationale.

Though clearly, if he was in this situation, he couldn't have had too many good ideas to begin with.

He hauled himself to his feet, gasping with the effort. His body ached, and somehow the smell of dust and age that permeated the hall seemed to make the sensation that much more acute. He found himself walking much more slowly than usual as he followed the hall of Sheffu's manse to a sealed door.

Khaliv spared him an impassive glance as he approached, but did not move away from the door as he leaned against it, arms folded.

"I need to talk to Sheffu now," Lenk said, trying to keep the breathlessness from his voice.

"Soon," the saccarii replied.

"I didn't say I needed to talk to him 'soon,' did I?" Lenk snarled, eyelid twitching.

"Ya didn't hear me say 'now,' did ya?" Khaliv looked less than impressed with Lenk's display of aggression, merely cocking a brow from behind his veil. "Ya don't look good, *shkainai*. Go to the *houn* with your pointy-eared friend and rest there. I'll send Eili down with some tea."

The thought of standing here before the saccarii, his wound throbbing beneath his bandages and his body begging to be off its feet, was not a tempting one. But the thought of being near Kataria right now was somehow even less so.

The route Denaos had led them through to Silktown had been harrowing. They had darted past squadrons of Karnerians, beneath flights of Sainite scraws, behind patrolling dragonmen. They had crept through thieves' alleys and old sewer passages in which shadows breathed and light was forbidden. No ordinary person could be blamed for finding the situation too tense for words.

But Kataria was far from ordinary. And she hadn't said a thing.

Not until Denaos saw them safely to Sheffu's house, at any rate, at which point she asked Eili for paper and excused herself to the *houn*. She hadn't once asked what Lenk was planning to ask Sheffu for. She hadn't cracked a single joke or commented on his human stupidity. She had looked at him only once during the entire trip.

She had stopped, dead in her tracks, and simply looked at him, just for a moment, before picking up and walking again.

And the thought of that look was enough to make him reach out and shove Khaliv aside.

The saccarii did not deign to pursue Lenk as the young man shouldered his way into the room. Old candles burned in bronze censers hanging overhead, filling the room with the scent of lilac incense and casting an orange glow upon the old stones. Lenk saw Sheffu—or rather, Sheffu's shadow—from behind a paper changing screen over which the fasha's robe hung.

"You could not wait?" Sheffu asked. Behind the screen, he poured a jug of water over himself.

"I needed to talk to you," Lenk said.

"And I needed to clean myself," Sheffu said. "And, to be fair, I was already in the bath when you arrived."

"It can wait," Lenk said. "If you hadn't noticed, your city's going to shit."

"*My* city?" Sheffu chuckled blackly. "Not so long ago, you wanted to call this city yours. Now that it's on fire, it's mine?" He poured more water over his head. "But yes, I had noticed. Long before it became fashionable to do so." His shadow tilted as he looked at Lenk through the screen. "And I hear you got yourself in a bit of trouble, hmm?"

Lenk sighed in exasperation. It hurt.

"Let's not drag this out," he said, rubbing his eyes. "You know what I want from you; I know what you want from me." When Sheffu did not answer, he allowed himself a mutter. And it *hurt*. "I need to get out of the city. They know me here and everyone thinks I did it."

"Did you?"

Kind of.

"No," he replied. "And I know I turned you down before about searching for Khoth-Kapira. But I can do it now, if you'll do this for me."

"And you think that's what I want?" Sheffu asked.

"I do."

"Then you were never listening in the first place." The fasha's voice took a hard edge. "I spoke of a demon who once ruled a world of his own design with an iron fist and whose word for 'mortal' was synonymous with 'slave' and 'food.' *You* speak of bargains and brokerings. I asked you to go out and bring me back a way to save a thousand lives. You ask me to save one."

"What's it matter?" Lenk demanded. "It gets done, doesn't it? Help me and my friend get out of the city and I'll do what you want."

"Before Khoth-Kapira was a demon, He was an Aeon, a servant of the Gods created to shepherd mankind. He was created to serve, He was ordered to watch, and He was given the power of a deity to do so. What did it matter, then? What did it matter until He used that power to become a tyrant? With demons, intent is *everything*, Lenk."

Sheffu's shadow reclined with a groan as he leaned against the edge of the bathtub.

"What is to stop you from simply fleeing once you leave the city?" he asked. "For that matter, why couldn't you just have the Jackal that brought you here get you out?"

"Denaos isn't—"

"Is that the name he goes by now?" Sheffu interrupted.

"Word will have spread beyond the walls soon," Lenk said. "Settlements from here to Muraska will know who I am before I even do. I don't just need your help getting out of the city, I need your help surviving once I'm outside it. I need *you*."

"And if you are caught, what then? Say you are tortured. Say you tell them I helped you. My influence here is shrinking. The other fashas already think me mad and useless. If they find an excuse to carve up what I have left up, they will not hesitate to do so. It is not enough to merely survive."

"Well, then, what the hell *is* enough?" Lenk shouted. "Why can't it be enough that I'm just willing to do this for you?"

"Because you are only willing to do it for *you*. Not me. Not for all the thousands who will die if you *don't*. But for you."

"You think you're some saint, then? Just because you know a bit about demons and doomsaying?" Lenk stormed toward the changing screen. "You think the world rests on your shoulders just because you read a book?" He grasped the screen, threw it aside. "Who gave you the—"

He recognized the amber eyes that stared up at him in alarm, but nothing else. The creature that lounged in the shallow water was not Fasha Sheffu. The creature that rose up, naked skin glistening, was not even human.

Sheffu was long and thin and gray beneath his robes, his skin patchy with rough spots of flesh reminiscent of scales. His left arm looked almost boneless, hanging at his side. And his right existed only as a hand, the rest of the limb fused to his body by webbed flesh. Hair clung to one side of his head, the other malformed by scaly flesh.

And when he spoke, a forked tongue slid between long fangs.

"Perhaps," he said, "my motives in finding Khoth-Kapira's powers are not wholly driven by selflessness." He stepped out of the tub, heedless of Lenk's terrified backward scramble as he passed. "On behalf of most saccarii, I am most intrigued by the legends regarding his powers of flesh-shaping."

Khaliv hurried forward, collecting Sheffu's dressing robe and wrapping it around him.

"I was not lying when I said Khoth-Kapira represents a threat to all," he continued. "I am not lying when I tell you that the lives of thousands rest on you. But if you and I benefit along with those thousands... perhaps that is not such a bad thing. Yes."

He looked quite shaky outside of his robes and veil, each step uncertain and shuddering as he made his way to the door. He ran a hand through his hair and scratched at the scaly patch of flesh across his scalp.

"I can get you out of the city, yes. I can get you to the mountains in the east. I can get you to Khoth-Kapira's seat of power." He looked over his shoulder. "And can you, Lenk, get me a way to save my people and yours?"

Lenk was stunned beyond words, beyond even nodding. Yet somehow, he found enough nerve to swallow hard and bob his head dumbly up and down.

"Good." Sheffu wandered out the door, into the hall. "Good." He walked away, his voice echoing off the stone. "Good."

— ·≺◆≻· —

At the second step from the top of the stairs, Lenk froze. He held his breath, steadied himself on one foot, and didn't even blink for fear that she might hear his eyelids close.

Kataria knelt near the doorway to Sheffu's *houn*, staring through Eili's veil and into her eyes. She was whispering something Lenk couldn't hear, and the little saccarii nodded at every word. Swiftly, Kataria slipped a folded-up scrap of paper into the girl's hand and patted her on the head. Eili tucked the paper into her robe, opened the door, and disappeared out into the streets.

The door slammed shut. Lenk let out a breath. Kataria's ears pricked up and she followed, leaping to her feet and whirling about with alarm in her eyes. Her expression softened as her breath left her.

"Don't sneak up on me like that," she said.

I could never sneak up on you. No one can sneak up on a shict. Isn't that what you always used to say? What happened?

He did not ask this, for he feared the answer.

"Everything all right?" he asked.

"Yeah," she said, nodding. "Everything's fine."

Everything isn't fine. The city's up in flames, they think I'm responsible, and you weren't there when it happened. It's just you and me now and we both know nothing's fine.

He did not say this, for he did not want her to confirm it.

"Did you talk to Sheffu?" she asked.

"Yeah, he..." He paused and rubbed the back of his neck. It ached. "He says he can get us out of the city. He just needs something from us in return."

She hesitated a moment, then nodded. "Okay."

It's not okay. Nothing is okay. He's going to send me out of one hell and into another and I did it because I don't know what I'm doing and I don't know what you're doing and I wish someone would just tell me where I fucked this all up.

He did not say this.

Instead, he said something much stupider.

"What did you write?" he asked.

She stiffened up and pressed herself against the doorway. "What?"

"In that note you just gave Eili," he said. "Where did she go?"

And Kataria looked at him again. Like she had on their way here. She paused, canted her head slightly to the side, and stared at him. Slowly, she closed her eyes and sighed.

"Do you want me here?" she asked.

He nodded.

"Well, I'm here," she replied.

Something in the tone of her voice, in the way her eyes lingered on him and her lips curled down at the edges, in the way she turned around and departed down the hall without looking back...

Something about her frightened him terribly at that moment.

"Wait. Come back. I don't care what it was, really. I mean, I do, but...if you don't want to tell me, that's fine. I just...I need you right now. I don't know what I'm doing anymore. I don't know if I ever did. I need you. Come back."

He did say this.

But if she heard him, she didn't return. Somewhere down the hall, a door slammed as she disappeared into a nearby bedroom.

He wanted very much to sleep, as well. But he couldn't. Deep down, some part of him knew that if he lay down to sleep now, he would never open his eyes.

So he contented himself with taking in Sheffu's *houn* with all its musty furniture, dusty tables, and frayed tapestries. Not so much "modest" as simply "given up," the room—a large square with wooden floors and drab gray walls—resembled something like a welcoming party at a mausoleum. Candles burned softly in sconces upon the wall, incense tried to cover the scent of dust and age, and the carpet lay drab on the floor.

Even the food that had been laid out upon a small table looked depressing. Granted, Sheffu hadn't been expecting them, but still, a fasha should have more than stale flatbread and fruits so dried they were like jerked beef. Still, eating was something to do instead of worrying, so Lenk reached down, plucked a piece of bread, and began to eat.

"I wouldn't, if I were you."

Lenk glanced up. He wasn't sure when Mocca had come in, or even if he had been there the whole time. The man in white smirked, easing back in a nearby chair.

"What are you doing here?" he asked, taking a bite.

"Sheffu decided to show his gratitude for my bravery back at Ghoukha's house by inviting me to stay for a while." Mocca gestured to the flatbread. "And I'm fairly certain the servants here scrape up the dust and ash and use it to bake with."

"Tastes fine," Lenk lied through a mouthful, though the grimace that followed his swallow betrayed him. "Better than eating a crossbow bolt, anyway."

"Yes, I heard about tonight's..." Mocca slid into a hum, making a vague gesture. "What would you call it? 'Debacle' is too tame a word; 'catastrophe' has a rather inappropriately playful connotation..."

Too tired to humor Mocca, Lenk fell back into the sofa and felt something cold brush against his leg. He looked down and saw his sword, exactly where he had left it propped when he had come in. It leaned against his leg, hilt staring up at him like an overaffectionate dog. Out of pure habit, he picked it up and drew it from its scabbard.

He hadn't looked it over in days; there were new nicks, scratches, a spot of blood he hadn't wiped away yet. His hand unconsciously reached for a napkin from the tray of fruit and began to rub the spot clean. Its rhythm felt so smooth, so natural, he hardly noticed doing it.

Just as he hardly noticed Mocca clearing his throat.

"Come now, Lenk," Mocca chided. "Is a chunk of steel really so much more entertaining than conversation with me?" He smiled teasingly. "You hold it like your child."

Lenk paused and looked at himself in its reflection. A dead man's tired eyes stared back at him and he sighed.

"When I left Steadbrook"—he caught himself—"what was left of Steadbrook, this sword was all I had. Parents gone, someone attacked in the night; I don't know. I sifted through the ashes the next morning, looking for their bodies, but all I found was the sword. I picked it up and started heading west. I guess I thought a man could find some coin so long as he had a blade.

"I found people. Found Denaos in Redgate, after I came out of the Silesrian, when he tried to rob me, found Asper when she tried to stop him. Picked up Dreadaeleon when he was thrown out of his tower, pulled Gariath out of a hole between there and Muraska." He bit his lower lip. "They weren't coin." He watched his face sink in the steel. "Lost them just as easily, though."

"And when did you meet her?" Mocca asked. "When did you meet Kataria?"

"The Silesrian. I found her first, actually." He shook his head.

"She found me, anyway. Four days in, food and water run out, sleeping on a bed of lichen with a rock for a pillow; and I wake up to her sitting on top of me, looking at me like I'm the weirdest thing she ever saw." He chuckled. "I guess maybe I was. She said I was so loud she could have found me miles away. In the dark. Blindfolded."

"In the dark..." Mocca furrowed his brow. "*And* blindfolded? That doesn't make any—"

"Yeah, I know; I thought it was weird, too. I thought *she* was weird. Hell, I was terrified. I remembered enough from my parents to know what they told me shicts did to humans on their land. But I couldn't get to my sword and she was sitting on me, so...you know."

"Of course. What happened next?"

"She led me out. Took another four days. She showed me deer trails, showed me where to find food and water, told me about her tribe, her life"—he hesitated—"her father. Wouldn't shut up about how easily she could kill me. You know, if she wanted to. She walked with me all the way to the edge of that dark forest, then kept right on walking out into the daylight with me."

When he looked up, he saw that Mocca's smirk had grown especially obnoxious.

"What?" he demanded.

"You're smiling," Mocca replied.

He caught a glimpse of himself in the steel, just in time to see a wistful smile flee from his features. Left in its wake was something soft, sad, and weary.

"Yeah, well..." He scabbarded his blade and tossed it onto the far end of the sofa. "She was with me then."

"She's with you now."

Lenk glanced down the hall where she had disappeared. "She says that."

"Do you believe her?"

"I don't know."

"Do you want to?"

He leaned forward and stared down at the floor, and the silence spoke for him. Mocca leaned back in his chair and steepled his fingers before him.

"Then," Mocca said softly, "that has to be enough."

Lenk's heart rose at the sound of footsteps coming down the hall. But when he looked at the doorway, it was only Sheffu who emerged from the darkness, wielding a small oil lamp in his hand.

"You are still up," Sheffu observed.

The fasha's composure seemed to have returned with his clothes. Once again, he was swaddled beneath layers of dingy silk robes and veils, leaving visible only amber eyes that flashed with their familiar enigma.

"Can't sleep," Lenk replied.

"Force yourself to," Sheffu said. "Tonight, the city bleeds. Tomorrow, it will stanch its wounds and start looking for someone to blame. Every way out of the city will be watched by a soldier or a thief, and all of them will be happy to claim your head. We must leave at dawn."

"Do we have a plan?" Lenk asked.

"My last source of revenue is a small rice farm a few miles from the city. It will serve, but not for long. There, you may rest a few days and recover your strength while I formulate what we must do next."

"And that is?"

"Forgotten cities of long-dead God-Kings, sadly, are not listed on many maps. I must find out where you are going and then find a way to secure passage for you and your shict. Getting two people into the Forbidden East is not a cheap endeavor."

"Then you're not going to enjoy finding passage for three," Lenk said.

"Pardon, *shkainai*?" Sheffu raised a single brow.

"I know I'm involved in this," Lenk said, "and I know that I can help fix it, if what you say is true; but there's no way I could have come this far without Mocca."

He glanced across to the chair and flashed his companion a smile. It seemed a tad odd, he thought, that Mocca should look as utterly panic-stricken as he did at that moment. But then again, being dragged into adventure always took one by surprise, didn't it?

And no one entered adventure ever, save by dragging.

"Wherever I go," Lenk said, folding his arms with an air of finality, "so does Mocca."

He hadn't expected that statement to go unchallenged. He expected Mocca to leap out of his chair and protest being inducted into this madness. He expected Sheffu to scoff at the idea of buying passage for three individuals. He expected himself to interrupt everyone and back out and go running into the streets, away from all of this.

What he hadn't expected was what Sheffu actually said.

"Who is Mocca?"

Lenk furrowed his brow. "Your guest?" He gestured at the chair. "You know?"

Sheffu looked at the chair for a long moment, his gaze completely blank. A long sigh sent his veil fluttering at he looked back at Lenk.

"Perhaps it is just the stress of tonight, yes?" Sheffu asked. "You are babbling nonsense, seeing things."

"No, I'm..." He looked intently at Mocca. Mocca, in turn, flashed a look somewhere between panic and a sheepish smirk. "I don't...but..."

"At dawn, Lenk," Sheffu said, turning to leave back down the hall. "Sleep well. Be less crazy in the morning."

The young man was left staring at the chair, mouth agape, blinking dumbly. The light was good in this room. Sheffu was not deranged. Had he just not seen Mocca? But then, why hadn't he recognized the name? Had Mocca given him a false one? Had Mocca been lying this whole time?

The questions came not as a flood, but as rocks upon which the water broke. Each one struck him, robbed him of his breath, made his head swim.

Why did he look at Mocca as though he wasn't there?

Why did he look at me as though I was crazy?

Why hasn't anyone ever acknowledged Mocca?

Why has Mocca never touched anything besides a chair?

And why, he thought, *did he know Kataria's name when I never told it to him?*

Out of pure habit, Lenk reached for his sword and drew it from its scabbard.

"I suppose," Mocca said slowly, in the way one would speak to a snarling animal, "you'll want an explanation for this. It's quite simple, you see—"

Lenk rose from his sofa, the sword naked in his hand. He drew it back. Mocca threw up his hands and shouted out.

"Now, Lenk, wait just a moment, I—"

Lenk leapt and thrust the blade. It drove through Mocca's chest, burst out between his shoulder blades, cut through the cloth and wood of the chair, and emerged out the back. He left it there, impaled through a man and a piece of furniture, and stepped back, speechless.

Mocca, without a single drop of blood upon him, stared back at Lenk. He leaned back in his chair and, for a moment, as a mote of dust burned in a candle's flame and the shadows shifted across his face, something about Mocca seemed very hard and very old.

"That," Mocca said through a long and tired sigh, "was unnecessary."

The man pulled himself out of the chair, passing through the blade as though it were as airy and insubstantial as he. He stepped away, not so much as a single thread of his robe out of place, and folded his hands in front of him.

Lenk stepped backward, tripped on the table, and collapsed. He couldn't feel his wound protest, couldn't feel his breath leave him, couldn't even feel the need to blink as he scrambled onto the couch and further away from Mocca.

Or whatever Mocca was.

"This is why I had hoped to explain it to you earlier," Mocca said, sighing. "To avoid all this—"he flitted a hand in Lenk's general direction—"melodrama."

"Stay back!" Lenk shouted.

"Or what? You'll ruin another awful piece of furniture and hope my aesthetics bleed?" He smiled softly at Lenk, exactly as he always did, yet now all Lenk could see were the shadows left by his grin. "I've been with you this whole time, Lenk, even when you couldn't see me. If I wanted you dead, I would have at least tried."

Lenk stared until his eyes and lungs could not take it. He shut his eyes, let out a slow, staggered breath, and gasped.

"Who are you?" he asked.

"You know who I am, Lenk."

He racked a brain that suddenly felt very feverish, trying to understand what was happening to him while at the same time trying to deny that it was happening to him. He shook his head, words and images tumbling through his skull, crashing off of each other; and all the while Mocca's smile grew broader and darker.

"Say it. It will make you feel better."

And then it hit him.

Such an innocuous sentence that had been uttered by Sheffu when he had first met the fasha and his book.

He speaks through visions.

Lenk swallowed hard. His mouth felt dry. The word pried itself out of his lips and simply fell to the floor.

"Khoth-Kapira."

Mocca inclined his head slowly, raised it. "Hello, Lenk."

"Disciple to His Will," Lenk babbled, unable to hold back the words spilling from mind to mouth, "God-King, Shaper of Flesh, Aeon, *demon!*"

"Shepherd of Men, Servant to Gods, and so on and so on." Mocca sighed. "So many names I've collected over the years. I like 'Mocca' the best."

Stunned silence hung between them. Or at least, stunned on Lenk's end. Mocca's quiescence was something softer, a considerate moment as if to let Lenk gather his wits. And yet Lenk still started when Mocca spoke, even if his voice was just as soft.

"Ask me," he said.

"Ask you . . . what?"

"You know what."

Lenk did know what. And yet he desperately did not want to know what. The words, he had to force from his lips now, he had to know.

"Is it true?" he asked.

"Yes," Mocca said.

"All of it? All of what Sheffu says?"

"Mostly," Mocca replied.

"Obviously," Lenk said, rubbing his head. "'*He speaks through visions.*' You've been in my head this whole time, just like the Khovura, turning me into some kind of lunatic fanatic, killing people through me."

"No." Mocca's voice was firm, his eyes hard. "I speak to you through visions, yes, as I speak to them. But I cannot control you, or them, or anyone. All those deaths, all this blood, was not my doing." He extended his hands. "All I can tell you is what you're already thinking."

"And what am I thinking, then?"

He regretted asking the moment the words left his lips, but did not truly fear doing so until he saw Mocca's smile return.

"You want me to fix things."

"I don't want a demon's help," Lenk said, rising up and moving to stalk away. After a moment, he turned and began to pace instead. "I've fought demons, I've killed demons. I *do* kill demons."

"Indeed, you do. Do you remember the first one you killed? The first one you *ever* killed?" Mocca watched him pace. "Do you remember how it cried out, like a child? How it wept and begged you to stop hurting it? It couldn't at all remember pain, and you reintroduced it. Did you hear that?" He smiled. "Because I did. I heard it echo through hell. That was the first time I heard your name." He shook his head. "But not the last."

"No?" Lenk whirled on him, stormed to the chair, and pulled his sword free. He held it up before him. "And what about your followers? Your Disciples? The Khovura? Did you hear it when I put this in them? Did you hear it when I killed them?"

Mocca's smile faded. His voice choked in his throat. "I did."

"And what about when they were howling for my blood? When those they killed were crying out? Did you hear that?"

"I heard it. I hear them all. I hear them now, wherever they are. They are screaming for me even now."

"Then go answer them. If you're a real God-King-Whatever, go deliver them."

"I am doing so," Mocca said. "When they speak to me, Lenk, they do not ask for power; they do not ask for wealth; they do not ask for blood. They ask of me what they asked of their Gods who did not listen." He turned and looked long out the window. "They ask 'save me.'"

"And you gave them fire and steel."

"This city is *dying*." Mocca whirled on Lenk, anger flashing in his eyes. "But not by flame or steel. It was dying long before that. It's just one tumor growing from a festering patch of disease. Tonight, there is fire, there is steel, and there is blood. But they have been screaming for much longer than one night. I have had eternity to hear them."

"I've met a lot of people promising deliverance," Lenk said. "I came here looking for it myself. If it's in this city, I couldn't find it."

"You looked with the edge of your sword," Mocca said. "Look now with your eyes. Look with your eyes. Look upon me." He gestured to himself. "And look upon salvation."

"Whose?"

"Everyone's. What Sheffu said is true. I did see my own end coming, as I saw my own resurrection. I was supposed to rise ten days ago, but something happened."

Lenk blinked. "That was the day I arrived."

"And I remembered your name," Mocca said. "And I saw you slay my Disciples and the people who cry out for me. And I know the demons who came before me, who tried to slay you and failed. So I stayed down in this pit and called out to you."

He stepped closer and reached out as if to touch Lenk. The young man flinched away and Mocca winced, as though struck. He regained his composure, folding his hands.

"I am coming back, Lenk. I won't be so arrogant as to suggest you can't stop me. If you wanted to, you could hurt me, possibly kill me, and certainly kill many of those who cry out to me. I come to you not as the God-King, nor even as Khoth-Kapira, but as Mocca."

He extended his hands to the side and bowed low before Lenk.

"And I am asking you to let me return."

"You're a demon," Lenk said. "I've seen what your kind does. I've seen what your monsters have done."

"And I do not blame you for slaying them, though it pains me. But how many have my followers slain, truly?"

"There was the Souk—" Lenk said.

"Where they waged war on a gang of thieves who bleed the city for coin."

"And Ghoukha's—"

"Where it was your companion who burned them alive."

"And tonight—"

"Where it is people who kill in the name of Gods, not demons." He shook his head. "My hands are not clean. I will not try to convince you otherwise. My people have killed in my name. But not nearly as many as others have killed in the name of loftier titles.

"Your priests have told you that this world was made by your Gods for you. That's not entirely a lie. But look at it now. Look at the city burning. See the armies drowning the streets in blood, see the people dying in squalor, see their lives coming and going like candles in the wind and watching them fall to their knees and praise the Gods for giving them this hell.

"Now imagine that across a single world and a thousand centuries. Clearly, somewhere in all that time, your Gods have failed you."

He clasped his hands and held them up before him.

"Let me fix this."

The intelligent thing to do, Lenk knew, would be to shut his ears to the words of a demon.

No, a *more* intelligent thing to do would be to go to Sheffu, explain all of this in slow, painstaking detail, twice, and then see what could be done about it.

And yet maybe the best thing of all would be to just go to Kataria's room, climb into bed beside her, breathe in her scent, sleep forever, and never wake up.

"Would you like to know what was on the note she wrote?"

Lenk's attention was seized by Mocca's words. The man smiled softly, encouragingly, all the malice having fled from his grin.

"Would you like to know what she's thinking? Who she's dreaming of? What her terrors are? What she wants to hear you say tomorrow to make it all better?"

"No!" Lenk had to restrain himself from swinging his sword at Mocca, if only because it would aggravate his wound. "You stay *out* of her head."

"As you like," Mocca said. "I don't need to be in it to know what you know. She walks with the knowledge that, no matter what, she's not one of you. She loves you, but not your people. You love her, but not the life she wants. You long for a world where you can walk with her and she with you and know that you will never need anything else."

Mocca slowly reached out and extended his hand.

"I can give you that, Lenk," he said. "I can give you, and everyone, a world like that. I ask you not to believe me . . . only to listen."

Lenk looked down and considered the hand offered to him.

His palm was calloused, worn, more fitting on a smith than a man of his stature. The sleeve of his robe slipped, leaving his arm and all its patterned scars bare. He hadn't noticed before—maybe he just hadn't been looking—but these were the scars of something so ingrained that they couldn't be removed or altered, even in a vision.

These were the scars of a maker. These were the scars of a demon.

The first mistake he had made since he had come here was in not walking away when he couldn't enter the city. He had made many more since then, spilled so much blood, struck so much steel, hurt so many people. Had each one been a mistake? Had they all led to this moment?

Lenk did not know.

Lenk did not know if it was a mistake now, as he reached out, as he wrapped his hand around Mocca's, as he felt the scars touch his.

And listened.

Young Man

On the fourth day of his meditation, shortly after the sun had awakened, Sekhlen felt it.

"Ah."

He opened his eyes, bleary against the breeze that rolled up the mountain and through his window. The sun was already climbing high, casting the mountain's shadow long over the forest, long to the desert beyond, long to the west.

Always west.

He rose from his knees to his feet, his old body protesting with popping joints and groaning muscle. He brushed the sand from his trousers, even though it pained him to bend over to do so. Age could not be accepted as a limitation any more than ignorance.

He took a moment to savor the breeze as it rolled in again, but only as long as it took him to feel the disease carried in on the wind. It was a shifting, nebulous sensation, at once both tiny and pronounced, like a needle inserted into the soft flesh of his eyelid.

Anyone else would have missed it.

As everyone else no doubt *had* missed it.

Which was why monasteries like this and men like Sekhlen existed.

He shuffled out of his tiny room carved into the mountain's face and descended down the stairs. Sand, too, littered the steps here. An entire forest and miles of rock rising high into the air, and it still wasn't far away enough to escape the desert.

He sighed, taking the steps one at a time. Halfway down, he paused before a crowd that looked up at him expectantly. The usual morning mob, feathers ruffled, beady eyes staring up at him expectantly, chirping various demands at him.

"Yes, yes," he said, "I'm only a *little* late today."

He reached into the pocket of his black shirt, pulled free a pouch, and emptied a fistful of seeds into his hand. As he sifted the handful gently out onto the steps, the mob of birds began to greedily—and ungratefully—peck up the seeds, allowing him to pass unmolested.

Sekhlen muttered gratitudes as he descended the steps to find his next nuisance. An initiate was busy sweeping the bottom of the stairs. A young man—Cheloe, if he recalled correctly—relatively new to the monastery. Yet they all came young, in spirit, if not in appearance. Cheloe had a young man's muscle, his black shirt and trousers tight on his body, but his hair hung gray as a mule's.

"Did you begin at the top?" Sekhlen asked.

Cheloe looked up from his duties. His eyes were a shade of such piercing blue that they would be breathtaking if Sekhlen hadn't seen such a shade every day, especially when he looked at his own reflection.

"I did not," Cheloe said.

"Have we not had this discussion before?"

"We have."

"And?"

Cheloe shouldered his broom like a spear, stood rigid, and began to recite. "I am an instrument of the Order, a blade ever-honed. I am the force of what must be, a storm ever-brewing. I am a slave to no God, no king, no man, a wind ever-moving. I am—"

"Yes, yes." Sekhlen interrupted with a sigh. Cheloe's unerring willingness to recite the oath was proof enough that, given time, he *could* actually remember things he had been told longer than a day. "If you would not mind attending to my meditation chamber? It's grown a tad dusty."

"I *just* swept that yesterday," Cheloe groaned.

A flash of a scowl was all it took to send the young man scurrying up the stairs, though. Cheloe had not yet been here long enough to grow unimpressed with the power of the eyes. Sekhlen lived in bitter dread of the day when that moment would come.

But that was a concern for another day.

He folded his hands behind his back as he continued through the courtyard. The other initiates went about their business: from the newer ones peeling rice and beating rugs to the older ones sharpening blades and bowing their heads in meditation.

Young, all of them.

Silver-haired, all of them.

Killers to a one, even the youngest having slain no less than three people before Sekhlen had found them.

"Sekhlen! Master Sekhlen!"

Shuro had slaughtered many before he had brought her here, beginning with her family. That wasn't so uncommon; so many of these poor young people began with their families. What was odd was how long she went on doing it, her body count a tragic fifteen when she had as many years.

He could still remember her, some skinny thing holed up in a barn somewhere in some northern shithole of a town, blue eyes wide and trembling, silver hair matted with blood, clutching a knife in her hand. She was such a frail thing, back then.

Far removed from the healthy, vibrant creature that came trotting up to him now. This girl—woman, he reminded himself; she was a young woman—was wiry with lean muscle, powerful beneath her black uniform, her hair done up in an elegant tail. Far stronger, far more confident than she had been so long ago.

And still so, so serious.

"Master Sekhlen," she said, sliding into a perfect posture as she came to a halt before him. Her chin, sharpened to a fine point like the rest of her features, angled up as she respectfully acknowledged him. "We have returned with the subject."

"You can call me 'Sekhlen,' you know," he replied. "I don't at all mind."

Her face, as honed as the blade she wore at her hip, twitched at that notion, such an impropriety completely beyond her comprehension. He sighed and made a gesture for her to lead.

"Show me."

The return to formality smoothed her again and she led him through the courtyard to the temple gates. Two other initiates, young men by the names of Calo and Fuma, surrounded another woman. They did little more than block her as she wandered this way and that and she tumbled away from them to stagger off in another direction, completely heedless of them.

She was not like them. Older, for one, and not having been spared the world of humanity like his initiates, her face was mapped with wrinkles that were exaggerated by the euphoric smile she wore across her face. Her hair hung about her in wild, greasy strands, framing eyes positively bulging with glee. The soles of her feet were completely black and her garments had been ripped, torn, and dirtied without any indication that she had ever even noticed.

Her wild gaze settled upon Sekhlen and she rushed toward him. Shuro immediately moved for her blade, but Sekhlen waved her off and let the wild woman come and seize his hand.

"Grandfather!" she all but shrieked. "How good to see you! You must hear the tremendous news! I heard it two weeks ago, saw it in my dreams." She nodded vigorously. "He came to me, Grandfather. All in white and smiling, he came to me and told me that all would be well. He told me my worries were at an end, that it wasn't my fault, that my husband did not die for nothing. He...he called to me...called to all of us, bade us to come to him. West. Always west. Oh, isn't it wonderful? He calls us home!"

Sekhlen nodded gently at her and pulled his hand from hers to rest it gently upon her brow. With his thumb, he moved a stray lock of hair from her eyes, smoothing it back behind her ear. Her smile grew wider at his touch and she just kept on smiling.

Even as he reached into his shirt, pulled out a dagger, and drew it cleanly across her throat.

Heavily, he watched her collapse to the ground and bleed out upon the temple stones. She hadn't deserved it, of course, neither the blade nor the visions. Such was his burden.

An instrument. A blade ever-honed.

"We discovered her at the edge of the forest with two others," Shuro said. "Both dead from exhaustion. We had to force water down her throat to keep her alive long enough to get here." The young woman's frown was as sharp as anything else about her. "They were heading west. To the city."

"Interesting," Sekhlen said. "Perhaps she came from a village. Or a trading caravan." He watched the woman's life leak out. "I wonder if there's anyone out there who wonders where she is."

"Does it matter?"

He cast a glance askew at Shuro.

So serious. So hard. So very different from that little girl. But who did he have to blame for that but himself?

"I suppose not," he said. "This confirms our fears, then." He looked out the temple gates, over the forest, and west to the desert. "Khoth-Kapira has made himself known."

"He has."

Sekhlen nodded, reached down, and took up both of Shuro's hands. He held them for a moment, noting just how cold she was, before releasing. And when he did, her fingers were bloodied by the blade he had left in her grasp.

"You know what to do, then," he said.

She stared down at the blade before looking up at him, eyes unwavering and blue and cold as ice. She nodded exactly once and spoke.

"I do."

THE END

extras

orbit

meet the author

Libbi Rich

SAM SYKES is the author of the acclaimed *Tome of the Undergates*, a vast and sprawling story of adventure, demons, madness and carnage. He lives in Arizona.

introducing

If you enjoyed
THE CITY STAINED RED
look out for

THE BLACK PRISM

Lightbringer: Book 1

by Brent Weeks

Gavin Guile is the Prism, the most powerful man in the world.
He is high priest and emperor, a man whose power, wit, and
charm are all that preserves a tenuous peace. But Prisms never last,
and Guile knows exactly how long he has left to live:
Five years to achieve five impossible goals.

But when Guile discovers he has a son, born in a far kingdom
after the war that put him in power, he must decide
how much he's willing to pay to protect a secret
that could tear his world apart.

CHAPTER 1

Kip crawled toward the battlefield in the darkness, the mist pressing down, blotting out sound, scattering starlight. Though the adults shunned it and the children were forbidden to come here, he'd played on the open field a hundred times—during the day. Tonight, his purpose was grimmer.

Reaching the top of the hill, Kip stood and hiked up his pants. The river behind him was hissing, or maybe that was the warriors beneath its surface, dead these sixteen years. He squared his shoulders, ignoring his imagination. The mists made him seem suspended, outside of time. But even if there was no evidence of it, the sun was coming. By the time it did, he had to get to the far side of the battlefield. Farther than he'd ever gone searching.

Even Ramir wouldn't come out here at night. Everyone knew Sundered Rock was haunted. But Ram didn't have to feed his family; *his* mother didn't smoke her wages.

Gripping his little belt knife tightly, Kip started walking. It wasn't just the unquiet dead that might pull him down to the evernight. A pack of giant javelinas had been seen roaming the night, tusks cruel, hooves sharp. They were good eating if you had a matchlock, iron nerves, and good aim, but since the Prisms' War had wiped out all the town's men, there weren't many people who braved death for a little bacon. Rekton was already a shell of what it had once been. The *alcaldesa* wasn't eager for any of her townspeople to throw their lives away. Besides, Kip didn't have a matchlock.

Nor were javelinas the only creatures that roamed the night. A mountain lion or a golden bear would also probably enjoy a well-marbled Kip.

A low howl cut the mist and the darkness hundreds of paces deeper into the battlefield. Kip froze. Oh, there were wolves too. How'd he forget wolves?

Another wolf answered, farther out. A haunting sound, the very voice of the wilderness. You couldn't help but freeze when you heard it. It was the kind of beauty that made you shit your pants.

Wetting his lips, Kip got moving. He had the distinct sensation of being followed. Stalked. He looked over his shoulder. There was nothing there. Of course. His mother always said he had too much imagination. Just walk, Kip. Places to be. Animals are more scared of you and all that. Besides, that was one of the tricks about a howl, it always sounded much closer than it really was. Those wolves were probably leagues away.

Before the Prisms' War, this had been excellent farmland. Right next to the Umber River, suitable for figs, grapes, pears, dewberries, asparagus—*everything* grew here. And it had been sixteen years since the final battle—a year before Kip was even born. But the plain was still torn and scarred. A few burnt timbers of old homes and barns poked out of the dirt. Deep furrows and craters remained from cannon shells. Filled now with swirling mist, those craters looked like lakes, tunnels, traps. Bottomless. Unfathomable.

Most of the magic used in the battle had dissolved sooner or later in the years of sun exposure, but here and there broken green luxin spears still glittered. Shards of solid yellow underfoot would cut through the toughest shoe leather.

Scavengers had long since taken all the valuable arms, mail, and luxin from the battlefield, but as the seasons passed and rains fell, more mysteries surfaced each year. That was what Kip was hoping for—and what he was seeking was most visible in the first rays of dawn.

The wolves stopped howling. Nothing was worse than hearing that chilling sound, but at least with the sound he knew where they were. Now...Kip swallowed on the hard knot in his throat.

As he walked in the valley of the shadow of two great unnatural hills—the remnant of two of the great funeral pyres where tens of thousands had burned—Kip saw something in the mist. His heart leapt into his throat. The curve of a mail cowl. A glint of eyes searching the darkness.

Then it was swallowed up in the roiling mists.

A ghost. Dear Orholam. Some spirit keeping watch at its grave.

Look on the bright side. Maybe wolves are scared of ghosts.

Kip realized he'd stopped walking, peering into the darkness. Move, fathead.

He moved, keeping low. He might be big, but he prided himself on being light on his feet. He tore his eyes away from the hill—still no sign of the ghost or man or whatever it was. He had that feeling again that he was being stalked. He looked back. Nothing.

A quick click, like someone dropping a small stone. And something at the corner of his eye. Kip shot a look up the hill. A click, a spark, the striking of flint against steel.

The mists illuminated for that briefest moment, Kip saw few details. Not a ghost—a soldier striking a flint, trying to light a slow-match. It caught fire, casting a red glow on the soldier's face, making his eyes seem to glow. He affixed the slow-match to the match-holder of his matchlock and spun, looking for targets in the darkness.

His night vision must have been ruined by staring at the brief flame on his match, now a smoldering red ember, because his eyes passed right over Kip.

The soldier turned again, sharply, paranoid. "The hell am I supposed to see out here, anyway? Swivin' wolves."

Very, very carefully, Kip started walking away. He had to get deeper into the mist and darkness before the soldier's night vision recovered, but if he made noise, the man might fire blindly. Kip walked on his toes, silently, his back itching, sure that a lead ball was going to tear through him at any moment.

But he made it. A hundred paces, more, and no one yelled. No shot cracked the night. Farther. Two hundred paces more, and he saw light off to his left, a campfire. It had burned so low it was barely more than coals now. Kip tried not to look directly at it to save his vision. There was no tent, no bedrolls nearby, just the fire.

Kip tried Master Danavis's trick for seeing in darkness. He let his focus relax and tried to view things from the periphery of his vision. Nothing but an irregularity, perhaps. He moved closer.

Two men lay on the cold ground. One was a soldier. Kip had seen his mother unconscious plenty of times; he knew instantly this man wasn't passed out. He was sprawled unnaturally, there were no blankets, and his mouth hung open, slack-jawed, eyes staring unblinking at the night. Next to the dead soldier lay another man, bound in chains but alive. He lay on his side, hands manacled behind his back, a black bag over his head and cinched tight around his neck.

The prisoner was alive, trembling. No, weeping. Kip looked around; there was no one else in sight.

"Why don't you just finish it, damn you?" the prisoner said.

Kip froze. He thought he'd approached silently.

"Coward," the prisoner said. "Just following your orders, I suppose? Orholam will smite you for what you're about to do to that little town."

Kip had no idea what the man was talking about.

Apparently his silence spoke for him.

"You're not one of them." A note of hope entered the prisoner's voice. "Please, help me!"

Kip stepped forward. The man was suffering. Then he stopped. Looked at the dead soldier. The front of the soldier's shirt was soaked with blood. Had this prisoner killed him? How?

"Please, leave me chained if you must. But please, I don't want to die in darkness."

Kip stayed back, though it felt cruel. "You killed him?"

"I'm supposed to be executed at first light. I got away. He chased me down and got the bag over my head before he died. If dawn's close, his replacement is coming anytime now."

Kip still wasn't putting it together. No one in Rekton trusted the soldiers who came through, and the alcaldesa had told the town's young people to give any soldiers a wide berth for a while— apparently the new satrap Garadul had declared himself free of the Chromeria's control. Now he was King Garadul, he said, but he wanted the usual levies from the town's young people. The alcaldesa had told his representative that if he wasn't the satrap anymore, he didn't have the right to raise levies. King or satrap, Garadul couldn't be happy with that, but Rekton was too small to bother with. Still, it would be wise to avoid his soldiers until this all blew over.

On the other hand, just because Rekton wasn't getting along with the satrap right now didn't make this man Kip's friend.

"So you *are* a criminal?" Kip asked.

"Of six shades to Sun Day," the man said. The hope leaked out of his voice. "Look, boy—you are a child, aren't you? You sound like one. I'm going to die today. I can't get away. Truth to tell, I don't want to. I've run enough. This time, I fight."

"I don't understand."

"You will. Take off my hood."

Though some vague doubt nagged Kip, he untied the half-knot around the man's neck and pulled off the hood.

At first, Kip had no idea what the prisoner was talking about. The man sat up, arms still bound behind his back. He was perhaps thirty years old, Tyrean like Kip but with a lighter complexion, his hair wavy rather than kinky, his limbs thin and muscular. Then Kip saw his eyes.

Men and women who could harness light and make luxin—drafters—always had unusual eyes. A little residue of whatever color they drafted ended up in their eyes. Over the course of their life, it would stain the entire iris red, or blue, or whatever their color was. The prisoner was a green drafter—or had been. Instead of the green being bound in a halo within the iris, it was shattered like crockery smashed to the floor. Little green fragments glowed even in the whites of his eyes. Kip gasped and shrank back.

"Please!" the man said. "Please, the madness isn't on me. I won't hurt you."

"You're a color wight."

"And now you know why I ran away from the Chromeria," the man said.

Because the Chromeria put down color wights like a farmer put down a beloved, rabid dog.

Kip was on the verge of bolting, but the man wasn't making any threatening moves. And besides, it was still dark. Even color wights needed light to draft. The mist did seem lighter, though, gray beginning to touch the horizon. It was crazy to talk to a madman, but maybe it wasn't too crazy. At least until dawn.

The color wight was looking at Kip oddly. "Blue eyes." He laughed.

Kip scowled. He hated his blue eyes. It was one thing when a foreigner like Master Danavis had blue eyes. They looked fine on him. Kip looked freakish.

"What's your name?" the color wight asked.

Kip swallowed, thinking he should probably run away.

"Oh, for Orholam's sake, you think I'm going to hex you with your name? How ignorant is this backwater? That isn't how chromaturgy works—"

"Kip."

The color wight grinned. "Kip. Well, Kip, have you ever wondered why you were stuck in such a small life? Have you ever gotten the feeling, Kip, that you're special?"

Kip said nothing. Yes, and yes.

"Do you know *why* you feel destined for something greater?"

"Why?" Kip asked, quiet, hopeful.

"Because you're an arrogant little shit." The color wight laughed.

Kip shouldn't have been taken off guard. His mother had said worse. Still, it took him a moment. A small failure. "Burn in hell, coward," he said. "You're not even good at running away. Caught by ironfoot soldiers."

The color wight laughed louder. "Oh, they didn't *catch* me. They recruited me."

Who would recruit madmen to join them? "They didn't know you were a—"

"Oh, they knew."

Dread like a weight dropped into Kip's stomach. "You said something about my town. Before. What are they planning to do?"

"You know, Orholam's got a sense of humor. Never realized that till now. Orphan, aren't you?"

"No. I've got a mother," Kip said. He instantly regretted giving the color wight even that much.

"Would you believe me if I told you there's a prophecy about you?"

"It wasn't funny the first time," Kip said. "What's going to happen to my town?" Dawn was coming, and Kip wasn't going to stick around. Not only would the guard's replacement come then, but Kip had no idea what the wight would do once he had light.

"You know," the wight said, "you're the reason I'm here. Not here here. Not like 'Why do I exist?' Not in Tyrea. In chains, I mean."

"What?" Kip asked.

"There's power in madness, Kip. Of course..." He trailed off, laughed at a private thought. Recovered. "Look, that soldier has a key in his breast pocket. I couldn't get it out, not with—" He shook his hands, bound and manacled behind his back.

"And I would help you why?" Kip asked.

"For a few straight answers before dawn."

Crazy, and cunning. *Perfect.* "Give me one first," Kip said.

"Shoot."

"What's the plan for Rekton?"

"Fire."

"What?" Kip asked.

"Sorry, you said one answer."

"That was no answer!"

"They're going to wipe out your village. Make an example so no one else defies King Garadul. Other villages defied the king too, of course. His rebellion against the Chromeria isn't popular everywhere. For every town burning to take vengeance on the Prism, there's another that wants nothing to do with war. Your village was chosen specially. Anyway, I had a little spasm of conscience and objected. Words were exchanged. I punched my superior. Not totally my fault. They know us greens don't do rules and hierarchy. Especially not once we've broken the halo." The color wight shrugged. "There, straight. I think that deserves the key, don't you?"

It was too much information to soak up at once—broken the halo?—but it *was* a straight answer. Kip walked over to the dead man. His skin was pallid in the rising light. Pull it together, Kip. Ask whatever you need to ask.

Kip could tell that dawn was coming. Eerie shapes were emerging from the night. The great twin looming masses of Sundered Rock itself were visible mostly as a place where stars were blotted out of the sky.

What do I need to ask?

He was hesitating, not wanting to touch the dead man. He knelt. "Why my town?" He poked through the dead man's pocket, careful not to touch skin. It was there, two keys.

"They think you have something that belongs to the king. I don't know what. I only picked up that much by eavesdropping."

"What would Rekton have that the king wants?" Kip asked.

"Not Rekton you. You you."

It took Kip a second. He touched his own chest. "Me? Me personally? I don't even own anything!"

The color wight gave a crazy grin, but Kip thought it was a pretense. "Tragic mistake, then. Their mistake, your tragedy."

"What, you think I'm lying?!" Kip asked. "You think I'd be out here scavenging luxin if I had any other choice?"

"I don't really care one way or the other. You going to bring that key over here, or do I need to ask real nice?"

It was a mistake to bring the keys over. Kip knew it. The color wight wasn't stable. He was dangerous. He'd admitted as much. But he had kept his word. How could Kip do less?

Kip unlocked the man's manacles, and then the padlock on the chains. He backed away carefully, as one would from a wild animal. The color wight pretended not to notice, simply rubbing his arms and stretching back and forth. He moved over to the guard and poked through his pockets again. His hand emerged with a pair of green spectacles with one cracked lens.

"You could come with me," Kip said. "If what you said is true—"

"How close do you think I'd get to your town before someone came running with a musket? Besides, once the sun comes up... I'm ready for it to be done." The color wight took a deep breath, staring at the horizon. "Tell me, Kip, if you've done bad things your whole life, but you die doing something good, do you think that makes up for all the bad?"

"No," Kip said, honestly, before he could stop himself.

"Me neither."

"But it's better than nothing," Kip said. "Orholam is merciful."

"Wonder if you'll say that after they're done with your village."

There were other questions Kip wanted to ask, but everything had happened in such a rush that he couldn't put his thoughts together.

In the rising light Kip saw what had been hidden in the fog and the darkness. Hundreds of tents were laid out in military precision. Soldiers. Lots of soldiers. And even as Kip stood, not two hundred paces from the nearest tent, the plain began winking. Glimmers sparkled as broken luxin gleamed, like stars scattered on the ground, answering their brethren in the sky.

It was what Kip had come for. Usually when a drafter released luxin, it simply dissolved, no matter what color it was. But in battle, there had been so much chaos, so many drafters, some sealed magic had been buried and protected from the sunlight that would break it down. The recent rain had uncovered more.

But Kip's eyes were pulled from the winking luxin by four soldiers and a man with a stark red cloak and red spectacles walking toward them from the camp.

"My name is Gaspar, by the by. Gaspar Elos." The color wight didn't look at Kip.

"What?"

"I'm not just some drafter. My father loved me. I had plans. A girl. A life."

"I don't—"

"You will." The color wight put the green spectacles on; they fit perfectly, tight to his face, lenses sweeping to either side so that wherever he looked, he would be looking through a green filter. "Now get out of here."

As the sun touched the horizon, Gaspar sighed. It was as if Kip had ceased to exist. It was like watching his mother take that first deep breath of haze. Between the sparkling spars of darker green, the whites of Gaspar's eyes swirled like droplets of green blood hitting water, first dispersing, then staining the whole. The emerald green of luxin ballooned through his eyes, thickened until it was solid, and then spread. Through his cheeks, up to his hairline, then down his neck, standing out starkly when it finally filled his lighter fingernails as if they'd been painted in radiant jade.

Gaspar started laughing. It was a low, unreasoning cackle, unrelenting. Mad. Not a pretense this time.

Kip ran.

He reached the funerary hill where the sentry had been, taking care to stay on the far side from the army. He had to get to Master Danavis. Master Danavis always knew what to do.

There was no sentry on the hill now. Kip turned around in time to see Gaspar change, transform. Green luxin spilled out of his hands onto his body, covering every part of him like a shell, like an enormous suit of armor. Kip couldn't see the soldiers or the red drafter approaching Gaspar, but he did see a fireball the size of his head streak toward the color wight, hit his chest, and burst apart, throwing flames everywhere.

Gaspar rammed through it, flaming red luxin sticking to his green armor. He was magnificent, terrible, powerful. He ran toward the soldiers, screaming defiance, and disappeared from Kip's view.

Kip fled, the vermilion sun setting fire to the mists.

introducing

If you enjoyed
THE CITY STAINED RED
look out for

PROMISE OF BLOOD

Book One of the Powder Mage Trilogy

by Brian McClellan

It's a bloody business overthrowing a king…

*Field Marshal Tamas's coup against his king sent corrupt
aristocrats to the guillotine and brought bread to the starving.
But it also provoked war with the Nine Nations, internal
attacks by royalist fanatics, and the greedy to scramble for money
and power by Tamas's supposed allies: the Church,
workers unions, and mercenary forces.*

It's up to a few…

*Stretched to his limit, Tamas is relying heavily on his few
remaining powder mages, including the embittered Taniel,
a brilliant marksman who also happens to be his estranged son,
and Adamat, a retired police inspector whose
loyalty is being tested by blackmail.*

But when gods are involved...

*Now, as attacks batter them from within and without,
the credulous are whispering about omens of death and destruction.
Just old peasant legends about the gods waking to walk
the earth. No modern educated man believes that sort of thing.
But they should...*

CHAPTER ONE

Adamat wore his coat tight, top buttons fastened against a wet night air that seemed to want to drown him. He tugged at his sleeves, trying to coax more length, and picked at the front of the jacket where it was too close by far around the waist. It'd been half a decade since he'd even seen this jacket, but when summons came from the king at this hour, there was no time to get his good one from the tailor. Yet this summer coat provided no defense against the chill snaking through the carriage window.

The morning was not far off but dawn would have a hard time scattering the fog. Adamat could feel it. It was humid even for early spring in Adopest, and chillier than Novi's frozen toes. The sooth-sayers in Noman's Alley said it was a bad omen. Yet who listened to soothsayers these days? Adamat reasoned it would give him a cold and wondered why he had been summoned out on a pit-made night like this.

The carriage approached the front gate of Skyline and moved on without a stop. Adamat clutched at his pantlegs and peered out the window. The guards were not at their posts. Odder still, as they continued along the wide path amid the fountains, there were no lights. Skyline had so many lanterns, it could be seen all the way from the city even on the cloudiest night. Tonight the gardens were dark.

Adamat was fine with this. Manhouch used enough of their taxes for his personal amusement. Adamat stared out into the gardens at the black maws where the hedge mazes began and imagined shapes flitting back and forth in the lawn. What was…ah, just a sculpture. Adamat sat back, took a deep breath. He could hear his heart beating, thumping, frightened, his stomach tightening. Perhaps they *should* light the garden lanterns…

A little part of him, the part that had once been a police inspector, prowling nights such as these for the thieves and pickpockets in dark alleys, laughed out from inside. *Still your heart, old man*, he said to himself. *You were once the eyes staring back from the darkness.*

The carriage jerked to a stop. Adamat waited for the coachman to open the door. He might have waited all night. The driver rapped on the roof. "You're here," a gruff voice said.

Rude.

Adamat stepped from the coach, just having time to snatch his hat and cane before the driver flicked the reins and was off, clattering into the night. Adamat uttered a quiet curse after the man and turned around, looking up at Skyline.

The nobility called Skyline Palace "the Jewel of Adro." It rested on a high hill east of Adopest so that the sun rose above it every morning. One particularly bold newspaper had compared it to a starving pauper wearing a diamond ring. It was an apt comparison in these lean times. A king's pride doesn't fill the people's bellies.

He was at the main entrance. By day, it was a grand avenue of marbled walks and fountains, all leading to a pair of giant, silver-plated doors, themselves dwarfed by the sheer façade of the biggest single building in Adro. Adamat listened for the soft footfalls of patrolling Hielmen. It was said the king's personal guard were everywhere in these gardens, watching every secluded corner, muskets always loaded, bayonets fixed, their gray-and-white sashes somber among the green-and-gold splendor. But there were no footfalls, nor were the fountains running. He'd heard once that the fountains only stopped for the death of the king. Surely he'd not have been summoned here if Manhouch were dead. He smoothed the front of his jacket. Here, next to the building, a few of the lanterns were lit.

A figure emerged from the darkness. Adamat tightened his grip on his cane, ready to draw the hidden sword inside at a moment's notice.

It was a man in uniform, but little could be discerned in such ill light. He held a rifle or a musket, trained loosely on Adamat, and wore a flat-topped forage cap with a stiff visor. Only one thing could be certain... he was not a Hielman. Their tall, plumed hats were easy to recognize, and they never went without them.

"You're alone?" a voice asked.

"Yes," Adamat said. He held up both hands and turned around.

"All right. Come on."

The soldier edged forward and yanked on one of the mighty silver doors. It rolled outward slowly, ponderously, despite the man putting his weight into it. Adamat moved closer and examined the soldier's jacket. It was dark blue with silver braiding. Adran military. In theory, the military reported to the king. In practice, one man held their leash: Field Marshal Tamas.

"Step back, friend," the soldier said. There was a note of impatience in his voice, some unseen stress—but that could have been the weight of the door. Adamat did as he was told, only coming forward again to slip through the entrance when the soldier gestured.

"Go ahead," the soldier directed. "Take a right at the diadem and head through the Diamond Hall. Keep walking until you find yourself in the Answering Room." The door inched shut behind him and closed with a muffled thump.

Adamat was alone in the palace vestibule. Adran military, he mused. Why would a soldier be here, on the grounds, without any sign of the Hielmen? The most frightening answer sprang to mind first. A power struggle. Had the military been called in to deal with a rebellion? There were a number of powerful factions within Adro: the Wings of Adom mercenaries, the royal cabal, the Mountainwatch, and the great noble families. Any one of them could have been giving Manhouch trouble. None of it made sense, though. If there had been a power struggle, the palace grounds would be a battlefield, or destroyed outright by the royal cabal.

Adamat passed the diadem—a giant facsimile of the Adran crown—and noted it was in as bad taste as rumor had it. He entered the Diamond Hall, where the walls and floor were of scarlet, accented in gold leaf, and thousands of tiny gems, which gave the room its name, glittered from the ceiling in the light of a single lit candelabra. The tiny flames of the candelabra flickered as if in the wind, and the room was cold.

Adamat's sense of unease deepened as he neared the far end of the gallery. Not a sign of life, and the only sound came from his own echoing footfalls on the marble floor. A window had been shattered, explaining the chill. The result of one of the king's famous temper tantrums? Or something else? He could hear his heart beating in his ears. There. Behind a curtain, a pair of boots? Adamat passed his hand before his eyes. A trick of the light. He stepped over to reassure himself and pulled back the curtain.

A body lay in the shadows. Adamat bent over it, touched the skin. It was warm, but the man was most certainly dead. He wore gray pants with a white stripe down the side and a matching jacket. A tall hat with a white plume lay on the floor some ways away. A Hielman. The shadows played on a young, clean-shaven face, peaceful except for a single hole in the side of his skull and the dark, wet stain on the floor.

He'd been right. A struggle of some kind. Had the Hielmen rebelled, and the military been brought in to deal with them? Again, it didn't make any sense. The Hielmen were fanatically loyal to the king, and any matters within Skyline Palace would have been dealt with by the royal cabal.

Adamat cursed silently. Every question compounded itself. He suspected he'd find some answers soon enough.

Adamat left the body behind the curtain. He lifted his cane and twisted, bared a few inches of steel, and approached a tall doorway flanked by two hooded, scepter-wielding sculptures. He paused between the ancient statues and took a deep breath, letting his eyes wander over a set of arcane script scrawled into the portal. He entered.

The Answering Room made the Hall of Diamonds look small. A pair of staircases, one to either side of him and each as wide across as three coaches, led to a high gallery that ran the length of the room on both sides. Few outside the king and his cabal of Privileged sorcerers ever entered this room.

In the center of the room was a single chair, on a dais a handbreadth off the floor, facing a collection of knee pillows, where the cabal acknowledged their liege. The room was well lit, though from no discernible source of light.

A man sat on the stairs to Adamat's right. He was older than Adamat, just into his sixtieth year with silver hair and a neatly trimmed mustache that still retained a hint of black. He had a strong but not overly large jaw and his cheekbones were well defined. His skin was darkened by the sun, and there were deep lines at the corners of his mouth and eyes. He wore a dark-blue soldier's uniform with a silver representation of a powder keg pinned above the heart and nine gold service stripes sewn on the right breast, one for every five years in the Adran military. His uniform lacked an officer's epaulettes, but the weary experience in the man's brown eyes left no question that he'd led armies on the battlefield. There was a single pistol, hammer cocked, on the stair next to him. He leaned on a sheathed small sword and watched as a stream of blood slowly trickled down each step, a dark line on the yellow-and-white marble.

"Field Marshal Tamas," Adamat said. He sheathed his cane sword and twisted until it clicked shut.

The man looked up. "I don't believe we've ever met."

"We have," Adamat said. "Fourteen years ago. A charity ball thrown by Lord Aumen."

"I have a terrible time with faces," the field marshal said. "I apologize."

Adamat couldn't take his eyes off the rivulet of blood. "Sir. I was summoned here. I wasn't told by whom, or for what reason."

"Yes," Tamas said. "I summoned you. On the recommendation of one of my Marked. Cenka. He said you served together on the police force in the twelfth district."

Adamat pictured Cenka in his mind. He was a short man with an unruly beard and a penchant for wines and fine food. He'd seen him last seven years ago. "I didn't know he was a powder mage."

"We try to find anyone with an affinity for it as soon as possible," Tamas said, "but Cenka was a late bloomer. In any case"—he waved a hand—"we've come upon a problem."

Adamat blinked. "You...want my help?"

The field marshal raised an eyebrow. "Is that such an unusual request? You were once a fine police investigator, a good servant of Adro, and Cenka tells me that you have a perfect memory."

"Still, sir."

"Eh?"

"I'm still an investigator. Not with the police, sir, but I still take jobs."

"Excellent. Then it's not so odd for me to seek your services?"

"Well, no," Adamat said, "but sir, this is Skyline Palace. There's a dead Hielman in the Diamond Hall and..." He pointed at the stream of blood on the stairs. "Where's the king?"

Tamas tilted his head to the side. "He's locked himself in the chapel."

"You've staged a coup," Adamat said. He caught a glimpse of movement with the corner of his eye, saw a soldier appear at the top of the stairs. The man was a Deliv, a dark-skinned northerner. He wore the same uniform as Tamas, with eight golden stripes on the right breast. The left breast of his uniform displayed a silver powder keg, the sign of a Marked. Another powder mage.

"We have a lot of bodies to move," the Deliv said.

Tamas gave his subordinate a glance. "I know, Sabon."

"Who's this?" Sabon asked.

"The inspector that Cenka requested."

"I don't like him being here," Sabon said. "It could compromise everything."

"Cenka trusted him."

"You've staged a coup," Adamat said again with certainty.

"I'll help with the bodies in a moment," Tamas said. "I'm old,

I need some rest now and then." The Deliv gave a sharp nod and disappeared.

"Sir!" Adamat said. "What have you done?" He tightened his grip on his cane sword.

Tamas pursed his lips. "Some say the Adran royal cabal had the most powerful Privileged sorcerers in all the Nine Nations, second only to Kez," he said quietly. "Yet I've just slaughtered every one of them. Do you think I'd have trouble with an old inspector and his cane sword?"

Adamat loosened his grip. He felt ill. "I suppose not."

"Cenka led me to believe that you were pragmatic. If that is the case, I would like to employ your services. If not, I'll kill you now and look for a solution elsewhere."

"You've staged a coup," Adamat said again.

Tamas sighed. "Must we keep coming back to that? Is it so shocking? Tell me, can you think of any fewer than a dozen factions within Adro with reason to dethrone the king?"

"I didn't think any of them had the skill," Adamat said. "Or the daring." His eyes returned to the blood on the stairs, before his mind traveled to his wife and children, asleep in their beds. He looked at the field marshal. His hair was tousled; there were drops of blood on his jacket—a lot, now that he thought to look. Tamas might as well have been sprayed with it. There were dark circles under his eyes and a weariness that spoke of more than just age.

"I will not agree to a job blindly," Adamat said. "Tell me what you want."

"We killed them in their sleep," Tamas said without preamble. "There's no easy way to kill a Privileged, but that's the best. A mistake was made and we had a fight on our hands." Tamas looked pained for a moment, and Adamat suspected that the fight had not gone as well as Tamas would have liked. "We prevailed. Yet upon the lips of the dying was one phrase."

Adamat waited.

"'You can't break Kresimir's Promise,'" Tamas said. "That's what the dying sorcerers said to me. Does it mean anything to you?"

Adamat smoothed the front of his coat and sought to recall old memories. "No. 'Kresimir's Promise'... 'Break'... 'Broken'... ait—'Kresimir's Broken Promise.'" He looked up. "It was the name of a street gang. Twenty... twenty-two years ago. Cenka couldn't remember that?"

Tamas continued. "Cenka thought it sounded familiar. He was certain you'd remember it."

"I don't forget things," Adamat said. "Kresimir's Broken Promise was a street gang with forty-three members. They were all young, some of them no more than children, the oldest not yet twenty. We were trying to round up some of the leaders to put a stop to a string of thefts. They were an odd lot—they broke into churches and robbed priests."

"What happened to them?"

Adamat couldn't help but look at the blood on the stairs. "One day they disappeared, every one of them—including our informants. We found the whole lot a few days later, forty-three bodies jammed into a drain culvert like pickled pigs' feet. They'd been massacred by powerful sorceries, with excessive brutality. The marks of the king's royal cabal. The investigation ended there." Adamat suppressed a shiver. He'd not once seen a thing like that, not before or since. He'd witnessed executions and riots and murder scenes that filled him with less dread.

The Deliv soldier appeared again at the top of the stairs. "We need you," he said to Tamas.

"Find out why these mages would utter those words with their final breath," Tamas said. "It may be connected to your street gang. Maybe not. Either way, find me an answer. I don't like the riddles of the dead." He got to his feet quickly, moving like a man twenty years younger, and jogged up the stairs after the Deliv. His boot splashed in the blood, leaving behind red prints. "Also," he called over his shoulder, "keep silent about what you have seen here until the execution. It will begin at noon."

"But..." Adamat said. "Where do I start? Can I speak with Cenka?"

Tamas paused near the top of the stairs and turned. "If you can speak with the dead, you're welcome to."

Adamat ground his teeth. "How did they say the words?" he said. "Was it a command, or a statement, or...?"

Tamas frowned. "An entreaty. As if the blood draining from their bodies was not their primary concern. I must go now."

"One more thing," Adamat said.

Tamas looked to be near the end of his patience.

"If I'm to help you, tell me why all of this?" He gestured to the blood on the stairs.

"I have things that require my attention," Tamas warned.

Adamat felt his jaw tighten. "Did you do this for power?"

"I did this for me," Tamas said. "And I did this for Adro. So that Manhouch wouldn't sign us all into slavery to the Kez with the Accords. I did it because those grumbling students of philosophy at the university only play at rebellion. The age of kings is dead, Adamat, and I have killed it."

Adamat examined Tamas's face. The Accords was a treaty to be signed with the king of Kez that would absolve all Adran debt but impose strict tax and regulation on Adro, making it little more than a Kez vassal. The field marshal had been outspoken about the Accords. But then, that was expected. The Kez had executed Tamas's late wife.

"It is," Adamat said.

"Then get me some bloody answers." The field marshal whirled and disappeared into the hallway above.

Adamat remembered the bodies of that street gang as they were being pulled from the drain in the wet and mud, remembered the horror etched upon their dead faces. *The answers may very well be bloody.*

⊶ ⊷

Nila paused for a moment to watch the fire burn beneath the big iron pot suspended in the fireplace. She rubbed her chapped hands together and warmed them over the flames. The water would boil soon, and she'd finish washing the laundry for everyone in the townhouse. There was a small pile of dirty laundry stacked by the pantry, but most of the family's clothes, as well as the servants' livery, had been soaking in the large vats of warm water and lye soap since last evening. They would need to be boiled, rinsed, and then hung out to dry, but first she needed to iron the duke's dress uniform. He had a meeting with the king at ten. That was still hours away, but all of it, the washing, rinsing, and ironing, had to be done before the cooks got up to make breakfast.

The door to the washroom opened and a boy of five came into the kitchen rubbing the sleep from his eyes.

"Can't sleep, young master?" Nila asked.

"No," he said. The only child of Duke Eldaminse, Jakob was very sickly. He had blond hair and a pale face with narrow cheeks. He was small for his age, but bright, and friendlier to the help than a duke's son ought to be. Nila had been thirteen and an apprentice laundress for the Eldaminse when he was born. From the time he could walk he'd taken a liking to her, much to the chagrin of his mother and governess.

"Have a seat here," Nila said, rearranging a clean, dry blanket near the fire for Jakob. "Only for a couple of minutes, then you need to go back to bed before Ganny awakes."

He settled onto the blanket and watched her heat the irons on the stove and lay out his father's clothes. His eyes soon began to droop and he settled onto his side.

Nila dragged a large washbasin over beside the iron pot. She was just about to pour in the water when the door opened again.

"Nila!" Ganny stood in the doorway, hands on her hips. She was twenty-six, and severe beyond her age; well suited to be the governess of a ducal heir. She wore her cocoa-colored hair up in a tight bun behind her head. Even in her nightclothes, Ganny seemed more proper than Nila with her plain dress and unruly auburn curls.

Nila put a finger to her lips.

"You know he's not supposed to be in here," Ganny said, lowering her voice.

"What should I do? Say no?"

"Of course!"

"Leave him be, he's finally asleep."

"He'll catch a cold down here."

"He's right next to the fire," Nila said.

"If the duchess finds him here, she'll be furious!" Ganny shook her finger at Nila. "I won't stick up for you when she turns you out on the street."

"And when have you ever stuck up for me?"

Ganny's lips took on a hard line. "I'll recommend your dismissal to the duchess tonight. You're nothing but a bad influence on Jakob."

"I will..." Nila took one look at the sleeping boy and closed her mouth. She had no family, no connections. The duchess already disliked her. Duke Eldaminse had a habit of bedding the help, and he'd been looking at her more often lately. Nila didn't need any trouble with Ganny, even if she was a bully. "I'm sorry, Ganny," Nila said. "I'll get him back to bed now. Do you have any clothes I can get the stains out of for you?"

"That's a better attitude," Ganny said. "Now..."

She was interrupted by a hammering on the front door, loud enough to be heard all the way at the back of the townhouse.

"Who is that at this early hour?" Ganny pulled her nightclothes tightly around her and headed into the hallway. "They'll wake up the lord and lady!"

Nila put her hands on her hips and looked at Jakob. "You'll get me in trouble, young master."

His eyes fluttered open. "Sorry," he said.

She knelt down beside him. "It's all right, go back to sleep. Let me carry you to bed."

She'd just lifted him up when she heard the scream from the front of the house. Shouts followed and then the hammering footsteps running up the stairs in the main hallway. She heard angry male voices that didn't belong to any of the house staff.

"What is that?" Jakob asked.

She set him on his feet so that he couldn't feel her hands shaking. "Quickly," she said. "In the washtub."

Jakob's bottom lip trembled. "Why, what's happening?"

"Hide!"

He climbed into the washtub. She dumped the dirty laundry on top of him and stacked it high and then hurried into the hallway.

She ran right into a soldier. The man shoved her back into the kitchen. He was soon joined by two other men, then another holding Ganny by the back of the neck. He shoved Ganny to the floor. The governess's eyes were full of fear mingled with indignation.

"These two will do," one of the soldiers said. He wore the dark blue of the Adran army, with two golden service stripes on his chest and a silver medal that indicated he'd served the crown overseas. He began to loosen his belt and stepped toward Nila.

Nila grabbed the hot iron from the stove and hit him hard across the face. He went down, to the shouts of his comrades.

Someone grabbed her arms, another her legs.

"Feisty," one said.

"That will leave a mark," said another.

"What is the meaning of this!" Ganny had finally gotten to her feet. "Do you know whose house this is?"

"Shut up." The soldier Nila had hit climbed to his feet, a swollen burn covering half of his face. He punched Ganny hard in the stomach. "We'll get to you soon enough." He turned to Nila.

Nila struggled against hands too strong for her. She turned to the washbasin, hoping Jakob would not see this, and closed her eyes to wait for the blow.

"Heathlo!" a voice barked.

She opened her eyes again when the hands that held her suddenly let up.

"What the pit you doing, soldier?" The man who spoke wore the same uniform as the others, only set apart by a gold triangle pinned to his silver lapel. He had sandy hair and a neatly trimmed beard. A cigarette hung out of the corner of his mouth. Nila had never seen a soldier with a beard before.

"Just having some fun, Sergeant." Heathlo gave Nila a menacing glare and turned toward the sergeant.

"Fun? No fun for us, soldier. This is the army. You heard the field marshal's orders."

"But, Sergeant..."

The sergeant leaned over and picked up the iron from where it lay on the floor. He looked at the bottom, then at the burn on the soldier's face. "You want me to give you a matching one on the other side?"

Heathlo's eyes hardened. "This bitch struck me."

"I'll hit you somewhere prettier than your face next time I see you try to rape an Adran citizen." The sergeant pointed his cigarette at Heathlo. "This isn't Gurla."

"I'll report this to the captain, sir," Heathlo sneered.

The sergeant shrugged.

"Heathlo," one of the other soldiers said. "Don't push him. Sorry, Sergeant, he's new to the company and all."

"Keep him in line," the sergeant said. "He's new, but I expect better from you two." He helped Ganny to her feet, then touched his finger to his forehead toward Nila. "Ma'am. We're looking for Duke Eldaminse's son."

Ganny looked at Nila. Nila could tell she was terrified. "He was with you," the governess said.

Nila forced herself to look into the sergeant's blue eyes. "I just carried him up to bed."

"Go on," the sergeant said to his soldiers. "Find him." They left the room quickly. He remained and gave a slow look around the kitchen. "He's not in his bed."

"He has a habit of wandering," Nila said. "I just put him to bed, but I'm sure he was scared by the noise. What is happening?" This was no accident. Those soldiers knew exactly whose house this was. The sergeant had mentioned a field marshal. Adro only had one man of that rank: Field Marshal Tamas.

"Duke Eldaminse and his family are under arrest for treason," the sergeant said.

Ganny blanched and looked as if she might faint.

Nila felt her stomach tighten. Treason. Accusations like that would see the whole staff put to the question. There was no escape. She'd heard a story once of an archduke, the Iron King's own cousin, who plotted against the throne. His family and every member of his staff had been sent to the guillotine.

"You're free to go," the sergeant said. "We're only here for the duke and his family." He stepped toward the washbasin, frowning. "You'll want to find new employment. In fact, if you can, you should leave the city for at least a few days." He put the cigarette between his lips and lifted a pair of trousers from the top of the washbasin.

"Olem!"

The sergeant turned his head as another soldier entered the room.

"They find the boy?" Olem said, the washbasin forgotten.

"No, but a summons came for you. From the field marshal."

"For me?" Olem sounded doubtful.

"Report to Commander Sabon immediately."

"All right," Olem said. He crushed his cigarette out on the kitchen table. "Keep an eye on Heathlo. Don't let him rough up any of the women. If you have to give the boys an armful of loot to keep 'em occupied, do it."

"But our orders—"

"The boys will break some of our orders one way or another. I'd rather they break the ones that won't see them hanged."

"Right."

Olem took one last look around the kitchen. "Get any valuables you have here and leave," he said. "The duke won't be coming back for anything, either..." He touched his forehead toward Ganny and Nila before leaving.

So take what you want. Nila finished the sentence in her head.

Ganny gave Nila one quick look before she ran into the hallway. Nila could hear her feet on the servants' stairs a moment later.

Nila fished the butler's key from its hiding place above the mantel and unlocked the silverware cabinet. Nothing she had hidden under her mattress upstairs was worth a fraction of the silver she now piled into a burlap bag.

She waited until she couldn't hear any of the soldiers in the hallway and pulled Jakob from the washbasin. She helped him pull his nightclothes over his head and handed him a pair of dirty trousers and a shirt from one of the serving boys. They'd be too big, but they'd do.

"What are we doing?" he asked.

"Taking you someplace safe."

"What about Miss Ganny?"

"I think she's gone for good," Nila said.

"Mother and father?"

"I don't know," Nila said. "They'll want you to come with me, I think." She took a handful of cool ashes from the corner of the fireplace and mixed them in her palm with water. "Hold still," she said, smearing the ashes in his hair and on his face. She took his hand, and with a sack full of pilfered silver over her shoulder, Nila headed out the back entrance.

Two soldiers watched the alley behind the townhouse. Nila walked toward them, head down.

"You there," one of the men said. "Whose child is this?"

"Mine," Nila said.

The soldier lifted Jakob's chin. "Doesn't look like a duke's son."

"Should we hold him till we find the boy?" the other said.

"Sergeant Olem said we could go," Nila said.

"Fine," the soldier said. "Off with you, then. We've a busy night."